LEGENDARY COMICS YA

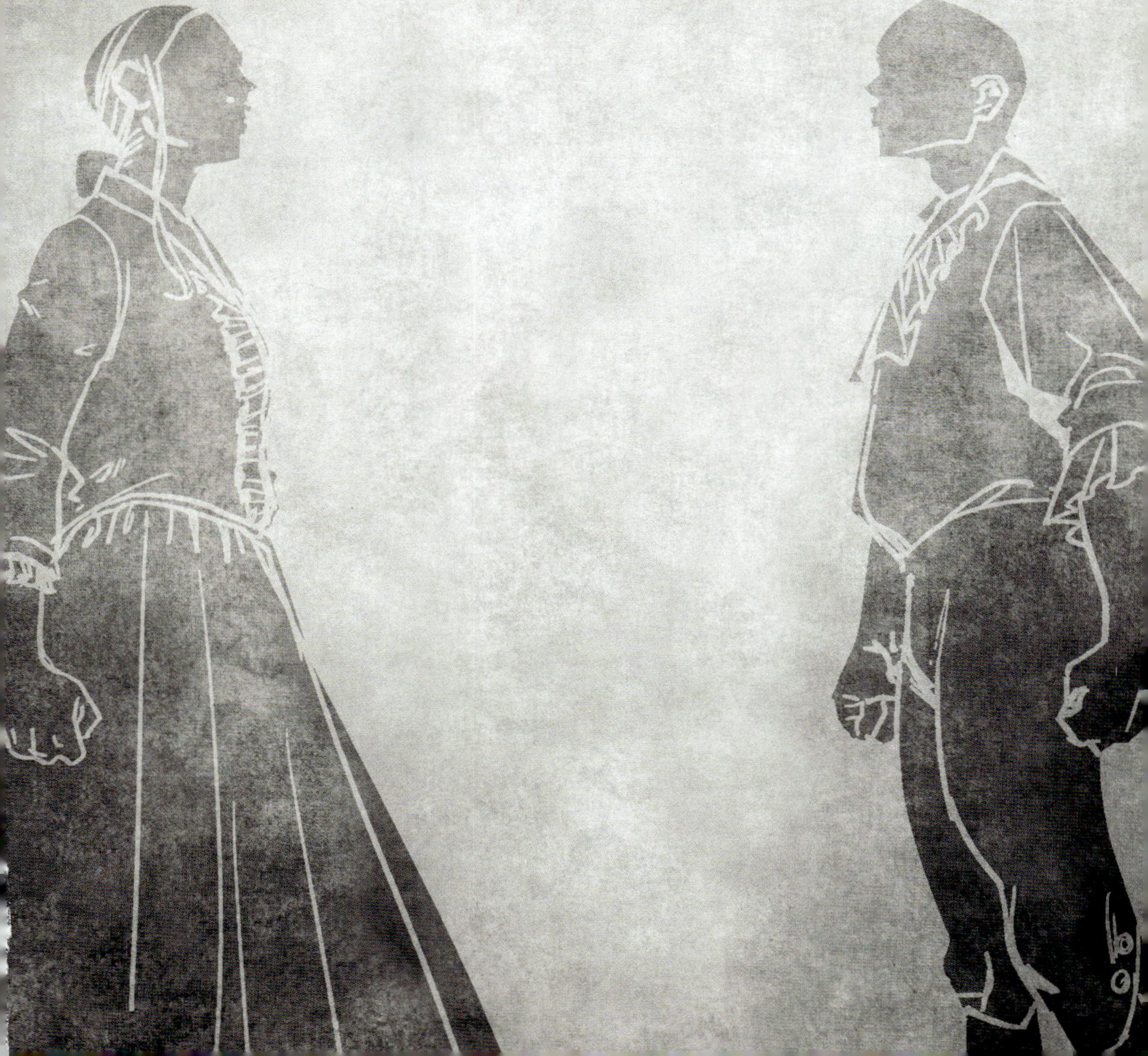

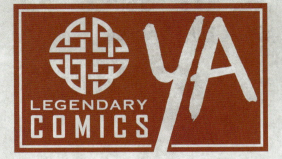

CHAMP

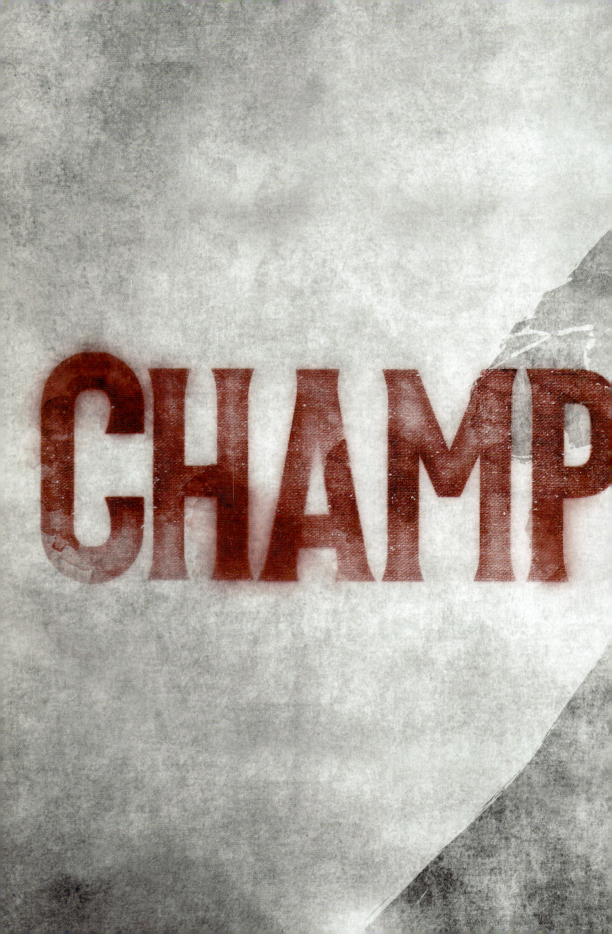

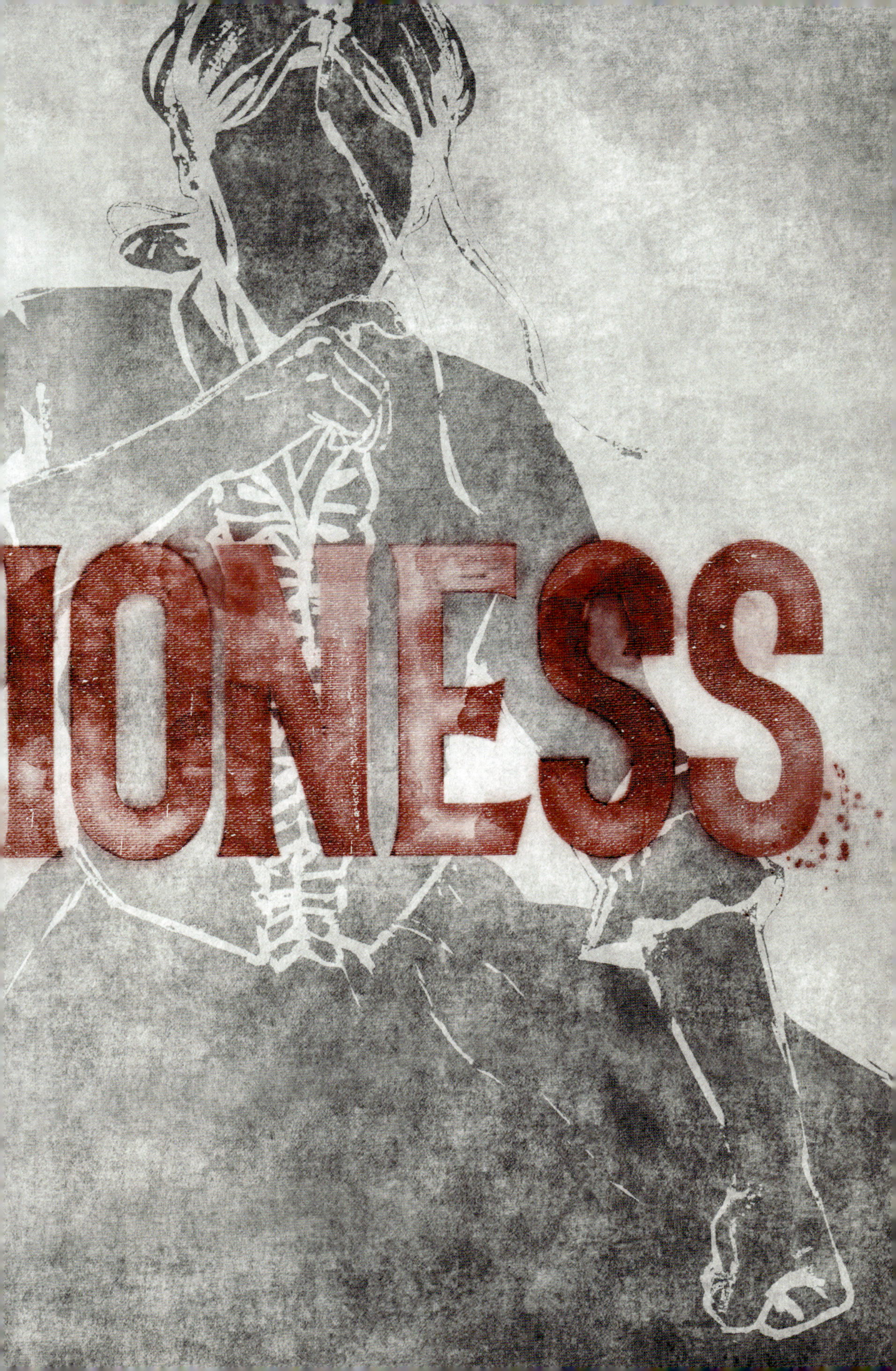
IONESS

KELLY ZEKAS & TARUN SHANKER
CREATORS/WRITERS

AMANDA PEREZ PUENTES
COVER AND INTERIOR ART

RICHARD STARKINGS & COMICRAFT'S JIMMY BETANCOURT
LETTERING

NIKITA KANNEKANTI
EDITOR

RICHARD STARKINGS & COMICRAFT'S TYLER SMITH
DESIGN

KATIE AGUILAR
CHAMPIONESS LOGO

LEGENDARY MARKETING LEGENDARY PUBLICITY
SPECIAL THANKS

✦ LEGENDARY

JOSHUA GRODE
Chief Executive Officer

MARY PARENT
Vice Chairman of Worldwide Production

CHRIS ALBRECHT
Managing Director, Legendary Television

RONALD HOHAUSER
Chief Financial Officer

BARNABY LEGG
SVP, Creative Strategy

MIKE ROSS
EVP, Business & Legal Affairs

KRISTINA HOLLIMAN
SVP, Business & Legal Affairs

BAYAN LAIRD
SVP, Business & Legal Affairs

ROBERT NAPTON SVP, Publishing • **NIKITA KANNEKANTI** Editor
JANN JONES Manager, Brand Development & Publishing Operations

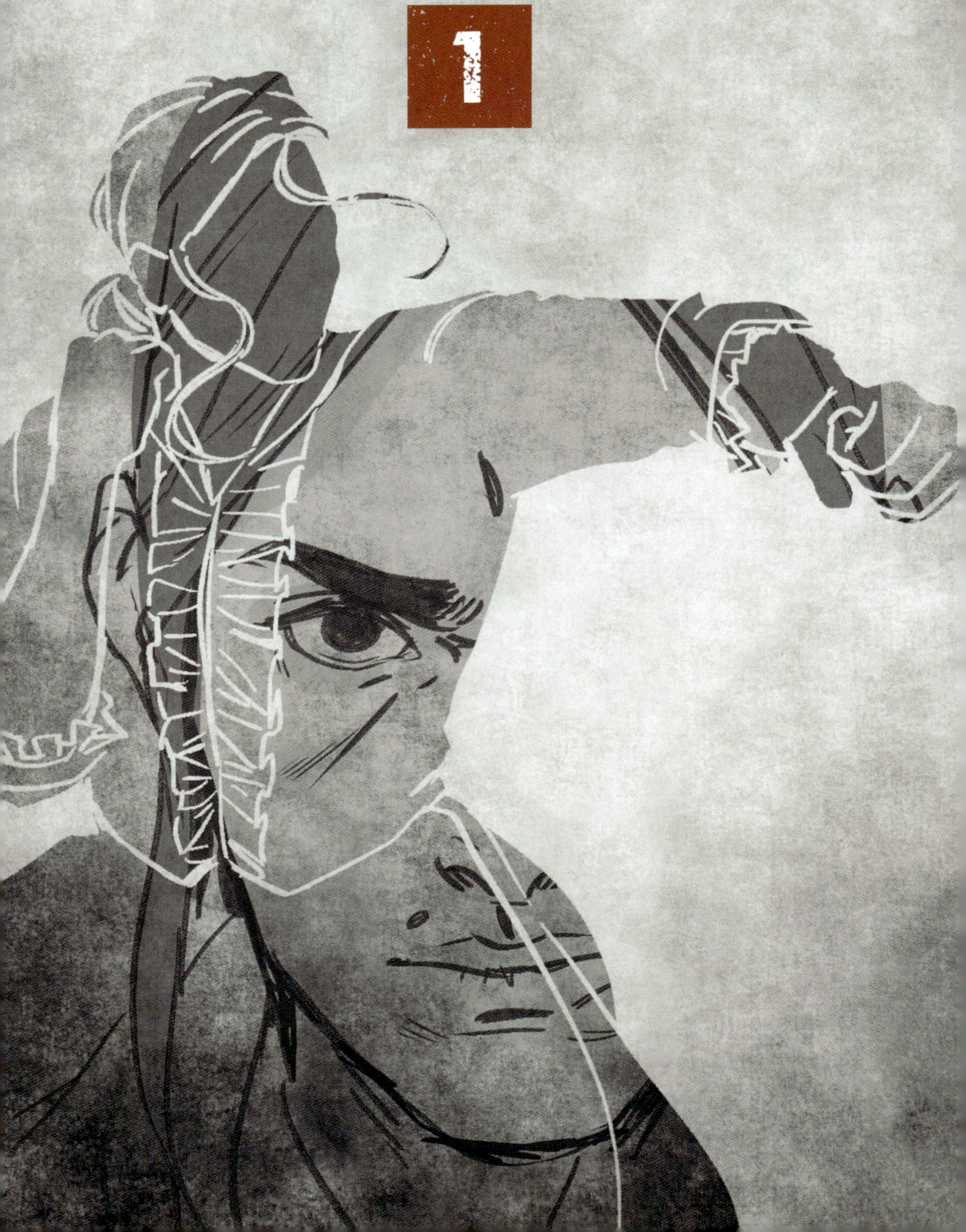
1

In 1743, Jack Broughton developed the first set of rules for the sport of boxing to prevent deaths from occurring in the ring. This story takes place twenty-one years earlier.

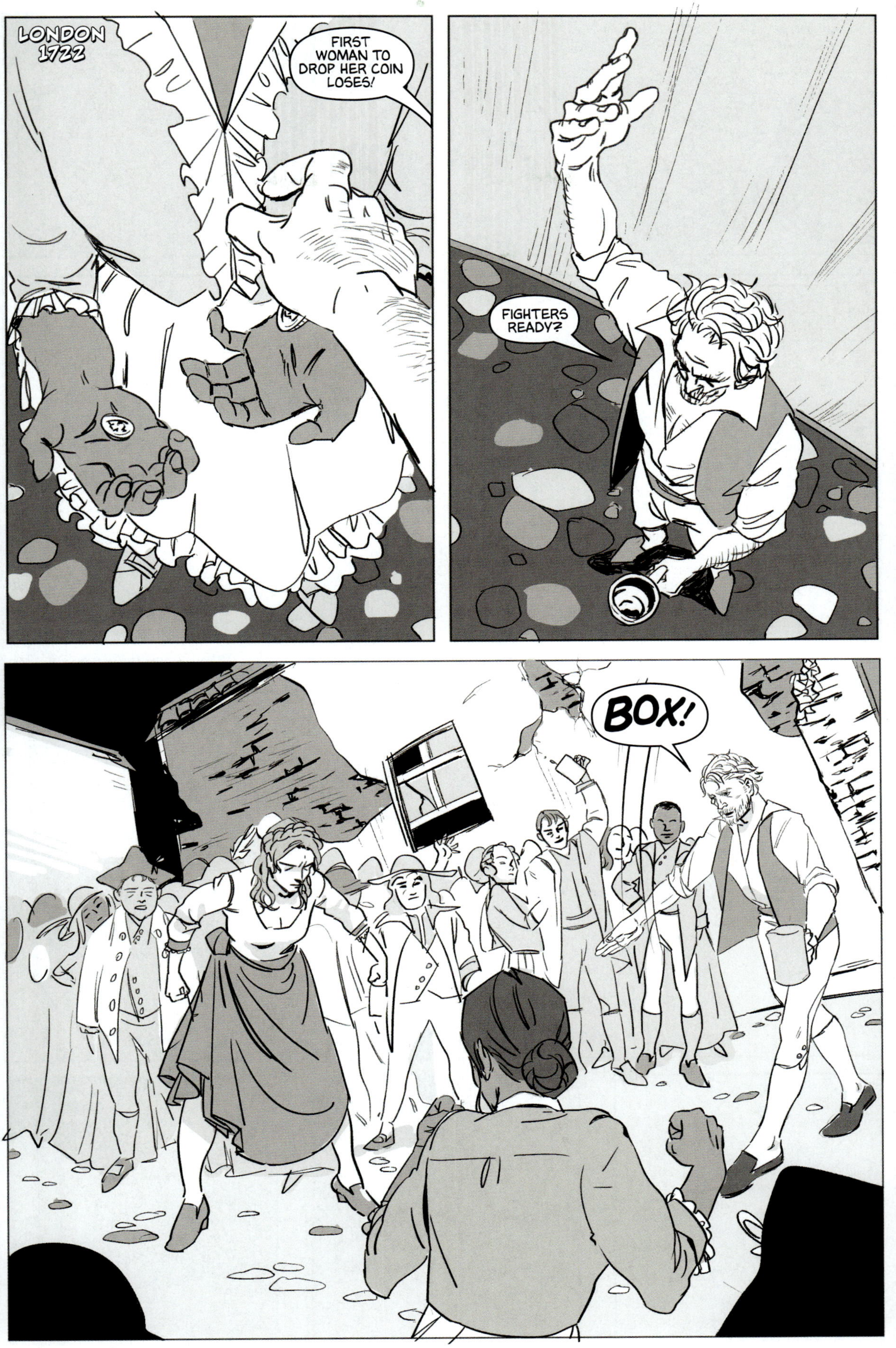
LONDON 1722
FIRST WOMAN TO DROP HER COIN LOSES!
FIGHTERS READY?
BOX!

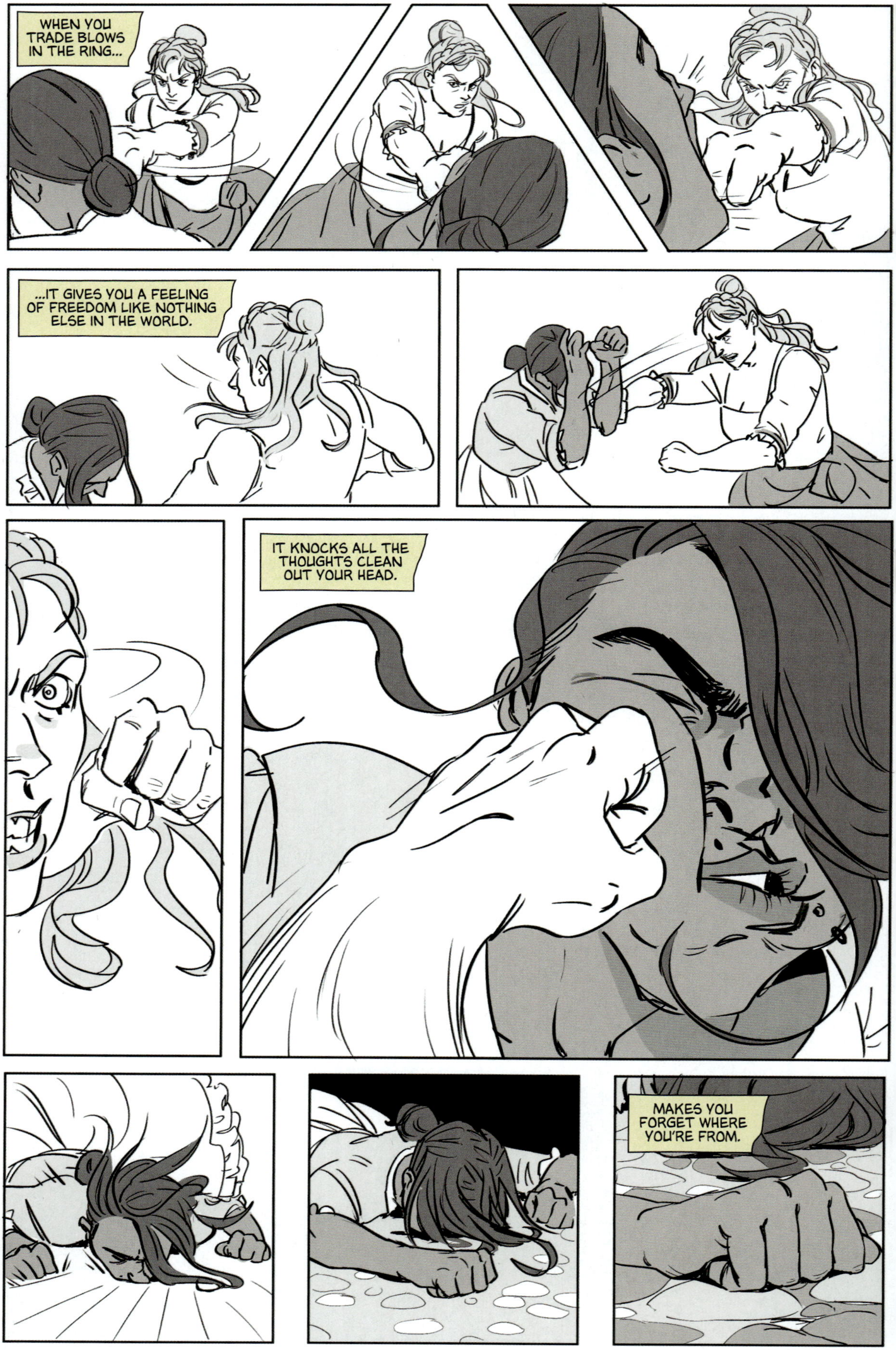
WHEN YOU TRADE BLOWS IN THE RING...
...IT GIVES YOU A FEELING OF FREEDOM LIKE NOTHING ELSE IN THE WORLD.
IT KNOCKS ALL THE THOUGHTS CLEAN OUT YOUR HEAD.
MAKES YOU FORGET WHERE YOU'RE FROM.

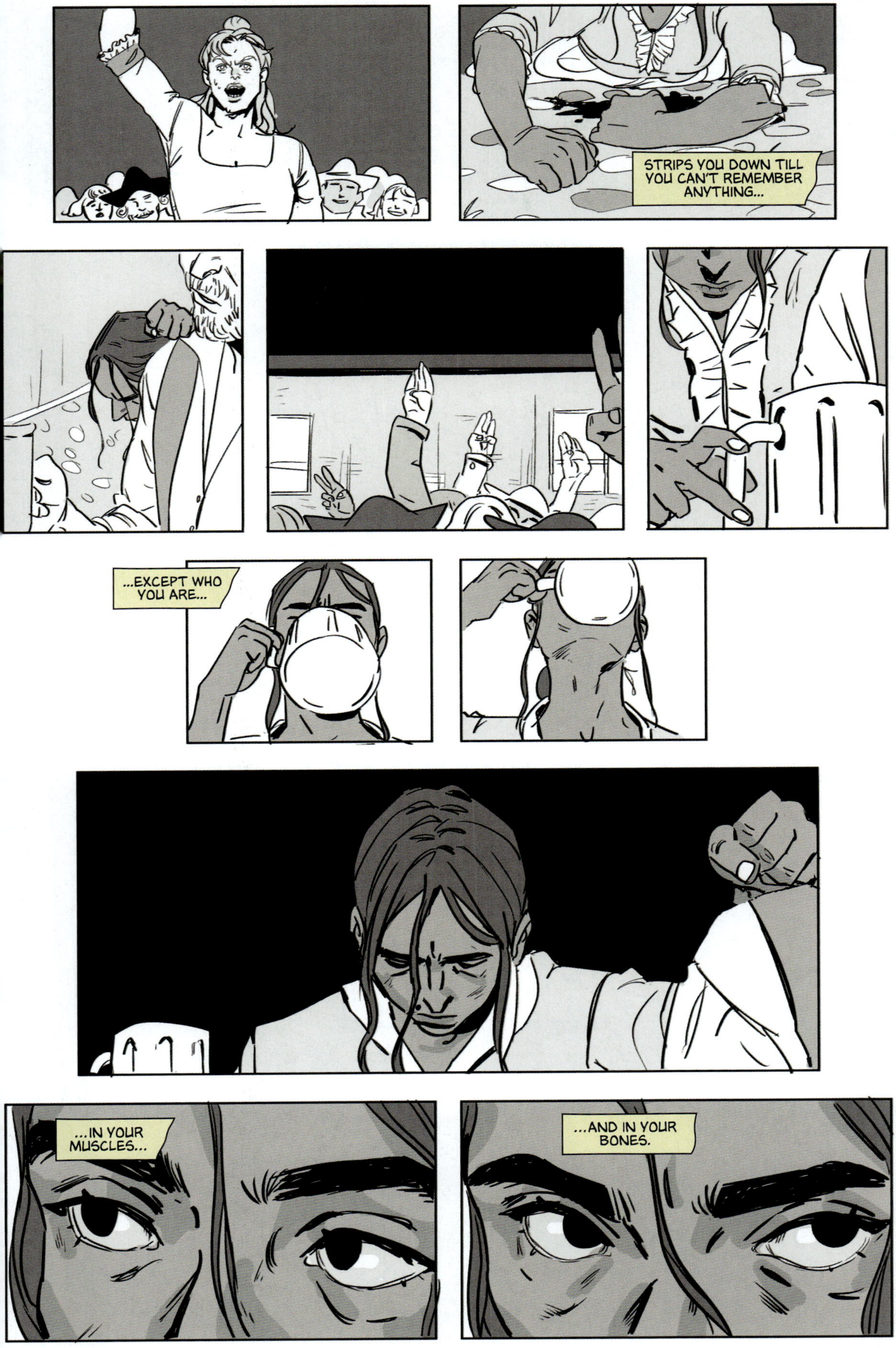
STRIPS YOU DOWN TILL YOU CAN'T REMEMBER ANYTHING...
...EXCEPT WHO YOU ARE...
...IN YOUR MUSCLES...
...AND IN YOUR BONES.

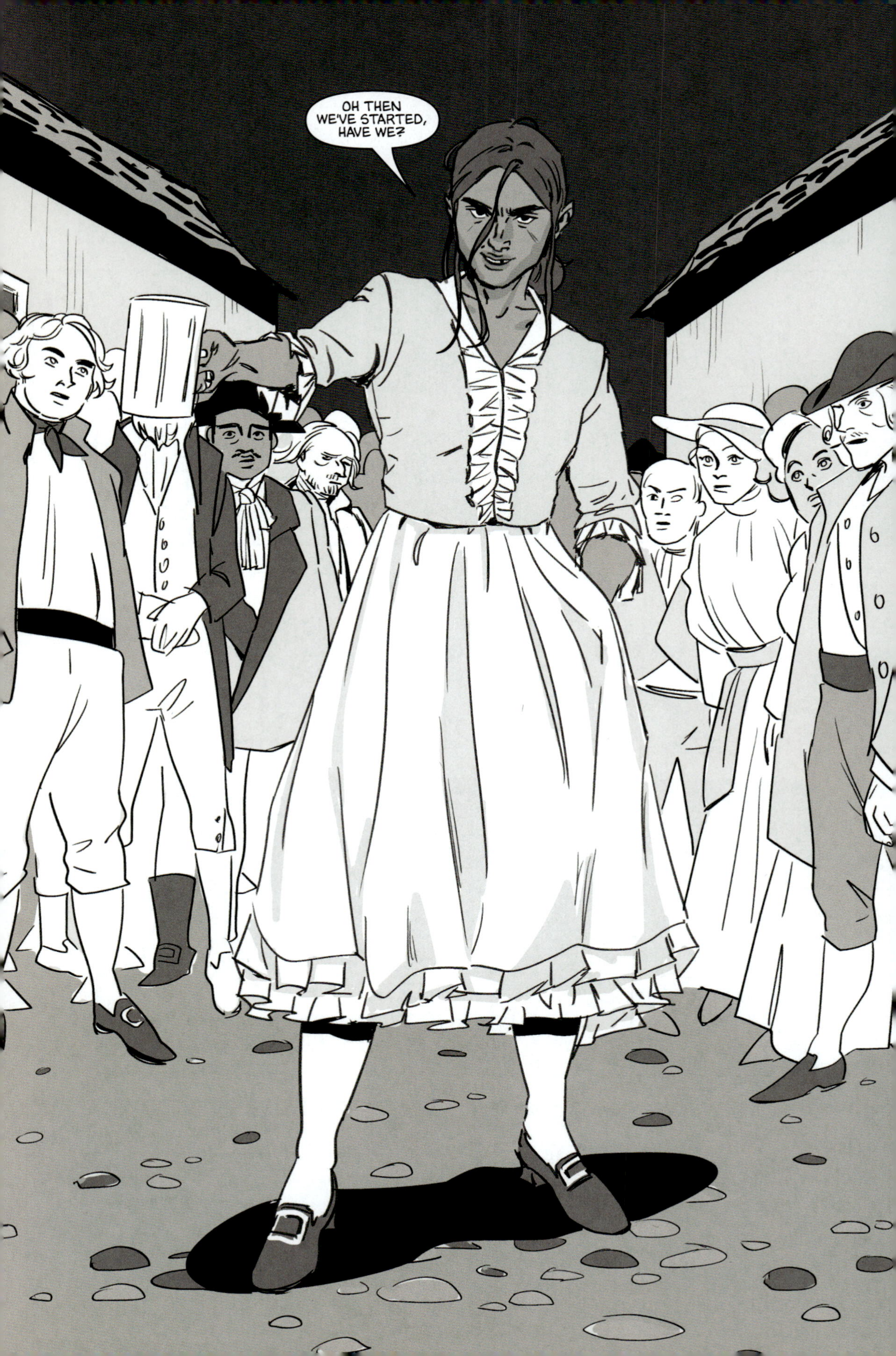
OH THEN WE'VE STARTED, HAVE WE?

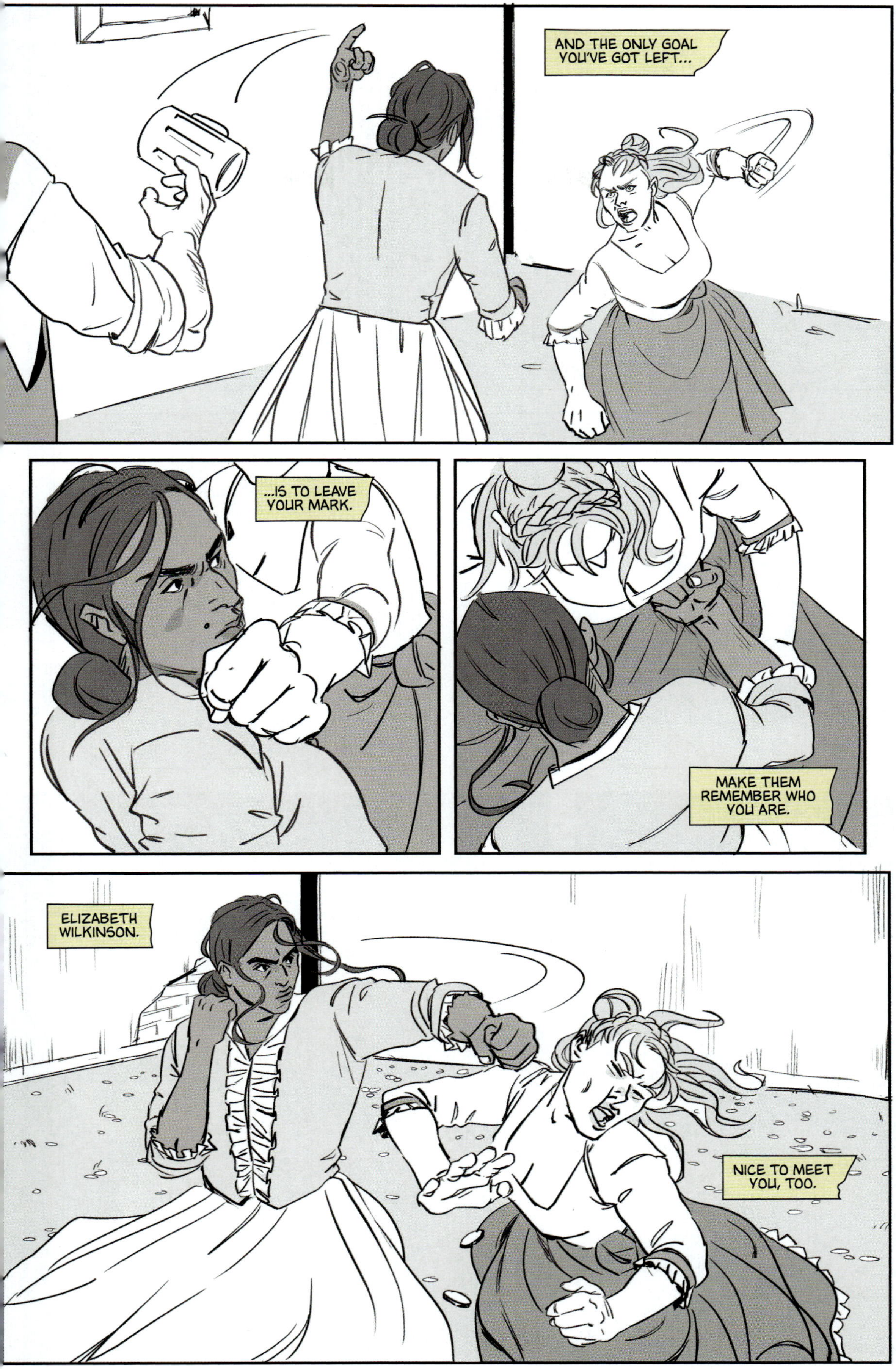
AND THE ONLY GOAL YOU'VE GOT LEFT...
...IS TO LEAVE YOUR MARK.
MAKE THEM REMEMBER WHO YOU ARE.
ELIZABETH WILKINSON.
NICE TO MEET YOU, TOO.

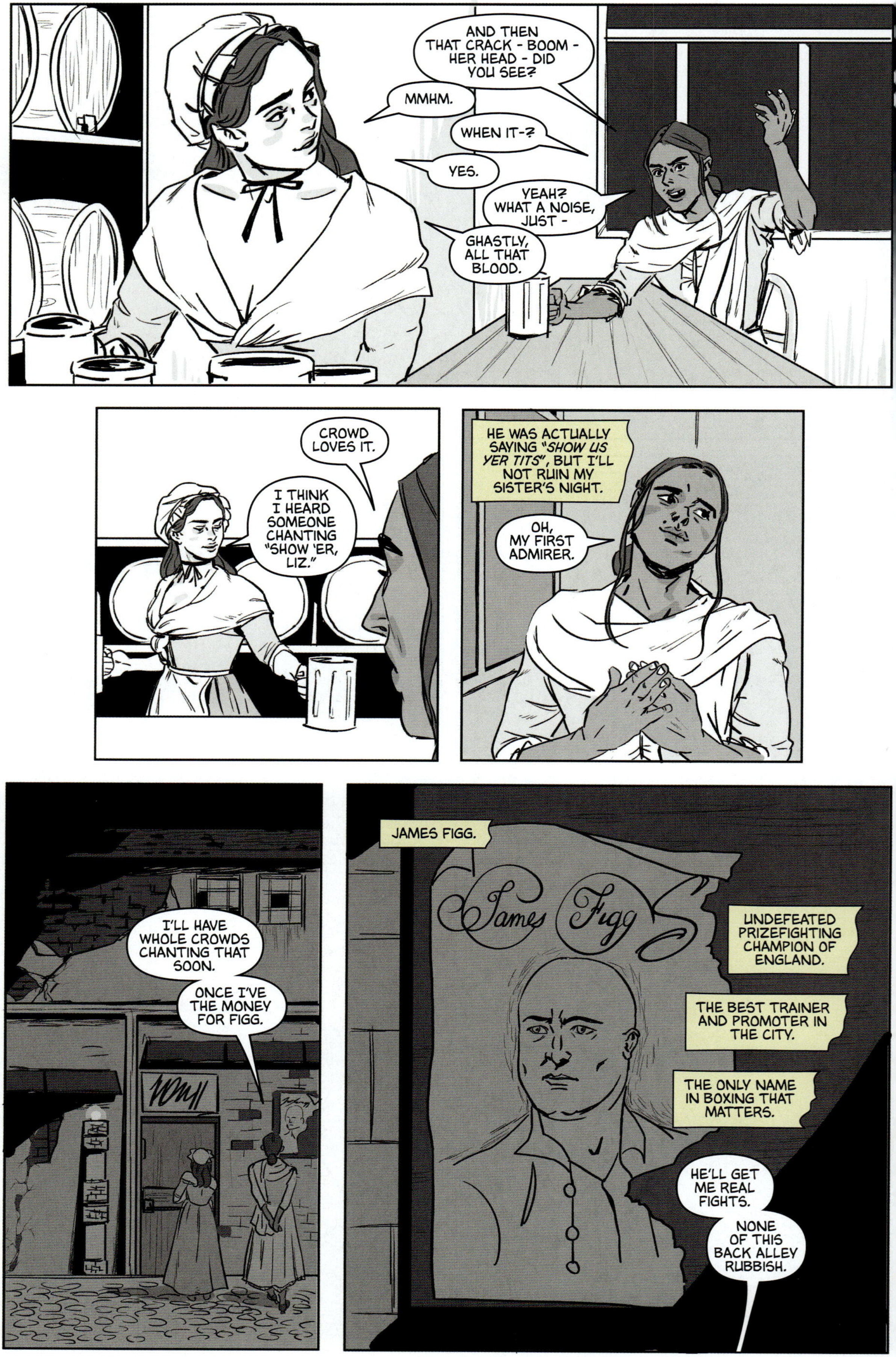
AND THEN THAT CRACK - BOOM - HER HEAD - DID YOU SEE?
MMHM.
WHEN IT-?
YES.
YEAH? WHAT A NOISE, JUST -
GHASTLY, ALL THAT BLOOD.
CROWD LOVES IT.
I THINK I HEARD SOMEONE CHANTING "SHOW 'ER, LIZ."
HE WAS ACTUALLY SAYING *"SHOW US YER TITS"*, BUT I'LL NOT RUIN MY SISTER'S NIGHT.
OH, MY FIRST ADMIRER.
I'LL HAVE WHOLE CROWDS CHANTING THAT SOON.
ONCE I'VE THE MONEY FOR FIGG.
JAMES FIGG.
James Figg
UNDEFEATED PRIZEFIGHTING CHAMPION OF ENGLAND.
THE BEST TRAINER AND PROMOTER IN THE CITY.
THE ONLY NAME IN BOXING THAT MATTERS.
HE'LL GET ME REAL FIGHTS.
NONE OF THIS BACK ALLEY RUBBISH.

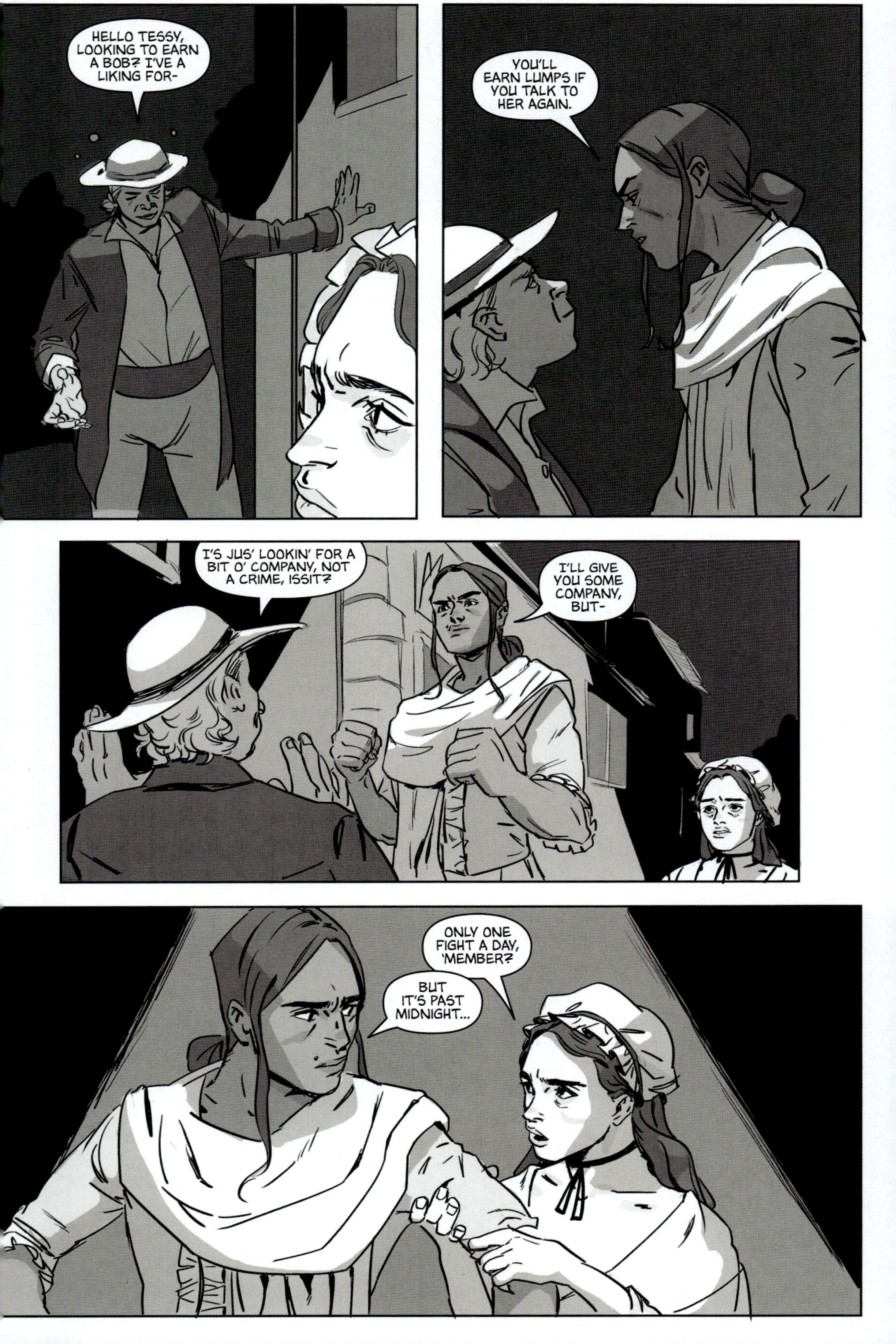
HELLO TESSY, LOOKING TO EARN A BOB? I'VE A LIKING FOR-
YOU'LL EARN LUMPS IF YOU TALK TO HER AGAIN.
I'S JUS' LOOKIN' FOR A BIT O' COMPANY, NOT A CRIME, ISSIT?
I'LL GIVE YOU SOME COMPANY, BUT-
ONLY ONE FIGHT A DAY, 'MEMBER?
BUT IT'S PAST MIDNIGHT...

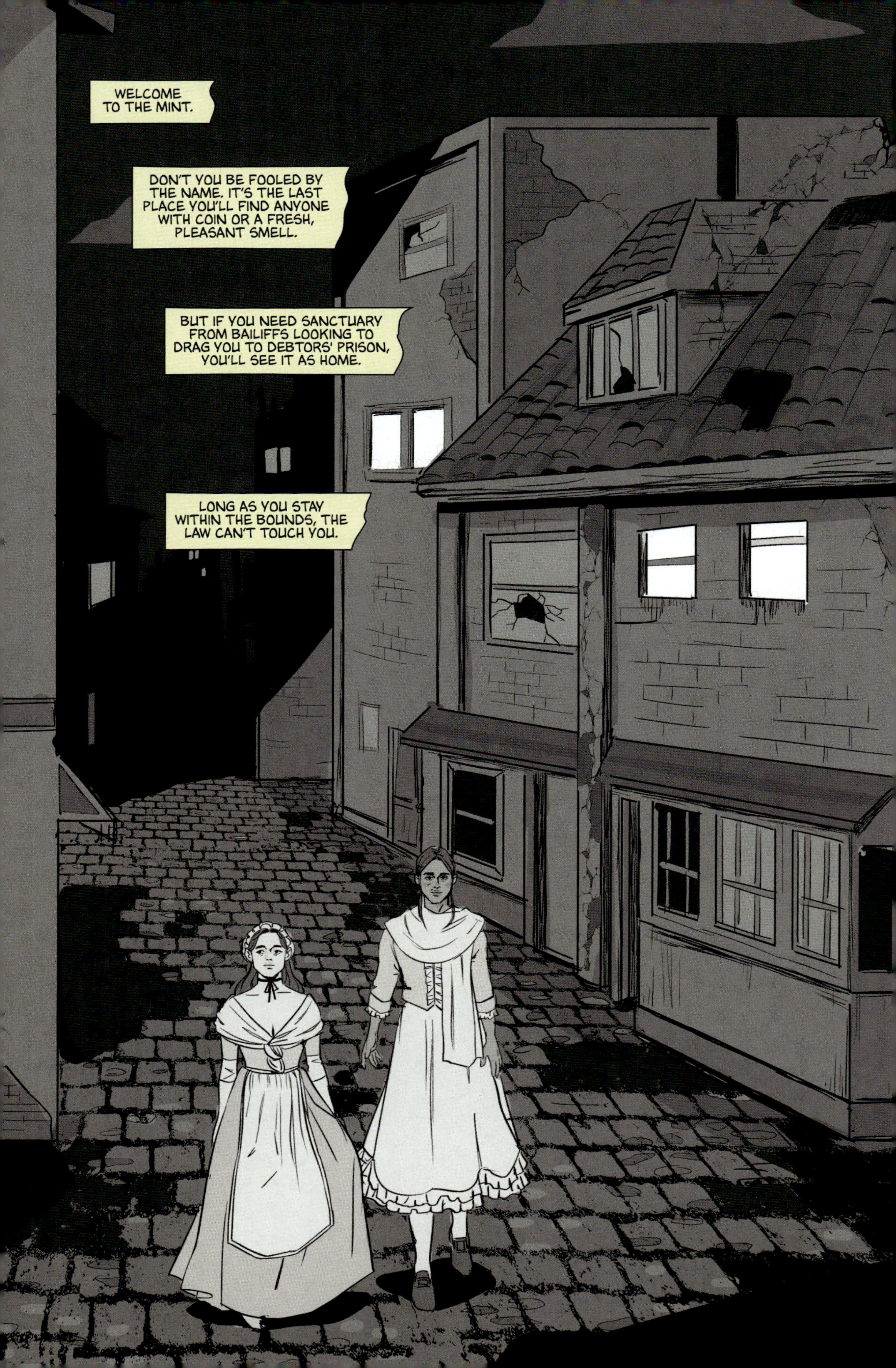
WELCOME TO THE MINT.
DON'T YOU BE FOOLED BY THE NAME. IT'S THE LAST PLACE YOU'LL FIND ANYONE WITH COIN OR A FRESH, PLEASANT SMELL.
BUT IF YOU NEED SANCTUARY FROM BAILIFFS LOOKING TO DRAG YOU TO DEBTORS' PRISON, YOU'LL SEE IT AS HOME.
LONG AS YOU STAY WITHIN THE BOUNDS, THE LAW CAN'T TOUCH YOU.

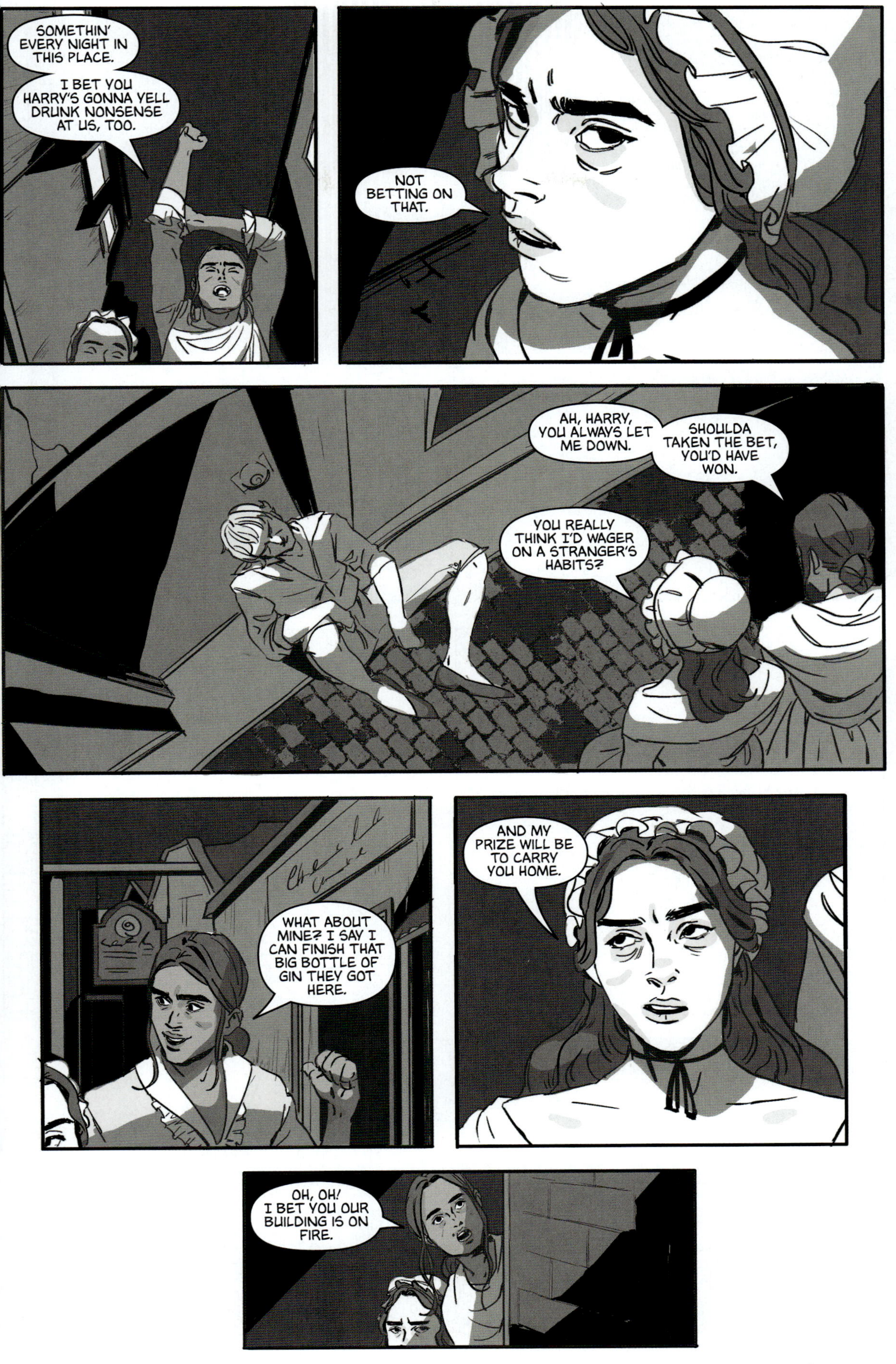

SOMETHIN' EVERY NIGHT IN THIS PLACE.
I BET YOU HARRY'S GONNA YELL DRUNK NONSENSE AT US, TOO.
NOT BETTING ON THAT.
AH, HARRY, YOU ALWAYS LET ME DOWN.
SHOULDA TAKEN THE BET, YOU'D HAVE WON.
YOU REALLY THINK I'D WAGER ON A STRANGER'S HABITS?
WHAT ABOUT MINE? I SAY I CAN FINISH THAT BIG BOTTLE OF GIN THEY GOT HERE.
AND MY PRIZE WILL BE TO CARRY YOU HOME.
OH, OH! I BET YOU OUR BUILDING IS ON FIRE.

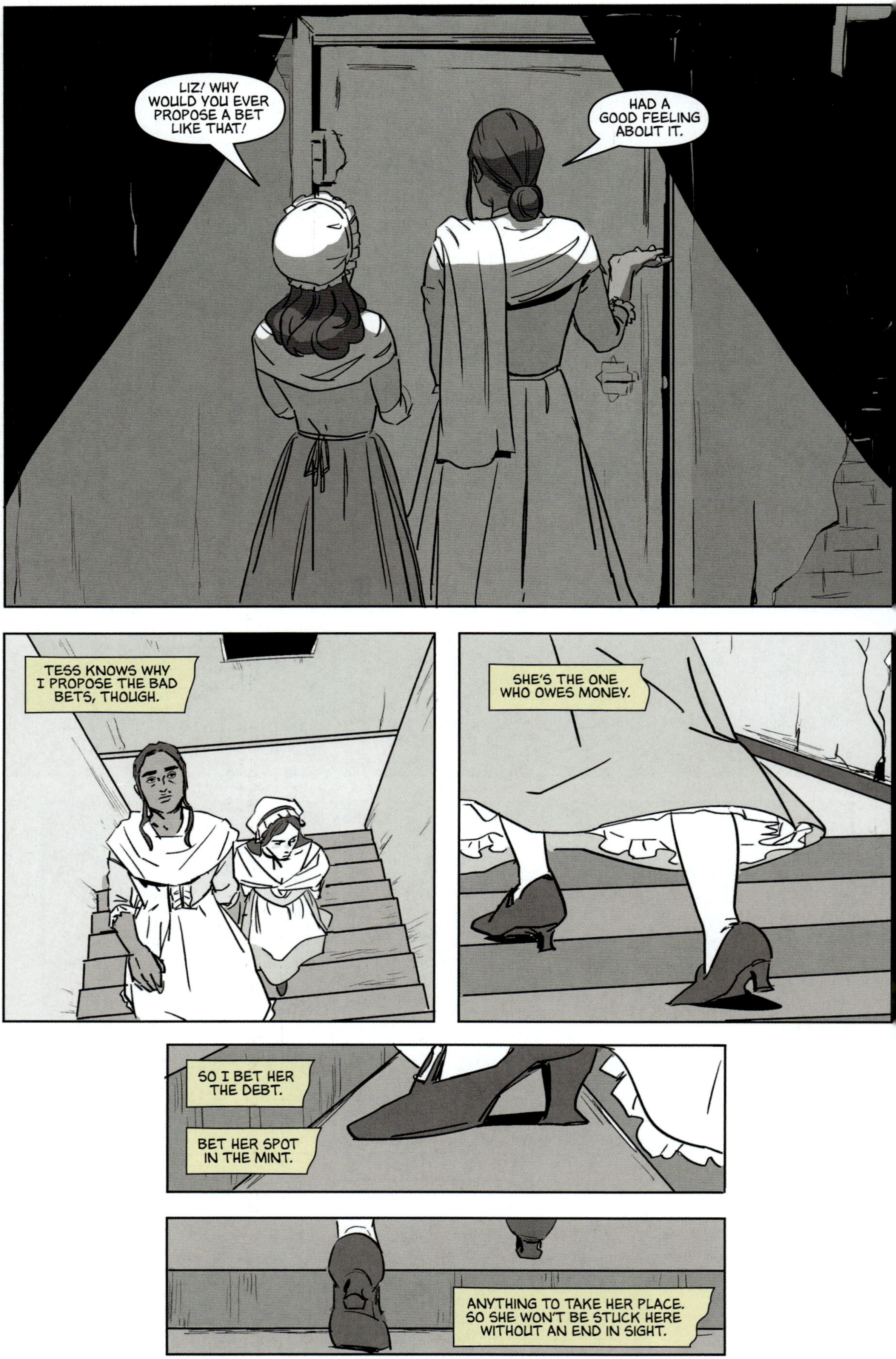
LIZ! WHY WOULD YOU EVER PROPOSE A BET LIKE THAT!
HAD A GOOD FEELING ABOUT IT.
TESS KNOWS WHY I PROPOSE THE BAD BETS, THOUGH.
SHE'S THE ONE WHO OWES MONEY.
SO I BET HER THE DEBT.
BET HER SPOT IN THE MINT.
ANYTHING TO TAKE HER PLACE. SO SHE WON'T BE STUCK HERE WITHOUT AN END IN SIGHT.

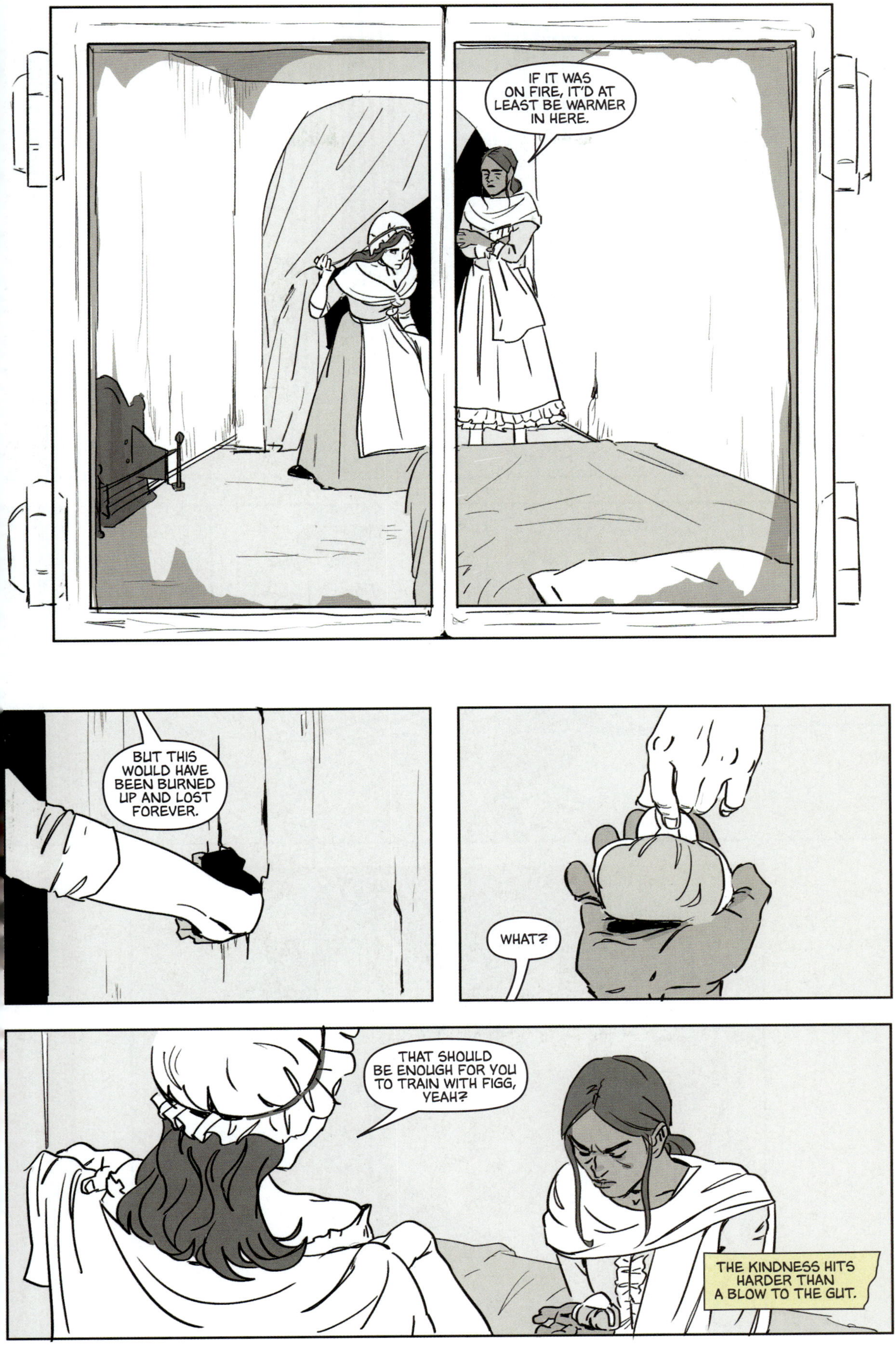
IF IT WAS ON FIRE, IT'D AT LEAST BE WARMER IN HERE.
BUT THIS WOULD HAVE BEEN BURNED UP AND LOST FOREVER.
WHAT?
THAT SHOULD BE ENOUGH FOR YOU TO TRAIN WITH FIGG, YEAH?
THE KINDNESS HITS HARDER THAN A BLOW TO THE GUT.

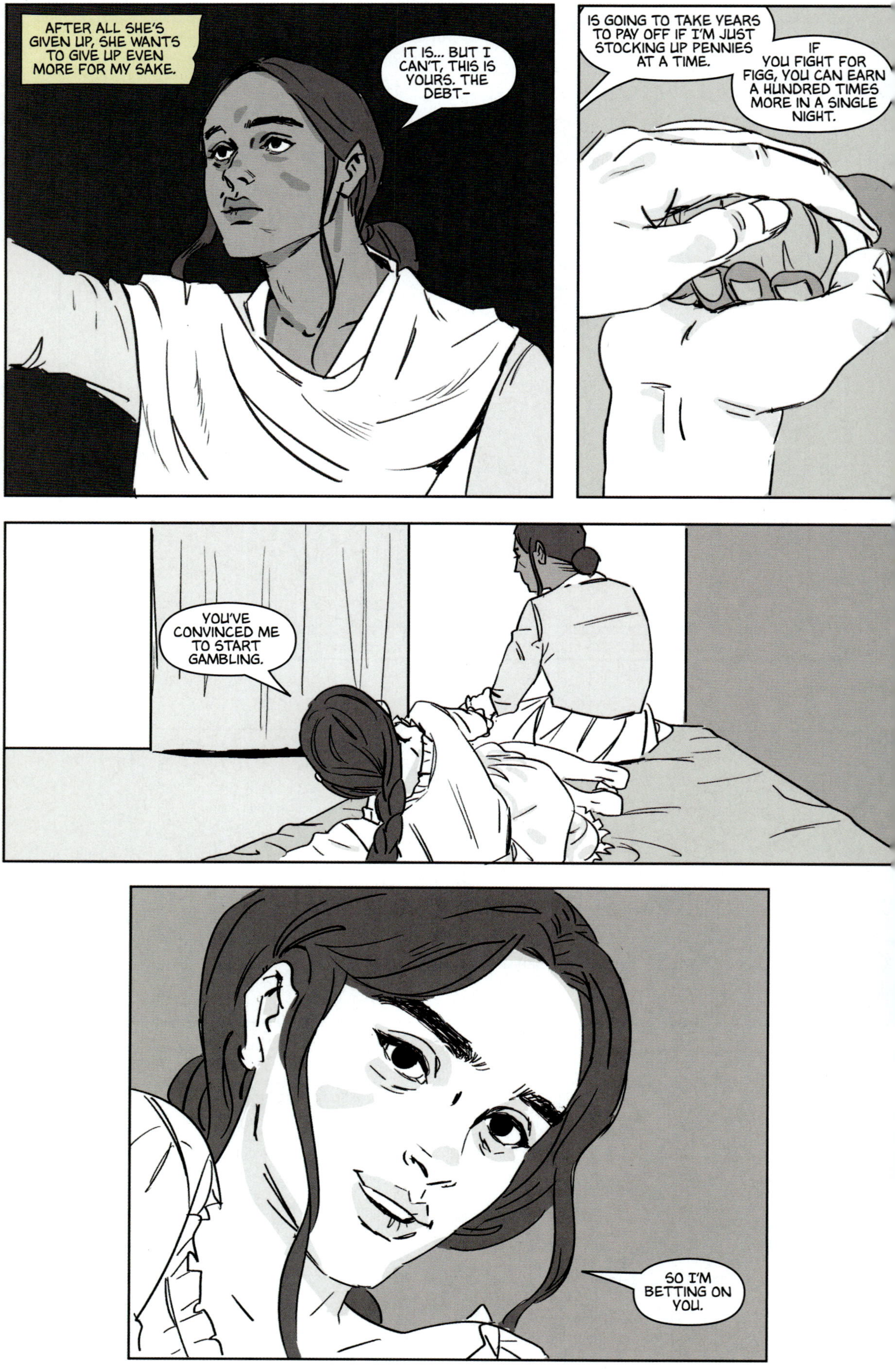

AFTER ALL SHE'S GIVEN UP, SHE WANTS TO GIVE UP EVEN MORE FOR MY SAKE.
IT IS... BUT I CAN'T, THIS IS YOURS. THE DEBT-
IS GOING TO TAKE YEARS TO PAY OFF IF I'M JUST STOCKING UP PENNIES AT A TIME.
IF YOU FIGHT FOR FIGG, YOU CAN EARN A HUNDRED TIMES MORE IN A SINGLE NIGHT.
YOU'VE CONVINCED ME TO START GAMBLING.
SO I'M BETTING ON YOU.

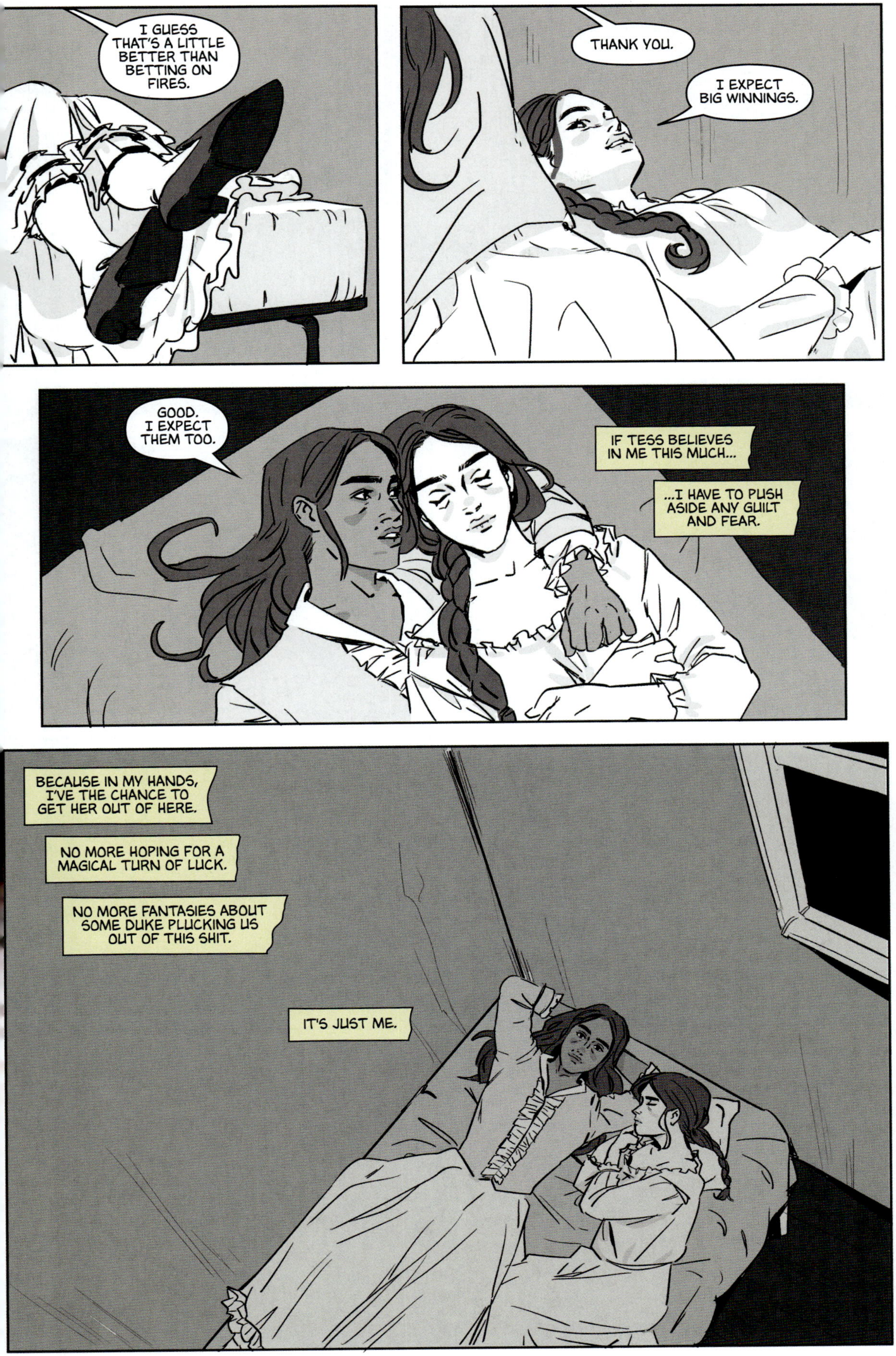
I GUESS THAT'S A LITTLE BETTER THAN BETTING ON FIRES.
THANK YOU.
I EXPECT BIG WINNINGS.
GOOD. I EXPECT THEM TOO.
IF TESS BELIEVES IN ME THIS MUCH...
...I HAVE TO PUSH ASIDE ANY GUILT AND FEAR.
BECAUSE IN MY HANDS, I'VE THE CHANCE TO GET HER OUT OF HERE.
NO MORE HOPING FOR A MAGICAL TURN OF LUCK.
NO MORE FANTASIES ABOUT SOME DUKE PLUCKING US OUT OF THIS SHIT.
IT'S JUST ME.

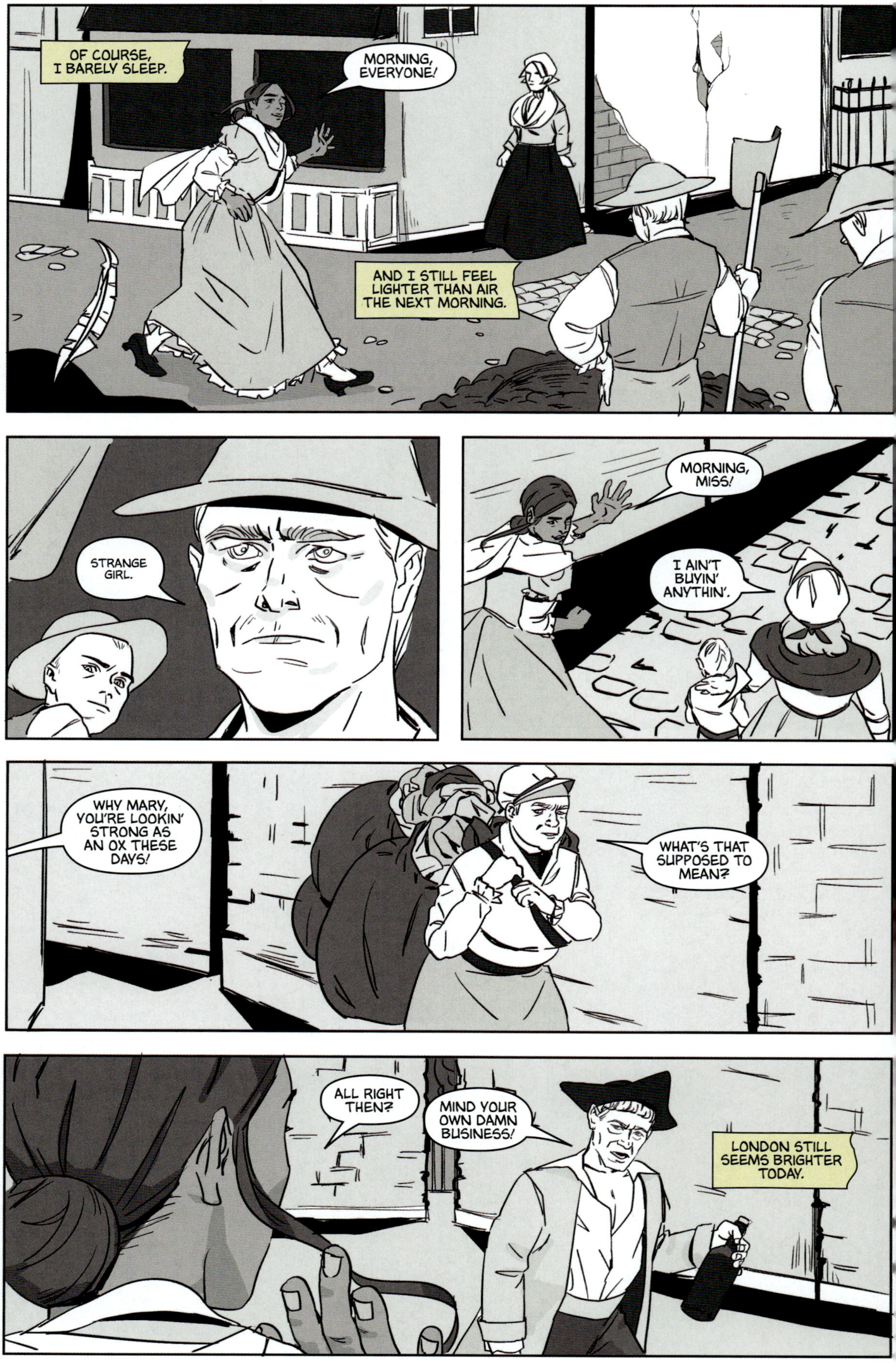
OF COURSE, I BARELY SLEEP.
MORNING, EVERYONE!
AND I STILL FEEL LIGHTER THAN AIR THE NEXT MORNING.
STRANGE GIRL.
MORNING, MISS!
I AIN'T BUYIN' ANYTHIN'.
WHY MARY, YOU'RE LOOKIN' STRONG AS AN OX THESE DAYS!
WHAT'S THAT SUPPOSED TO MEAN?
ALL RIGHT THEN?
MIND YOUR OWN DAMN BUSINESS!
LONDON STILL SEEMS BRIGHTER TODAY.

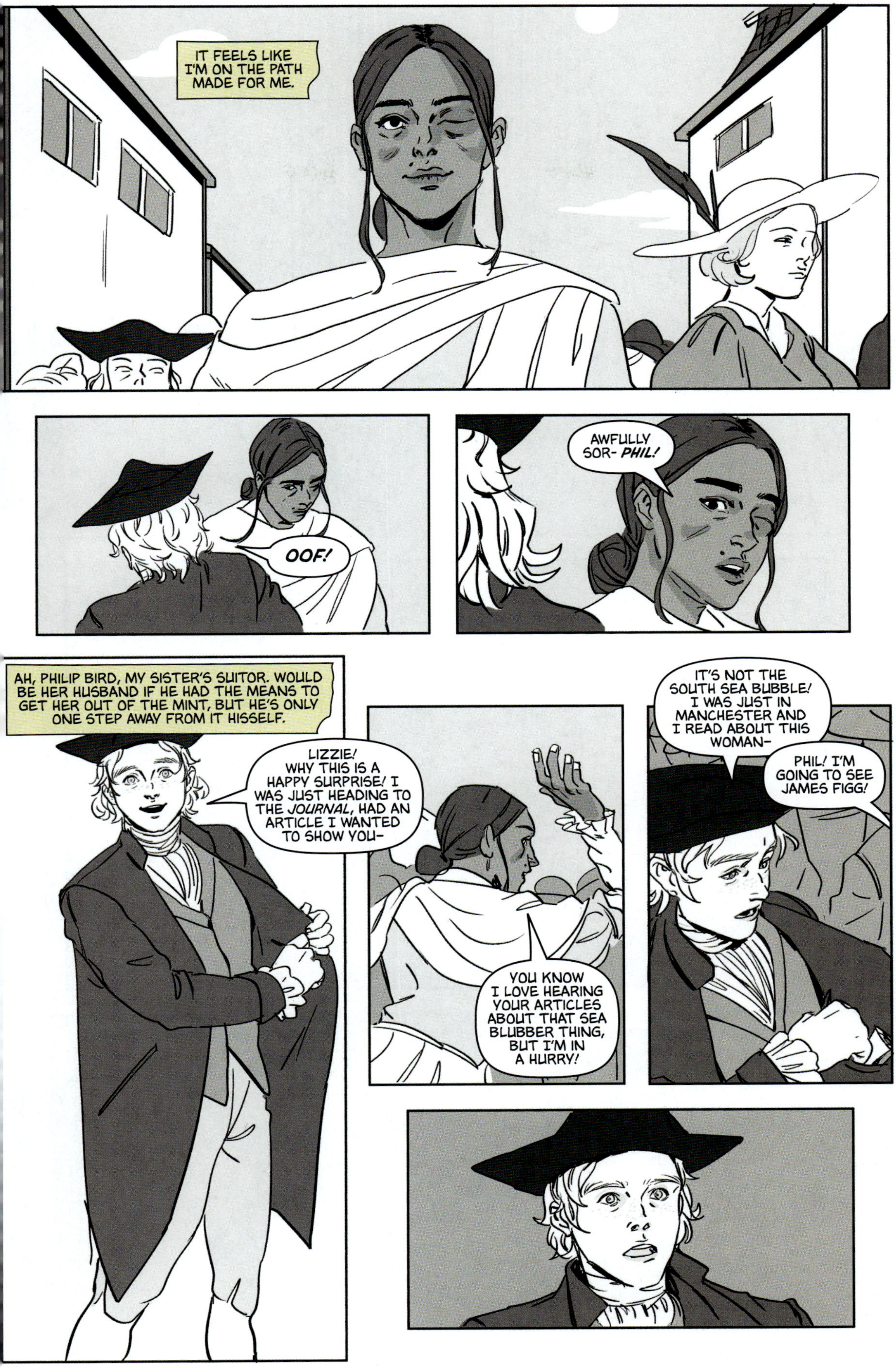

IT FEELS LIKE I'M ON THE PATH MADE FOR ME.
OOF!
AWFULLY SOR- *PHIL!*
AH, PHILIP BIRD, MY SISTER'S SUITOR. WOULD BE HER HUSBAND IF HE HAD THE MEANS TO GET HER OUT OF THE MINT, BUT HE'S ONLY ONE STEP AWAY FROM IT HISSELF.
LIZZIE! WHY THIS IS A HAPPY SURPRISE! I WAS JUST HEADING TO THE *JOURNAL*, HAD AN ARTICLE I WANTED TO SHOW YOU-
YOU KNOW I LOVE HEARING YOUR ARTICLES ABOUT THAT SEA BLUBBER THING, BUT I'M IN A HURRY!
IT'S NOT THE SOUTH SEA BUBBLE! I WAS JUST IN MANCHESTER AND I READ ABOUT THIS WOMAN-
PHIL! I'M GOING TO SEE JAMES FIGG!

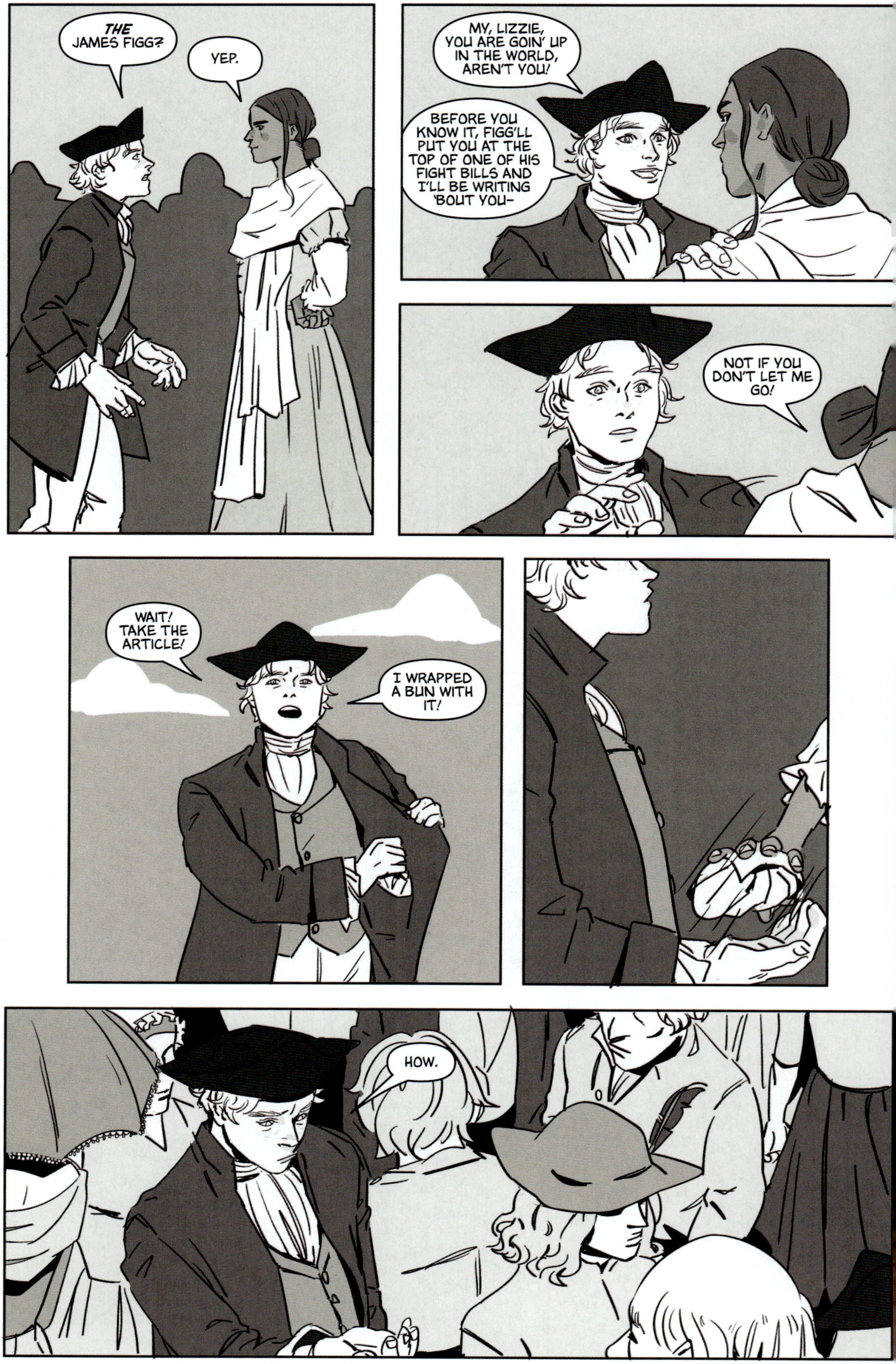
THE JAMES FIGG?
YEP.
MY, LIZZIE, YOU ARE GOIN' UP IN THE WORLD, AREN'T YOU!
BEFORE YOU KNOW IT, FIGG'LL PUT YOU AT THE TOP OF ONE OF HIS FIGHT BILLS AND I'LL BE WRITING 'BOUT YOU-
NOT IF YOU DON'T LET ME GO!
WAIT! TAKE THE ARTICLE!
I WRAPPED A BUN WITH IT!
HOW.

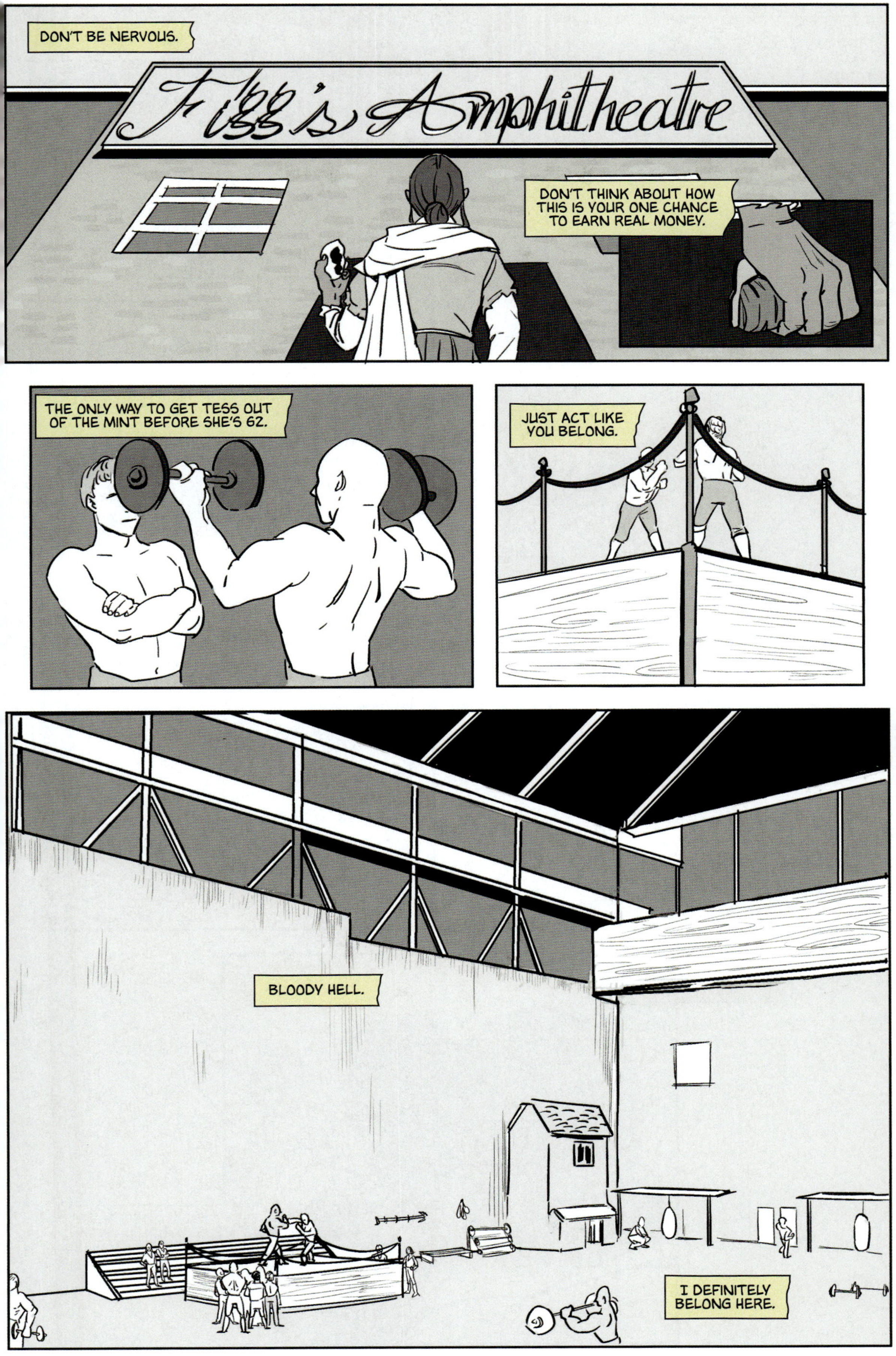
DON'T BE NERVOUS.
Figg's Amphitheatre
DON'T THINK ABOUT HOW THIS IS YOUR ONE CHANCE TO EARN REAL MONEY.
THE ONLY WAY TO GET TESS OUT OF THE MINT BEFORE SHE'S 62.
JUST ACT LIKE YOU BELONG.
BLOODY HELL.
I DEFINITELY BELONG HERE.

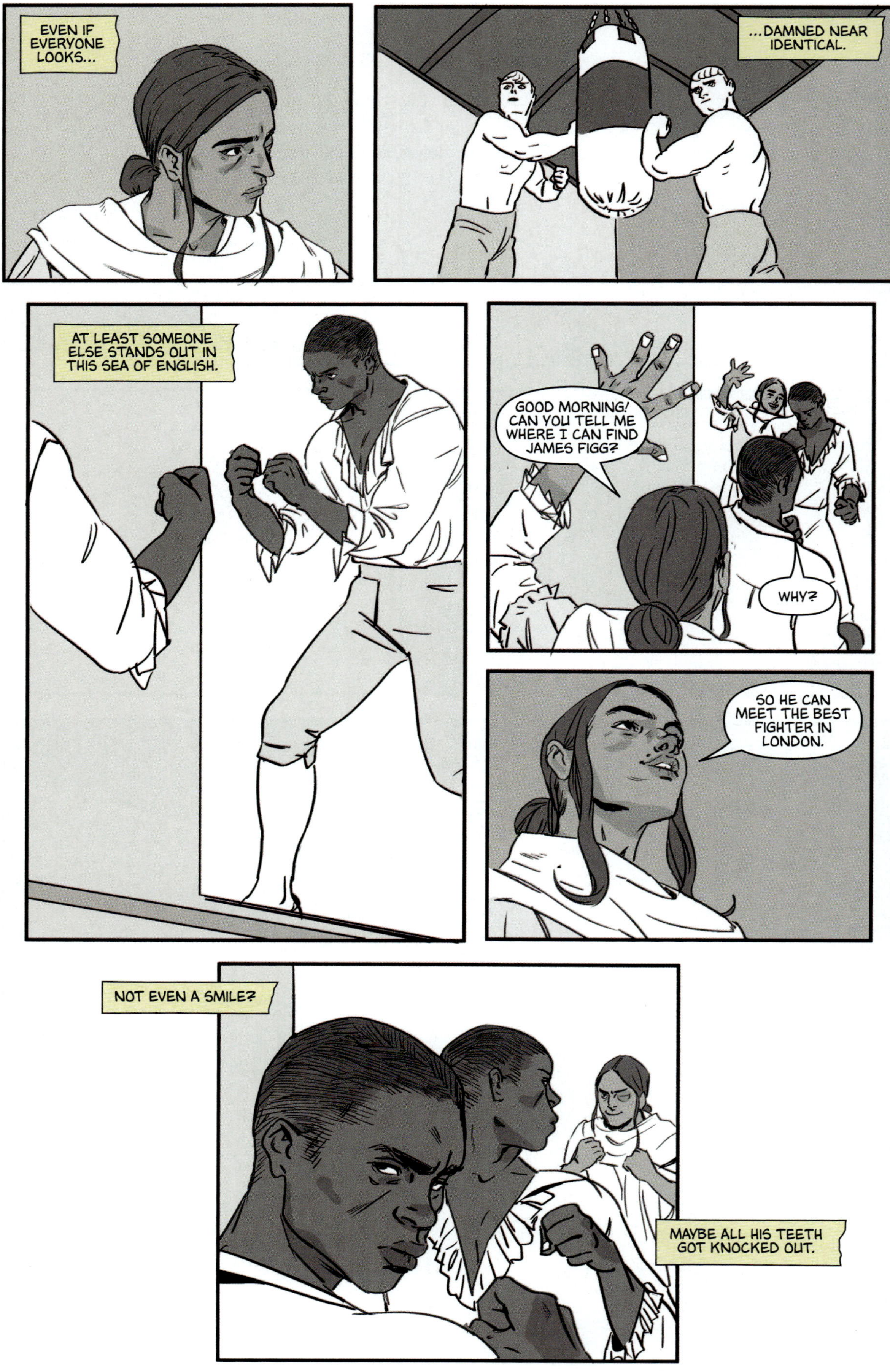
EVEN IF EVERYONE LOOKS...
...DAMNED NEAR IDENTICAL.
AT LEAST SOMEONE ELSE STANDS OUT IN THIS SEA OF ENGLISH.
GOOD MORNING! CAN YOU TELL ME WHERE I CAN FIND JAMES FIGG?
WHY?
SO HE CAN MEET THE BEST FIGHTER IN LONDON.
NOT EVEN A SMILE?
MAYBE ALL HIS TEETH GOT KNOCKED OUT.

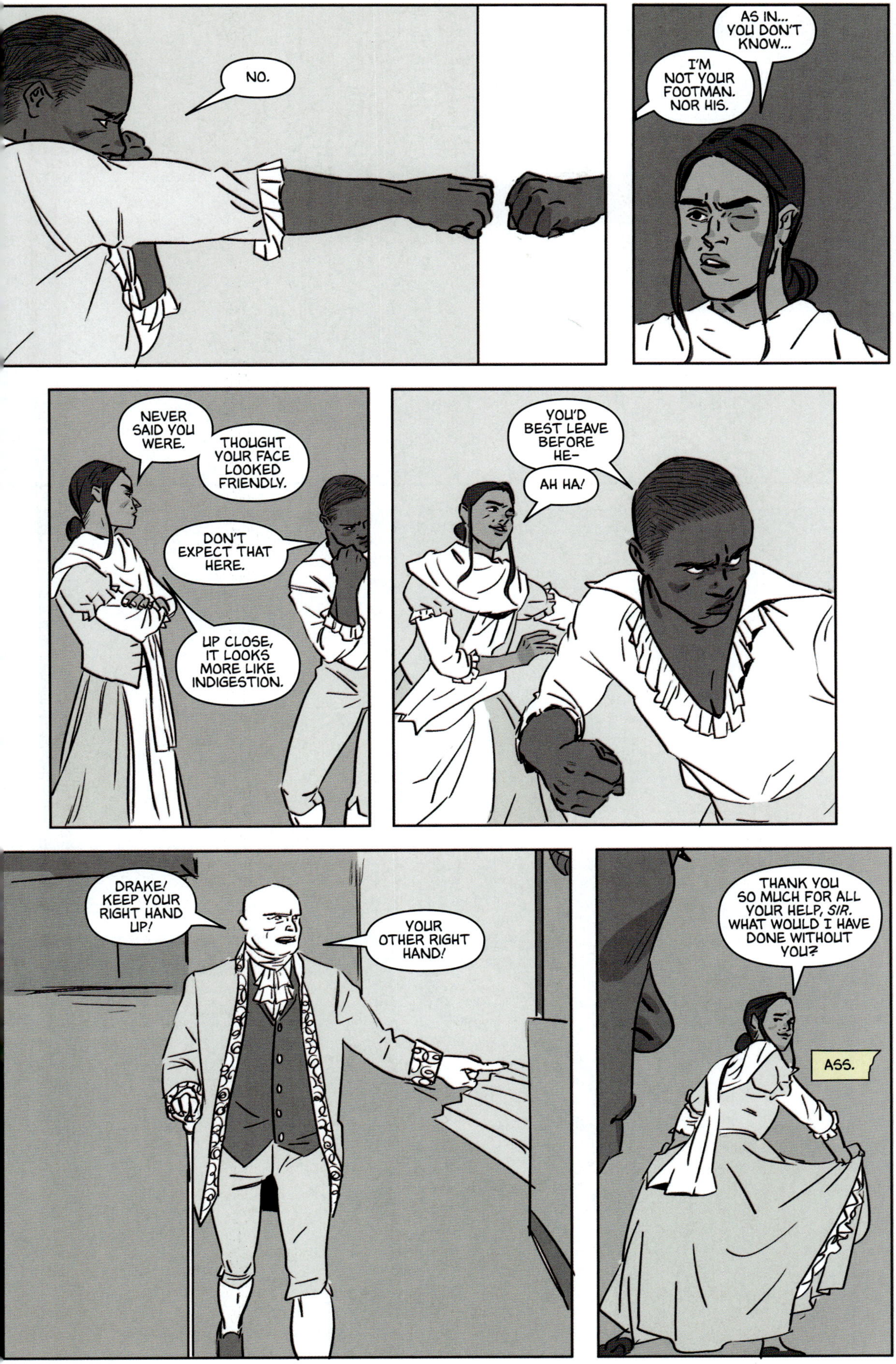
NO.
I'M NOT YOUR FOOTMAN. NOR HIS.
AS IN... YOU DON'T KNOW...
NEVER SAID YOU WERE.
THOUGHT YOUR FACE LOOKED FRIENDLY.
DON'T EXPECT THAT HERE.
UP CLOSE, IT LOOKS MORE LIKE INDIGESTION.
YOU'D BEST LEAVE BEFORE HE–
AH HA!
DRAKE! KEEP YOUR RIGHT HAND UP!
YOUR OTHER RIGHT HAND!
THANK YOU SO MUCH FOR ALL YOUR HELP, *SIR.* WHAT WOULD I HAVE DONE WITHOUT YOU?
ASS.

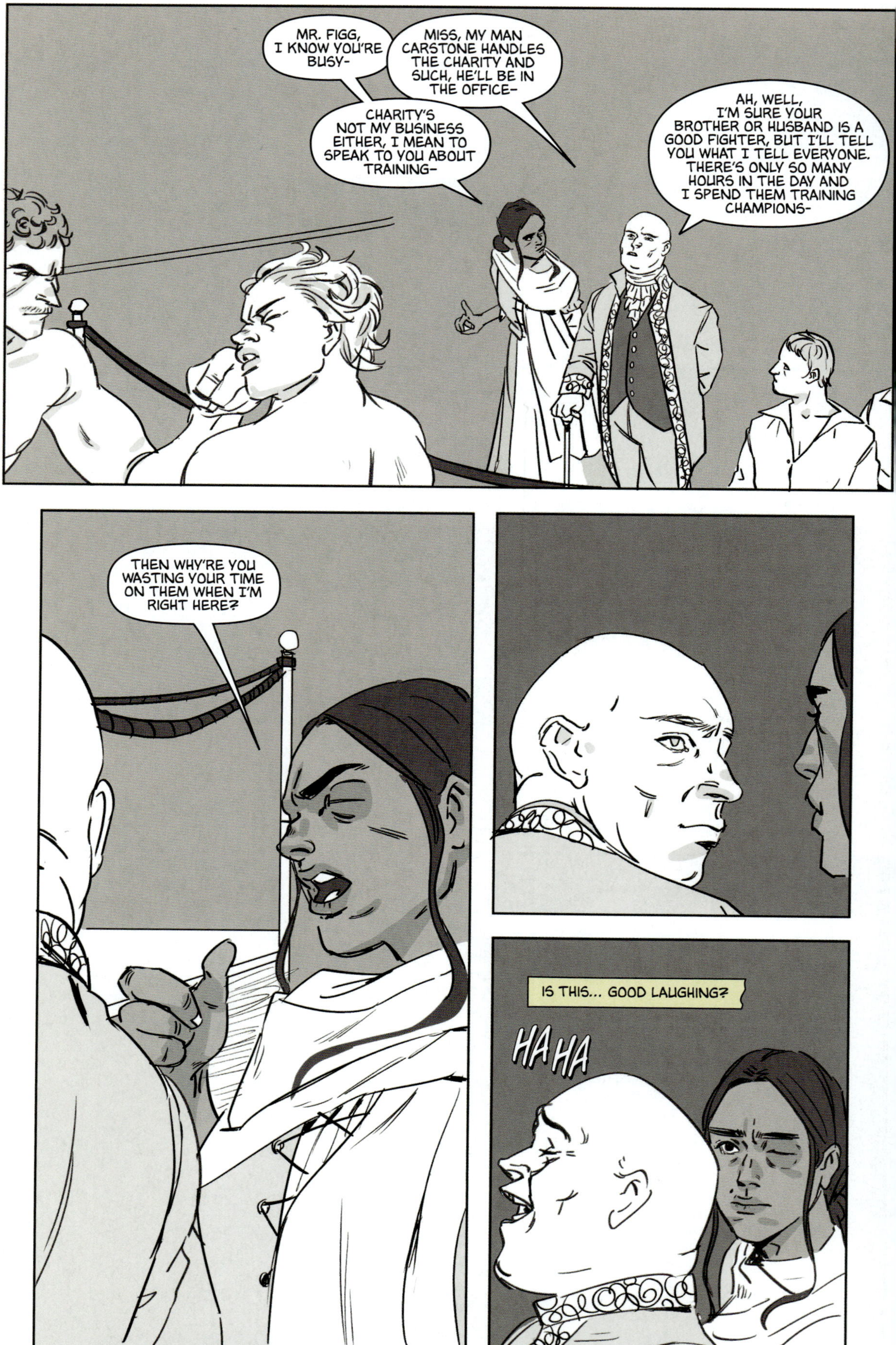

MR. FIGG, I KNOW YOU'RE BUSY-
MISS, MY MAN CARSTONE HANDLES THE CHARITY AND SUCH, HE'LL BE IN THE OFFICE-
CHARITY'S NOT MY BUSINESS EITHER, I MEAN TO SPEAK TO YOU ABOUT TRAINING-
AH, WELL, I'M SURE YOUR BROTHER OR HUSBAND IS A GOOD FIGHTER, BUT I'LL TELL YOU WHAT I TELL EVERYONE. THERE'S ONLY SO MANY HOURS IN THE DAY AND I SPEND THEM TRAINING CHAMPIONS-
THEN WHY'RE YOU WASTING YOUR TIME ON THEM WHEN I'M RIGHT HERE?
IS THIS... GOOD LAUGHING?
HA HA

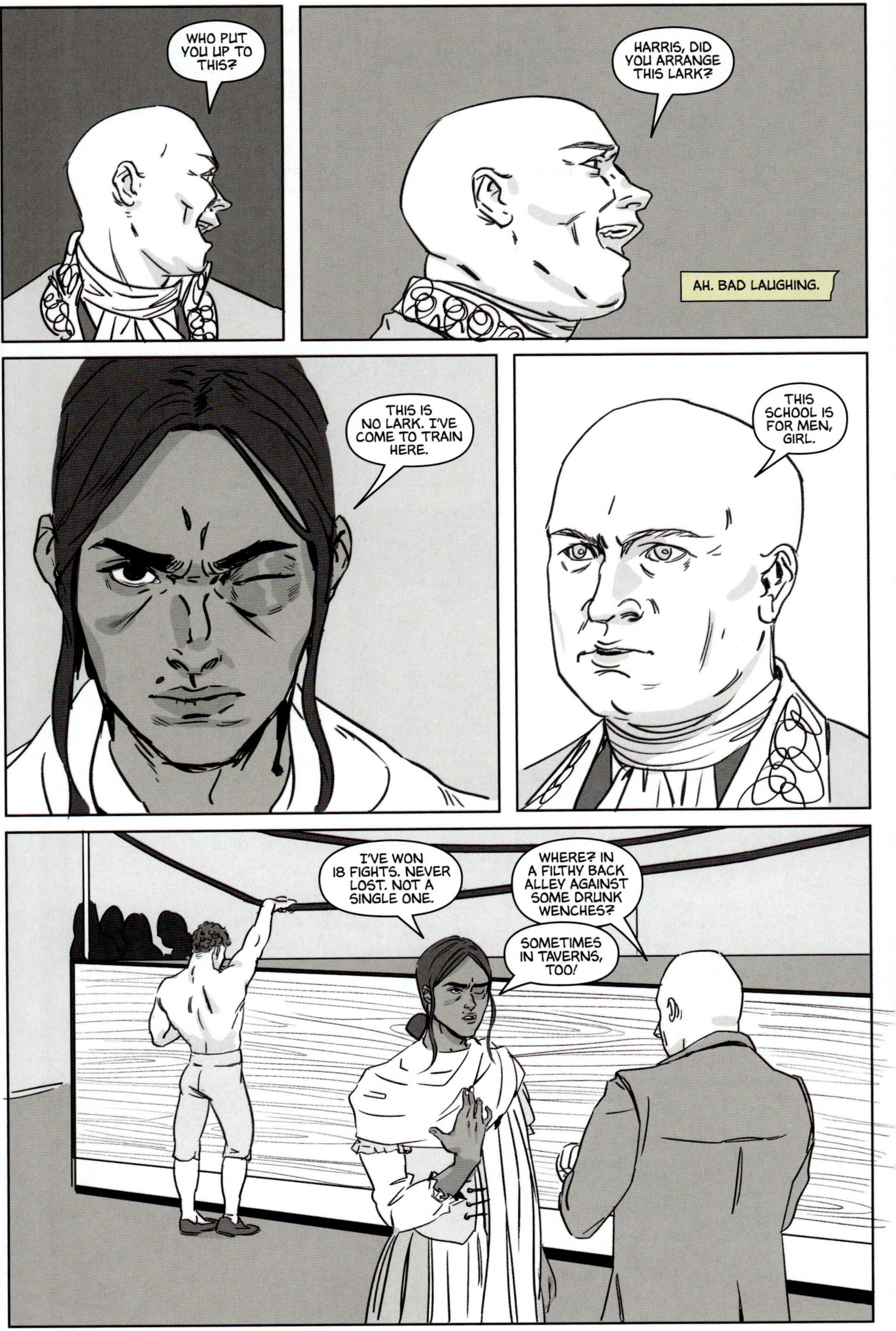
WHO PUT YOU UP TO THIS?
HARRIS, DID YOU ARRANGE THIS LARK?
AH. BAD LAUGHING.
THIS IS NO LARK. I'VE COME TO TRAIN HERE.
THIS SCHOOL IS FOR MEN, GIRL.
I'VE WON 18 FIGHTS. NEVER LOST. NOT A SINGLE ONE.
WHERE? IN A FILTHY BACK ALLEY AGAINST SOME DRUNK WENCHES?
SOMETIMES IN TAVERNS, TOO!

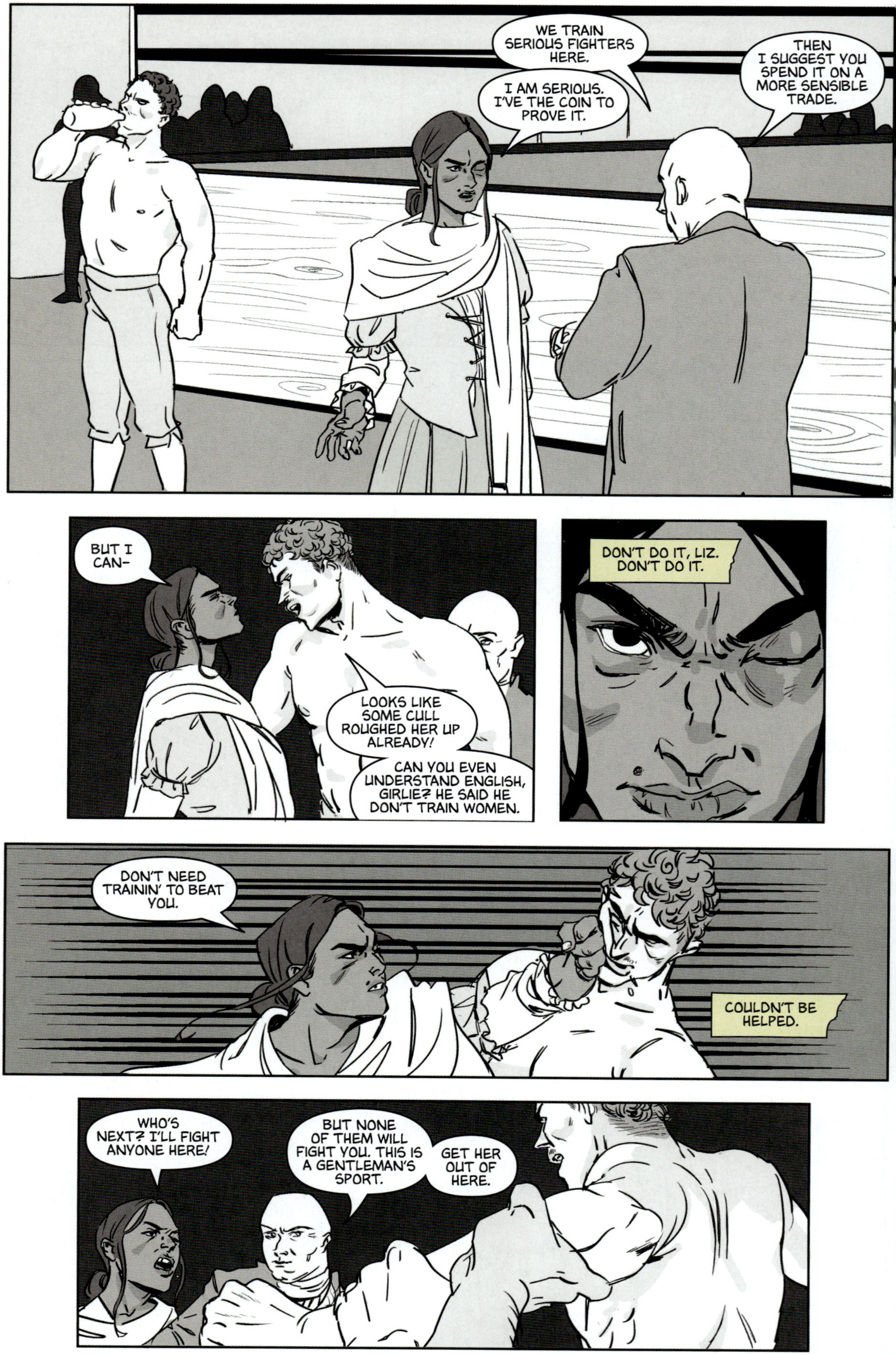
WE TRAIN SERIOUS FIGHTERS HERE.
I AM SERIOUS. I'VE THE COIN TO PROVE IT.
THEN I SUGGEST YOU SPEND IT ON A MORE SENSIBLE TRADE.
BUT I CAN-
LOOKS LIKE SOME CULL ROUGHED HER UP ALREADY!
CAN YOU EVEN UNDERSTAND ENGLISH, GIRLIE? HE SAID HE DON'T TRAIN WOMEN.
DON'T DO IT, LIZ. DON'T DO IT.
DON'T NEED TRAININ' TO BEAT YOU.
COULDN'T BE HELPED.
WHO'S NEXT? I'LL FIGHT ANYONE HERE!
BUT NONE OF THEM WILL FIGHT YOU. THIS IS A GENTLEMAN'S SPORT.
GET HER OUT OF HERE.

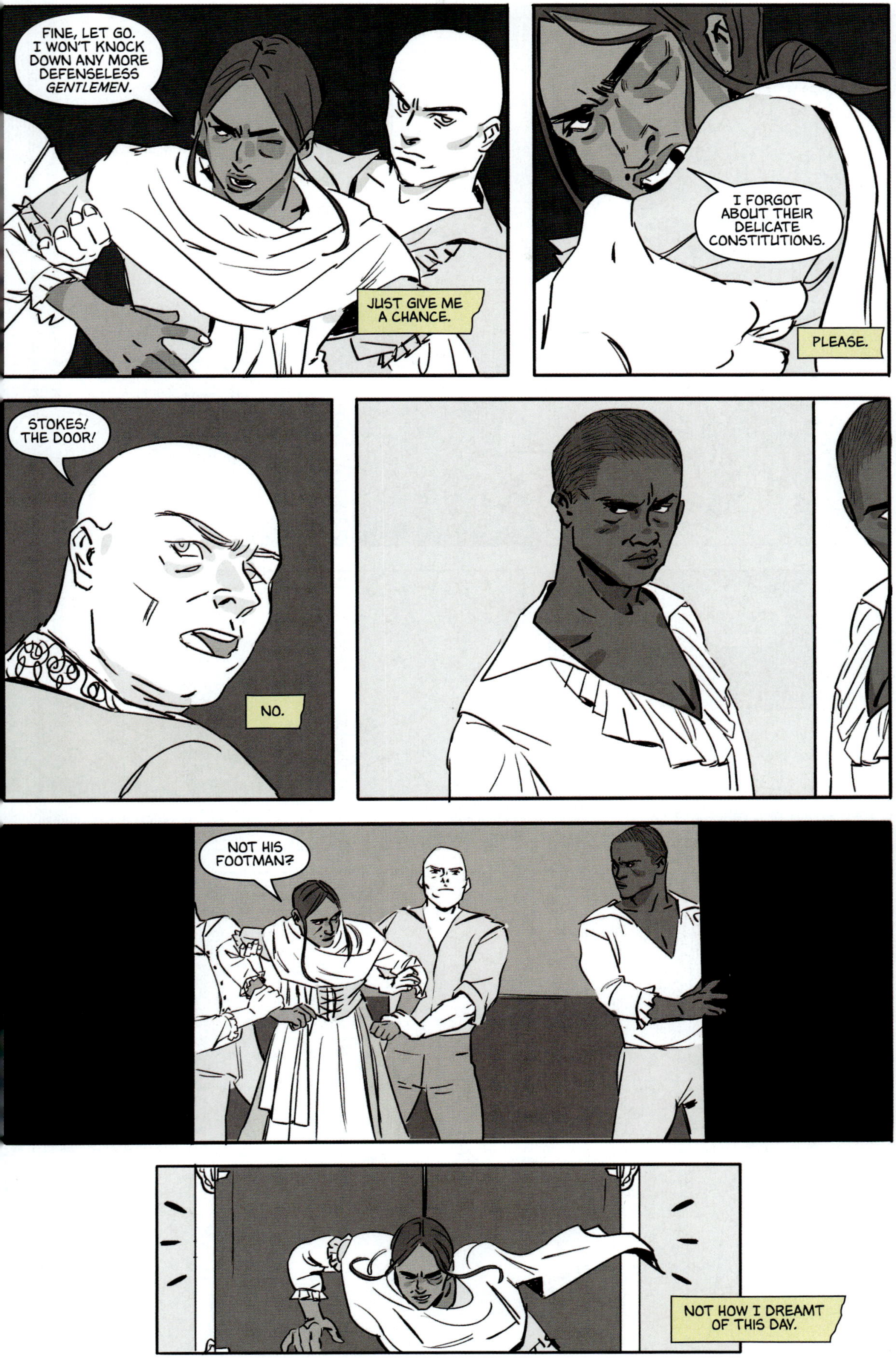

FINE, LET GO. I WON'T KNOCK DOWN ANY MORE DEFENSELESS *GENTLEMEN*.
JUST GIVE ME A CHANCE.
I FORGOT ABOUT THEIR DELICATE CONSTITUTIONS.
PLEASE.
STOKES! THE DOOR!
NO.
NOT HIS FOOTMAN?
NOT HOW I DREAMT OF THIS DAY.

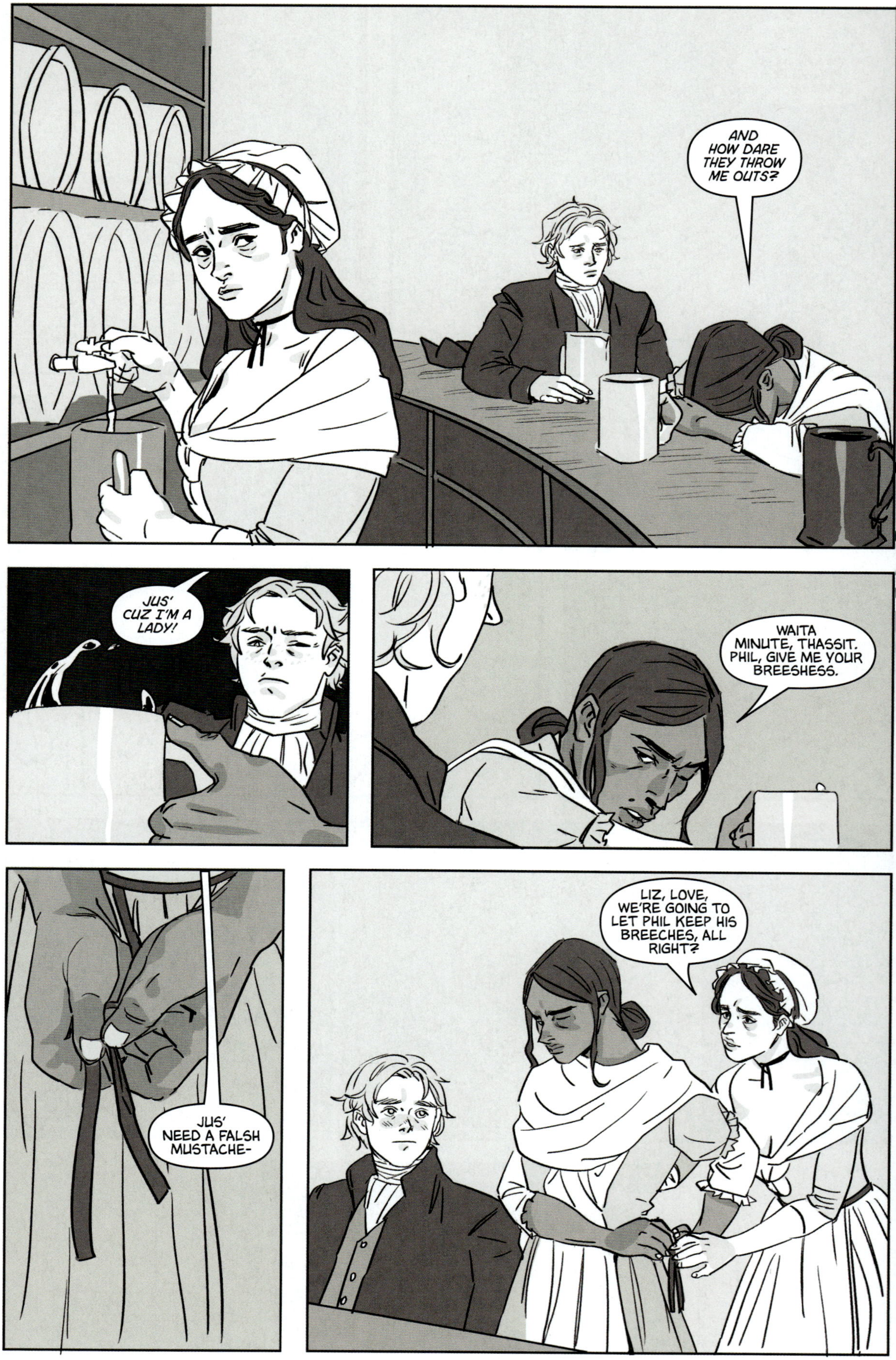
AND HOW DARE THEY THROW ME OUTS?
JUS' CUZ I'M A LADY!
WAITA MINUTE, THASSIT. PHIL, GIVE ME YOUR BREESHESS.
JUS' NEED A FALSH MUSTACHE-
LIZ, LOVE, WE'RE GOING TO LET PHIL KEEP HIS BREECHES, ALL RIGHT?

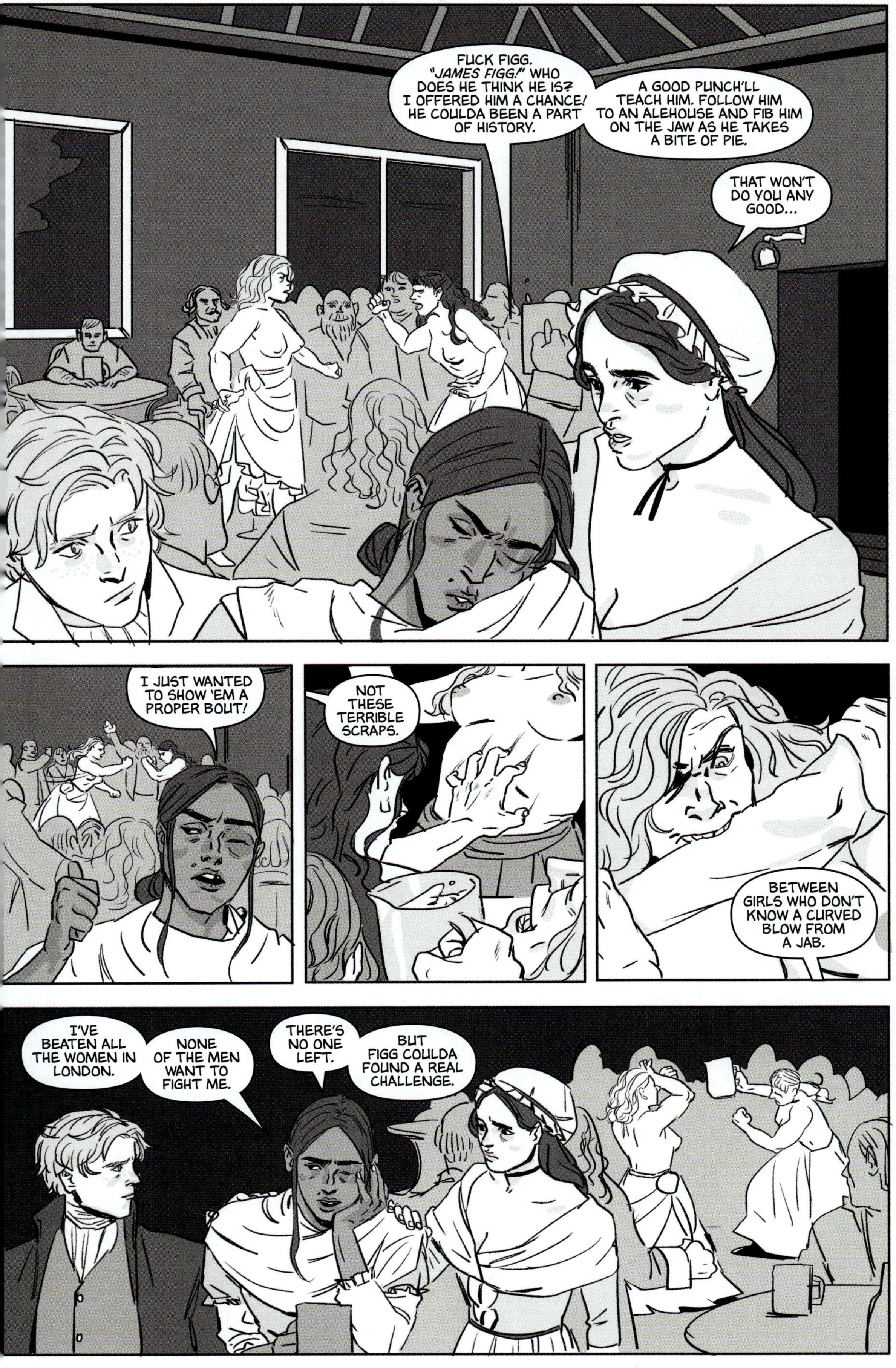
FUCK FIGG. "JAMES FIGG!" WHO DOES HE THINK HE IS? I OFFERED HIM A CHANCE! HE COULDA BEEN A PART OF HISTORY.
A GOOD PUNCH'LL TEACH HIM. FOLLOW HIM TO AN ALEHOUSE AND FIB HIM ON THE JAW AS HE TAKES A BITE OF PIE.
THAT WON'T DO YOU ANY GOOD...
I JUST WANTED TO SHOW 'EM A PROPER BOUT!
NOT THESE TERRIBLE SCRAPS.
BETWEEN GIRLS WHO DON'T KNOW A CURVED BLOW FROM A JAB.
I'VE BEATEN ALL THE WOMEN IN LONDON.
NONE OF THE MEN WANT TO FIGHT ME.
THERE'S NO ONE LEFT.
BUT FIGG COULDA FOUND A REAL CHALLENGE.

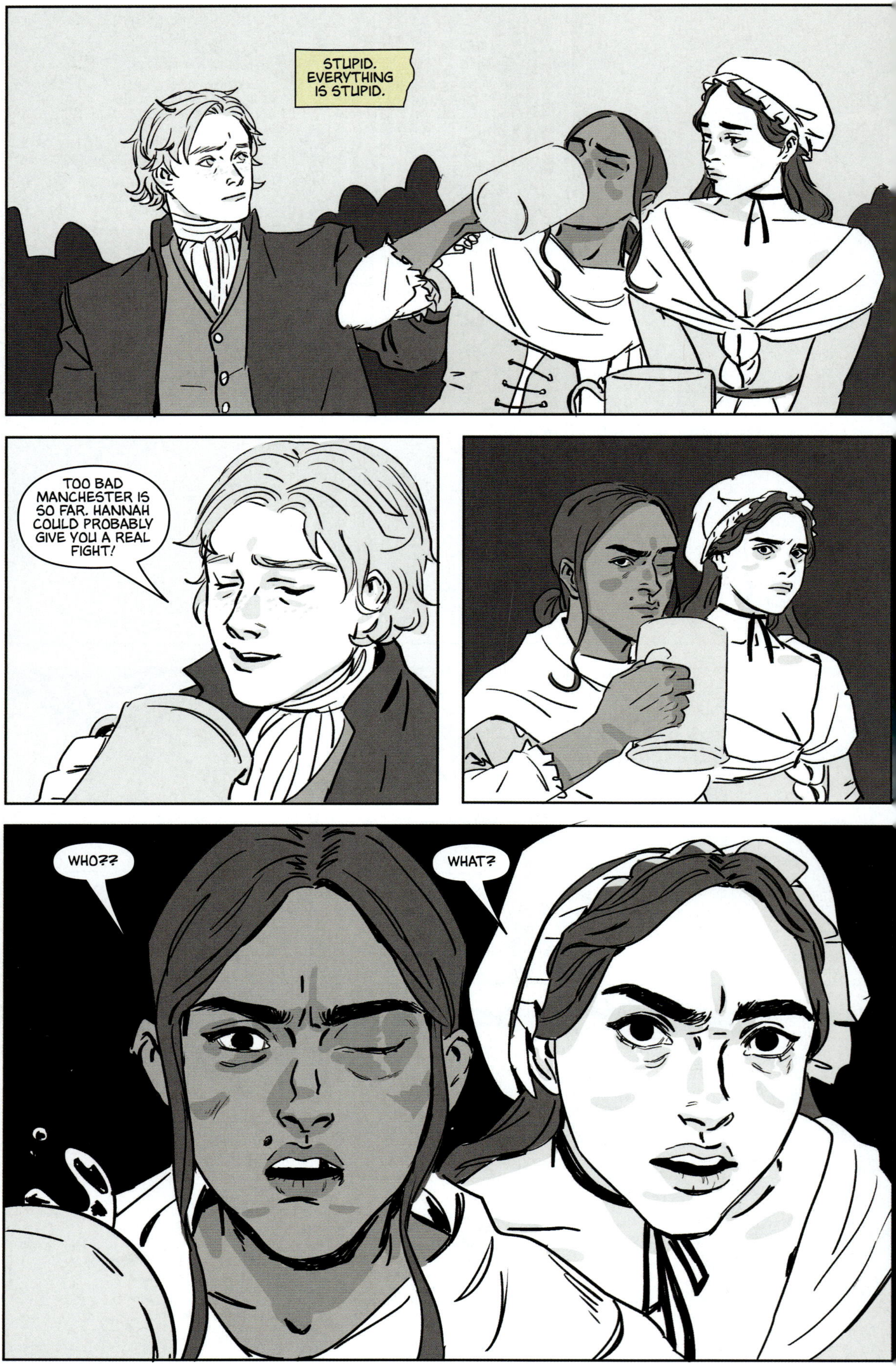
STUPID. EVERYTHING IS STUPID.
TOO BAD MANCHESTER IS SO FAR. HANNAH COULD PROBABLY GIVE YOU A REAL FIGHT!
WHO??
WHAT?

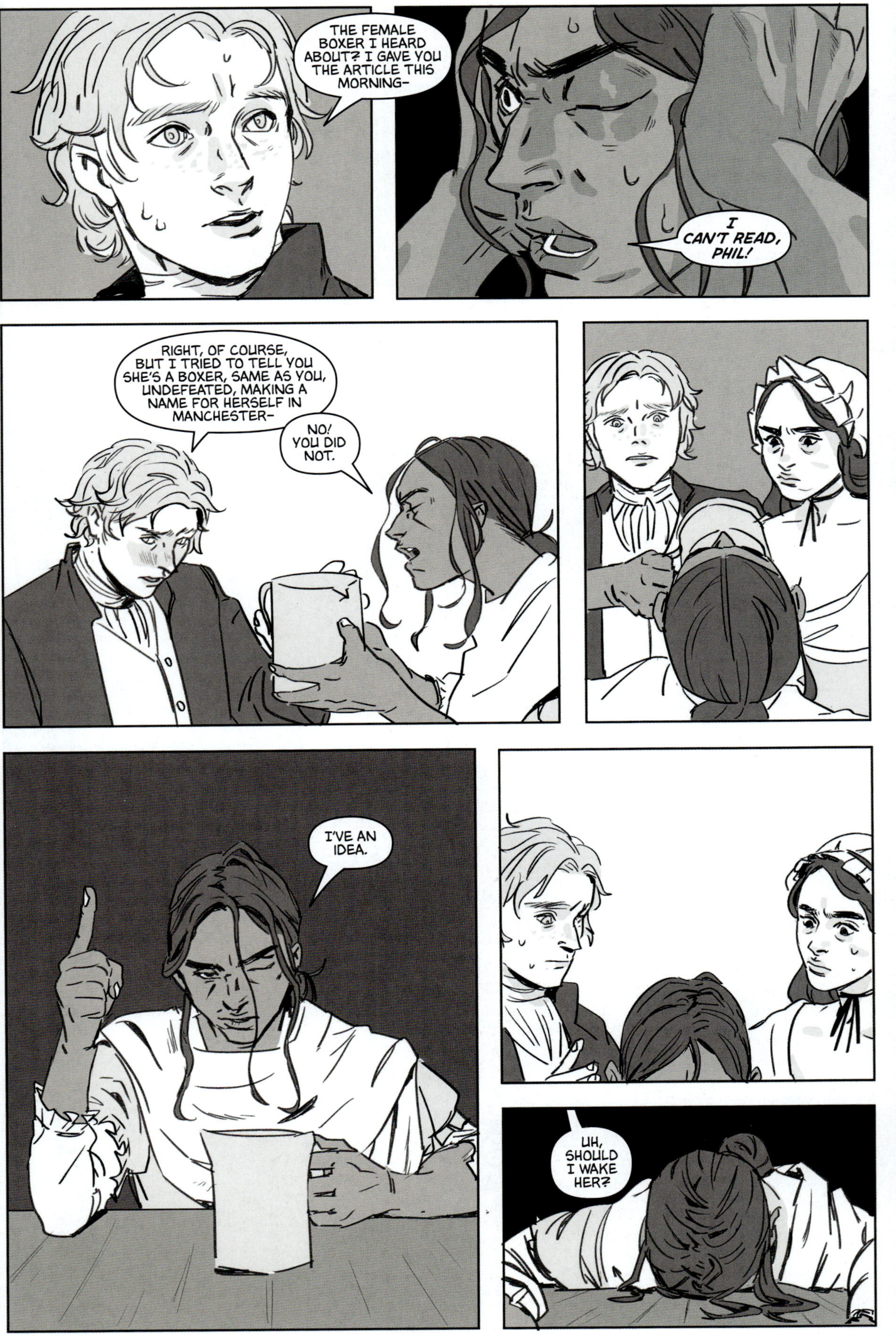
THE FEMALE BOXER I HEARD ABOUT? I GAVE YOU THE ARTICLE THIS MORNING–
I CAN'T READ, PHIL!
RIGHT, OF COURSE, BUT I TRIED TO TELL YOU SHE'S A BOXER, SAME AS YOU, UNDEFEATED, MAKING A NAME FOR HERSELF IN MANCHESTER–
NO! YOU DID NOT.
I'VE AN IDEA.
UH, SHOULD I WAKE HER?

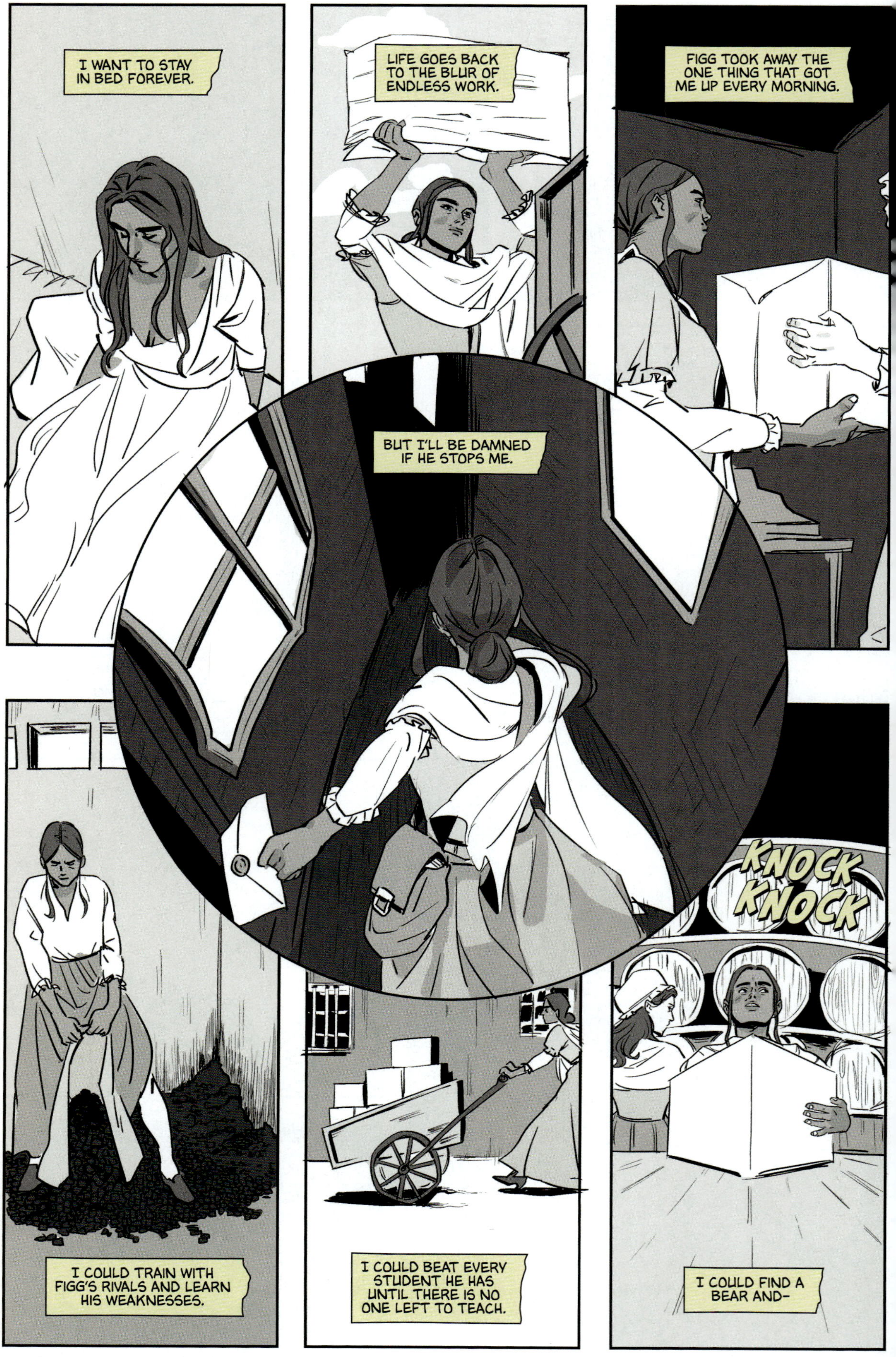
I WANT TO STAY IN BED FOREVER.
LIFE GOES BACK TO THE BLUR OF ENDLESS WORK.
FIGG TOOK AWAY THE ONE THING THAT GOT ME UP EVERY MORNING.
BUT I'LL BE DAMNED IF HE STOPS ME.
I COULD TRAIN WITH FIGG'S RIVALS AND LEARN HIS WEAKNESSES.
I COULD BEAT EVERY STUDENT HE HAS UNTIL THERE IS NO ONE LEFT TO TEACH.
KNOCK KNOCK
I COULD FIND A BEAR AND–

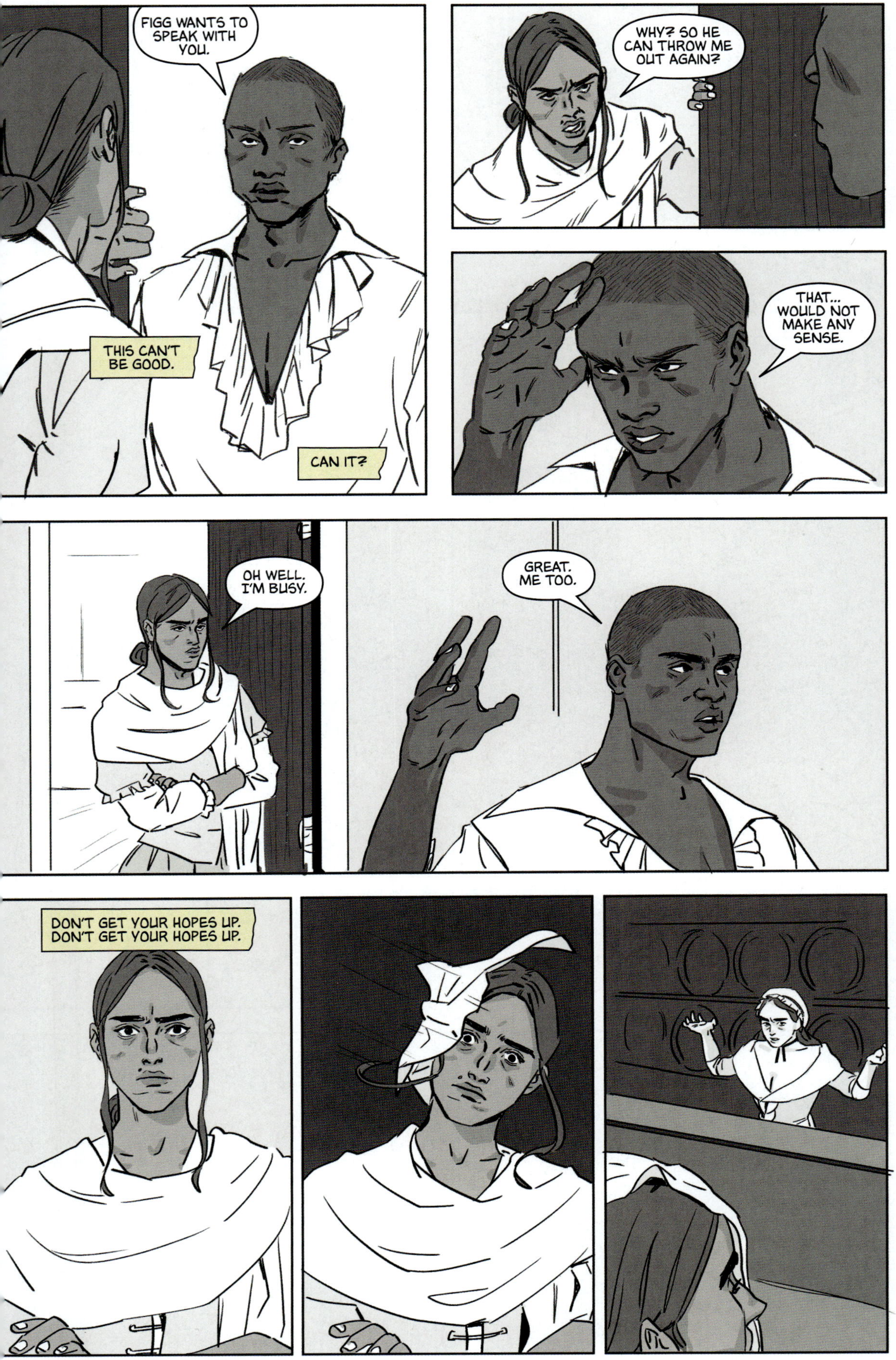
FIGG WANTS TO SPEAK WITH YOU.
THIS CAN'T BE GOOD.
CAN IT?
WHY? SO HE CAN THROW ME OUT AGAIN?
THAT... WOULD NOT MAKE ANY SENSE.
OH WELL. I'M BUSY.
GREAT. ME TOO.
DON'T GET YOUR HOPES UP. DON'T GET YOUR HOPES UP.

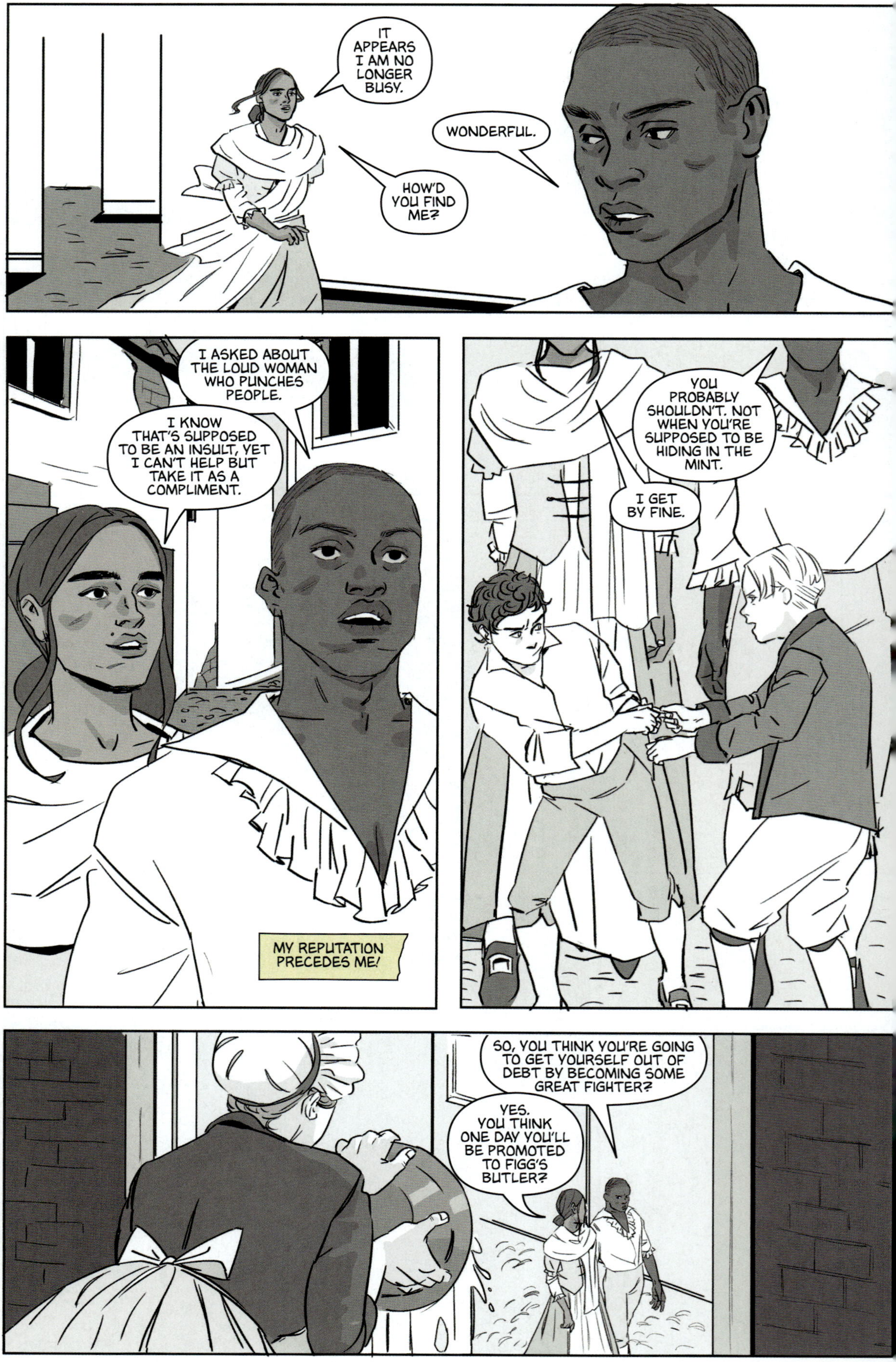
IT APPEARS I AM NO LONGER BUSY.
WONDERFUL.
HOW'D YOU FIND ME?
I ASKED ABOUT THE LOUD WOMAN WHO PUNCHES PEOPLE.
I KNOW THAT'S SUPPOSED TO BE AN INSULT, YET I CAN'T HELP BUT TAKE IT AS A COMPLIMENT.
MY REPUTATION PRECEDES ME!
YOU PROBABLY SHOULDN'T. NOT WHEN YOU'RE SUPPOSED TO BE HIDING IN THE MINT.
I GET BY FINE.
SO, YOU THINK YOU'RE GOING TO GET YOURSELF OUT OF DEBT BY BECOMING SOME GREAT FIGHTER?
YES. YOU THINK ONE DAY YOU'LL BE PROMOTED TO FIGG'S BUTLER?

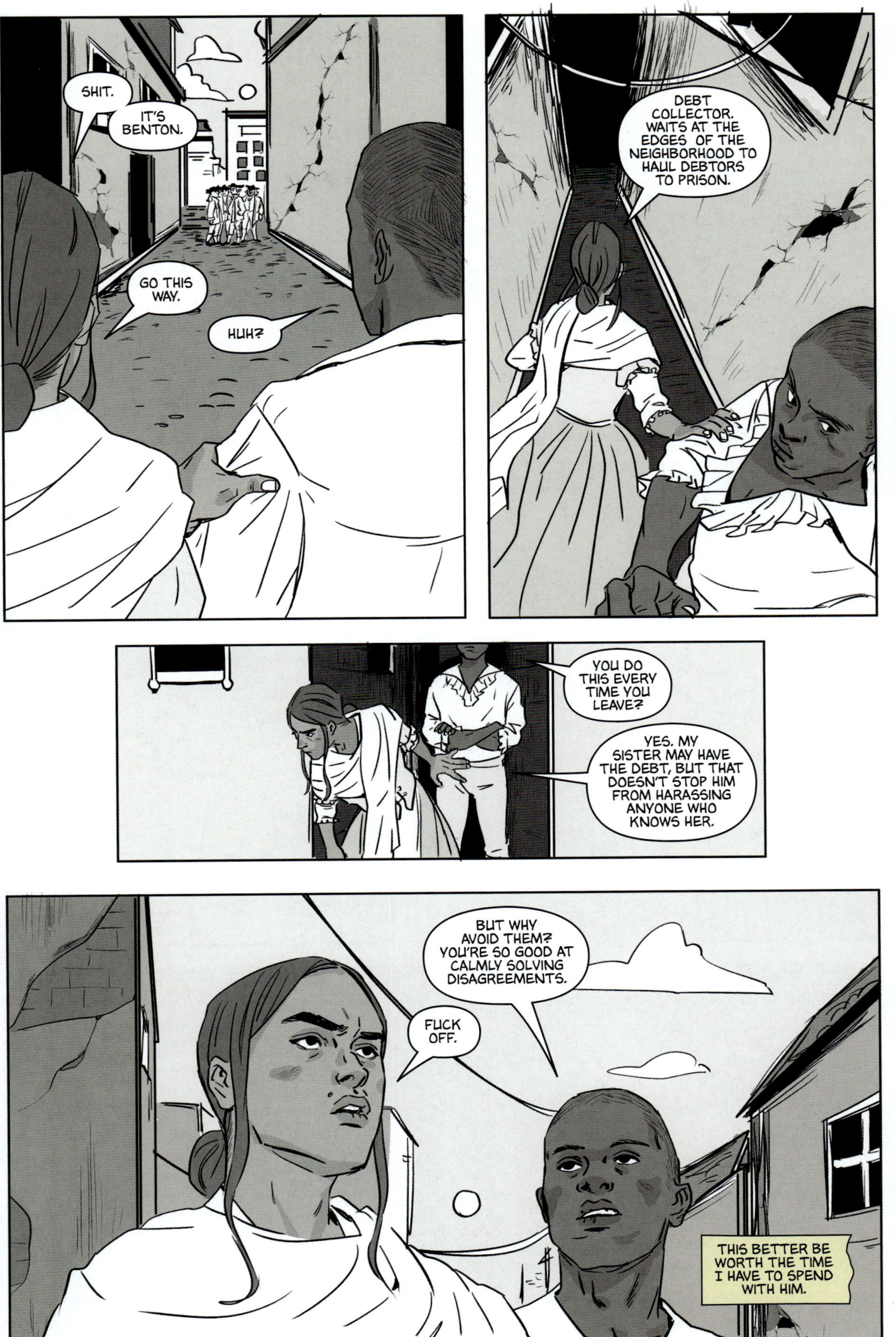
SHIT.
IT'S BENTON.
GO THIS WAY.
HUH?
DEBT COLLECTOR. WAITS AT THE EDGES OF THE NEIGHBORHOOD TO HAUL DEBTORS TO PRISON.
YOU DO THIS EVERY TIME YOU LEAVE?
YES. MY SISTER MAY HAVE THE DEBT, BUT THAT DOESN'T STOP HIM FROM HARASSING ANYONE WHO KNOWS HER.
BUT WHY AVOID THEM? YOU'RE SO GOOD AT CALMLY SOLVING DISAGREEMENTS.
FUCK OFF.
THIS BETTER BE WORTH THE TIME I HAVE TO SPEND WITH HIM.

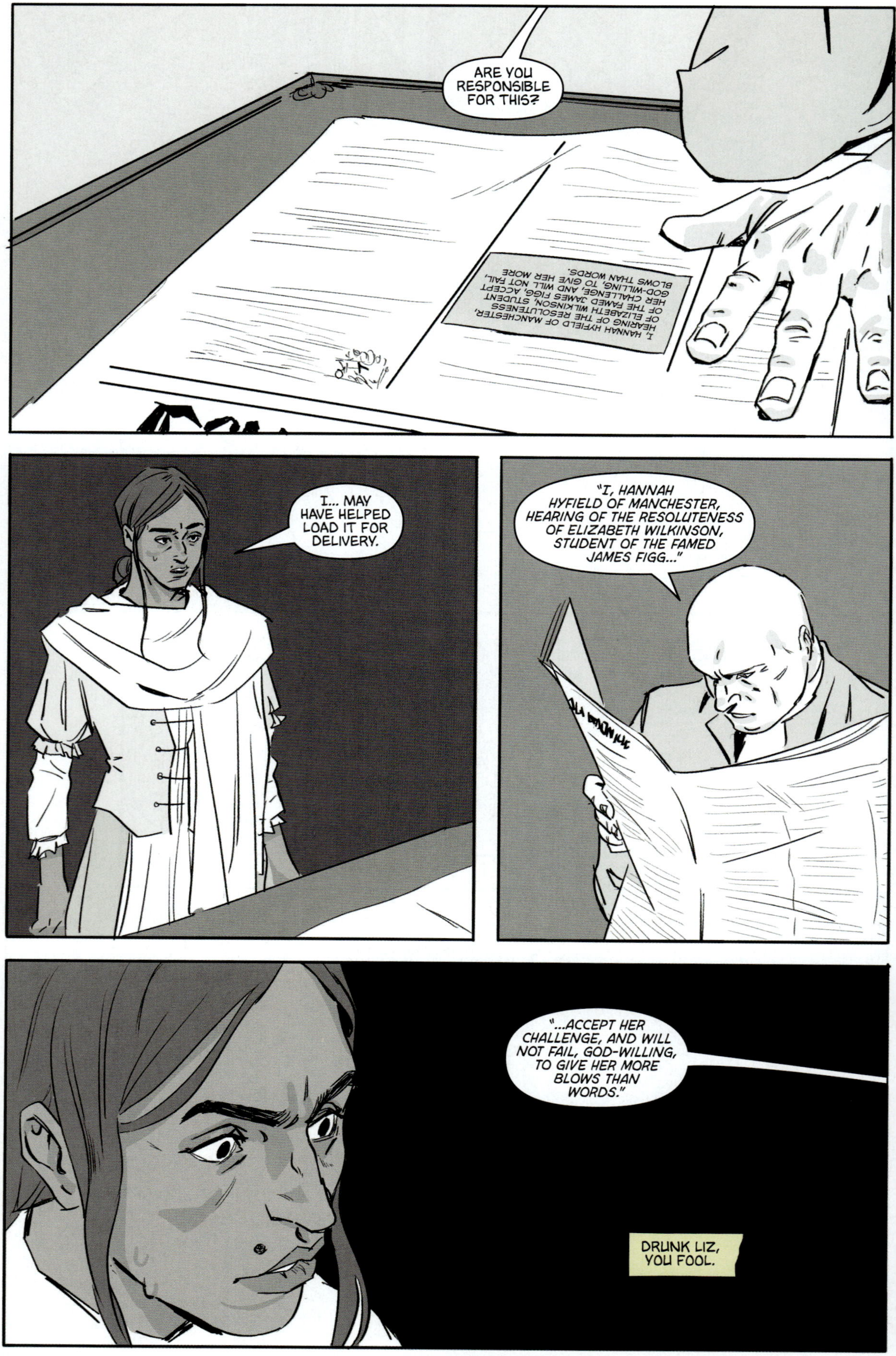

ARE YOU RESPONSIBLE FOR THIS?
I, HANNAH HYFIELD OF MANCHESTER, HEARING OF THE RESOLUTENESS OF ELIZABETH WILKINSON, STUDENT OF THE FAMED JAMES FIGG, ACCEPT HER CHALLENGE, AND WILL NOT FAIL, GOD-WILLING, TO GIVE HER MORE BLOWS THAN WORDS.
I... MAY HAVE HELPED LOAD IT FOR DELIVERY.
"I, HANNAH HYFIELD OF MANCHESTER, HEARING OF THE RESOLUTENESS OF ELIZABETH WILKINSON, STUDENT OF THE FAMED JAMES FIGG..."
"...ACCEPT HER CHALLENGE, AND WILL NOT FAIL, GOD-WILLING, TO GIVE HER MORE BLOWS THAN WORDS."
DRUNK LIZ, YOU FOOL.

A PUBLIC CHALLENGE. CLEVER.

PHIL TRULY TOOK OUT THE ADVERTISEMENT TO CHALLENGE THAT MANCHESTER WOMAN.

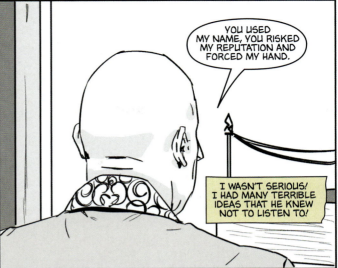

YOU USED MY NAME, YOU RISKED MY REPUTATION AND FORCED MY HAND.

I WASN'T SERIOUS! I HAD MANY TERRIBLE IDEAS THAT HE KNEW NOT TO LISTEN TO!

THIS IS A DISASTER.

YOU BETTER HOPE YOU STAY CLEVER.

WHAT?

YOUR FIGHT'S IN THREE WEEKS.

DRUNK LIZ, YOU GENIUS.

"I, Elizabeth Wilkinson, of Clerkenwell, having had some words with Hannah Hyfield, and requiring satisfaction, do invite her to meet me upon the stage, and box me for three guineas; each woman holding half-a-crown in each hand, and the first woman that drops the money to lose the battle."

(Original challenge printed in the Daily Post, 1722)

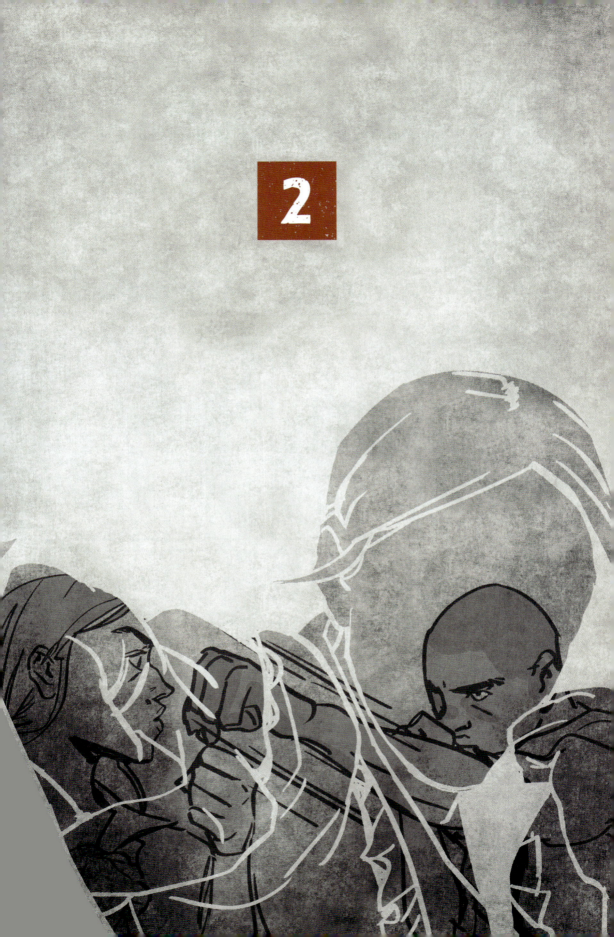

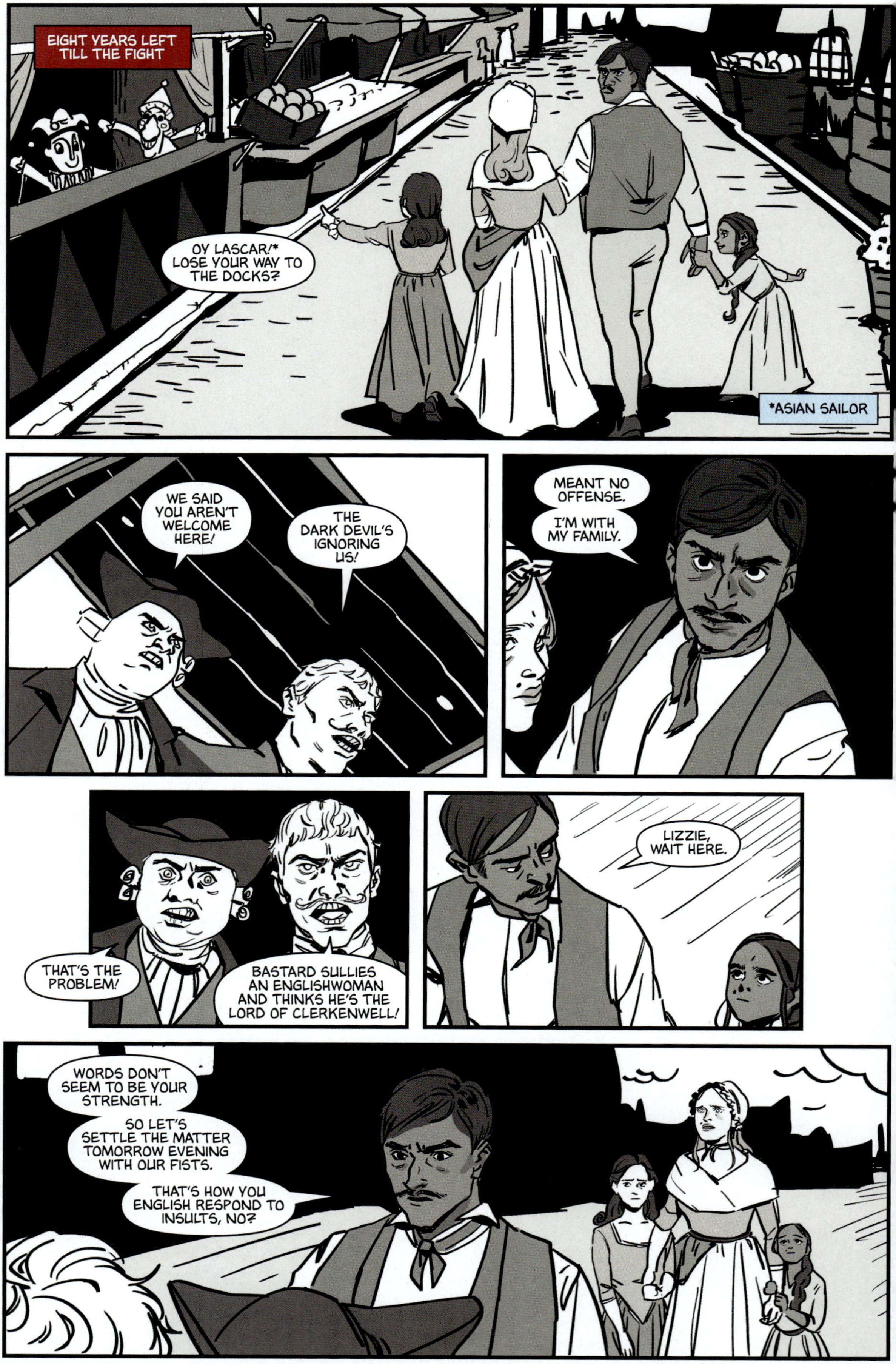
EIGHT YEARS LEFT TILL THE FIGHT
OY LASCAR!* LOSE YOUR WAY TO THE DOCKS?
*ASIAN SAILOR
WE SAID YOU AREN'T WELCOME HERE!
THE DARK DEVIL'S IGNORING US!
MEANT NO OFFENSE.
I'M WITH MY FAMILY.
THAT'S THE PROBLEM!
BASTARD SULLIES AN ENGLISHWOMAN AND THINKS HE'S THE LORD OF CLERKENWELL!
LIZZIE, WAIT HERE.
WORDS DON'T SEEM TO BE YOUR STRENGTH.
SO LET'S SETTLE THE MATTER TOMORROW EVENING WITH OUR FISTS.
THAT'S HOW YOU ENGLISH RESPOND TO INSULTS, NO?

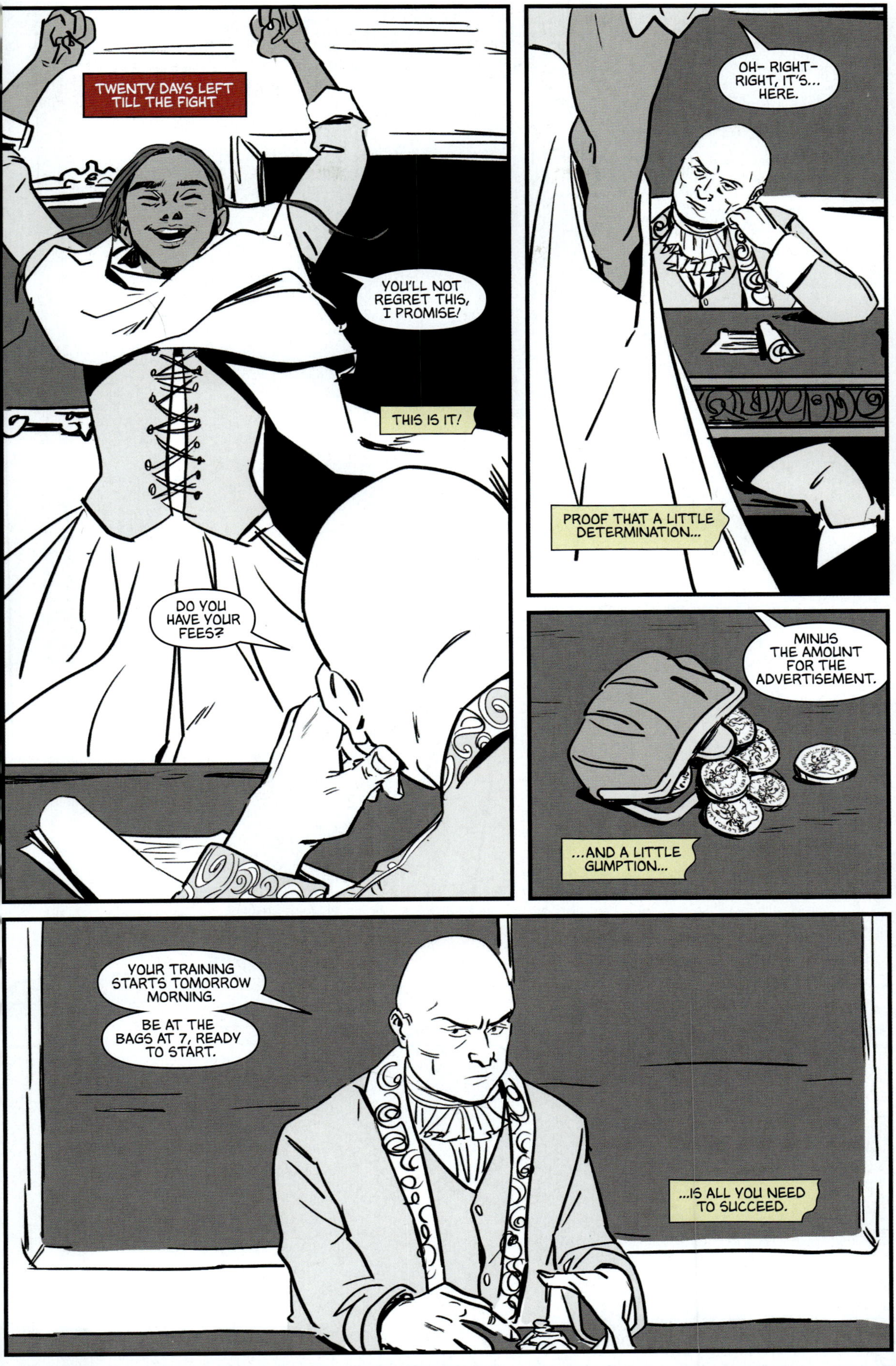
TWENTY DAYS LEFT TILL THE FIGHT
YOU'LL NOT REGRET THIS, I PROMISE!
THIS IS IT!
DO YOU HAVE YOUR FEES?
OH- RIGHT- RIGHT, IT'S... HERE.
PROOF THAT A LITTLE DETERMINATION...
MINUS THE AMOUNT FOR THE ADVERTISEMENT.
...AND A LITTLE GUMPTION...
YOUR TRAINING STARTS TOMORROW MORNING.
BE AT THE BAGS AT 7, READY TO START.
...IS ALL YOU NEED TO SUCCEED.

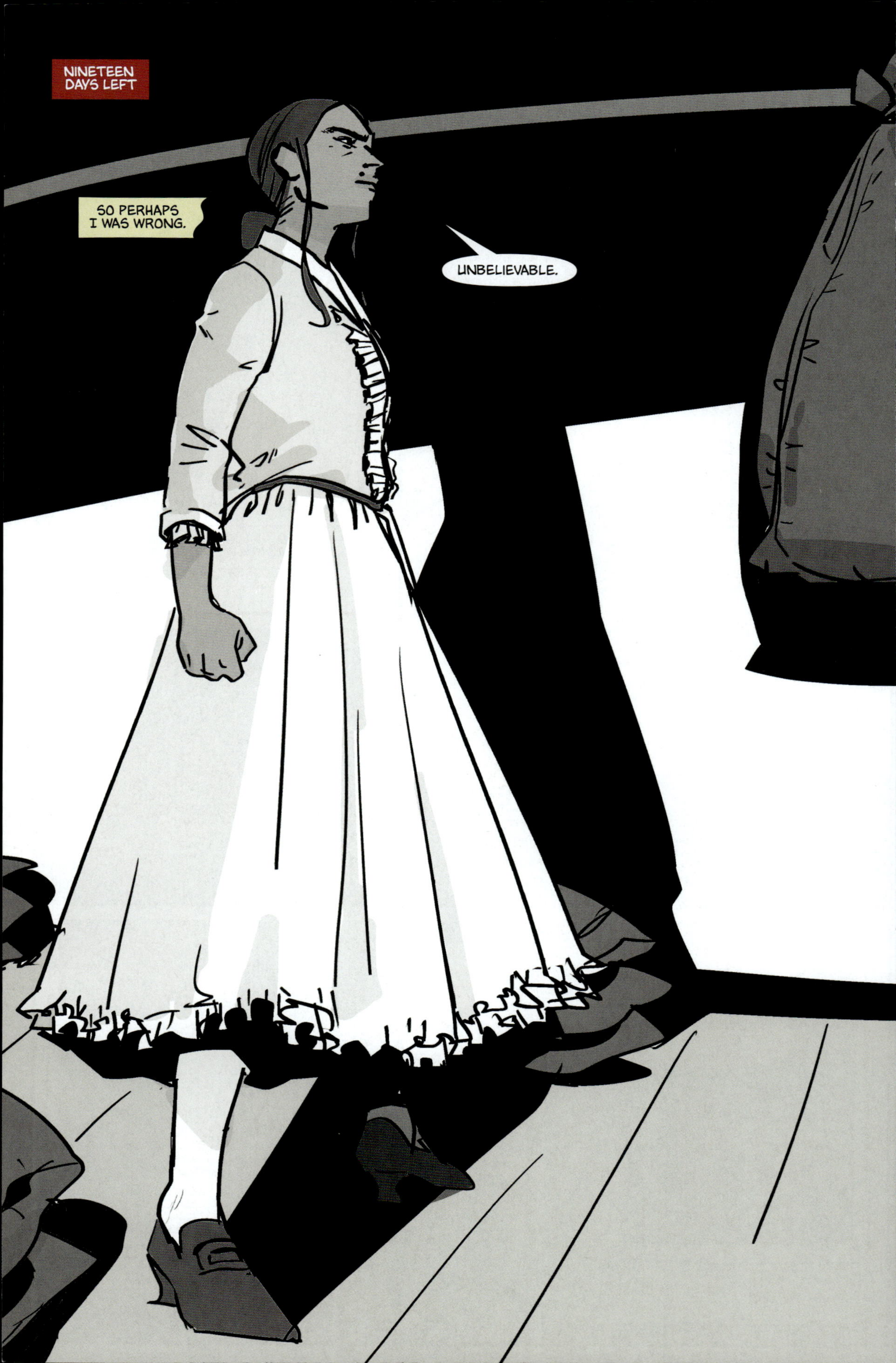
NINETEEN DAYS LEFT
SO PERHAPS I WAS WRONG.
UNBELIEVABLE.

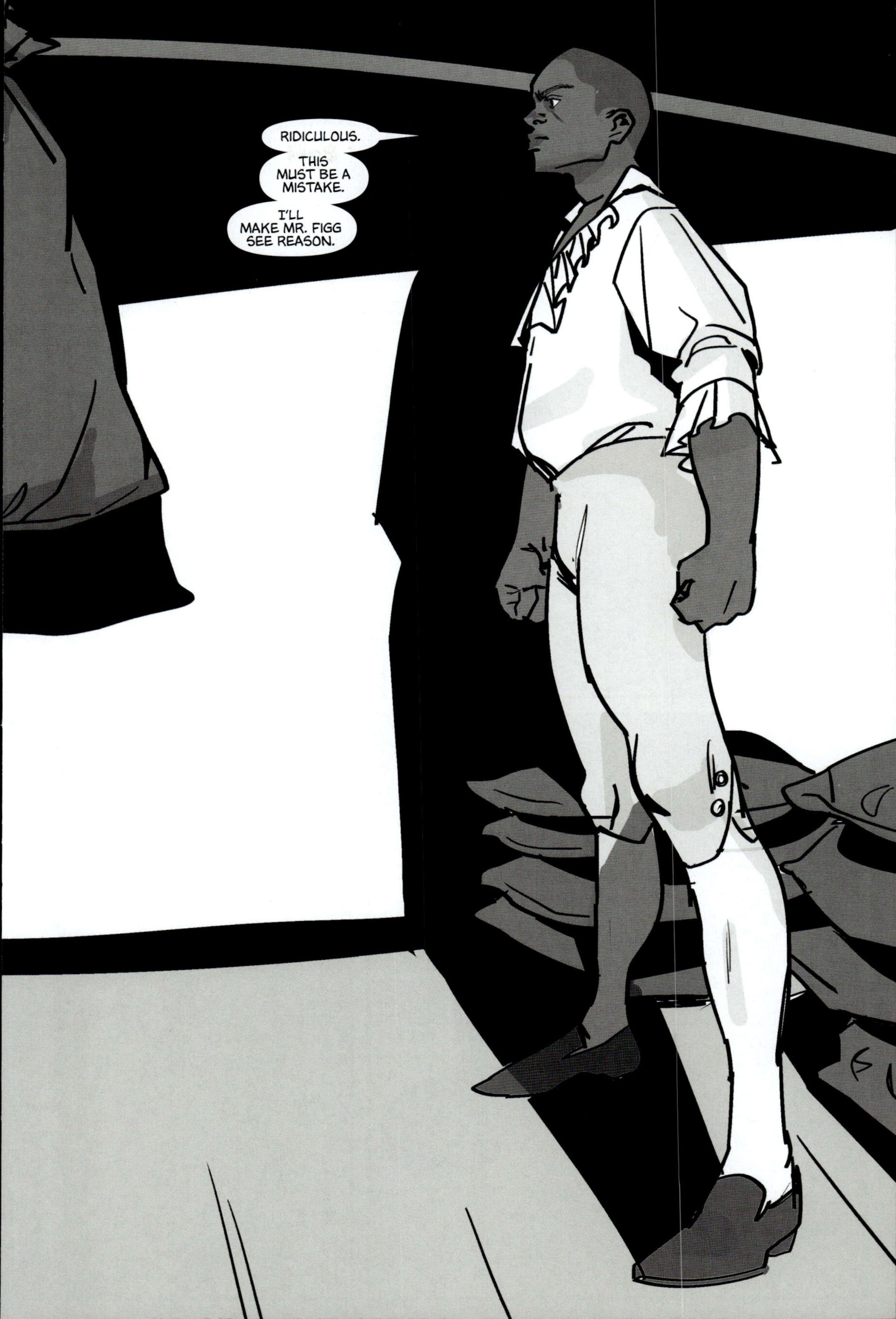
RIDICULOUS.
THIS MUST BE A MISTAKE.
I'LL MAKE MR. FIGG SEE REASON.

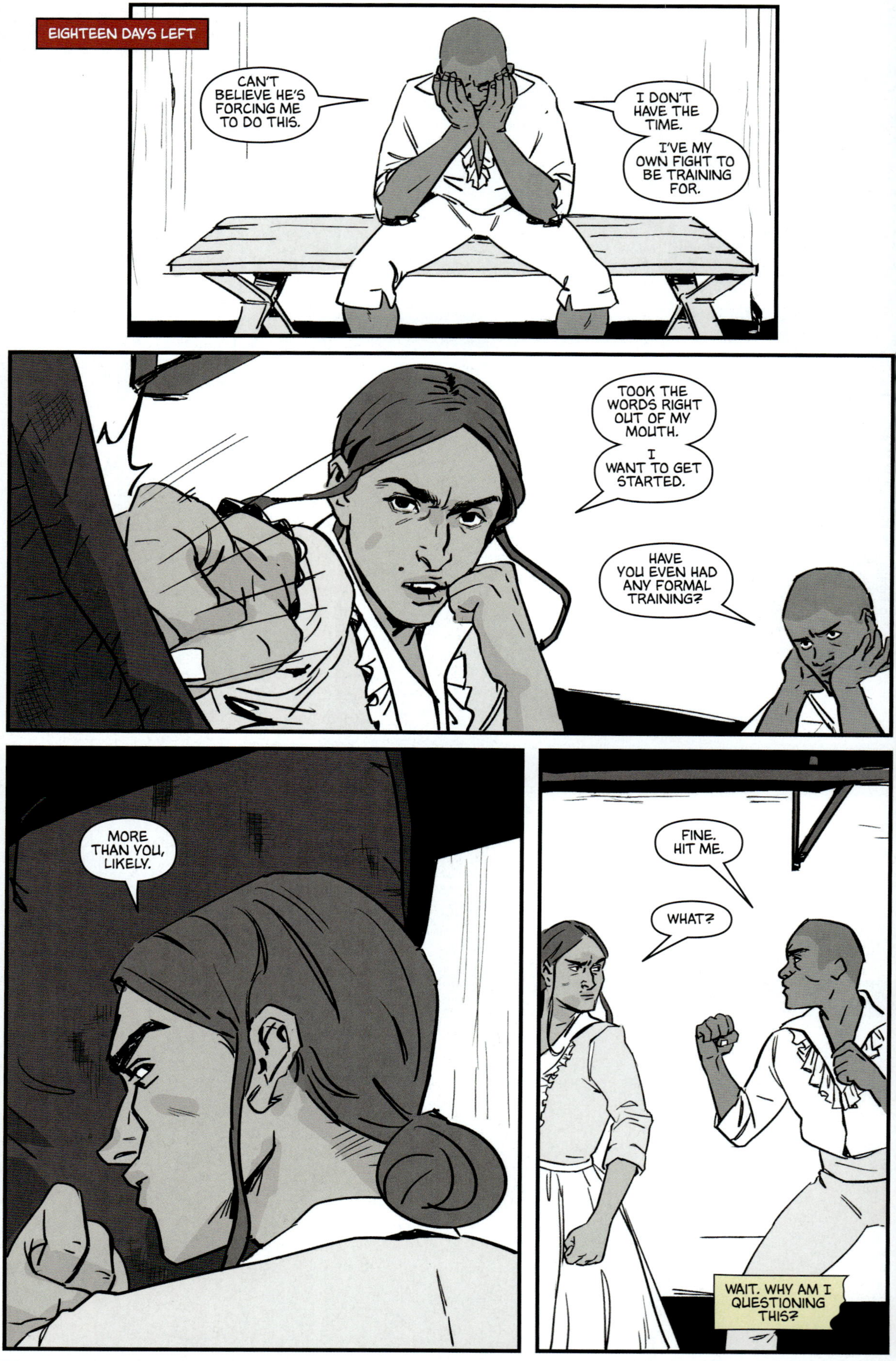
EIGHTEEN DAYS LEFT
CAN'T BELIEVE HE'S FORCING ME TO DO THIS.
I DON'T HAVE THE TIME.
I'VE MY OWN FIGHT TO BE TRAINING FOR.
TOOK THE WORDS RIGHT OUT OF MY MOUTH.
I WANT TO GET STARTED.
HAVE YOU EVEN HAD ANY FORMAL TRAINING?
MORE THAN YOU, LIKELY.
FINE. HIT ME.
WHAT?
WAIT. WHY AM I QUESTIONING THIS?

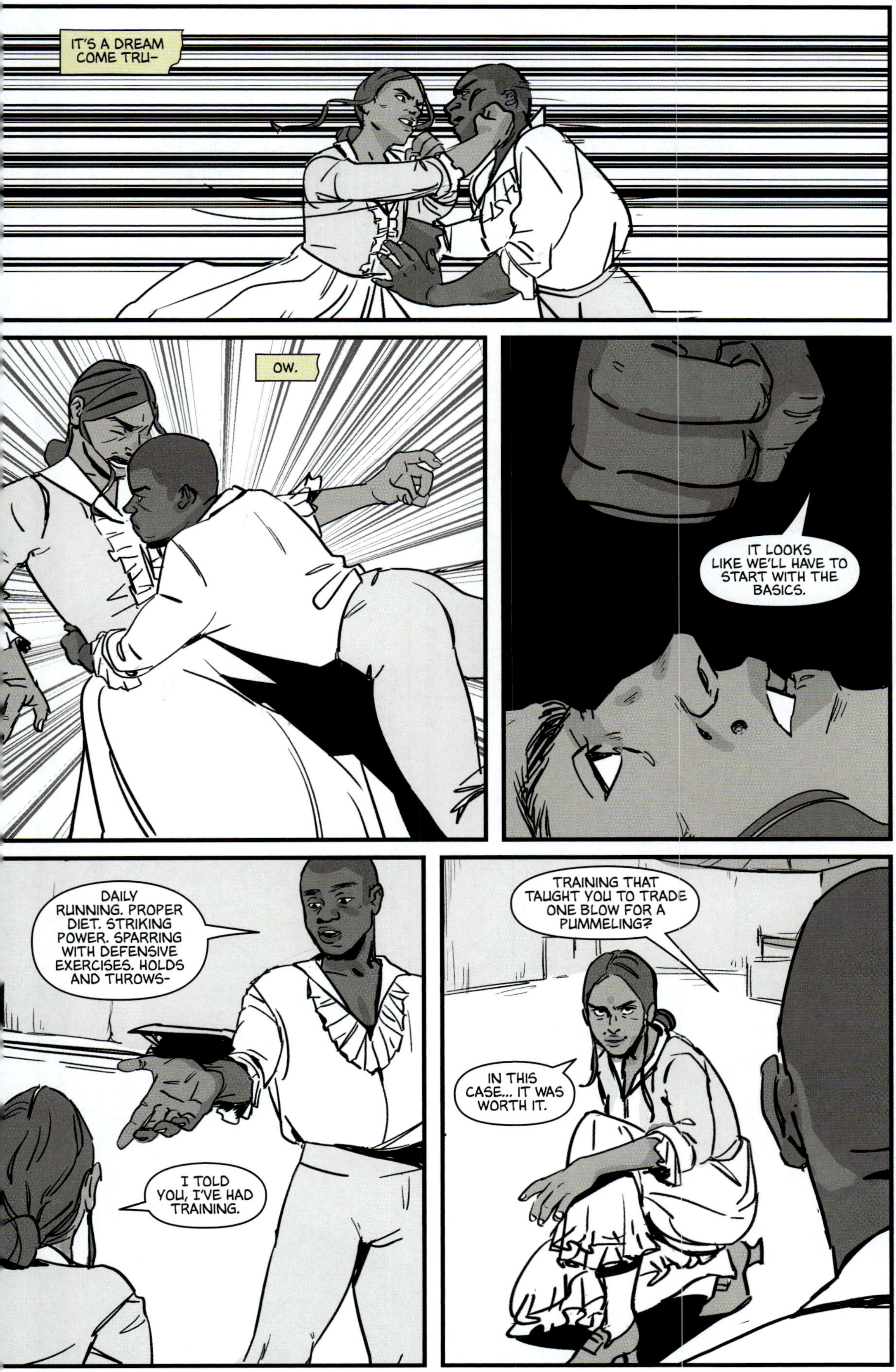
IT'S A DREAM COME TRU-
OW.
IT LOOKS LIKE WE'LL HAVE TO START WITH THE BASICS.
DAILY RUNNING. PROPER DIET. STRIKING POWER. SPARRING WITH DEFENSIVE EXERCISES. HOLDS AND THROWS-
I TOLD YOU, I'VE HAD TRAINING.
TRAINING THAT TAUGHT YOU TO TRADE ONE BLOW FOR A PUMMELING?
IN THIS CASE... IT WAS WORTH IT.

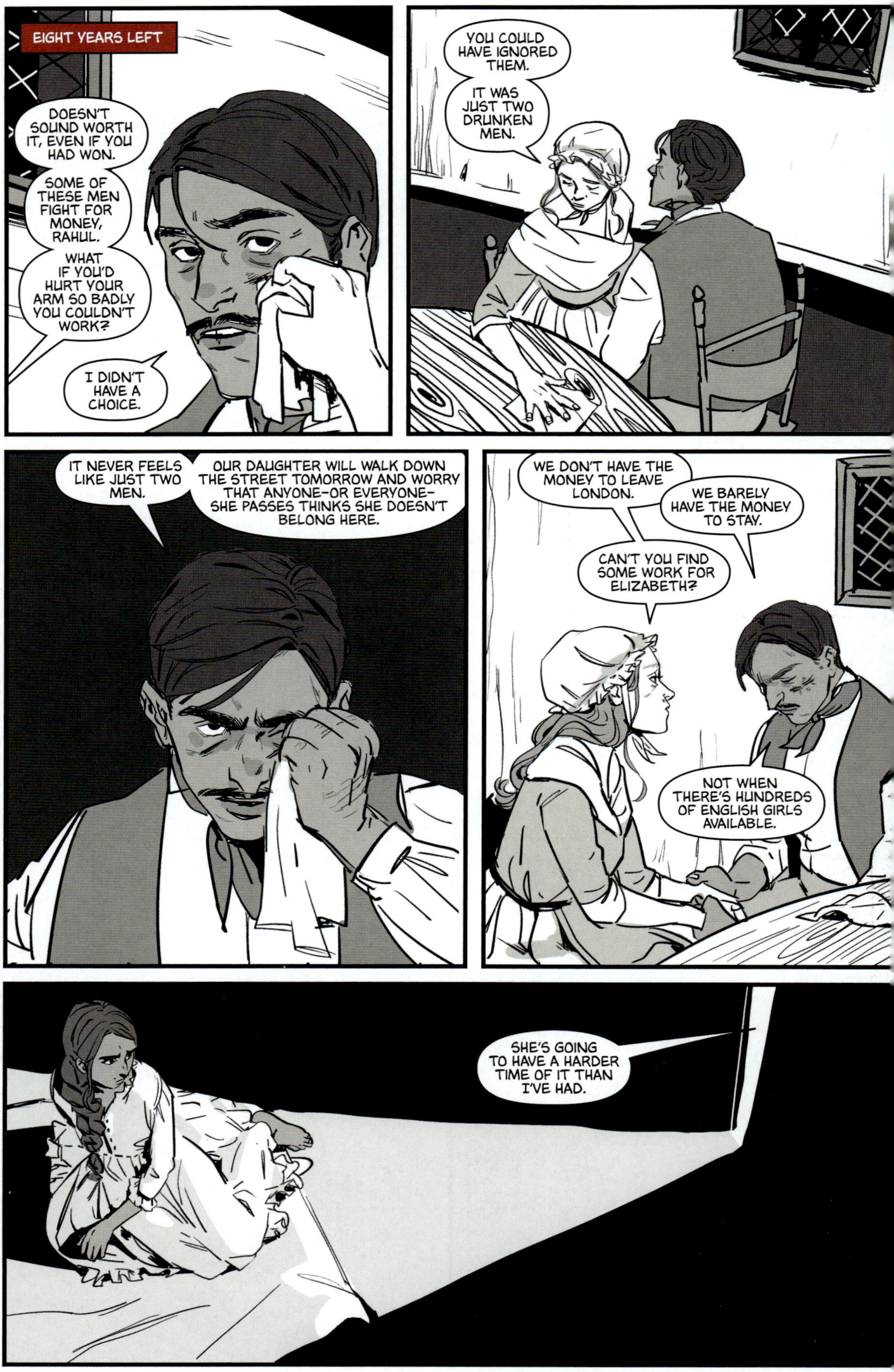
EIGHT YEARS LEFT
DOESN'T SOUND WORTH IT, EVEN IF YOU HAD WON.
SOME OF THESE MEN FIGHT FOR MONEY, RAHUL.
WHAT IF YOU'D HURT YOUR ARM SO BADLY YOU COULDN'T WORK?
I DIDN'T HAVE A CHOICE.
YOU COULD HAVE IGNORED THEM.
IT WAS JUST TWO DRUNKEN MEN.
IT NEVER FEELS LIKE JUST TWO MEN.
OUR DAUGHTER WILL WALK DOWN THE STREET TOMORROW AND WORRY THAT ANYONE–OR EVERYONE–SHE PASSES THINKS SHE DOESN'T BELONG HERE.
WE DON'T HAVE THE MONEY TO LEAVE LONDON.
WE BARELY HAVE THE MONEY TO STAY.
CAN'T YOU FIND SOME WORK FOR ELIZABETH?
NOT WHEN THERE'S HUNDREDS OF ENGLISH GIRLS AVAILABLE.
SHE'S GOING TO HAVE A HARDER TIME OF IT THAN I'VE HAD.

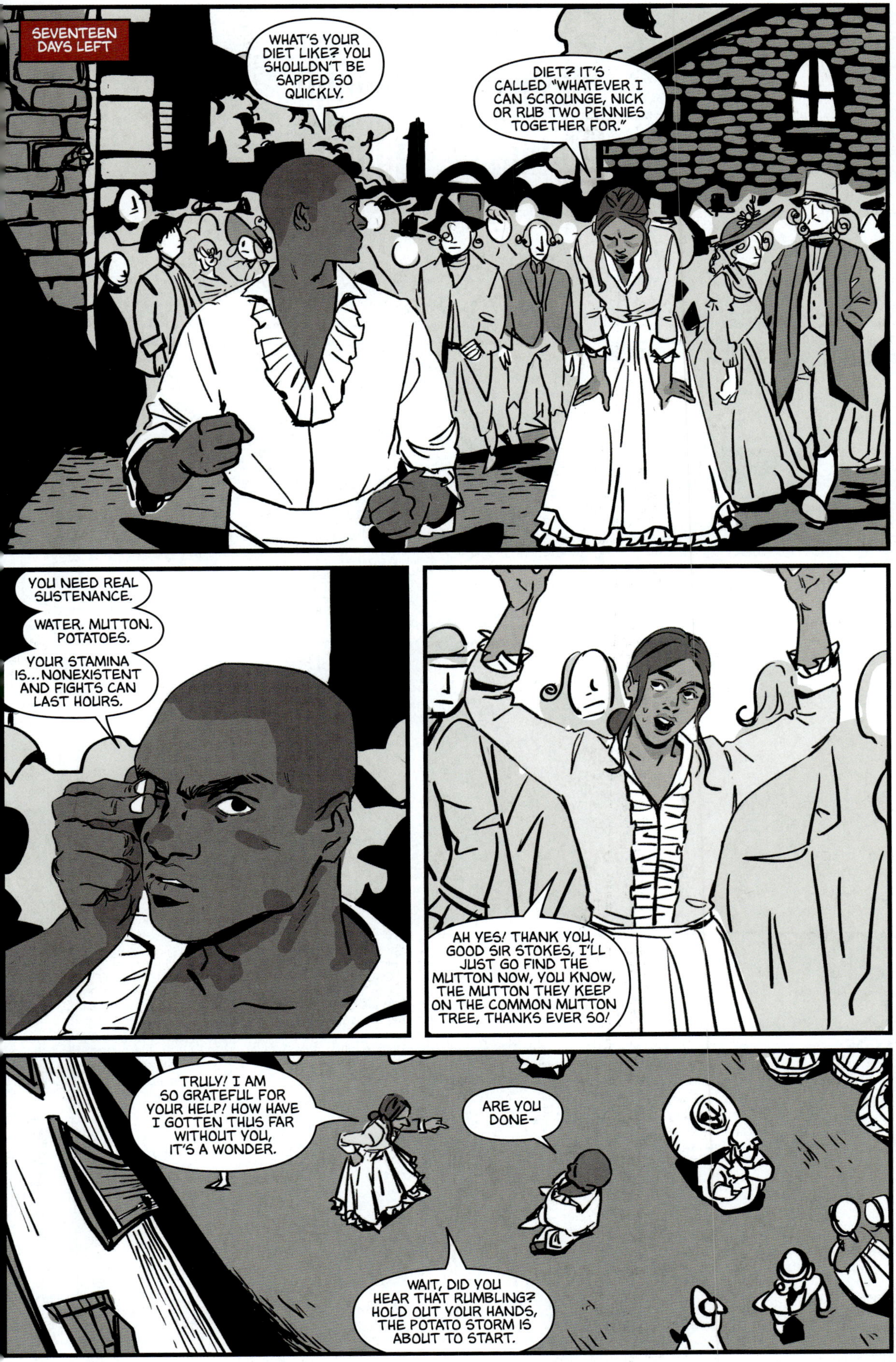
SEVENTEEN DAYS LEFT
WHAT'S YOUR DIET LIKE? YOU SHOULDN'T BE SAPPED SO QUICKLY.
DIET? IT'S CALLED "WHATEVER I CAN SCROUNGE, NICK OR RUB TWO PENNIES TOGETHER FOR."
YOU NEED REAL SUSTENANCE.
WATER. MUTTON. POTATOES.
YOUR STAMINA IS...NONEXISTENT AND FIGHTS CAN LAST HOURS.
AH YES! THANK YOU, GOOD SIR STOKES, I'LL JUST GO FIND THE MUTTON NOW, YOU KNOW, THE MUTTON THEY KEEP ON THE COMMON MUTTON TREE, THANKS EVER SO!
TRULY! I AM SO GRATEFUL FOR YOUR HELP! HOW HAVE I GOTTEN THUS FAR WITHOUT YOU, IT'S A WONDER.
ARE YOU DONE-
WAIT, DID YOU HEAR THAT RUMBLING? HOLD OUT YOUR HANDS, THE POTATO STORM IS ABOUT TO START.

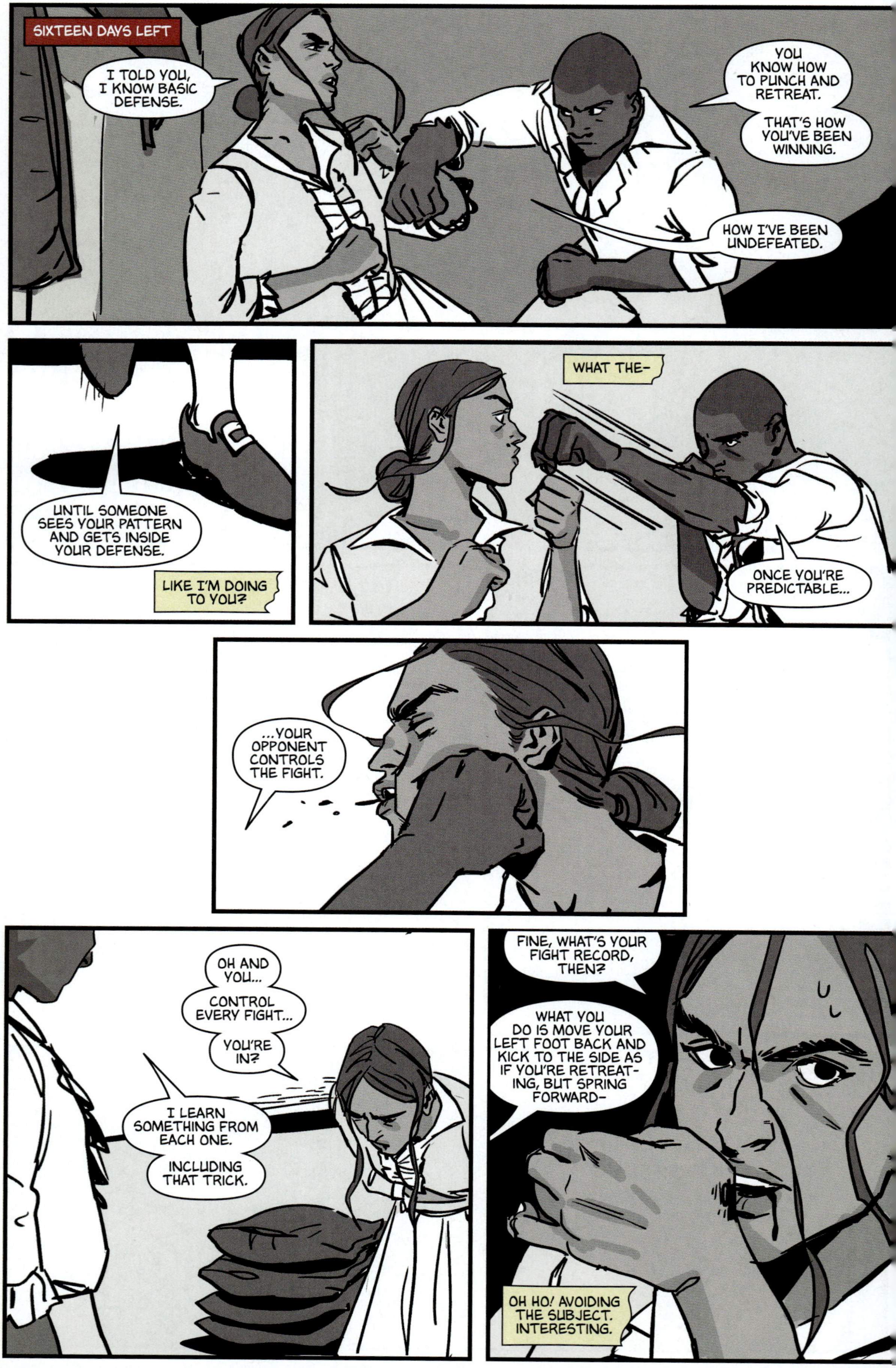
SIXTEEN DAYS LEFT
I TOLD YOU, I KNOW BASIC DEFENSE.
YOU KNOW HOW TO PUNCH AND RETREAT.
THAT'S HOW YOU'VE BEEN WINNING.
HOW I'VE BEEN UNDEFEATED.
UNTIL SOMEONE SEES YOUR PATTERN AND GETS INSIDE YOUR DEFENSE.
LIKE I'M DOING TO YOU?
WHAT THE-
ONCE YOU'RE PREDICTABLE...
...YOUR OPPONENT CONTROLS THE FIGHT.
OH AND YOU...
CONTROL EVERY FIGHT...
YOU'RE IN?
I LEARN SOMETHING FROM EACH ONE.
INCLUDING THAT TRICK.
FINE, WHAT'S YOUR FIGHT RECORD, THEN?
WHAT YOU DO IS MOVE YOUR LEFT FOOT BACK AND KICK TO THE SIDE AS IF YOU'RE RETREAT-ING, BUT SPRING FORWARD-
OH HO! AVOIDING THE SUBJECT. INTERESTING.

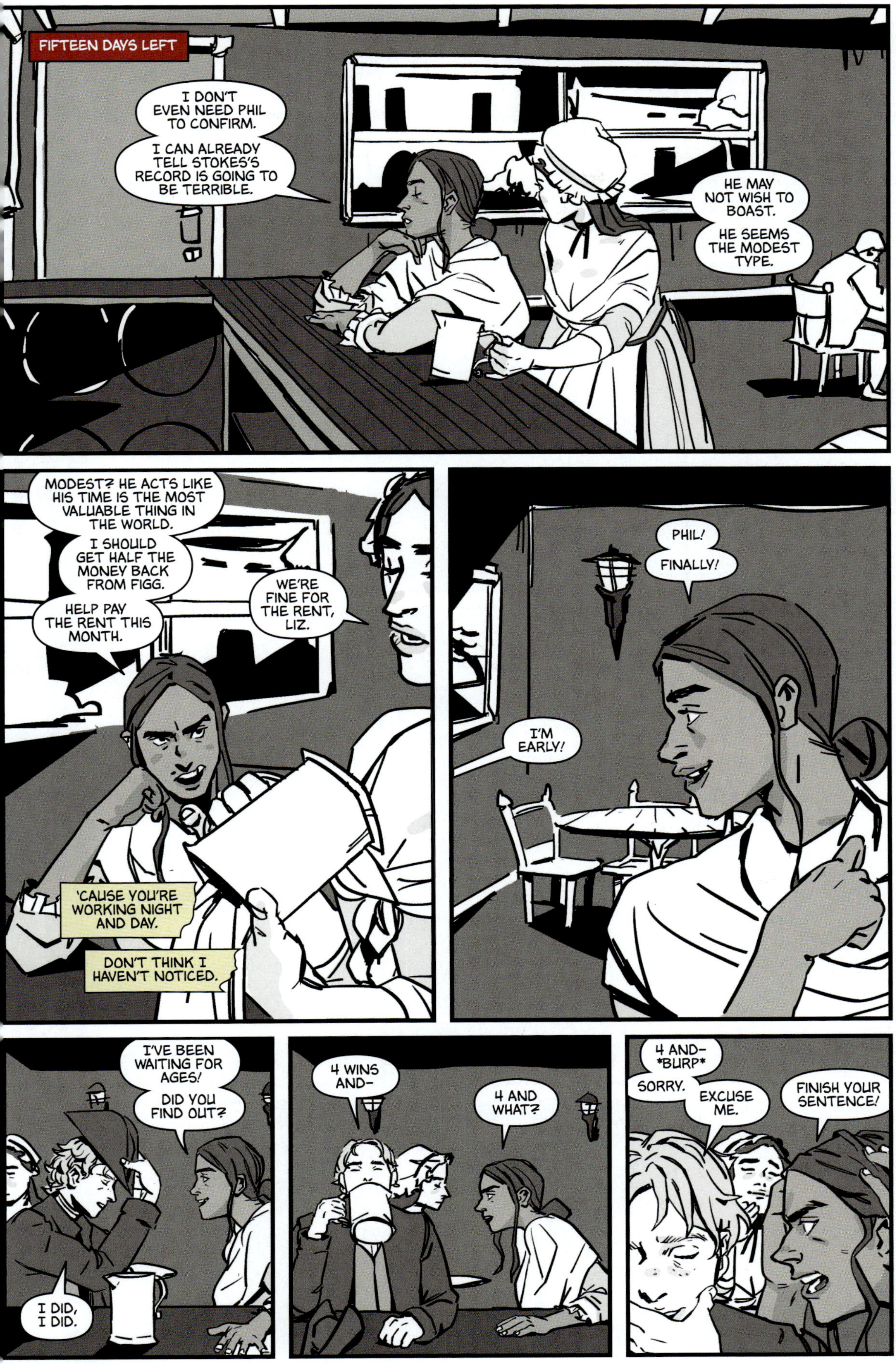
FIFTEEN DAYS LEFT
I DON'T EVEN NEED PHIL TO CONFIRM.
I CAN ALREADY TELL STOKES'S RECORD IS GOING TO BE TERRIBLE.
HE MAY NOT WISH TO BOAST.
HE SEEMS THE MODEST TYPE.
MODEST? HE ACTS LIKE HIS TIME IS THE MOST VALUABLE THING IN THE WORLD.
I SHOULD GET HALF THE MONEY BACK FROM FIGG.
HELP PAY THE RENT THIS MONTH.
WE'RE FINE FOR THE RENT, LIZ.
'CAUSE YOU'RE WORKING NIGHT AND DAY.
DON'T THINK I HAVEN'T NOTICED.
PHIL!
FINALLY!
I'M EARLY!
I'VE BEEN WAITING FOR AGES!
DID YOU FIND OUT?
I DID, I DID.
4 WINS AND-
4 AND WHAT?
4 AND- *BURP*
SORRY.
EXCUSE ME.
FINISH YOUR SENTENCE!

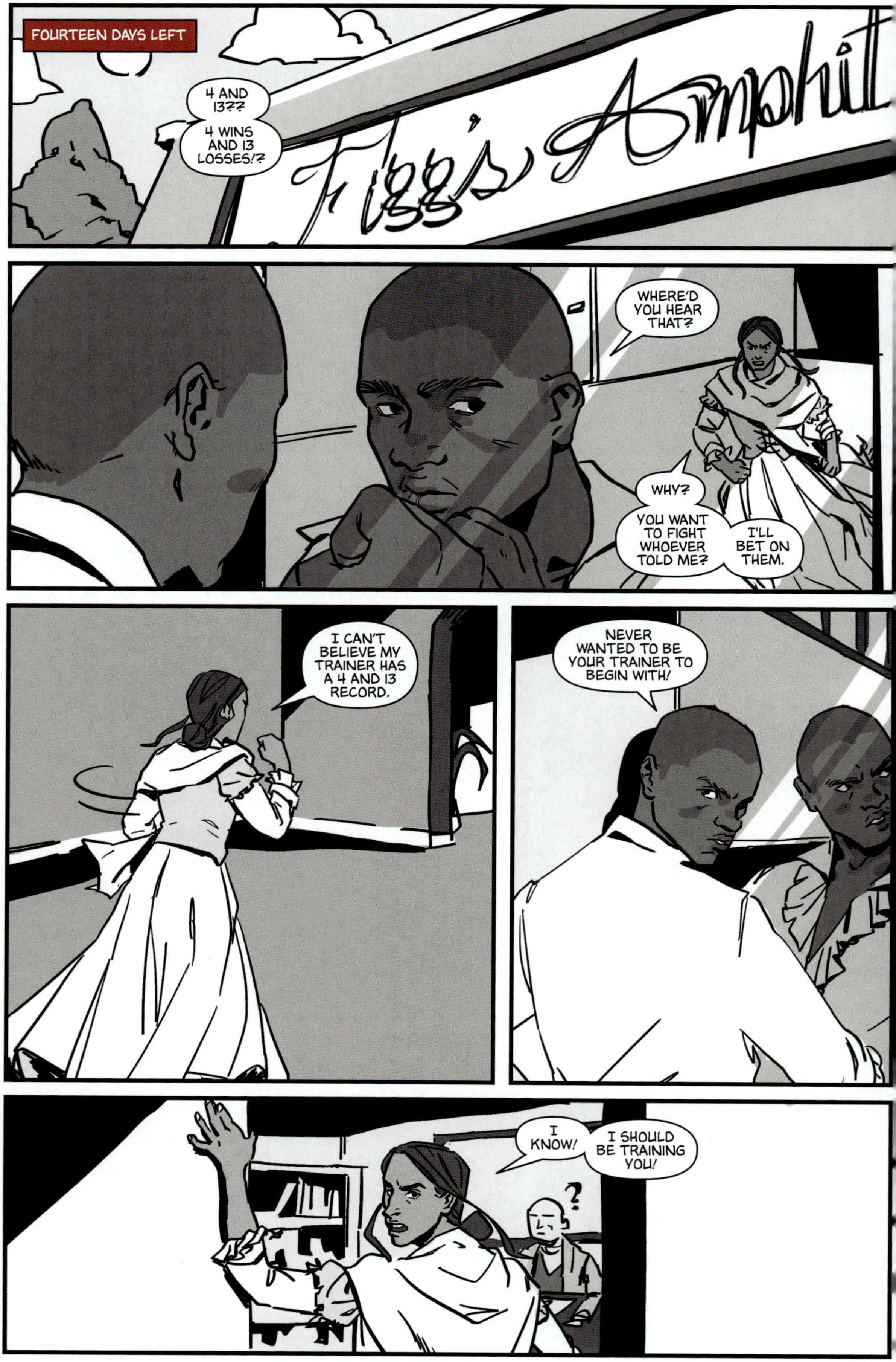
FOURTEEN DAYS LEFT
4 AND 13??
4 WINS AND 13 LOSSES!?
WHERE'D YOU HEAR THAT?
WHY?
YOU WANT TO FIGHT WHOEVER TOLD ME?
I'LL BET ON THEM.
I CAN'T BELIEVE MY TRAINER HAS A 4 AND 13 RECORD.
NEVER WANTED TO BE YOUR TRAINER TO BEGIN WITH!
I KNOW!
I SHOULD BE TRAINING YOU!
?

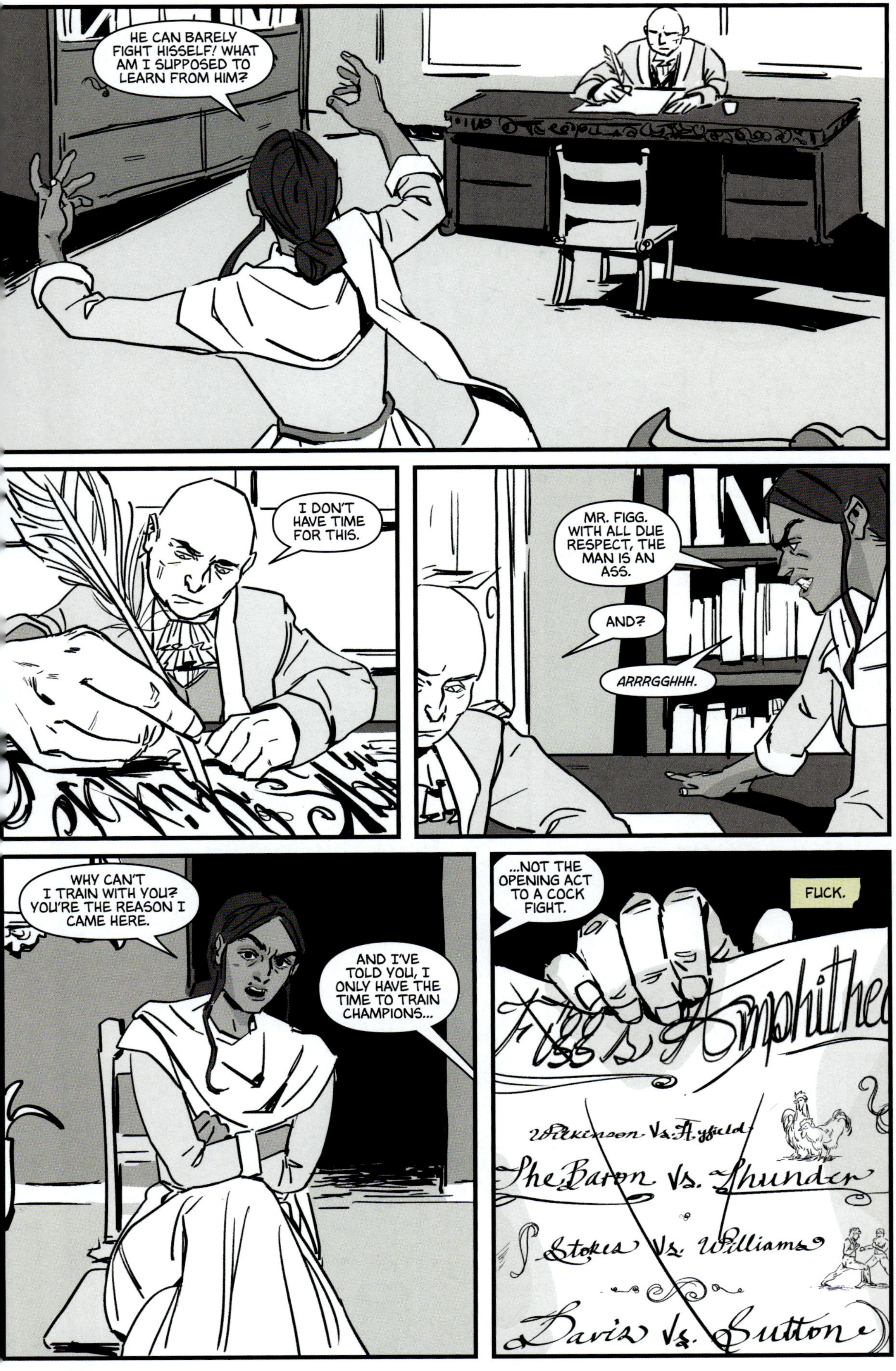
HE CAN BARELY FIGHT HISSELF! WHAT AM I SUPPOSED TO LEARN FROM HIM?
I DON'T HAVE TIME FOR THIS.
MR. FIGG. WITH ALL DUE RESPECT, THE MAN IS AN ASS.
AND?
ARRRGGHHH.
WHY CAN'T I TRAIN WITH YOU? YOU'RE THE REASON I CAME HERE.
AND I'VE TOLD YOU, I ONLY HAVE THE TIME TO TRAIN CHAMPIONS...
...NOT THE OPENING ACT TO A COCK FIGHT.
FUCK.
The Baron Vs. Thunder
Stokes Vs. Williams
Davis Vs. Sutton

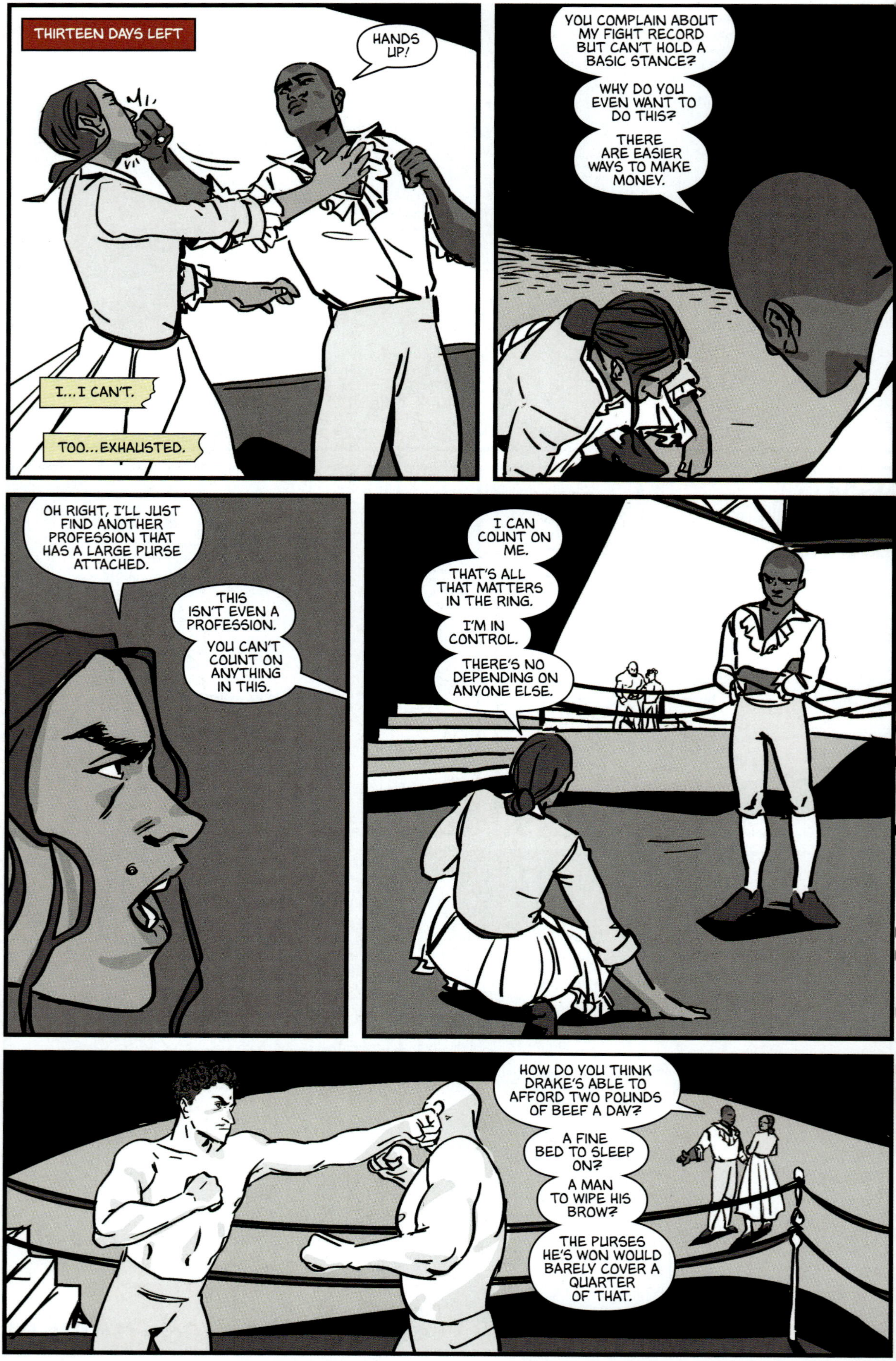
THIRTEEN DAYS LEFT
HANDS UP!
I...I CAN'T.
TOO...EXHAUSTED.
YOU COMPLAIN ABOUT MY FIGHT RECORD BUT CAN'T HOLD A BASIC STANCE?
WHY DO YOU EVEN WANT TO DO THIS?
THERE ARE EASIER WAYS TO MAKE MONEY.
OH RIGHT, I'LL JUST FIND ANOTHER PROFESSION THAT HAS A LARGE PURSE ATTACHED.
THIS ISN'T EVEN A PROFESSION.
YOU CAN'T COUNT ON ANYTHING IN THIS.
I CAN COUNT ON ME.
THAT'S ALL THAT MATTERS IN THE RING.
I'M IN CONTROL.
THERE'S NO DEPENDING ON ANYONE ELSE.
HOW DO YOU THINK DRAKE'S ABLE TO AFFORD TWO POUNDS OF BEEF A DAY?
A FINE BED TO SLEEP ON?
A MAN TO WIPE HIS BROW?
THE PURSES HE'S WON WOULD BARELY COVER A QUARTER OF THAT.

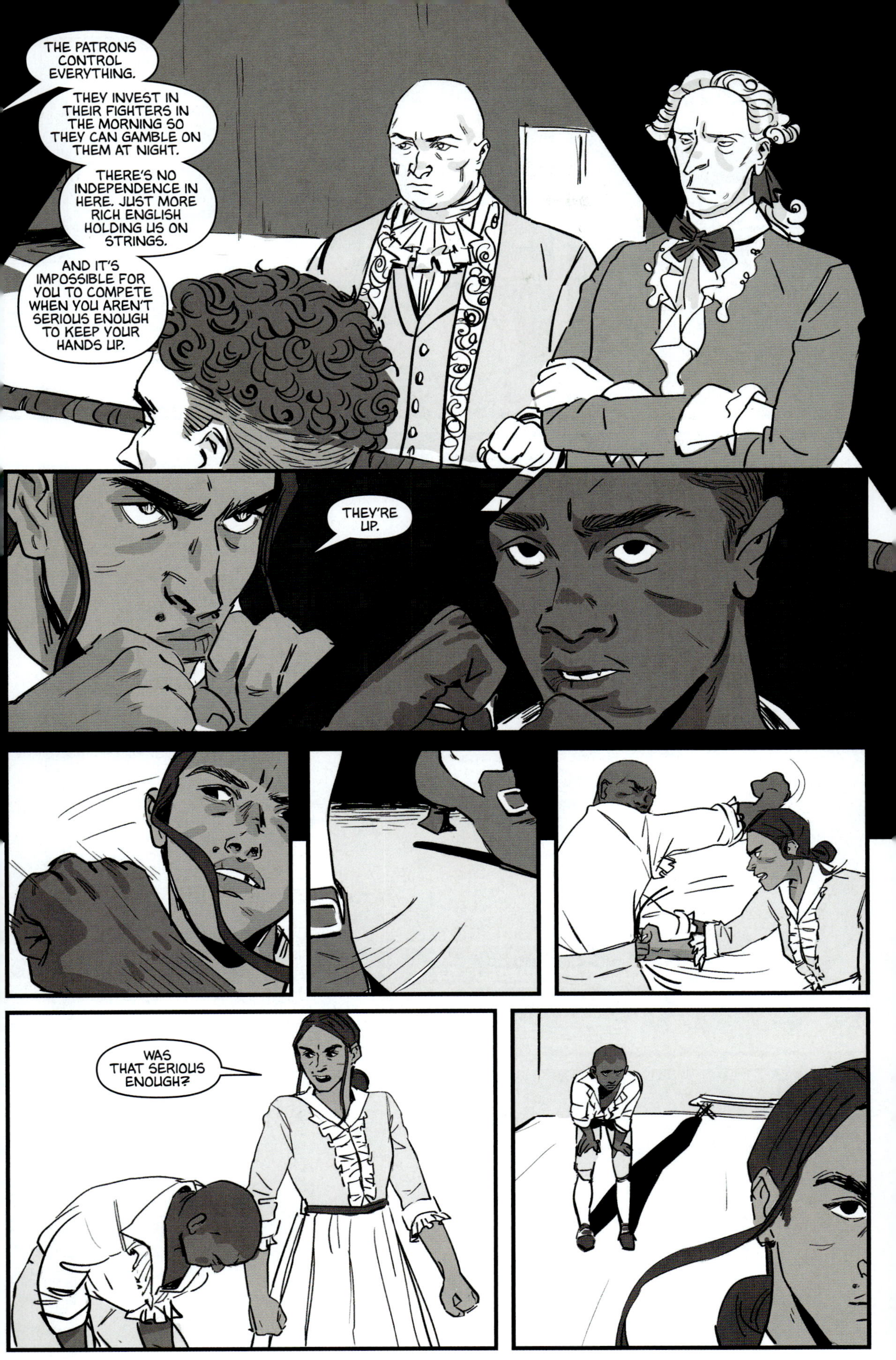
THE PATRONS CONTROL EVERYTHING.
THEY INVEST IN THEIR FIGHTERS IN THE MORNING SO THEY CAN GAMBLE ON THEM AT NIGHT.
THERE'S NO INDEPENDENCE IN HERE. JUST MORE RICH ENGLISH HOLDING US ON STRINGS.
AND IT'S IMPOSSIBLE FOR YOU TO COMPETE WHEN YOU AREN'T SERIOUS ENOUGH TO KEEP YOUR HANDS UP.
THEY'RE UP.
WAS THAT SERIOUS ENOUGH?

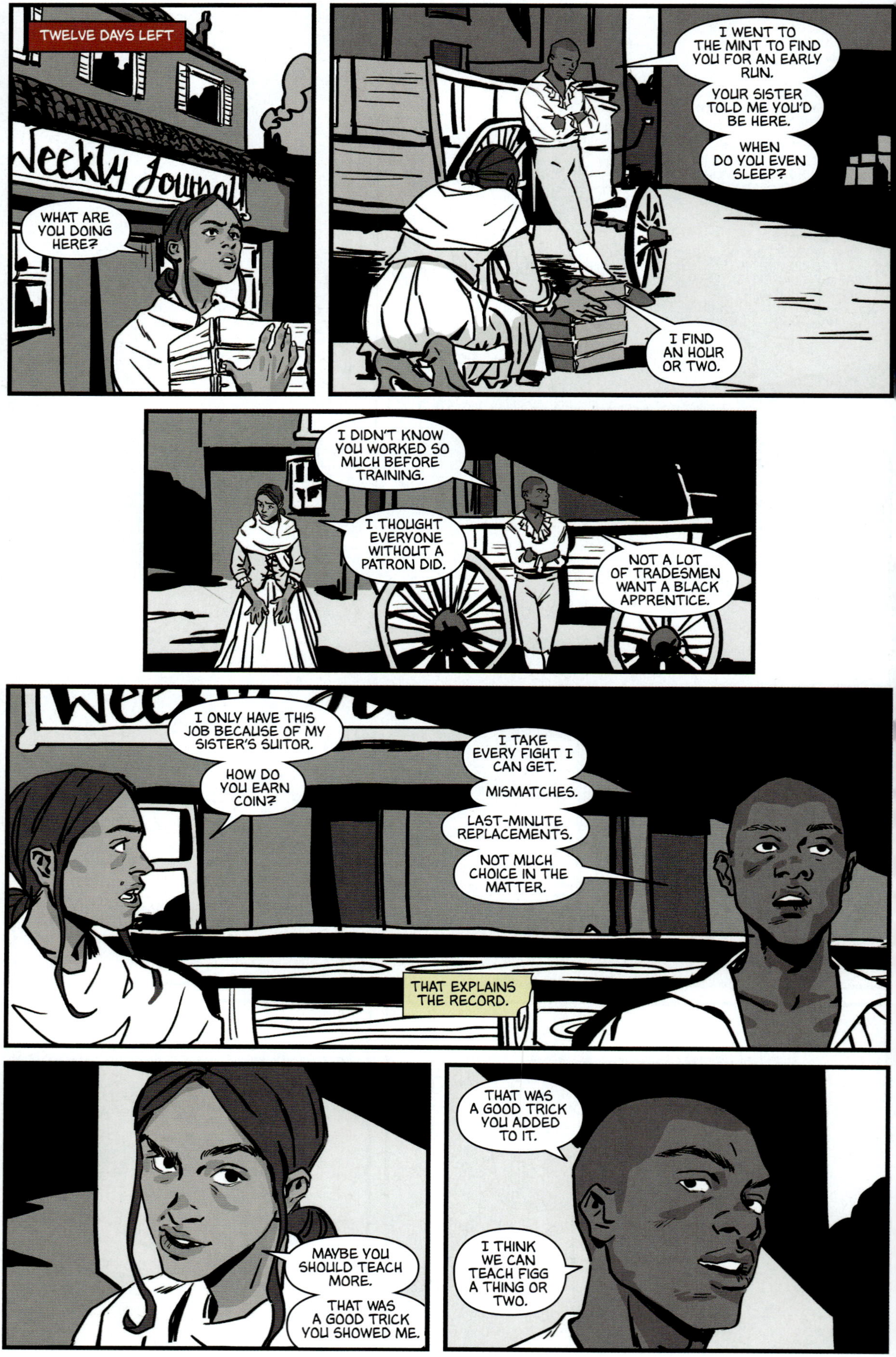
TWELVE DAYS LEFT
Weekly Journal
WHAT ARE YOU DOING HERE?
I WENT TO THE MINT TO FIND YOU FOR AN EARLY RUN.
YOUR SISTER TOLD ME YOU'D BE HERE.
WHEN DO YOU EVEN SLEEP?
I FIND AN HOUR OR TWO.
I DIDN'T KNOW YOU WORKED SO MUCH BEFORE TRAINING.
I THOUGHT EVERYONE WITHOUT A PATRON DID.
NOT A LOT OF TRADESMEN WANT A BLACK APPRENTICE.
I ONLY HAVE THIS JOB BECAUSE OF MY SISTER'S SUITOR.
HOW DO YOU EARN COIN?
I TAKE EVERY FIGHT I CAN GET.
MISMATCHES.
LAST-MINUTE REPLACEMENTS.
NOT MUCH CHOICE IN THE MATTER.
THAT EXPLAINS THE RECORD.
MAYBE YOU SHOULD TEACH MORE.
THAT WAS A GOOD TRICK YOU SHOWED ME.
THAT WAS A GOOD TRICK YOU ADDED TO IT.
I THINK WE CAN TEACH FIGG A THING OR TWO.

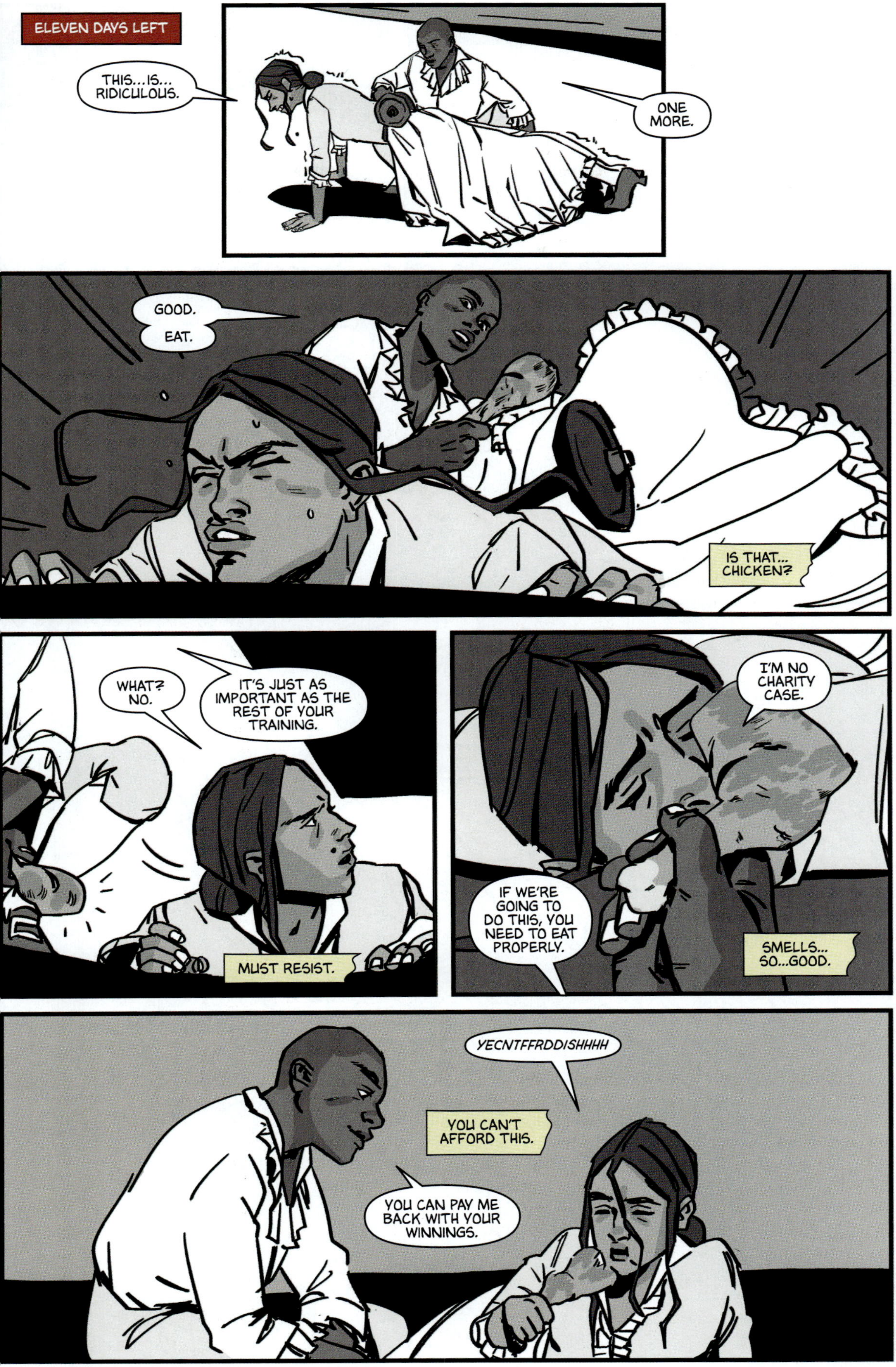

ELEVEN DAYS LEFT
THIS...IS... RIDICULOUS.
ONE MORE.
GOOD.
EAT.
IS THAT... CHICKEN?
WHAT? NO.
IT'S JUST AS IMPORTANT AS THE REST OF YOUR TRAINING.
MUST RESIST.
I'M NO CHARITY CASE.
IF WE'RE GOING TO DO THIS, YOU NEED TO EAT PROPERLY.
SMELLS... SO...GOOD.
YECNTFFRDDISHHHH
YOU CAN'T AFFORD THIS.
YOU CAN PAY ME BACK WITH YOUR WINNINGS.

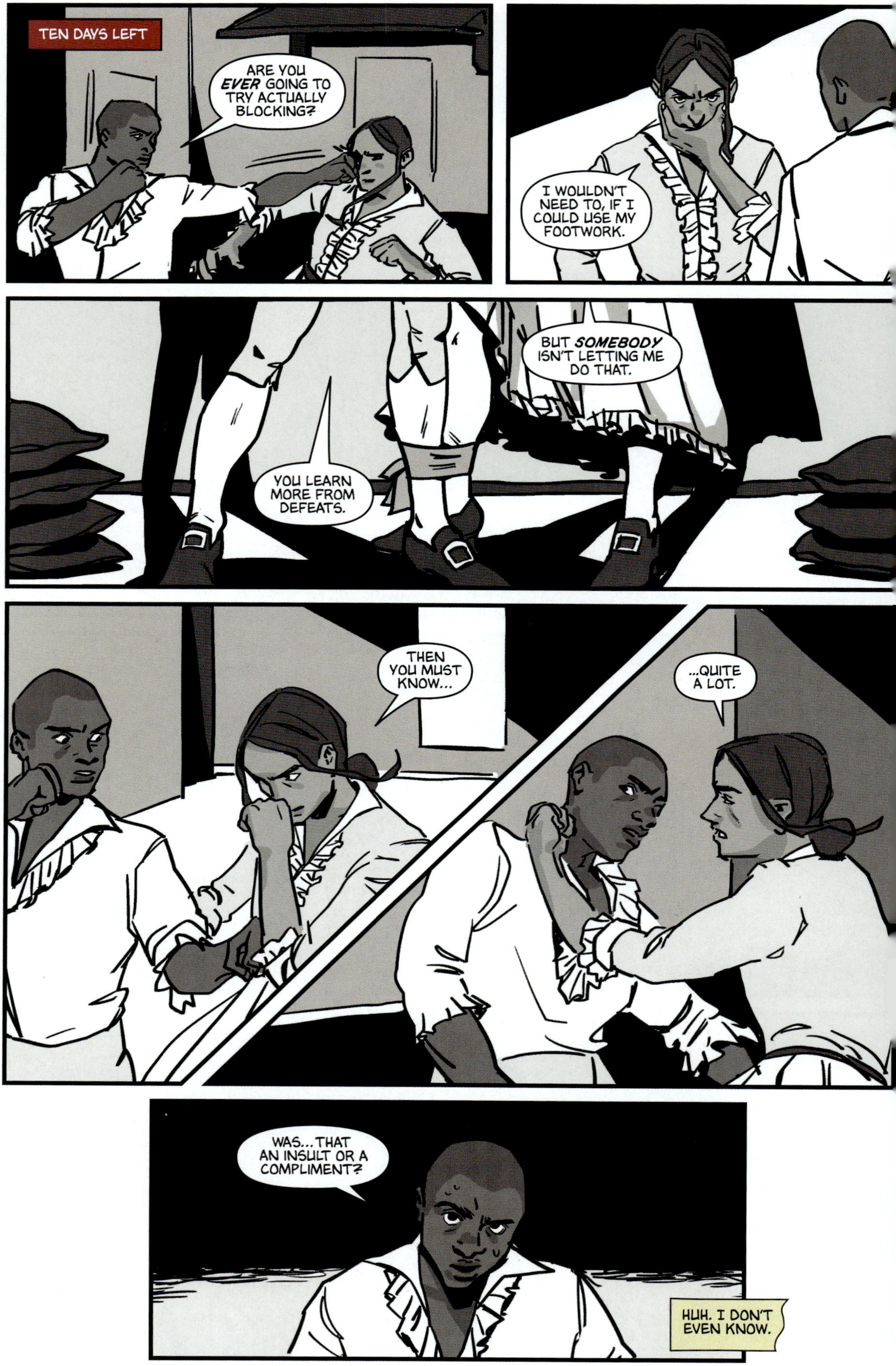
TEN DAYS LEFT
ARE YOU *EVER* GOING TO TRY ACTUALLY BLOCKING?
I WOULDN'T NEED TO, IF I COULD USE MY FOOTWORK.
BUT *SOMEBODY* ISN'T LETTING ME DO THAT.
YOU LEARN MORE FROM DEFEATS.
THEN YOU MUST KNOW...
...QUITE A LOT.
WAS... THAT AN INSULT OR A COMPLIMENT?
HUH. I DON'T EVEN KNOW.

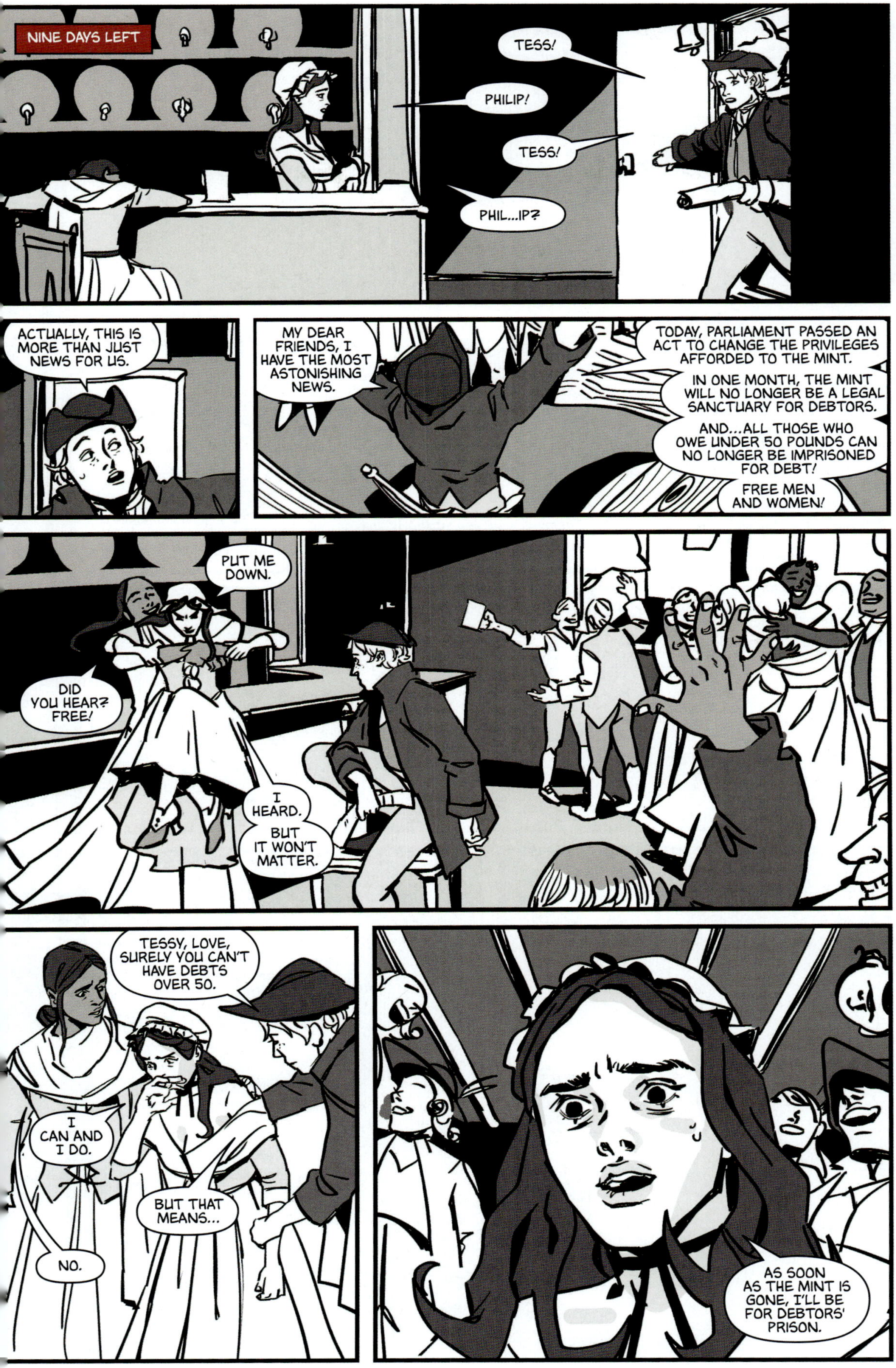
NINE DAYS LEFT
TESS!
PHILIP!
TESS!
PHIL...IP?
ACTUALLY, THIS IS MORE THAN JUST NEWS FOR US.
MY DEAR FRIENDS, I HAVE THE MOST ASTONISHING NEWS.
TODAY, PARLIAMENT PASSED AN ACT TO CHANGE THE PRIVILEGES AFFORDED TO THE MINT.
IN ONE MONTH, THE MINT WILL NO LONGER BE A LEGAL SANCTUARY FOR DEBTORS.
AND...ALL THOSE WHO OWE UNDER 50 POUNDS CAN NO LONGER BE IMPRISONED FOR DEBT!
FREE MEN AND WOMEN!
PUT ME DOWN.
DID YOU HEAR? FREE!
I HEARD.
BUT IT WON'T MATTER.
TESSY, LOVE, SURELY YOU CAN'T HAVE DEBTS OVER 50.
I CAN AND I DO.
BUT THAT MEANS...
NO.
AS SOON AS THE MINT IS GONE, I'LL BE FOR DEBTORS' PRISON.

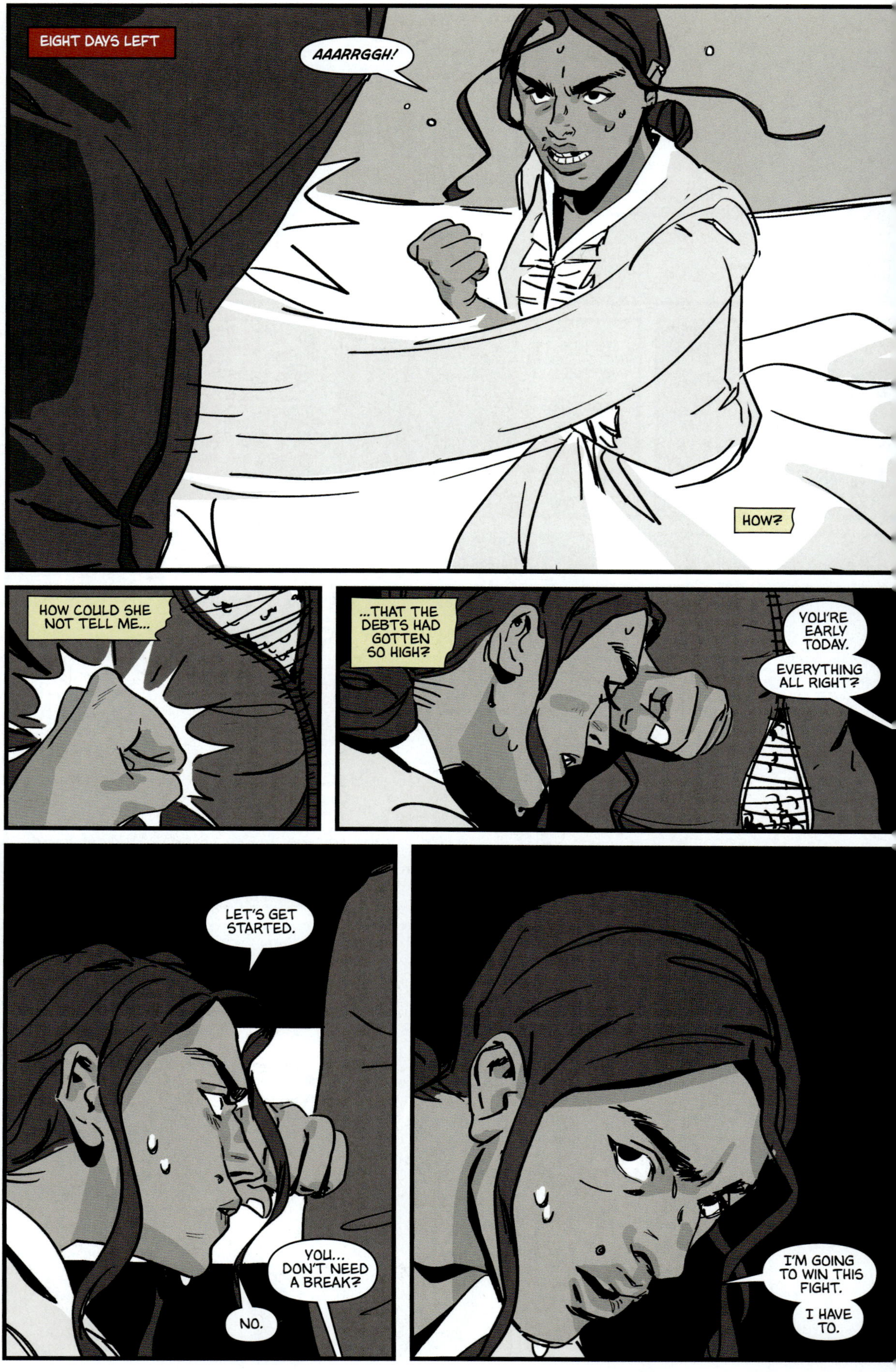

EIGHT DAYS LEFT
AAARRGGH!
HOW?
HOW COULD SHE NOT TELL ME...
...THAT THE DEBTS HAD GOTTEN SO HIGH?
YOU'RE EARLY TODAY.
EVERYTHING ALL RIGHT?
LET'S GET STARTED.
YOU... DON'T NEED A BREAK?
NO.
I'M GOING TO WIN THIS FIGHT.
I HAVE TO.

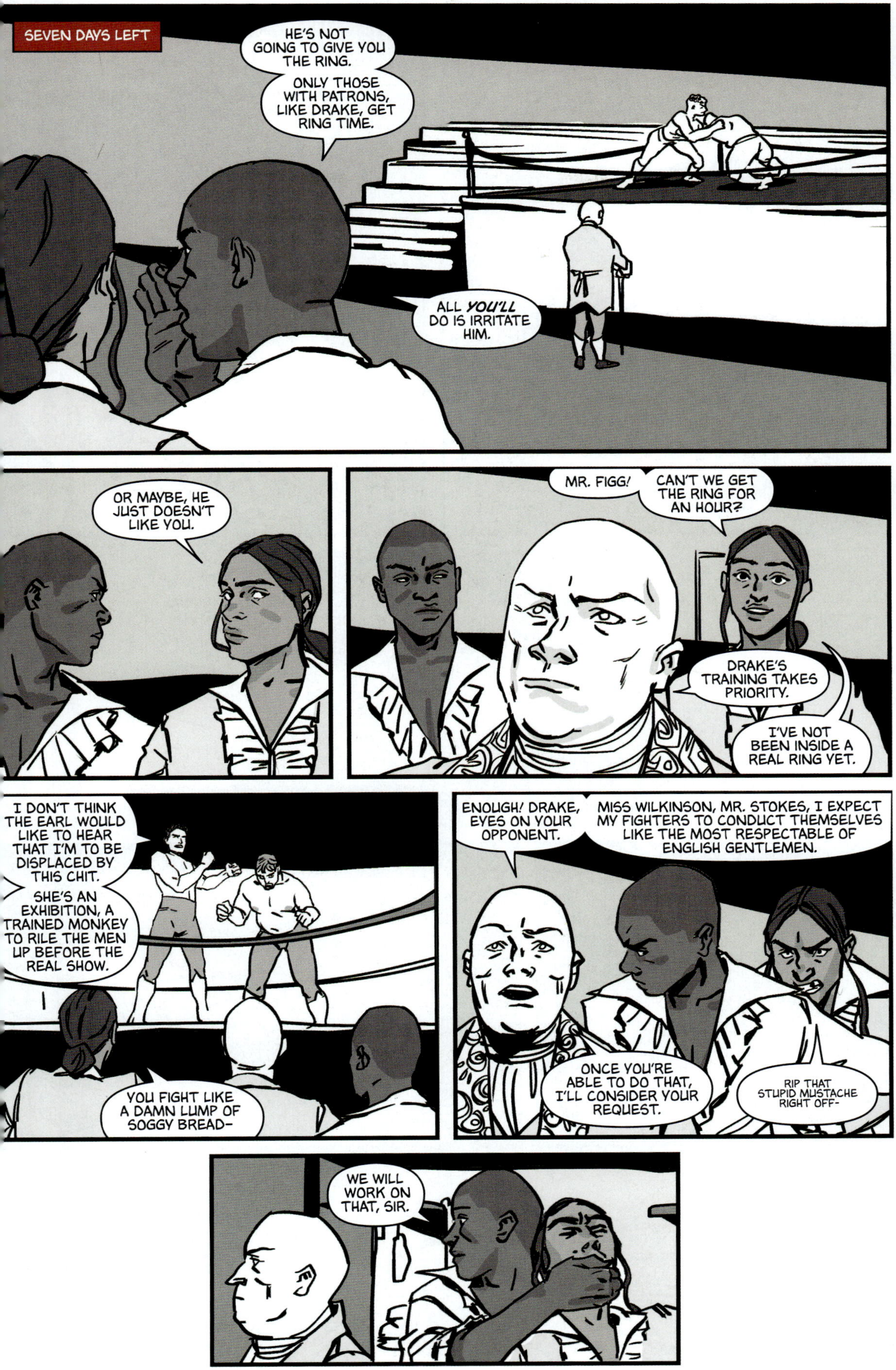
SEVEN DAYS LEFT
HE'S NOT GOING TO GIVE YOU THE RING.
ONLY THOSE WITH PATRONS, LIKE DRAKE, GET RING TIME.
ALL YOU'LL DO IS IRRITATE HIM.
OR MAYBE, HE JUST DOESN'T LIKE YOU.
MR. FIGG!
CAN'T WE GET THE RING FOR AN HOUR?
DRAKE'S TRAINING TAKES PRIORITY.
I'VE NOT BEEN INSIDE A REAL RING YET.
I DON'T THINK THE EARL WOULD LIKE TO HEAR THAT I'M TO BE DISPLACED BY THIS CHIT.
SHE'S AN EXHIBITION, A TRAINED MONKEY TO RILE THE MEN UP BEFORE THE REAL SHOW.
YOU FIGHT LIKE A DAMN LUMP OF SOGGY BREAD–
ENOUGH! DRAKE, EYES ON YOUR OPPONENT.
MISS WILKINSON, MR. STOKES, I EXPECT MY FIGHTERS TO CONDUCT THEMSELVES LIKE THE MOST RESPECTABLE OF ENGLISH GENTLEMEN.
ONCE YOU'RE ABLE TO DO THAT, I'LL CONSIDER YOUR REQUEST.
RIP THAT STUPID MUSTACHE RIGHT OFF–
WE WILL WORK ON THAT, SIR.

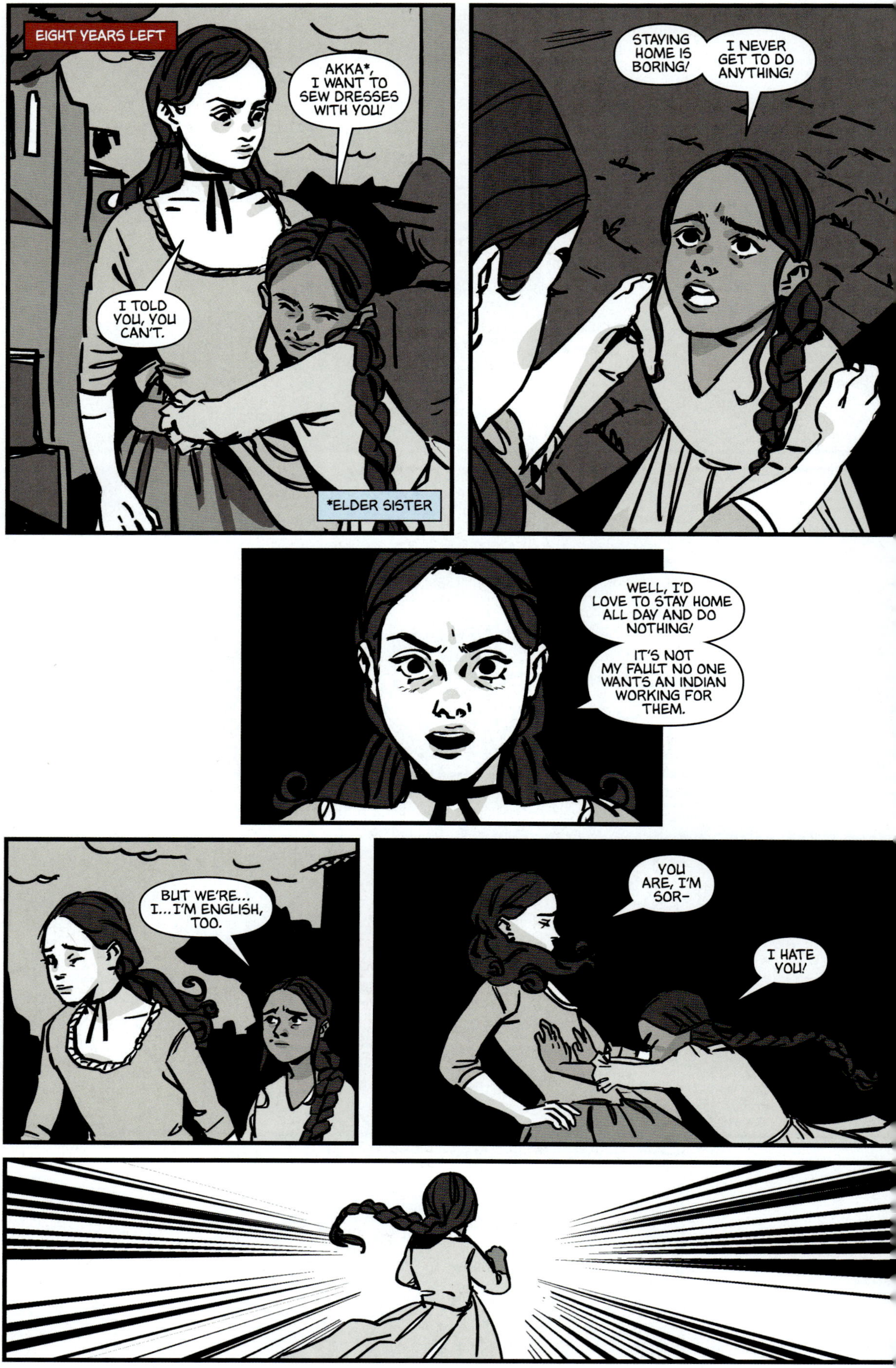
EIGHT YEARS LEFT
AKKA*, I WANT TO SEW DRESSES WITH YOU!
I TOLD YOU, YOU CAN'T.
*ELDER SISTER
STAYING HOME IS BORING!
I NEVER GET TO DO ANYTHING!
WELL, I'D LOVE TO STAY HOME ALL DAY AND DO NOTHING!
IT'S NOT MY FAULT NO ONE WANTS AN INDIAN WORKING FOR THEM.
BUT WE'RE... I...I'M ENGLISH, TOO.
YOU ARE, I'M SOR-
I HATE YOU!

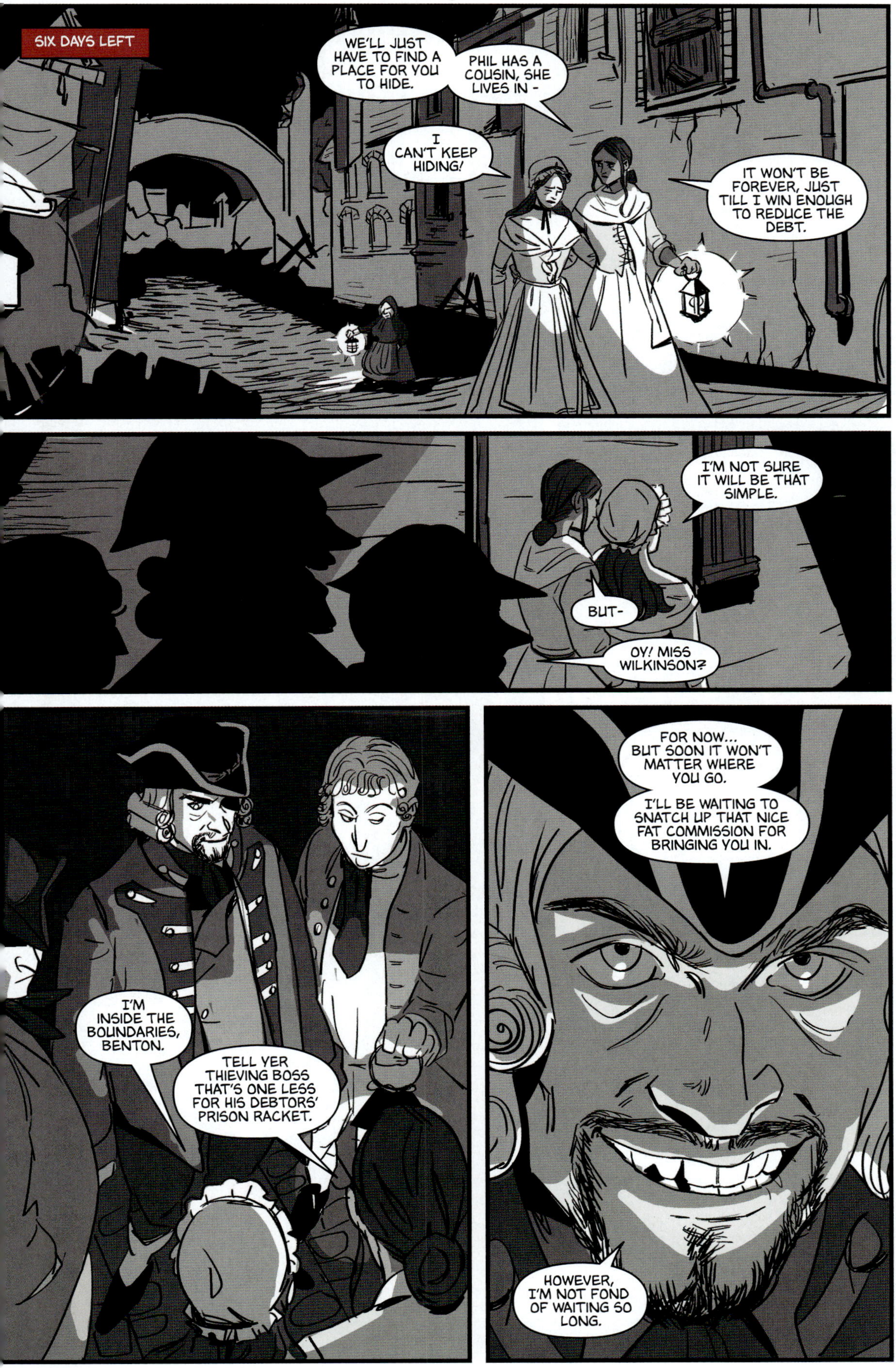
SIX DAYS LEFT
WE'LL JUST HAVE TO FIND A PLACE FOR YOU TO HIDE.
PHIL HAS A COUSIN, SHE LIVES IN -
I CAN'T KEEP HIDING!
IT WON'T BE FOREVER, JUST TILL I WIN ENOUGH TO REDUCE THE DEBT.
I'M NOT SURE IT WILL BE THAT SIMPLE.
BUT-
OY! MISS WILKINSON?
I'M INSIDE THE BOUNDARIES, BENTON.
TELL YER THIEVING BOSS THAT'S ONE LESS FOR HIS DEBTORS' PRISON RACKET.
FOR NOW... BUT SOON IT WON'T MATTER WHERE YOU GO.
I'LL BE WAITING TO SNATCH UP THAT NICE FAT COMMISSION FOR BRINGING YOU IN.
HOWEVER, I'M NOT FOND OF WAITING SO LONG.

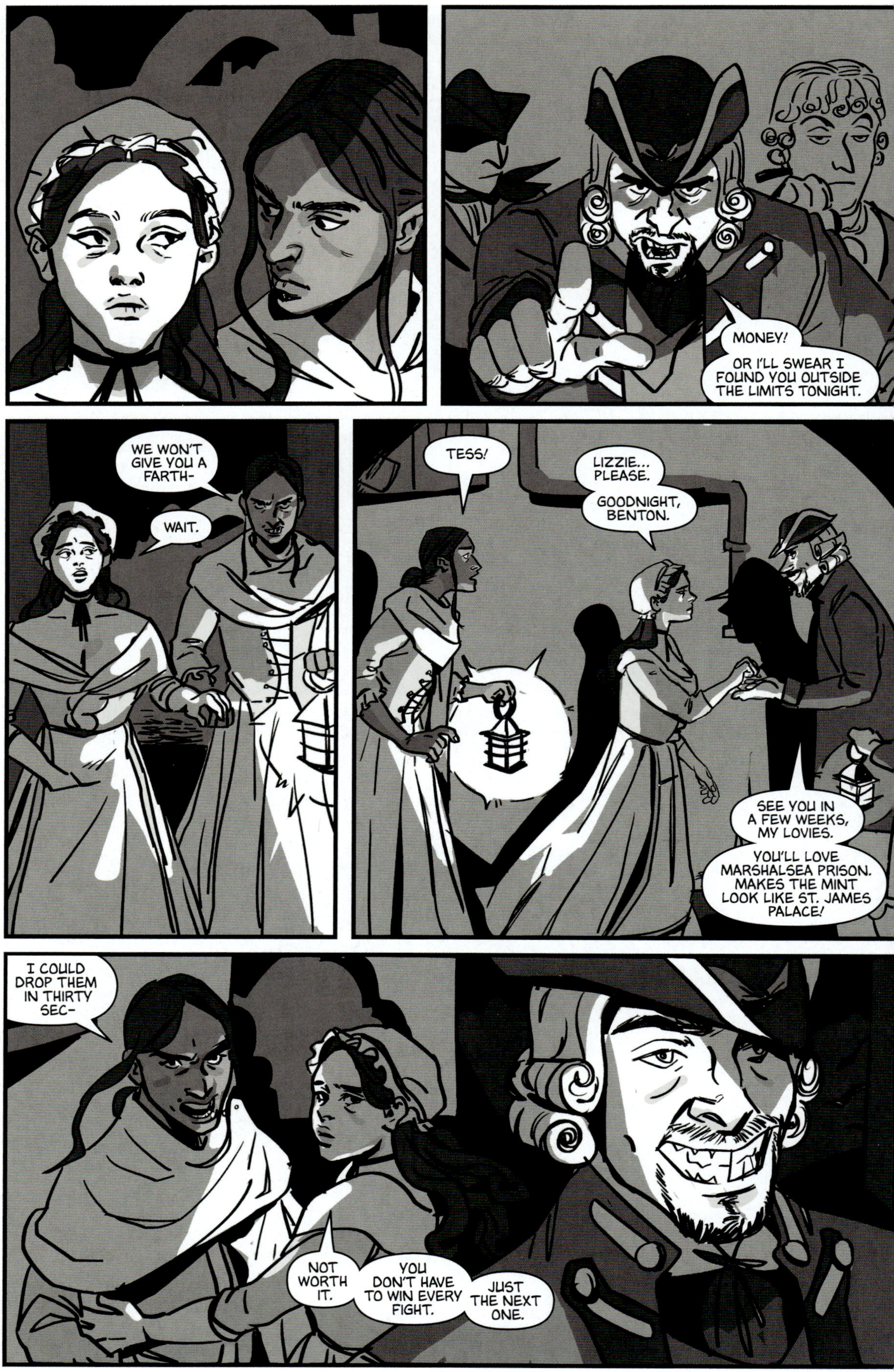
MONEY!
OR I'LL SWEAR I FOUND YOU OUTSIDE THE LIMITS TONIGHT.
WE WON'T GIVE YOU A FARTH-
WAIT.
TESS!
LIZZIE... PLEASE.
GOODNIGHT, BENTON.
SEE YOU IN A FEW WEEKS, MY LOVIES.
YOU'LL LOVE MARSHALSEA PRISON. MAKES THE MINT LOOK LIKE ST. JAMES PALACE!
I COULD DROP THEM IN THIRTY SEC-
NOT WORTH IT.
YOU DON'T HAVE TO WIN EVERY FIGHT.
JUST THE NEXT ONE.

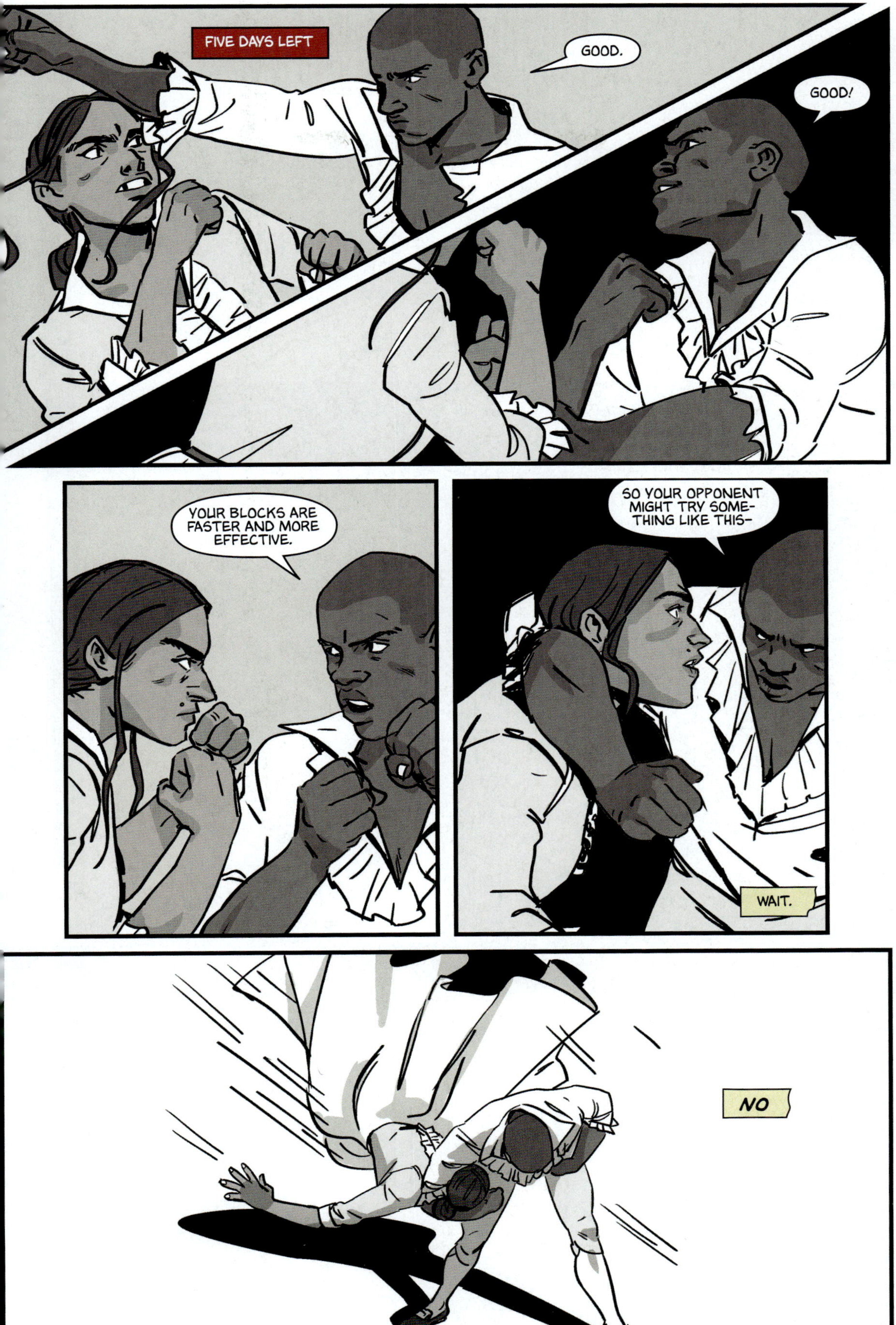
FIVE DAYS LEFT
GOOD.
GOOD!
YOUR BLOCKS ARE FASTER AND MORE EFFECTIVE.
SO YOUR OPPONENT MIGHT TRY SOME-THING LIKE THIS-
WAIT.
NO

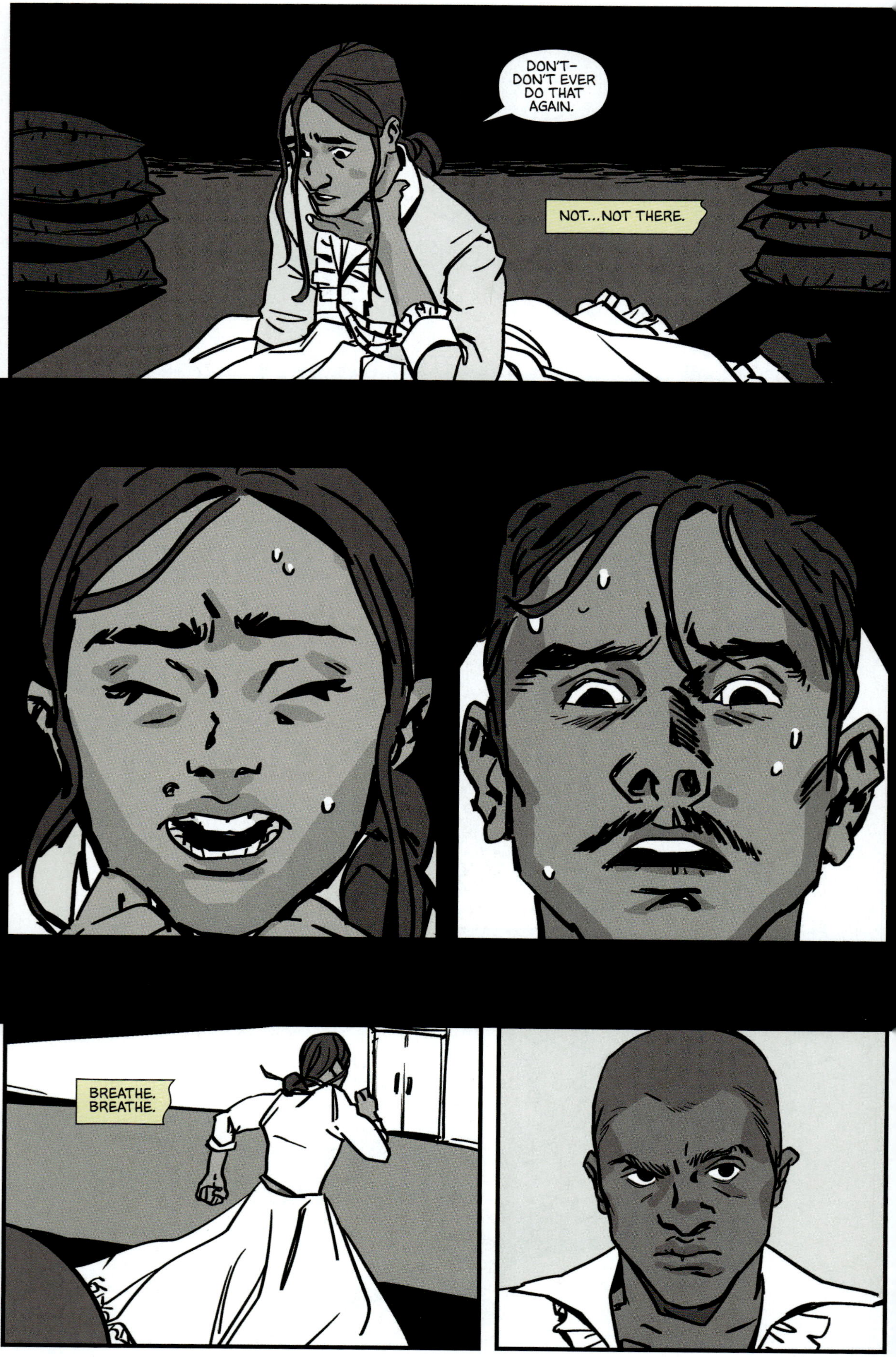
DON'T-
DON'T EVER
DO THAT
AGAIN.
NOT...NOT THERE.
BREATHE.
BREATHE.

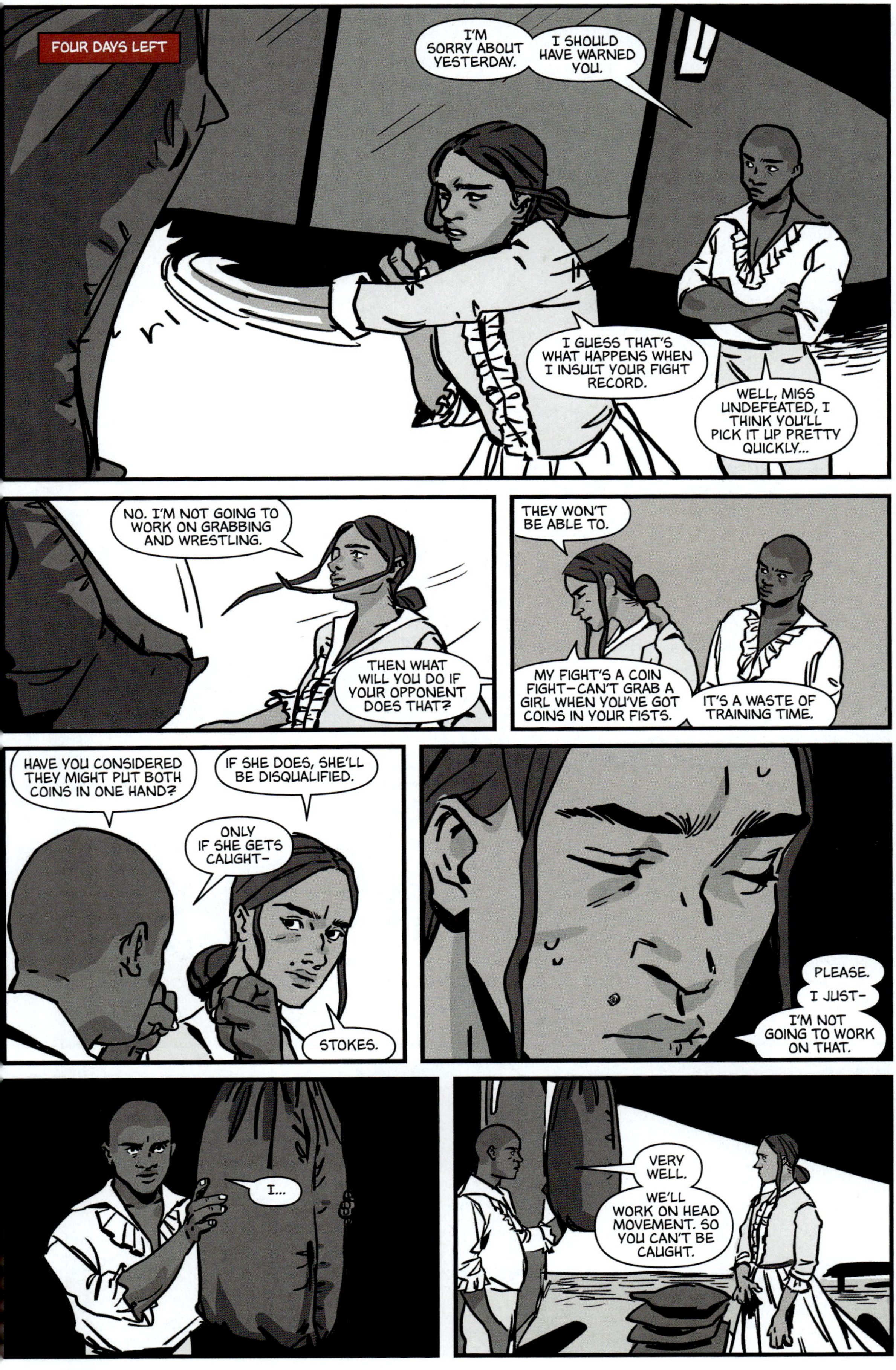
FOUR DAYS LEFT
I'M SORRY ABOUT YESTERDAY.
I SHOULD HAVE WARNED YOU.
I GUESS THAT'S WHAT HAPPENS WHEN I INSULT YOUR FIGHT RECORD.
WELL, MISS UNDEFEATED, I THINK YOU'LL PICK IT UP PRETTY QUICKLY...
NO. I'M NOT GOING TO WORK ON GRABBING AND WRESTLING.
THEN WHAT WILL YOU DO IF YOUR OPPONENT DOES THAT?
THEY WON'T BE ABLE TO.
MY FIGHT'S A COIN FIGHT—CAN'T GRAB A GIRL WHEN YOU'VE GOT COINS IN YOUR FISTS.
IT'S A WASTE OF TRAINING TIME.
HAVE YOU CONSIDERED THEY MIGHT PUT BOTH COINS IN ONE HAND?
IF SHE DOES, SHE'LL BE DISQUALIFIED.
ONLY IF SHE GETS CAUGHT-
STOKES.
PLEASE.
I JUST-
I'M NOT GOING TO WORK ON THAT.
I...
VERY WELL.
WE'LL WORK ON HEAD MOVEMENT. SO YOU CAN'T BE CAUGHT.

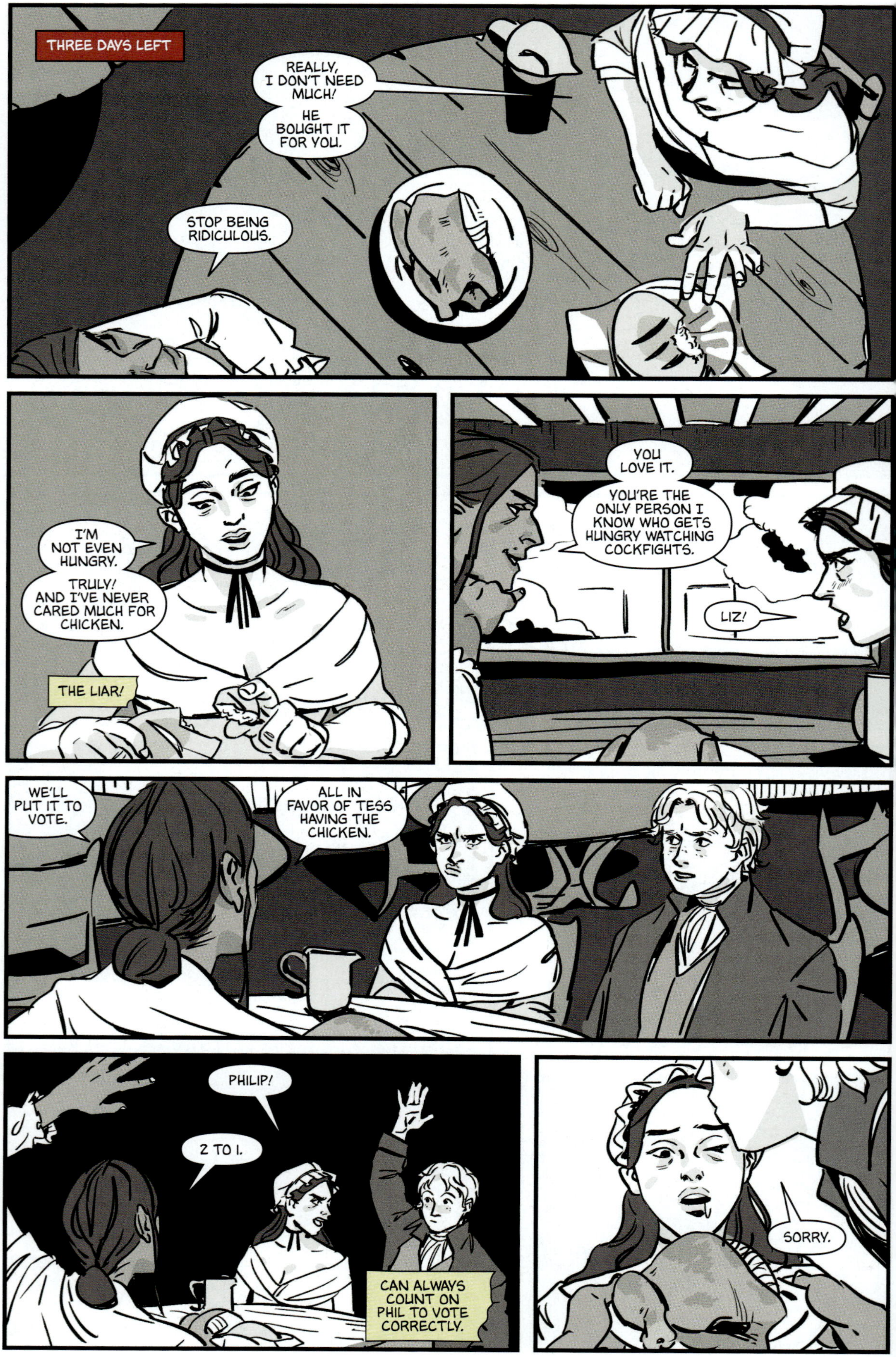
THREE DAYS LEFT
REALLY, I DON'T NEED MUCH!
HE BOUGHT IT FOR YOU.
STOP BEING RIDICULOUS.
I'M NOT EVEN HUNGRY.
TRULY! AND I'VE NEVER CARED MUCH FOR CHICKEN.
THE LIAR!
YOU LOVE IT.
YOU'RE THE ONLY PERSON I KNOW WHO GETS HUNGRY WATCHING COCKFIGHTS.
LIZ!
WE'LL PUT IT TO VOTE.
ALL IN FAVOR OF TESS HAVING THE CHICKEN.
PHILIP!
2 TO 1.
CAN ALWAYS COUNT ON PHIL TO VOTE CORRECTLY.
SORRY.

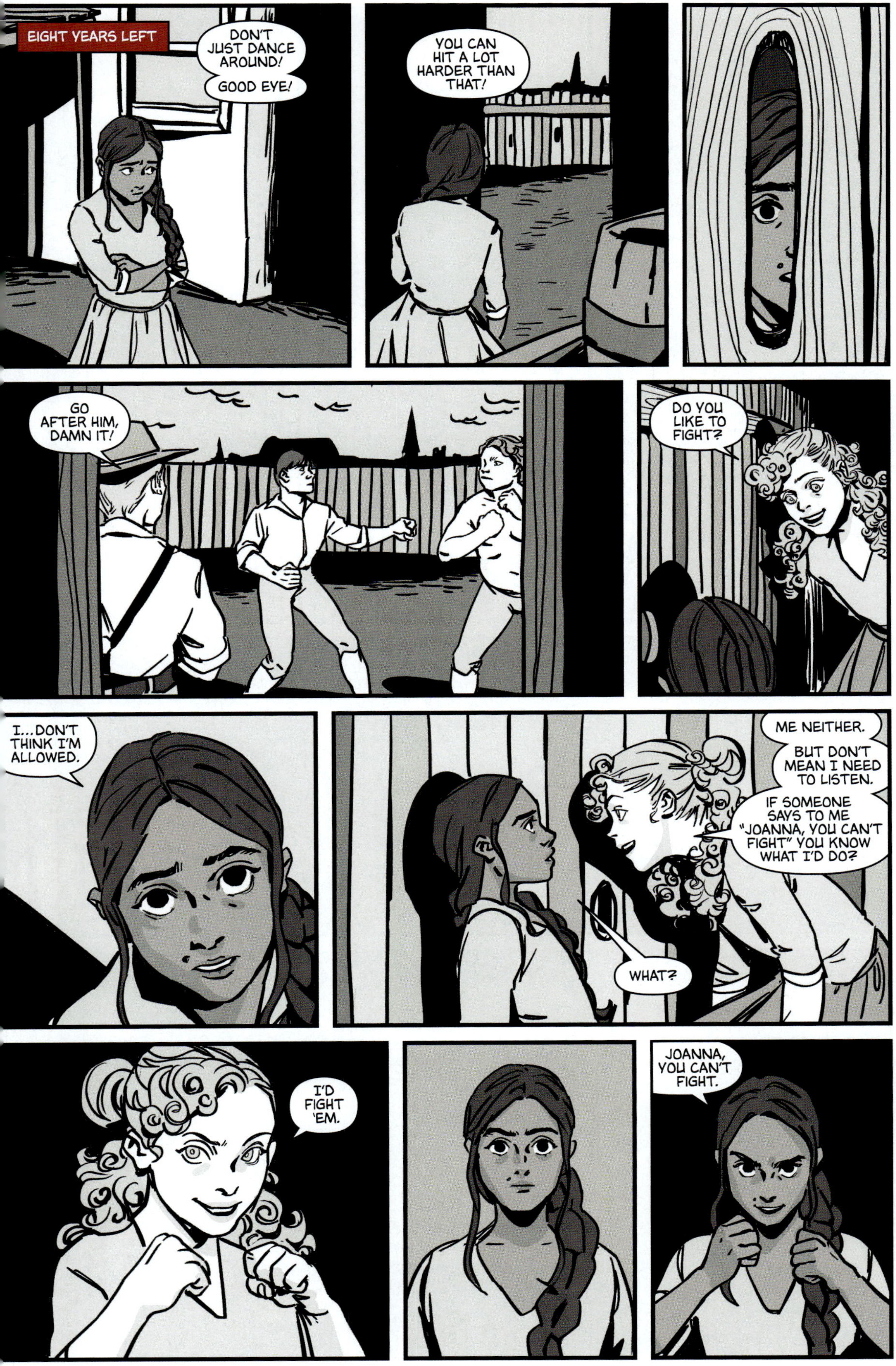
EIGHT YEARS LEFT
DON'T JUST DANCE AROUND!
GOOD EYE!
YOU CAN HIT A LOT HARDER THAN THAT!
GO AFTER HIM, DAMN IT!
DO YOU LIKE TO FIGHT?
I...DON'T THINK I'M ALLOWED.
ME NEITHER.
BUT DON'T MEAN I NEED TO LISTEN.
IF SOMEONE SAYS TO ME "JOANNA, YOU CAN'T FIGHT" YOU KNOW WHAT I'D DO?
WHAT?
I'D FIGHT 'EM.
JOANNA, YOU CAN'T FIGHT.

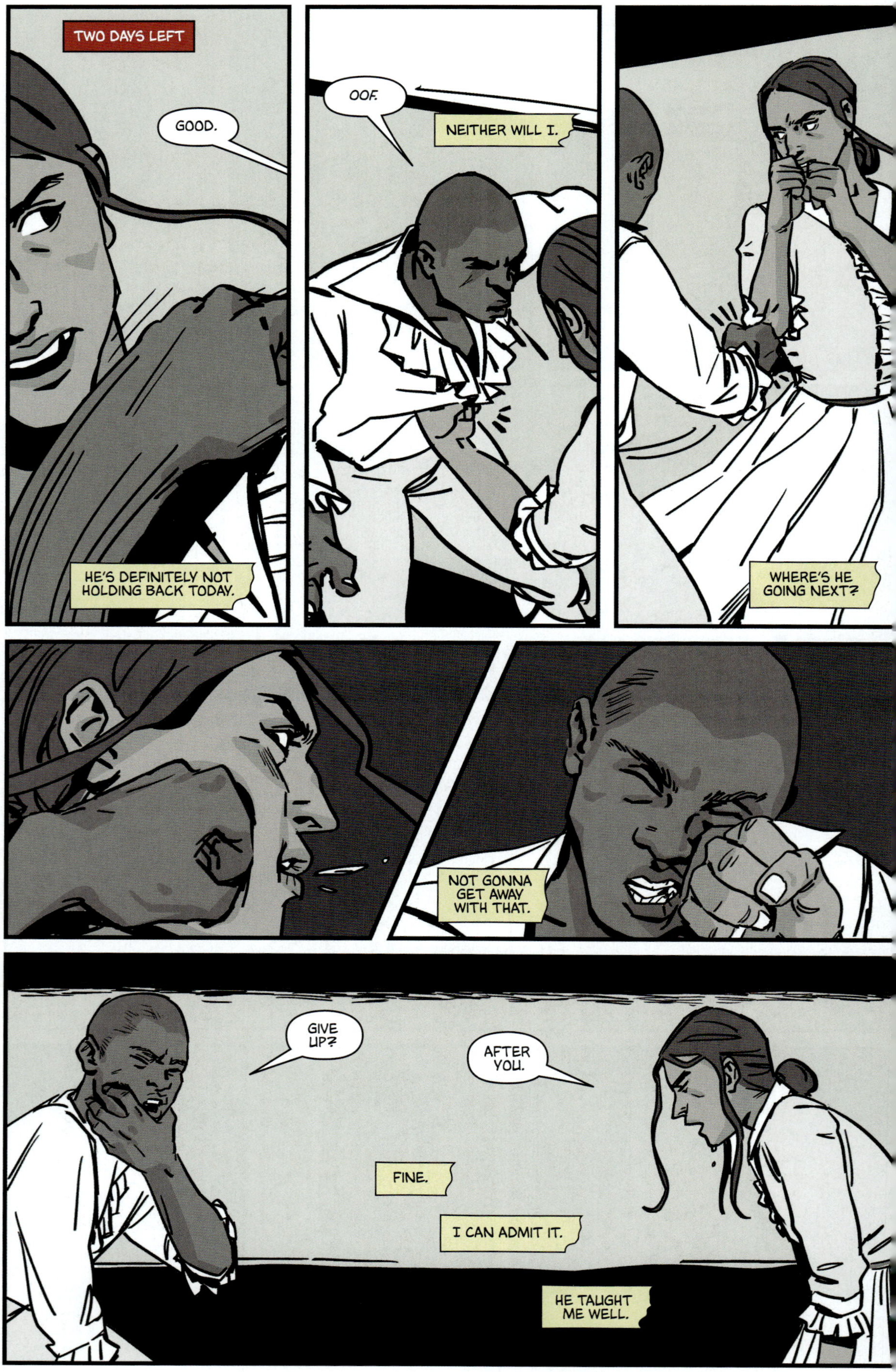
TWO DAYS LEFT
GOOD.
HE'S DEFINITELY NOT HOLDING BACK TODAY.
OOF.
NEITHER WILL I.
WHERE'S HE GOING NEXT?
NOT GONNA GET AWAY WITH THAT.
GIVE UP?
AFTER YOU.
FINE.
I CAN ADMIT IT.
HE TAUGHT ME WELL.

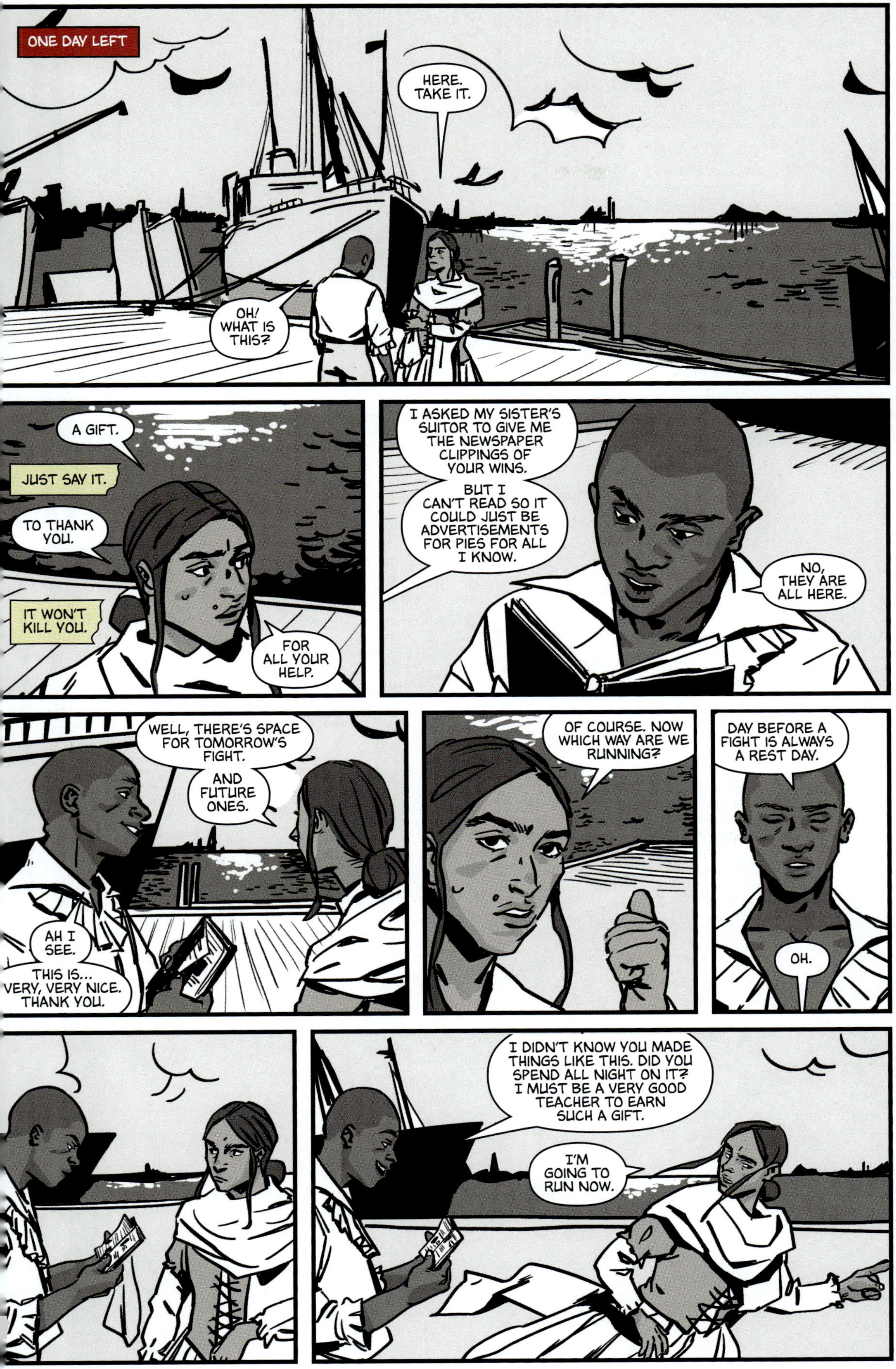
ONE DAY LEFT
HERE. TAKE IT.
OH! WHAT IS THIS?
A GIFT.
JUST SAY IT.
TO THANK YOU.
IT WON'T KILL YOU.
FOR ALL YOUR HELP.
I ASKED MY SISTER'S SUITOR TO GIVE ME THE NEWSPAPER CLIPPINGS OF YOUR WINS.
BUT I CAN'T READ SO IT COULD JUST BE ADVERTISEMENTS FOR PIES FOR ALL I KNOW.
NO, THEY ARE ALL HERE.
WELL, THERE'S SPACE FOR TOMORROW'S FIGHT.
AND FUTURE ONES.
AH I SEE.
THIS IS... VERY, VERY NICE. THANK YOU.
OF COURSE. NOW WHICH WAY ARE WE RUNNING?
DAY BEFORE A FIGHT IS ALWAYS A REST DAY.
OH.
I DIDN'T KNOW YOU MADE THINGS LIKE THIS. DID YOU SPEND ALL NIGHT ON IT? I MUST BE A VERY GOOD TEACHER TO EARN SUCH A GIFT.
I'M GOING TO RUN NOW.

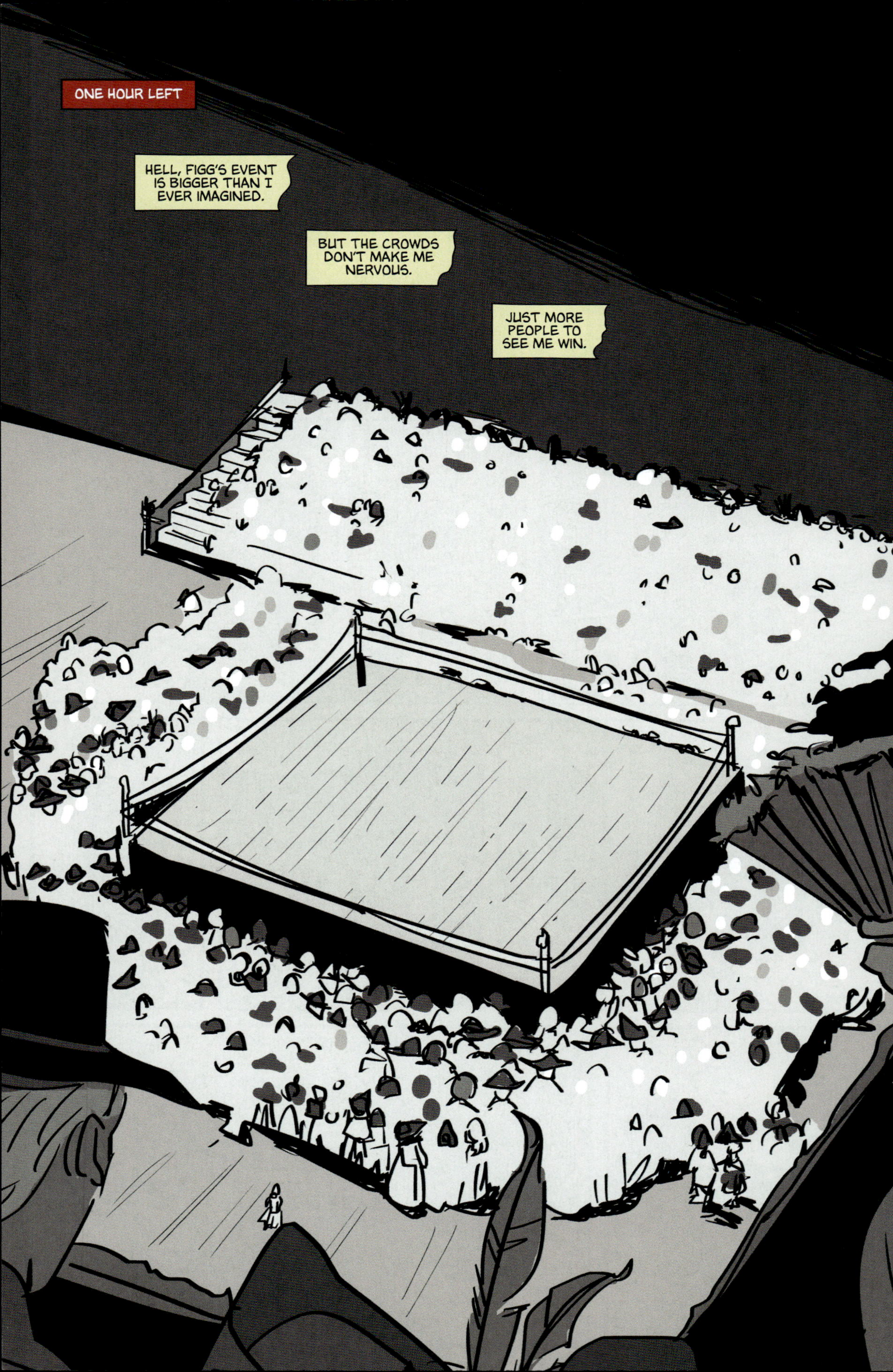
ONE HOUR LEFT
HELL, FIGG'S EVENT IS BIGGER THAN I EVER IMAGINED.
BUT THE CROWDS DON'T MAKE ME NERVOUS.
JUST MORE PEOPLE TO SEE ME WIN.

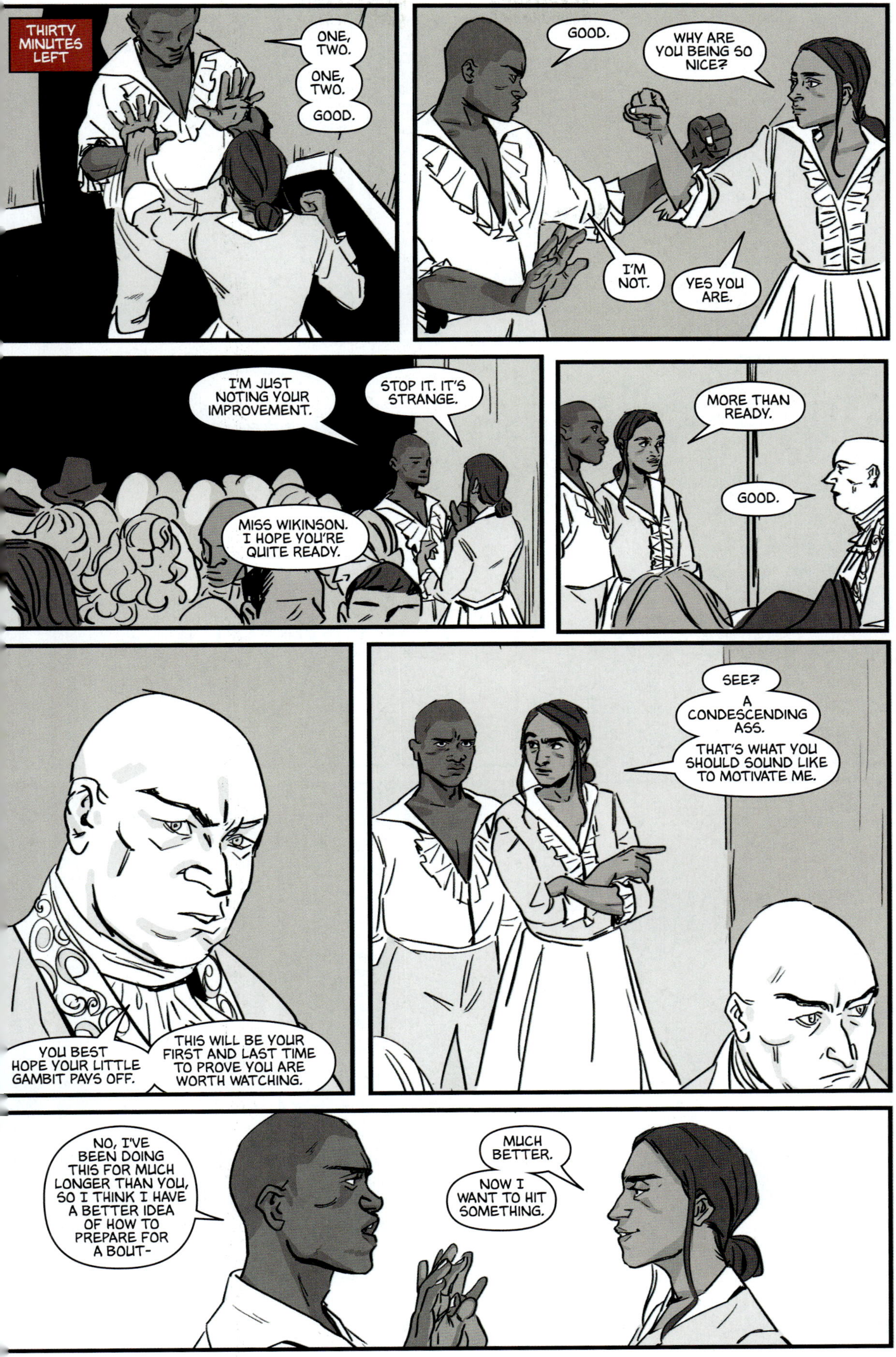
THIRTY MINUTES LEFT
ONE, TWO.
ONE, TWO.
GOOD.
GOOD.
WHY ARE YOU BEING SO NICE?
I'M NOT.
YES YOU ARE.
I'M JUST NOTING YOUR IMPROVEMENT.
STOP IT. IT'S STRANGE.
MISS WIKINSON. I HOPE YOU'RE QUITE READY.
MORE THAN READY.
GOOD.
YOU BEST HOPE YOUR LITTLE GAMBIT PAYS OFF.
THIS WILL BE YOUR FIRST AND LAST TIME TO PROVE YOU ARE WORTH WATCHING.
SEE?
A CONDESCENDING ASS.
THAT'S WHAT YOU SHOULD SOUND LIKE TO MOTIVATE ME.
NO, I'VE BEEN DOING THIS FOR MUCH LONGER THAN YOU, SO I THINK I HAVE A BETTER IDEA OF HOW TO PREPARE FOR A BOUT-
MUCH BETTER.
NOW I WANT TO HIT SOMETHING.

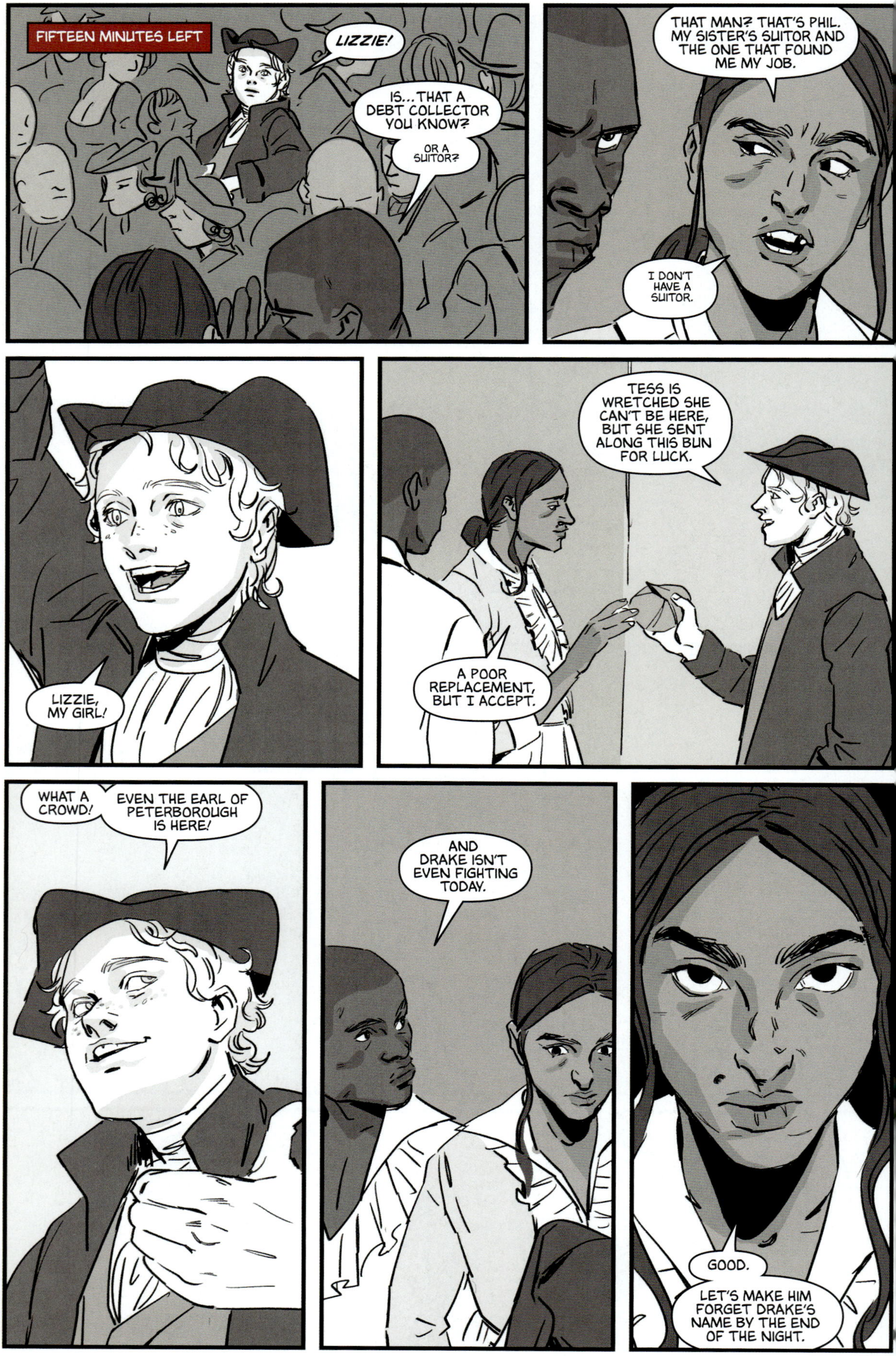
FIFTEEN MINUTES LEFT
LIZZIE!
IS...THAT A DEBT COLLECTOR YOU KNOW?
OR A SUITOR?
THAT MAN? THAT'S PHIL. MY SISTER'S SUITOR AND THE ONE THAT FOUND ME MY JOB.
I DON'T HAVE A SUITOR.
LIZZIE, MY GIRL!
TESS IS WRETCHED SHE CAN'T BE HERE, BUT SHE SENT ALONG THIS BUN FOR LUCK.
A POOR REPLACEMENT, BUT I ACCEPT.
WHAT A CROWD!
EVEN THE EARL OF PETERBOROUGH IS HERE!
AND DRAKE ISN'T EVEN FIGHTING TODAY.
GOOD.
LET'S MAKE HIM FORGET DRAKE'S NAME BY THE END OF THE NIGHT.

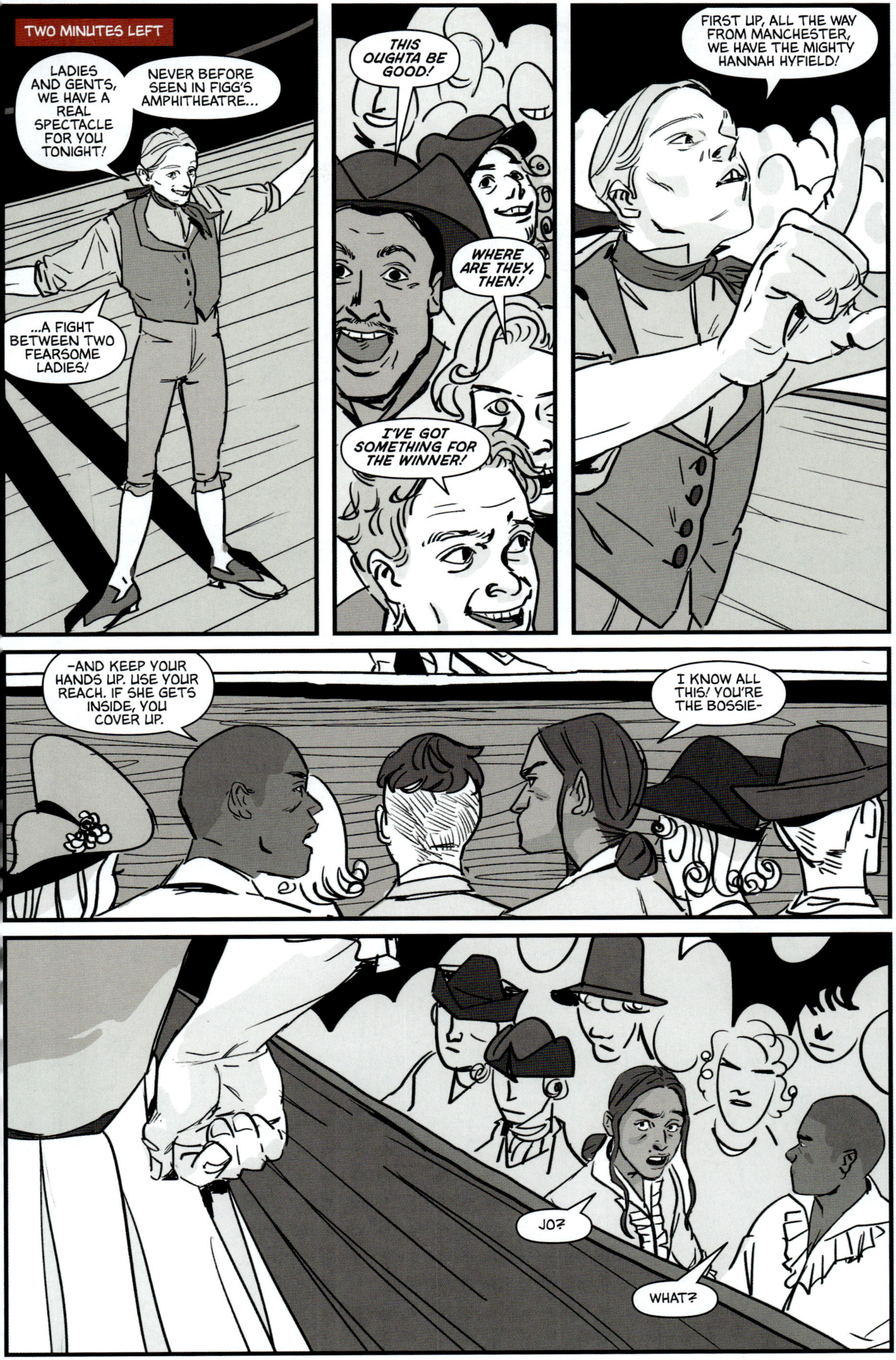
TWO MINUTES LEFT
LADIES AND GENTS, WE HAVE A REAL SPECTACLE FOR YOU TONIGHT!
NEVER BEFORE SEEN IN FIGG'S AMPHITHEATRE...
...A FIGHT BETWEEN TWO FEARSOME LADIES!
THIS OUGHTA BE GOOD!
WHERE ARE THEY, THEN!
I'VE GOT SOMETHING FOR THE WINNER!
FIRST UP, ALL THE WAY FROM MANCHESTER, WE HAVE THE MIGHTY HANNAH HYFIELD!
-AND KEEP YOUR HANDS UP. USE YOUR REACH. IF SHE GETS INSIDE, YOU COVER UP.
I KNOW ALL THIS! YOU'RE THE BOSSIE-
JO?
WHAT?

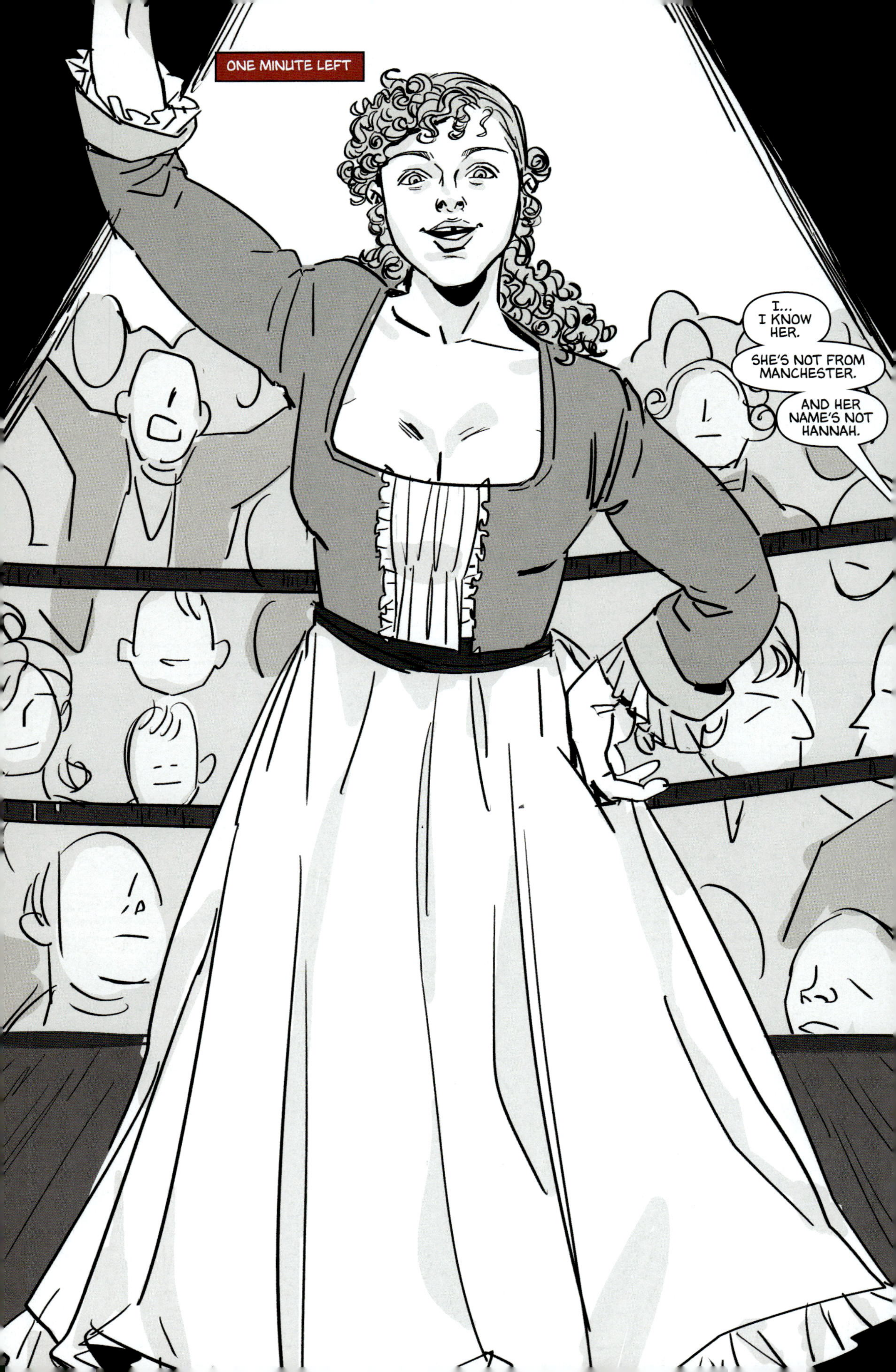

ONE MINUTE LEFT
I... I KNOW HER.
SHE'S NOT FROM MANCHESTER.
AND HER NAME'S NOT HANNAH.

3

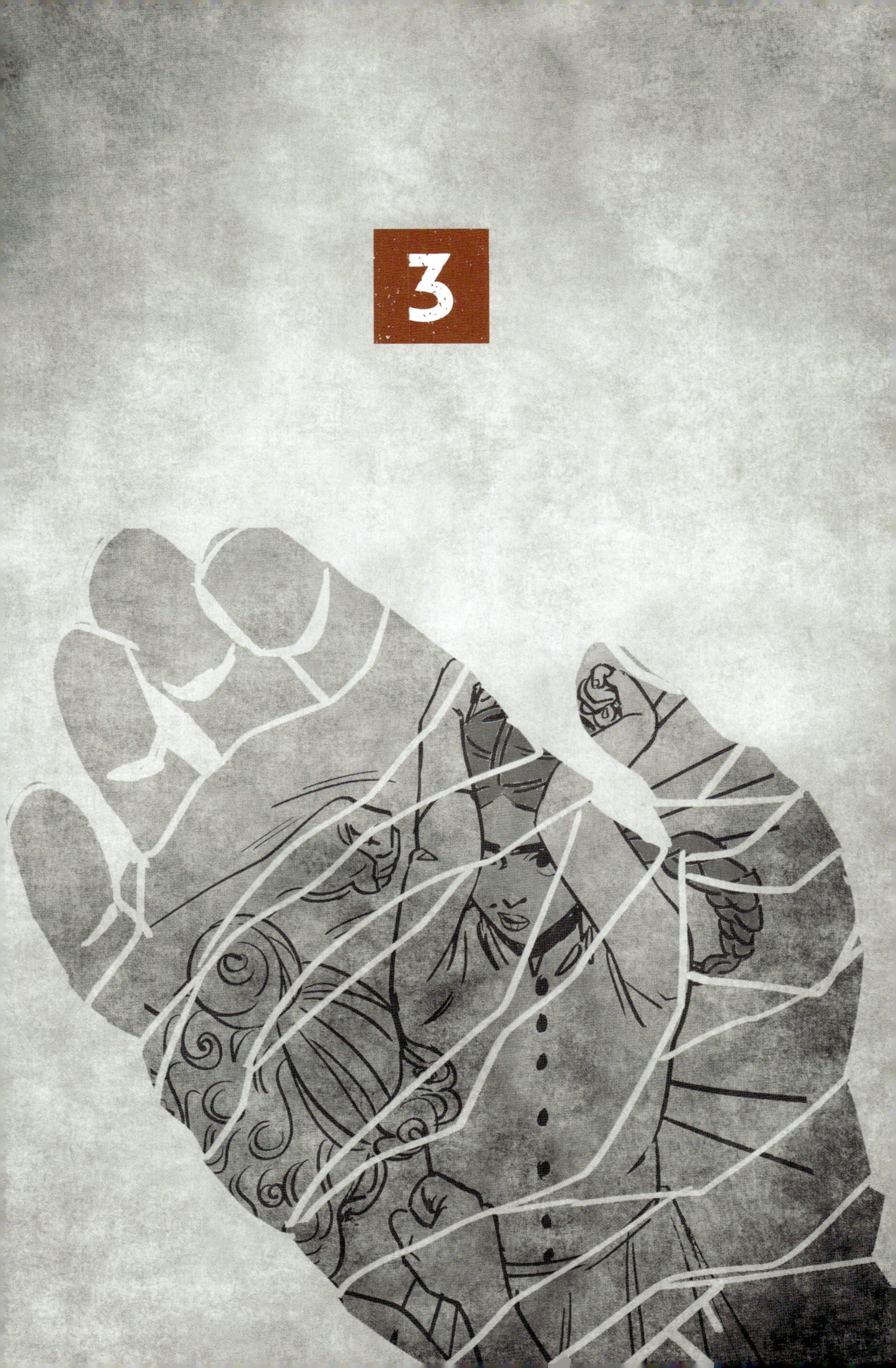

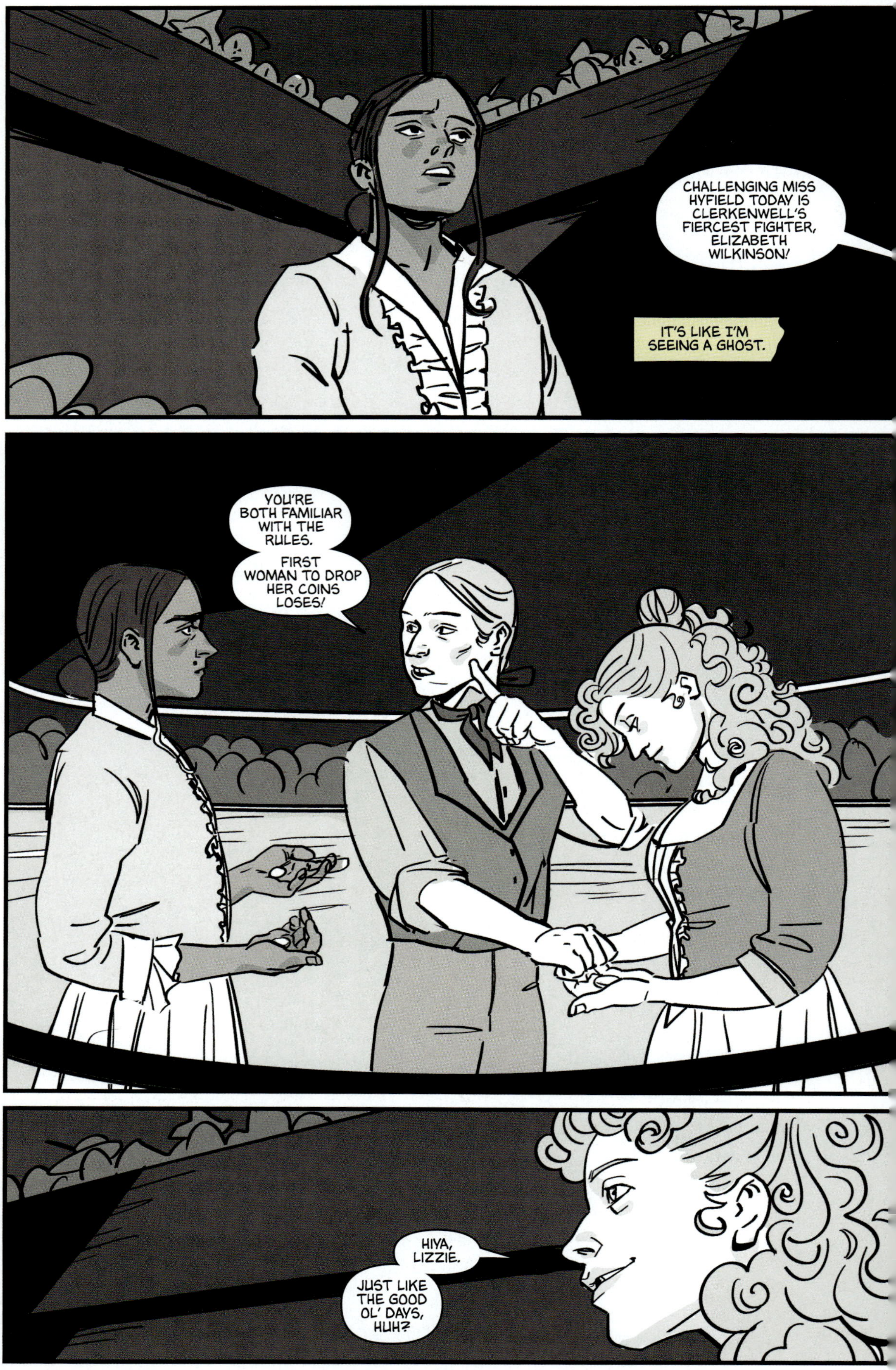
CHALLENGING MISS HYFIELD TODAY IS CLERKENWELL'S FIERCEST FIGHTER, ELIZABETH WILKINSON!
IT'S LIKE I'M SEEING A GHOST.
YOU'RE BOTH FAMILIAR WITH THE RULES.
FIRST WOMAN TO DROP HER COINS LOSES!
HIYA, LIZZIE.
JUST LIKE THE GOOD OL' DAYS, HUH?

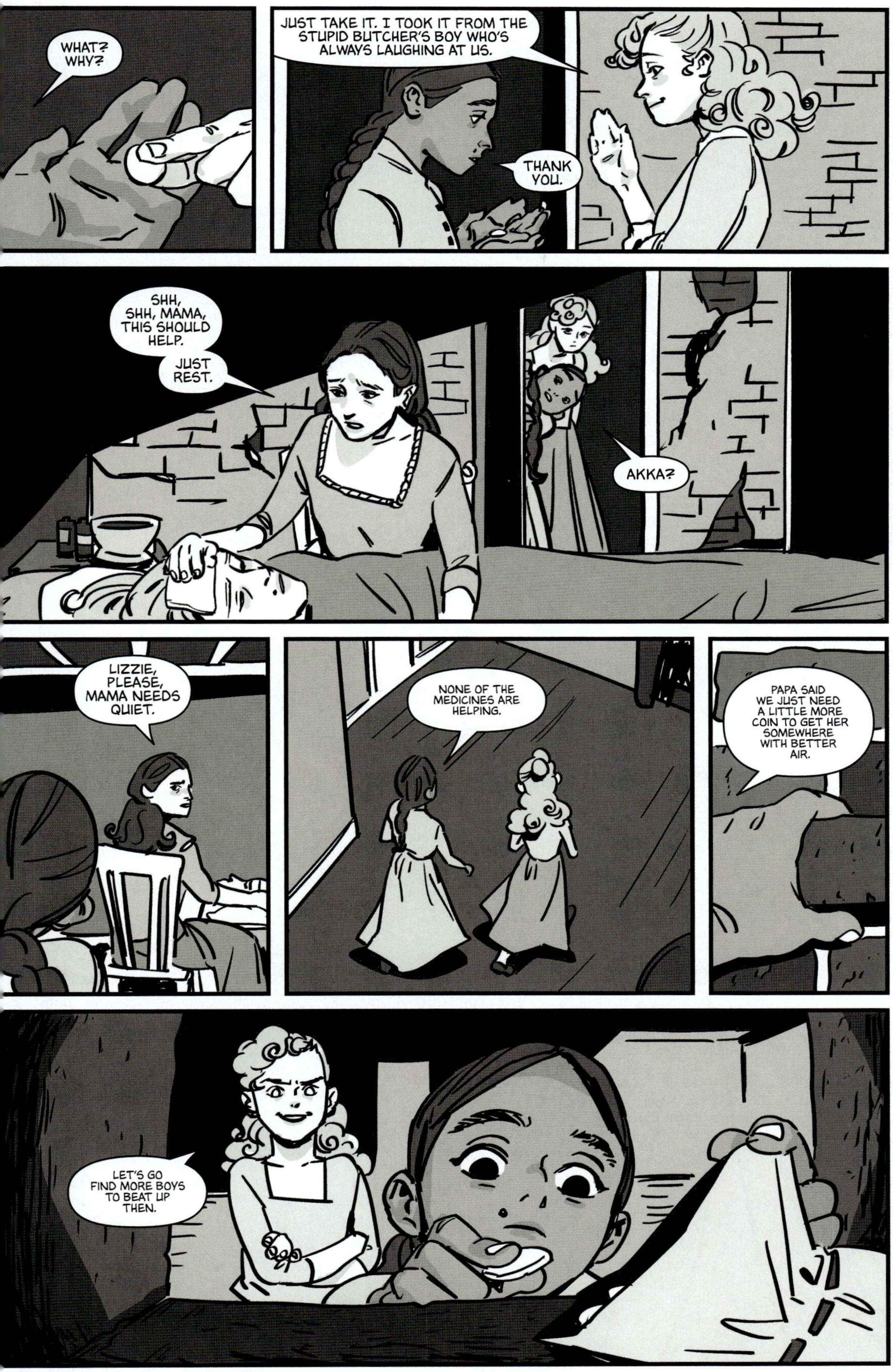
WHAT? WHY?
JUST TAKE IT. I TOOK IT FROM THE STUPID BUTCHER'S BOY WHO'S ALWAYS LAUGHING AT US.
THANK YOU.
SHH, SHH, MAMA, THIS SHOULD HELP.
JUST REST.
AKKA?
LIZZIE, PLEASE, MAMA NEEDS QUIET.
NONE OF THE MEDICINES ARE HELPING.
PAPA SAID WE JUST NEED A LITTLE MORE COIN TO GET HER SOMEWHERE WITH BETTER AIR.
LET'S GO FIND MORE BOYS TO BEAT UP THEN.

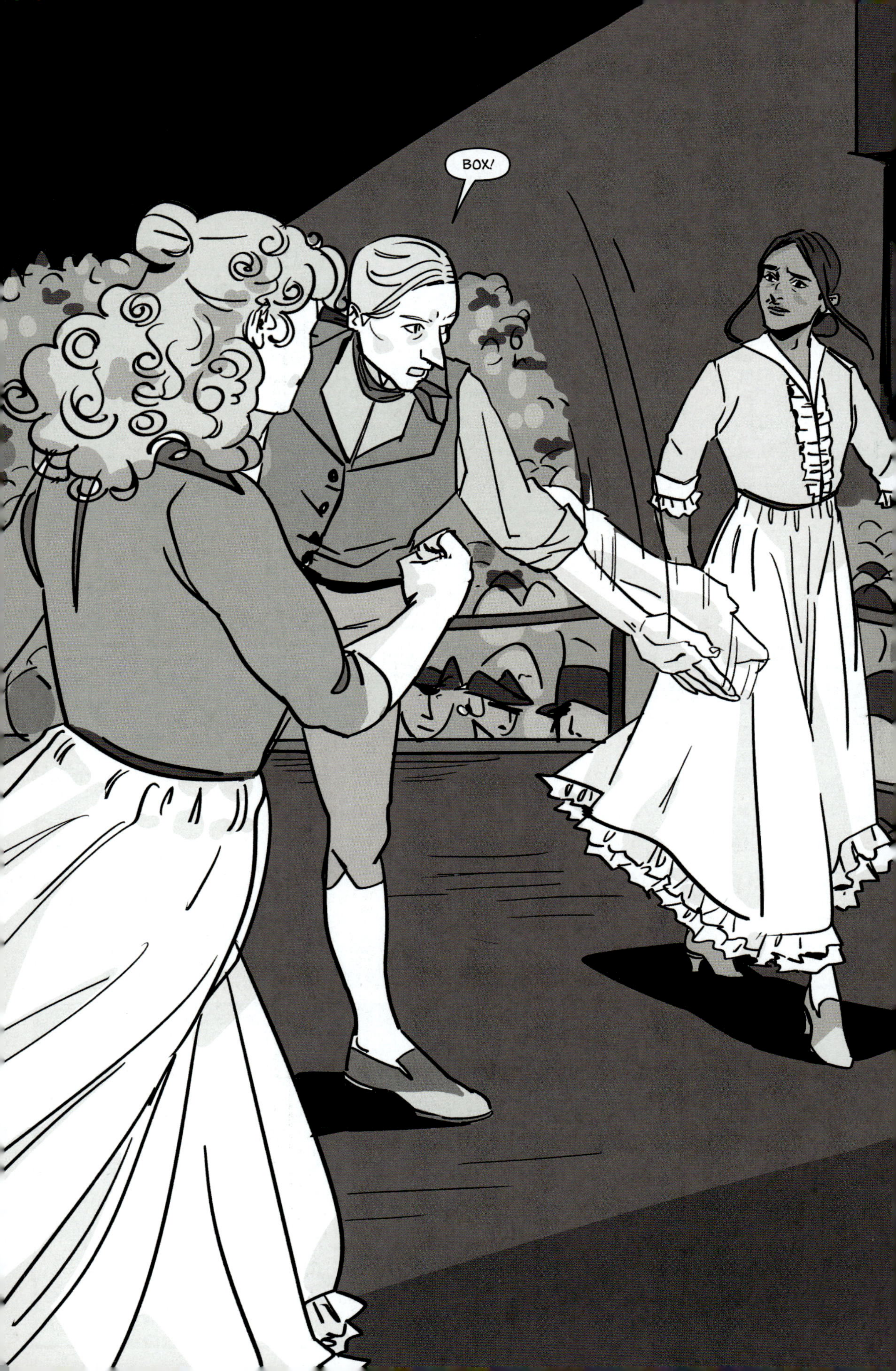
BOX!

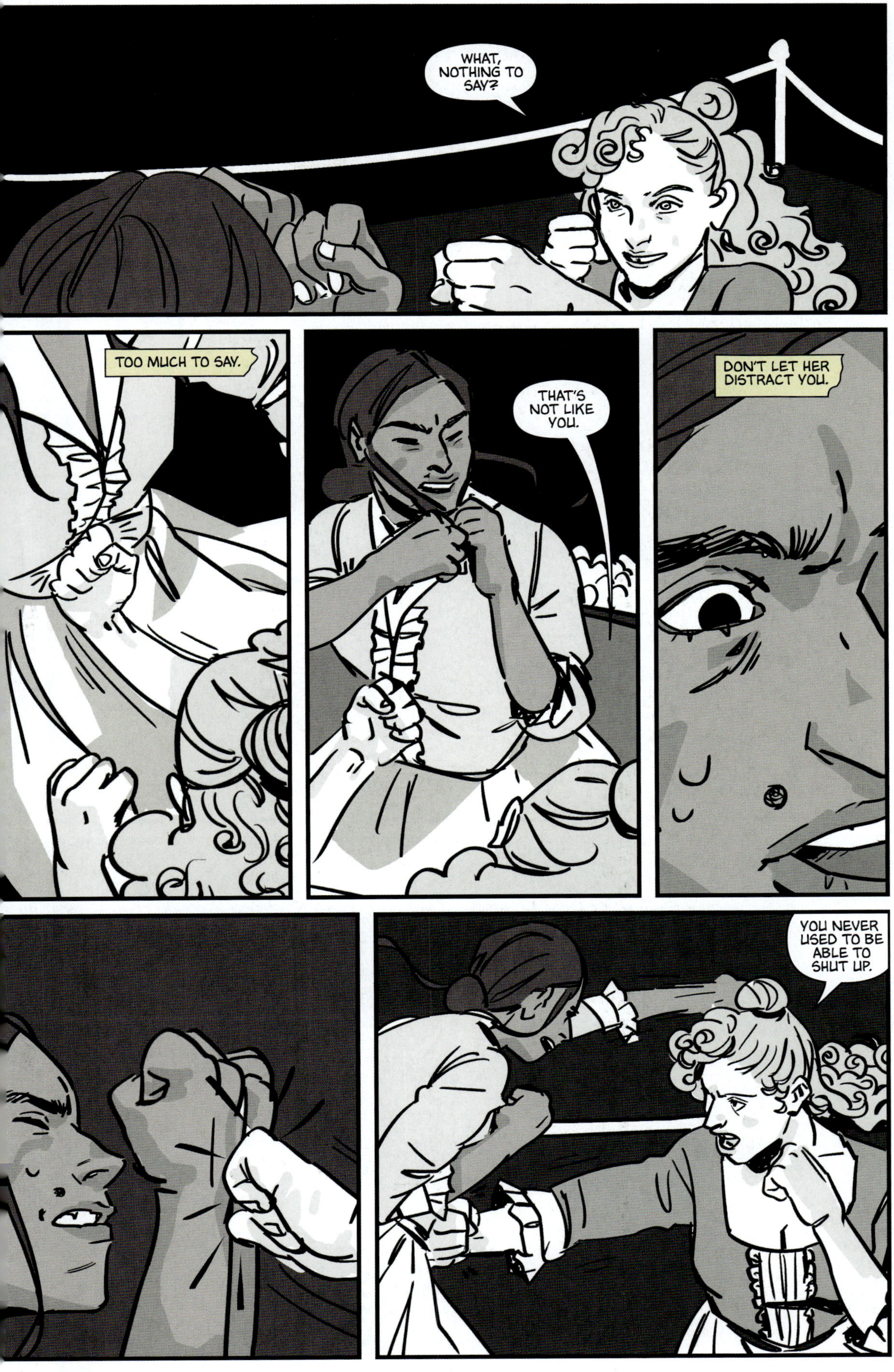
WHAT, NOTHING TO SAY?
TOO MUCH TO SAY.
THAT'S NOT LIKE YOU.
DON'T LET HER DISTRACT YOU.
YOU NEVER USED TO BE ABLE TO SHUT UP.

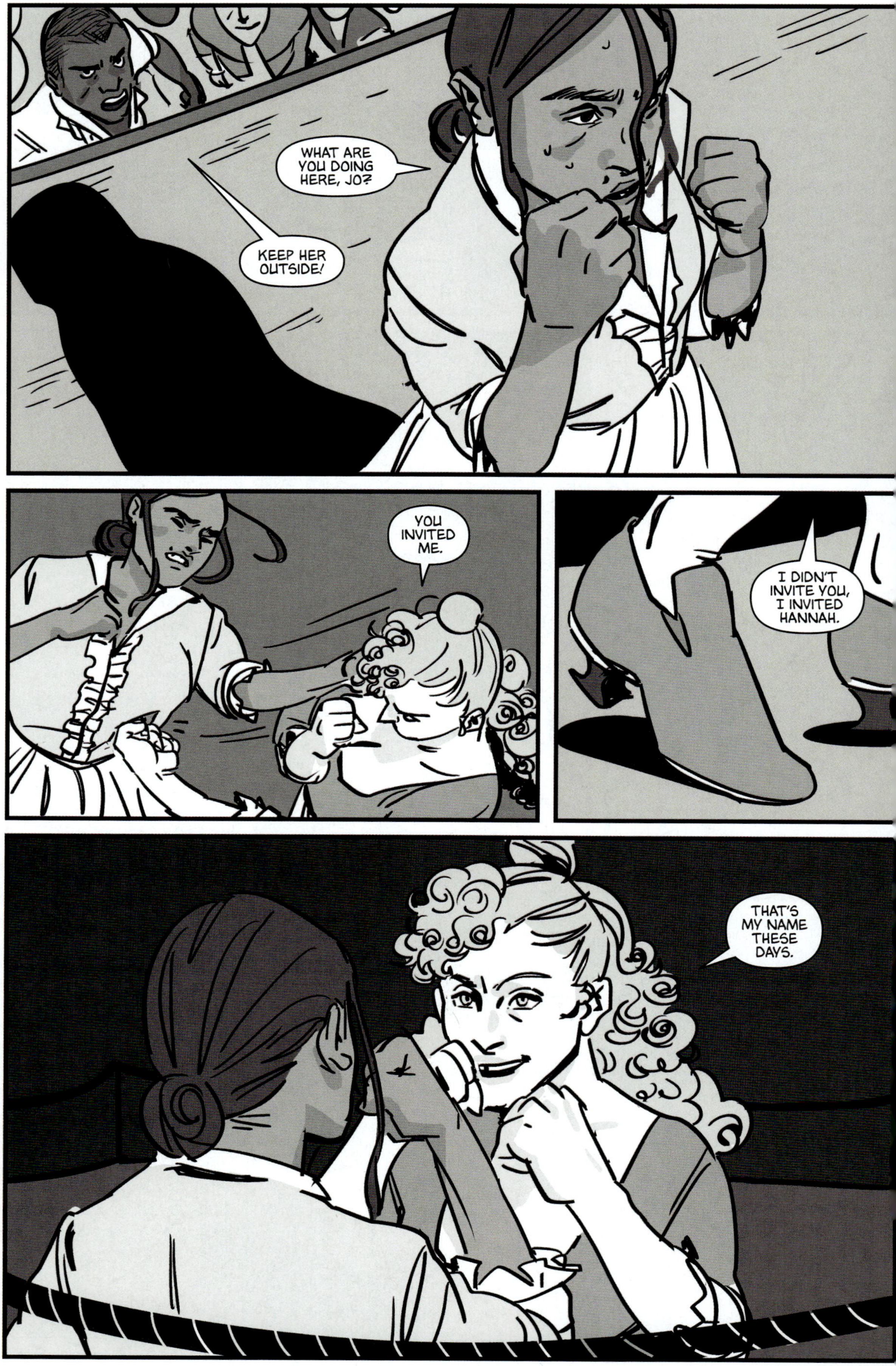
WHAT ARE YOU DOING HERE, JO?
KEEP HER OUTSIDE!
YOU INVITED ME.
I DIDN'T INVITE YOU, I INVITED HANNAH.
THAT'S MY NAME THESE DAYS.

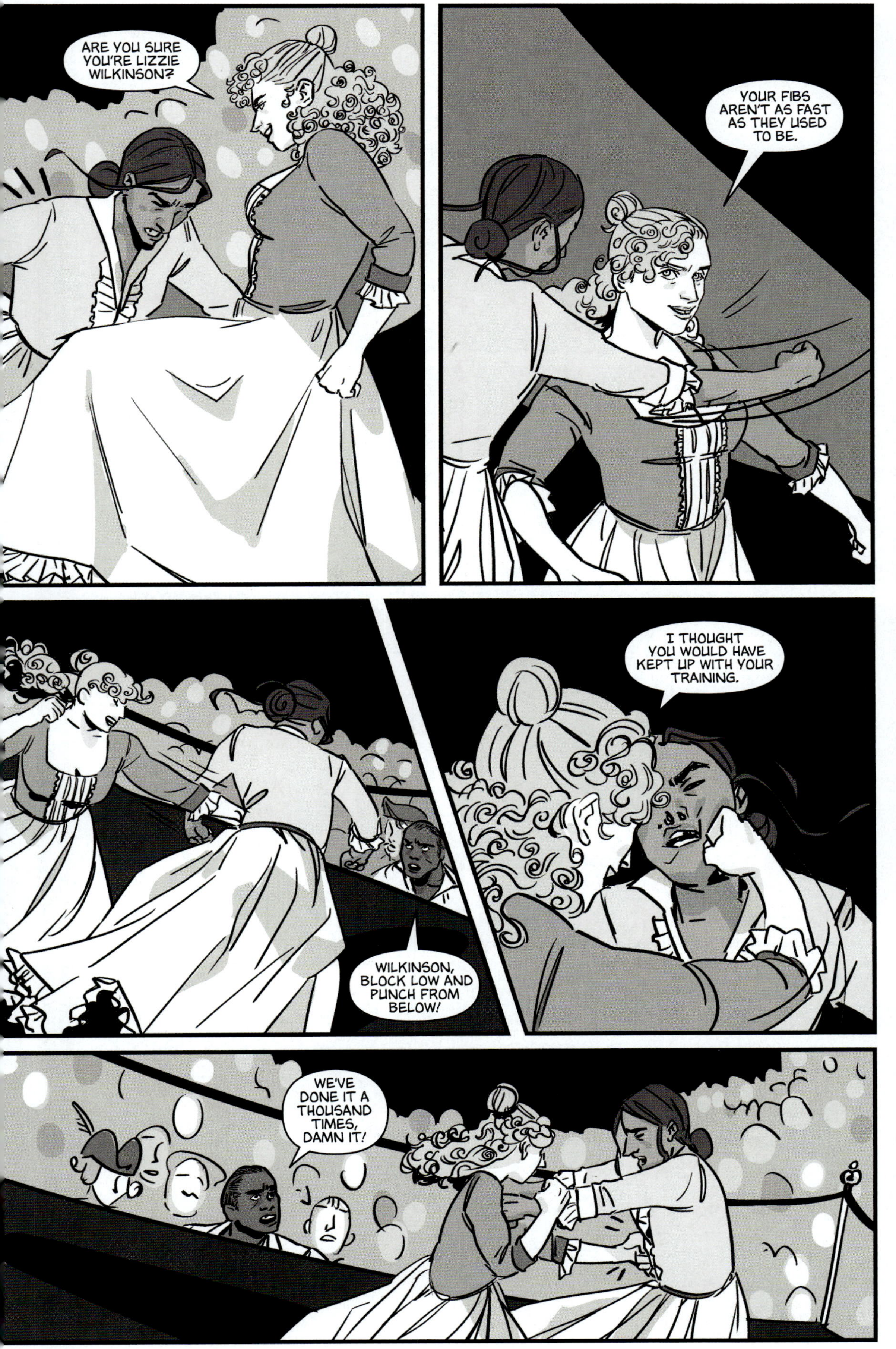
ARE YOU SURE YOU'RE LIZZIE WILKINSON?
YOUR FIBS AREN'T AS FAST AS THEY USED TO BE.
WILKINSON, BLOCK LOW AND PUNCH FROM BELOW!
I THOUGHT YOU WOULD HAVE KEPT UP WITH YOUR TRAINING.
WE'VE DONE IT A THOUSAND TIMES, DAMN IT!

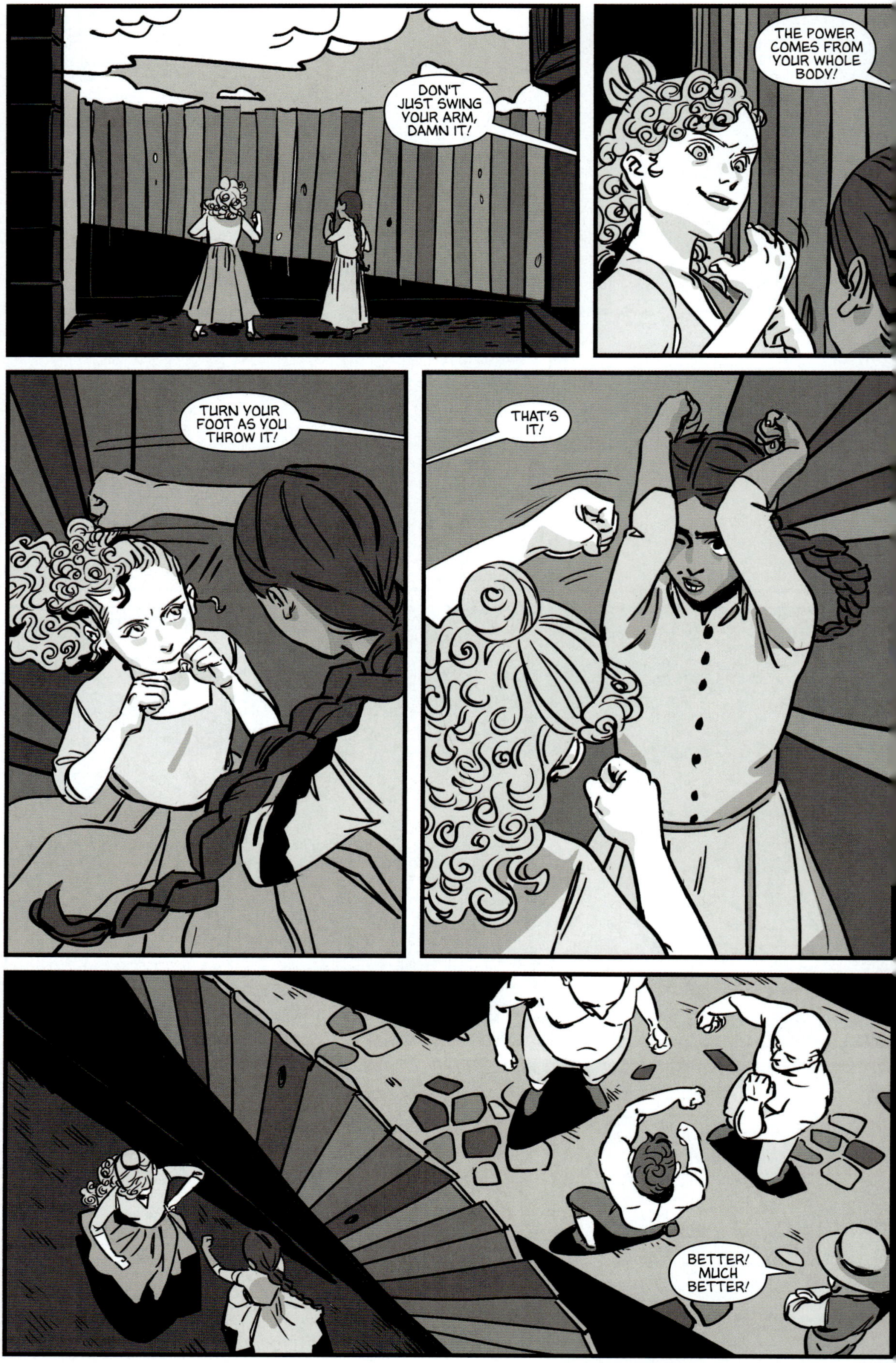
DON'T JUST SWING YOUR ARM, DAMN IT!
THE POWER COMES FROM YOUR WHOLE BODY!
TURN YOUR FOOT AS YOU THROW IT!
THAT'S IT!
BETTER! MUCH BETTER!

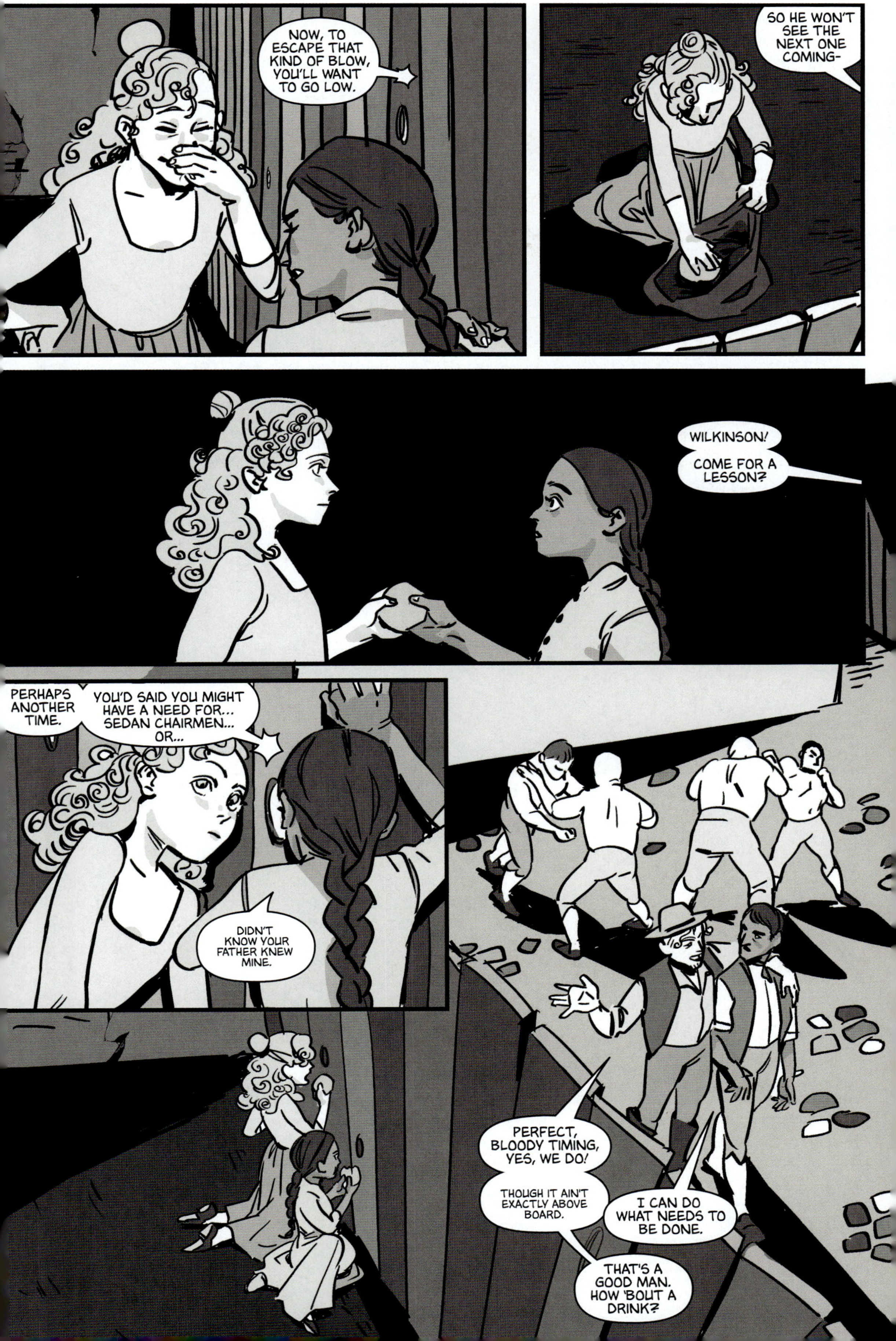
NOW, TO ESCAPE THAT KIND OF BLOW, YOU'LL WANT TO GO LOW.
SO HE WON'T SEE THE NEXT ONE COMING-
WILKINSON!
COME FOR A LESSON?
PERHAPS ANOTHER TIME.
YOU'D SAID YOU MIGHT HAVE A NEED FOR... SEDAN CHAIRMEN... OR...
DIDN'T KNOW YOUR FATHER KNEW MINE.
PERFECT, BLOODY TIMING, YES, WE DO!
THOUGH IT AIN'T EXACTLY ABOVE BOARD.
I CAN DO WHAT NEEDS TO BE DONE.
THAT'S A GOOD MAN. HOW 'BOUT A DRINK?

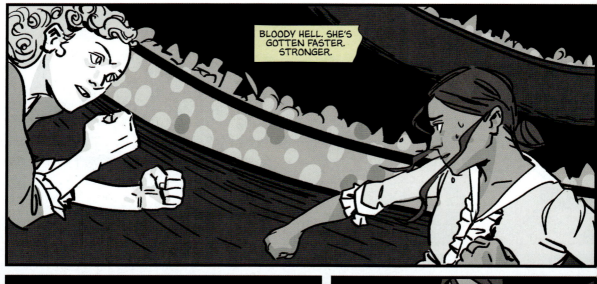

BLOODY HELL. SHE'S GOTTEN FASTER. STRONGER.

BUT.

SO.

HAVE.

I.

KEEP THE CENTER!

I'M NOT THAT HELPLESS LITTLE GIRL ANYMORE.

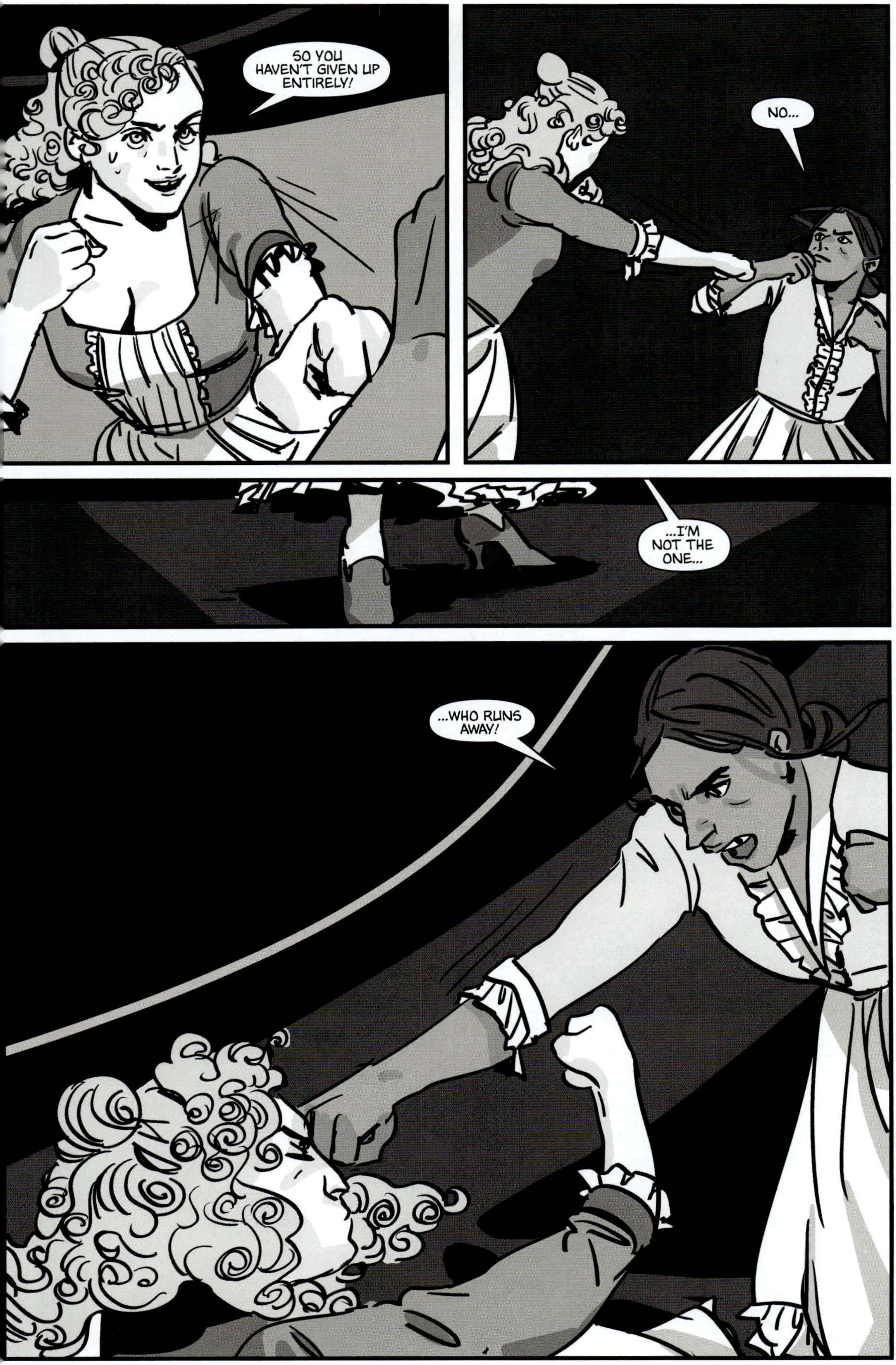
SO YOU HAVEN'T GIVEN UP ENTIRELY!
NO...
...I'M NOT THE ONE...
...WHO RUNS AWAY!

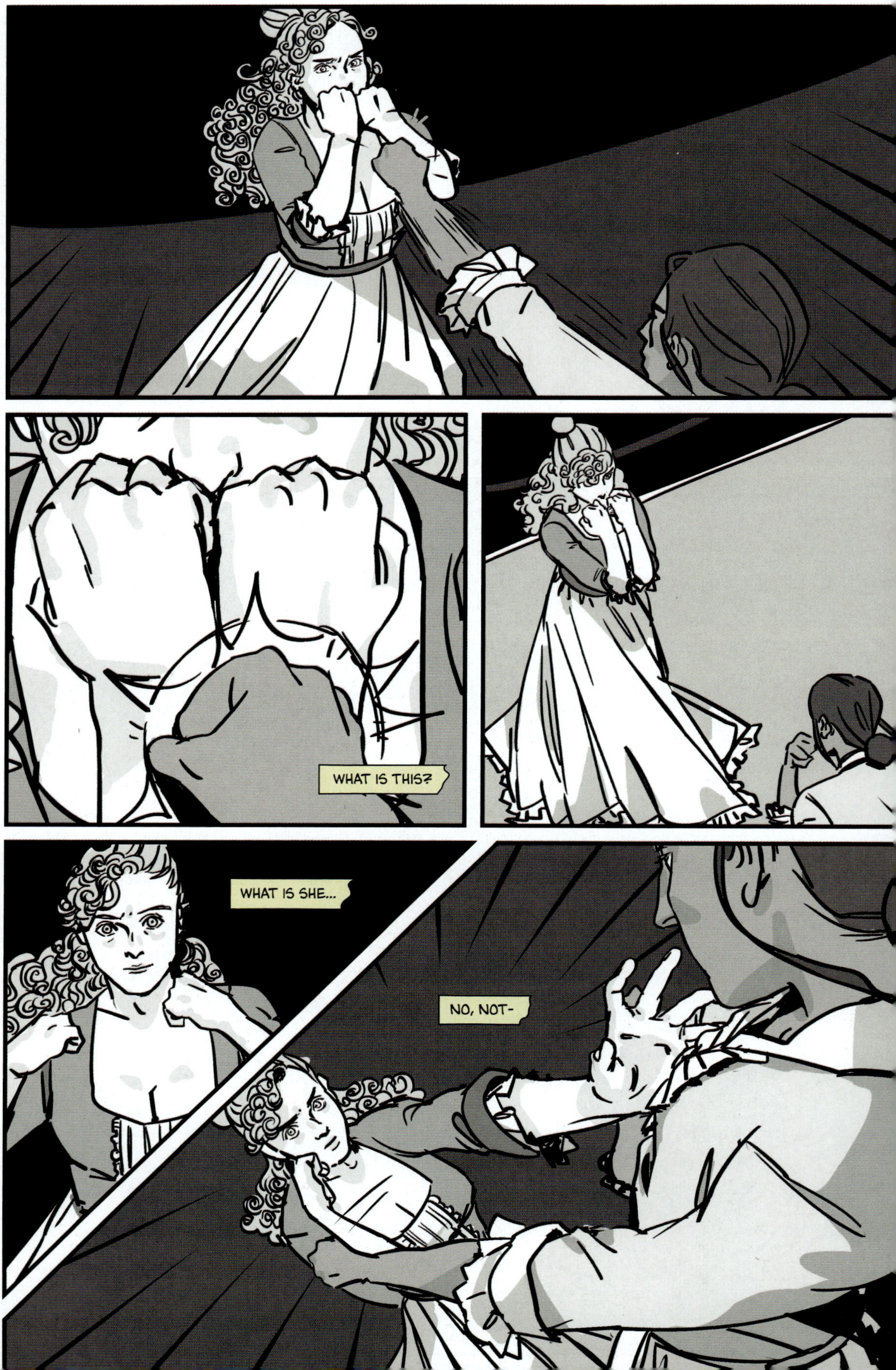
WHAT IS THIS?
WHAT IS SHE...
NO, NOT-

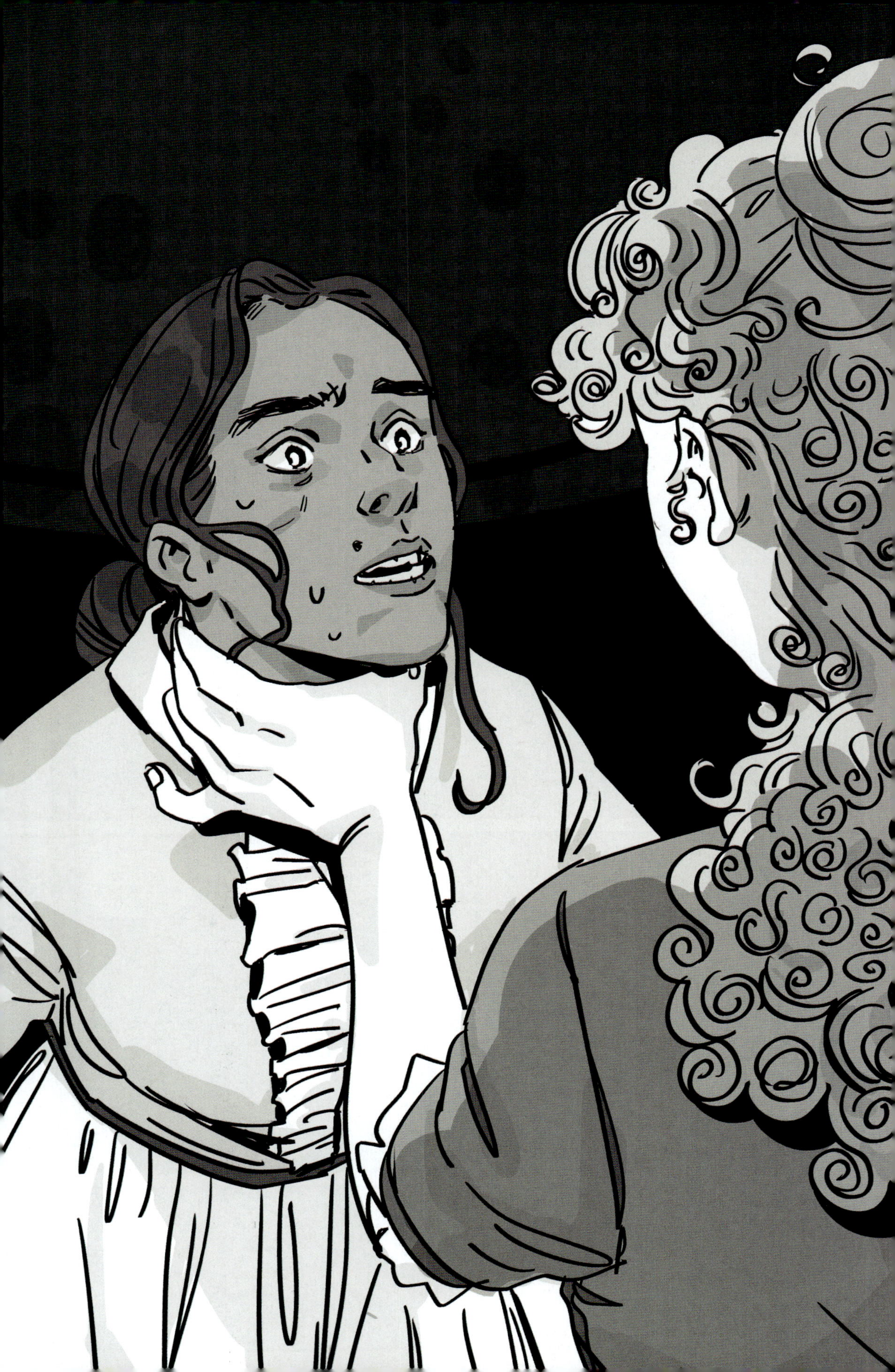

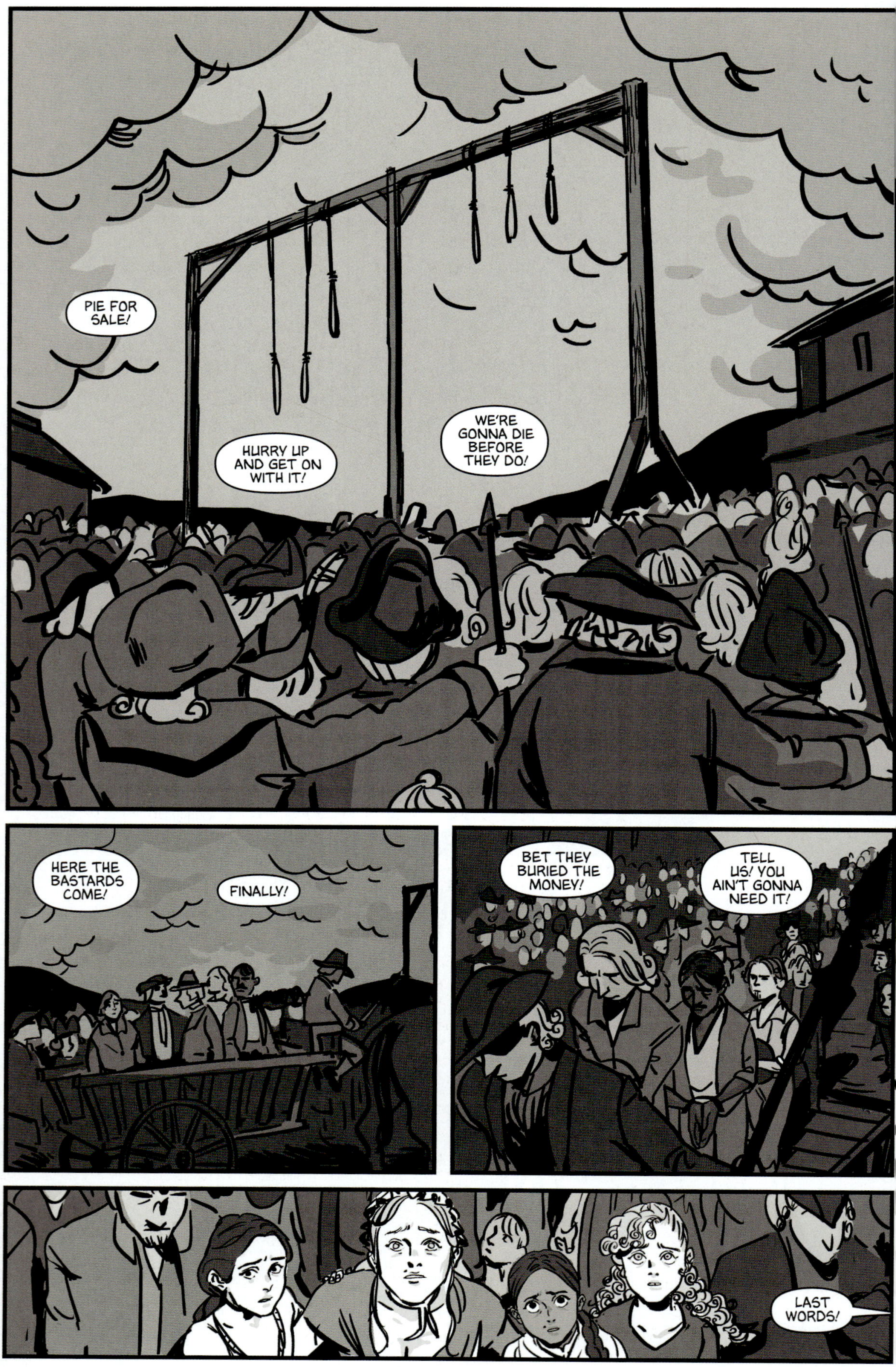
PIE FOR SALE!
HURRY UP AND GET ON WITH IT!
WE'RE GONNA DIE BEFORE THEY DO!
HERE THE BASTARDS COME!
FINALLY!
BET THEY BURIED THE MONEY!
TELL US! YOU AIN'T GONNA NEED IT!
LAST WORDS!

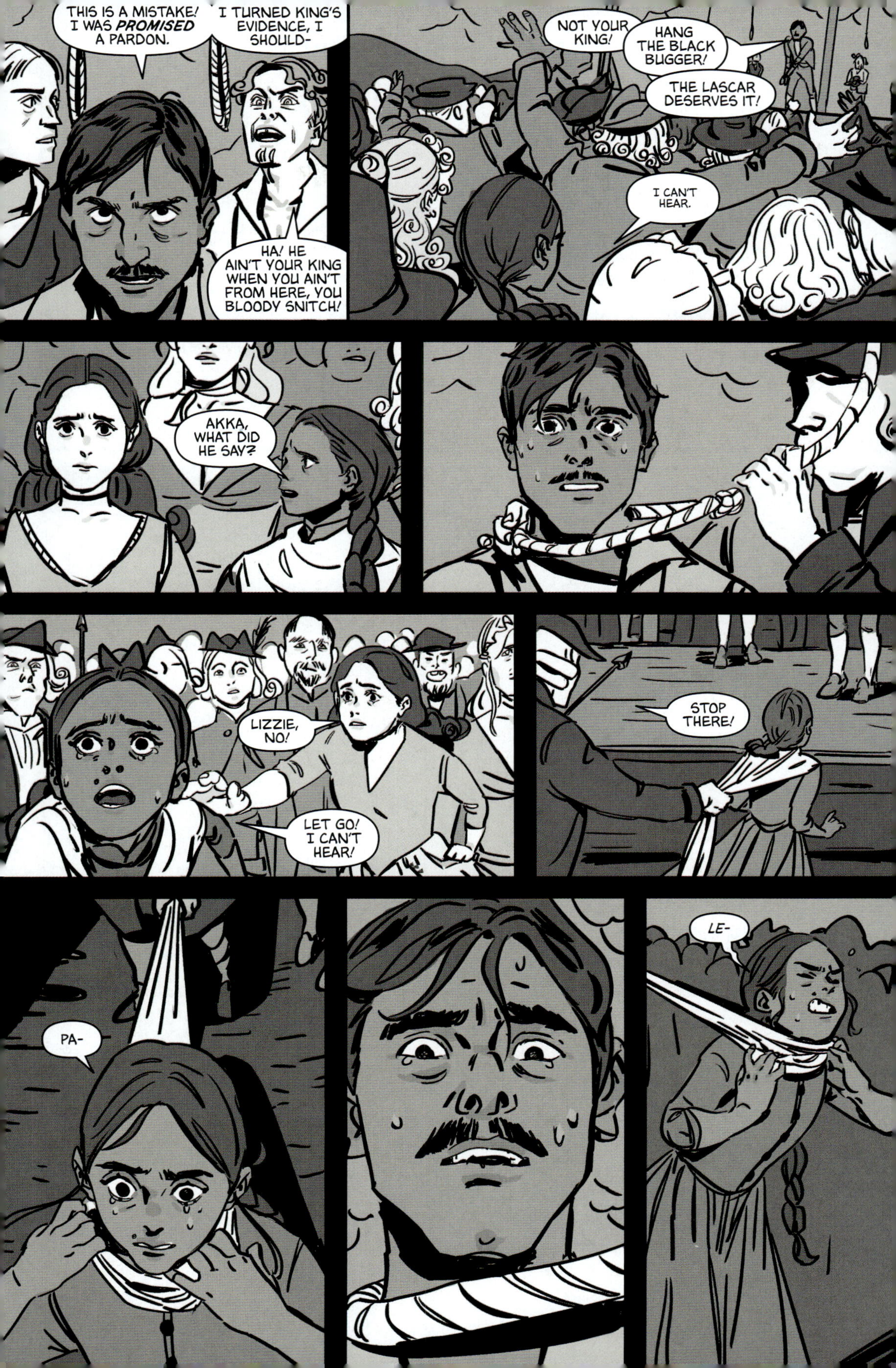
THIS IS A MISTAKE! I WAS *PROMISED* A PARDON.
I TURNED KING'S EVIDENCE, I SHOULD-
HA! HE AIN'T YOUR KING WHEN YOU AIN'T FROM HERE, YOU BLOODY SNITCH!
NOT YOUR KING!
HANG THE BLACK BUGGER!
THE LASCAR DESERVES IT!
I CAN'T HEAR.
AKKA, WHAT DID HE SAY?
LIZZIE, NO!
LET GO! I CAN'T HEAR!
STOP THERE!
PA-
LE-

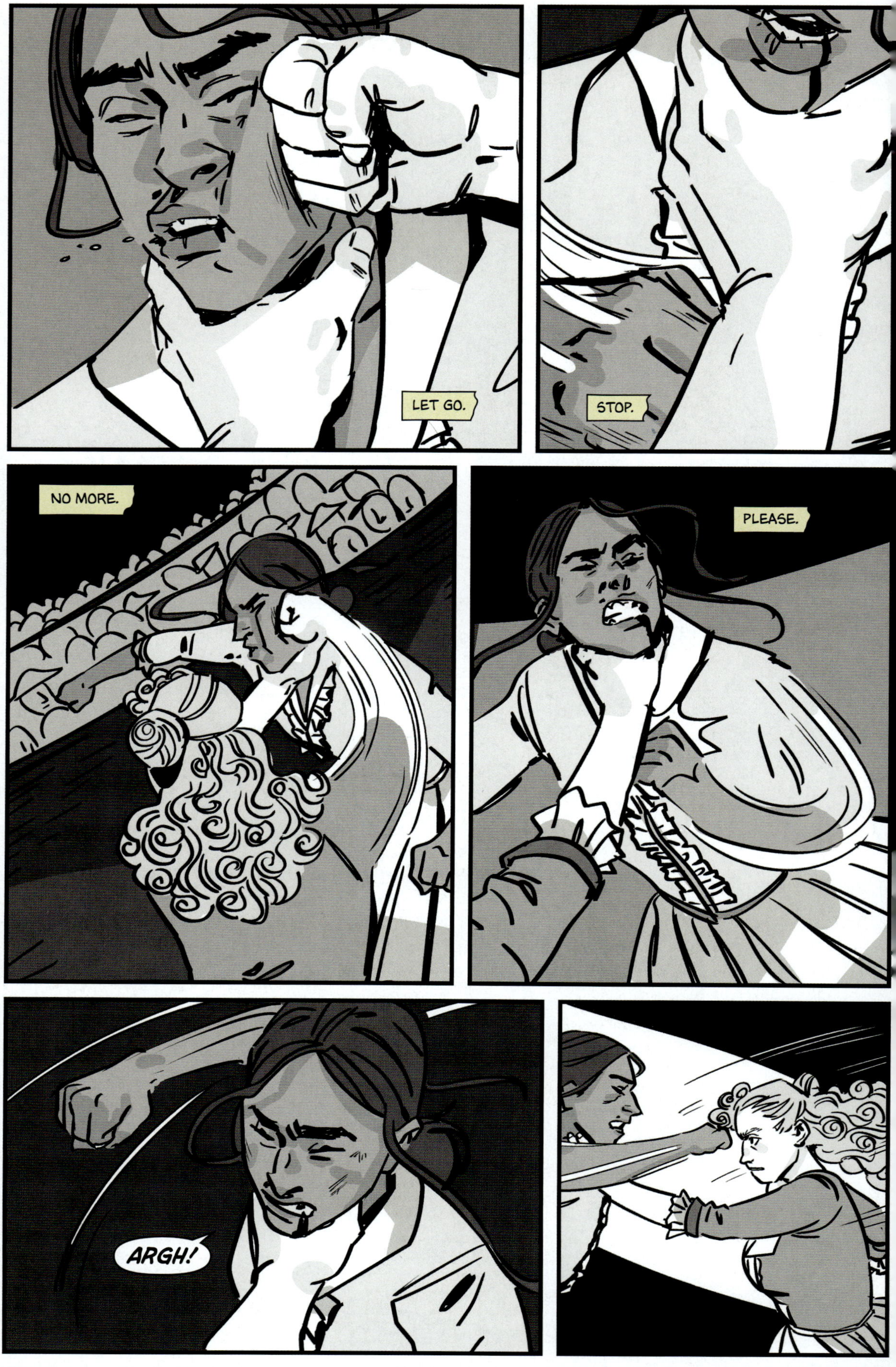
LET GO.
STOP.
NO MORE.
PLEASE.
ARGH!

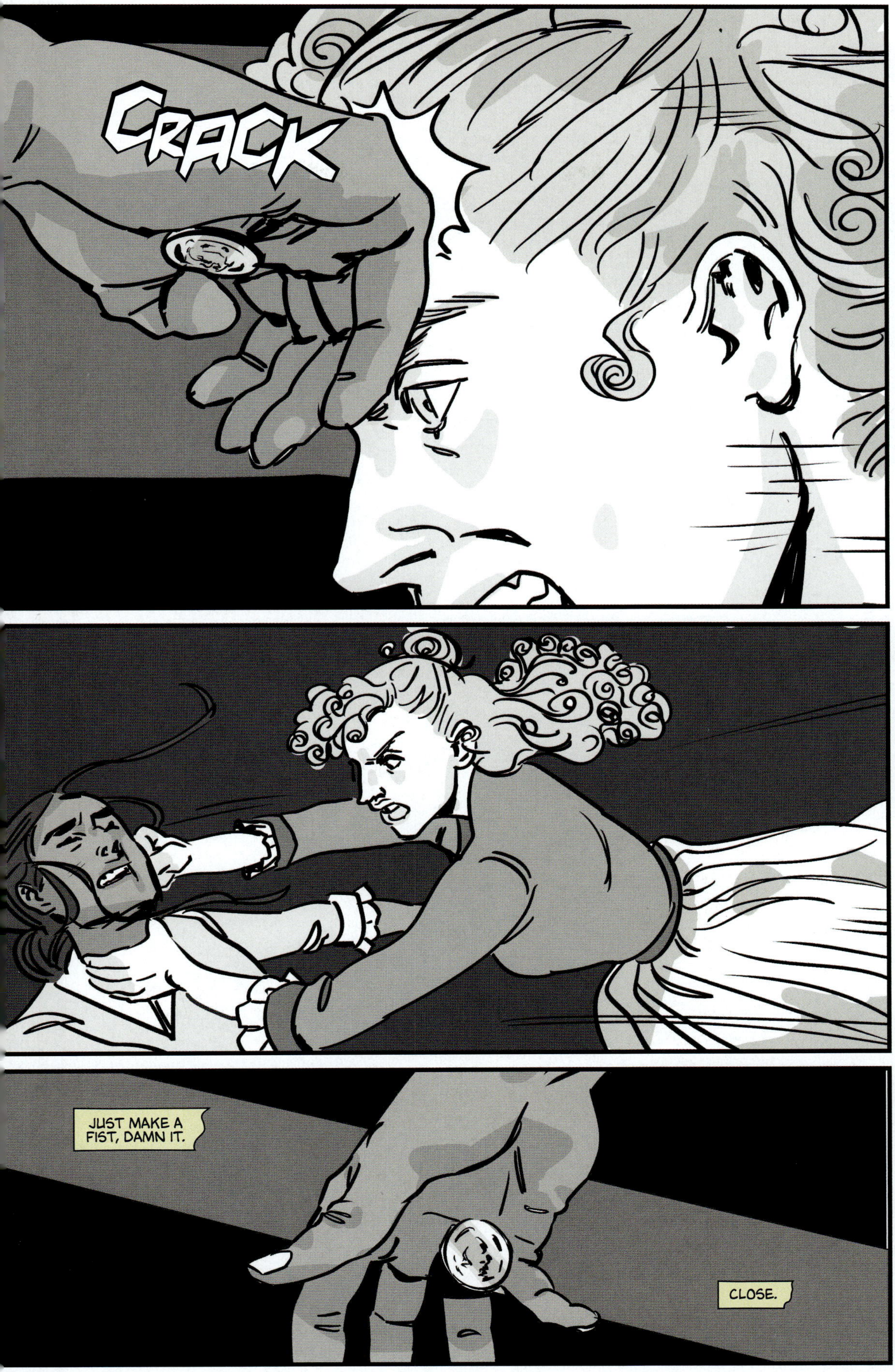
CRACK
JUST MAKE A FIST, DAMN IT.
CLOSE.

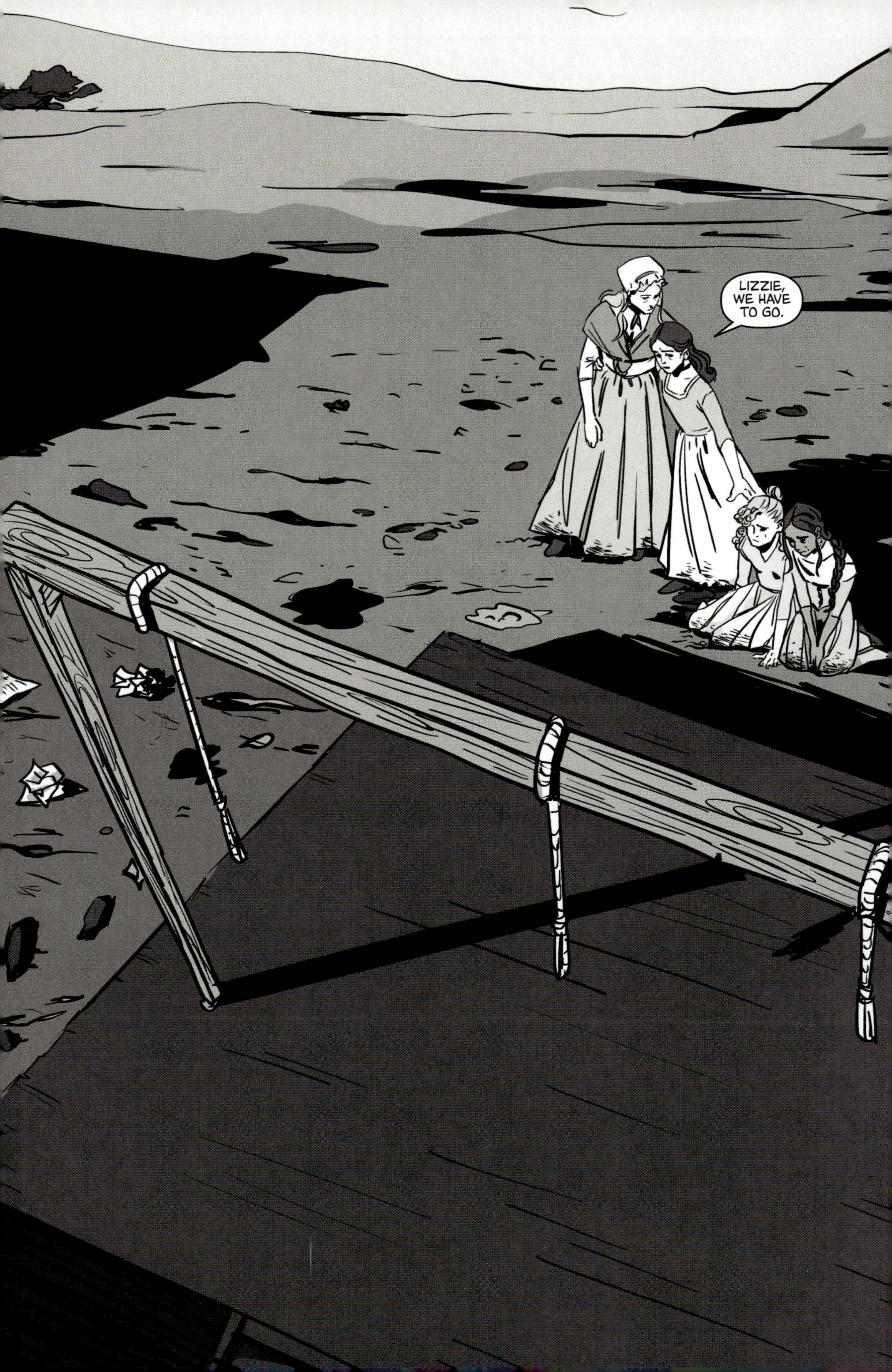
LIZZIE, WE HAVE TO GO.

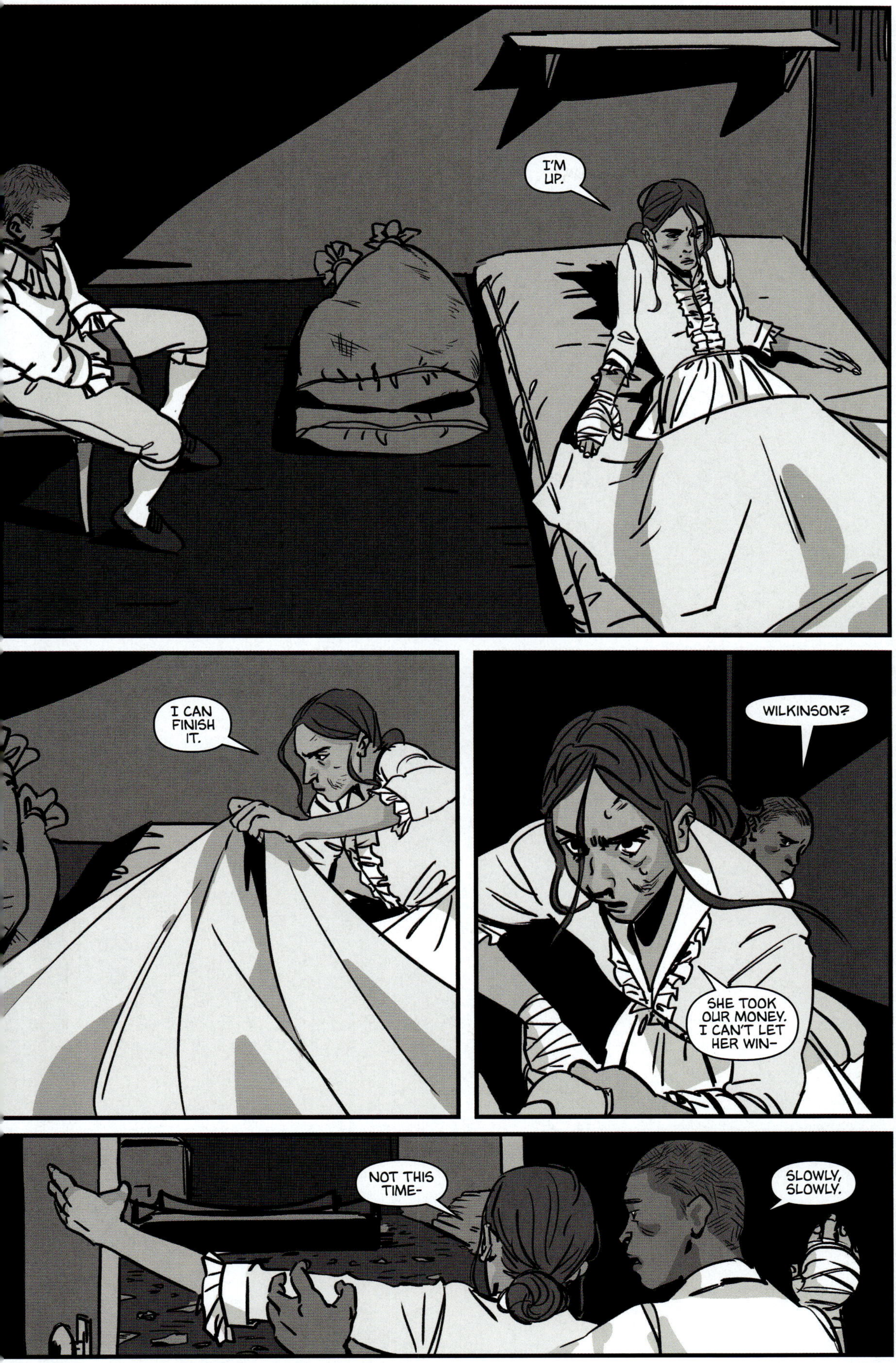
I'M UP.
I CAN FINISH IT.
WILKINSON?
SHE TOOK OUR MONEY. I CAN'T LET HER WIN-
NOT THIS TIME-
SLOWLY, SLOWLY.

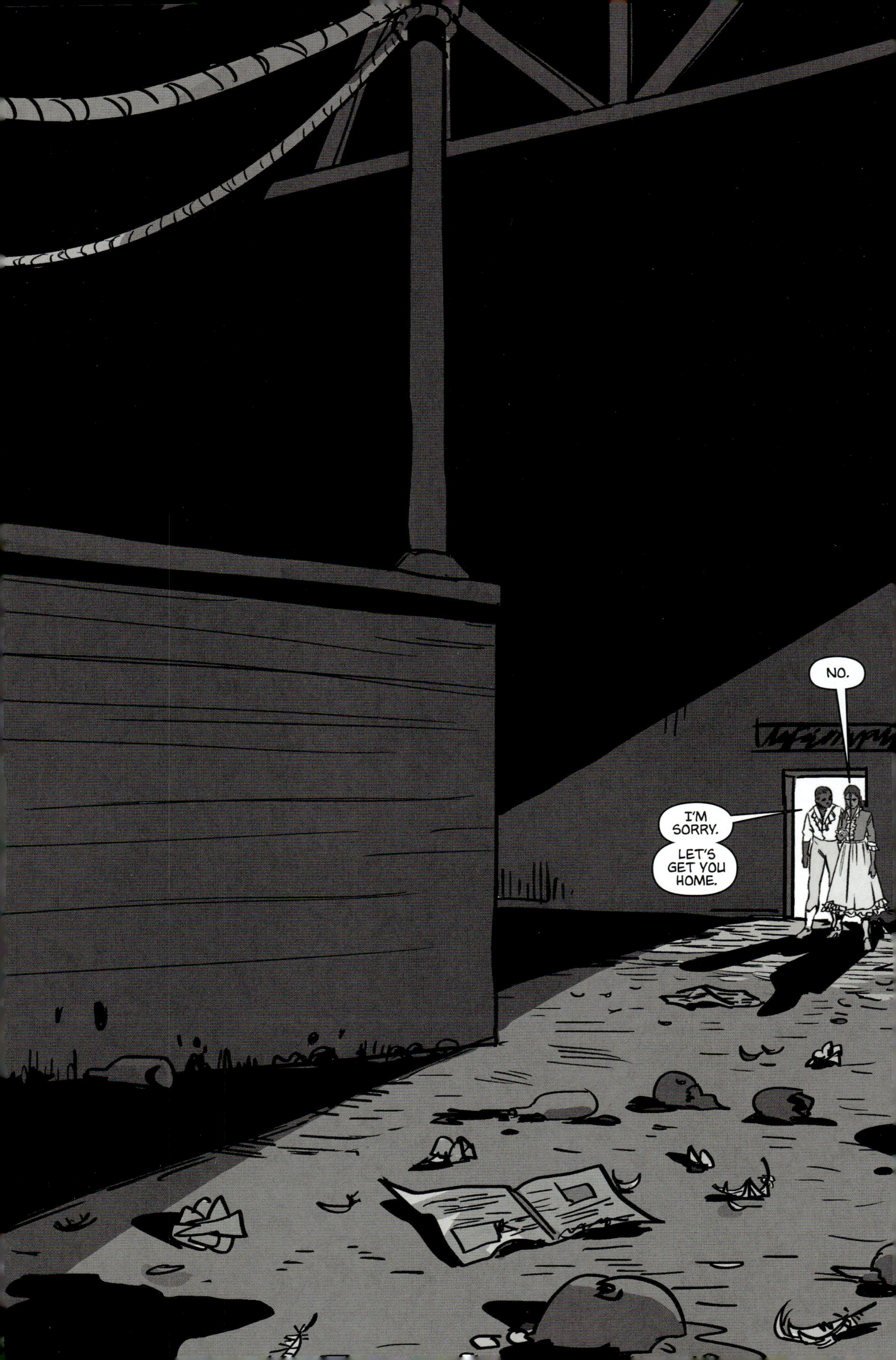
NO.
I'M SORRY.
LET'S GET YOU HOME.

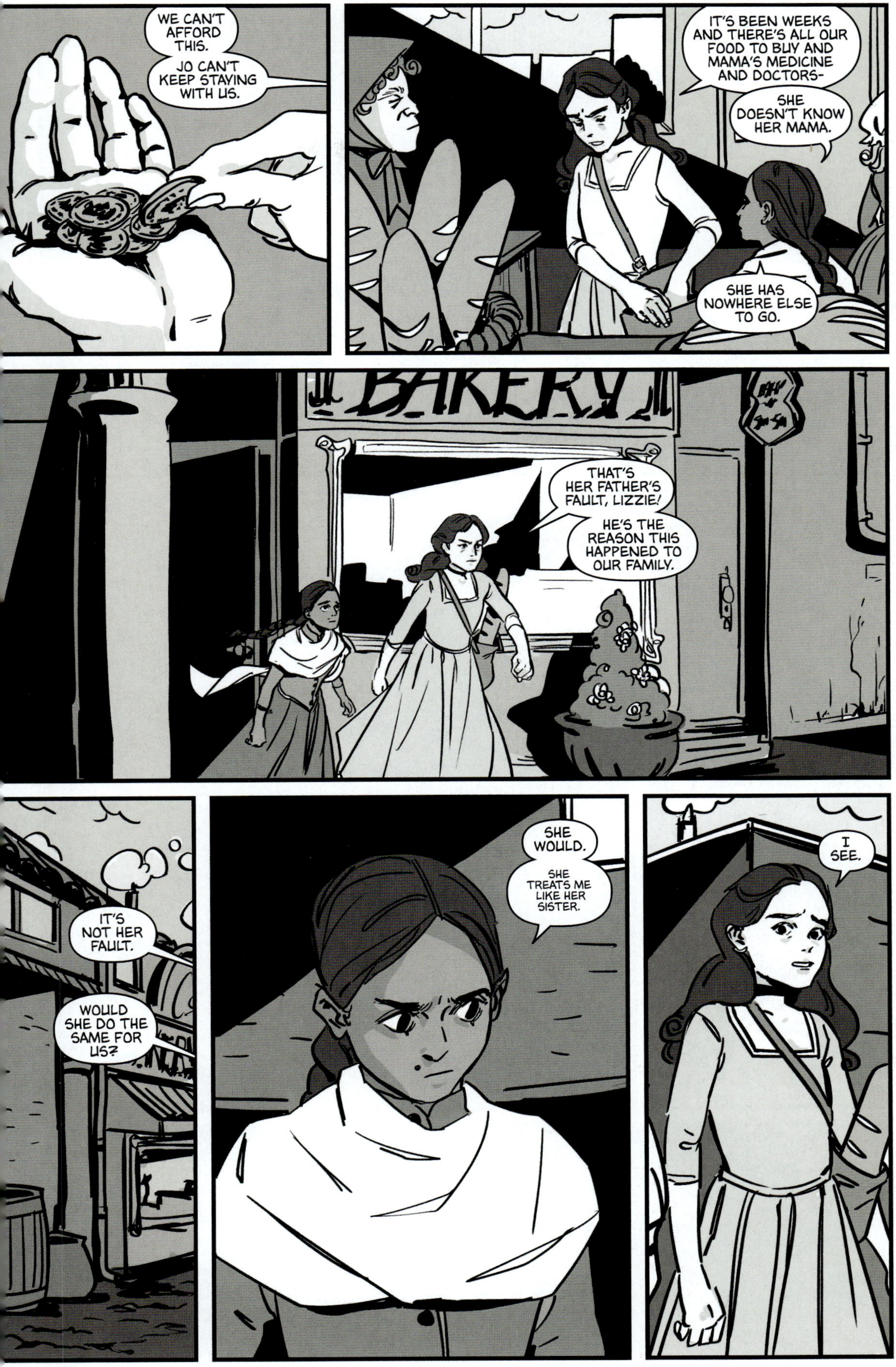
WE CAN'T AFFORD THIS.
JO CAN'T KEEP STAYING WITH US.
IT'S BEEN WEEKS AND THERE'S ALL OUR FOOD TO BUY AND MAMA'S MEDICINE AND DOCTORS-
SHE DOESN'T KNOW HER MAMA.
SHE HAS NOWHERE ELSE TO GO.
BAKERY
THAT'S HER FATHER'S FAULT, LIZZIE!
HE'S THE REASON THIS HAPPENED TO OUR FAMILY.
IT'S NOT HER FAULT.
WOULD SHE DO THE SAME FOR US?
SHE WOULD.
SHE TREATS ME LIKE HER SISTER.
I SEE.

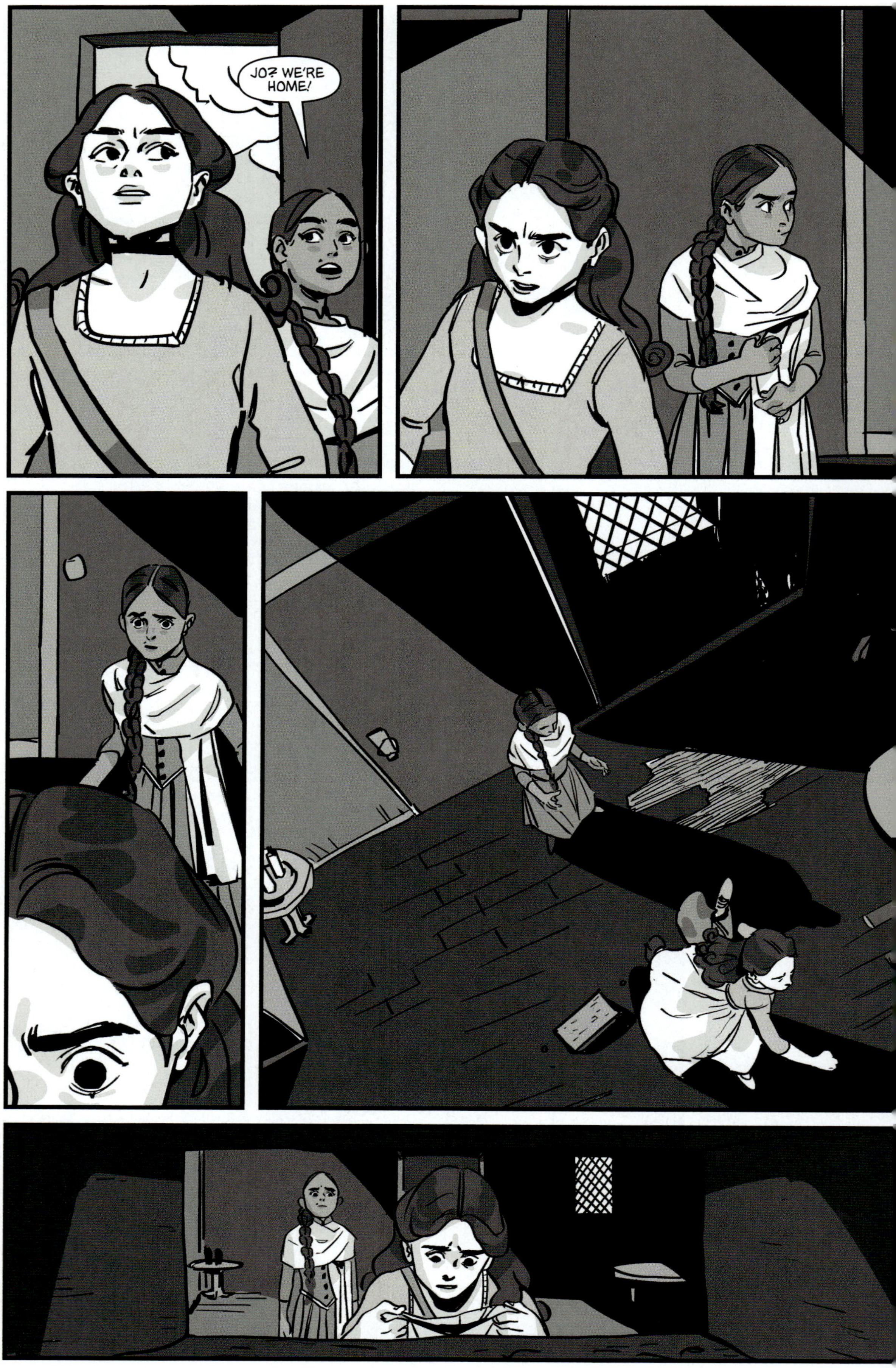
JO? WE'RE HOME!

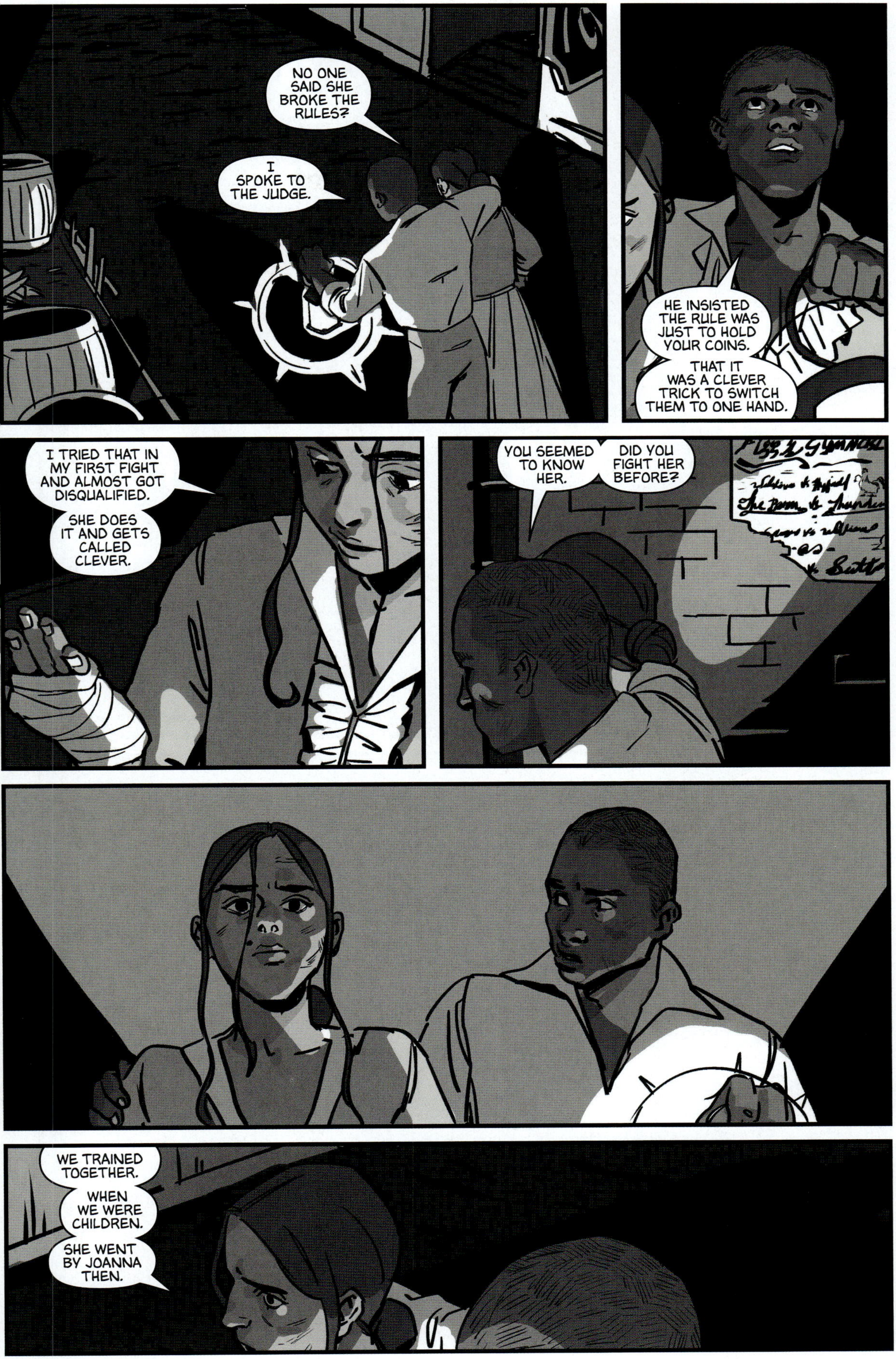
NO ONE SAID SHE BROKE THE RULES?
I SPOKE TO THE JUDGE.
HE INSISTED THE RULE WAS JUST TO HOLD YOUR COINS.
THAT IT WAS A CLEVER TRICK TO SWITCH THEM TO ONE HAND.
I TRIED THAT IN MY FIRST FIGHT AND ALMOST GOT DISQUALIFIED.
SHE DOES IT AND GETS CALLED CLEVER.
YOU SEEMED TO KNOW HER.
DID YOU FIGHT HER BEFORE?
WE TRAINED TOGETHER.
WHEN WE WERE CHILDREN.
SHE WENT BY JOANNA THEN.

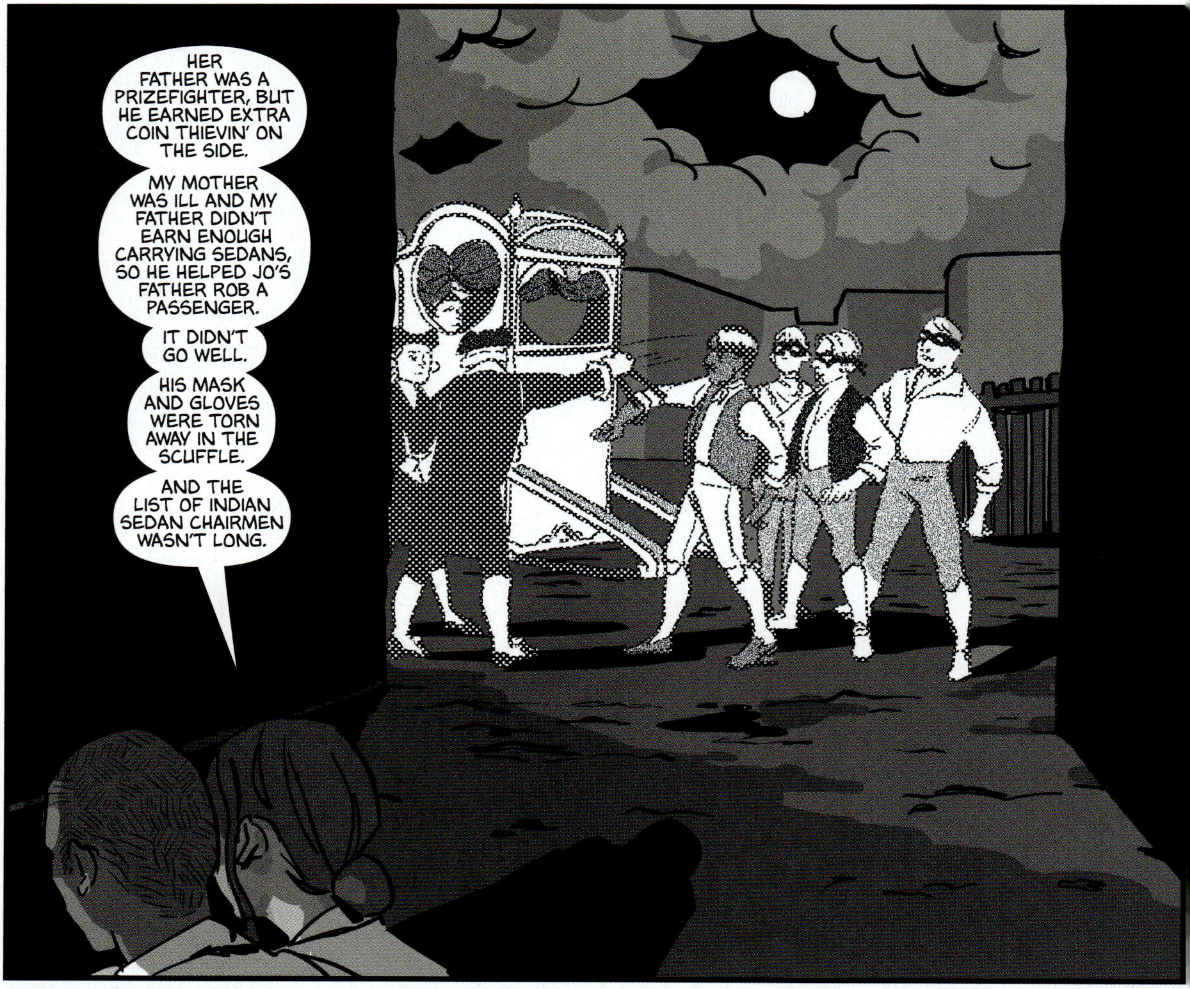
HER FATHER WAS A PRIZEFIGHTER, BUT HE EARNED EXTRA COIN THIEVIN' ON THE SIDE.
MY MOTHER WAS ILL AND MY FATHER DIDN'T EARN ENOUGH CARRYING SEDANS, SO HE HELPED JO'S FATHER ROB A PASSENGER.
IT DIDN'T GO WELL.
HIS MASK AND GLOVES WERE TORN AWAY IN THE SCUFFLE.
AND THE LIST OF INDIAN SEDAN CHAIRMEN WASN'T LONG.

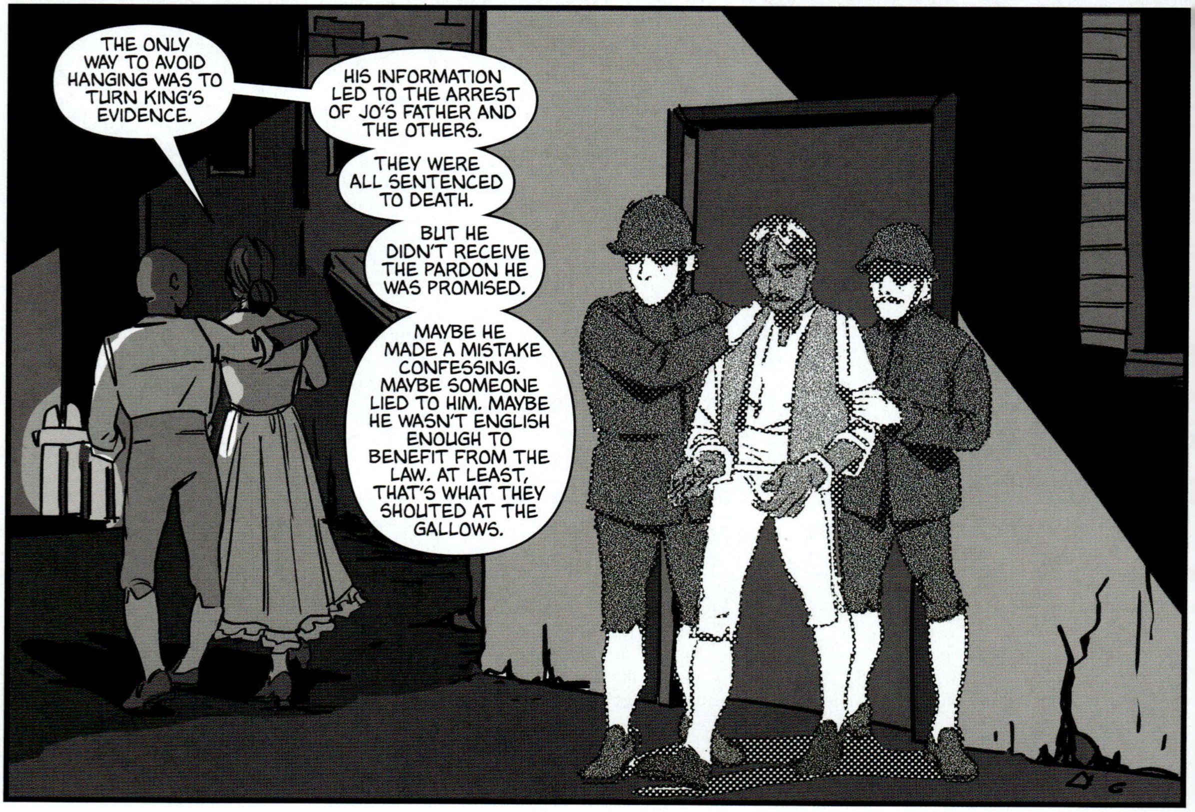
THE ONLY WAY TO AVOID HANGING WAS TO TURN KING'S EVIDENCE.
HIS INFORMATION LED TO THE ARREST OF JO'S FATHER AND THE OTHERS.
THEY WERE ALL SENTENCED TO DEATH.
BUT HE DIDN'T RECEIVE THE PARDON HE WAS PROMISED.
MAYBE HE MADE A MISTAKE CONFESSING. MAYBE SOMEONE LIED TO HIM. MAYBE HE WASN'T ENGLISH ENOUGH TO BENEFIT FROM THE LAW. AT LEAST, THAT'S WHAT THEY SHOUTED AT THE GALLOWS.

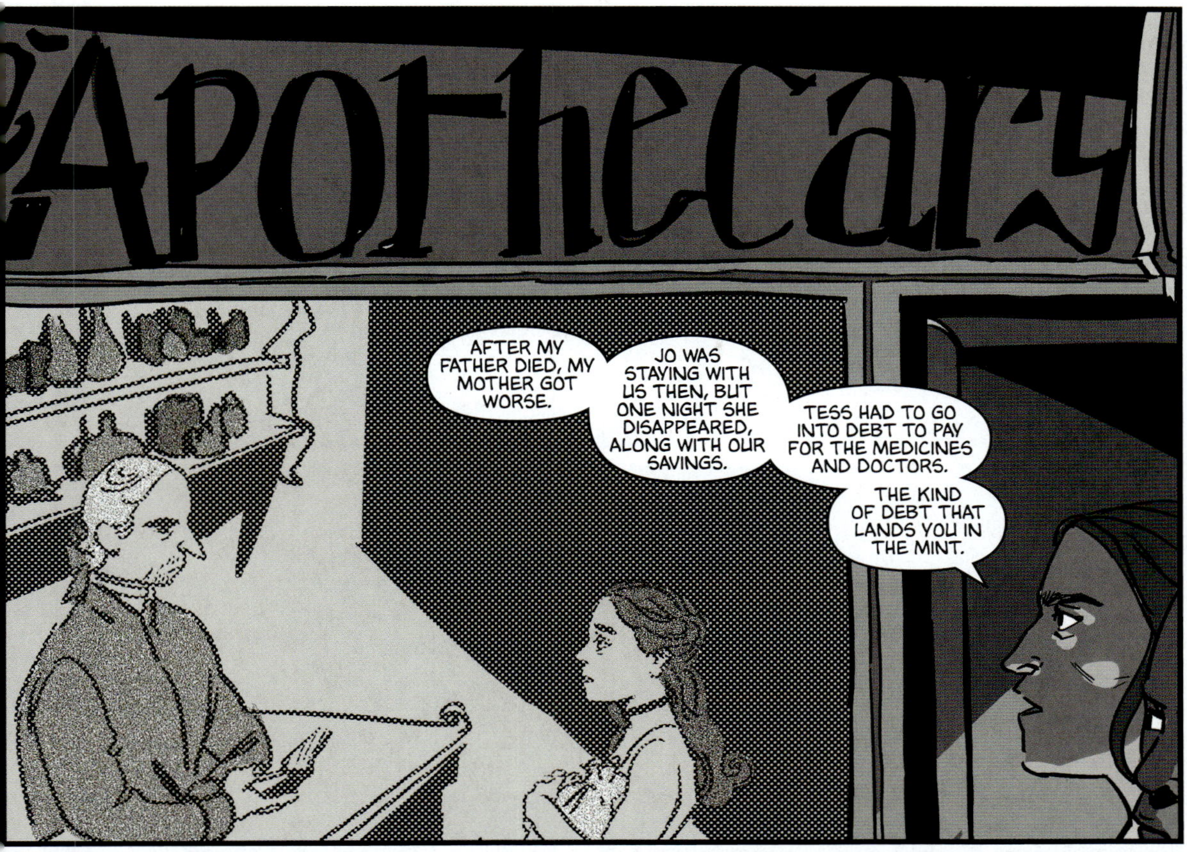
Apothecary
AFTER MY FATHER DIED, MY MOTHER GOT WORSE.
JO WAS STAYING WITH US THEN, BUT ONE NIGHT SHE DISAPPEARED, ALONG WITH OUR SAVINGS.
TESS HAD TO GO INTO DEBT TO PAY FOR THE MEDICINES AND DOCTORS.
THE KIND OF DEBT THAT LANDS YOU IN THE MINT.
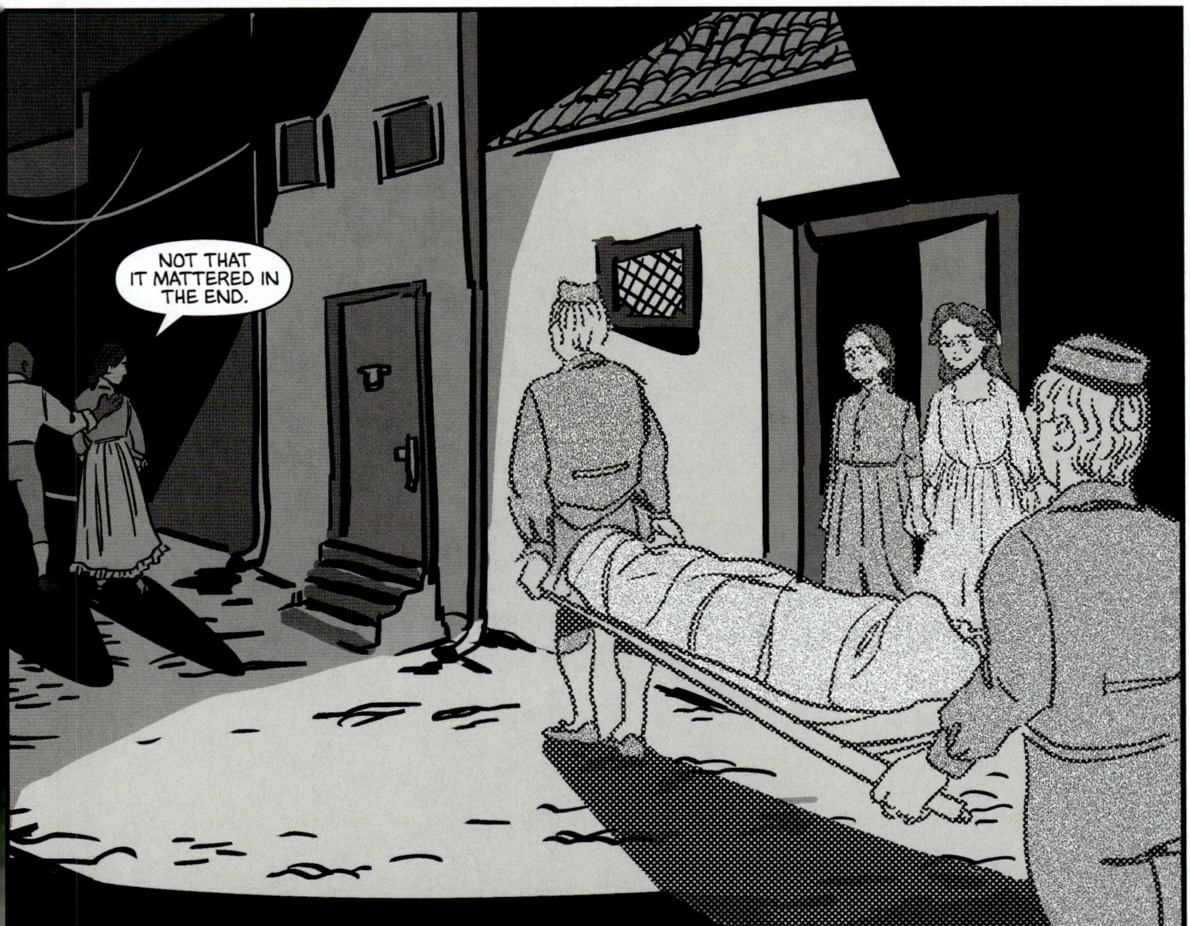
NOT THAT IT MATTERED IN THE END.

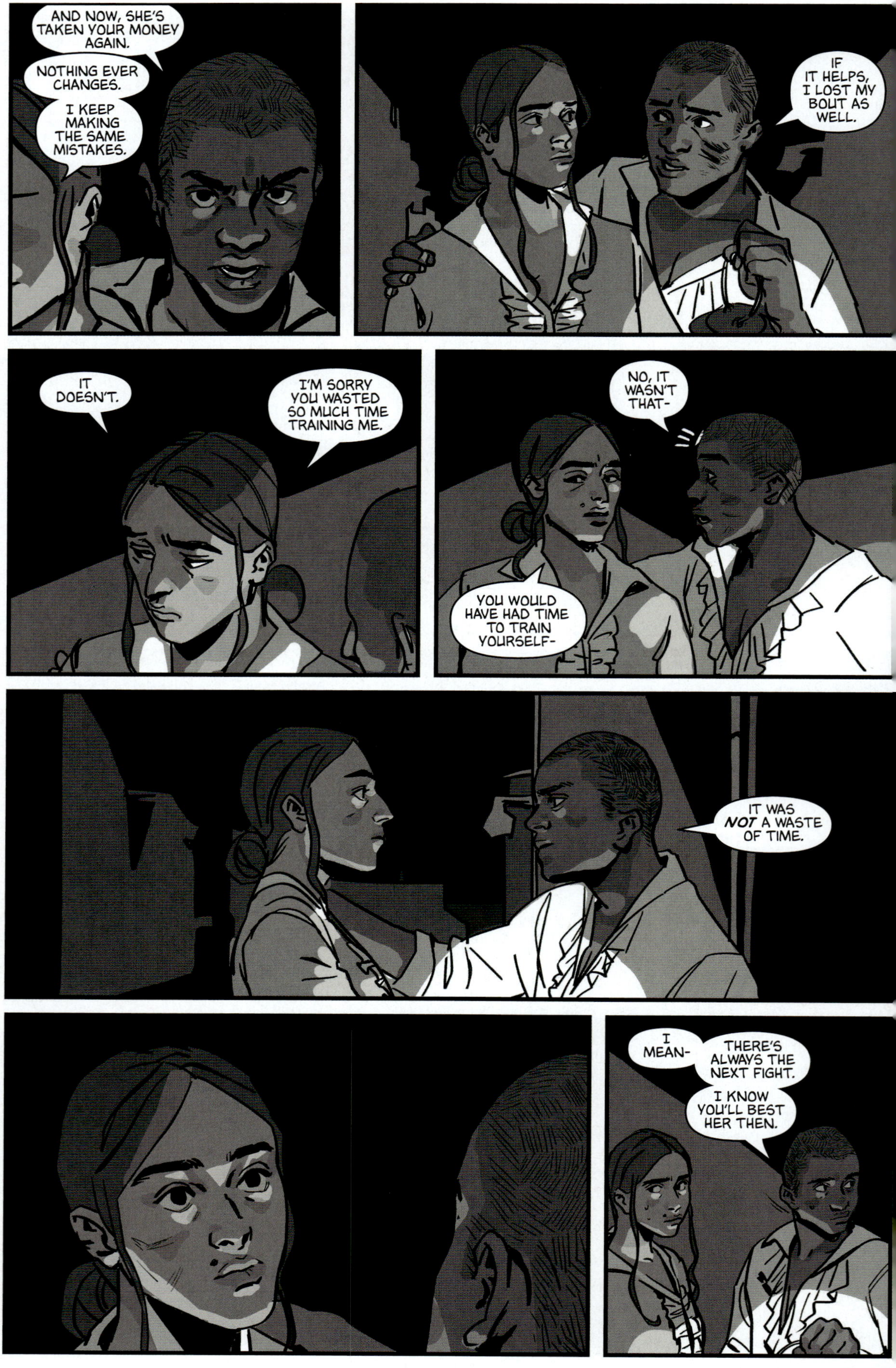
AND NOW, SHE'S TAKEN YOUR MONEY AGAIN.
NOTHING EVER CHANGES.
I KEEP MAKING THE SAME MISTAKES.
IF IT HELPS, I LOST MY BOUT AS WELL.
IT DOESN'T.
I'M SORRY YOU WASTED SO MUCH TIME TRAINING ME.
NO, IT WASN'T THAT-
YOU WOULD HAVE HAD TIME TO TRAIN YOURSELF-
IT WAS *NOT* A WASTE OF TIME.
I MEAN-
THERE'S ALWAYS THE NEXT FIGHT.
I KNOW YOU'LL BEST HER THEN.

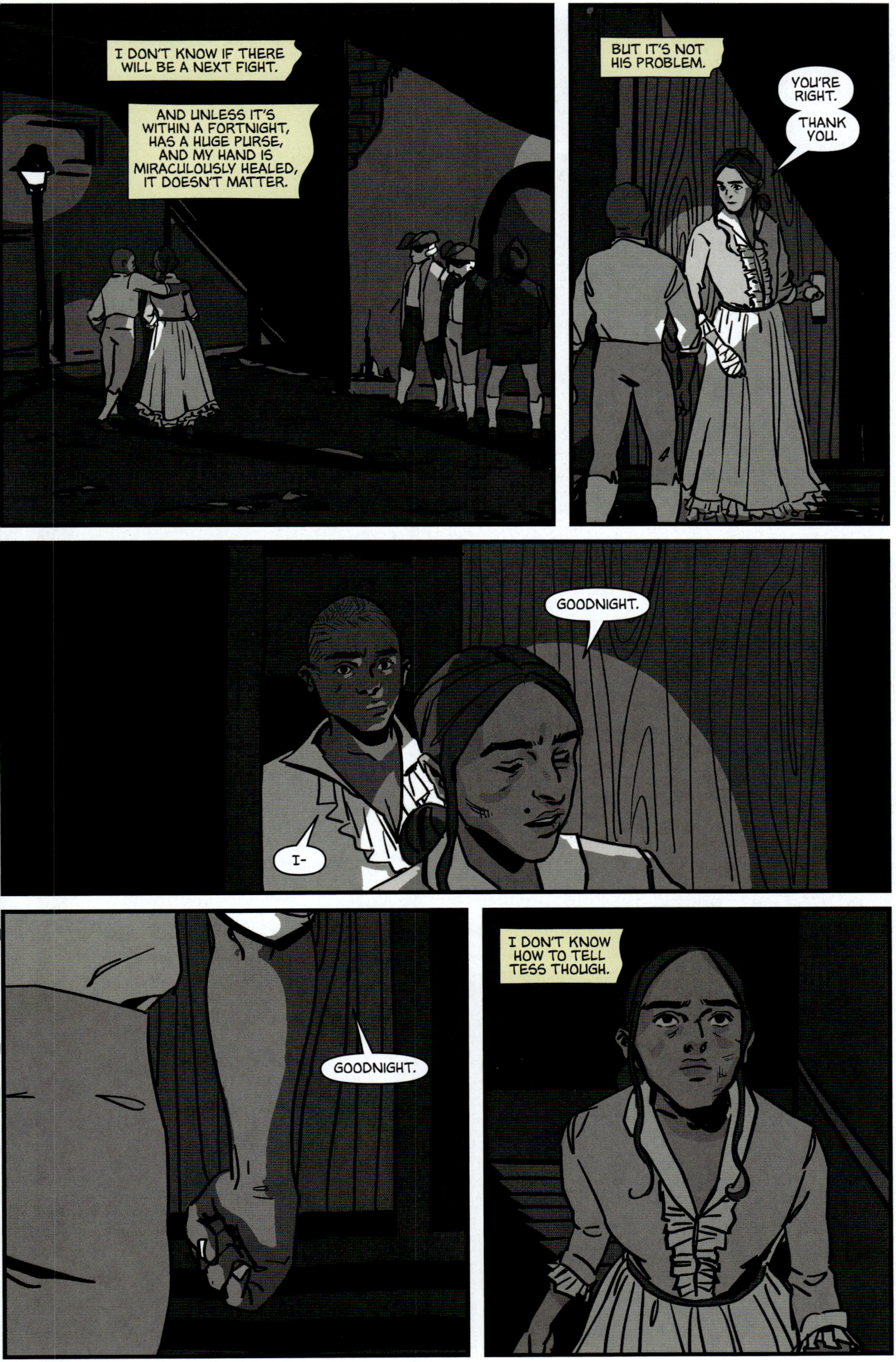

I DON'T KNOW IF THERE WILL BE A NEXT FIGHT.
AND UNLESS IT'S WITHIN A FORTNIGHT, HAS A HUGE PURSE, AND MY HAND IS MIRACULOUSLY HEALED, IT DOESN'T MATTER.
BUT IT'S NOT HIS PROBLEM.
YOU'RE RIGHT.
THANK YOU.
GOODNIGHT.
I-
GOODNIGHT.
I DON'T KNOW HOW TO TELL TESS THOUGH.

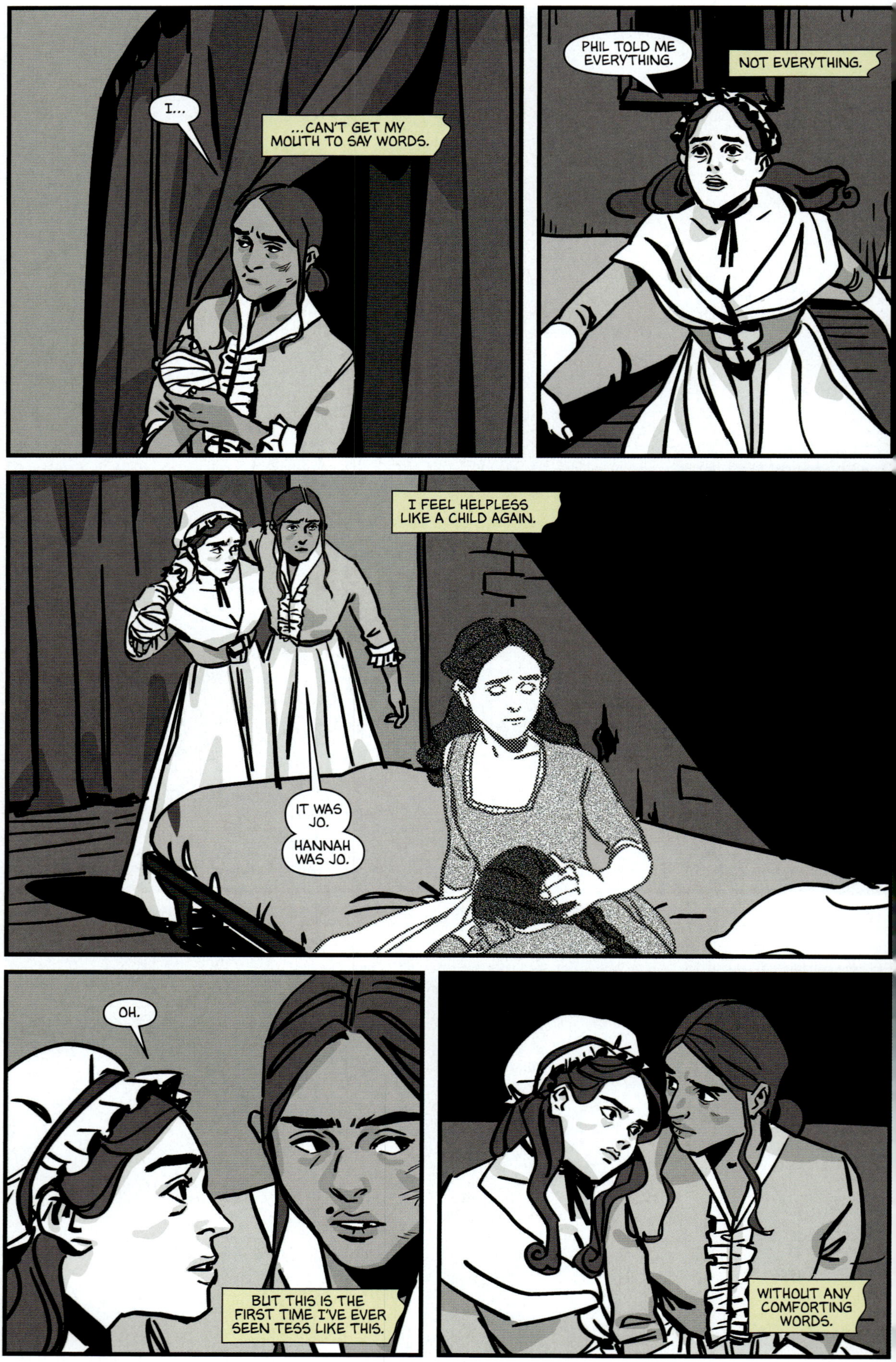
I...
...CAN'T GET MY MOUTH TO SAY WORDS.
PHIL TOLD ME EVERYTHING.
NOT EVERYTHING.
I FEEL HELPLESS LIKE A CHILD AGAIN.
IT WAS JO.
HANNAH WAS JO.
OH.
BUT THIS IS THE FIRST TIME I'VE EVER SEEN TESS LIKE THIS.
WITHOUT ANY COMFORTING WORDS.

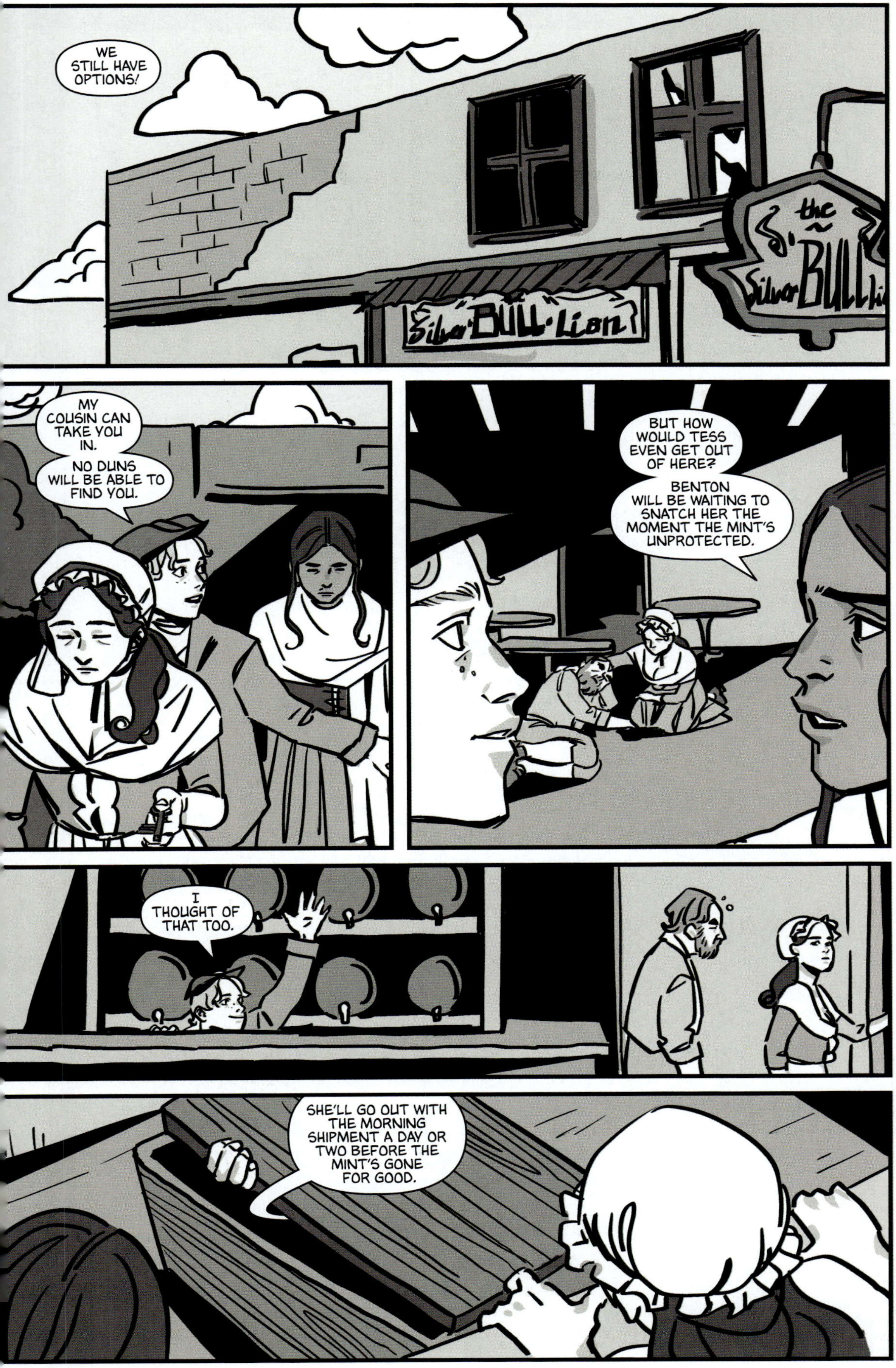
WE STILL HAVE OPTIONS!
the Silver BULL-lion
Silver BULL-Lion
MY COUSIN CAN TAKE YOU IN.
NO DUNS WILL BE ABLE TO FIND YOU.
BUT HOW WOULD TESS EVEN GET OUT OF HERE?
BENTON WILL BE WAITING TO SNATCH HER THE MOMENT THE MINT'S UNPROTECTED.
I THOUGHT OF THAT TOO.
SHE'LL GO OUT WITH THE MORNING SHIPMENT A DAY OR TWO BEFORE THE MINT'S GONE FOR GOOD.

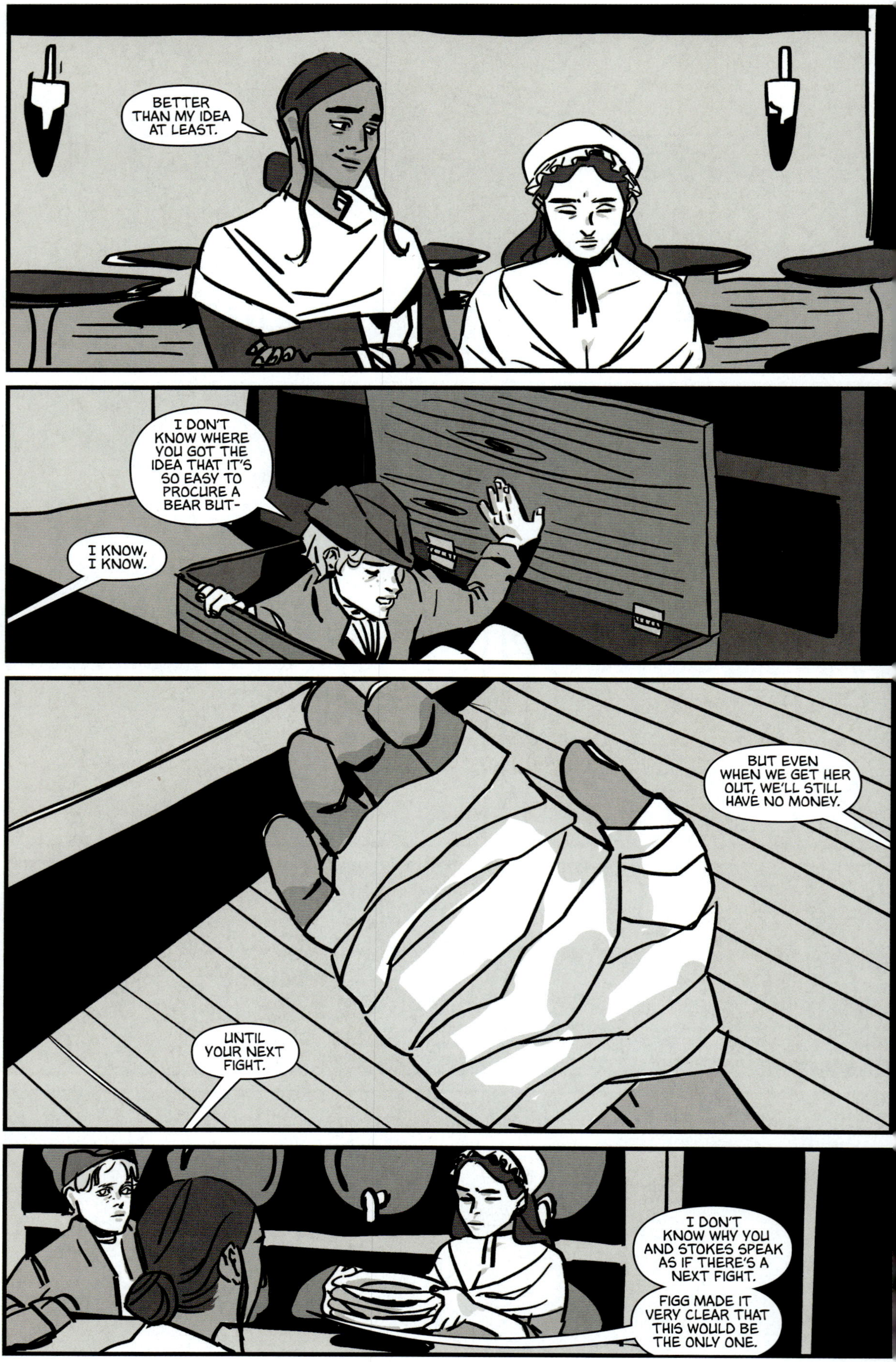
BETTER THAN MY IDEA AT LEAST.
I DON'T KNOW WHERE YOU GOT THE IDEA THAT IT'S SO EASY TO PROCURE A BEAR BUT-
I KNOW, I KNOW.
BUT EVEN WHEN WE GET HER OUT, WE'LL STILL HAVE NO MONEY.
UNTIL YOUR NEXT FIGHT.
I DON'T KNOW WHY YOU AND STOKES SPEAK AS IF THERE'S A NEXT FIGHT.
FIGG MADE IT VERY CLEAR THAT THIS WOULD BE THE ONLY ONE.

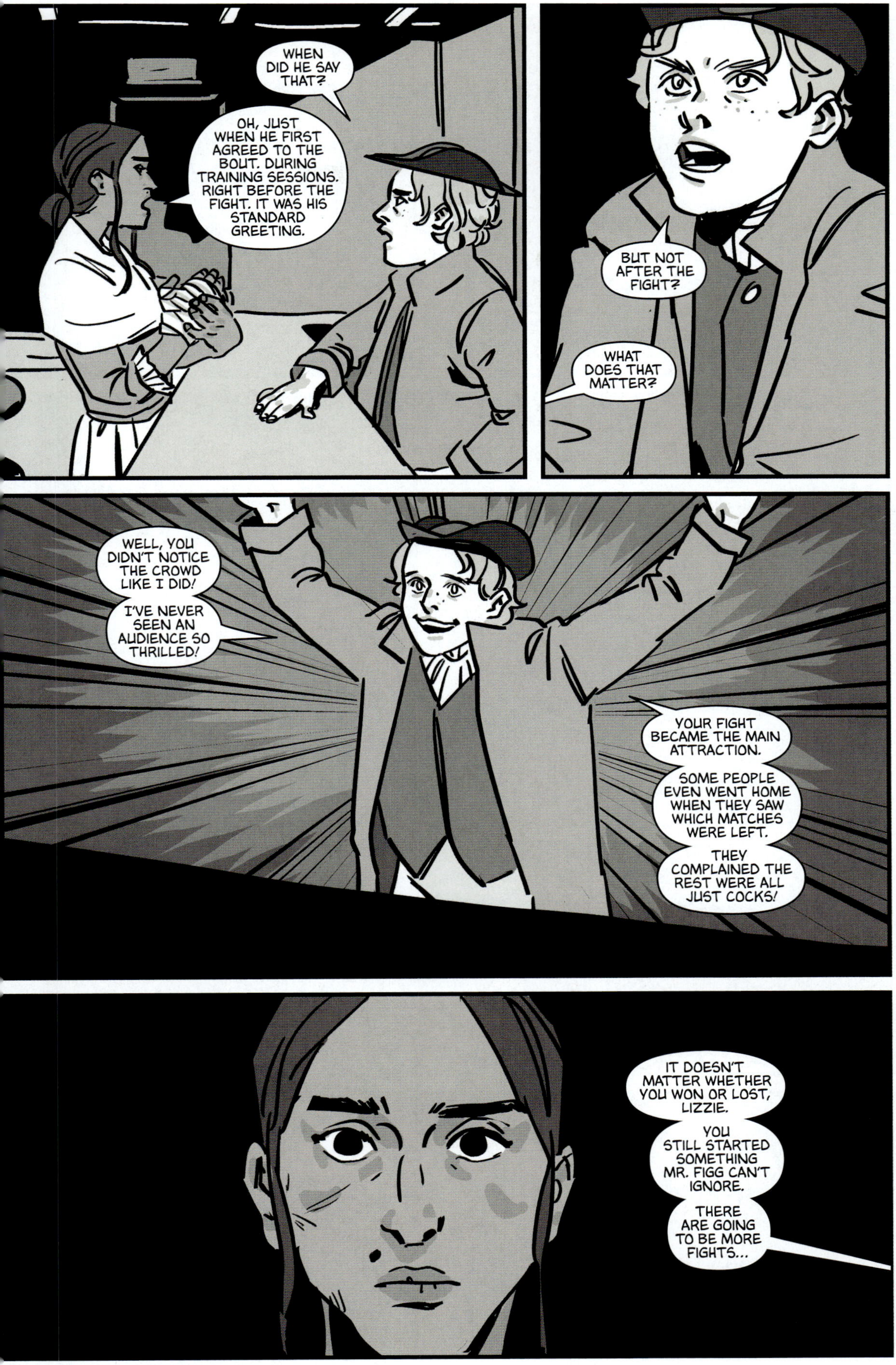
WHEN DID HE SAY THAT?
OH, JUST WHEN HE FIRST AGREED TO THE BOUT. DURING TRAINING SESSIONS. RIGHT BEFORE THE FIGHT. IT WAS HIS STANDARD GREETING.
BUT NOT AFTER THE FIGHT?
WHAT DOES THAT MATTER?
WELL, YOU DIDN'T NOTICE THE CROWD LIKE I DID!
I'VE NEVER SEEN AN AUDIENCE SO THRILLED!
YOUR FIGHT BECAME THE MAIN ATTRACTION.
SOME PEOPLE EVEN WENT HOME WHEN THEY SAW WHICH MATCHES WERE LEFT.
THEY COMPLAINED THE REST WERE ALL JUST COCKS!
IT DOESN'T MATTER WHETHER YOU WON OR LOST, LIZZIE.
YOU STILL STARTED SOMETHING MR. FIGG CAN'T IGNORE.
THERE ARE GOING TO BE MORE FIGHTS...

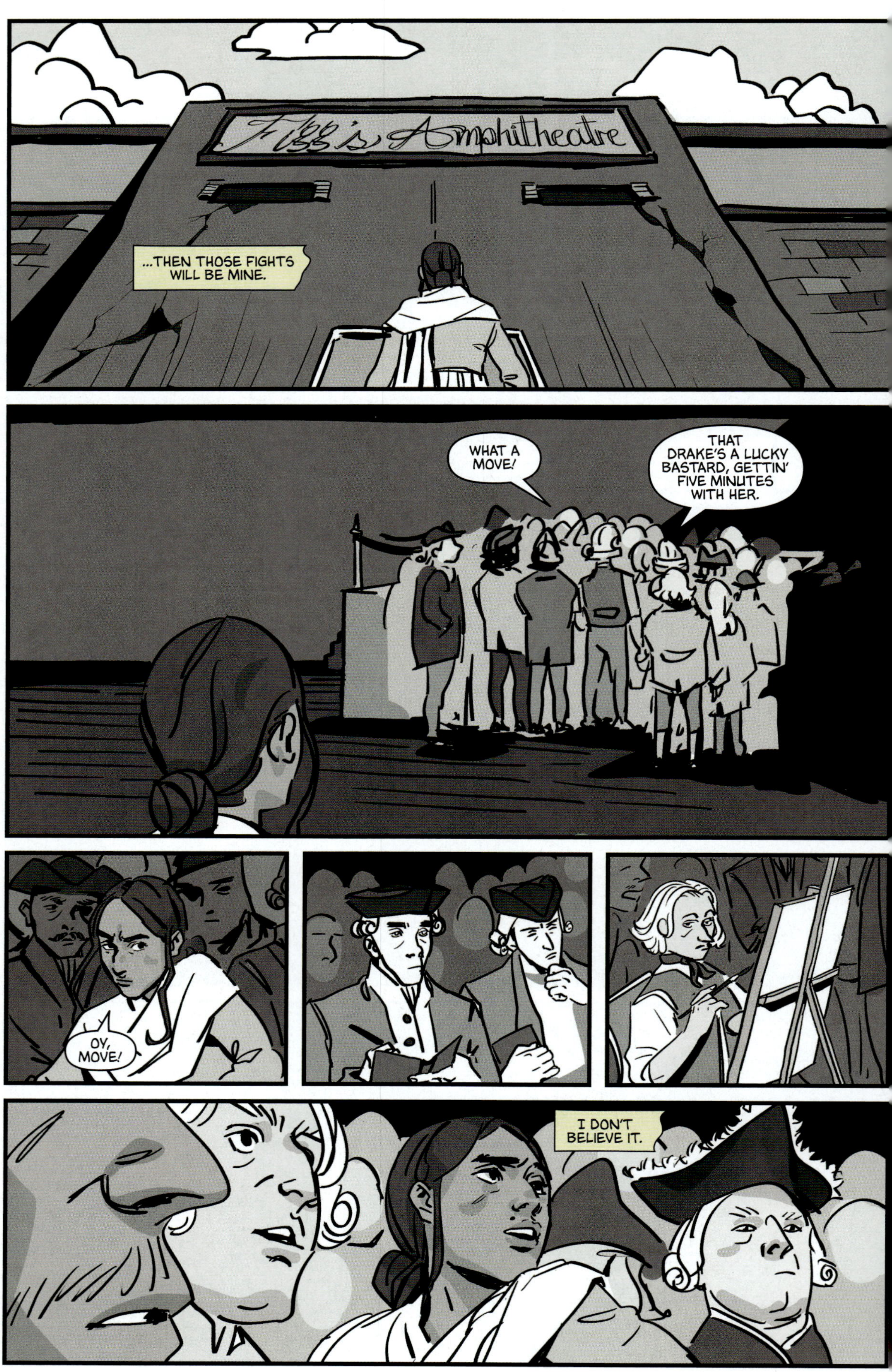
Figg's Amphitheatre
...THEN THOSE FIGHTS WILL BE MINE.
WHAT A MOVE!
THAT DRAKE'S A LUCKY BASTARD, GETTIN' FIVE MINUTES WITH HER.
OY, MOVE!
I DON'T BELIEVE IT.

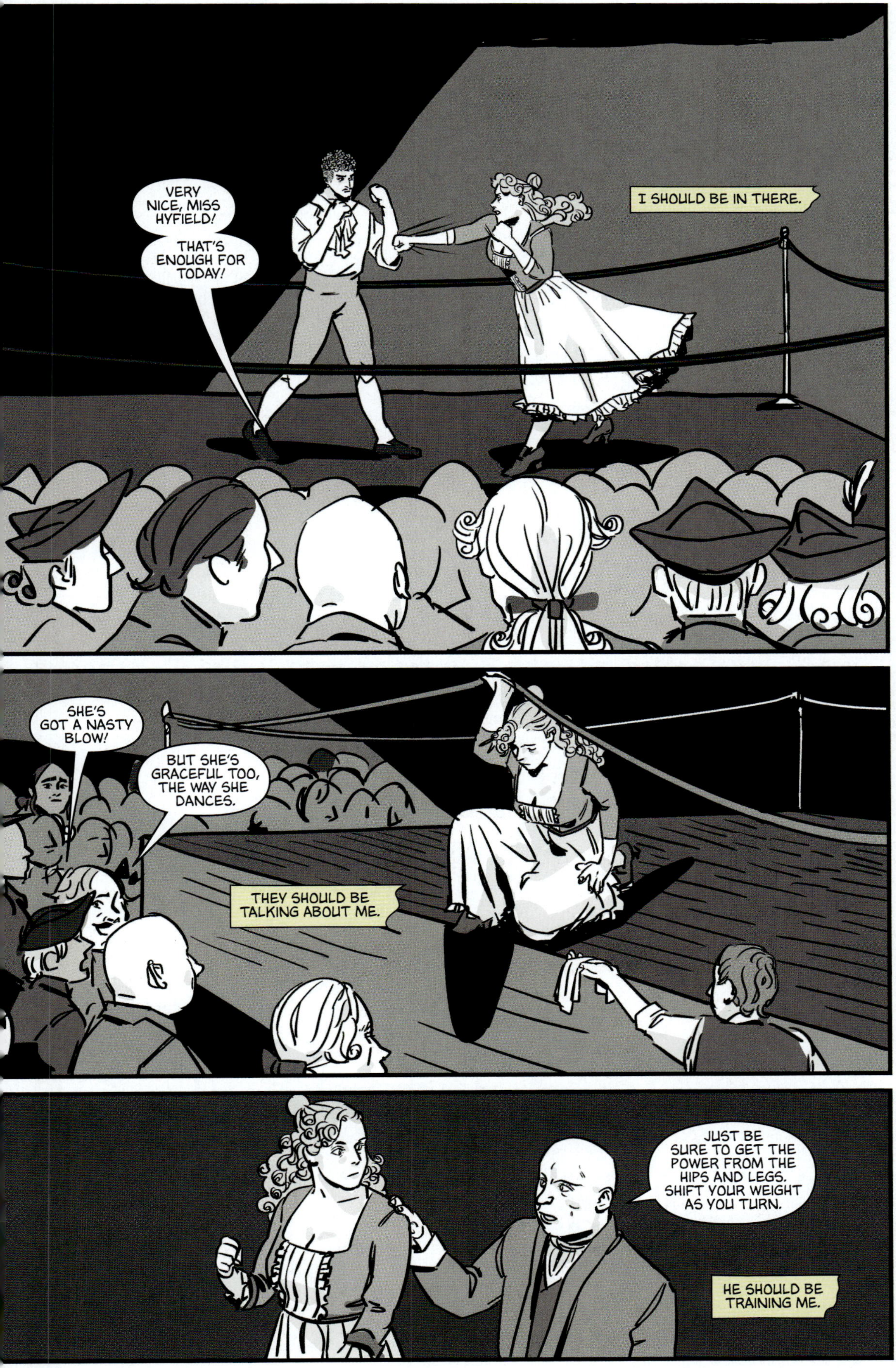

VERY NICE, MISS HYFIELD!
THAT'S ENOUGH FOR TODAY!
I SHOULD BE IN THERE.
SHE'S GOT A NASTY BLOW!
BUT SHE'S GRACEFUL TOO, THE WAY SHE DANCES.
THEY SHOULD BE TALKING ABOUT ME.
JUST BE SURE TO GET THE POWER FROM THE HIPS AND LEGS. SHIFT YOUR WEIGHT AS YOU TURN.
HE SHOULD BE TRAINING ME.

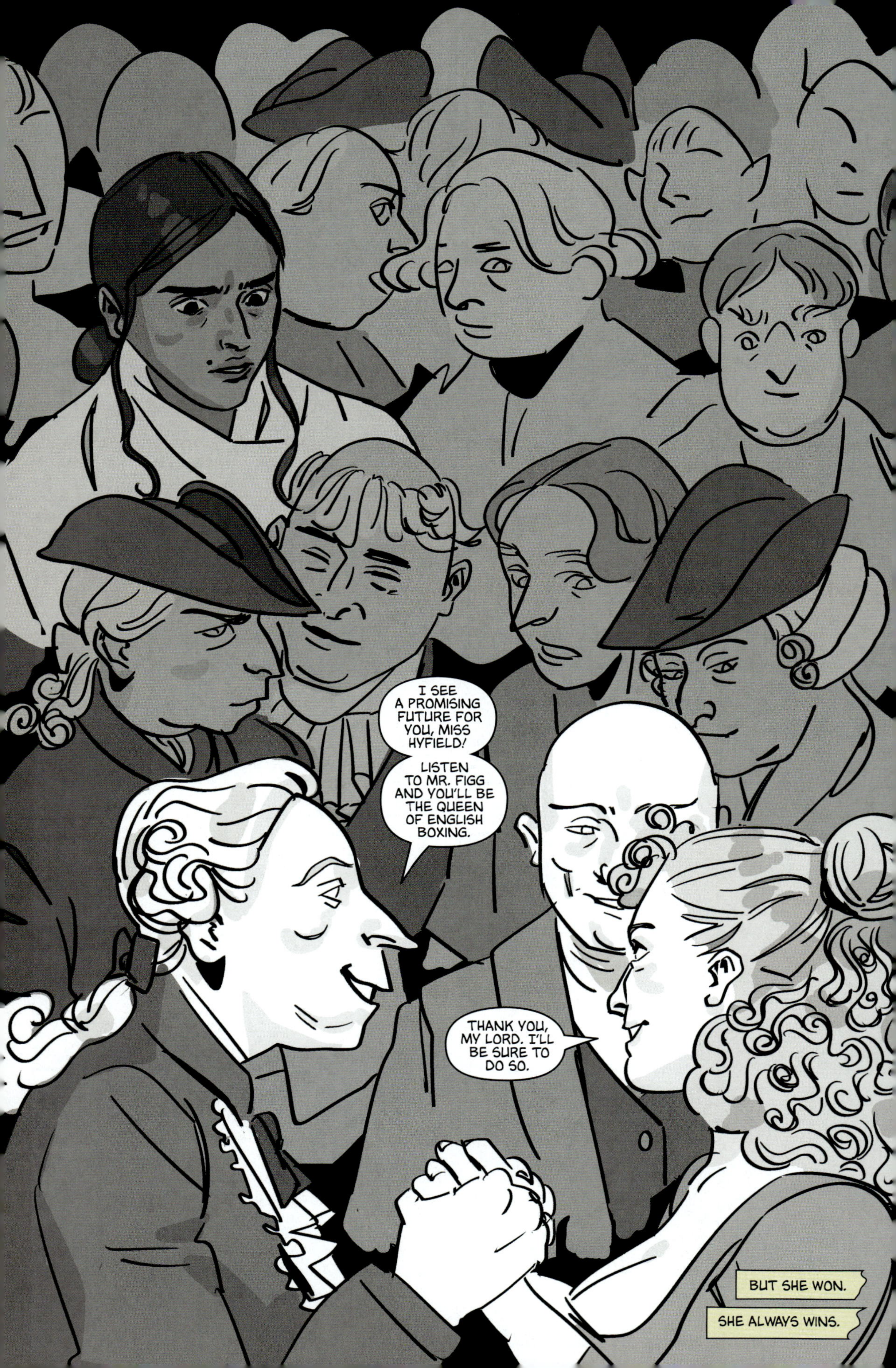
I SEE A PROMISING FUTURE FOR YOU, MISS HYFIELD!
LISTEN TO MR. FIGG AND YOU'LL BE THE QUEEN OF ENGLISH BOXING.
THANK YOU, MY LORD. I'LL BE SURE TO DO SO.
BUT SHE WON.
SHE ALWAYS WINS.

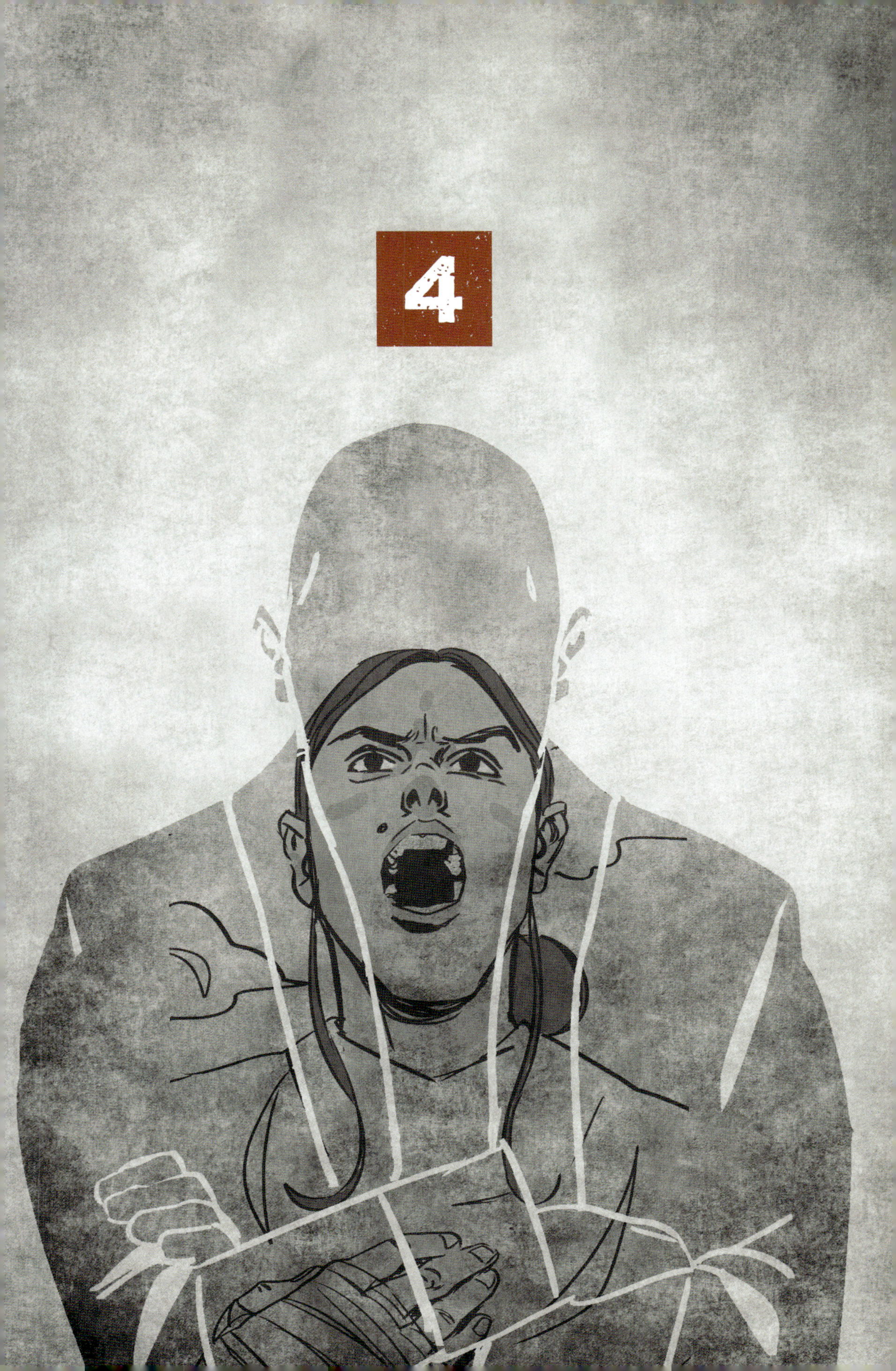
4

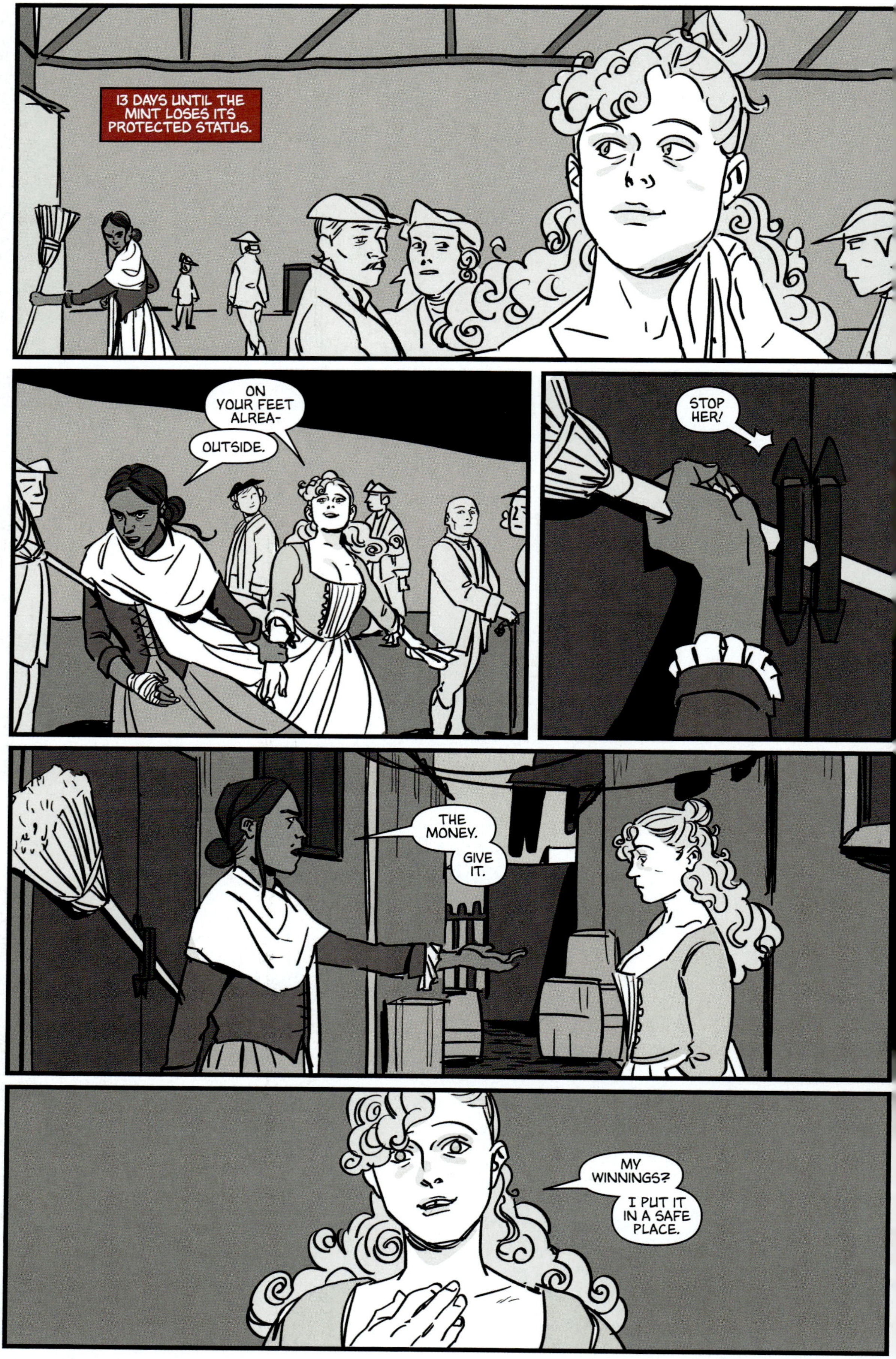
13 DAYS UNTIL THE MINT LOSES ITS PROTECTED STATUS.
ON YOUR FEET ALREA-
OUTSIDE.
STOP HER!
THE MONEY.
GIVE IT.
MY WINNINGS?
I PUT IT IN A SAFE PLACE.

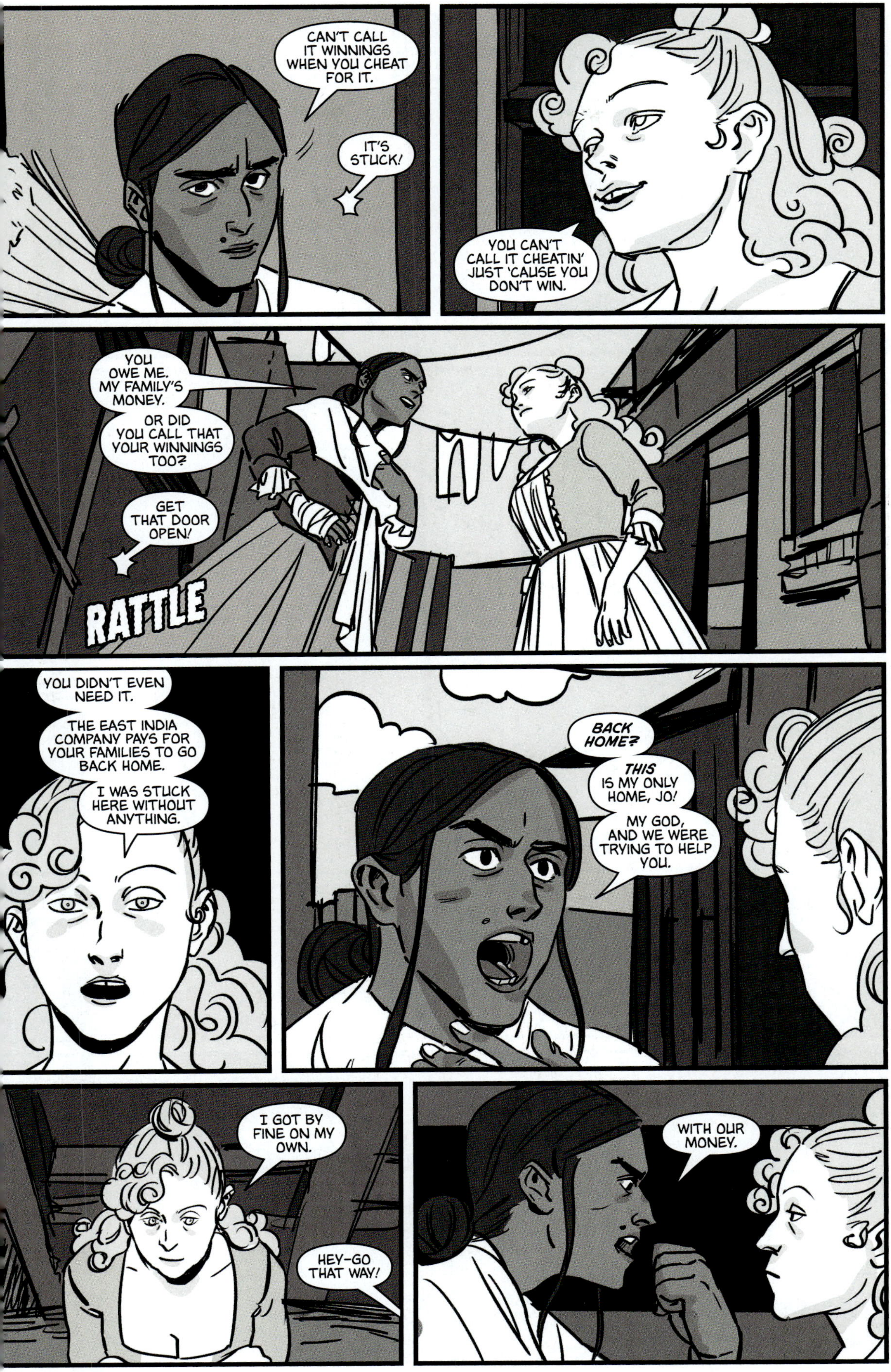
CAN'T CALL IT WINNINGS WHEN YOU CHEAT FOR IT.
IT'S STUCK!
YOU CAN'T CALL IT CHEATIN' JUST 'CAUSE YOU DON'T WIN.
YOU OWE ME. MY FAMILY'S MONEY.
OR DID YOU CALL THAT YOUR WINNINGS TOO?
GET THAT DOOR OPEN!
RATTLE
YOU DIDN'T EVEN NEED IT.
THE EAST INDIA COMPANY PAYS FOR YOUR FAMILIES TO GO BACK HOME.
I WAS STUCK HERE WITHOUT ANYTHING.
BACK HOME?
THIS IS MY ONLY HOME, JO!
MY GOD, AND WE WERE TRYING TO HELP YOU.
I GOT BY FINE ON MY OWN.
HEY–GO THAT WAY!
WITH OUR MONEY.

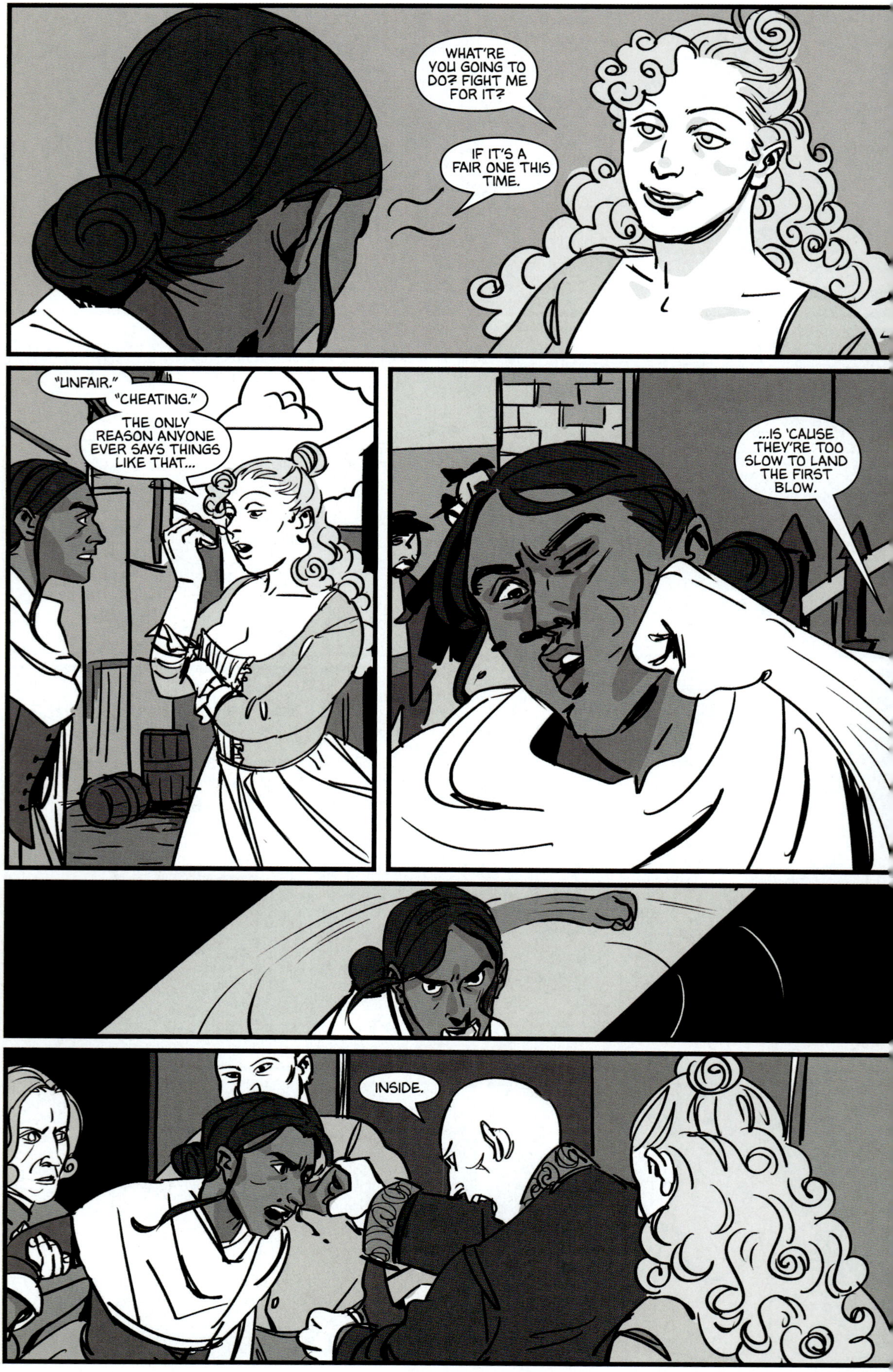
WHAT'RE YOU GOING TO DO? FIGHT ME FOR IT?
IF IT'S A FAIR ONE THIS TIME.
"UNFAIR."
"CHEATING."
THE ONLY REASON ANYONE EVER SAYS THINGS LIKE THAT...
...IS 'CAUSE THEY'RE TOO SLOW TO LAND THE FIRST BLOW.
INSIDE.

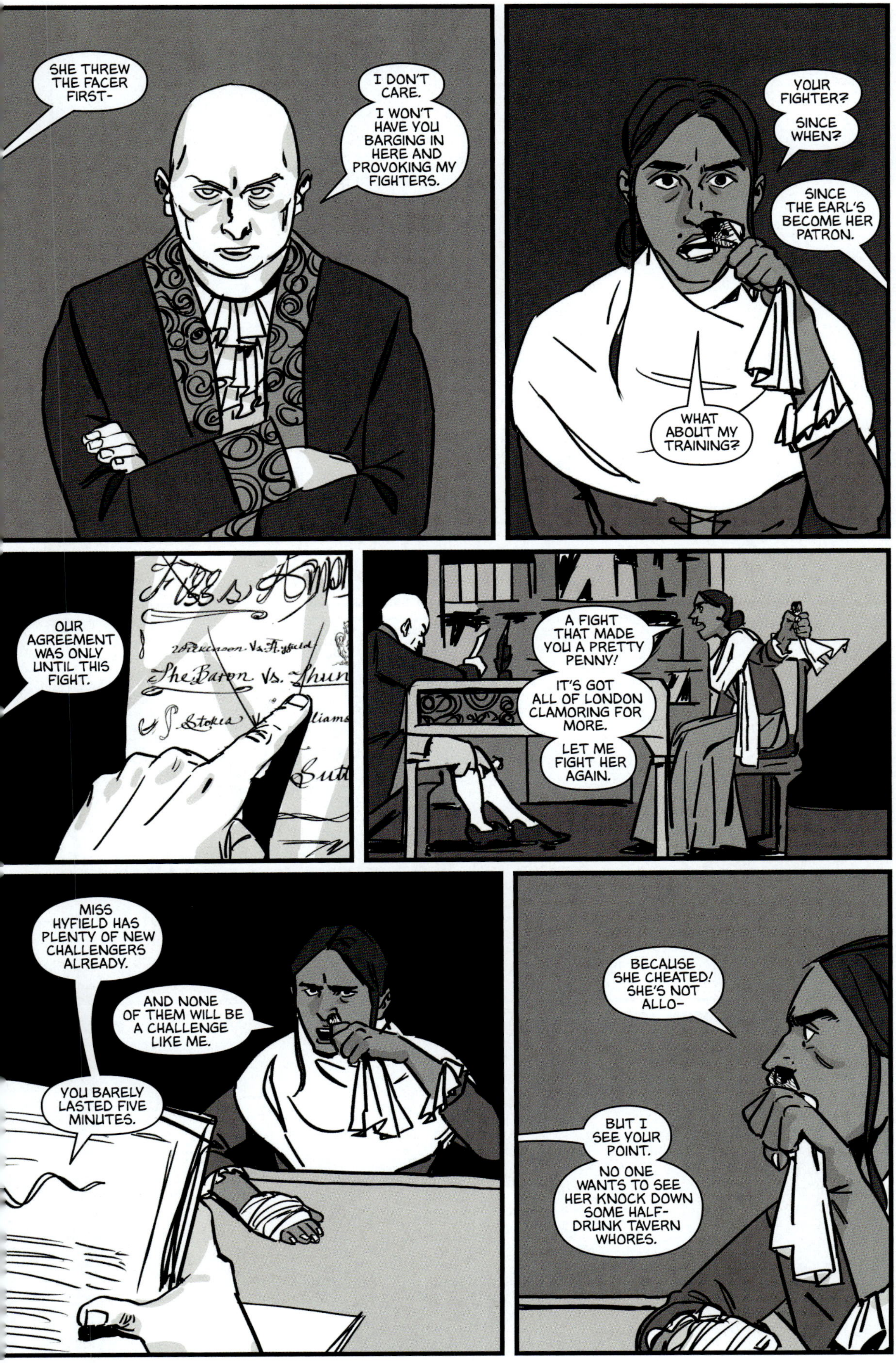
SHE THREW THE FACER FIRST-
I DON'T CARE.
I WON'T HAVE YOU BARGING IN HERE AND PROVOKING MY FIGHTERS.
YOUR FIGHTER?
SINCE WHEN?
SINCE THE EARL'S BECOME HER PATRON.
WHAT ABOUT MY TRAINING?
OUR AGREEMENT WAS ONLY UNTIL THIS FIGHT.
A FIGHT THAT MADE YOU A PRETTY PENNY!
IT'S GOT ALL OF LONDON CLAMORING FOR MORE.
LET ME FIGHT HER AGAIN.
MISS HYFIELD HAS PLENTY OF NEW CHALLENGERS ALREADY.
AND NONE OF THEM WILL BE A CHALLENGE LIKE ME.
YOU BARELY LASTED FIVE MINUTES.
BECAUSE SHE CHEATED! SHE'S NOT ALLO-
BUT I SEE YOUR POINT.
NO ONE WANTS TO SEE HER KNOCK DOWN SOME HALF-DRUNK TAVERN WHORES.

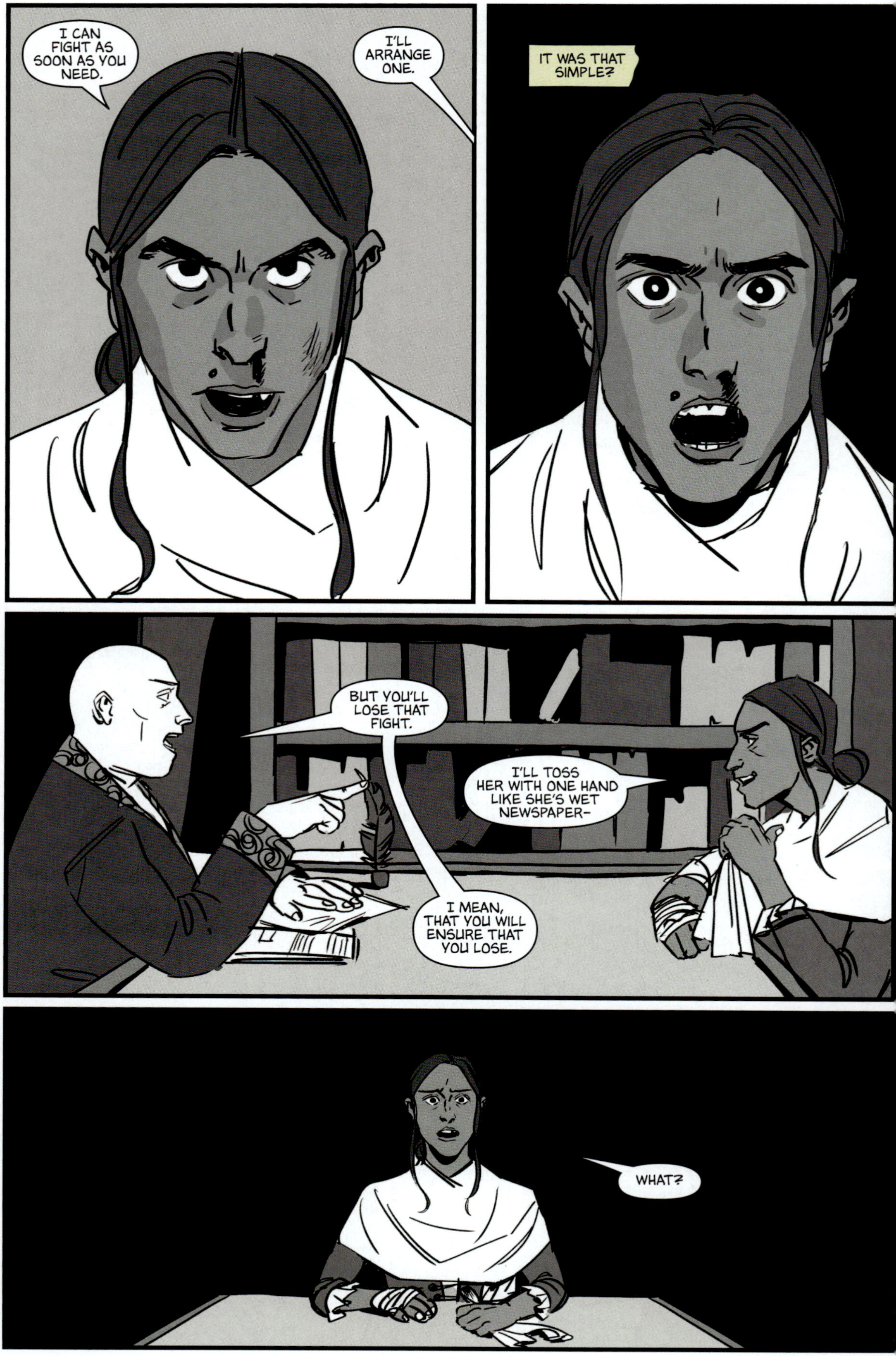
I CAN FIGHT AS SOON AS YOU NEED.
I'LL ARRANGE ONE.
IT WAS THAT SIMPLE?
BUT YOU'LL LOSE THAT FIGHT.
I'LL TOSS HER WITH ONE HAND LIKE SHE'S WET NEWSPAPER-
I MEAN, THAT YOU WILL ENSURE THAT YOU LOSE.
WHAT?

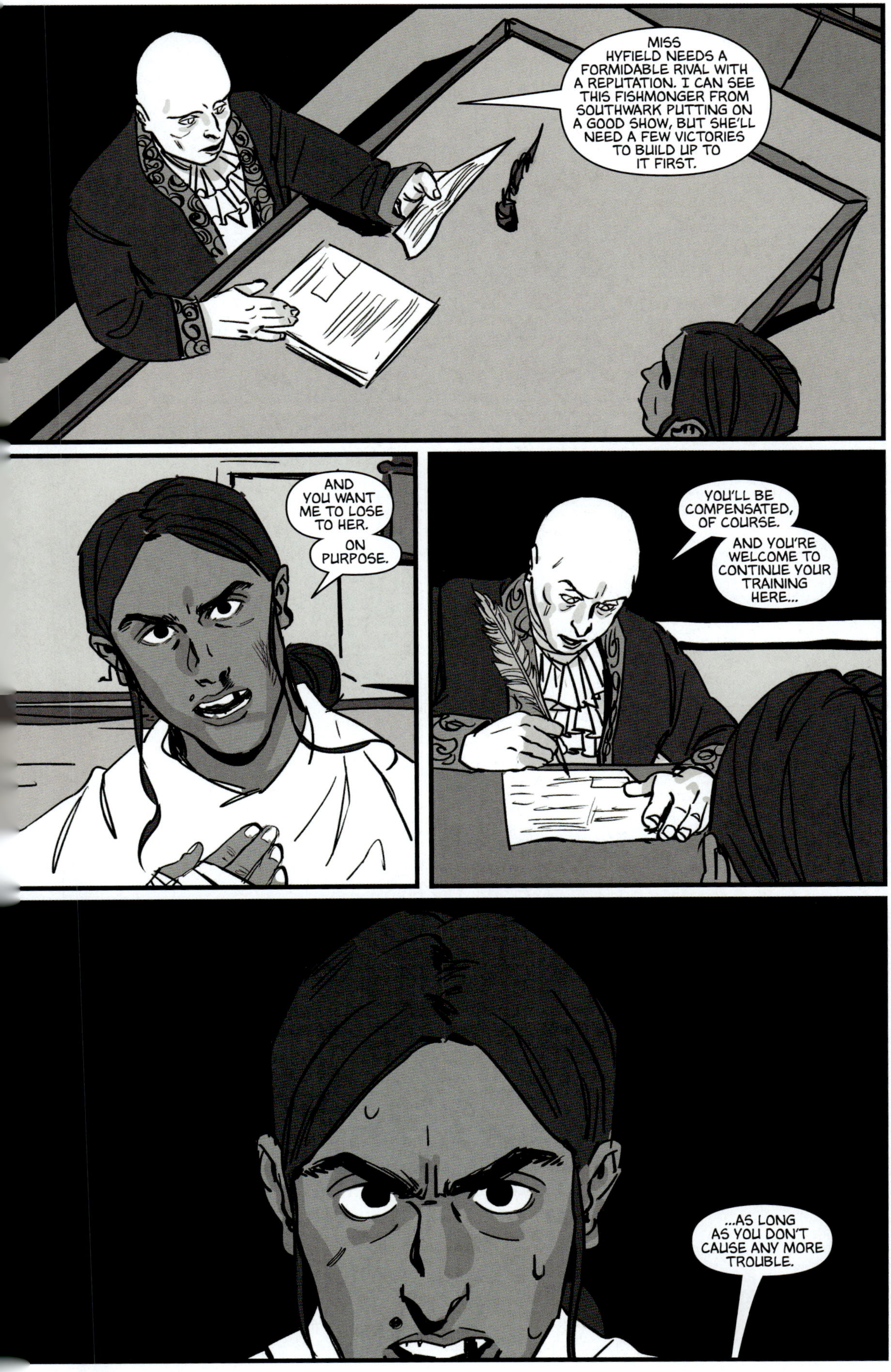
MISS HYFIELD NEEDS A FORMIDABLE RIVAL WITH A REPUTATION. I CAN SEE THIS FISHMONGER FROM SOUTHWARK PUTTING ON A GOOD SHOW, BUT SHE'LL NEED A FEW VICTORIES TO BUILD UP TO IT FIRST.
AND YOU WANT ME TO LOSE TO HER.
ON PURPOSE.
YOU'LL BE COMPENSATED, OF COURSE.
AND YOU'RE WELCOME TO CONTINUE YOUR TRAINING HERE...
...AS LONG AS YOU DON'T CAUSE ANY MORE TROUBLE.

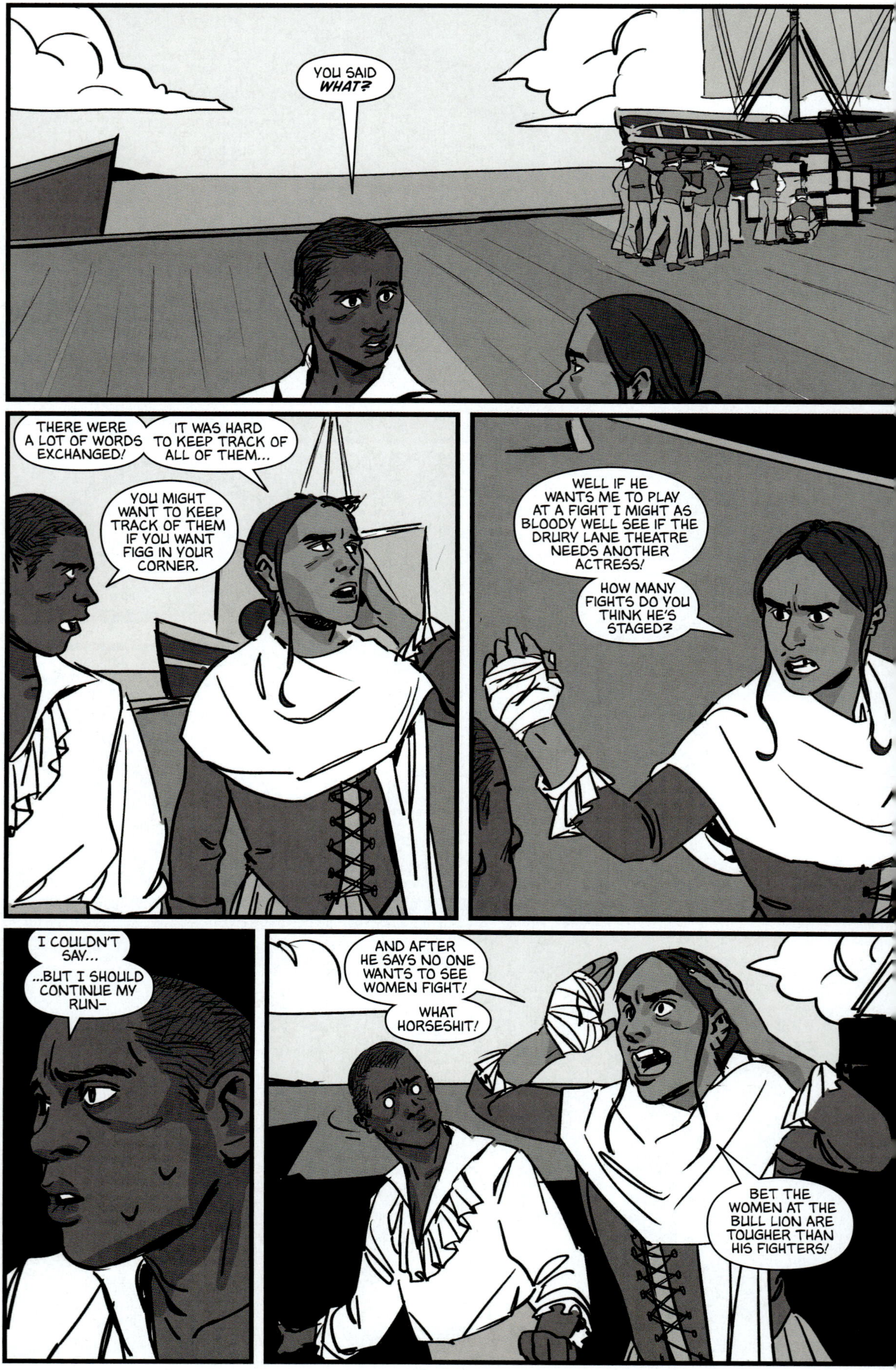
YOU SAID *WHAT?*
THERE WERE A LOT OF WORDS EXCHANGED!
IT WAS HARD TO KEEP TRACK OF ALL OF THEM...
YOU MIGHT WANT TO KEEP TRACK OF THEM IF YOU WANT FIGG IN YOUR CORNER.
WELL IF HE WANTS ME TO PLAY AT A FIGHT I MIGHT AS BLOODY WELL SEE IF THE DRURY LANE THEATRE NEEDS ANOTHER ACTRESS!
HOW MANY FIGHTS DO YOU THINK HE'S STAGED?
I COULDN'T SAY...
...BUT I SHOULD CONTINUE MY RUN-
AND AFTER HE SAYS NO ONE WANTS TO SEE WOMEN FIGHT!
WHAT HORSESHIT!
BET THE WOMEN AT THE BULL LION ARE TOUGHER THAN HIS FIGHTERS!

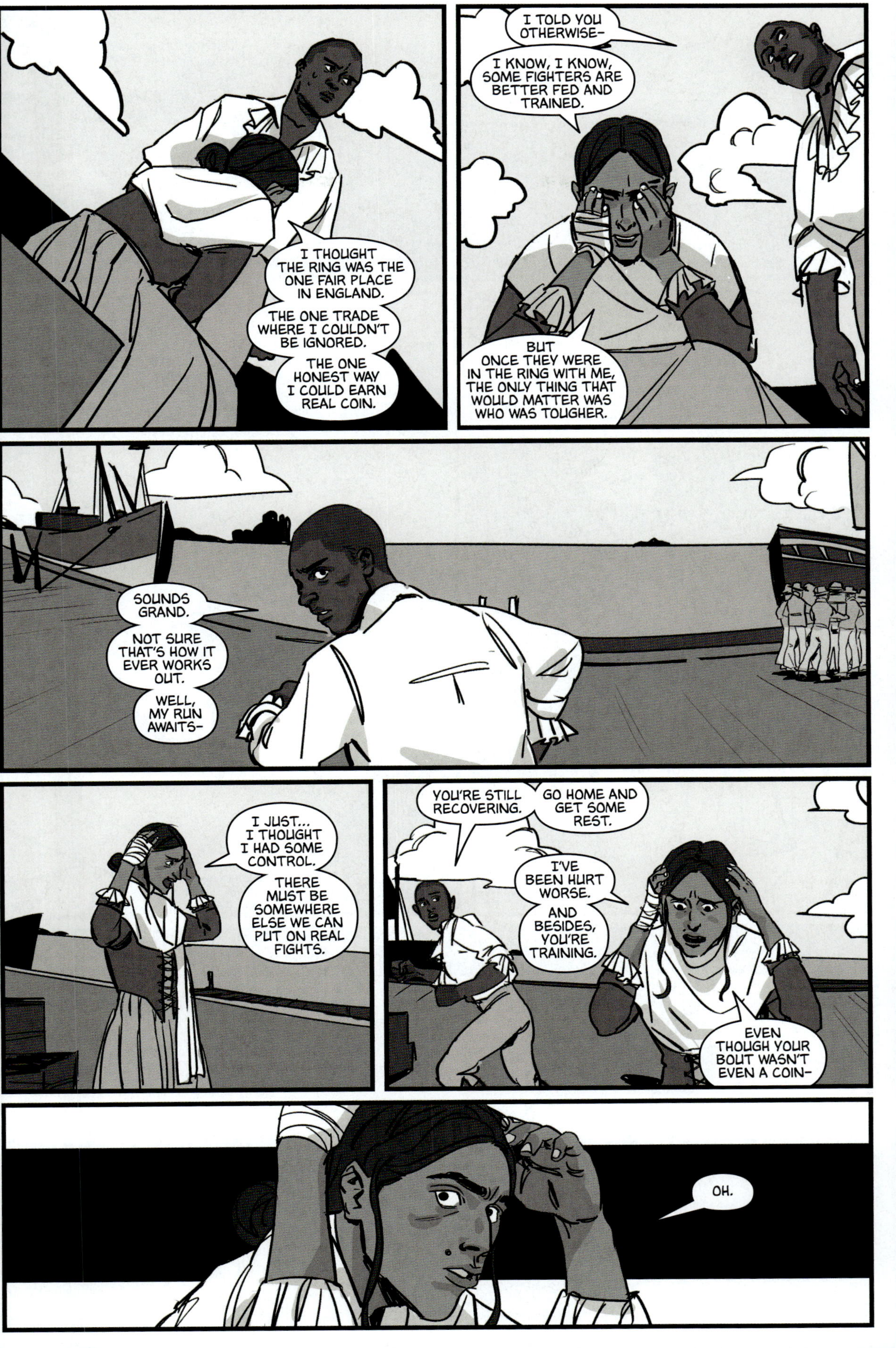
I THOUGHT THE RING WAS THE ONE FAIR PLACE IN ENGLAND.
THE ONE TRADE WHERE I COULDN'T BE IGNORED.
THE ONE HONEST WAY I COULD EARN REAL COIN.
I TOLD YOU OTHERWISE-
I KNOW, I KNOW, SOME FIGHTERS ARE BETTER FED AND TRAINED.
BUT ONCE THEY WERE IN THE RING WITH ME, THE ONLY THING THAT WOULD MATTER WAS WHO WAS TOUGHER.
SOUNDS GRAND.
NOT SURE THAT'S HOW IT EVER WORKS OUT.
WELL, MY RUN AWAITS-
I JUST... I THOUGHT I HAD SOME CONTROL.
THERE MUST BE SOMEWHERE ELSE WE CAN PUT ON REAL FIGHTS.
YOU'RE STILL RECOVERING.
GO HOME AND GET SOME REST.
I'VE BEEN HURT WORSE.
AND BESIDES, YOU'RE TRAINING.
EVEN THOUGH YOUR BOUT WASN'T EVEN A COIN-
OH.

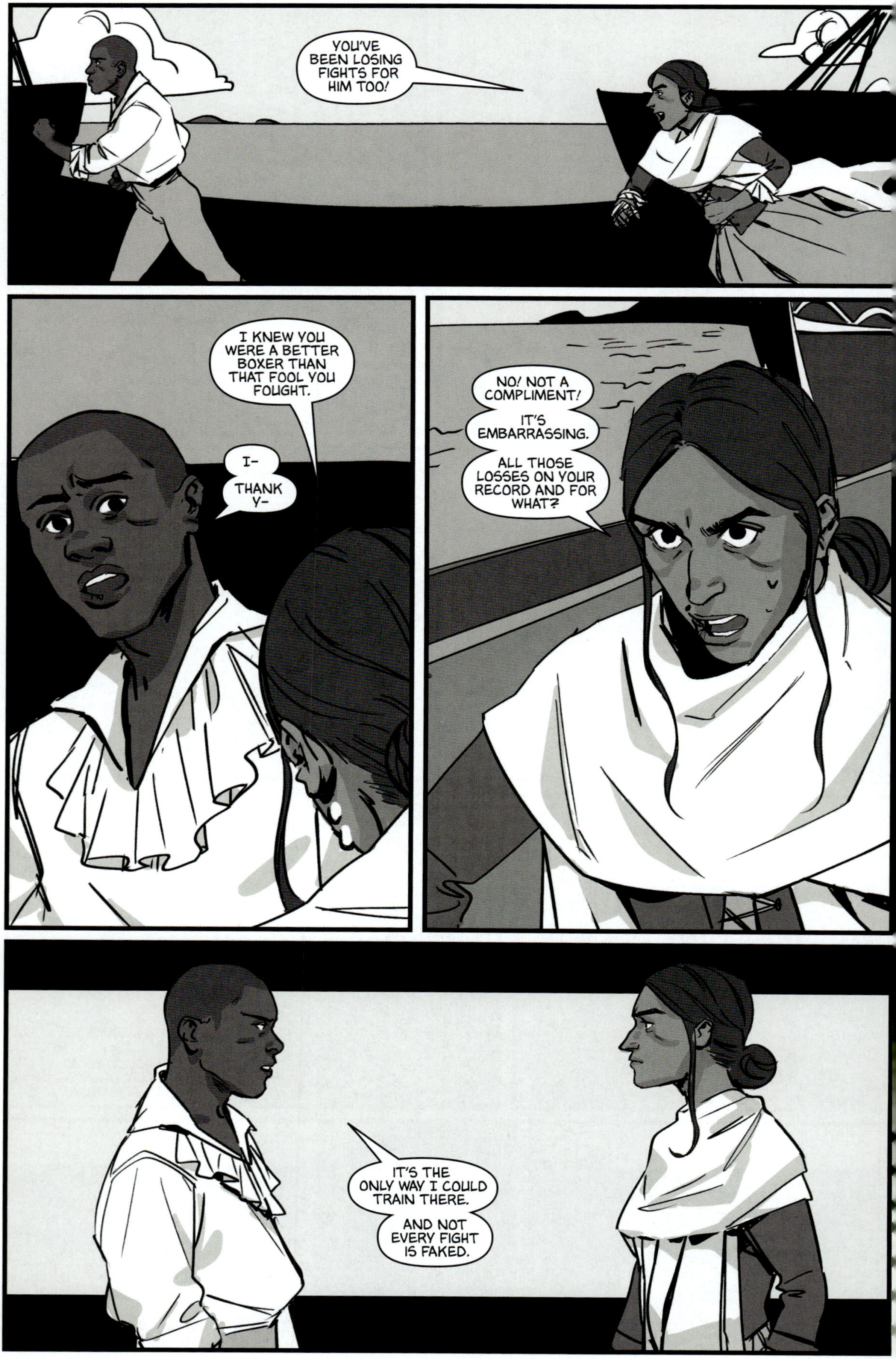
YOU'VE BEEN LOSING FIGHTS FOR HIM TOO!
I KNEW YOU WERE A BETTER BOXER THAN THAT FOOL YOU FOUGHT.
I-
THANK Y-
NO! NOT A COMPLIMENT!
IT'S EMBARRASSING.
ALL THOSE LOSSES ON YOUR RECORD AND FOR WHAT?
IT'S THE ONLY WAY I COULD TRAIN THERE.
AND NOT EVERY FIGHT IS FAKED.

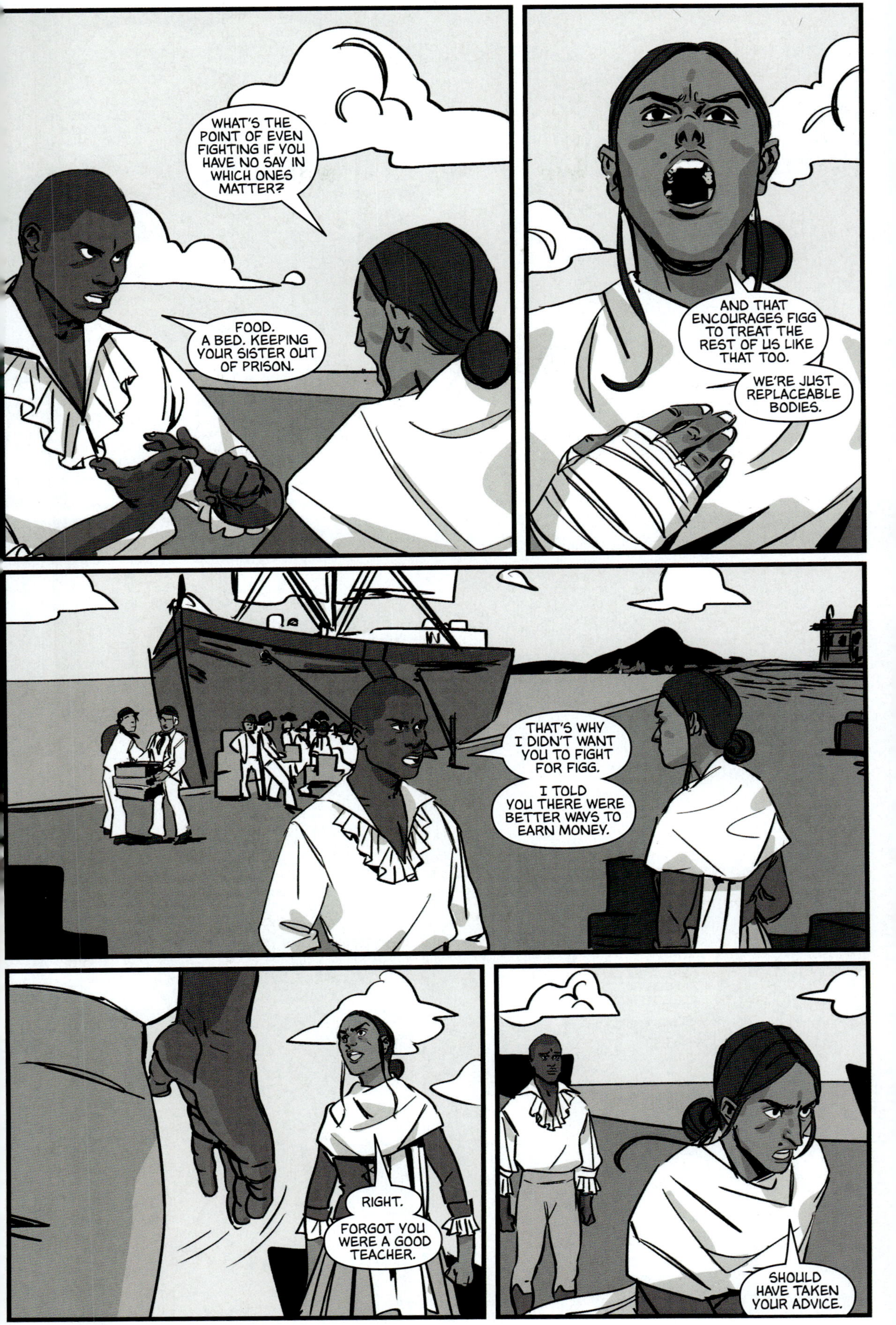
WHAT'S THE POINT OF EVEN FIGHTING IF YOU HAVE NO SAY IN WHICH ONES MATTER?
FOOD. A BED. KEEPING YOUR SISTER OUT OF PRISON.
AND THAT ENCOURAGES FIGG TO TREAT THE REST OF US LIKE THAT TOO.
WE'RE JUST REPLACEABLE BODIES.
THAT'S WHY I DIDN'T WANT YOU TO FIGHT FOR FIGG.
I TOLD YOU THERE WERE BETTER WAYS TO EARN MONEY.
RIGHT.
FORGOT YOU WERE A GOOD TEACHER.
SHOULD HAVE TAKEN YOUR ADVICE.

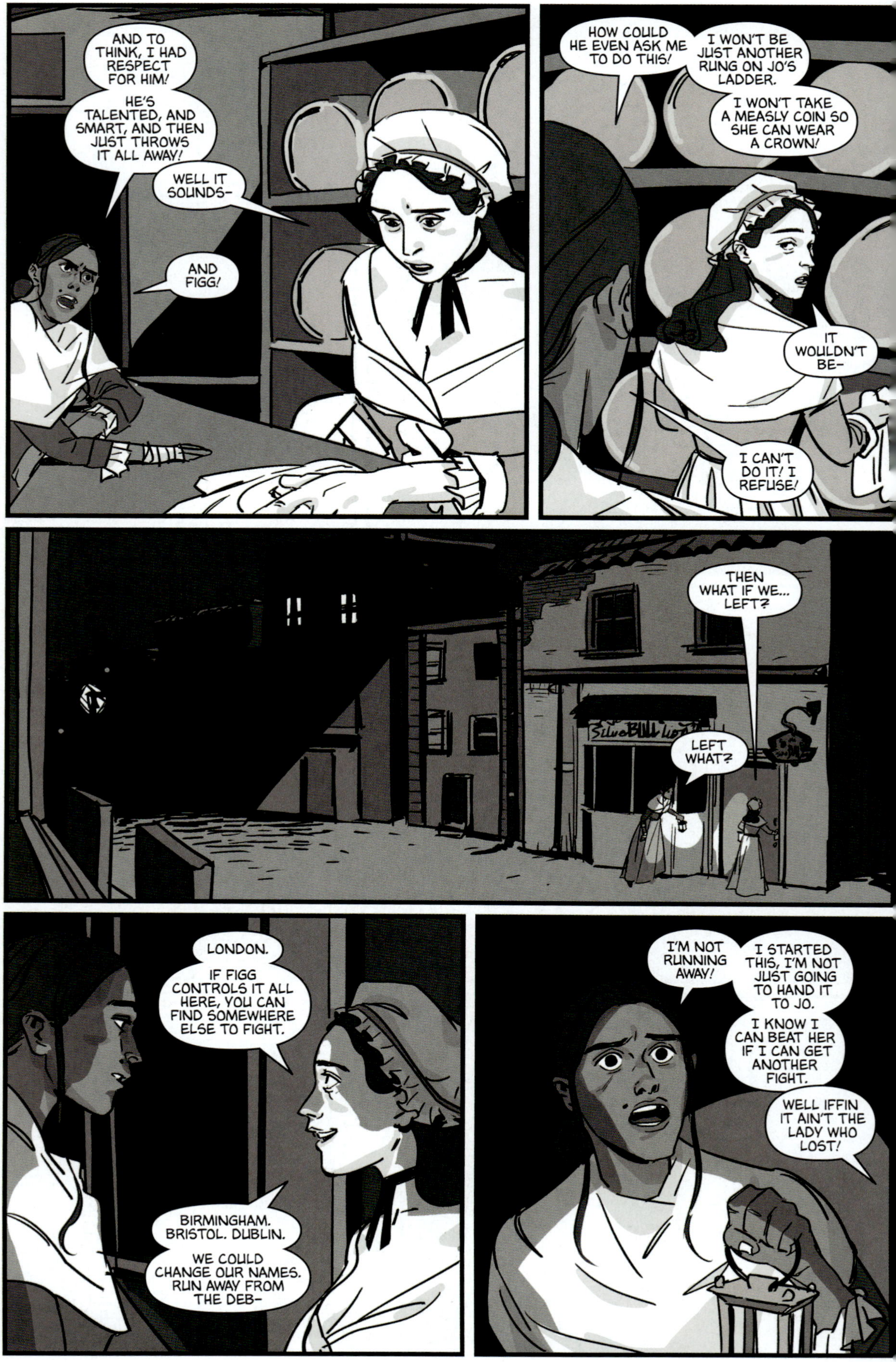
AND TO THINK, I HAD RESPECT FOR HIM!
HE'S TALENTED, AND SMART, AND THEN JUST THROWS IT ALL AWAY!
WELL IT SOUNDS-
AND FIGG!
HOW COULD HE EVEN ASK ME TO DO THIS!
I WON'T BE JUST ANOTHER RUNG ON JO'S LADDER.
I WON'T TAKE A MEASLY COIN SO SHE CAN WEAR A CROWN!
IT WOULDN'T BE-
I CAN'T DO IT! I REFUSE!
THEN WHAT IF WE... LEFT?
LEFT WHAT?
LONDON.
IF FIGG CONTROLS IT ALL HERE, YOU CAN FIND SOMEWHERE ELSE TO FIGHT.
BIRMINGHAM. BRISTOL. DUBLIN.
WE COULD CHANGE OUR NAMES. RUN AWAY FROM THE DEB-
I'M NOT RUNNING AWAY!
I STARTED THIS, I'M NOT JUST GOING TO HAND IT TO JO.
I KNOW I CAN BEAT HER IF I CAN GET ANOTHER FIGHT.
WELL IFFIN IT AIN'T THE LADY WHO LOST!

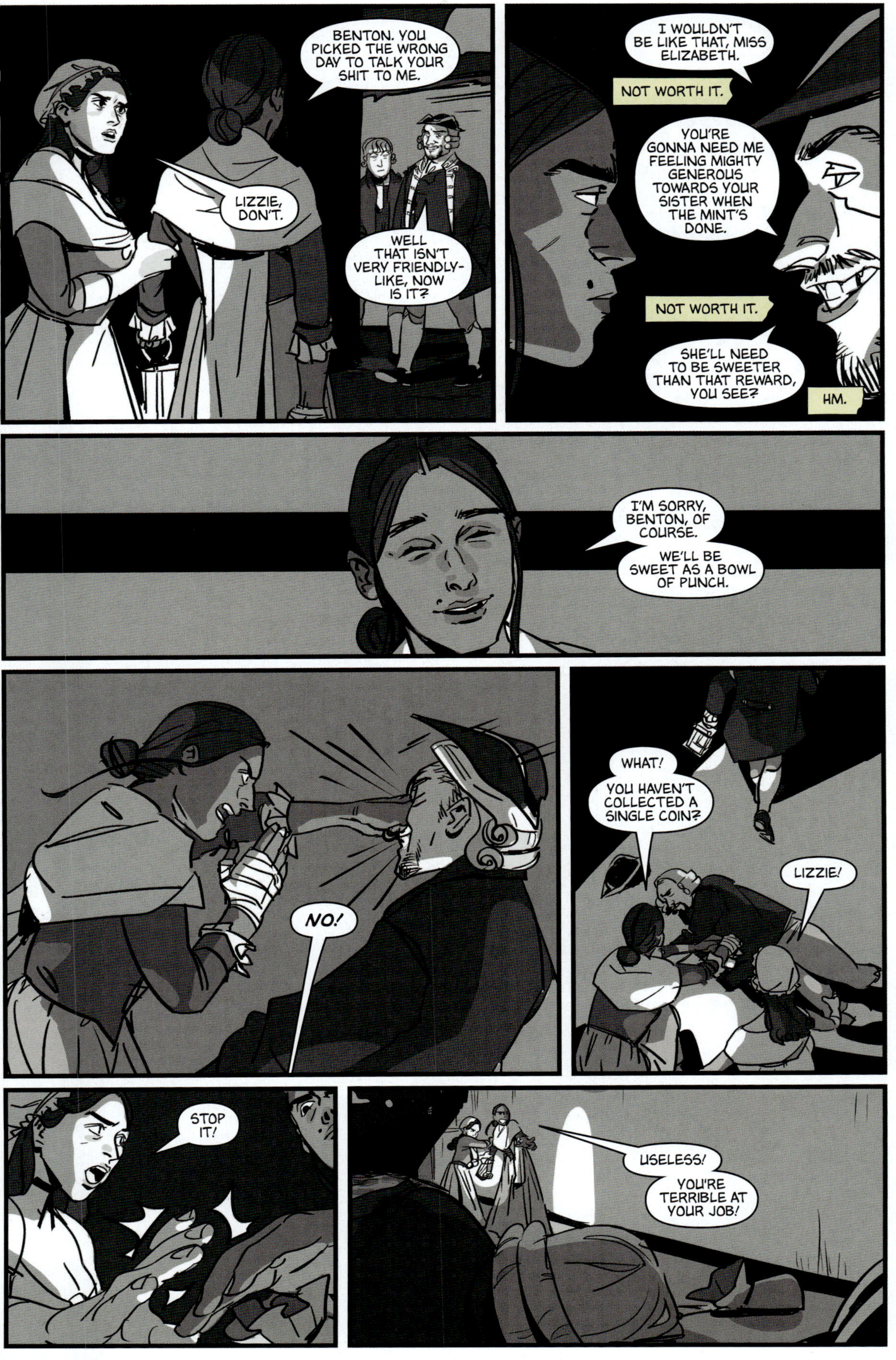

BENTON. YOU PICKED THE WRONG DAY TO TALK YOUR SHIT TO ME.
LIZZIE, DON'T.
WELL THAT ISN'T VERY FRIENDLY-LIKE, NOW IS IT?
I WOULDN'T BE LIKE THAT, MISS ELIZABETH.
NOT WORTH IT.
YOU'RE GONNA NEED ME FEELING MIGHTY GENEROUS TOWARDS YOUR SISTER WHEN THE MINT'S DONE.
NOT WORTH IT.
SHE'LL NEED TO BE SWEETER THAN THAT REWARD, YOU SEE?
HM.
I'M SORRY, BENTON, OF COURSE.
WE'LL BE SWEET AS A BOWL OF PUNCH.
NO!
WHAT!
YOU HAVEN'T COLLECTED A SINGLE COIN?
LIZZIE!
STOP IT!
USELESS!
YOU'RE TERRIBLE AT YOUR JOB!

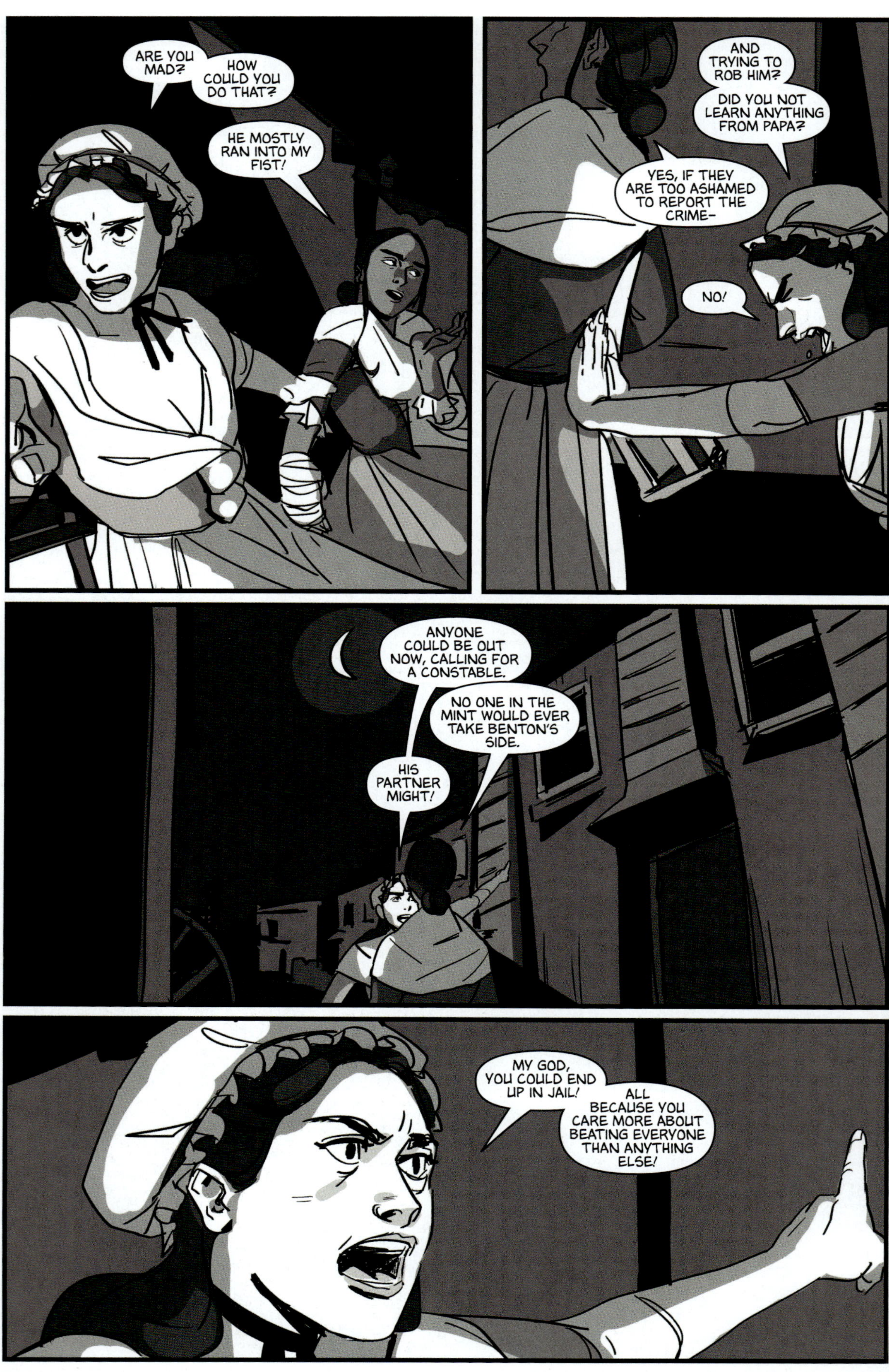
ARE YOU MAD?
HOW COULD YOU DO THAT?
HE MOSTLY RAN INTO MY FIST!
AND TRYING TO ROB HIM?
DID YOU NOT LEARN ANYTHING FROM PAPA?
YES, IF THEY ARE TOO ASHAMED TO REPORT THE CRIME–
NO!
ANYONE COULD BE OUT NOW, CALLING FOR A CONSTABLE.
NO ONE IN THE MINT WOULD EVER TAKE BENTON'S SIDE.
HIS PARTNER MIGHT!
MY GOD, YOU COULD END UP IN JAIL!
ALL BECAUSE YOU CARE MORE ABOUT BEATING EVERYONE THAN ANYTHING ELSE!

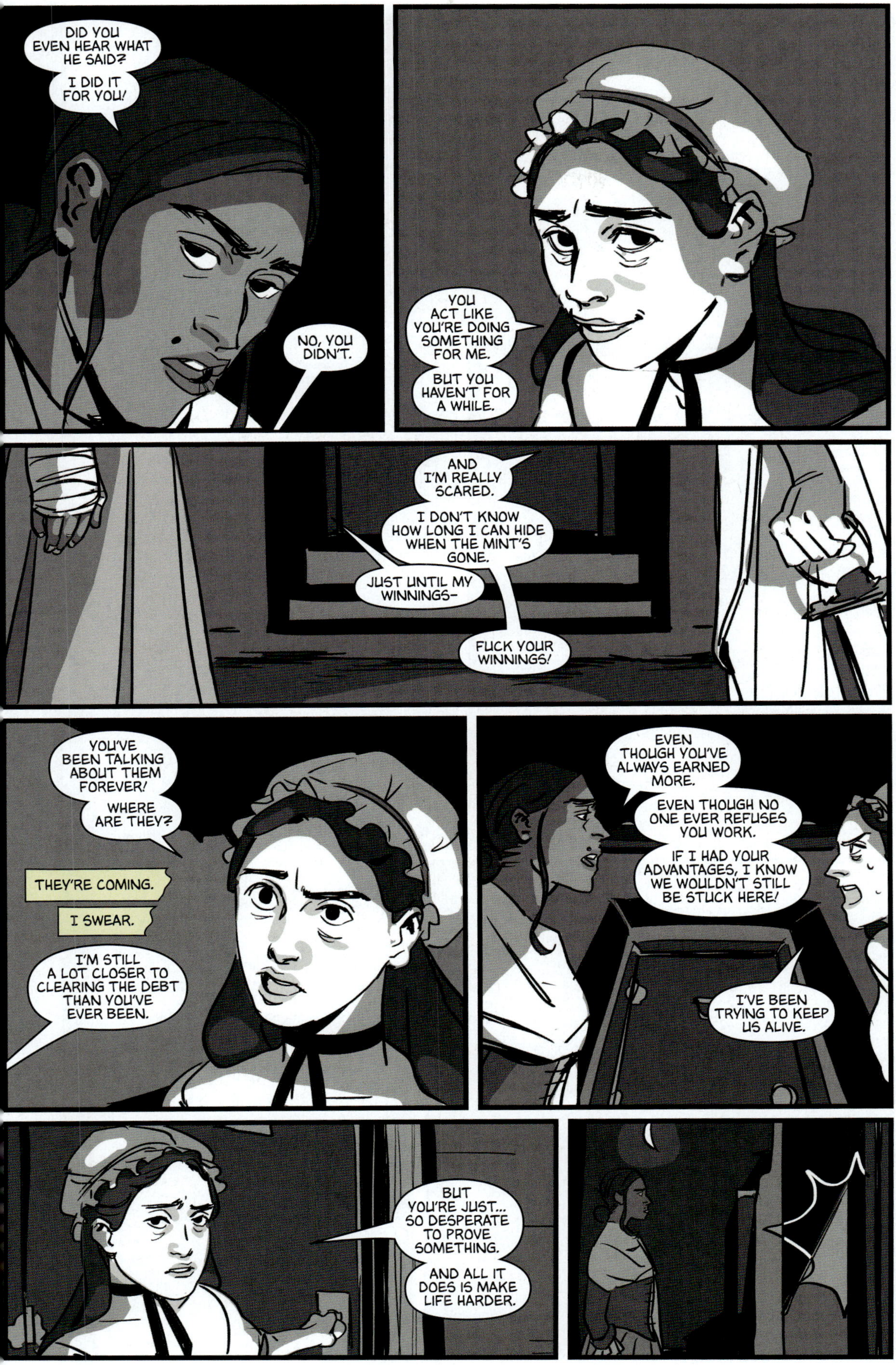
DID YOU EVEN HEAR WHAT HE SAID?
I DID IT FOR YOU!
NO, YOU DIDN'T.
YOU ACT LIKE YOU'RE DOING SOMETHING FOR ME.
BUT YOU HAVEN'T FOR A WHILE.
AND I'M REALLY SCARED.
I DON'T KNOW HOW LONG I CAN HIDE WHEN THE MINT'S GONE.
JUST UNTIL MY WINNINGS–
FUCK YOUR WINNINGS!
YOU'VE BEEN TALKING ABOUT THEM FOREVER!
WHERE ARE THEY?
THEY'RE COMING.
I SWEAR.
I'M STILL A LOT CLOSER TO CLEARING THE DEBT THAN YOU'VE EVER BEEN.
EVEN THOUGH YOU'VE ALWAYS EARNED MORE.
EVEN THOUGH NO ONE EVER REFUSES YOU WORK.
IF I HAD YOUR ADVANTAGES, I KNOW WE WOULDN'T STILL BE STUCK HERE!
I'VE BEEN TRYING TO KEEP US ALIVE.
BUT YOU'RE JUST... SO DESPERATE TO PROVE SOMETHING.
AND ALL IT DOES IS MAKE LIFE HARDER.

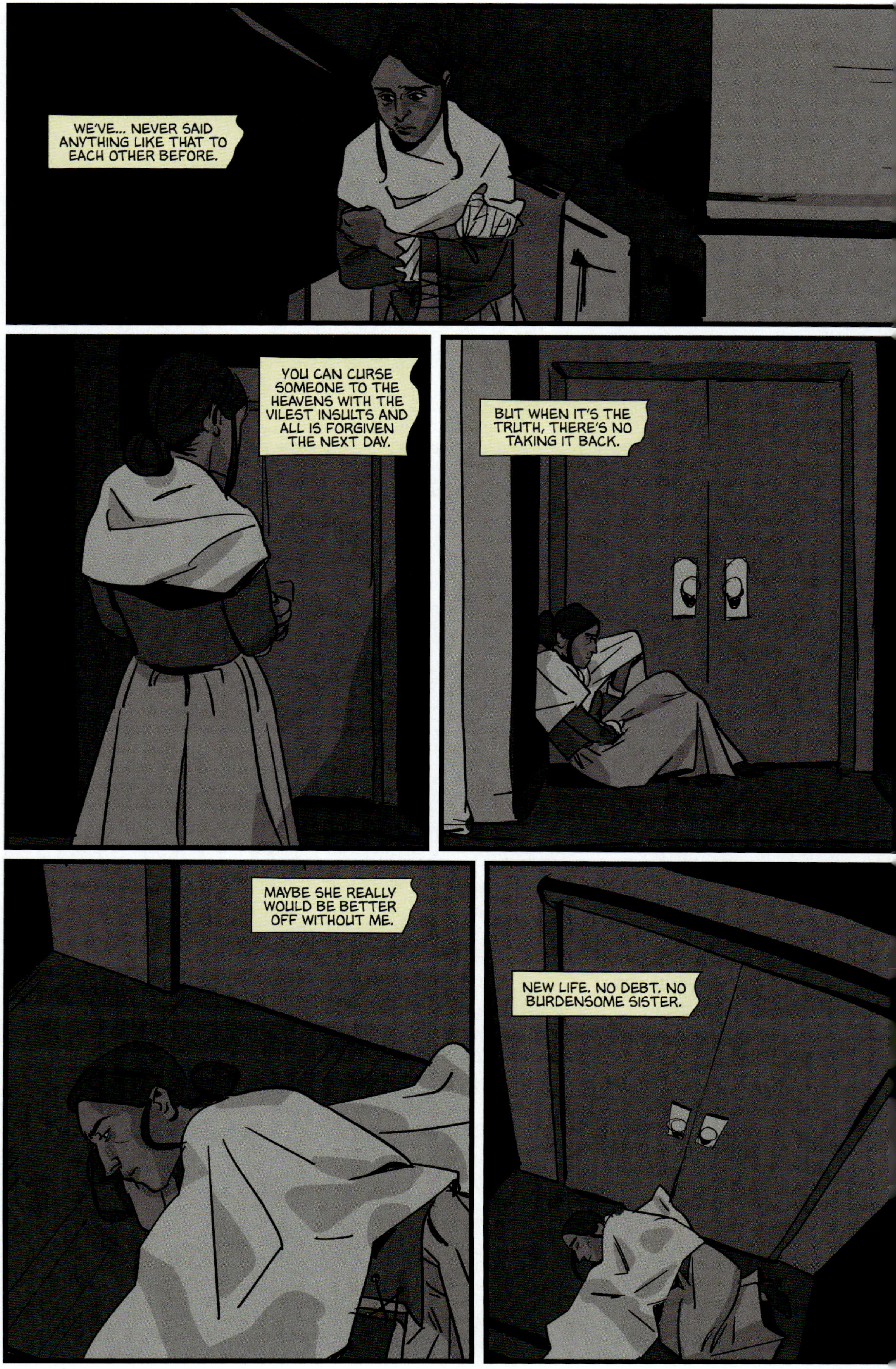
WE'VE... NEVER SAID ANYTHING LIKE THAT TO EACH OTHER BEFORE.
YOU CAN CURSE SOMEONE TO THE HEAVENS WITH THE VILEST INSULTS AND ALL IS FORGIVEN THE NEXT DAY.
BUT WHEN IT'S THE TRUTH, THERE'S NO TAKING IT BACK.
MAYBE SHE REALLY WOULD BE BETTER OFF WITHOUT ME.
NEW LIFE. NO DEBT. NO BURDENSOME SISTER.

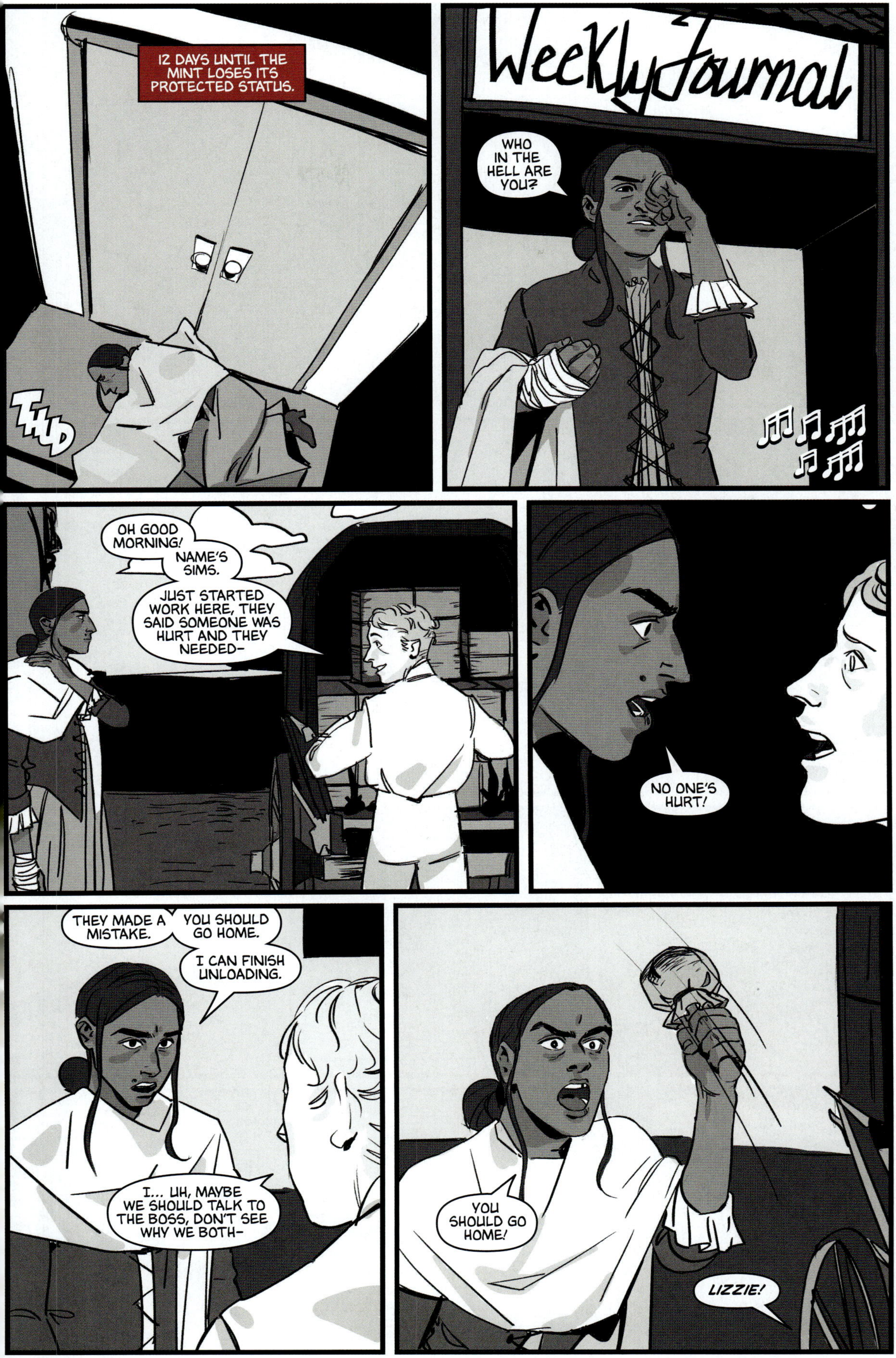
12 DAYS UNTIL THE MINT LOSES ITS PROTECTED STATUS.
THUD
WeeklyJournal
WHO IN THE HELL ARE YOU?
OH GOOD MORNING!
NAME'S SIMS.
JUST STARTED WORK HERE, THEY SAID SOMEONE WAS HURT AND THEY NEEDED-
NO ONE'S HURT!
THEY MADE A MISTAKE.
YOU SHOULD GO HOME.
I CAN FINISH UNLOADING.
I... UH, MAYBE WE SHOULD TALK TO THE BOSS, DON'T SEE WHY WE BOTH-
YOU SHOULD GO HOME!
LIZZIE!

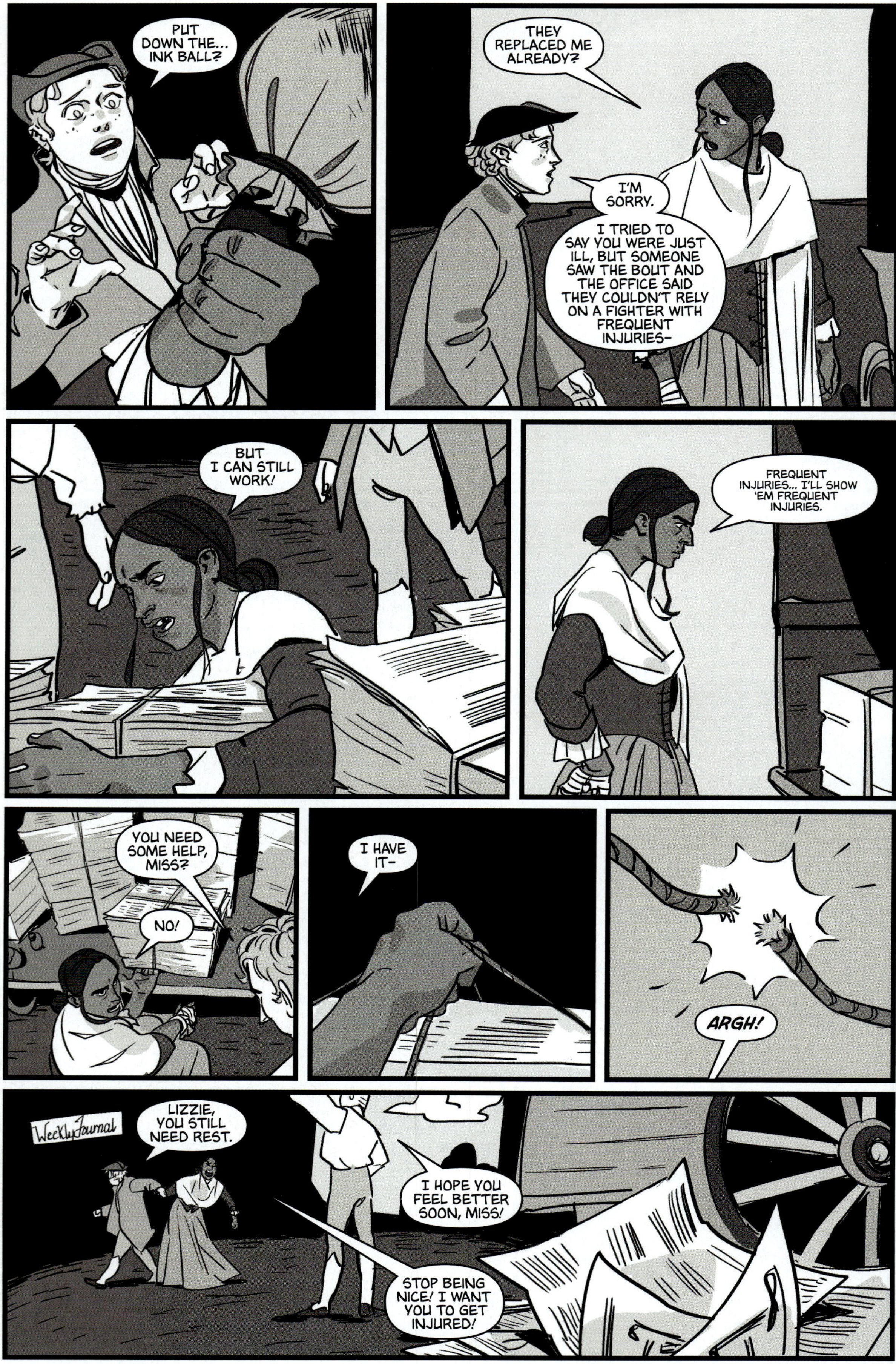
PUT DOWN THE... INK BALL?
THEY REPLACED ME ALREADY?
I'M SORRY.
I TRIED TO SAY YOU WERE JUST ILL, BUT SOMEONE SAW THE BOUT AND THE OFFICE SAID THEY COULDN'T RELY ON A FIGHTER WITH FREQUENT INJURIES–
BUT I CAN STILL WORK!
FREQUENT INJURIES... I'LL SHOW 'EM FREQUENT INJURIES.
YOU NEED SOME HELP, MISS?
NO!
I HAVE IT–
ARGH!
Weekly Journal
LIZZIE, YOU STILL NEED REST.
I HOPE YOU FEEL BETTER SOON, MISS!
STOP BEING NICE! I WANT YOU TO GET INJURED!

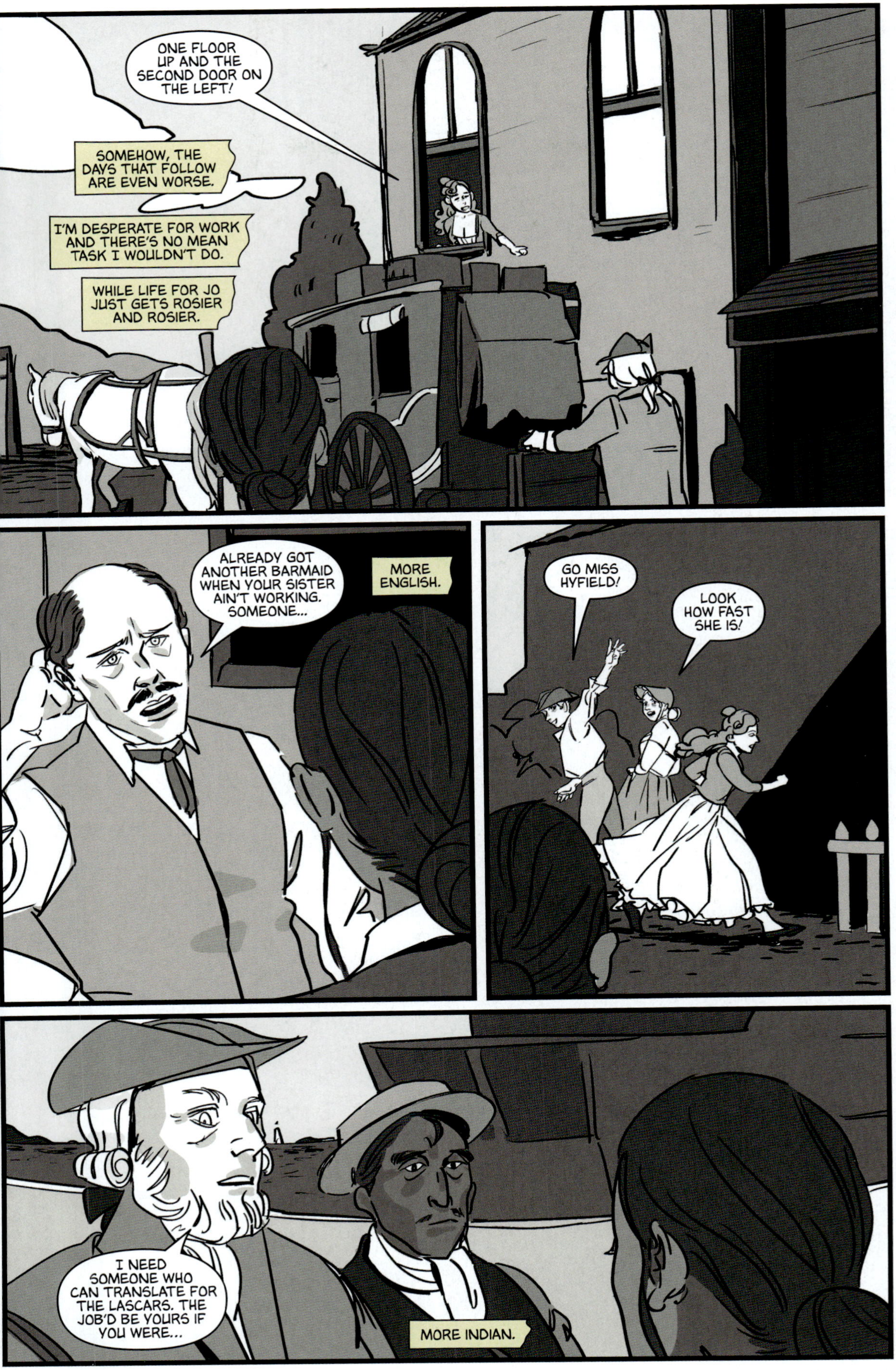
ONE FLOOR UP AND THE SECOND DOOR ON THE LEFT!
SOMEHOW, THE DAYS THAT FOLLOW ARE EVEN WORSE.
I'M DESPERATE FOR WORK AND THERE'S NO MEAN TASK I WOULDN'T DO.
WHILE LIFE FOR JO JUST GETS ROSIER AND ROSIER.
ALREADY GOT ANOTHER BARMAID WHEN YOUR SISTER AIN'T WORKING. SOMEONE...
MORE ENGLISH.
GO MISS HYFIELD!
LOOK HOW FAST SHE IS!
I NEED SOMEONE WHO CAN TRANSLATE FOR THE LASCARS. THE JOB'D BE YOURS IF YOU WERE...
MORE INDIAN.

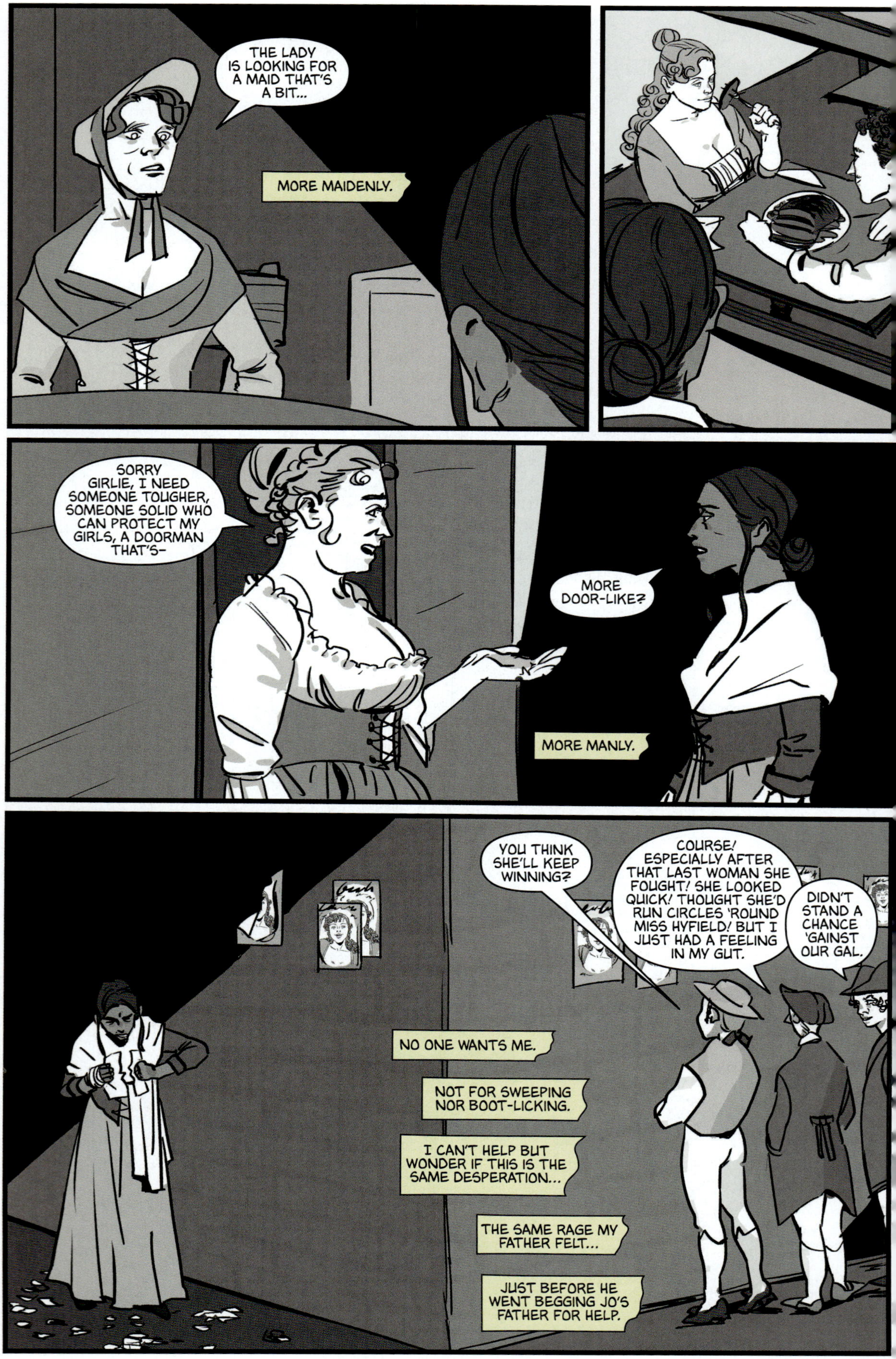
THE LADY IS LOOKING FOR A MAID THAT'S A BIT...
MORE MAIDENLY.
SORRY GIRLIE, I NEED SOMEONE TOUGHER, SOMEONE SOLID WHO CAN PROTECT MY GIRLS, A DOORMAN THAT'S-
MORE DOOR-LIKE?
MORE MANLY.
YOU THINK SHE'LL KEEP WINNING?
COURSE! ESPECIALLY AFTER THAT LAST WOMAN SHE FOUGHT! SHE LOOKED QUICK! THOUGHT SHE'D RUN CIRCLES 'ROUND MISS HYFIELD! BUT I JUST HAD A FEELING IN MY GUT.
DIDN'T STAND A CHANCE 'GAINST OUR GAL.
NO ONE WANTS ME.
NOT FOR SWEEPING NOR BOOT-LICKING.
I CAN'T HELP BUT WONDER IF THIS IS THE SAME DESPERATION...
THE SAME RAGE MY FATHER FELT...
JUST BEFORE HE WENT BEGGING JO'S FATHER FOR HELP.

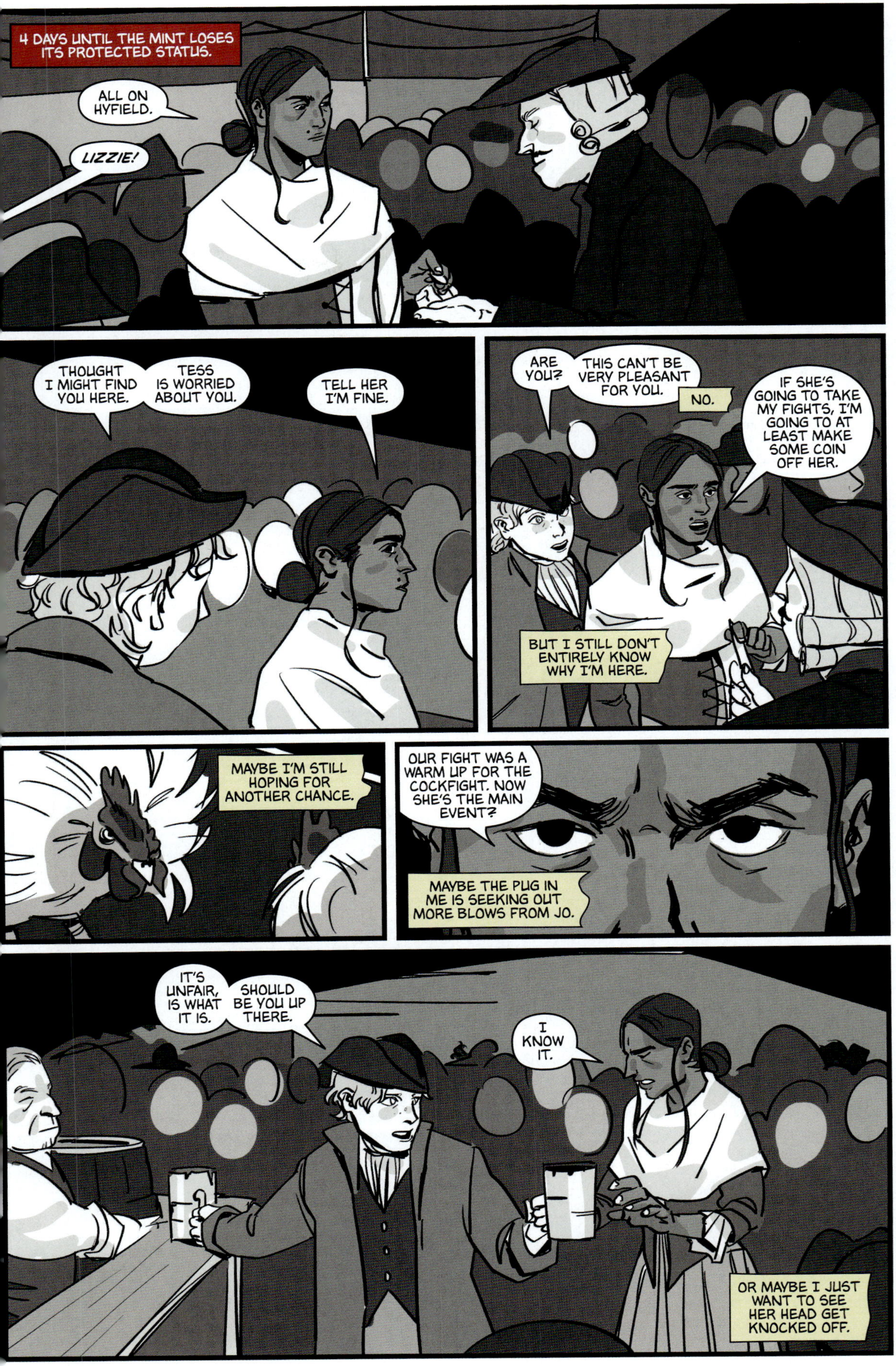

4 DAYS UNTIL THE MINT LOSES ITS PROTECTED STATUS.
ALL ON HYFIELD.
LIZZIE!
THOUGHT I MIGHT FIND YOU HERE.
TESS IS WORRIED ABOUT YOU.
TELL HER I'M FINE.
ARE YOU?
THIS CAN'T BE VERY PLEASANT FOR YOU.
NO.
IF SHE'S GOING TO TAKE MY FIGHTS, I'M GOING TO AT LEAST MAKE SOME COIN OFF HER.
BUT I STILL DON'T ENTIRELY KNOW WHY I'M HERE.
MAYBE I'M STILL HOPING FOR ANOTHER CHANCE.
OUR FIGHT WAS A WARM UP FOR THE COCKFIGHT. NOW SHE'S THE MAIN EVENT?
MAYBE THE PUG IN ME IS SEEKING OUT MORE BLOWS FROM JO.
IT'S UNFAIR, IS WHAT IT IS.
SHOULD BE YOU UP THERE.
I KNOW IT.
OR MAYBE I JUST WANT TO SEE HER HEAD GET KNOCKED OFF.

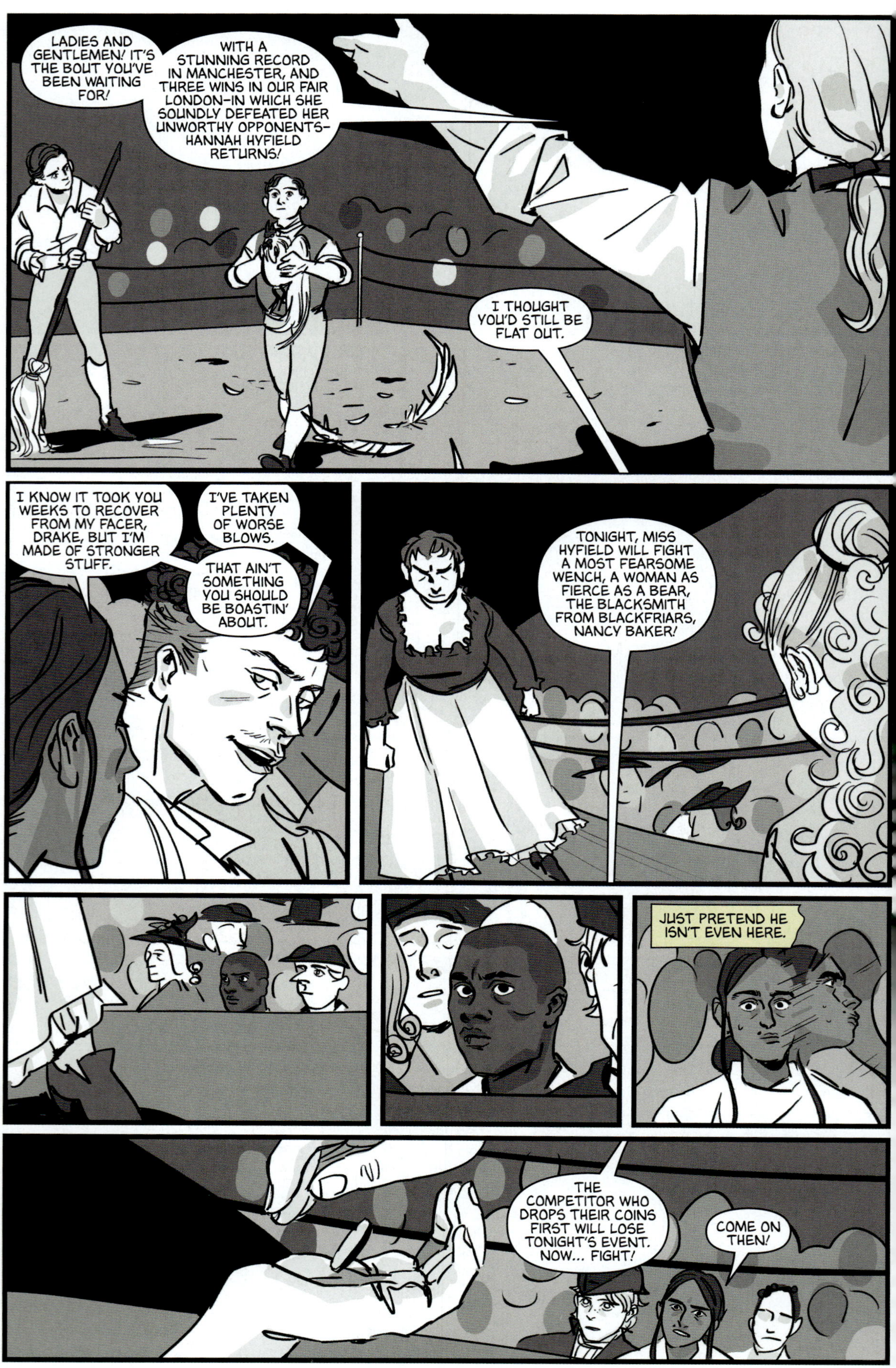
LADIES AND GENTLEMEN! IT'S THE BOUT YOU'VE BEEN WAITING FOR!
WITH A STUNNING RECORD IN MANCHESTER, AND THREE WINS IN OUR FAIR LONDON—IN WHICH SHE SOUNDLY DEFEATED HER UNWORTHY OPPONENTS—HANNAH HYFIELD RETURNS!
I THOUGHT YOU'D STILL BE FLAT OUT.
I KNOW IT TOOK YOU WEEKS TO RECOVER FROM MY FACER, DRAKE, BUT I'M MADE OF STRONGER STUFF.
I'VE TAKEN PLENTY OF WORSE BLOWS.
THAT AIN'T SOMETHING YOU SHOULD BE BOASTIN' ABOUT.
TONIGHT, MISS HYFIELD WILL FIGHT A MOST FEARSOME WENCH, A WOMAN AS FIERCE AS A BEAR, THE BLACKSMITH FROM BLACKFRIARS, NANCY BAKER!
JUST PRETEND HE ISN'T EVEN HERE.
THE COMPETITOR WHO DROPS THEIR COINS FIRST WILL LOSE TONIGHT'S EVENT. NOW... FIGHT!
COME ON THEN!

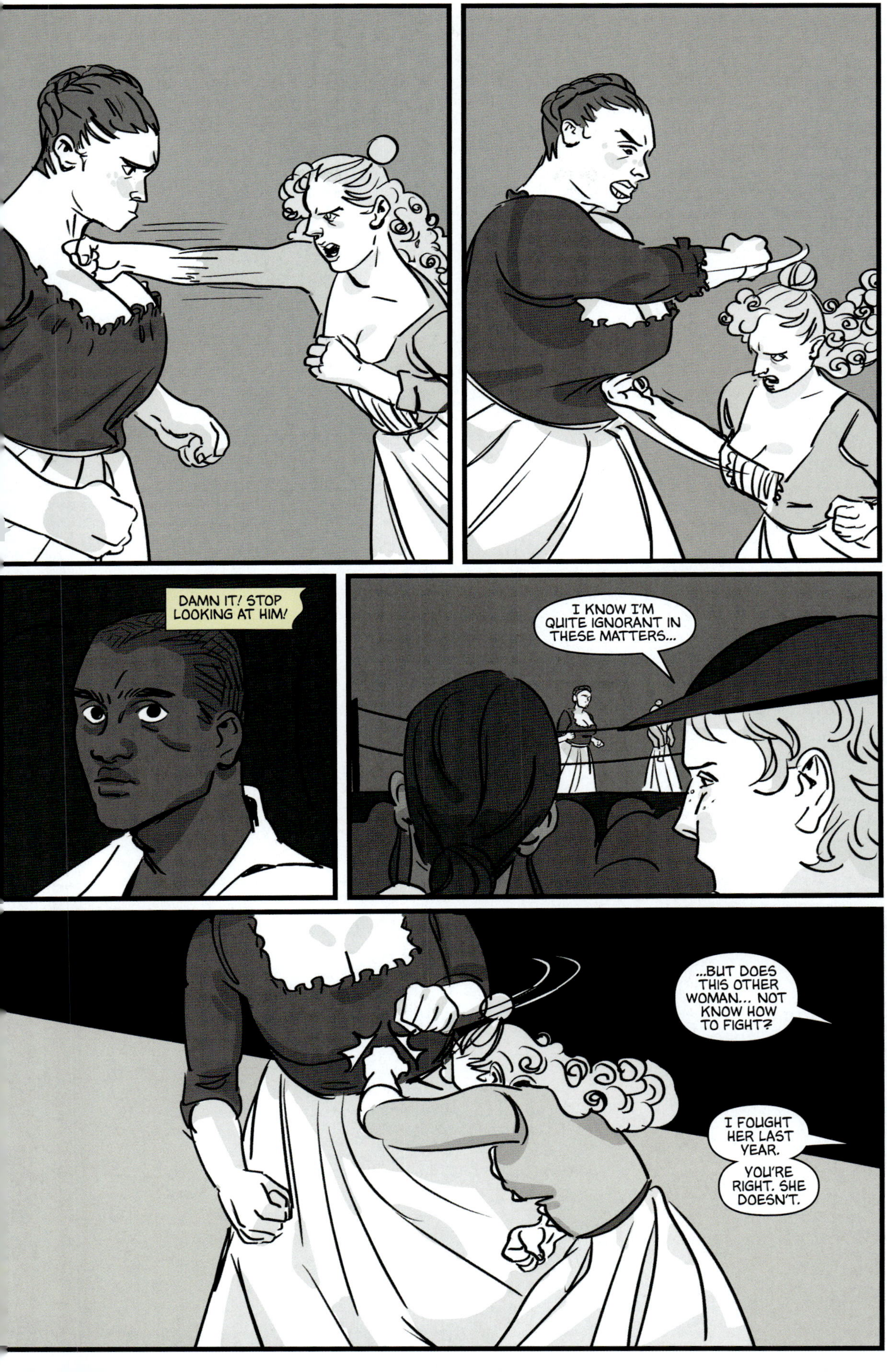
DAMN IT! STOP LOOKING AT HIM!
I KNOW I'M QUITE IGNORANT IN THESE MATTERS...
...BUT DOES THIS OTHER WOMAN... NOT KNOW HOW TO FIGHT?
I FOUGHT HER LAST YEAR.
YOU'RE RIGHT. SHE DOESN'T.

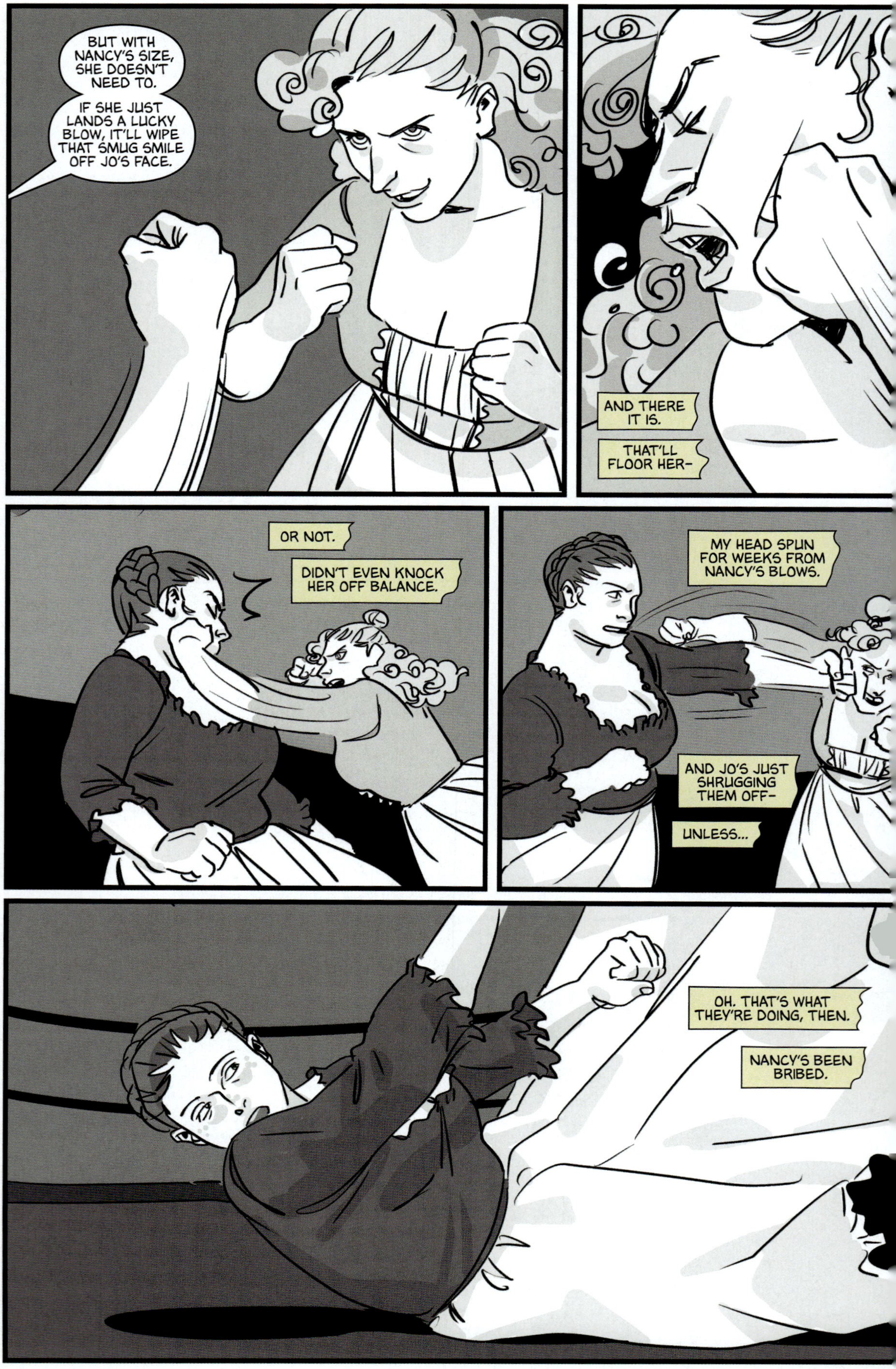

BUT WITH NANCY'S SIZE, SHE DOESN'T NEED TO.
IF SHE JUST LANDS A LUCKY BLOW, IT'LL WIPE THAT SMUG SMILE OFF JO'S FACE.
AND THERE IT IS.
THAT'LL FLOOR HER-
OR NOT.
DIDN'T EVEN KNOCK HER OFF BALANCE.
MY HEAD SPUN FOR WEEKS FROM NANCY'S BLOWS.
AND JO'S JUST SHRUGGING THEM OFF-
UNLESS...
OH. THAT'S WHAT THEY'RE DOING, THEN.
NANCY'S BEEN BRIBED.

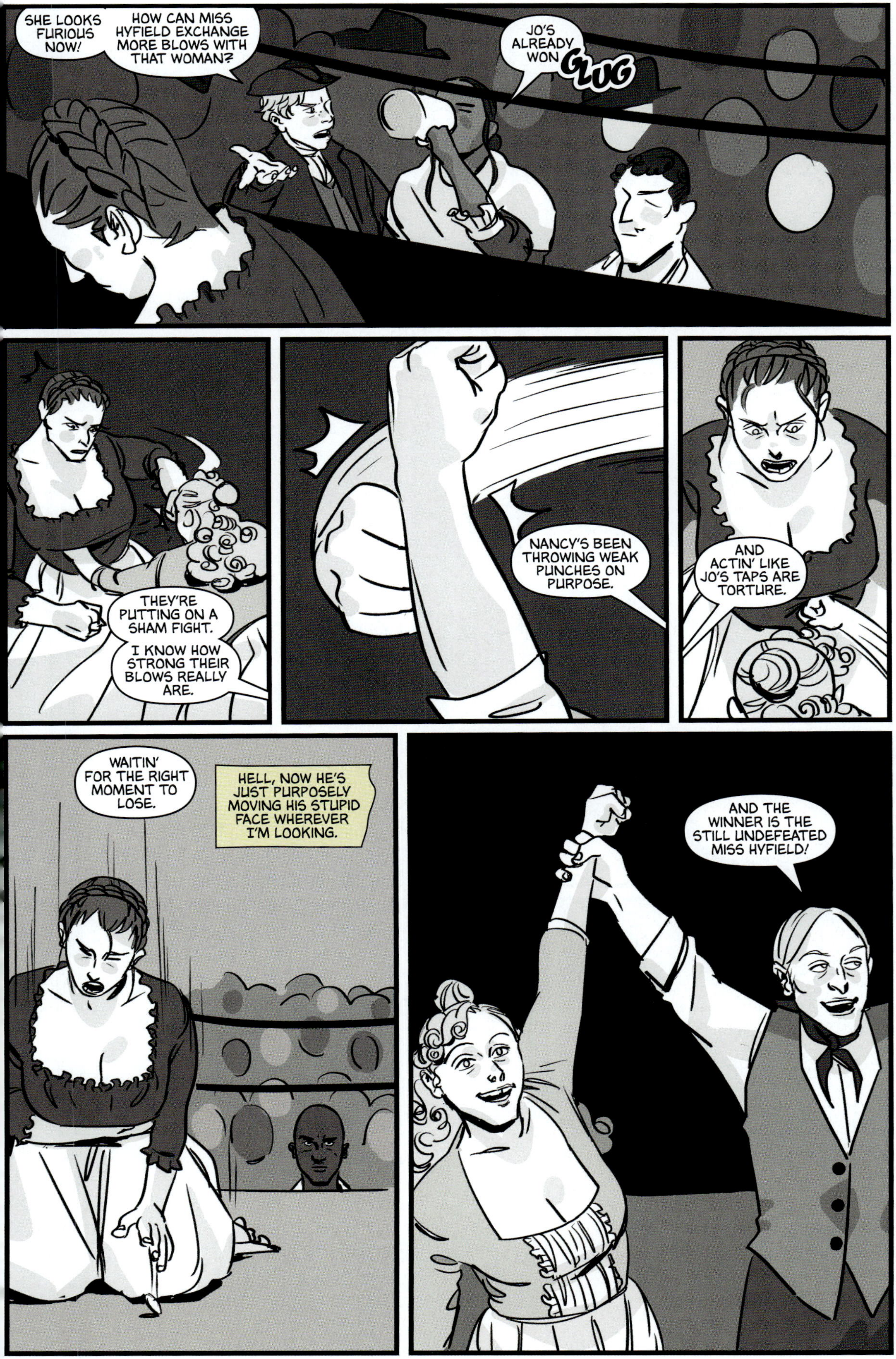
SHE LOOKS FURIOUS NOW!
HOW CAN MISS HYFIELD EXCHANGE MORE BLOWS WITH THAT WOMAN?
JO'S ALREADY WON
GLUG
THEY'RE PUTTING ON A SHAM FIGHT.
I KNOW HOW STRONG THEIR BLOWS REALLY ARE.
NANCY'S BEEN THROWING WEAK PUNCHES ON PURPOSE.
AND ACTIN' LIKE JO'S TAPS ARE TORTURE.
WAITIN' FOR THE RIGHT MOMENT TO LOSE.
HELL, NOW HE'S JUST PURPOSELY MOVING HIS STUPID FACE WHEREVER I'M LOOKING.
AND THE WINNER IS THE STILL UNDEFEATED MISS HYFIELD!

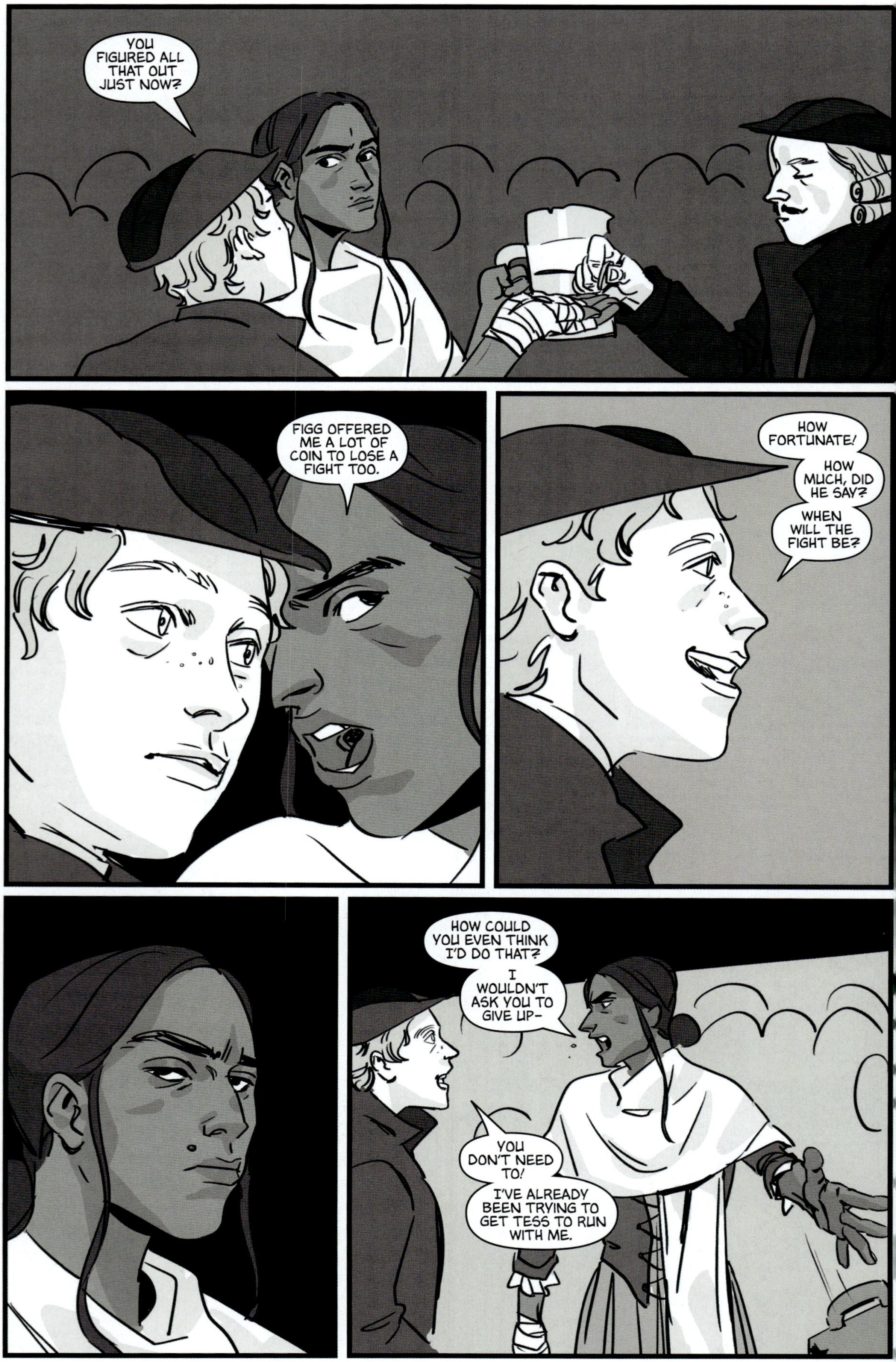
YOU FIGURED ALL THAT OUT JUST NOW?
FIGG OFFERED ME A LOT OF COIN TO LOSE A FIGHT TOO.
HOW FORTUNATE!
HOW MUCH, DID HE SAY?
WHEN WILL THE FIGHT BE?
HOW COULD YOU EVEN THINK I'D DO THAT?
I WOULDN'T ASK YOU TO GIVE UP-
YOU DON'T NEED TO!
I'VE ALREADY BEEN TRYING TO GET TESS TO RUN WITH ME.

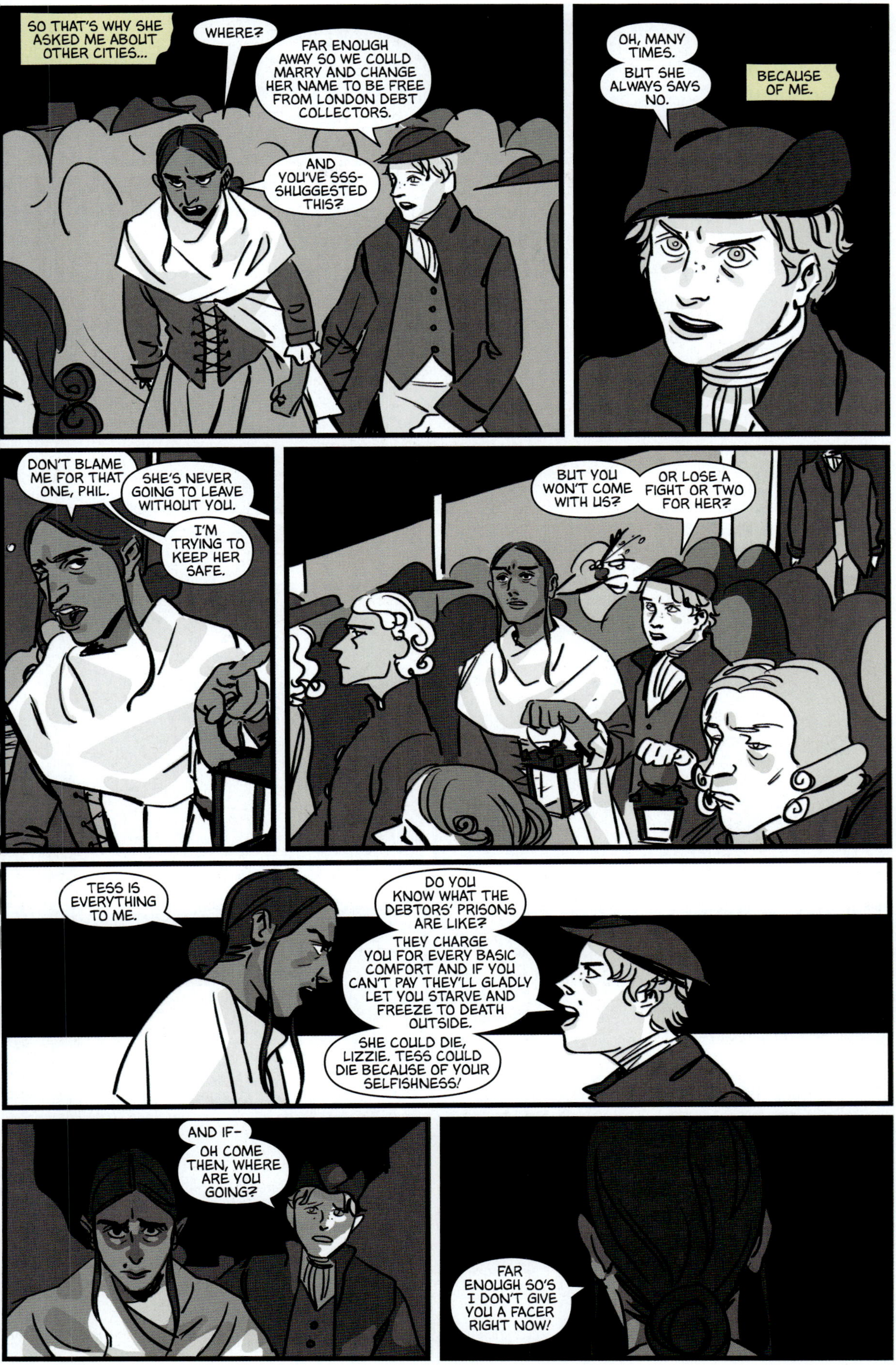

SO THAT'S WHY SHE ASKED ME ABOUT OTHER CITIES...
WHERE?
FAR ENOUGH AWAY SO WE COULD MARRY AND CHANGE HER NAME TO BE FREE FROM LONDON DEBT COLLECTORS.
AND YOU'VE SSS-SHUGGESTED THIS?
OH, MANY TIMES.
BUT SHE ALWAYS SAYS NO.
BECAUSE OF ME.
DON'T BLAME ME FOR THAT ONE, PHIL.
SHE'S NEVER GOING TO LEAVE WITHOUT YOU.
I'M TRYING TO KEEP HER SAFE.
BUT YOU WON'T COME WITH US?
OR LOSE A FIGHT OR TWO FOR HER?
TESS IS EVERYTHING TO ME.
DO YOU KNOW WHAT THE DEBTORS' PRISONS ARE LIKE?
THEY CHARGE YOU FOR EVERY BASIC COMFORT AND IF YOU CAN'T PAY THEY'LL GLADLY LET YOU STARVE AND FREEZE TO DEATH OUTSIDE.
SHE COULD DIE, LIZZIE. TESS COULD DIE BECAUSE OF YOUR SELFISHNESS!
AND IF-
OH COME THEN, WHERE ARE YOU GOING?
FAR ENOUGH SO'S I DON'T GIVE YOU A FACER RIGHT NOW!

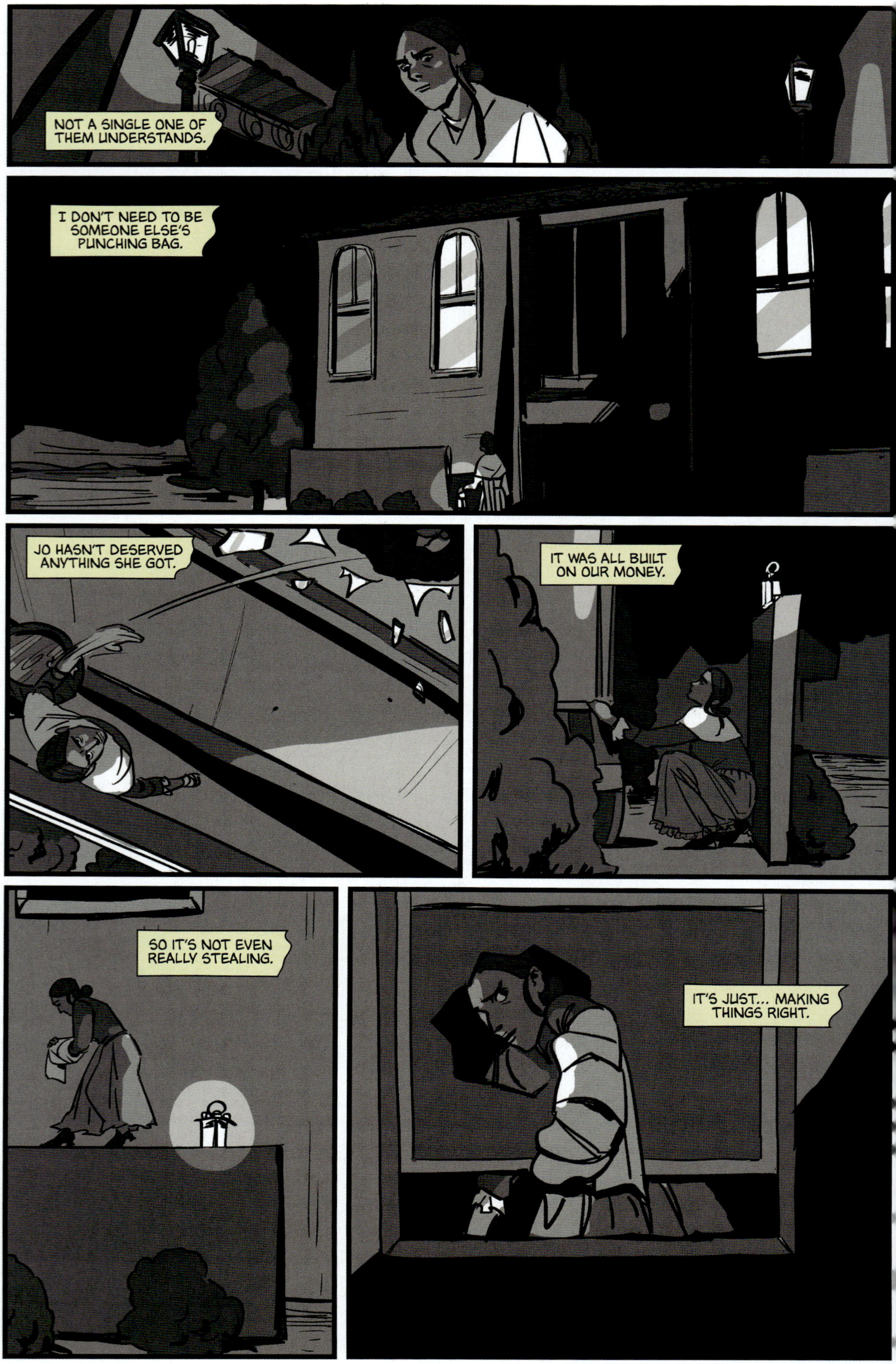

NOT A SINGLE ONE OF THEM UNDERSTANDS.
I DON'T NEED TO BE SOMEONE ELSE'S PUNCHING BAG.
JO HASN'T DESERVED ANYTHING SHE GOT.
IT WAS ALL BUILT ON OUR MONEY.
SO IT'S NOT EVEN REALLY STEALING.
IT'S JUST... MAKING THINGS RIGHT.

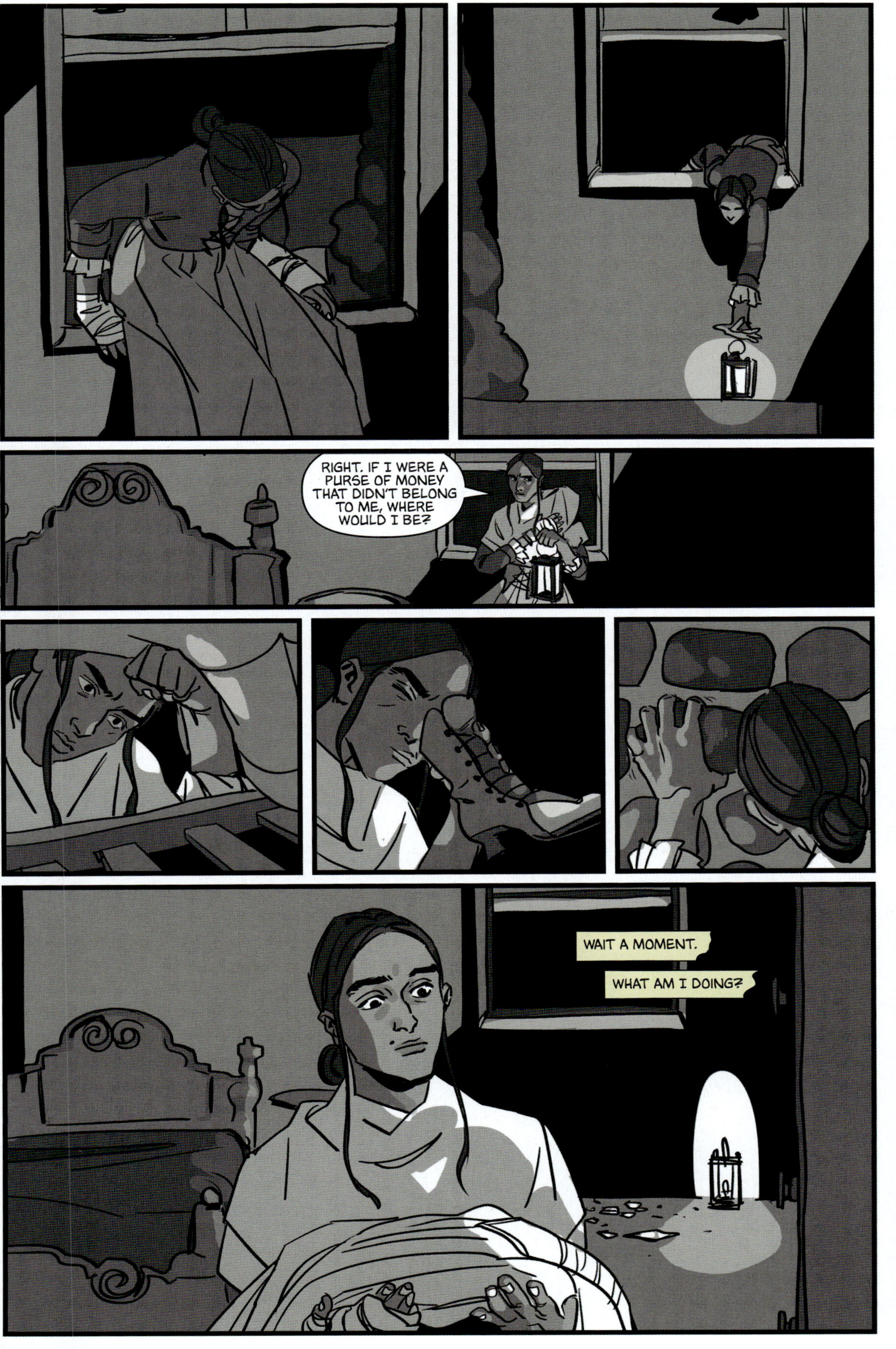
RIGHT. IF I WERE A PURSE OF MONEY THAT DIDN'T BELONG TO ME, WHERE WOULD I BE?
WAIT A MOMENT.
WHAT AM I DOING?

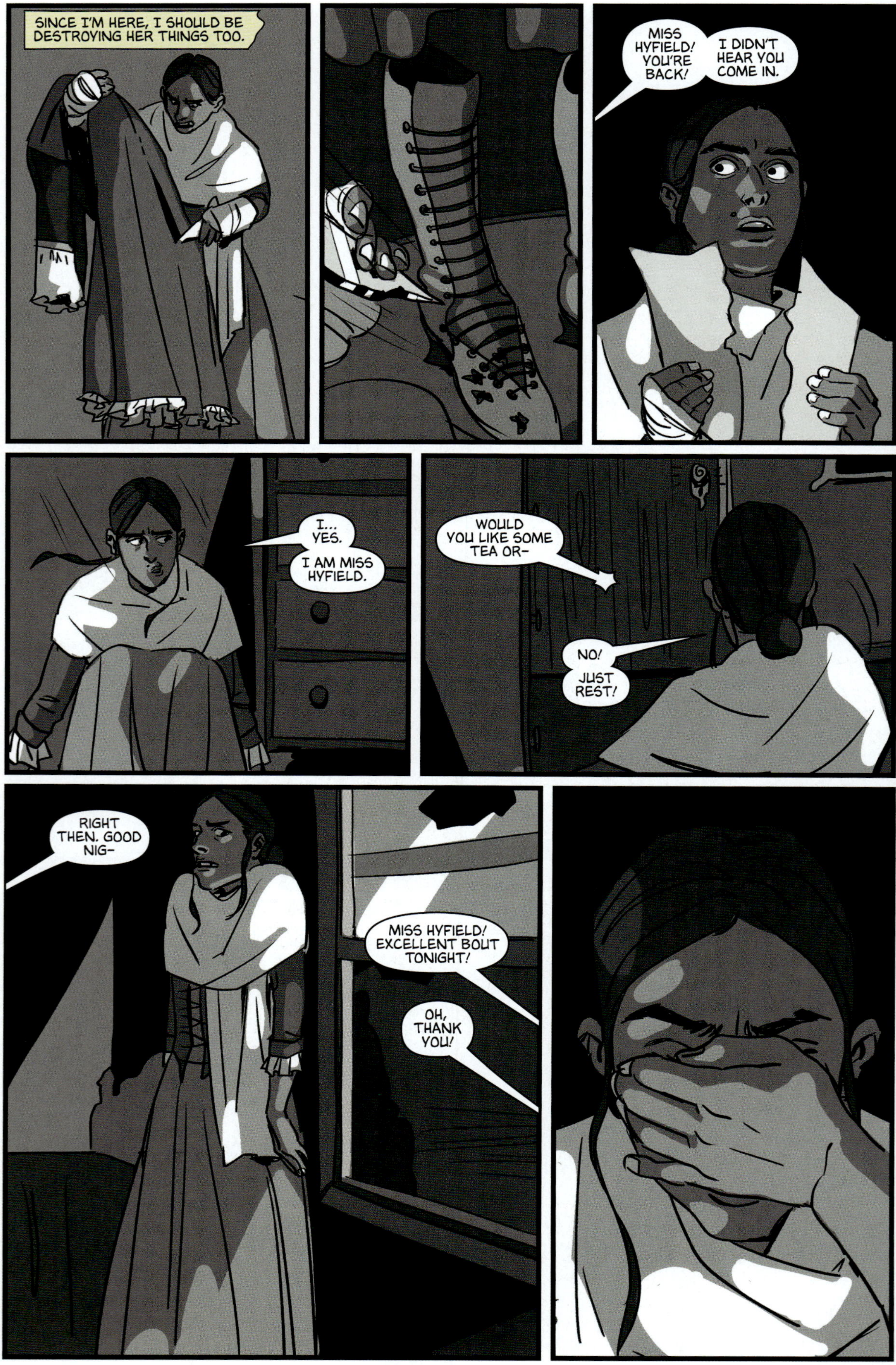
SINCE I'M HERE, I SHOULD BE DESTROYING HER THINGS TOO.
MISS HYFIELD! YOU'RE BACK!
I DIDN'T HEAR YOU COME IN.
I... YES.
I AM MISS HYFIELD.
WOULD YOU LIKE SOME TEA OR-
NO!
JUST REST!
RIGHT THEN. GOOD NIG-
MISS HYFIELD! EXCELLENT BOUT TONIGHT!
OH, THANK YOU!

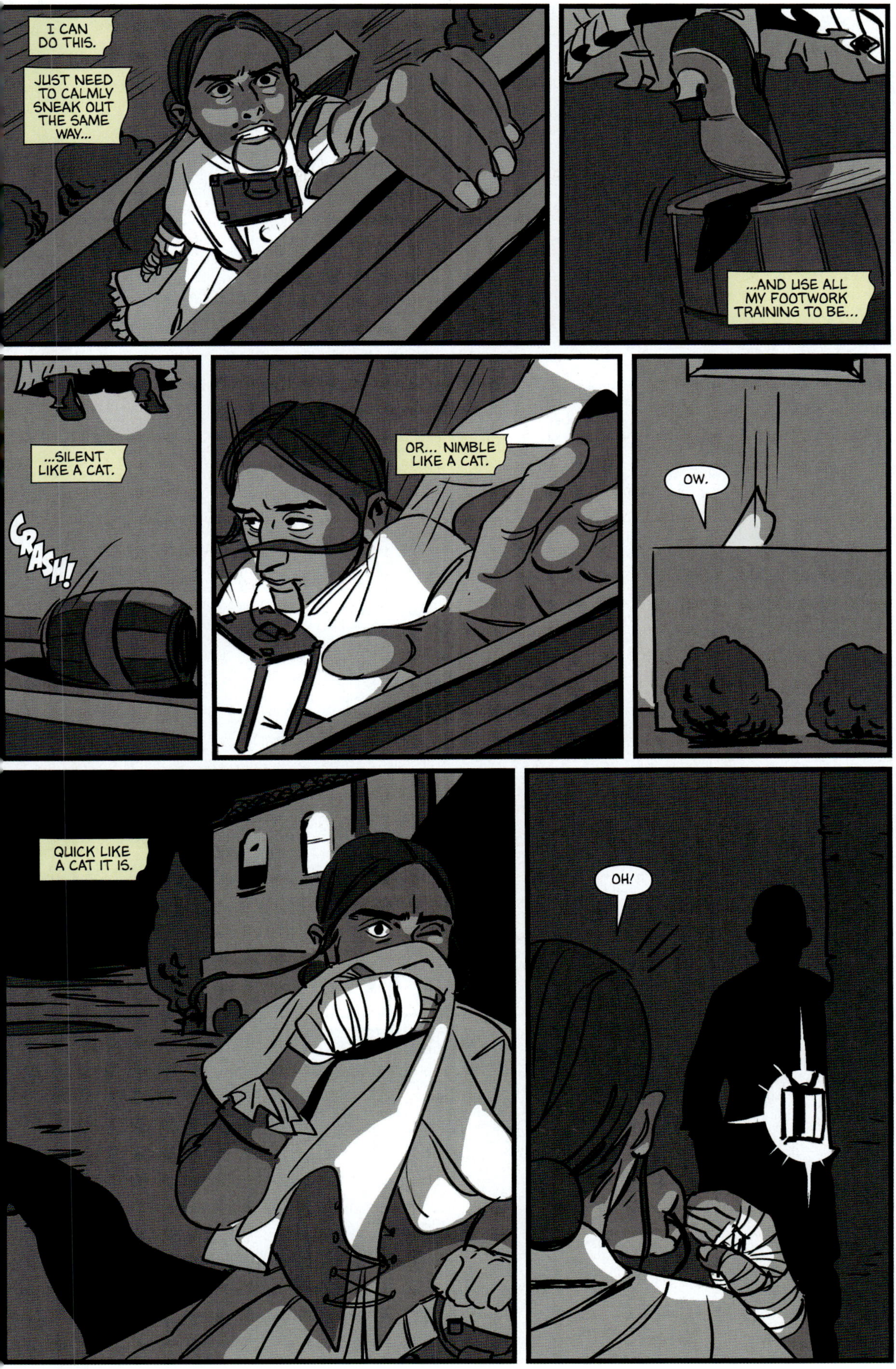
I CAN DO THIS.
JUST NEED TO CALMLY SNEAK OUT THE SAME WAY...
...AND USE ALL MY FOOTWORK TRAINING TO BE...
...SILENT LIKE A CAT.
CRASH!
OR... NIMBLE LIKE A CAT.
OW.
QUICK LIKE A CAT IT IS.
OH!

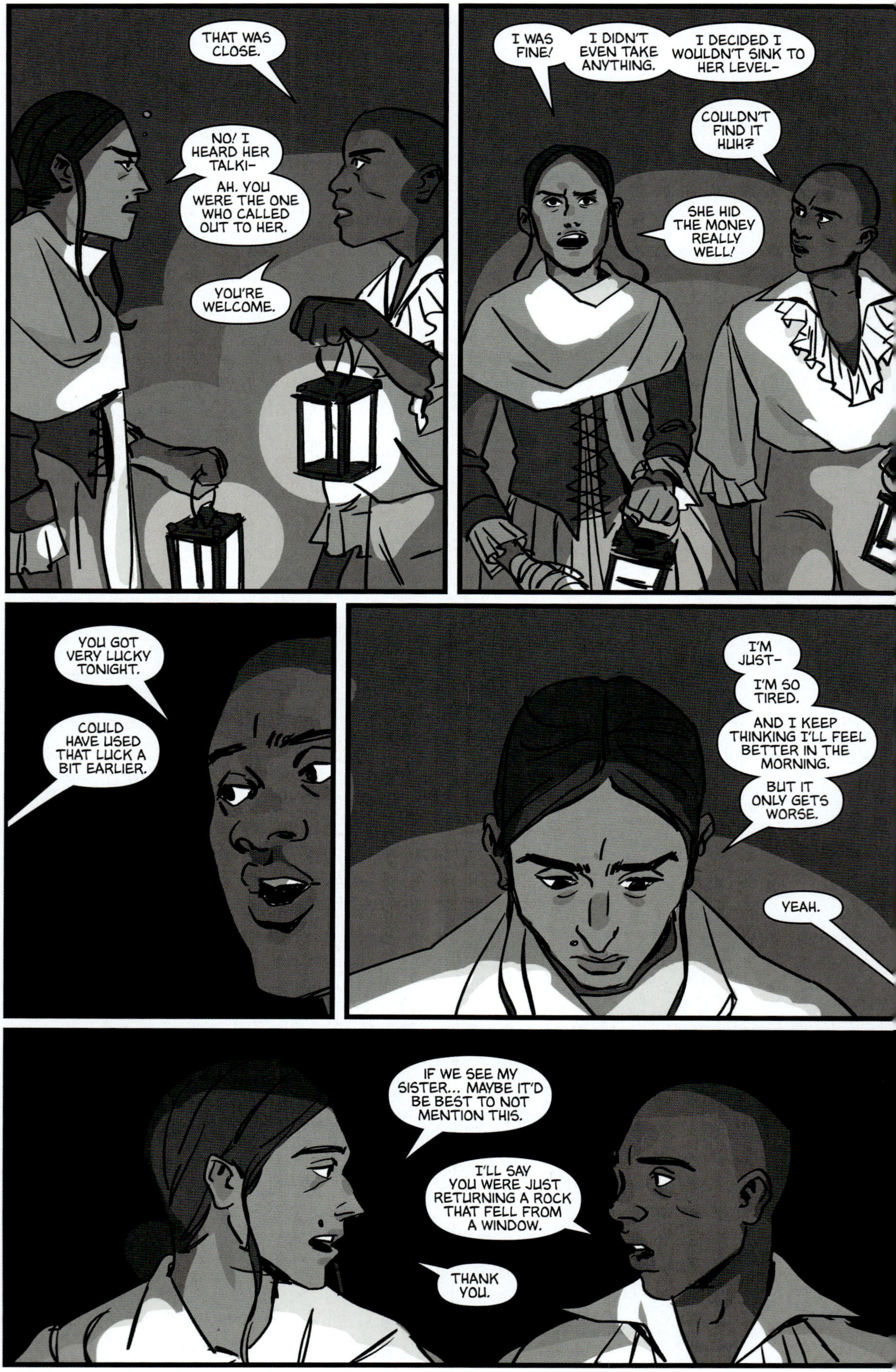
THAT WAS CLOSE.
NO! I HEARD HER TALKI–
AH. YOU WERE THE ONE WHO CALLED OUT TO HER.
YOU'RE WELCOME.
I WAS FINE!
I DIDN'T EVEN TAKE ANYTHING.
I DECIDED I WOULDN'T SINK TO HER LEVEL–
COULDN'T FIND IT HUH?
SHE HID THE MONEY REALLY WELL!
YOU GOT VERY LUCKY TONIGHT.
COULD HAVE USED THAT LUCK A BIT EARLIER.
I'M JUST–
I'M SO TIRED.
AND I KEEP THINKING I'LL FEEL BETTER IN THE MORNING.
BUT IT ONLY GETS WORSE.
YEAH.
IF WE SEE MY SISTER... MAYBE IT'D BE BEST TO NOT MENTION THIS.
I'LL SAY YOU WERE JUST RETURNING A ROCK THAT FELL FROM A WINDOW.
THANK YOU.

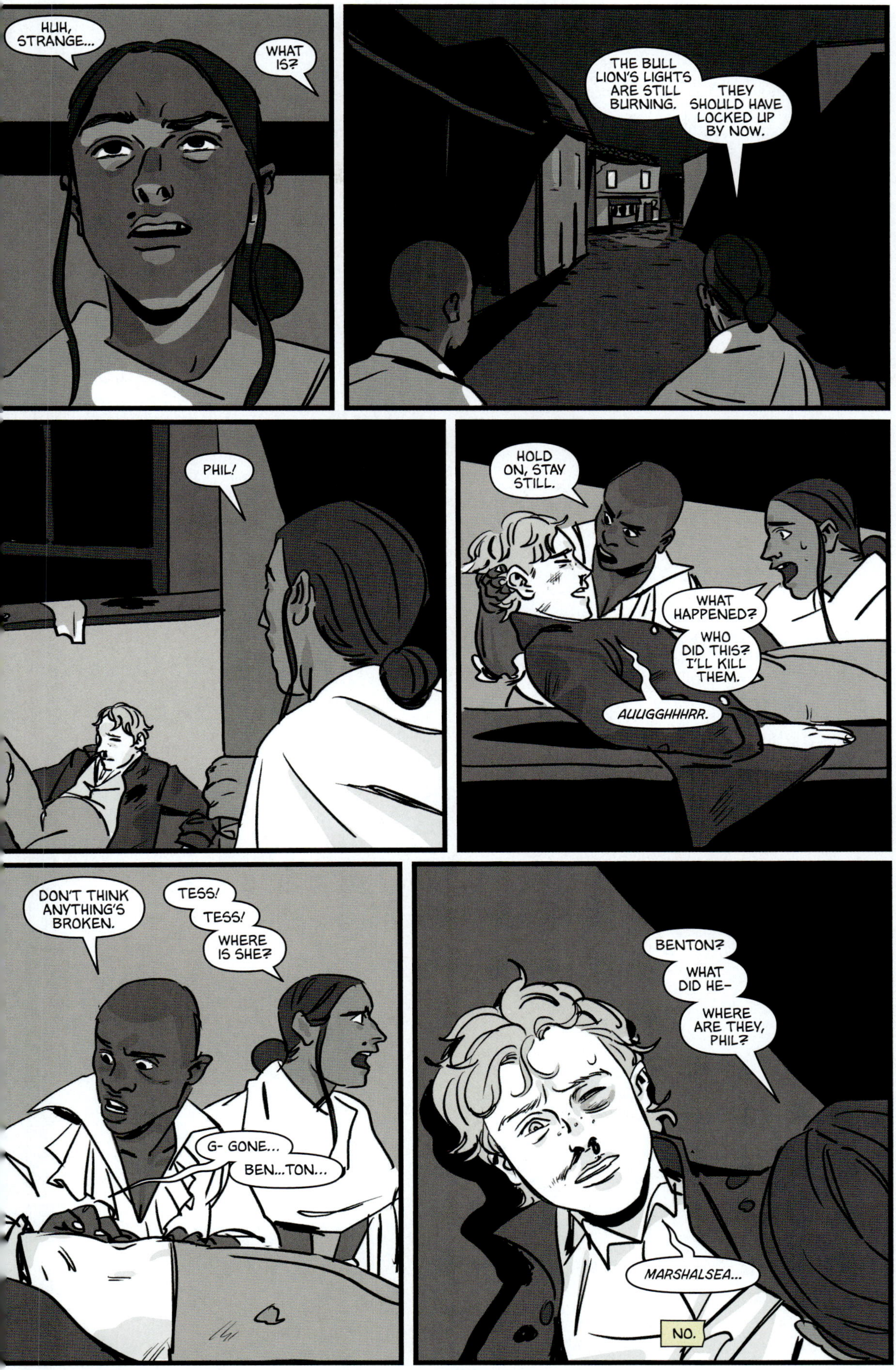
HUH, STRANGE...
WHAT IS?
THE BULL LION'S LIGHTS ARE STILL BURNING.
THEY SHOULD HAVE LOCKED UP BY NOW.
PHIL!
HOLD ON, STAY STILL.
WHAT HAPPENED?
WHO DID THIS? I'LL KILL THEM.
AUUGGHHHRR.
DON'T THINK ANYTHING'S BROKEN.
TESS!
TESS!
WHERE IS SHE?
G- GONE...
BEN...TON...
BENTON?
WHAT DID HE-
WHERE ARE THEY, PHIL?
MARSHALSEA...
NO.

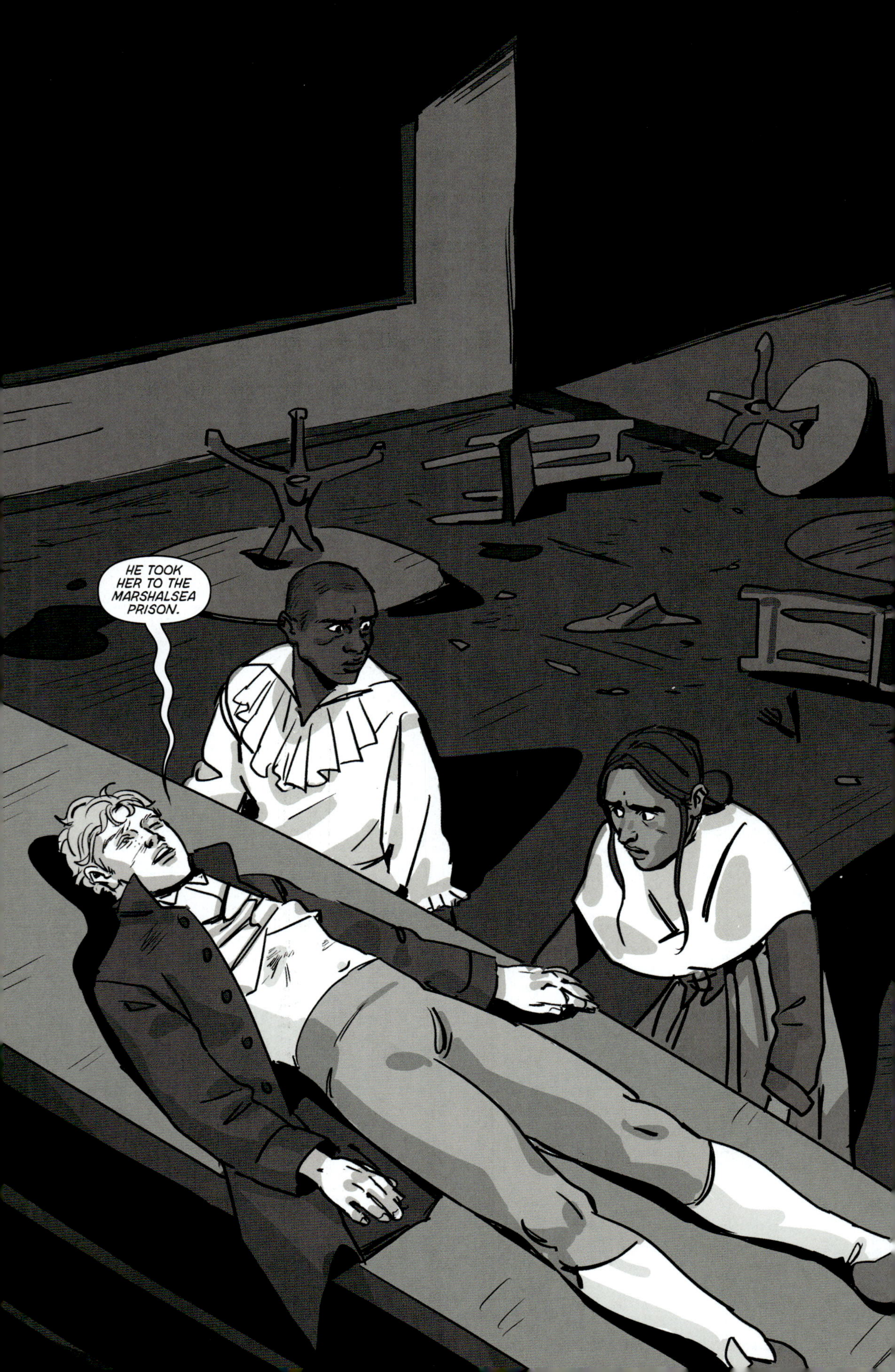
HE TOOK HER TO THE MARSHALSEA PRISON.

5

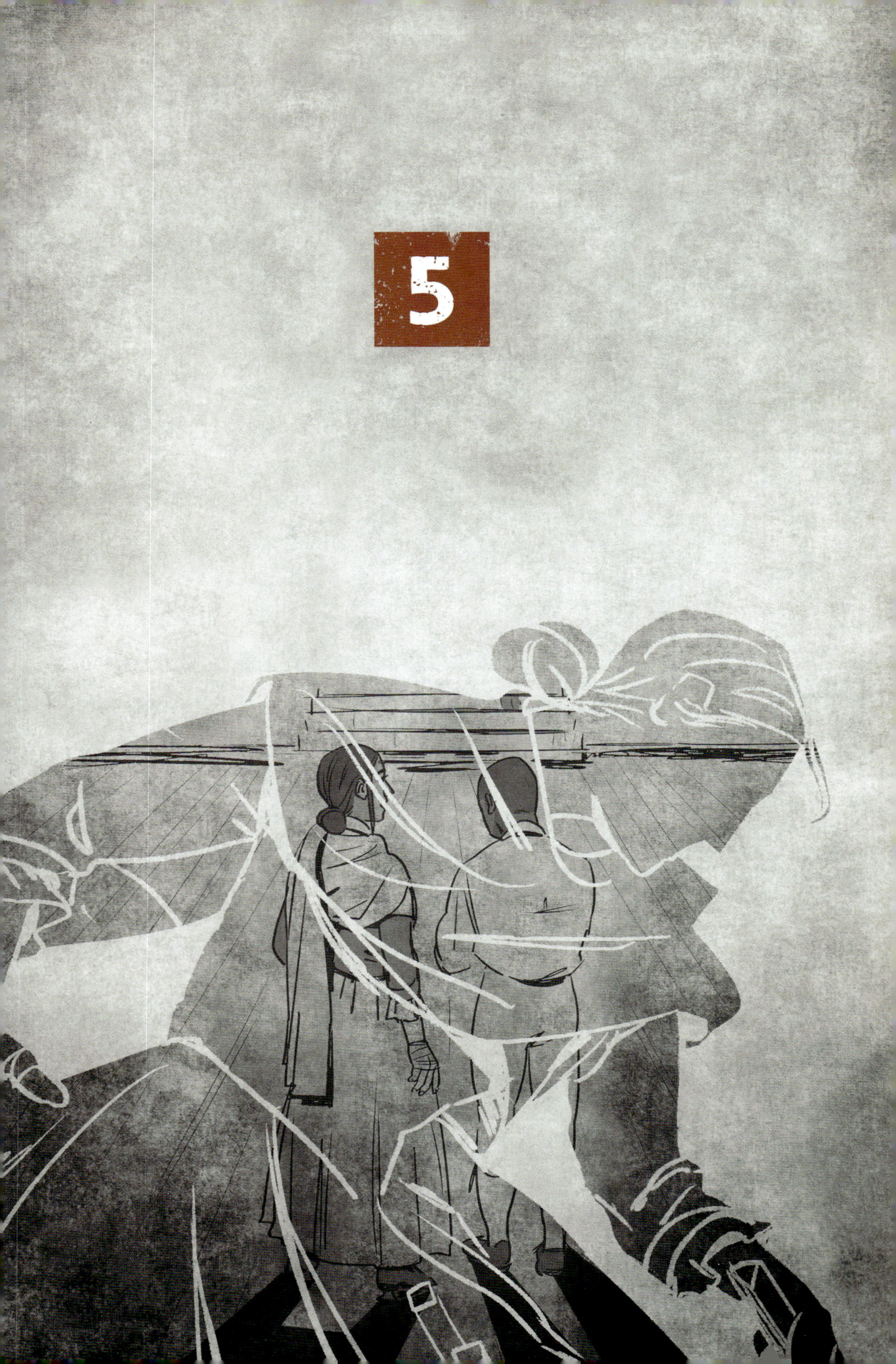

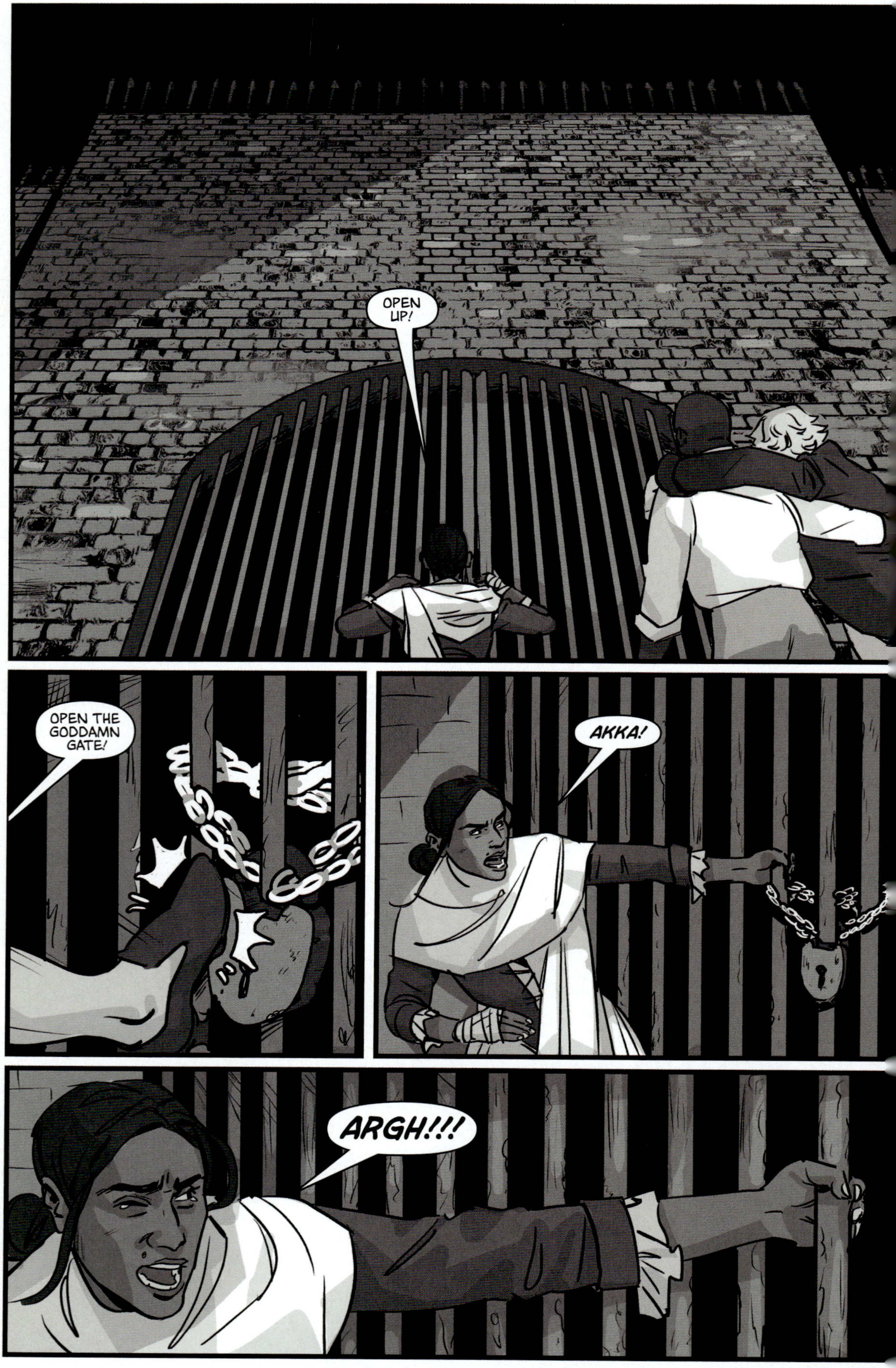
OPEN UP!
OPEN THE GODDAMN GATE!
AKKA!
ARGH!!!

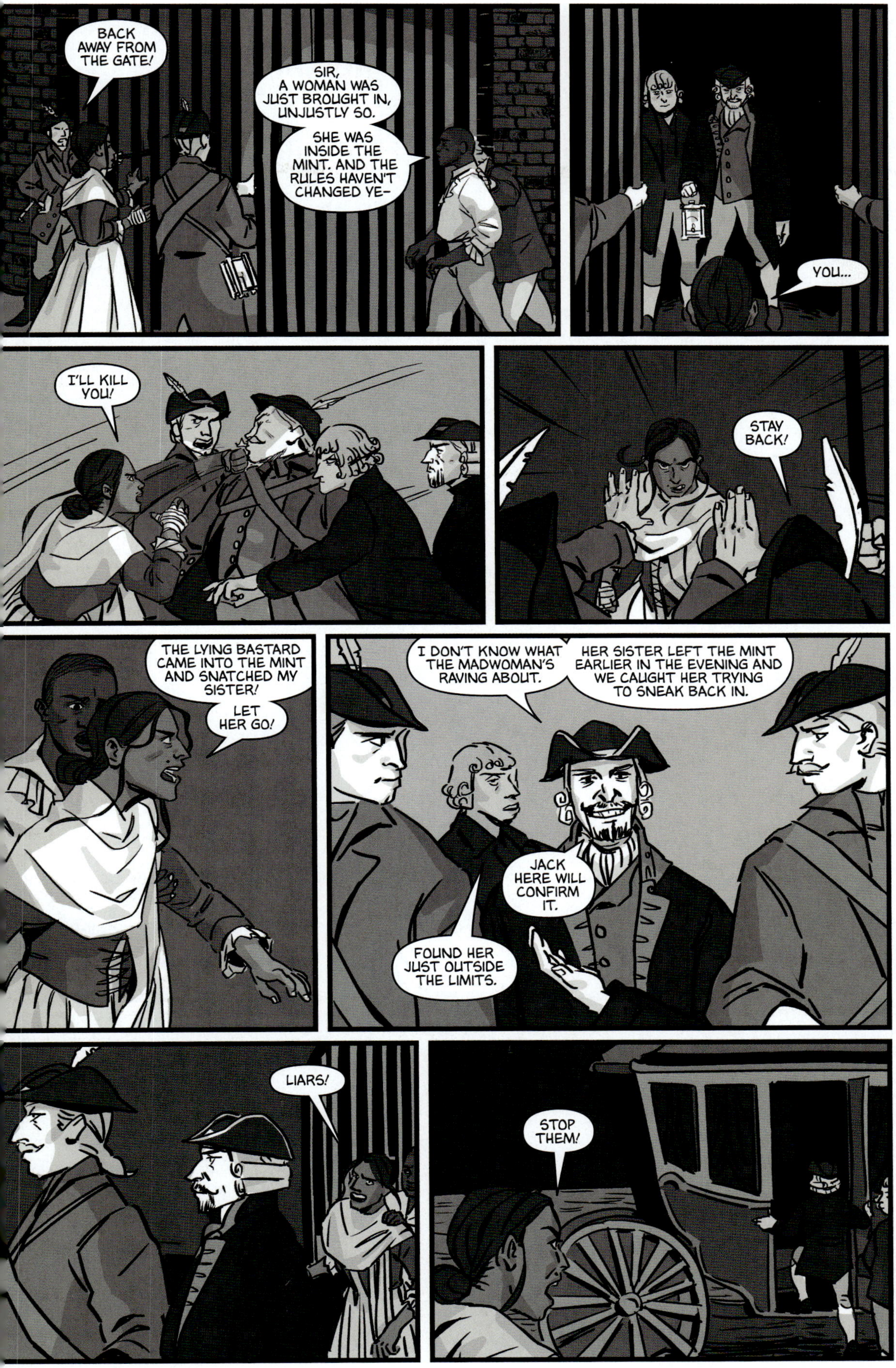
BACK AWAY FROM THE GATE!
SIR, A WOMAN WAS JUST BROUGHT IN, UNJUSTLY SO.
SHE WAS INSIDE THE MINT. AND THE RULES HAVEN'T CHANGED YE-
YOU...
I'LL KILL YOU!
STAY BACK!
THE LYING BASTARD CAME INTO THE MINT AND SNATCHED MY SISTER!
LET HER GO!
I DON'T KNOW WHAT THE MADWOMAN'S RAVING ABOUT.
HER SISTER LEFT THE MINT EARLIER IN THE EVENING AND WE CAUGHT HER TRYING TO SNEAK BACK IN.
JACK HERE WILL CONFIRM IT.
FOUND HER JUST OUTSIDE THE LIMITS.
LIARS!
STOP THEM!

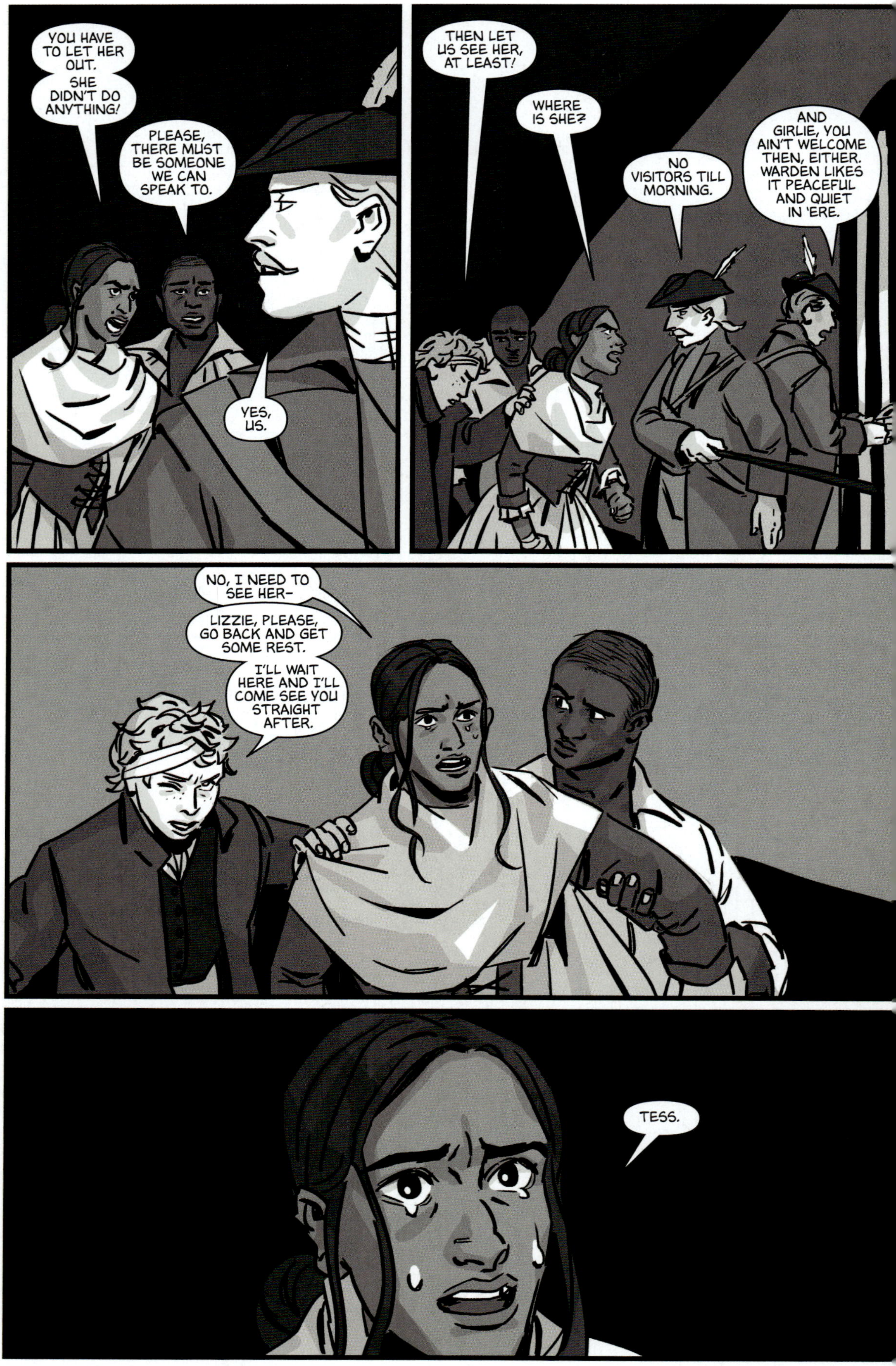
YOU HAVE TO LET HER OUT.
SHE DIDN'T DO ANYTHING!
PLEASE, THERE MUST BE SOMEONE WE CAN SPEAK TO.
YES, US.
THEN LET US SEE HER, AT LEAST!
WHERE IS SHE?
NO VISITORS TILL MORNING.
AND GIRLIE, YOU AIN'T WELCOME THEN, EITHER. WARDEN LIKES IT PEACEFUL AND QUIET IN 'ERE.
NO, I NEED TO SEE HER–
LIZZIE, PLEASE, GO BACK AND GET SOME REST.
I'LL WAIT HERE AND I'LL COME SEE YOU STRAIGHT AFTER.
TESS.

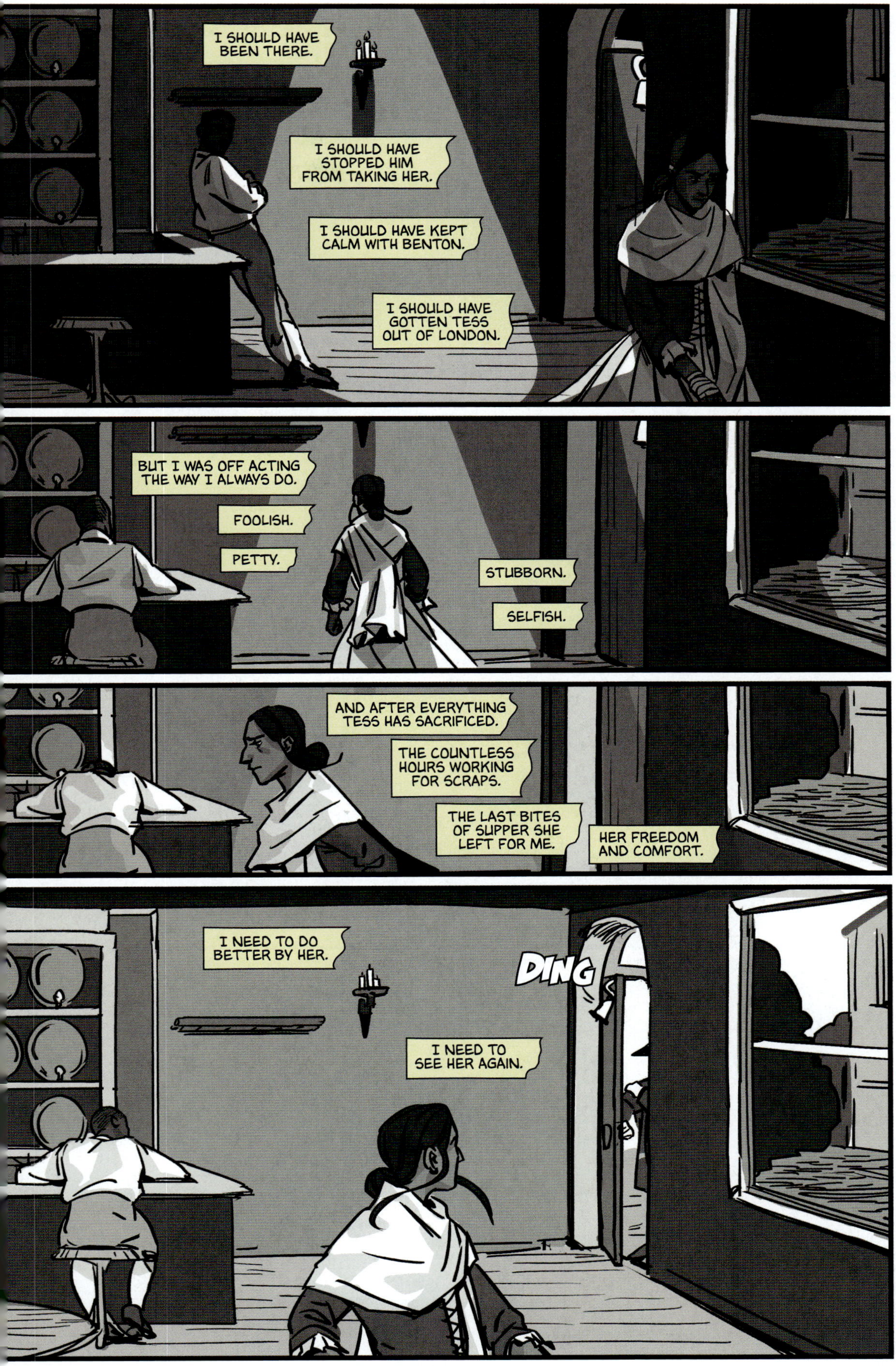
I SHOULD HAVE BEEN THERE.
I SHOULD HAVE STOPPED HIM FROM TAKING HER.
I SHOULD HAVE KEPT CALM WITH BENTON.
I SHOULD HAVE GOTTEN TESS OUT OF LONDON.
BUT I WAS OFF ACTING THE WAY I ALWAYS DO.
FOOLISH.
PETTY.
STUBBORN.
SELFISH.
AND AFTER EVERYTHING TESS HAS SACRIFICED.
THE COUNTLESS HOURS WORKING FOR SCRAPS.
THE LAST BITES OF SUPPER SHE LEFT FOR ME.
HER FREEDOM AND COMFORT.
I NEED TO DO BETTER BY HER.
DING
I NEED TO SEE HER AGAIN.

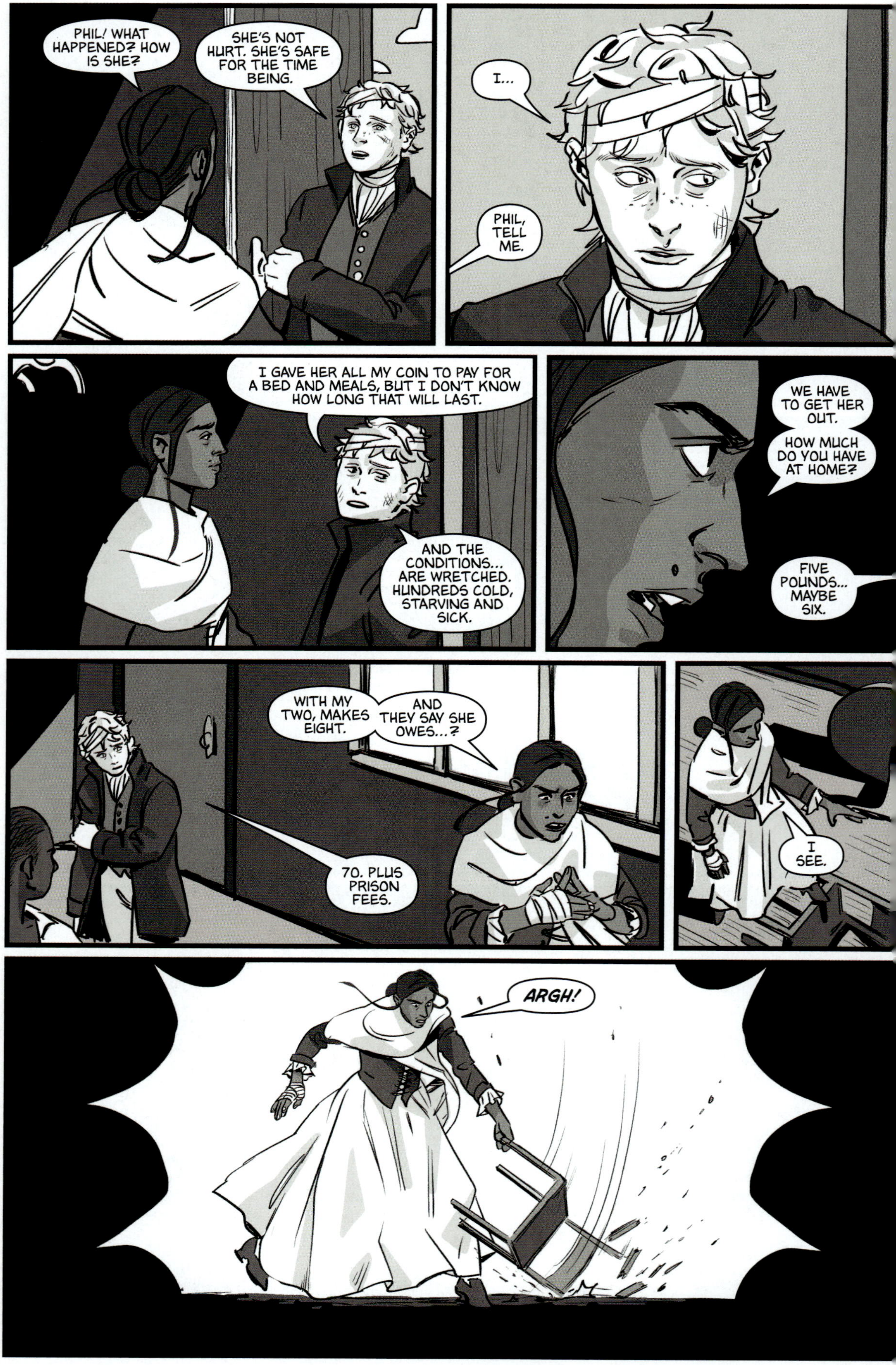
PHIL! WHAT HAPPENED? HOW IS SHE?
SHE'S NOT HURT. SHE'S SAFE FOR THE TIME BEING.
I...
PHIL, TELL ME.
I GAVE HER ALL MY COIN TO PAY FOR A BED AND MEALS, BUT I DON'T KNOW HOW LONG THAT WILL LAST.
AND THE CONDITIONS... ARE WRETCHED. HUNDREDS COLD, STARVING AND SICK.
WE HAVE TO GET HER OUT.
HOW MUCH DO YOU HAVE AT HOME?
FIVE POUNDS... MAYBE SIX.
WITH MY TWO, MAKES EIGHT.
AND THEY SAY SHE OWES...?
70. PLUS PRISON FEES.
I SEE.
ARGH!

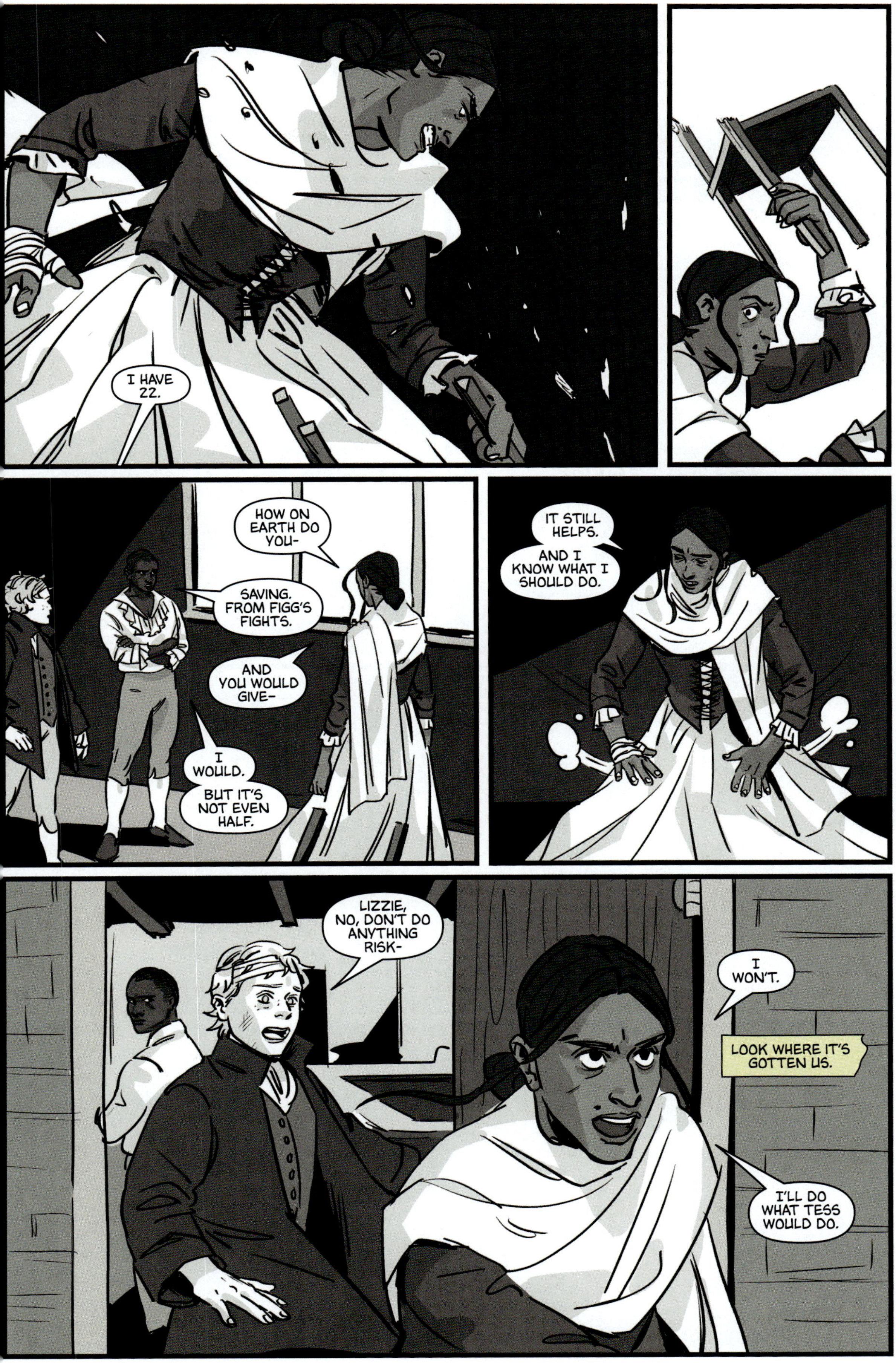
I HAVE 22.
HOW ON EARTH DO YOU-
SAVING. FROM FIGG'S FIGHTS.
AND YOU WOULD GIVE-
I WOULD.
BUT IT'S NOT EVEN HALF.
IT STILL HELPS.
AND I KNOW WHAT I SHOULD DO.
LIZZIE, NO, DON'T DO ANYTHING RISK-
I WON'T.
LOOK WHERE IT'S GOTTEN US.
I'LL DO WHAT TESS WOULD DO.

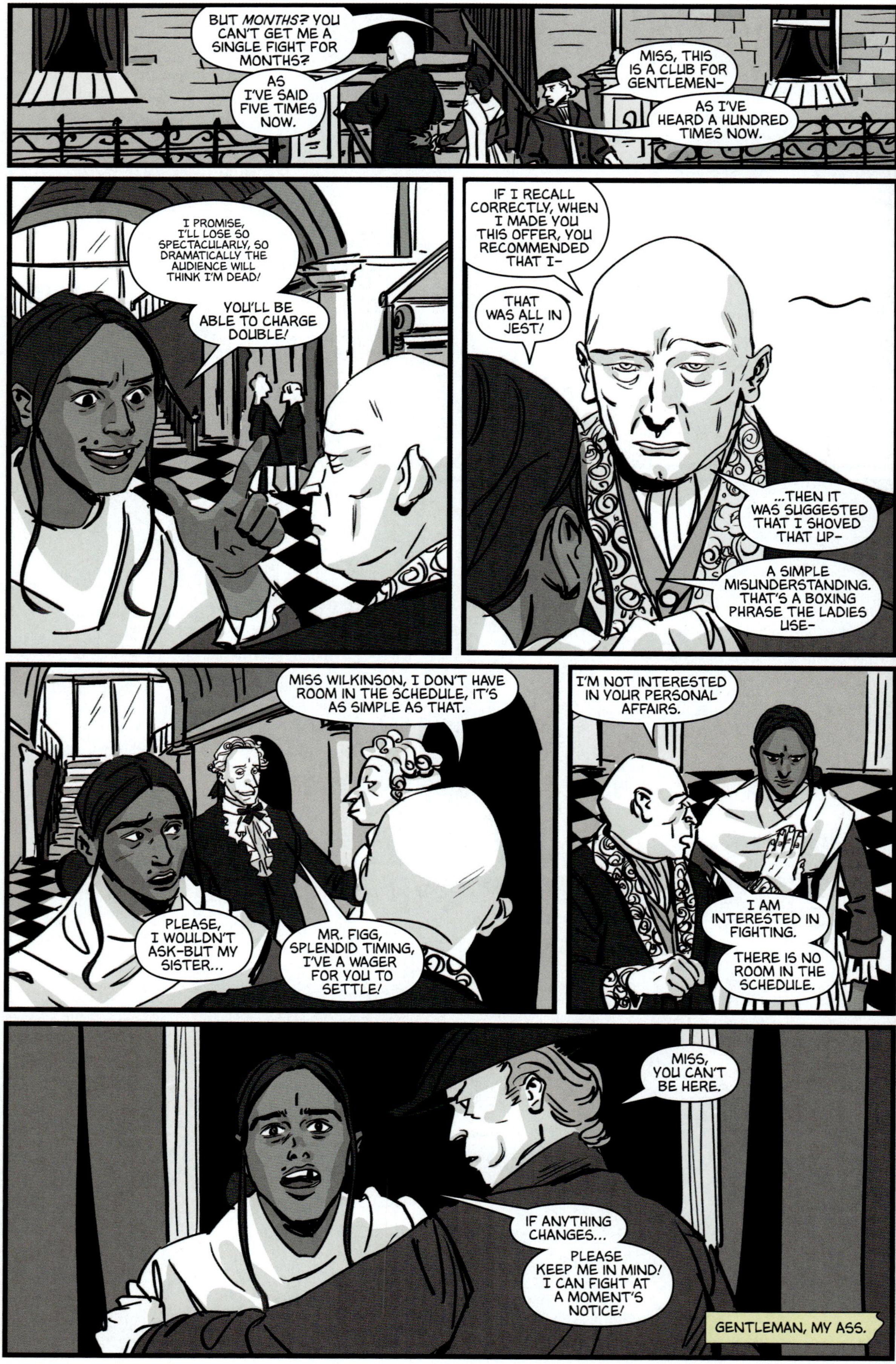
BUT *MONTHS?* YOU CAN'T GET ME A SINGLE FIGHT FOR MONTHS?
AS I'VE SAID FIVE TIMES NOW.
MISS, THIS IS A CLUB FOR GENTLEMEN–
AS I'VE HEARD A HUNDRED TIMES NOW.
I PROMISE, I'LL LOSE SO SPECTACULARLY, SO DRAMATICALLY THE AUDIENCE WILL THINK I'M DEAD!
YOU'LL BE ABLE TO CHARGE DOUBLE!
IF I RECALL CORRECTLY, WHEN I MADE YOU THIS OFFER, YOU RECOMMENDED THAT I–
THAT WAS ALL IN JEST!
...THEN IT WAS SUGGESTED THAT I SHOVED THAT UP–
A SIMPLE MISUNDERSTANDING. THAT'S A BOXING PHRASE THE LADIES USE–
MISS WILKINSON, I DON'T HAVE ROOM IN THE SCHEDULE, IT'S AS SIMPLE AS THAT.
PLEASE, I WOULDN'T ASK–BUT MY SISTER...
MR. FIGG, SPLENDID TIMING, I'VE A WAGER FOR YOU TO SETTLE!
I'M NOT INTERESTED IN YOUR PERSONAL AFFAIRS.
I AM INTERESTED IN FIGHTING.
THERE IS NO ROOM IN THE SCHEDULE.
MISS, YOU CAN'T BE HERE.
IF ANYTHING CHANGES...
PLEASE KEEP ME IN MIND! I CAN FIGHT AT A MOMENT'S NOTICE!
GENTLEMAN, MY ASS.

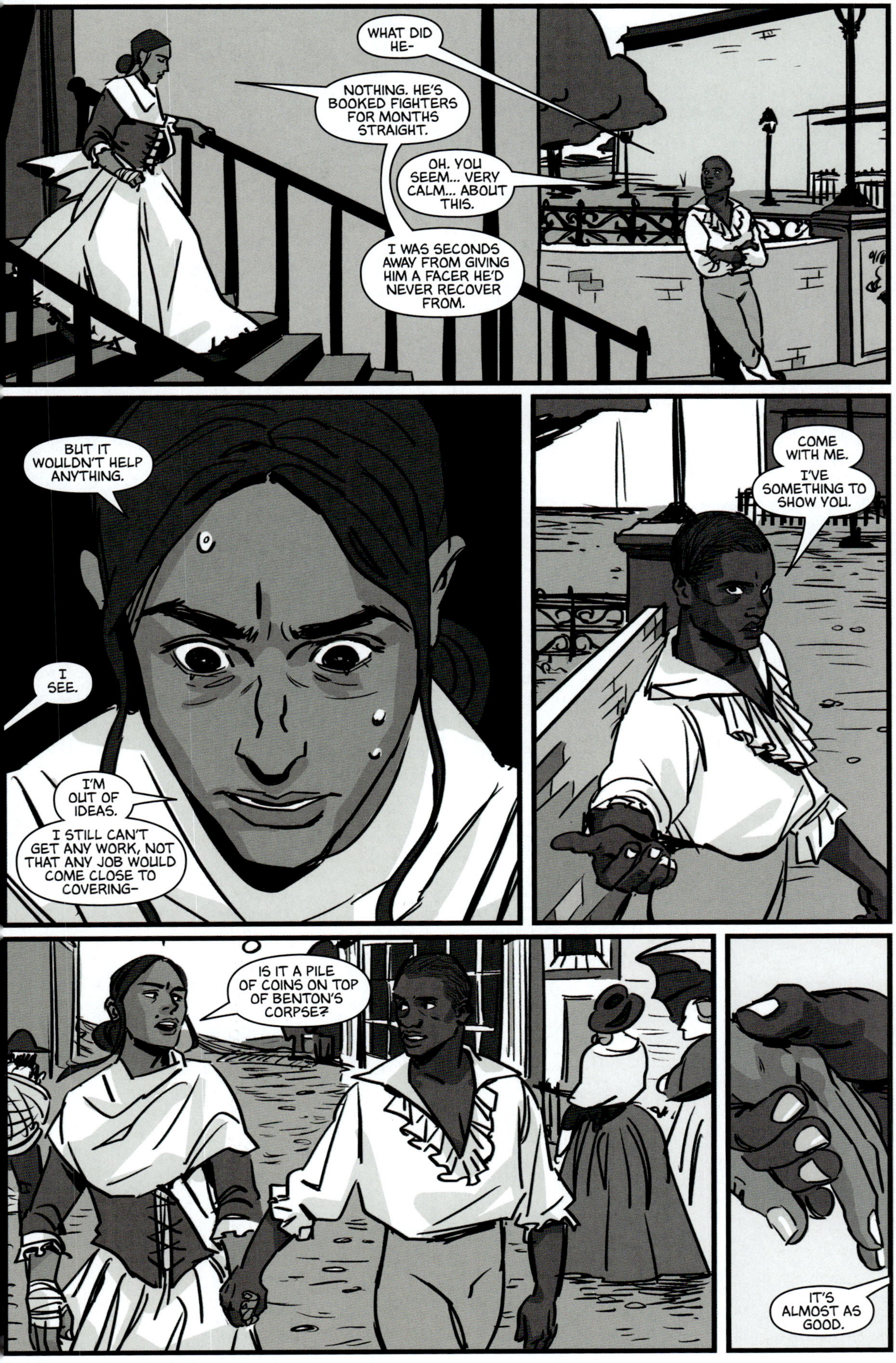
WHAT DID HE-
NOTHING. HE'S BOOKED FIGHTERS FOR MONTHS STRAIGHT.
OH. YOU SEEM... VERY CALM... ABOUT THIS.
I WAS SECONDS AWAY FROM GIVING HIM A FACER HE'D NEVER RECOVER FROM.
BUT IT WOULDN'T HELP ANYTHING.
I SEE.
I'M OUT OF IDEAS.
I STILL CAN'T GET ANY WORK, NOT THAT ANY JOB WOULD COME CLOSE TO COVERING-
COME WITH ME.
I'VE SOMETHING TO SHOW YOU.
IS IT A PILE OF COINS ON TOP OF BENTON'S CORPSE?
IT'S ALMOST AS GOOD.

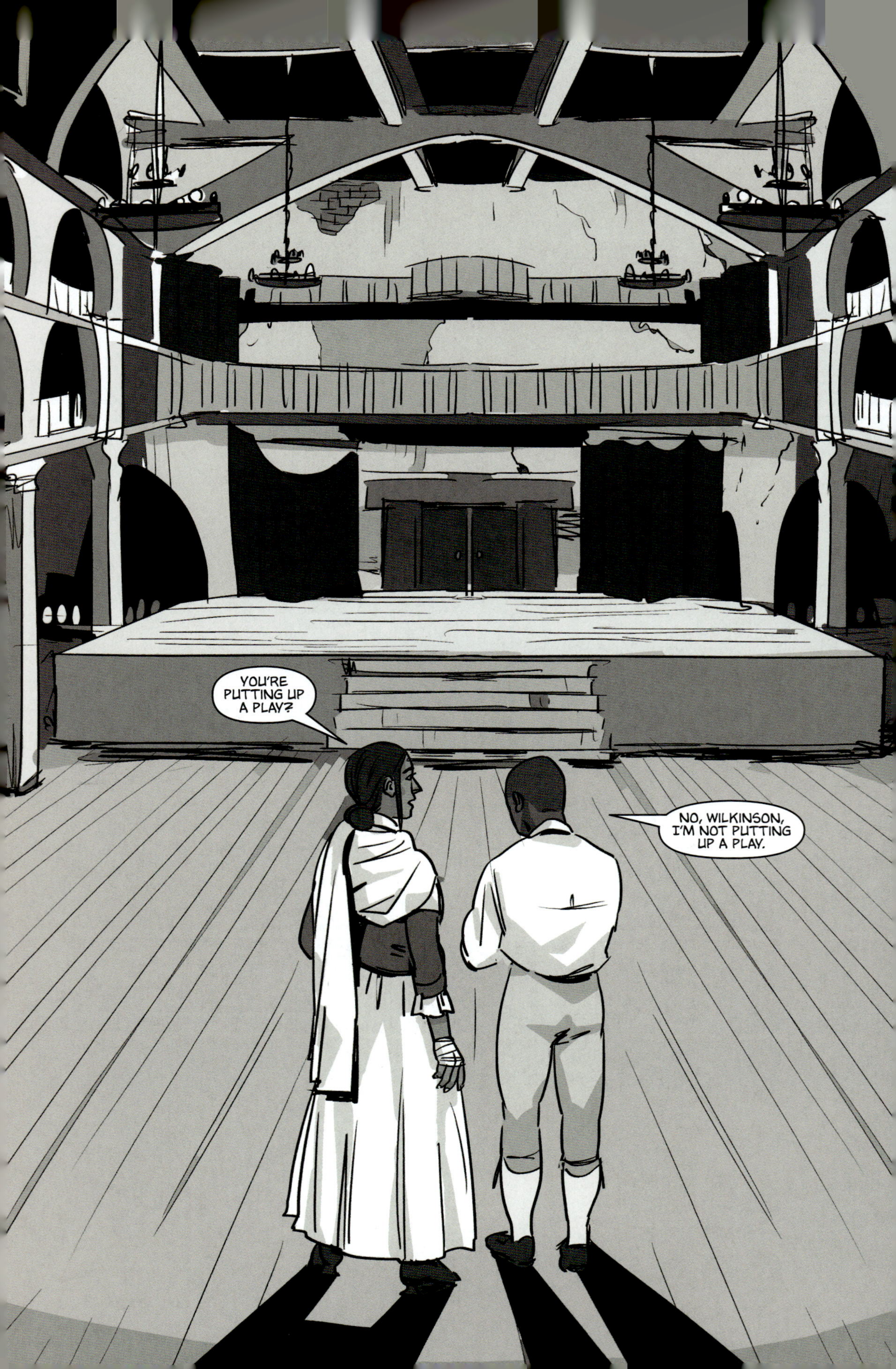
YOU'RE PUTTING UP A PLAY?
NO, WILKINSON, I'M NOT PUTTING UP A PLAY.

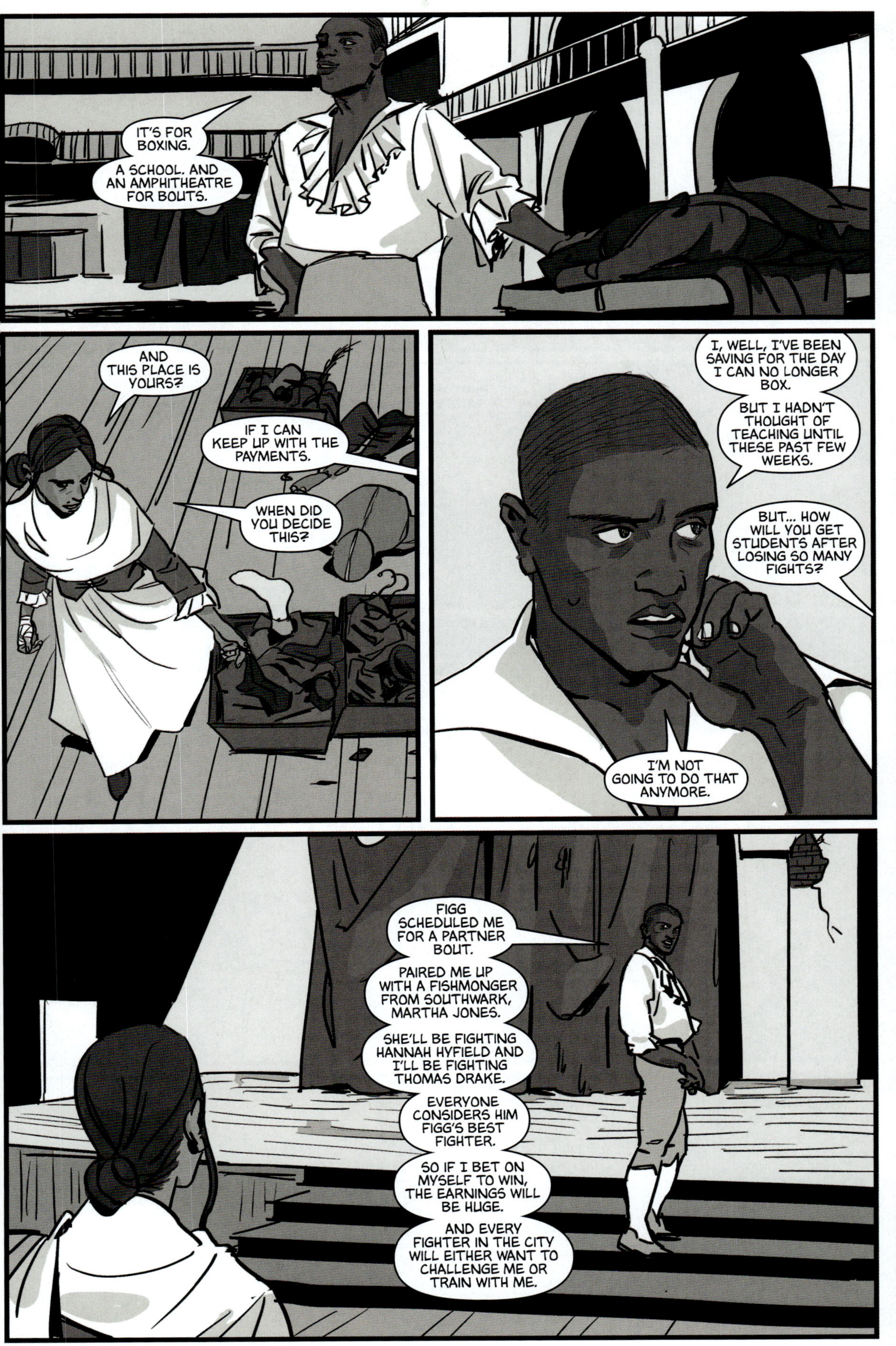
IT'S FOR BOXING.
A SCHOOL. AND AN AMPHITHEATRE FOR BOUTS.
AND THIS PLACE IS YOURS?
IF I CAN KEEP UP WITH THE PAYMENTS.
WHEN DID YOU DECIDE THIS?
I, WELL, I'VE BEEN SAVING FOR THE DAY I CAN NO LONGER BOX.
BUT I HADN'T THOUGHT OF TEACHING UNTIL THESE PAST FEW WEEKS.
BUT... HOW WILL YOU GET STUDENTS AFTER LOSING SO MANY FIGHTS?
I'M NOT GOING TO DO THAT ANYMORE.
FIGG SCHEDULED ME FOR A PARTNER BOUT.
PAIRED ME UP WITH A FISHMONGER FROM SOUTHWARK, MARTHA JONES.
SHE'LL BE FIGHTING HANNAH HYFIELD AND I'LL BE FIGHTING THOMAS DRAKE.
EVERYONE CONSIDERS HIM FIGG'S BEST FIGHTER.
SO IF I BET ON MYSELF TO WIN, THE EARNINGS WILL BE HUGE.
AND EVERY FIGHTER IN THE CITY WILL EITHER WANT TO CHALLENGE ME OR TRAIN WITH ME.

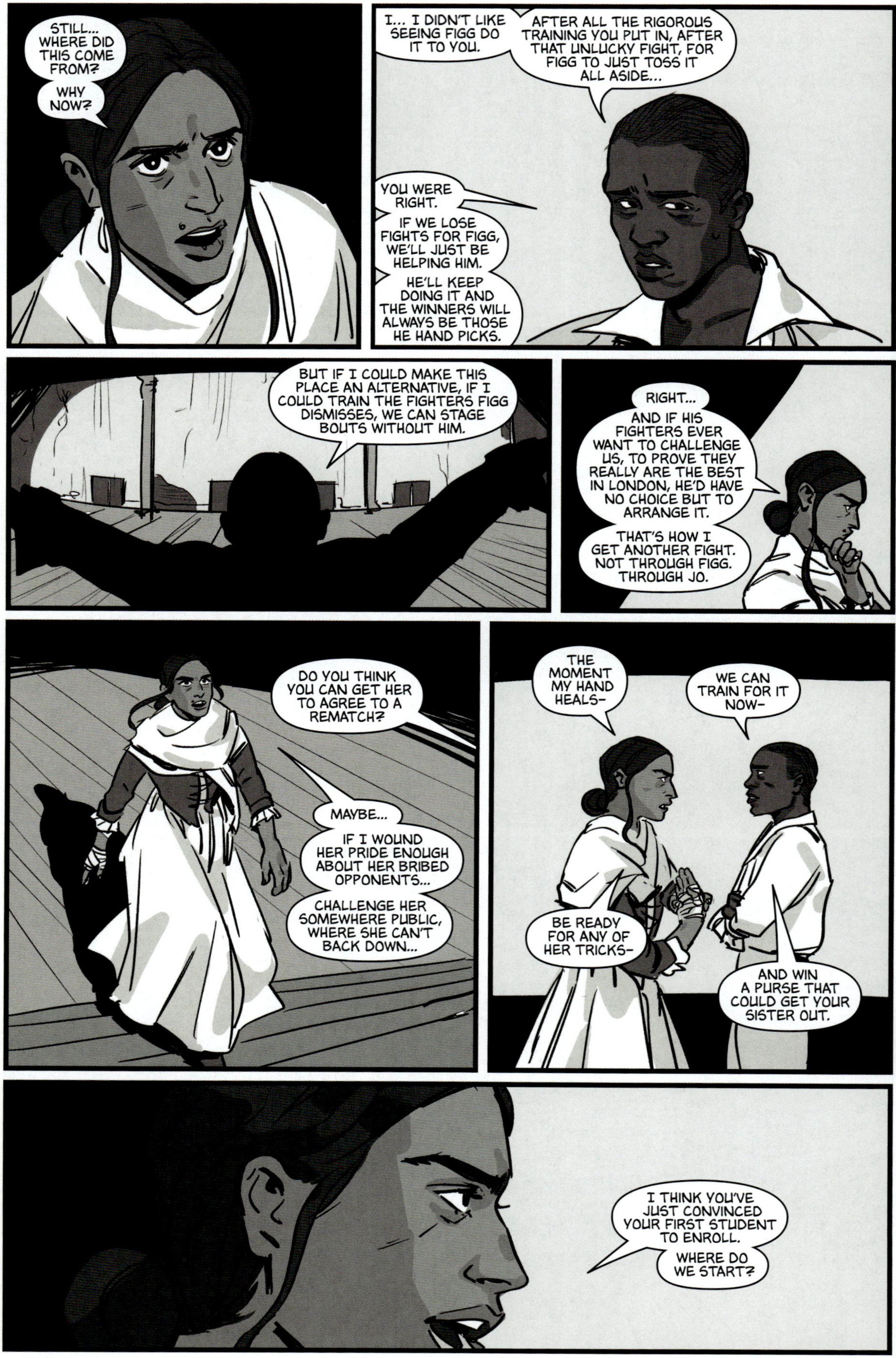
STILL... WHERE DID THIS COME FROM?
WHY NOW?
I... I DIDN'T LIKE SEEING FIGG DO IT TO YOU.
AFTER ALL THE RIGOROUS TRAINING YOU PUT IN, AFTER THAT UNLUCKY FIGHT, FOR FIGG TO JUST TOSS IT ALL ASIDE...
YOU WERE RIGHT.
IF WE LOSE FIGHTS FOR FIGG, WE'LL JUST BE HELPING HIM.
HE'LL KEEP DOING IT AND THE WINNERS WILL ALWAYS BE THOSE HE HAND PICKS.
BUT IF I COULD MAKE THIS PLACE AN ALTERNATIVE, IF I COULD TRAIN THE FIGHTERS FIGG DISMISSES, WE CAN STAGE BOUTS WITHOUT HIM.
RIGHT...
AND IF HIS FIGHTERS EVER WANT TO CHALLENGE US, TO PROVE THEY REALLY ARE THE BEST IN LONDON, HE'D HAVE NO CHOICE BUT TO ARRANGE IT.
THAT'S HOW I GET ANOTHER FIGHT. NOT THROUGH FIGG. THROUGH JO.
DO YOU THINK YOU CAN GET HER TO AGREE TO A REMATCH?
MAYBE...
IF I WOUND HER PRIDE ENOUGH ABOUT HER BRIBED OPPONENTS...
CHALLENGE HER SOMEWHERE PUBLIC, WHERE SHE CAN'T BACK DOWN...
THE MOMENT MY HAND HEALS-
WE CAN TRAIN FOR IT NOW-
BE READY FOR ANY OF HER TRICKS-
AND WIN A PURSE THAT COULD GET YOUR SISTER OUT.
I THINK YOU'VE JUST CONVINCED YOUR FIRST STUDENT TO ENROLL.
WHERE DO WE START?

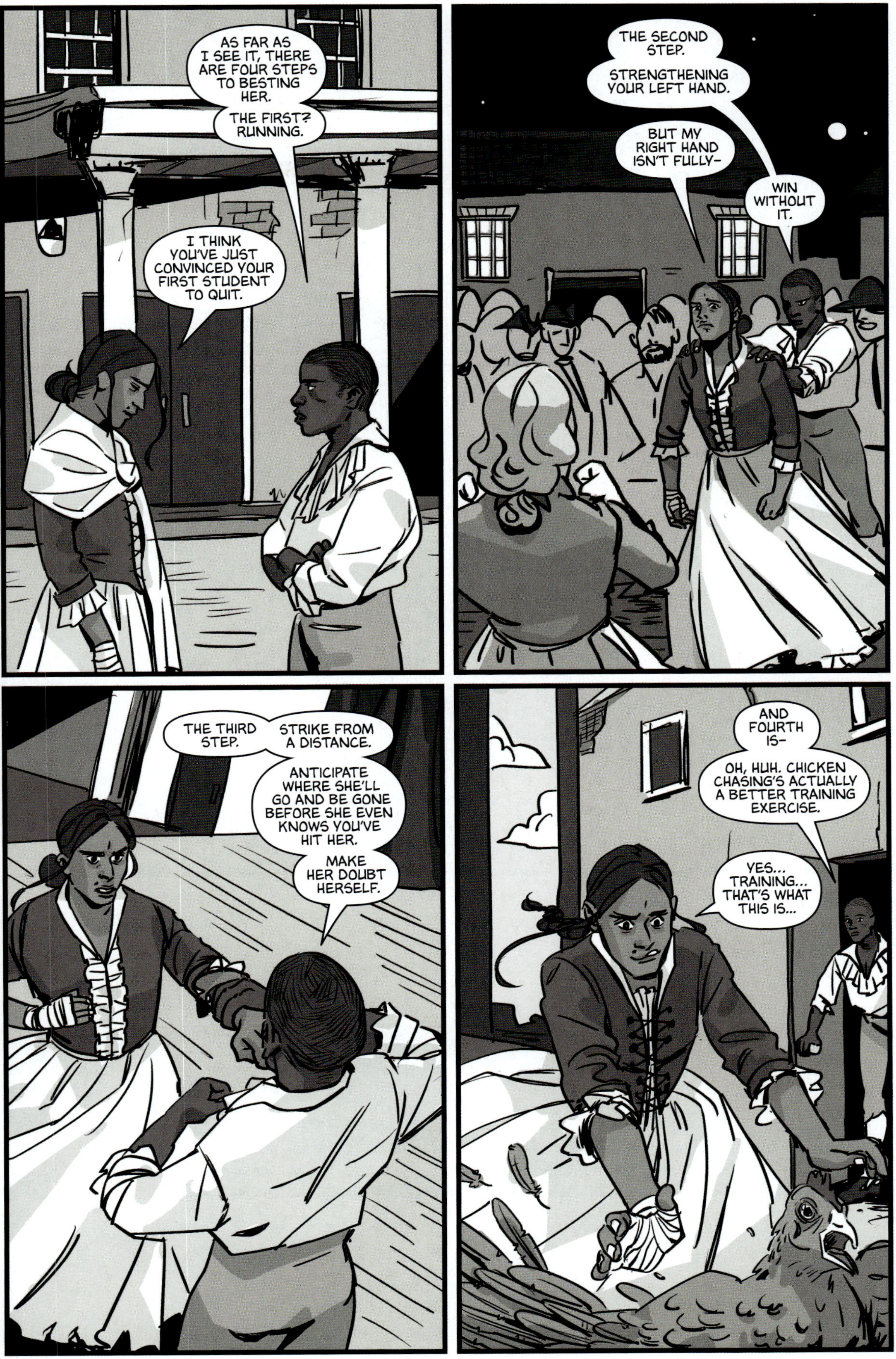
AS FAR AS I SEE IT, THERE ARE FOUR STEPS TO BESTING HER.
THE FIRST? RUNNING.
I THINK YOU'VE JUST CONVINCED YOUR FIRST STUDENT TO QUIT.
THE SECOND STEP.
STRENGTHENING YOUR LEFT HAND.
BUT MY RIGHT HAND ISN'T FULLY–
WIN WITHOUT IT.
THE THIRD STEP.
STRIKE FROM A DISTANCE.
ANTICIPATE WHERE SHE'LL GO AND BE GONE BEFORE SHE EVEN KNOWS YOU'VE HIT HER.
MAKE HER DOUBT HERSELF.
AND FOURTH IS–
OH, HUH. CHICKEN CHASING'S ACTUALLY A BETTER TRAINING EXERCISE.
YES... TRAINING... THAT'S WHAT THIS IS...

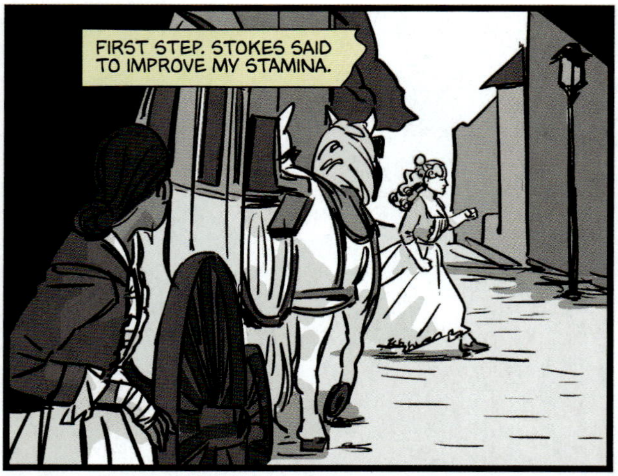
FIRST STEP. STOKES SAID TO IMPROVE MY STAMINA.

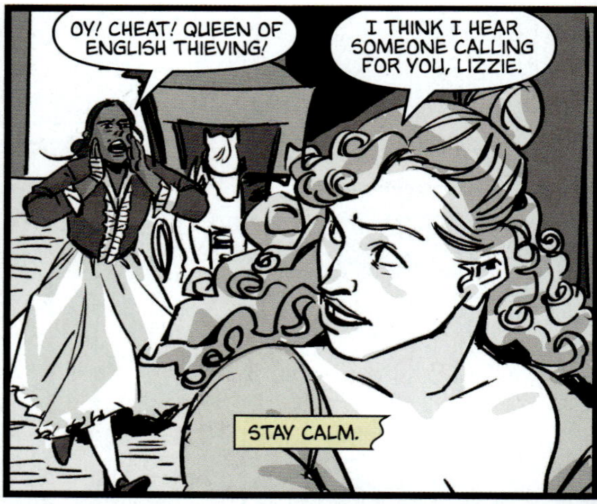
OY! CHEAT! QUEEN OF ENGLISH THIEVING!
I THINK I HEAR SOMEONE CALLING FOR YOU, LIZZIE.
STAY CALM.

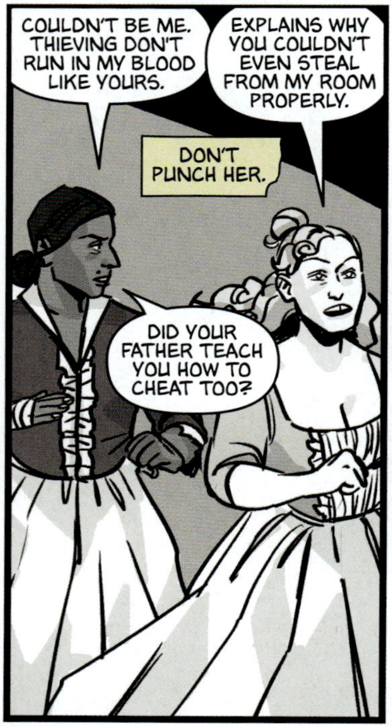
COULDN'T BE ME. THIEVING DON'T RUN IN MY BLOOD LIKE YOURS.
EXPLAINS WHY YOU COULDN'T EVEN STEAL FROM MY ROOM PROPERLY.
DON'T PUNCH HER.
DID YOUR FATHER TEACH YOU HOW TO CHEAT TOO?

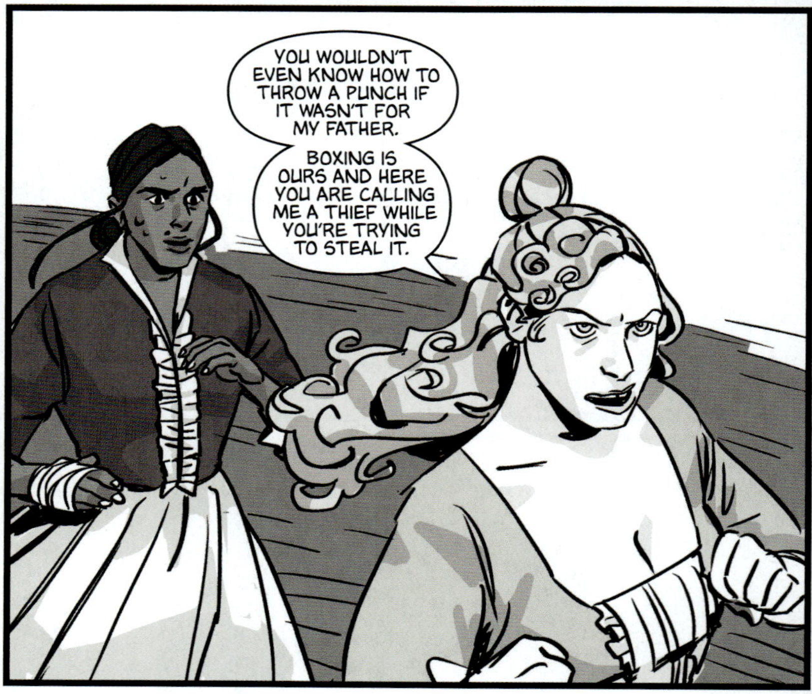
YOU WOULDN'T EVEN KNOW HOW TO THROW A PUNCH IF IT WASN'T FOR MY FATHER.
BOXING IS OURS AND HERE YOU ARE CALLING ME A THIEF WHILE YOU'RE TRYING TO STEAL IT.

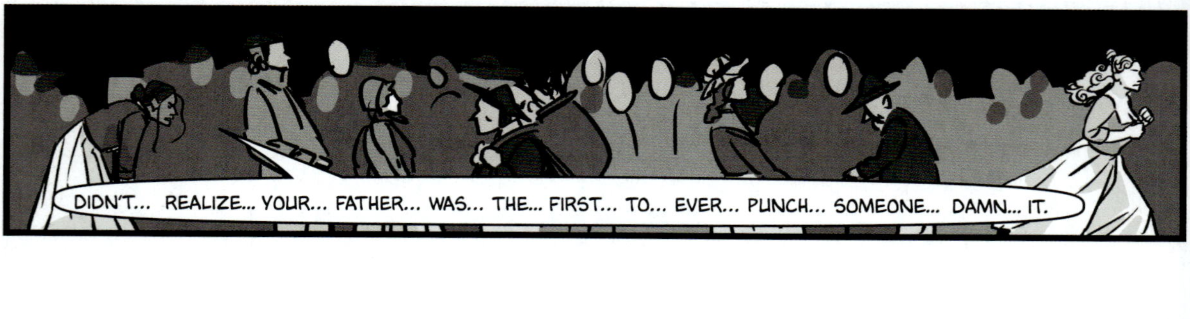
DIDN'T... REALIZE... YOUR... FATHER... WAS... THE... FIRST... TO... EVER... PUNCH... SOMEONE... DAMN... IT.

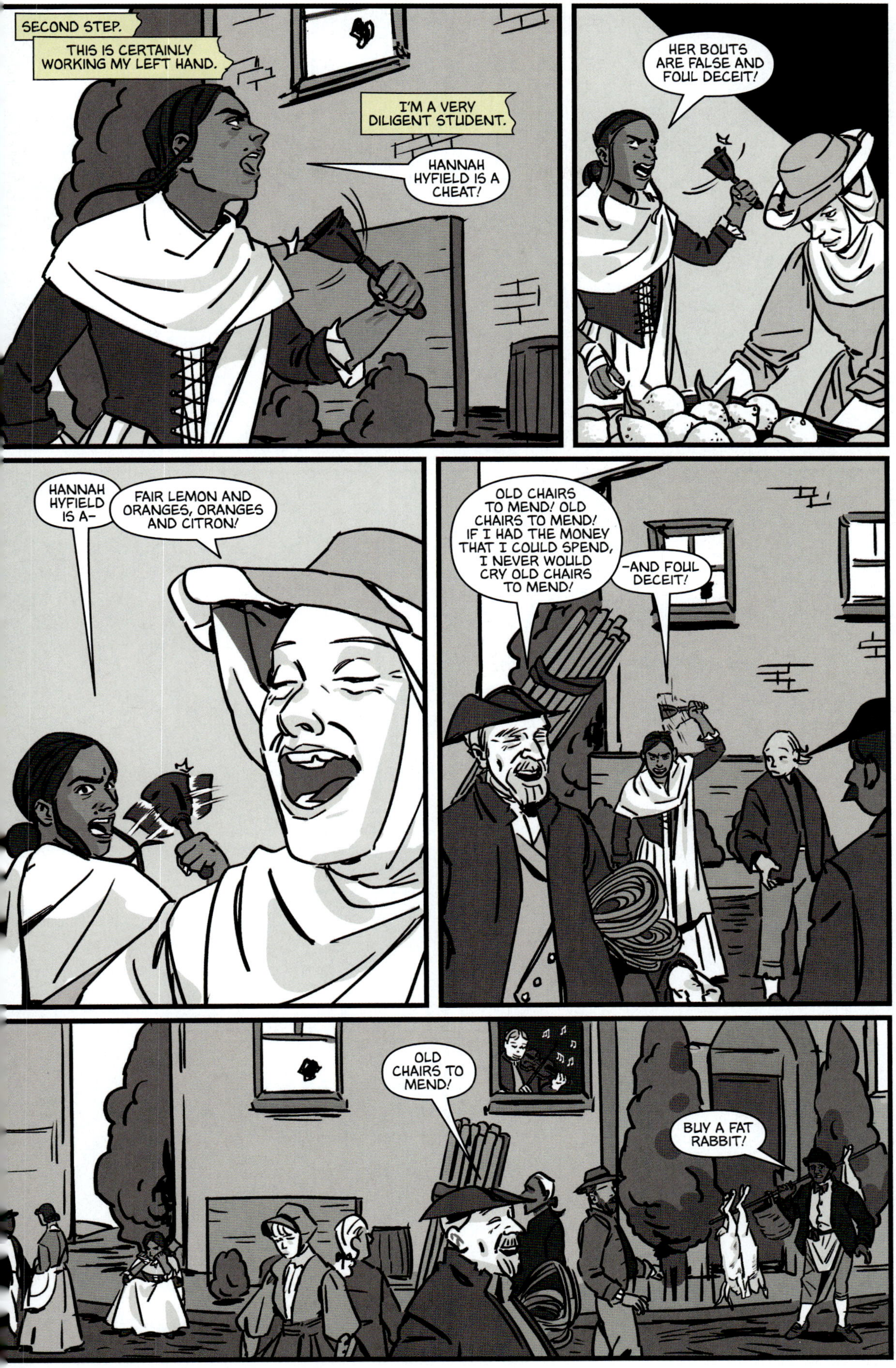
SECOND STEP.
THIS IS CERTAINLY WORKING MY LEFT HAND.
I'M A VERY DILIGENT STUDENT.
HANNAH HYFIELD IS A CHEAT!
HER BOUTS ARE FALSE AND FOUL DECEIT!
HANNAH HYFIELD IS A-
FAIR LEMON AND ORANGES, ORANGES AND CITRON!
OLD CHAIRS TO MEND! OLD CHAIRS TO MEND! IF I HAD THE MONEY THAT I COULD SPEND, I NEVER WOULD CRY OLD CHAIRS TO MEND!
-AND FOUL DECEIT!
OLD CHAIRS TO MEND!
BUY A FAT RABBIT!

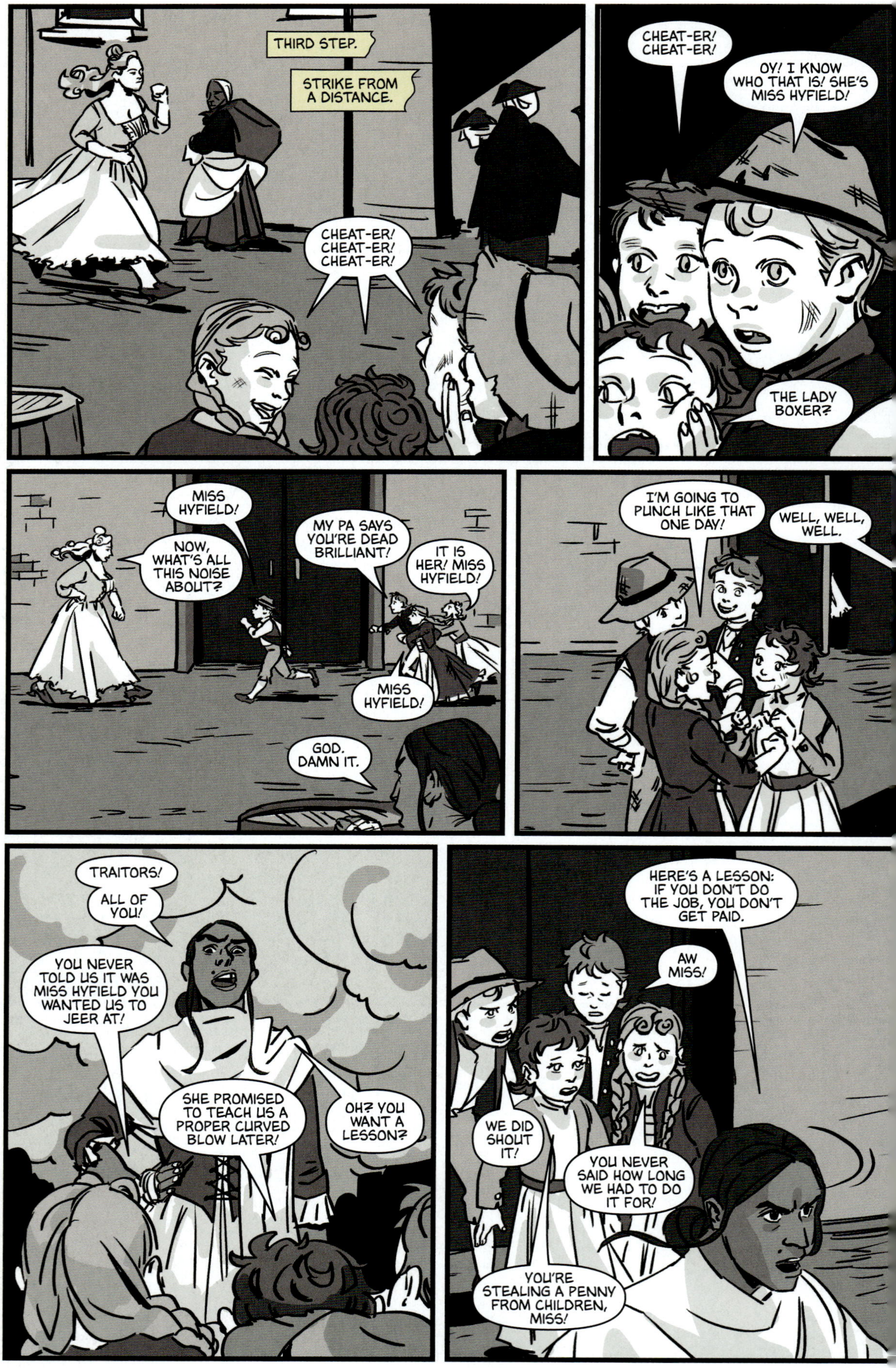
THIRD STEP.
STRIKE FROM A DISTANCE.
CHEAT-ER! CHEAT-ER! CHEAT-ER!
CHEAT-ER! CHEAT-ER!
OY! I KNOW WHO THAT IS! SHE'S MISS HYFIELD!
THE LADY BOXER?
MISS HYFIELD!
NOW, WHAT'S ALL THIS NOISE ABOUT?
MY PA SAYS YOU'RE DEAD BRILLIANT!
IT IS HER! MISS HYFIELD!
MISS HYFIELD!
GOD. DAMN IT.
I'M GOING TO PUNCH LIKE THAT ONE DAY!
WELL, WELL, WELL.
TRAITORS!
ALL OF YOU!
YOU NEVER TOLD US IT WAS MISS HYFIELD YOU WANTED US TO JEER AT!
SHE PROMISED TO TEACH US A PROPER CURVED BLOW LATER!
OH? YOU WANT A LESSON?
HERE'S A LESSON: IF YOU DON'T DO THE JOB, YOU DON'T GET PAID.
AW MISS!
WE DID SHOUT IT!
YOU NEVER SAID HOW LONG WE HAD TO DO IT FOR!
YOU'RE STEALING A PENNY FROM CHILDREN, MISS!

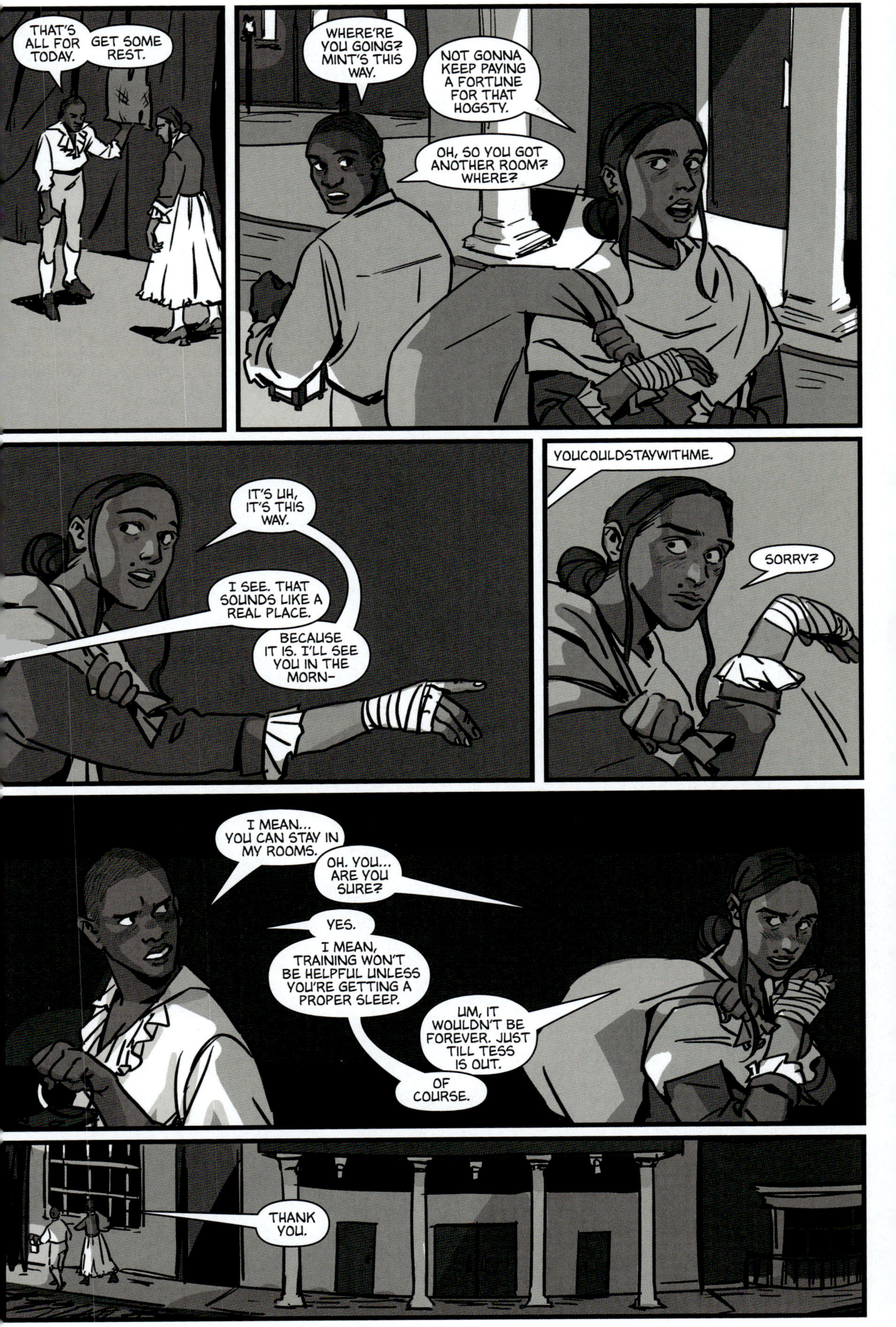
THAT'S ALL FOR TODAY.
GET SOME REST.
WHERE'RE YOU GOING? MINT'S THIS WAY.
NOT GONNA KEEP PAYING A FORTUNE FOR THAT HOGSTY.
OH, SO YOU GOT ANOTHER ROOM? WHERE?
IT'S UH, IT'S THIS WAY.
I SEE. THAT SOUNDS LIKE A REAL PLACE.
BECAUSE IT IS. I'LL SEE YOU IN THE MORN-
YOUCOULDSTAYWITHME.
SORRY?
I MEAN... YOU CAN STAY IN MY ROOMS.
OH. YOU... ARE YOU SURE?
YES.
I MEAN, TRAINING WON'T BE HELPFUL UNLESS YOU'RE GETTING A PROPER SLEEP.
UM, IT WOULDN'T BE FOREVER. JUST TILL TESS IS OUT.
OF COURSE.
THANK YOU.

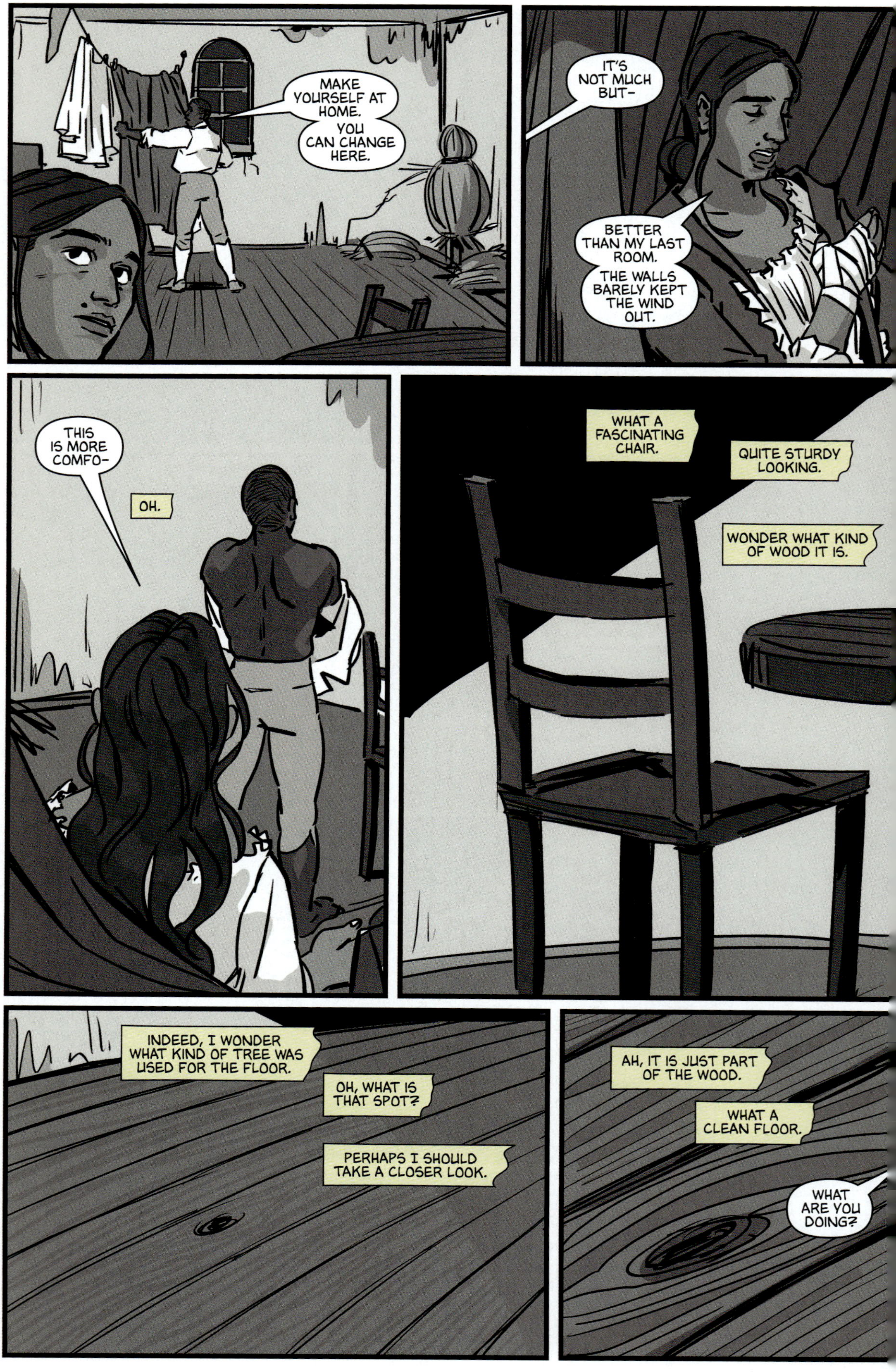
MAKE YOURSELF AT HOME.
YOU CAN CHANGE HERE.
IT'S NOT MUCH BUT-
BETTER THAN MY LAST ROOM.
THE WALLS BARELY KEPT THE WIND OUT.
THIS IS MORE COMFO-
OH.
WHAT A FASCINATING CHAIR.
QUITE STURDY LOOKING.
WONDER WHAT KIND OF WOOD IT IS.
INDEED, I WONDER WHAT KIND OF TREE WAS USED FOR THE FLOOR.
OH, WHAT IS THAT SPOT?
PERHAPS I SHOULD TAKE A CLOSER LOOK.
AH, IT IS JUST PART OF THE WOOD.
WHAT A CLEAN FLOOR.
WHAT ARE YOU DOING?

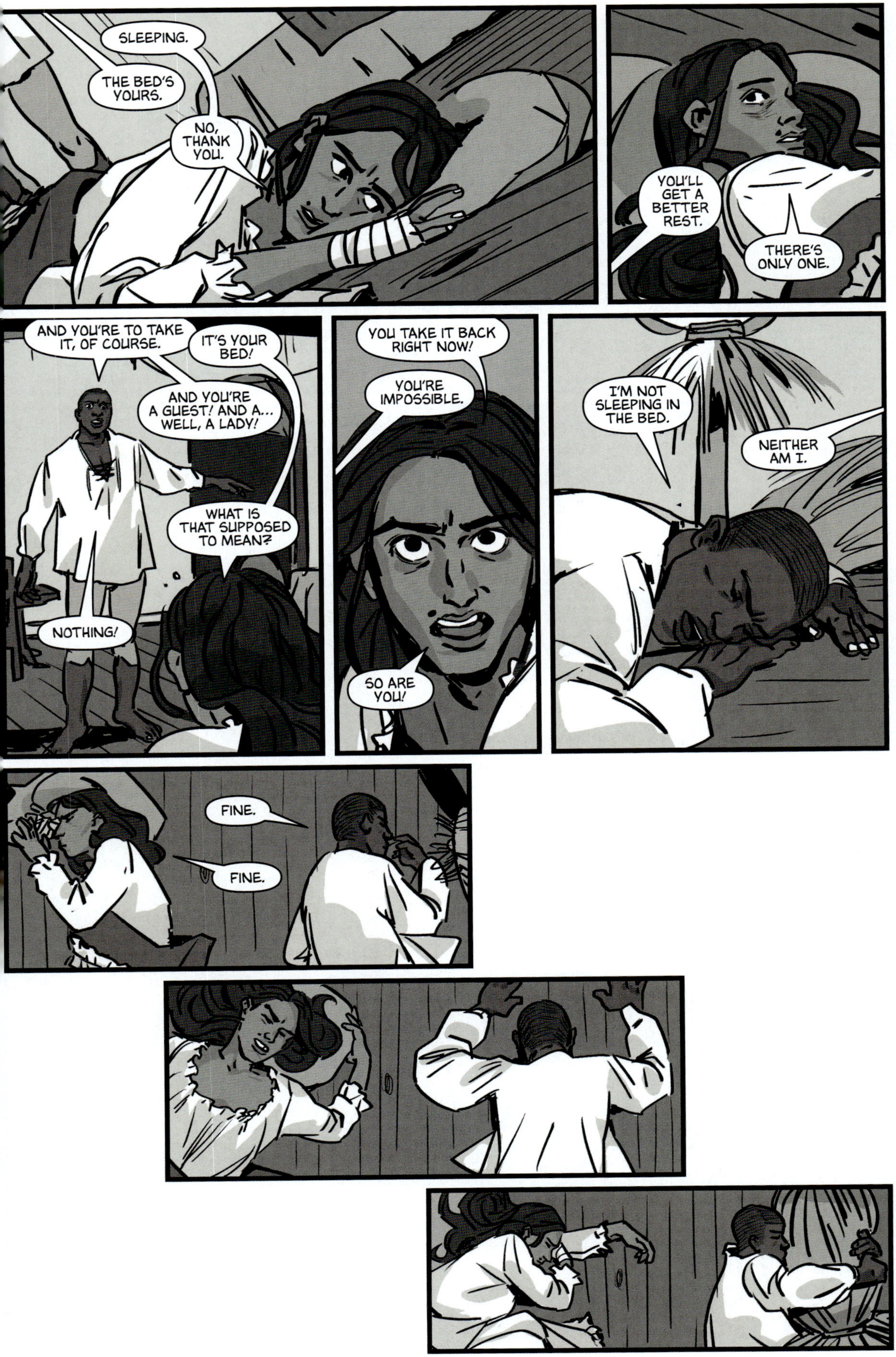
SLEEPING.
THE BED'S YOURS.
NO, THANK YOU.
YOU'LL GET A BETTER REST.
THERE'S ONLY ONE.
AND YOU'RE TO TAKE IT, OF COURSE.
IT'S YOUR BED!
AND YOU'RE A GUEST! AND A... WELL, A LADY!
WHAT IS THAT SUPPOSED TO MEAN?
NOTHING!
YOU TAKE IT BACK RIGHT NOW!
YOU'RE IMPOSSIBLE.
SO ARE YOU!
I'M NOT SLEEPING IN THE BED.
NEITHER AM I.
FINE.
FINE.

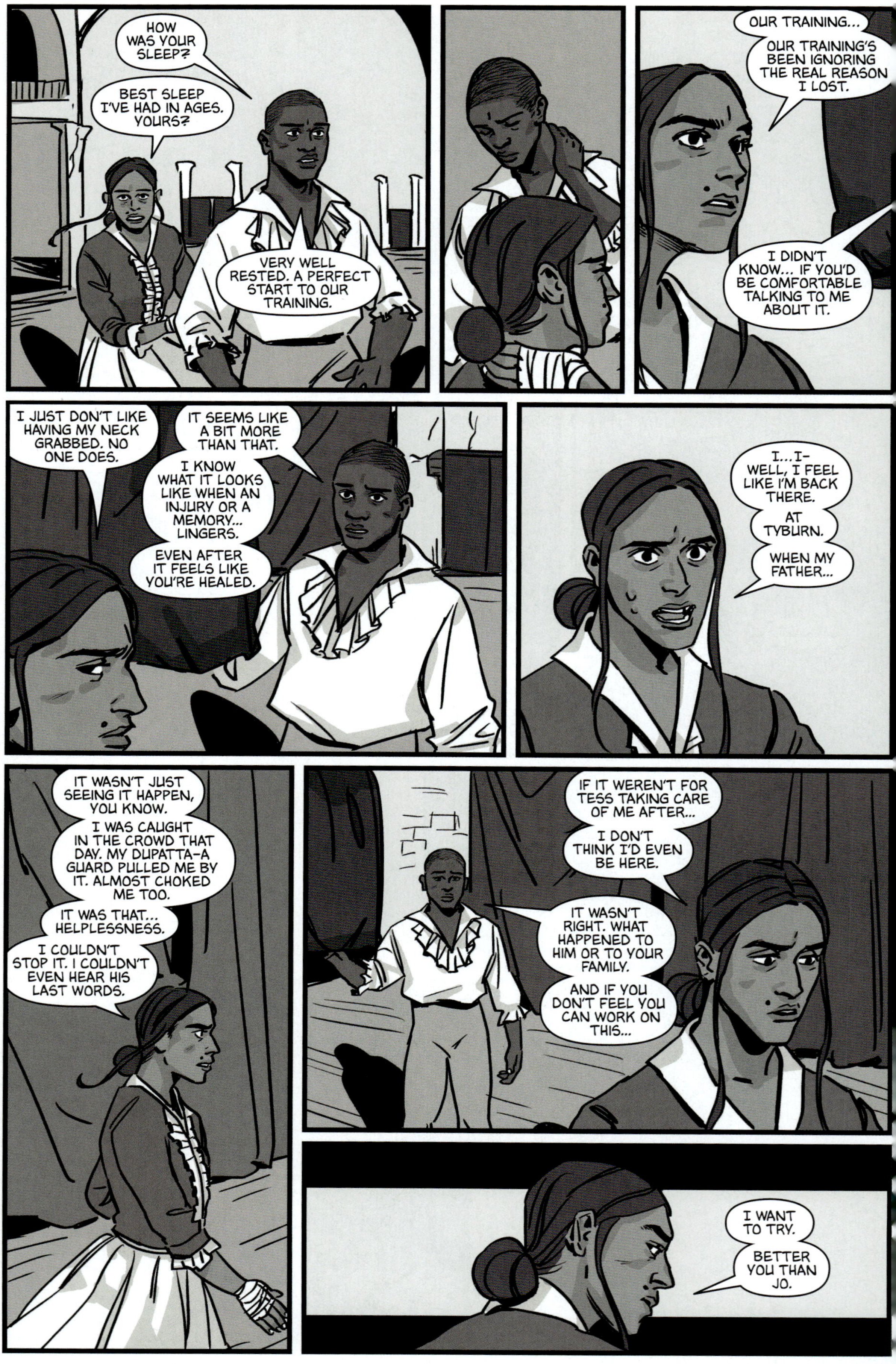
HOW WAS YOUR SLEEP?
BEST SLEEP I'VE HAD IN AGES. YOURS?
VERY WELL RESTED. A PERFECT START TO OUR TRAINING.
OUR TRAINING...
OUR TRAINING'S BEEN IGNORING THE REAL REASON I LOST.
I DIDN'T KNOW... IF YOU'D BE COMFORTABLE TALKING TO ME ABOUT IT.
I JUST DON'T LIKE HAVING MY NECK GRABBED. NO ONE DOES.
IT SEEMS LIKE A BIT MORE THAN THAT.
I KNOW WHAT IT LOOKS LIKE WHEN AN INJURY OR A MEMORY... LINGERS.
EVEN AFTER IT FEELS LIKE YOU'RE HEALED.
I... I- WELL, I FEEL LIKE I'M BACK THERE.
AT TYBURN.
WHEN MY FATHER...
IT WASN'T JUST SEEING IT HAPPEN, YOU KNOW.
I WAS CAUGHT IN THE CROWD THAT DAY. MY DUPATTA–A GUARD PULLED ME BY IT. ALMOST CHOKED ME TOO.
IT WAS THAT... HELPLESSNESS.
I COULDN'T STOP IT. I COULDN'T EVEN HEAR HIS LAST WORDS.
IF IT WEREN'T FOR TESS TAKING CARE OF ME AFTER...
I DON'T THINK I'D EVEN BE HERE.
IT WASN'T RIGHT. WHAT HAPPENED TO HIM OR TO YOUR FAMILY.
AND IF YOU DON'T FEEL YOU CAN WORK ON THIS...
I WANT TO TRY.
BETTER YOU THAN JO.

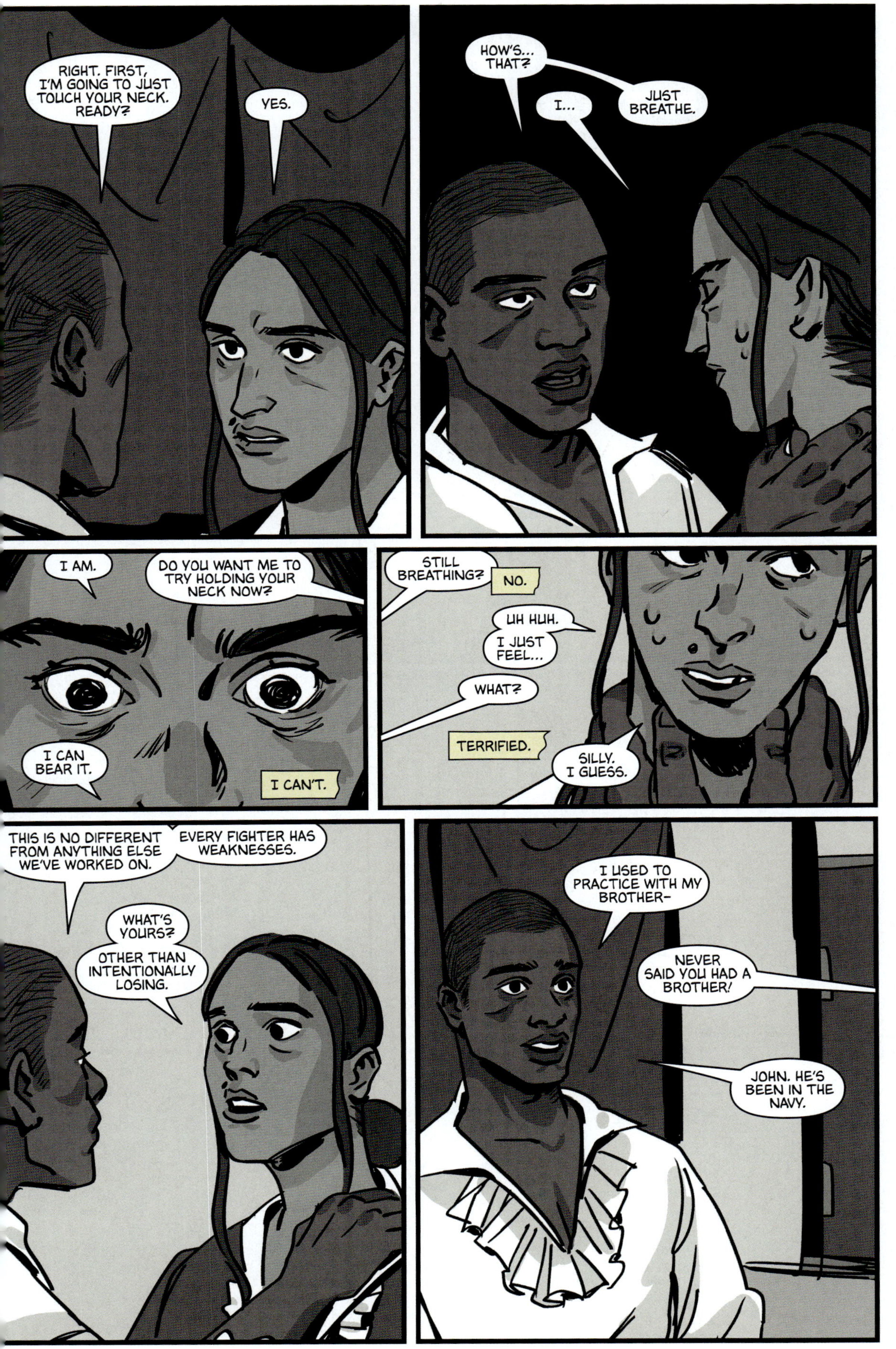
RIGHT. FIRST, I'M GOING TO JUST TOUCH YOUR NECK. READY?
YES.
HOW'S... THAT?
I...
JUST BREATHE.
I AM.
DO YOU WANT ME TO TRY HOLDING YOUR NECK NOW?
I CAN BEAR IT.
I CAN'T.
STILL BREATHING?
NO.
UH HUH.
I JUST FEEL...
WHAT?
TERRIFIED.
SILLY. I GUESS.
THIS IS NO DIFFERENT FROM ANYTHING ELSE WE'VE WORKED ON.
EVERY FIGHTER HAS WEAKNESSES.
WHAT'S YOURS?
OTHER THAN INTENTIONALLY LOSING.
I USED TO PRACTICE WITH MY BROTHER–
NEVER SAID YOU HAD A BROTHER!
JOHN. HE'S BEEN IN THE NAVY.

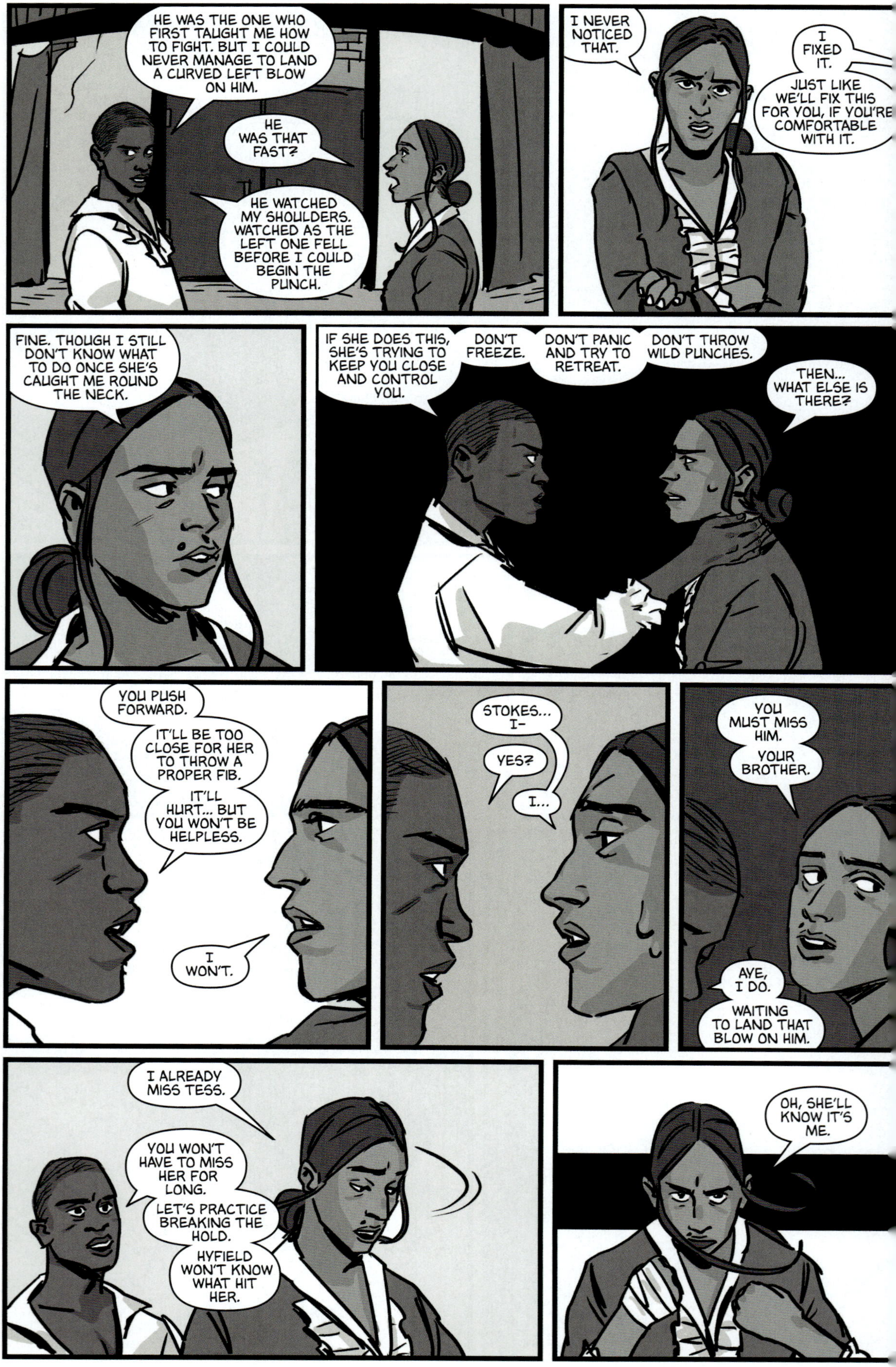
HE WAS THE ONE WHO FIRST TAUGHT ME HOW TO FIGHT. BUT I COULD NEVER MANAGE TO LAND A CURVED LEFT BLOW ON HIM.
HE WAS THAT FAST?
HE WATCHED MY SHOULDERS. WATCHED AS THE LEFT ONE FELL BEFORE I COULD BEGIN THE PUNCH.
I NEVER NOTICED THAT.
I FIXED IT.
JUST LIKE WE'LL FIX THIS FOR YOU, IF YOU'RE COMFORTABLE WITH IT.
FINE. THOUGH I STILL DON'T KNOW WHAT TO DO ONCE SHE'S CAUGHT ME ROUND THE NECK.
IF SHE DOES THIS, SHE'S TRYING TO KEEP YOU CLOSE AND CONTROL YOU.
DON'T FREEZE.
DON'T PANIC AND TRY TO RETREAT.
DON'T THROW WILD PUNCHES.
THEN... WHAT ELSE IS THERE?
YOU PUSH FORWARD.
IT'LL BE TOO CLOSE FOR HER TO THROW A PROPER FIB.
IT'LL HURT... BUT YOU WON'T BE HELPLESS.
I WON'T.
STOKES... I-
YES?
I...
YOU MUST MISS HIM.
YOUR BROTHER.
AYE, I DO.
WAITING TO LAND THAT BLOW ON HIM.
I ALREADY MISS TESS.
YOU WON'T HAVE TO MISS HER FOR LONG.
LET'S PRACTICE BREAKING THE HOLD.
HYFIELD WON'T KNOW WHAT HIT HER.
OH, SHE'LL KNOW IT'S ME.

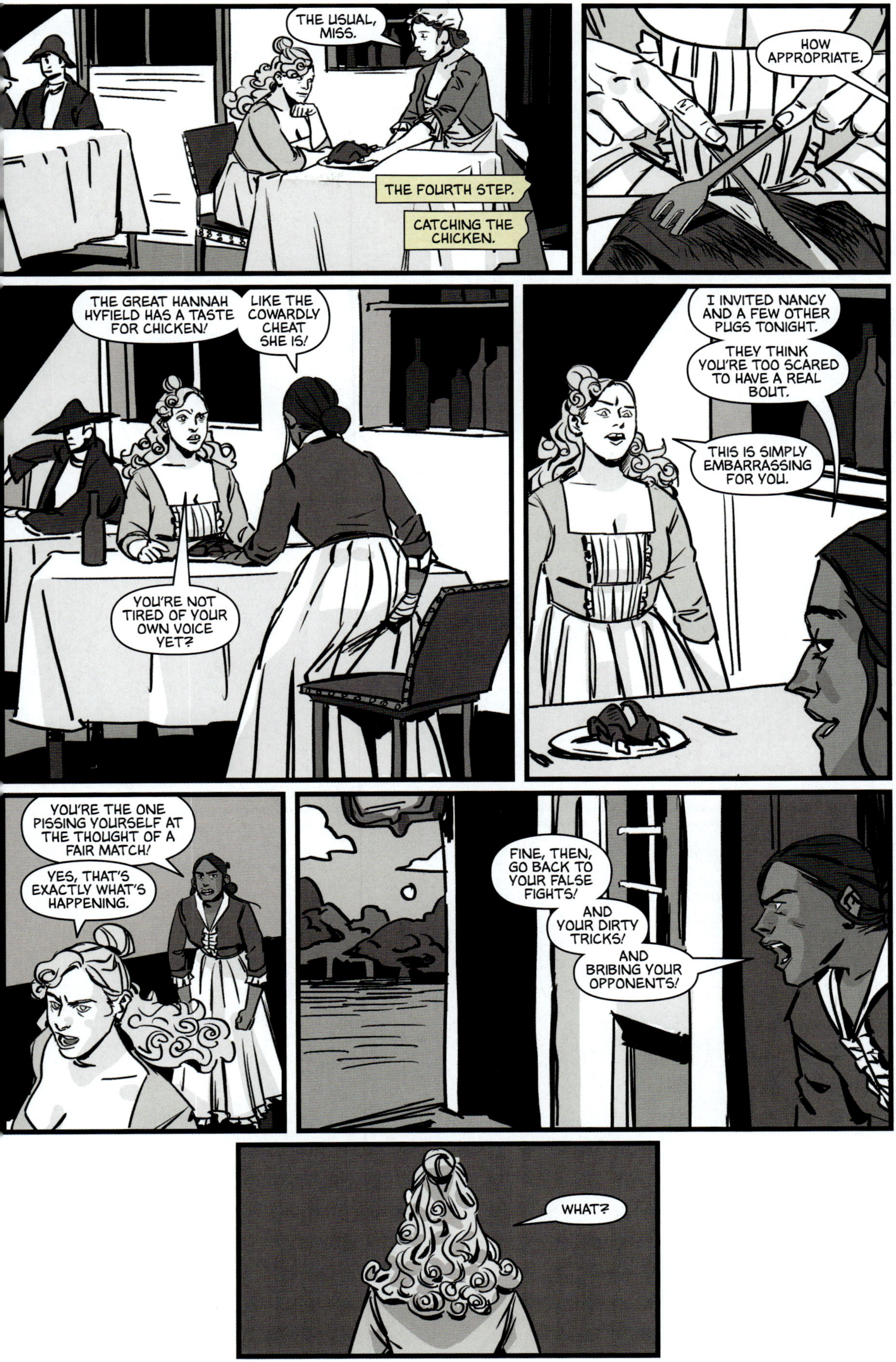
THE USUAL, MISS.
THE FOURTH STEP.
CATCHING THE CHICKEN.
HOW APPROPRIATE.
THE GREAT HANNAH HYFIELD HAS A TASTE FOR CHICKEN!
LIKE THE COWARDLY CHEAT SHE IS!
YOU'RE NOT TIRED OF YOUR OWN VOICE YET?
I INVITED NANCY AND A FEW OTHER PUGS TONIGHT.
THEY THINK YOU'RE TOO SCARED TO HAVE A REAL BOUT.
THIS IS SIMPLY EMBARRASSING FOR YOU.
YOU'RE THE ONE PISSING YOURSELF AT THE THOUGHT OF A FAIR MATCH!
YES, THAT'S EXACTLY WHAT'S HAPPENING.
FINE, THEN, GO BACK TO YOUR FALSE FIGHTS!
AND YOUR DIRTY TRICKS!
AND BRIBING YOUR OPPONENTS!
WHAT?

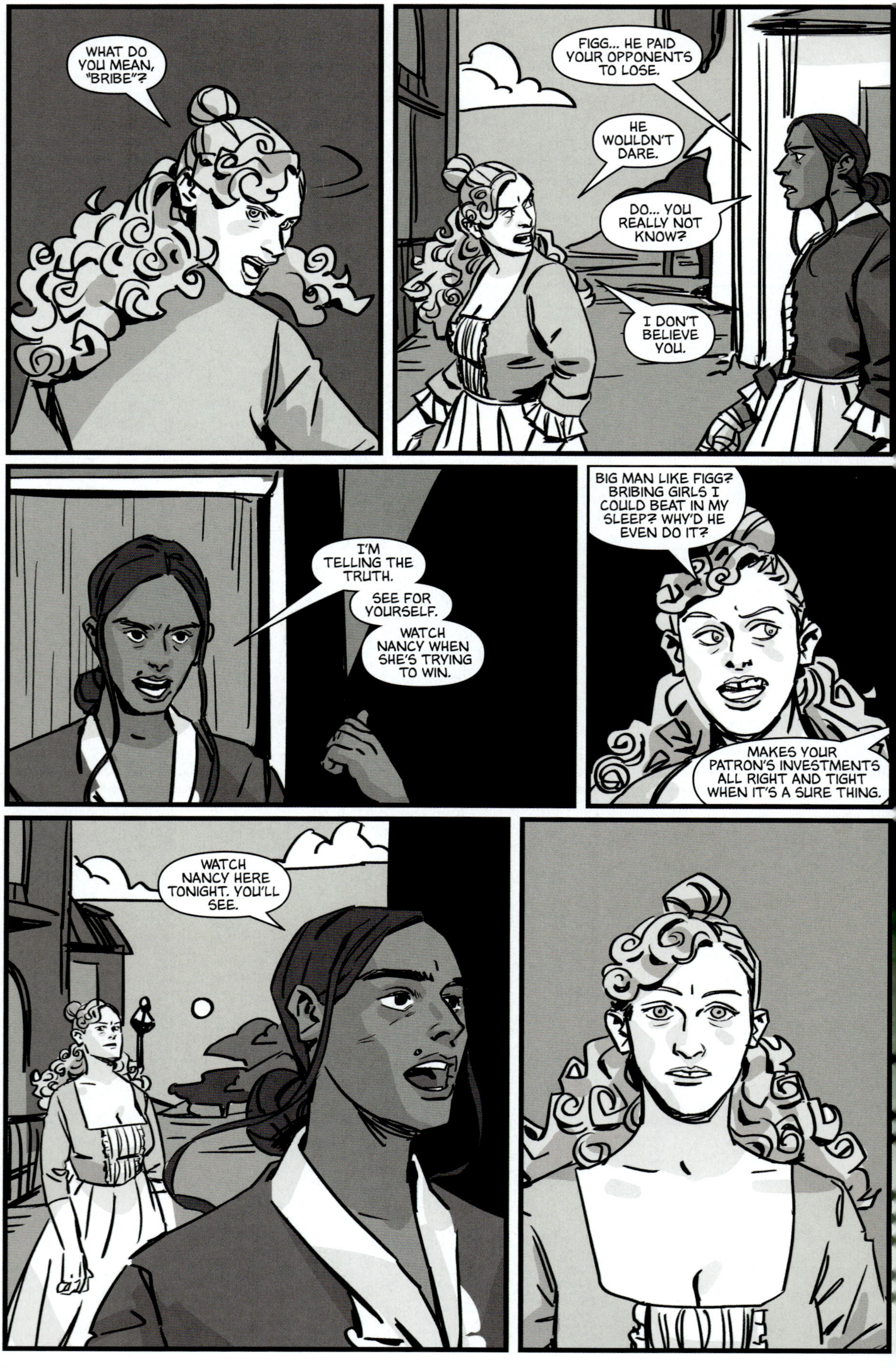
WHAT DO YOU MEAN, "BRIBE"?
FIGG... HE PAID YOUR OPPONENTS TO LOSE.
HE WOULDN'T DARE.
DO... YOU REALLY NOT KNOW?
I DON'T BELIEVE YOU.
I'M TELLING THE TRUTH.
SEE FOR YOURSELF.
WATCH NANCY WHEN SHE'S TRYING TO WIN.
BIG MAN LIKE FIGG? BRIBING GIRLS I COULD BEAT IN MY SLEEP? WHY'D HE EVEN DO IT?
MAKES YOUR PATRON'S INVESTMENTS ALL RIGHT AND TIGHT WHEN IT'S A SURE THING.
WATCH NANCY HERE TONIGHT. YOU'LL SEE.

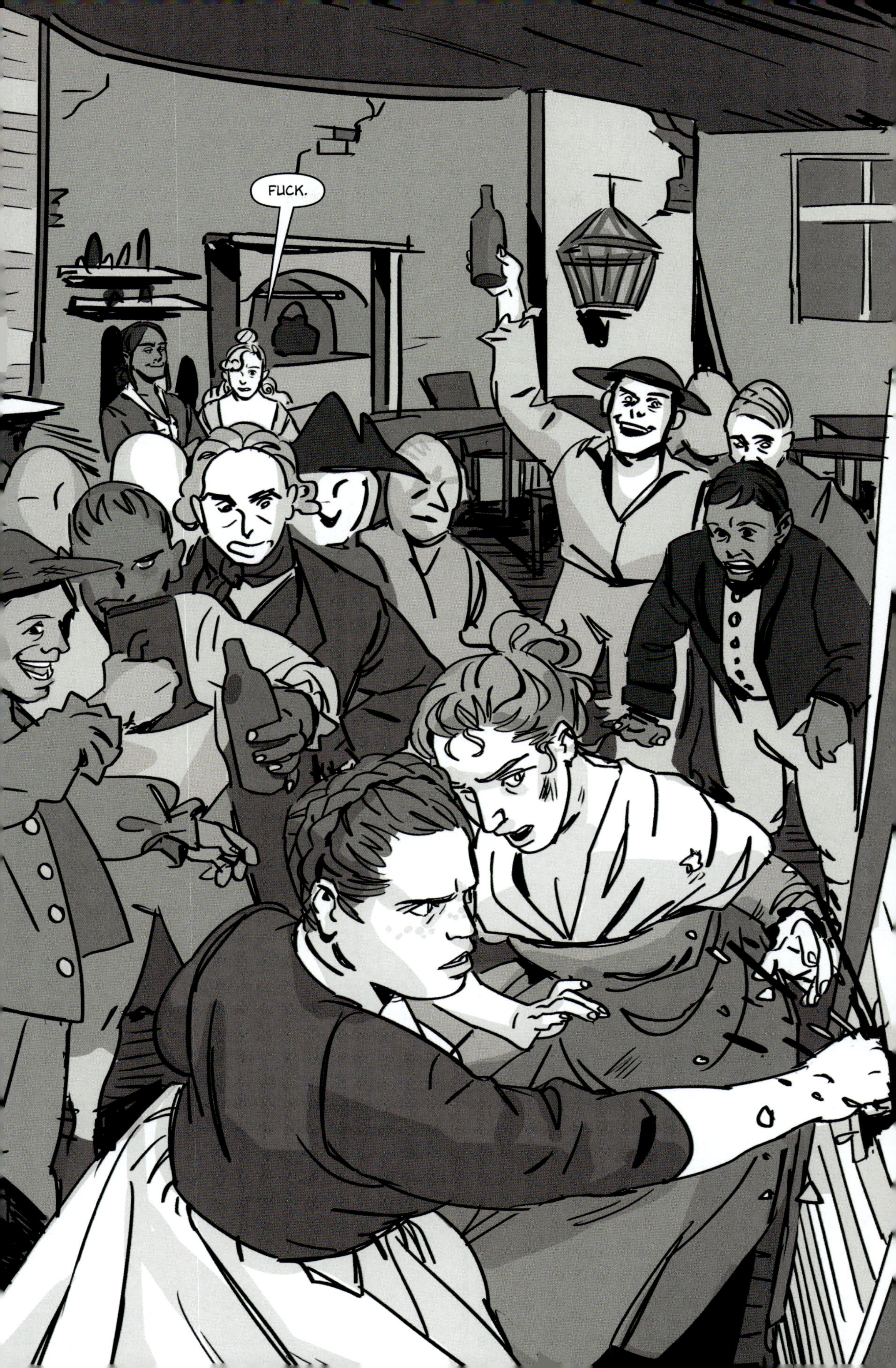
FUCK.

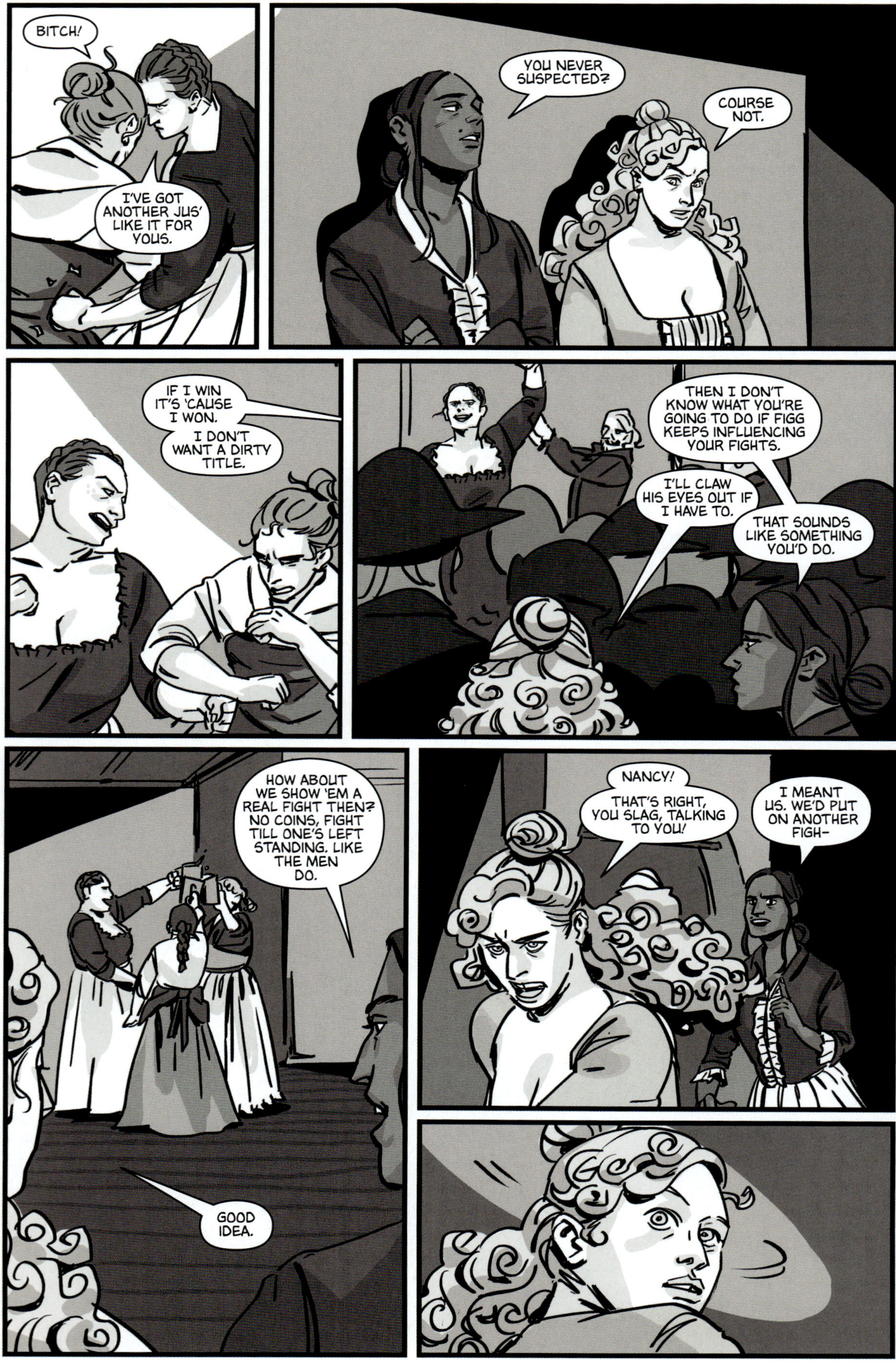
BITCH!
I'VE GOT ANOTHER JUS' LIKE IT FOR YOUS.
YOU NEVER SUSPECTED?
COURSE NOT.
IF I WIN IT'S 'CAUSE I WON.
I DON'T WANT A DIRTY TITLE.
THEN I DON'T KNOW WHAT YOU'RE GOING TO DO IF FIGG KEEPS INFLUENCING YOUR FIGHTS.
I'LL CLAW HIS EYES OUT IF I HAVE TO.
THAT SOUNDS LIKE SOMETHING YOU'D DO.
HOW ABOUT WE SHOW 'EM A REAL FIGHT THEN? NO COINS, FIGHT TILL ONE'S LEFT STANDING. LIKE THE MEN DO.
GOOD IDEA.
NANCY!
THAT'S RIGHT, YOU SLAG, TALKING TO YOU!
I MEANT US. WE'D PUT ON ANOTHER FIGH–

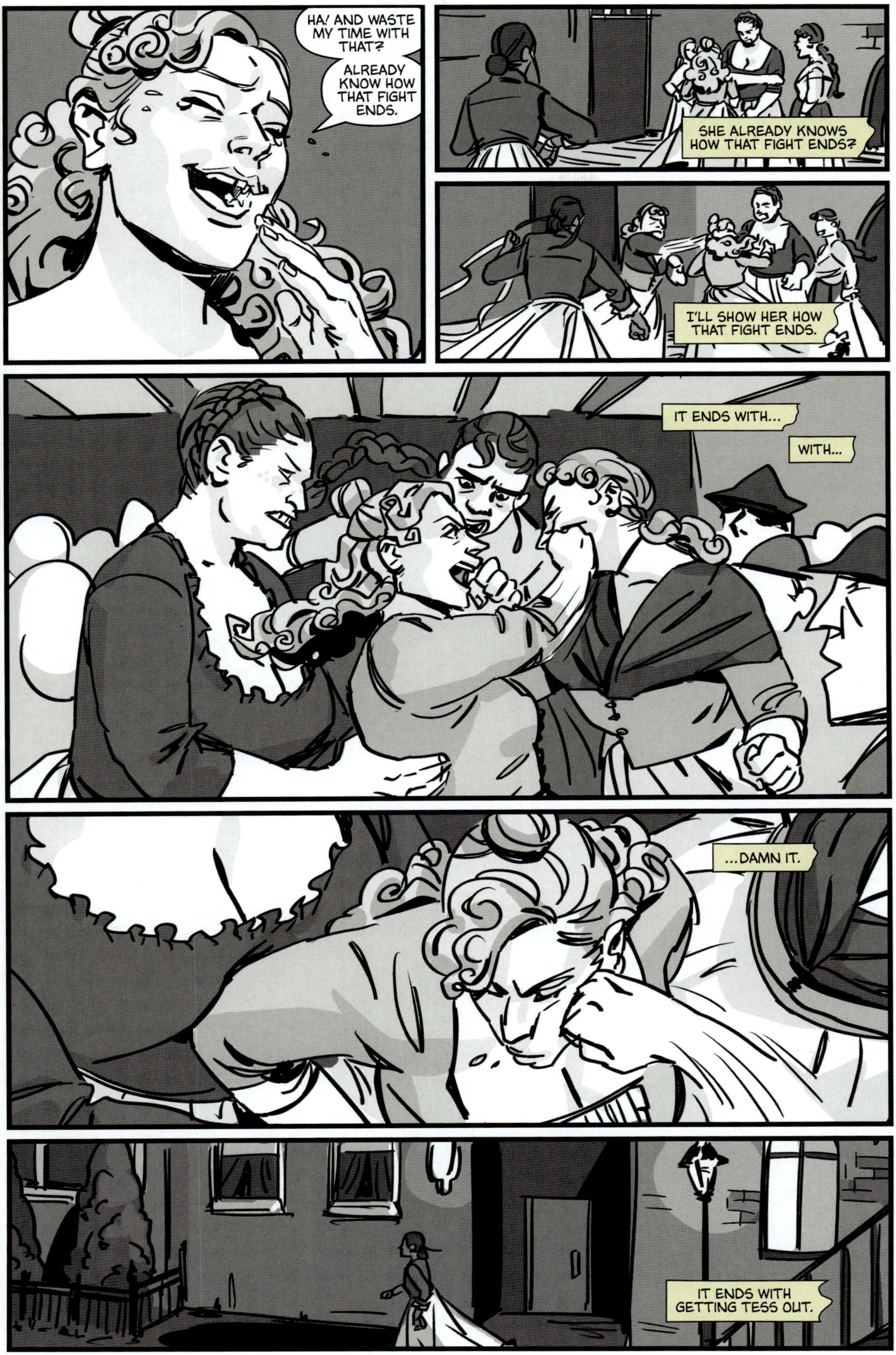
HA! AND WASTE MY TIME WITH THAT?
ALREADY KNOW HOW THAT FIGHT ENDS.
SHE ALREADY KNOWS HOW THAT FIGHT ENDS?
I'LL SHOW HER HOW THAT FIGHT ENDS.
IT ENDS WITH...
WITH...
...DAMN IT.
IT ENDS WITH GETTING TESS OUT.

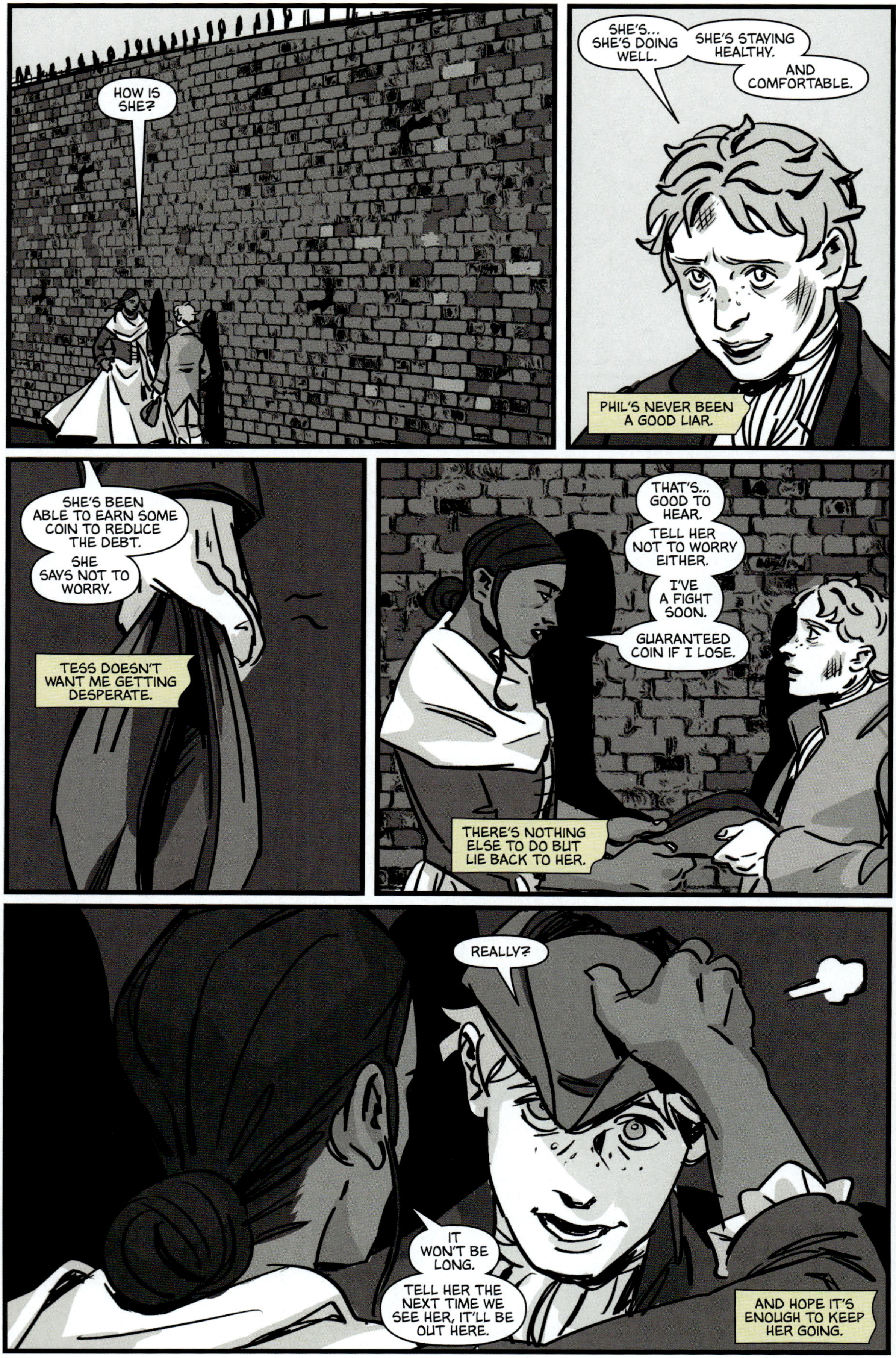
HOW IS SHE?
SHE'S... SHE'S DOING WELL.
SHE'S STAYING HEALTHY.
AND COMFORTABLE.
PHIL'S NEVER BEEN A GOOD LIAR.
SHE'S BEEN ABLE TO EARN SOME COIN TO REDUCE THE DEBT.
SHE SAYS NOT TO WORRY.
TESS DOESN'T WANT ME GETTING DESPERATE.
THAT'S... GOOD TO HEAR.
TELL HER NOT TO WORRY EITHER.
I'VE A FIGHT SOON.
GUARANTEED COIN IF I LOSE.
THERE'S NOTHING ELSE TO DO BUT LIE BACK TO HER.
REALLY?
IT WON'T BE LONG.
TELL HER THE NEXT TIME WE SEE HER, IT'LL BE OUT HERE.
AND HOPE IT'S ENOUGH TO KEEP HER GOING.

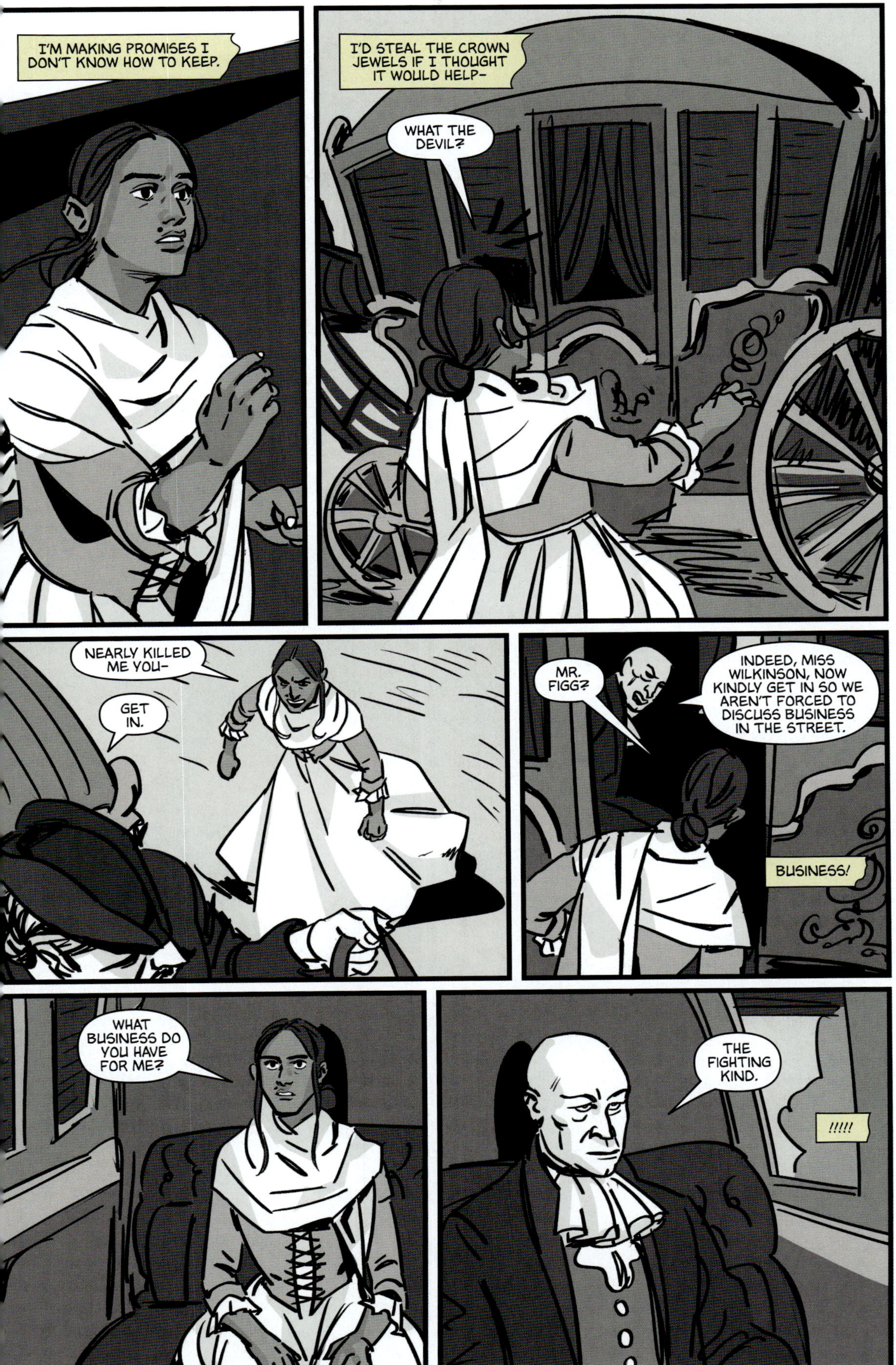
I'M MAKING PROMISES I DON'T KNOW HOW TO KEEP.
I'D STEAL THE CROWN JEWELS IF I THOUGHT IT WOULD HELP–
WHAT THE DEVIL?
NEARLY KILLED ME YOU–
GET IN.
MR. FIGG?
INDEED, MISS WILKINSON, NOW KINDLY GET IN SO WE AREN'T FORCED TO DISCUSS BUSINESS IN THE STREET.
BUSINESS!
WHAT BUSINESS DO YOU HAVE FOR ME?
THE FIGHTING KIND.
!!!!!

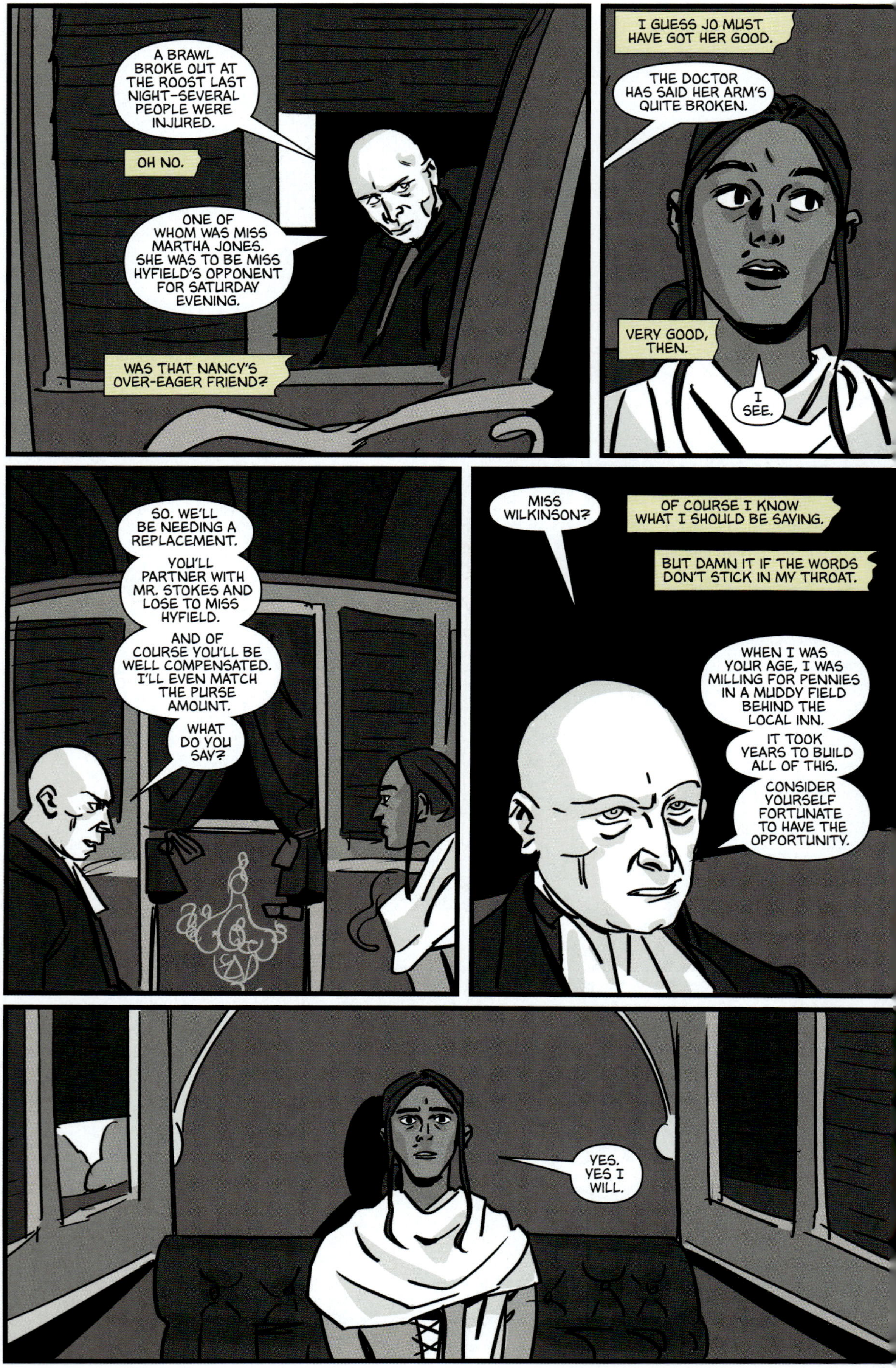
A BRAWL BROKE OUT AT THE ROOST LAST NIGHT—SEVERAL PEOPLE WERE INJURED.
OH NO.
ONE OF WHOM WAS MISS MARTHA JONES. SHE WAS TO BE MISS HYFIELD'S OPPONENT FOR SATURDAY EVENING.
WAS THAT NANCY'S OVER-EAGER FRIEND?
I GUESS JO MUST HAVE GOT HER GOOD.
THE DOCTOR HAS SAID HER ARM'S QUITE BROKEN.
VERY GOOD, THEN.
I SEE.
SO. WE'LL BE NEEDING A REPLACEMENT.
YOU'LL PARTNER WITH MR. STOKES AND LOSE TO MISS HYFIELD.
AND OF COURSE YOU'LL BE WELL COMPENSATED. I'LL EVEN MATCH THE PURSE AMOUNT.
WHAT DO YOU SAY?
MISS WILKINSON?
OF COURSE I KNOW WHAT I SHOULD BE SAYING.
BUT DAMN IT IF THE WORDS DON'T STICK IN MY THROAT.
WHEN I WAS YOUR AGE, I WAS MILLING FOR PENNIES IN A MUDDY FIELD BEHIND THE LOCAL INN.
IT TOOK YEARS TO BUILD ALL OF THIS.
CONSIDER YOURSELF FORTUNATE TO HAVE THE OPPORTUNITY.
YES. YES I WILL.

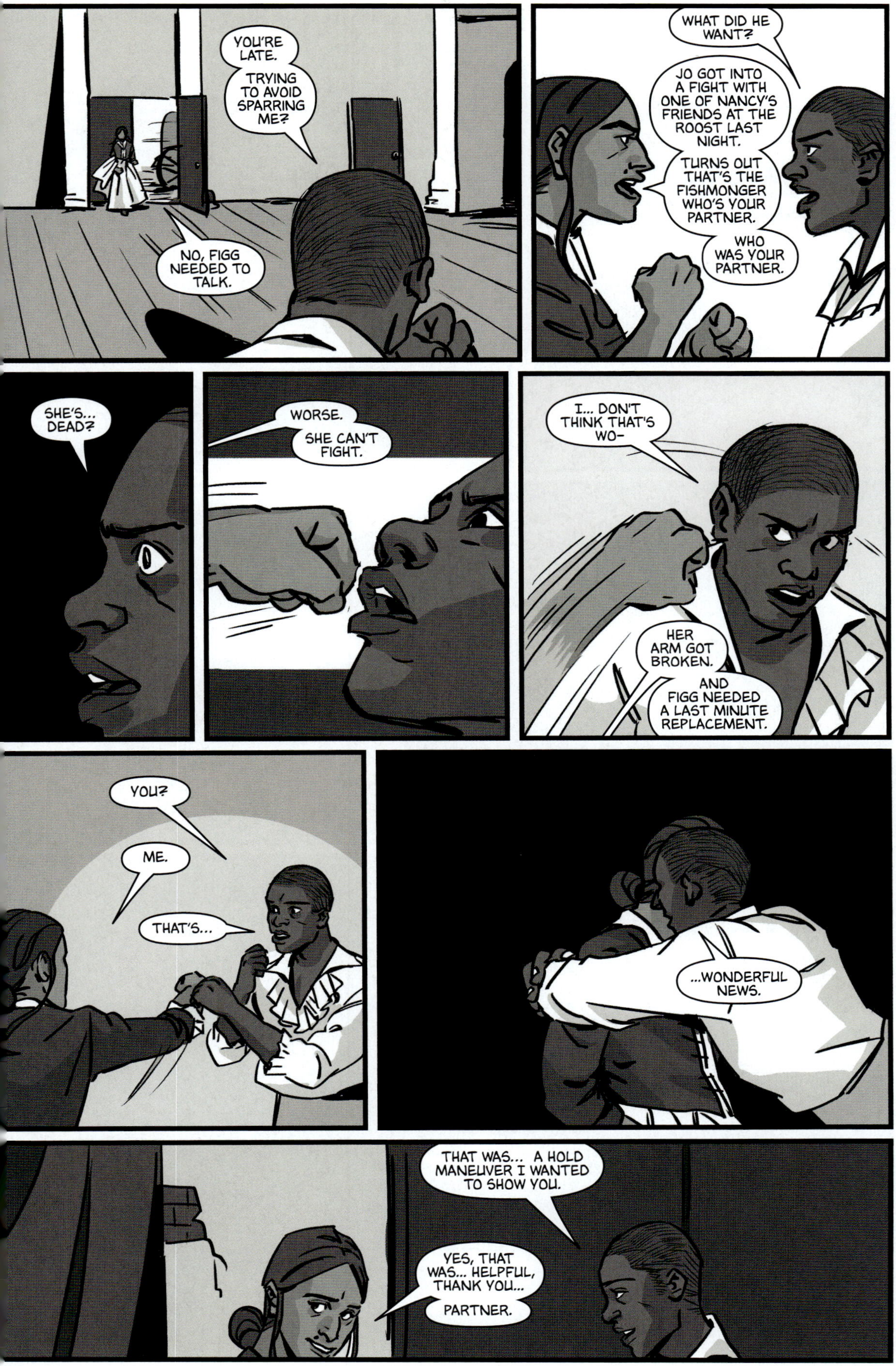
YOU'RE LATE.
TRYING TO AVOID SPARRING ME?
NO, FIGG NEEDED TO TALK.
WHAT DID HE WANT?
JO GOT INTO A FIGHT WITH ONE OF NANCY'S FRIENDS AT THE ROOST LAST NIGHT.
TURNS OUT THAT'S THE FISHMONGER WHO'S YOUR PARTNER.
WHO WAS YOUR PARTNER.
SHE'S... DEAD?
WORSE.
SHE CAN'T FIGHT.
I... DON'T THINK THAT'S WO-
HER ARM GOT BROKEN.
AND FIGG NEEDED A LAST MINUTE REPLACEMENT.
YOU?
ME.
THAT'S...
...WONDERFUL NEWS.
THAT WAS... A HOLD MANEUVER I WANTED TO SHOW YOU.
YES, THAT WAS... HELPFUL, THANK YOU...
PARTNER.

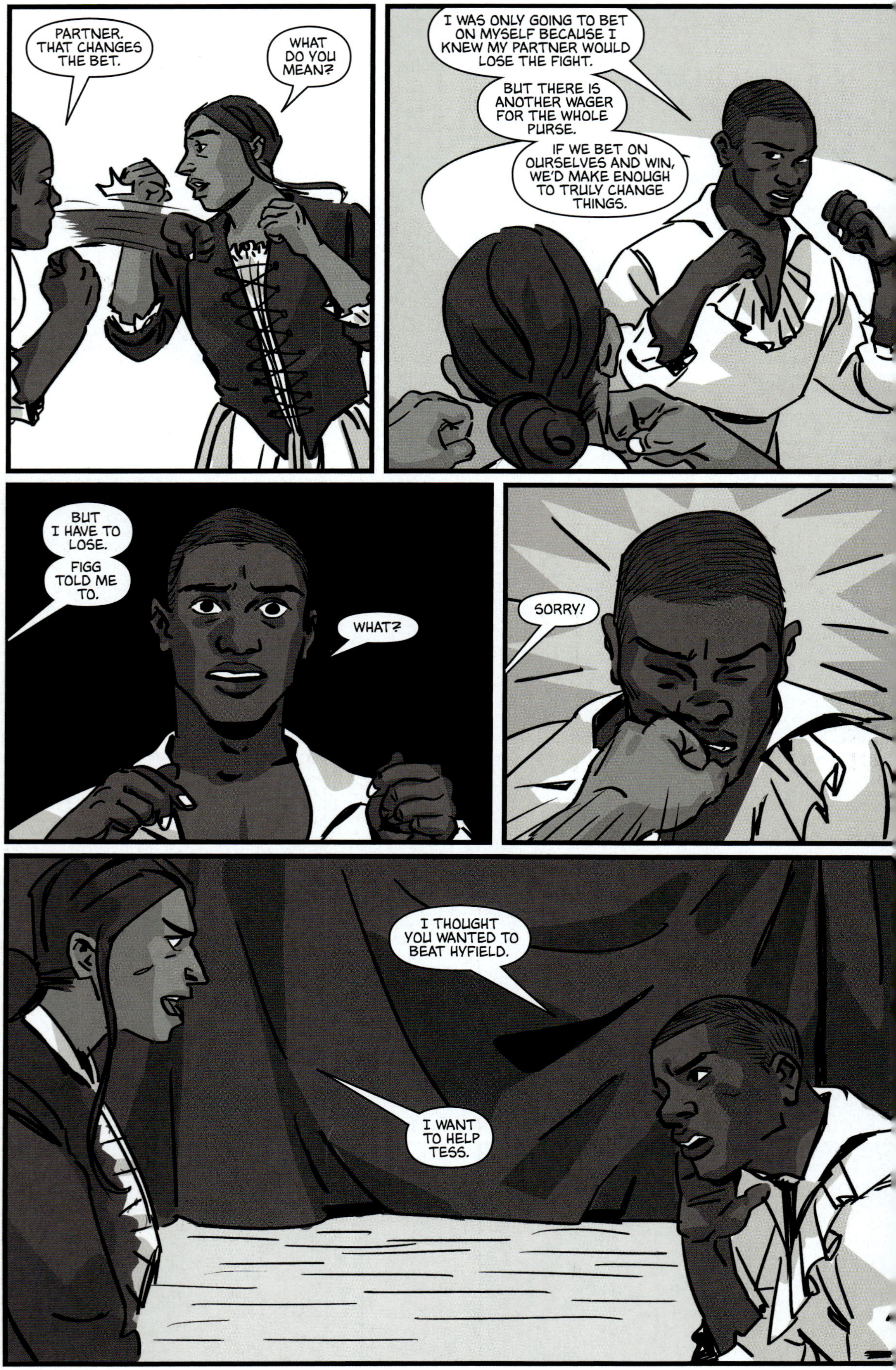
PARTNER. THAT CHANGES THE BET.
WHAT DO YOU MEAN?
I WAS ONLY GOING TO BET ON MYSELF BECAUSE I KNEW MY PARTNER WOULD LOSE THE FIGHT.
BUT THERE IS ANOTHER WAGER FOR THE WHOLE PURSE.
IF WE BET ON OURSELVES AND WIN, WE'D MAKE ENOUGH TO TRULY CHANGE THINGS.
BUT I HAVE TO LOSE.
FIGG TOLD ME TO.
WHAT?
SORRY!
I THOUGHT YOU WANTED TO BEAT HYFIELD.
I WANT TO HELP TESS.

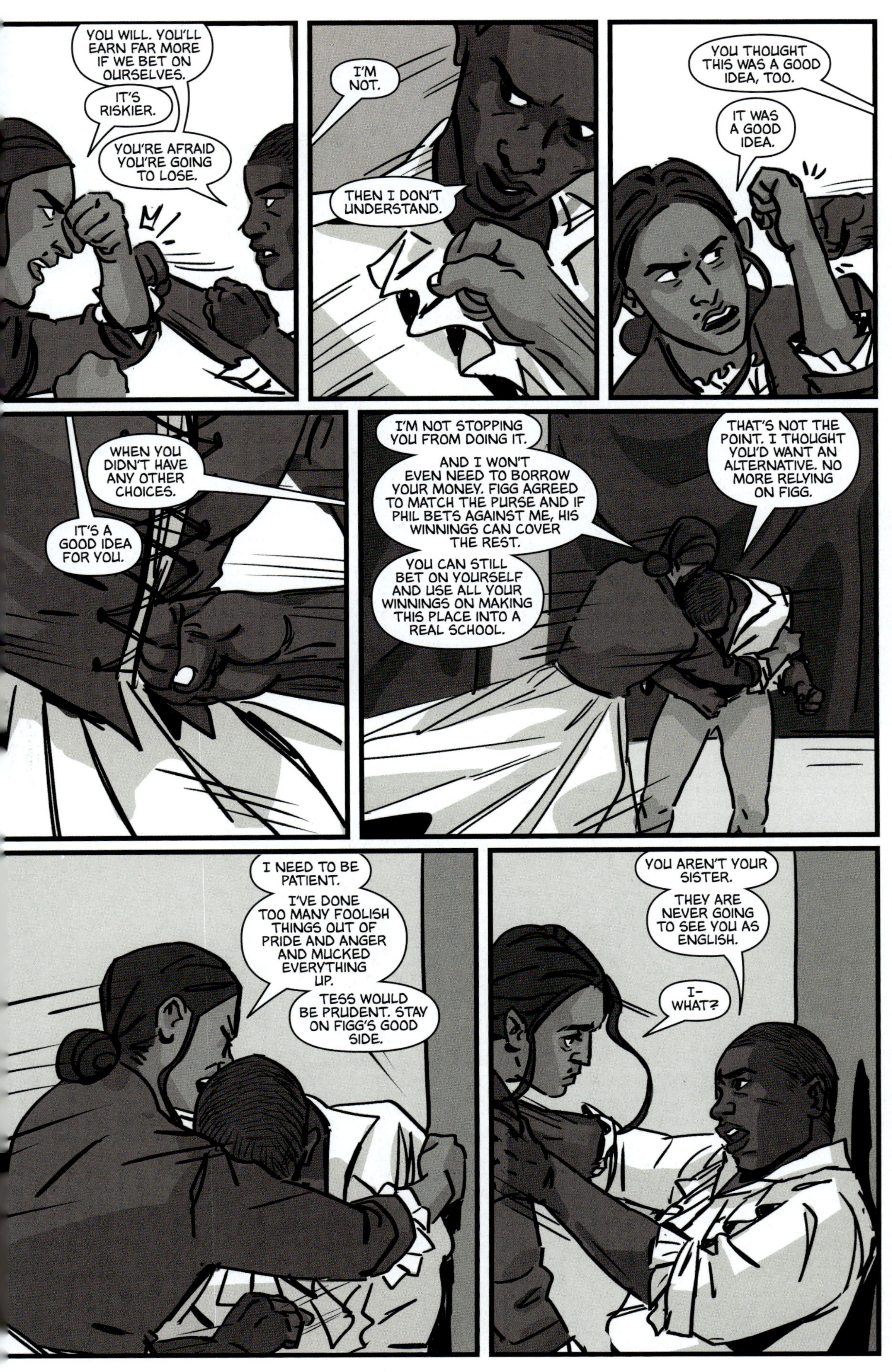
YOU WILL. YOU'LL EARN FAR MORE IF WE BET ON OURSELVES.
IT'S RISKIER.
YOU'RE AFRAID YOU'RE GOING TO LOSE.
I'M NOT.
THEN I DON'T UNDERSTAND.
YOU THOUGHT THIS WAS A GOOD IDEA, TOO.
IT WAS A GOOD IDEA.
WHEN YOU DIDN'T HAVE ANY OTHER CHOICES.
IT'S A GOOD IDEA FOR YOU.
I'M NOT STOPPING YOU FROM DOING IT.
AND I WON'T EVEN NEED TO BORROW YOUR MONEY. FIGG AGREED TO MATCH THE PURSE AND IF PHIL BETS AGAINST ME, HIS WINNINGS CAN COVER THE REST.
YOU CAN STILL BET ON YOURSELF AND USE ALL YOUR WINNINGS ON MAKING THIS PLACE INTO A REAL SCHOOL.
THAT'S NOT THE POINT. I THOUGHT YOU'D WANT AN ALTERNATIVE. NO MORE RELYING ON FIGG.
I NEED TO BE PATIENT.
I'VE DONE TOO MANY FOOLISH THINGS OUT OF PRIDE AND ANGER AND MUCKED EVERYTHING UP.
TESS WOULD BE PRUDENT. STAY ON FIGG'S GOOD SIDE.
YOU AREN'T YOUR SISTER.
THEY ARE NEVER GOING TO SEE YOU AS ENGLISH.
I- WHAT?

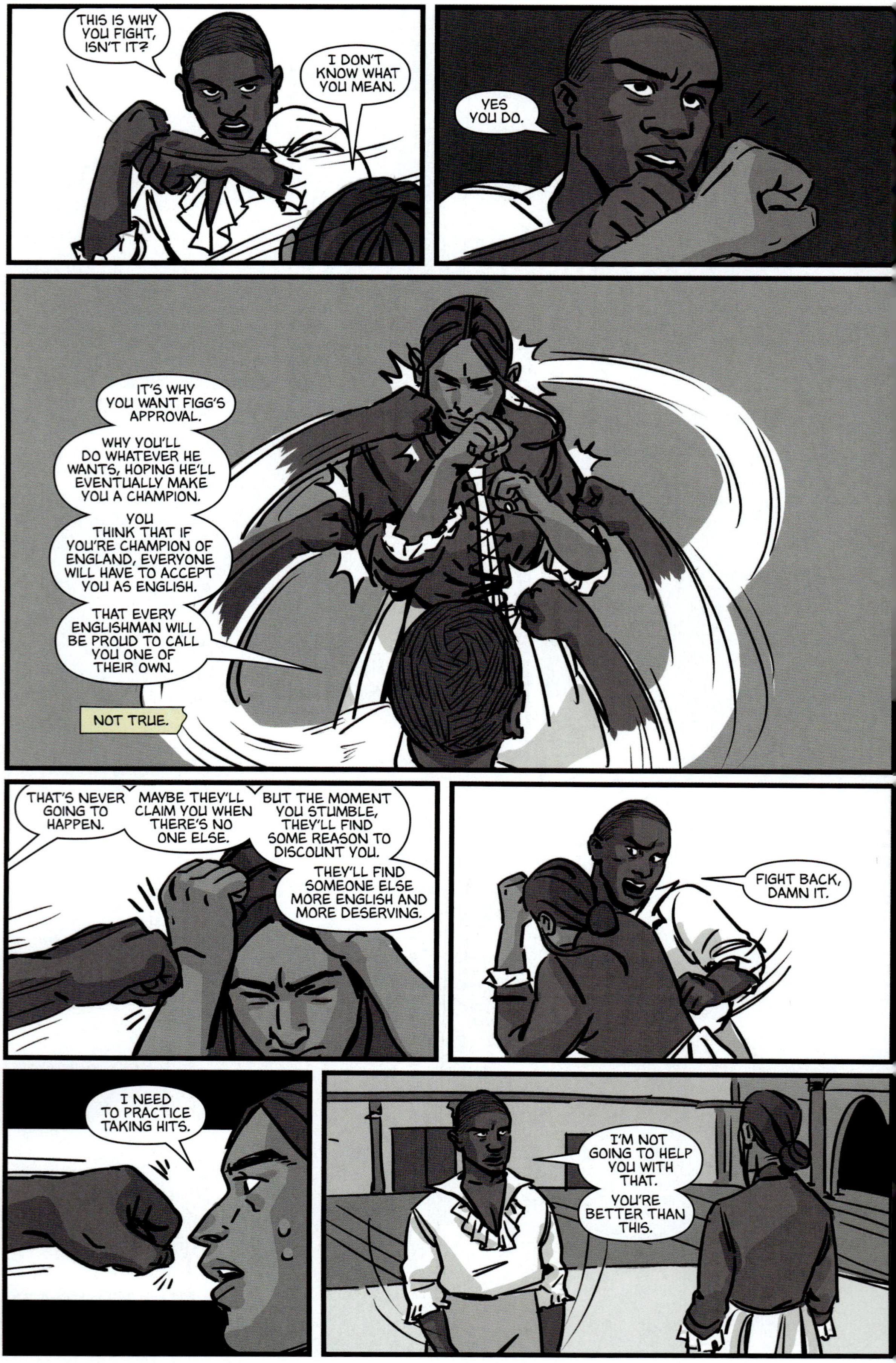
THIS IS WHY YOU FIGHT, ISN'T IT?
I DON'T KNOW WHAT YOU MEAN.
YES YOU DO.
IT'S WHY YOU WANT FIGG'S APPROVAL.
WHY YOU'LL DO WHATEVER HE WANTS, HOPING HE'LL EVENTUALLY MAKE YOU A CHAMPION.
YOU THINK THAT IF YOU'RE CHAMPION OF ENGLAND, EVERYONE WILL HAVE TO ACCEPT YOU AS ENGLISH.
THAT EVERY ENGLISHMAN WILL BE PROUD TO CALL YOU ONE OF THEIR OWN.
NOT TRUE.
THAT'S NEVER GOING TO HAPPEN.
MAYBE THEY'LL CLAIM YOU WHEN THERE'S NO ONE ELSE.
BUT THE MOMENT YOU STUMBLE, THEY'LL FIND SOME REASON TO DISCOUNT YOU.
THEY'LL FIND SOMEONE ELSE MORE ENGLISH AND MORE DESERVING.
FIGHT BACK, DAMN IT.
I NEED TO PRACTICE TAKING HITS.
I'M NOT GOING TO HELP YOU WITH THAT.
YOU'RE BETTER THAN THIS.

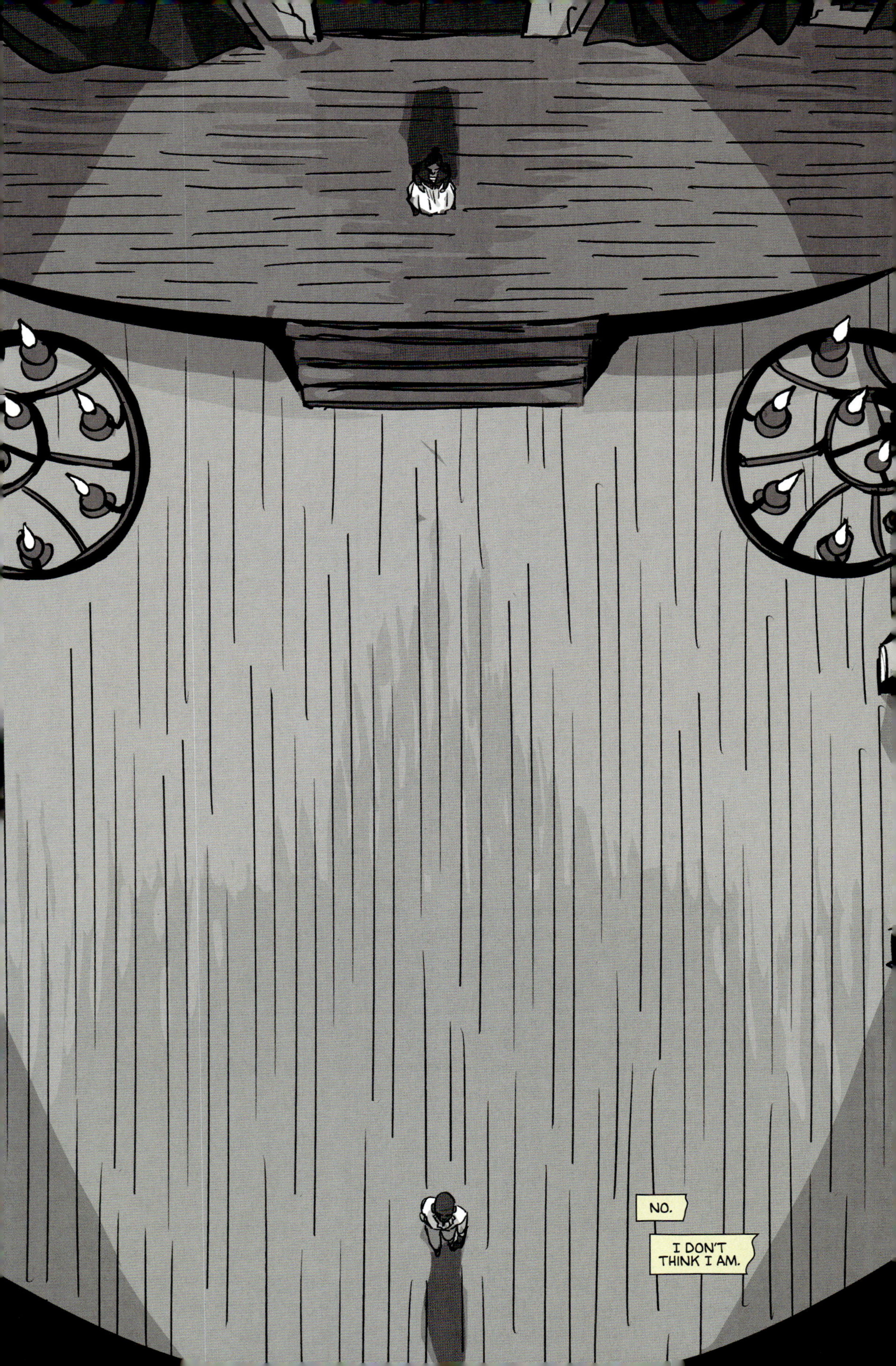
NO.
I DON'T THINK I AM.

6

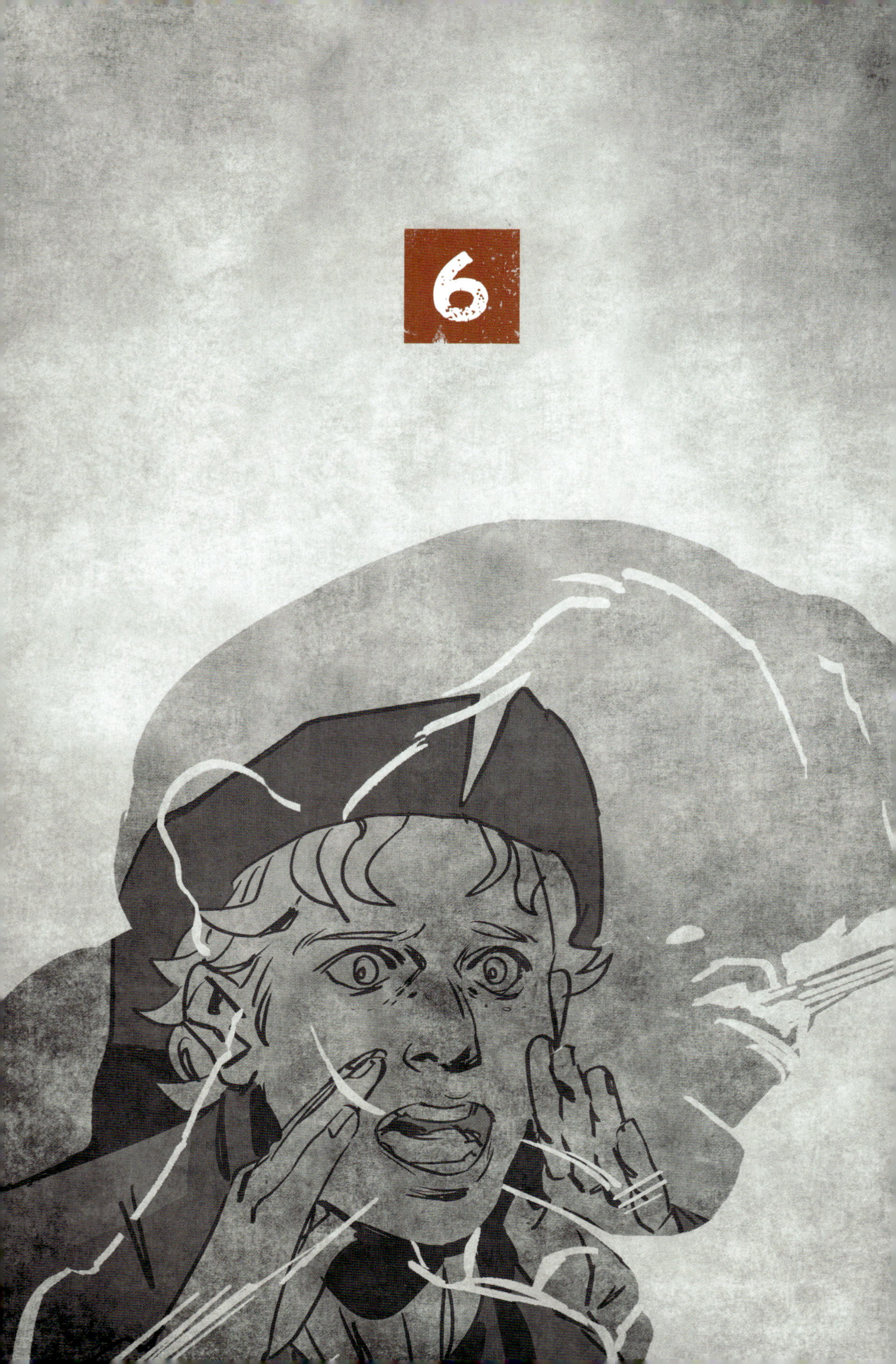

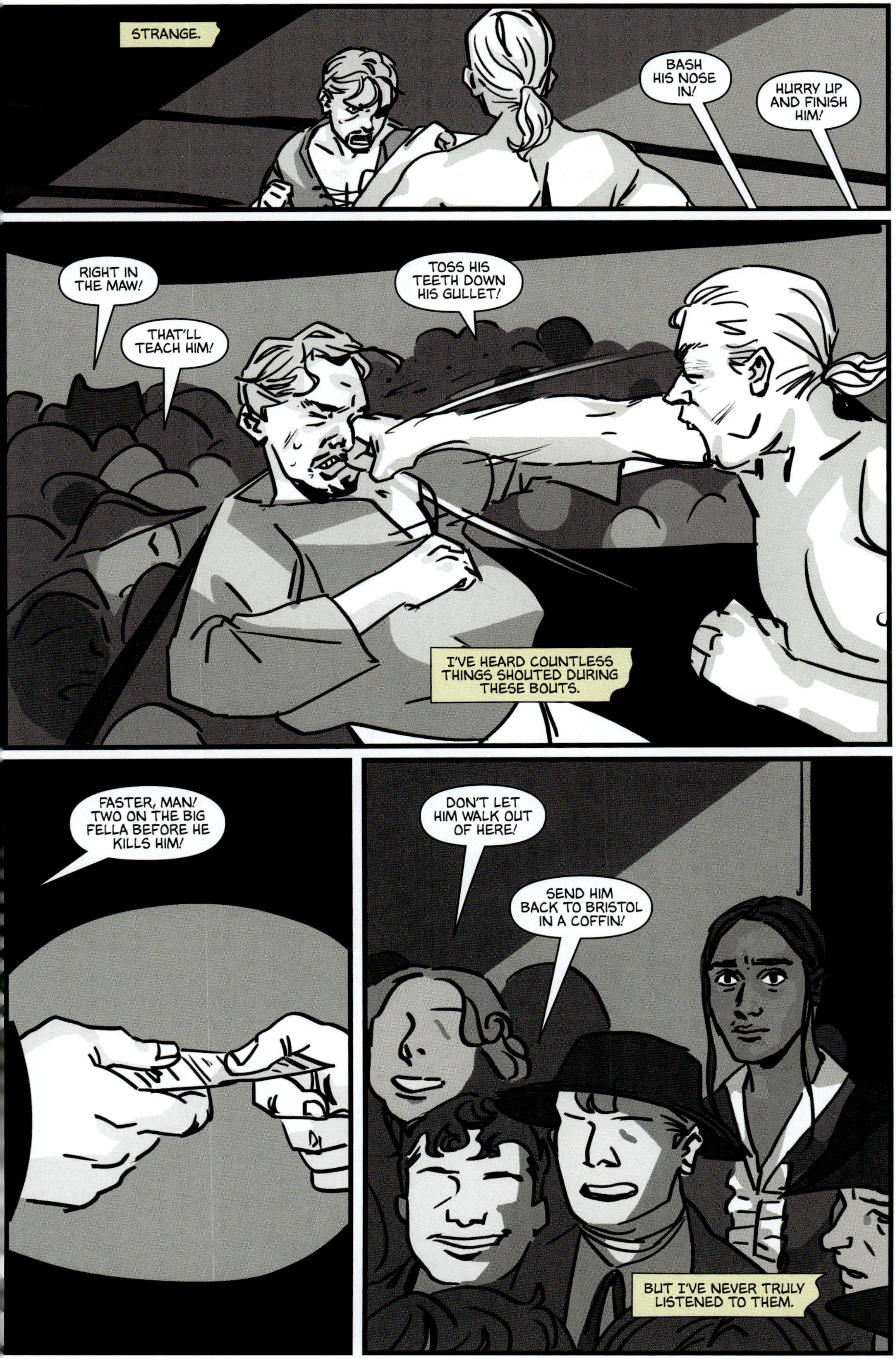
STRANGE.
BASH HIS NOSE IN!
HURRY UP AND FINISH HIM!
RIGHT IN THE MAW!
THAT'LL TEACH HIM!
TOSS HIS TEETH DOWN HIS GULLET!
I'VE HEARD COUNTLESS THINGS SHOUTED DURING THESE BOUTS.
FASTER, MAN! TWO ON THE BIG FELLA BEFORE HE KILLS HIM!
DON'T LET HIM WALK OUT OF HERE!
SEND HIM BACK TO BRISTOL IN A COFFIN!
BUT I'VE NEVER TRULY LISTENED TO THEM.

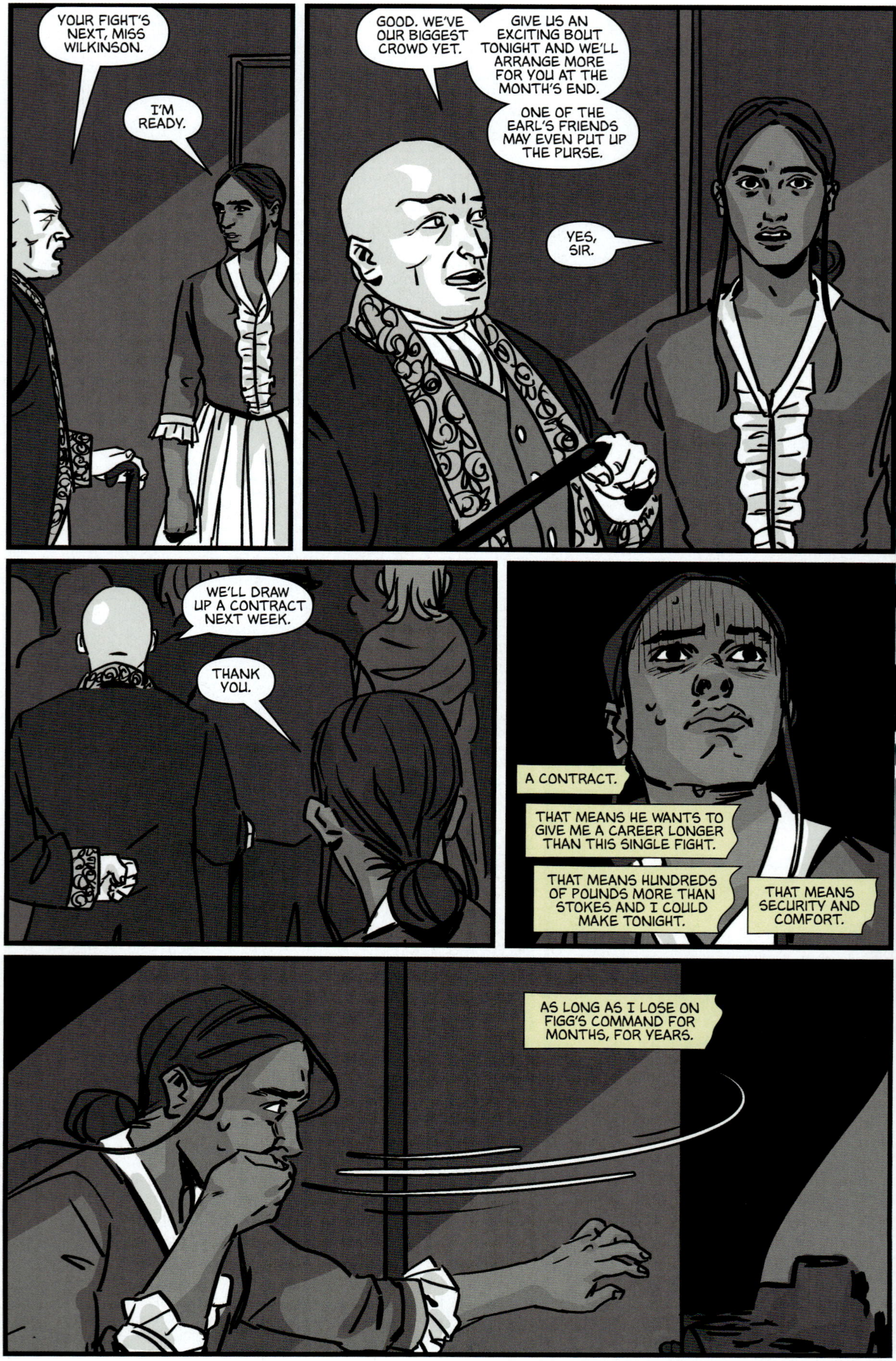
YOUR FIGHT'S NEXT, MISS WILKINSON.
I'M READY.
GOOD. WE'VE OUR BIGGEST CROWD YET.
GIVE US AN EXCITING BOUT TONIGHT AND WE'LL ARRANGE MORE FOR YOU AT THE MONTH'S END.
ONE OF THE EARL'S FRIENDS MAY EVEN PUT UP THE PURSE.
YES, SIR.
WE'LL DRAW UP A CONTRACT NEXT WEEK.
THANK YOU.
A CONTRACT.
THAT MEANS HE WANTS TO GIVE ME A CAREER LONGER THAN THIS SINGLE FIGHT.
THAT MEANS HUNDREDS OF POUNDS MORE THAN STOKES AND I COULD MAKE TONIGHT.
THAT MEANS SECURITY AND COMFORT.
AS LONG AS I LOSE ON FIGG'S COMMAND FOR MONTHS, FOR YEARS.

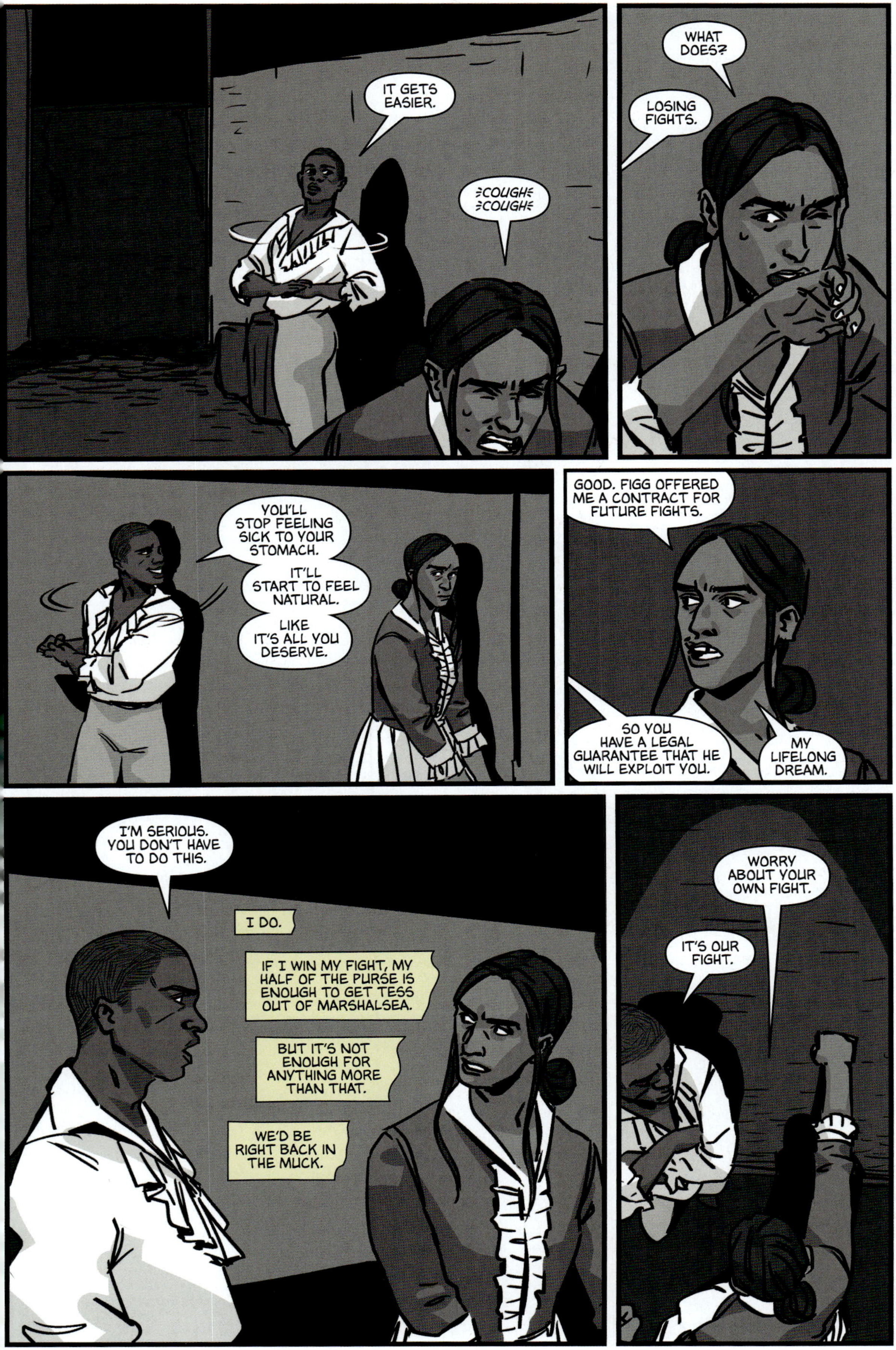
IT GETS EASIER.
≷COUGH≷ ≷COUGH≷
WHAT DOES?
LOSING FIGHTS.
YOU'LL STOP FEELING SICK TO YOUR STOMACH.
IT'LL START TO FEEL NATURAL.
LIKE IT'S ALL YOU DESERVE.
GOOD. FIGG OFFERED ME A CONTRACT FOR FUTURE FIGHTS.
SO YOU HAVE A LEGAL GUARANTEE THAT HE WILL EXPLOIT YOU.
MY LIFELONG DREAM.
I'M SERIOUS. YOU DON'T HAVE TO DO THIS.
I DO.
IF I WIN MY FIGHT, MY HALF OF THE PURSE IS ENOUGH TO GET TESS OUT OF MARSHALSEA.
BUT IT'S NOT ENOUGH FOR ANYTHING MORE THAN THAT.
WE'D BE RIGHT BACK IN THE MUCK.
WORRY ABOUT YOUR OWN FIGHT.
IT'S OUR FIGHT.

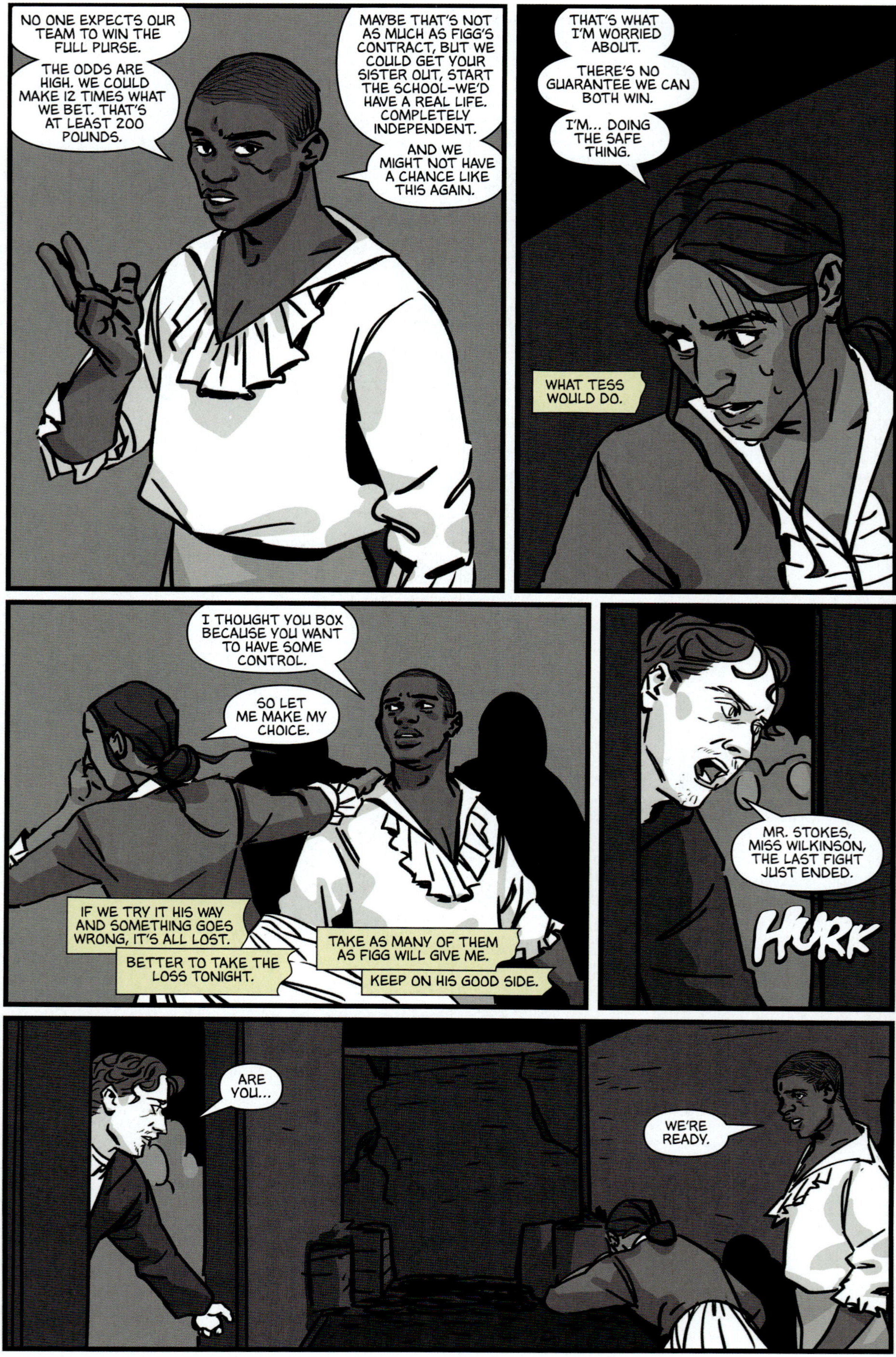
NO ONE EXPECTS OUR TEAM TO WIN THE FULL PURSE.
THE ODDS ARE HIGH. WE COULD MAKE 12 TIMES WHAT WE BET. THAT'S AT LEAST 200 POUNDS.
MAYBE THAT'S NOT AS MUCH AS FIGG'S CONTRACT, BUT WE COULD GET YOUR SISTER OUT, START THE SCHOOL—WE'D HAVE A REAL LIFE. COMPLETELY INDEPENDENT.
AND WE MIGHT NOT HAVE A CHANCE LIKE THIS AGAIN.
THAT'S WHAT I'M WORRIED ABOUT.
THERE'S NO GUARANTEE WE CAN BOTH WIN.
I'M... DOING THE SAFE THING.
WHAT TESS WOULD DO.
I THOUGHT YOU BOX BECAUSE YOU WANT TO HAVE SOME CONTROL.
SO LET ME MAKE MY CHOICE.
IF WE TRY IT HIS WAY AND SOMETHING GOES WRONG, IT'S ALL LOST.
BETTER TO TAKE THE LOSS TONIGHT.
TAKE AS MANY OF THEM AS FIGG WILL GIVE ME.
KEEP ON HIS GOOD SIDE.
MR. STOKES, MISS WILKINSON, THE LAST FIGHT JUST ENDED.
HURK
ARE YOU...
WE'RE READY.

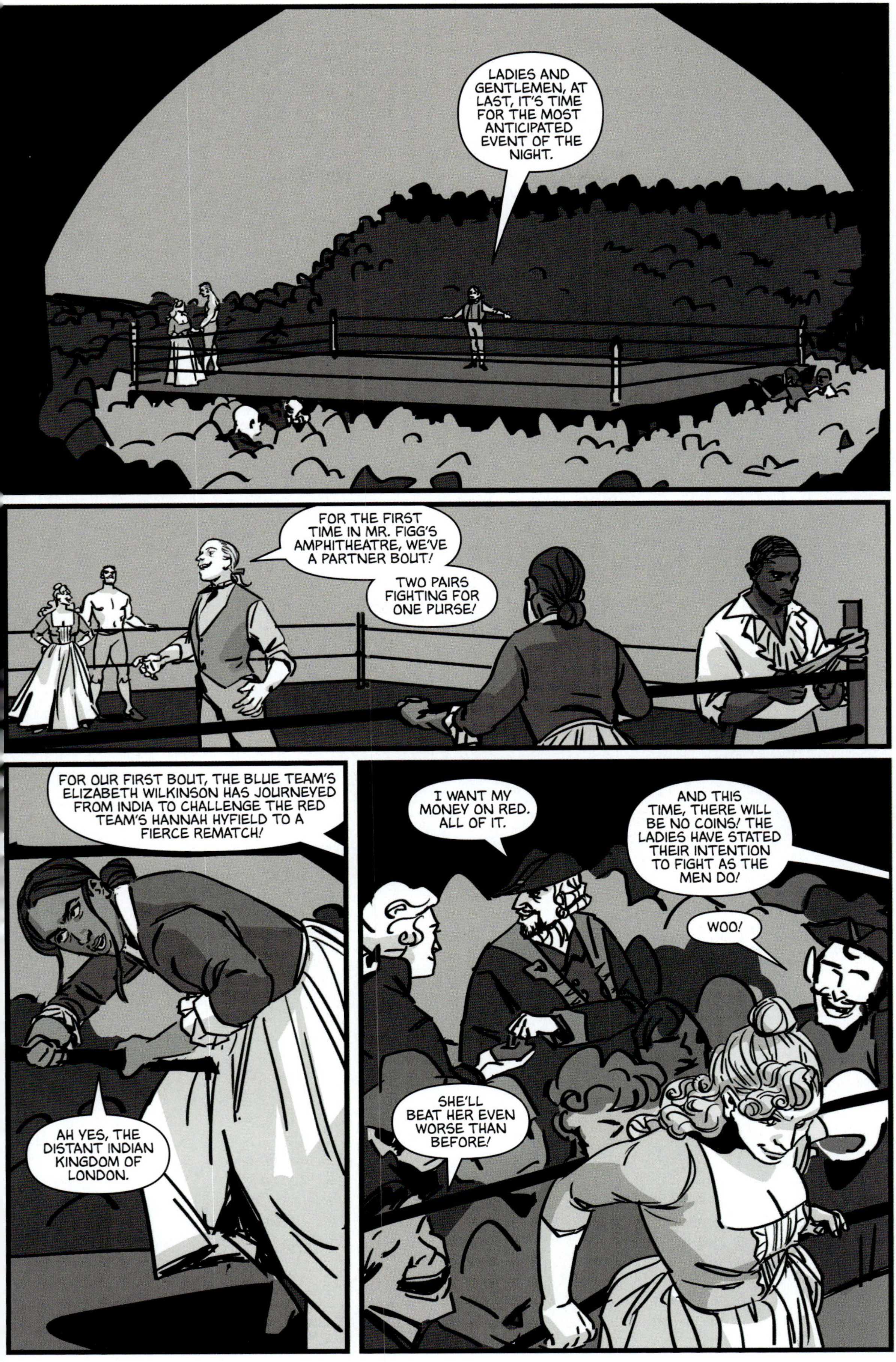
LADIES AND GENTLEMEN, AT LAST, IT'S TIME FOR THE MOST ANTICIPATED EVENT OF THE NIGHT.
FOR THE FIRST TIME IN MR. FIGG'S AMPHITHEATRE, WE'VE A PARTNER BOUT!
TWO PAIRS FIGHTING FOR ONE PURSE!
FOR OUR FIRST BOUT, THE BLUE TEAM'S ELIZABETH WILKINSON HAS JOURNEYED FROM INDIA TO CHALLENGE THE RED TEAM'S HANNAH HYFIELD TO A FIERCE REMATCH!
AH YES, THE DISTANT INDIAN KINGDOM OF LONDON.
I WANT MY MONEY ON RED. ALL OF IT.
AND THIS TIME, THERE WILL BE NO COINS! THE LADIES HAVE STATED THEIR INTENTION TO FIGHT AS THE MEN DO!
WOO!
SHE'LL BEAT HER EVEN WORSE THAN BEFORE!

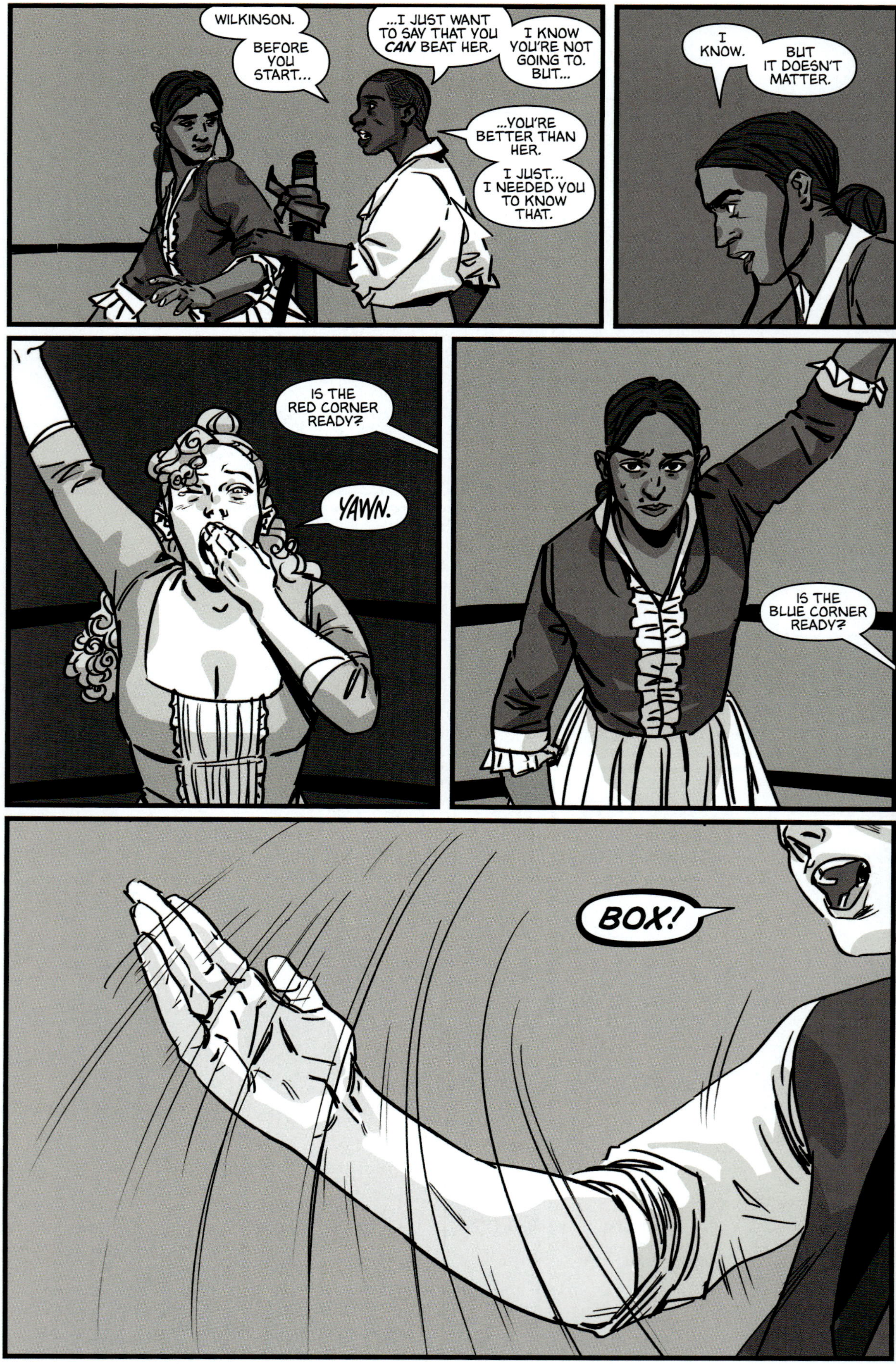
WILKINSON.
BEFORE YOU START...
...I JUST WANT TO SAY THAT YOU *CAN* BEAT HER.
I KNOW YOU'RE NOT GOING TO. BUT...
...YOU'RE BETTER THAN HER.
I JUST... I NEEDED YOU TO KNOW THAT.
I KNOW.
BUT IT DOESN'T MATTER.
IS THE RED CORNER READY?
YAWN.
IS THE BLUE CORNER READY?
BOX!

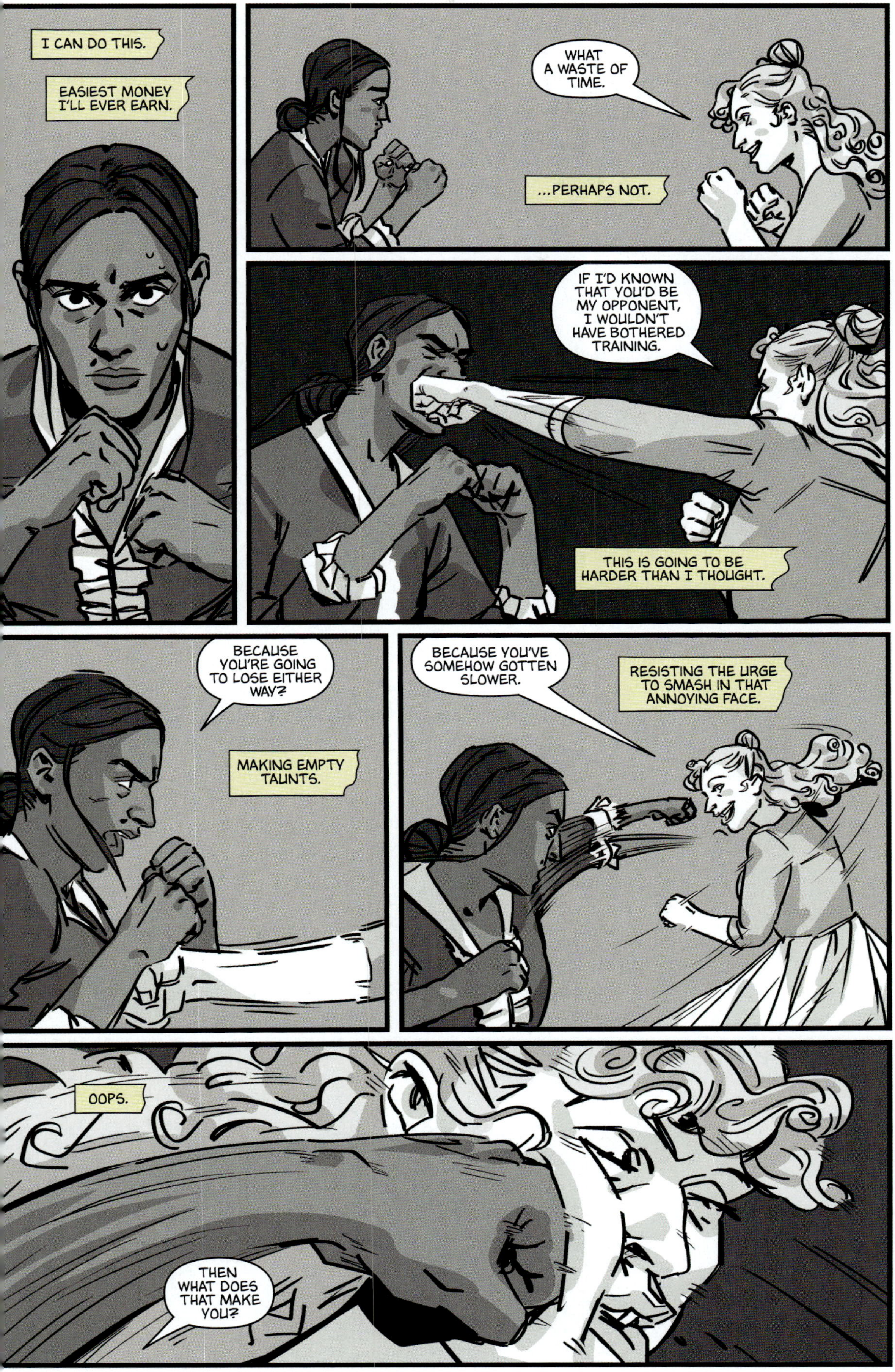

I CAN DO THIS.
EASIEST MONEY I'LL EVER EARN.
WHAT A WASTE OF TIME.
...PERHAPS NOT.
IF I'D KNOWN THAT YOU'D BE MY OPPONENT, I WOULDN'T HAVE BOTHERED TRAINING.
THIS IS GOING TO BE HARDER THAN I THOUGHT.
BECAUSE YOU'RE GOING TO LOSE EITHER WAY?
MAKING EMPTY TAUNTS.
BECAUSE YOU'VE SOMEHOW GOTTEN SLOWER.
RESISTING THE URGE TO SMASH IN THAT ANNOYING FACE.
OOPS.
THEN WHAT DOES THAT MAKE YOU?

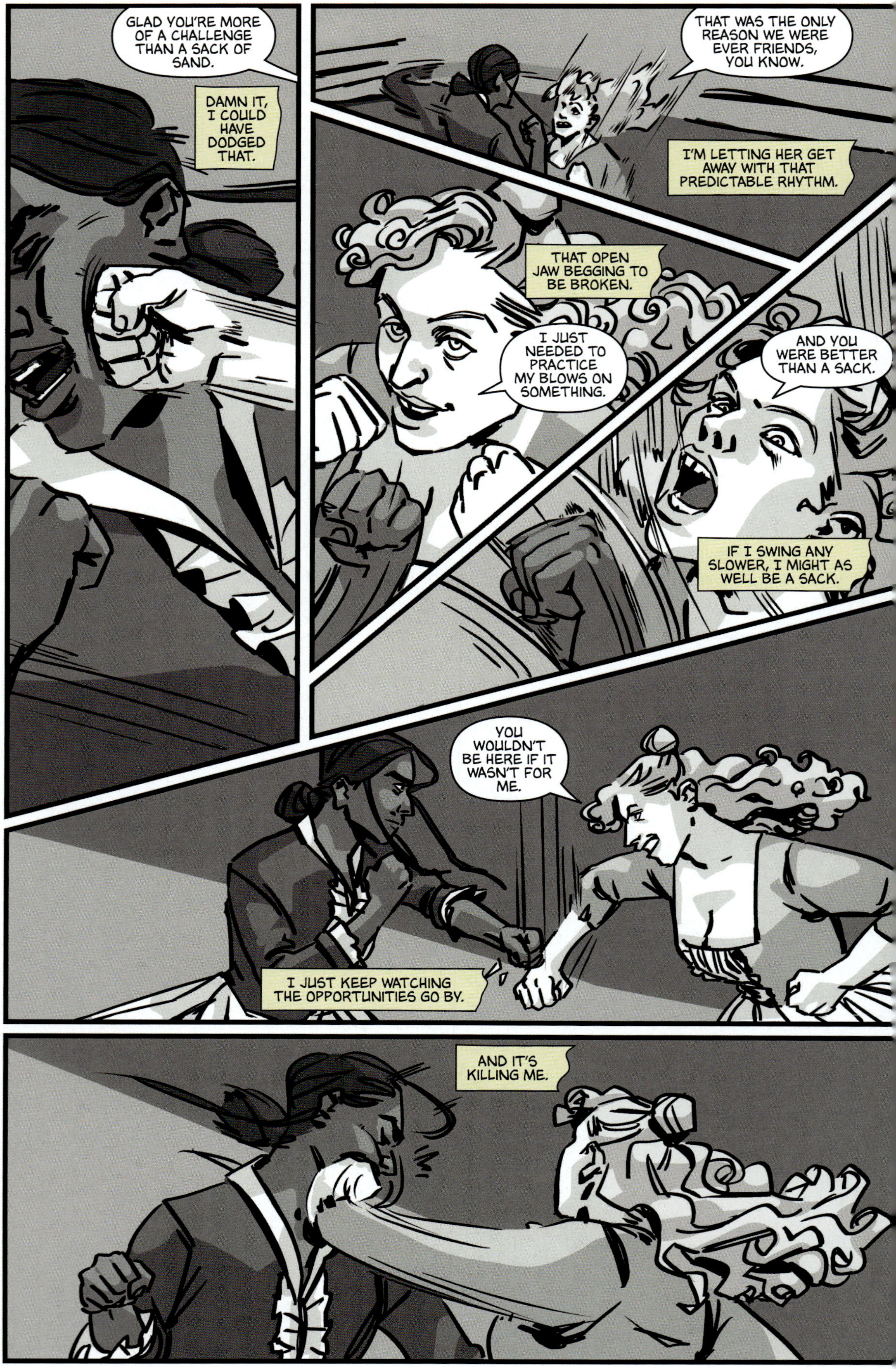
GLAD YOU'RE MORE OF A CHALLENGE THAN A SACK OF SAND.
DAMN IT, I COULD HAVE DODGED THAT.
THAT WAS THE ONLY REASON WE WERE EVER FRIENDS, YOU KNOW.
I'M LETTING HER GET AWAY WITH THAT PREDICTABLE RHYTHM.
THAT OPEN JAW BEGGING TO BE BROKEN.
I JUST NEEDED TO PRACTICE MY BLOWS ON SOMETHING.
AND YOU WERE BETTER THAN A SACK.
IF I SWING ANY SLOWER, I MIGHT AS WELL BE A SACK.
YOU WOULDN'T BE HERE IF IT WASN'T FOR ME.
I JUST KEEP WATCHING THE OPPORTUNITIES GO BY.
AND IT'S KILLING ME.

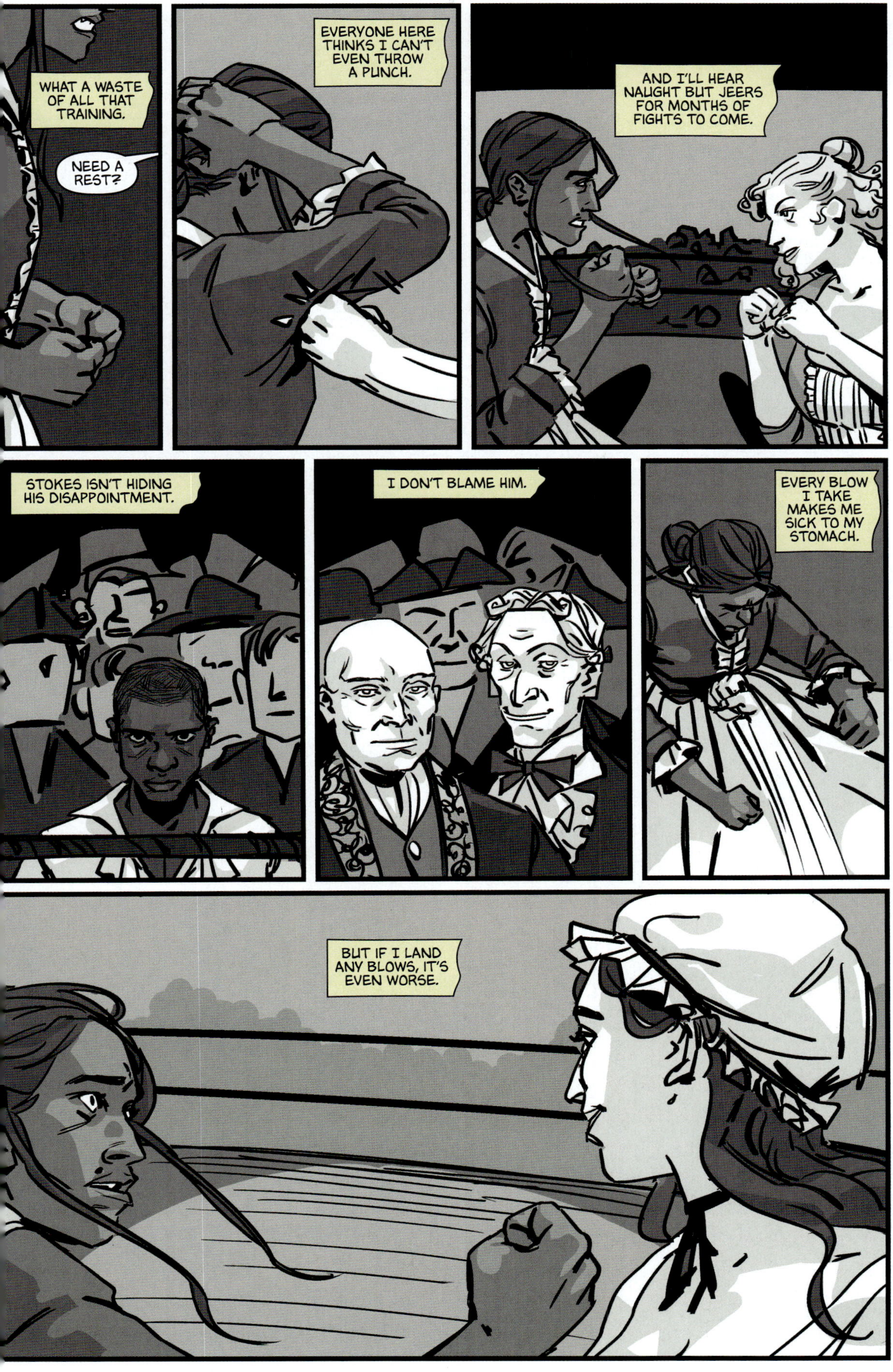
WHAT A WASTE OF ALL THAT TRAINING.
NEED A REST?
EVERYONE HERE THINKS I CAN'T EVEN THROW A PUNCH.
AND I'LL HEAR NAUGHT BUT JEERS FOR MONTHS OF FIGHTS TO COME.
STOKES ISN'T HIDING HIS DISAPPOINTMENT.
I DON'T BLAME HIM.
EVERY BLOW I TAKE MAKES ME SICK TO MY STOMACH.
BUT IF I LAND ANY BLOWS, IT'S EVEN WORSE.

SO I PICTURE MY FAMILY, THE LAST PEOPLE I WANT TO HURT.

MY FATHER, TOO SCARED TO EVEN MOVE.

MY MOTHER, TOO SICK TO EVEN SPEAK.

MY SISTER, TOO DISAPPOINTED TO EVEN LOOK AT ME.

THEY GAVE UP EVERYTHING.

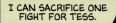

I CAN SACRIFICE ONE FIGHT FOR TESS.

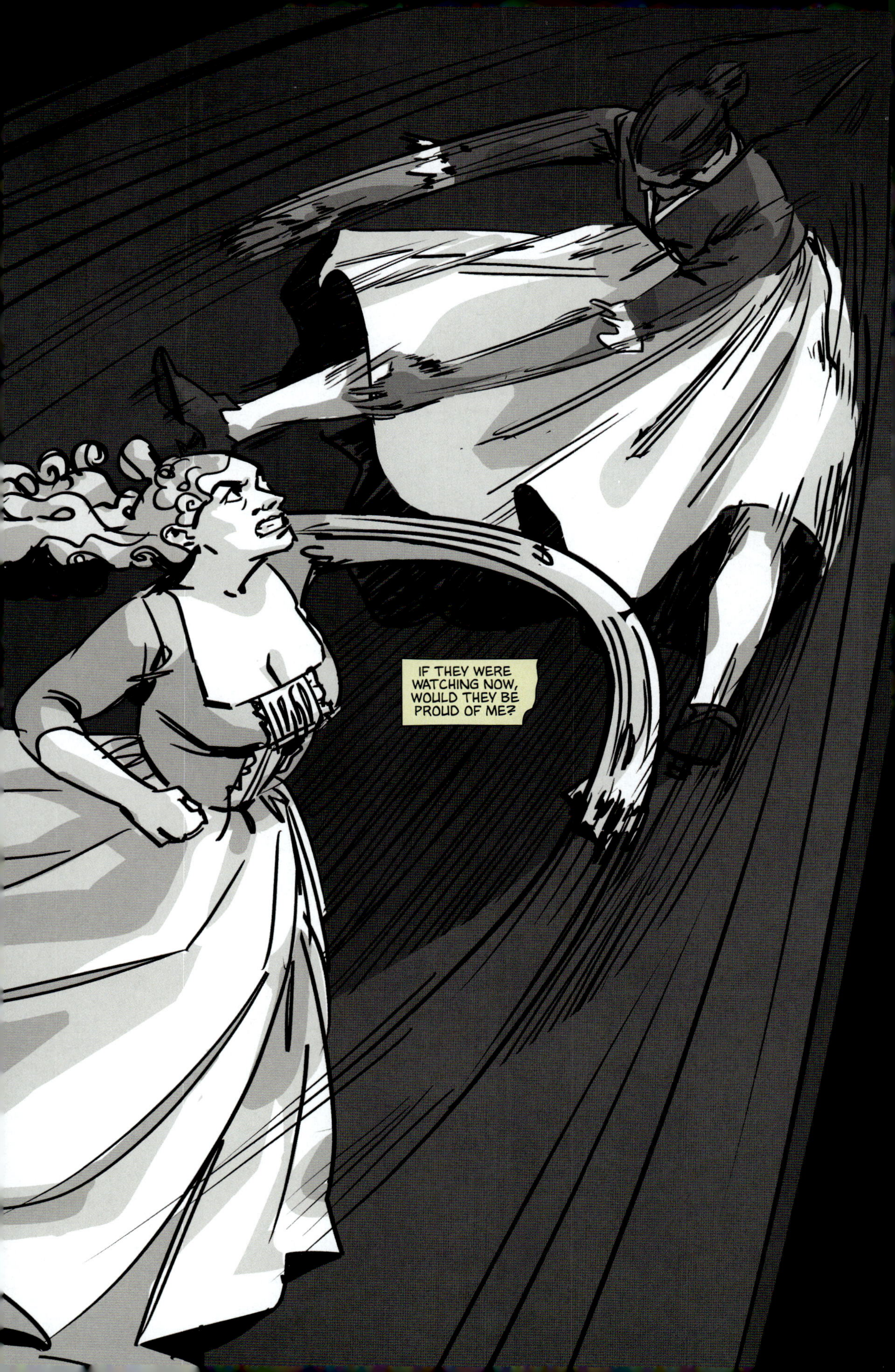
IF THEY WERE WATCHING NOW, WOULD THEY BE PROUD OF ME?

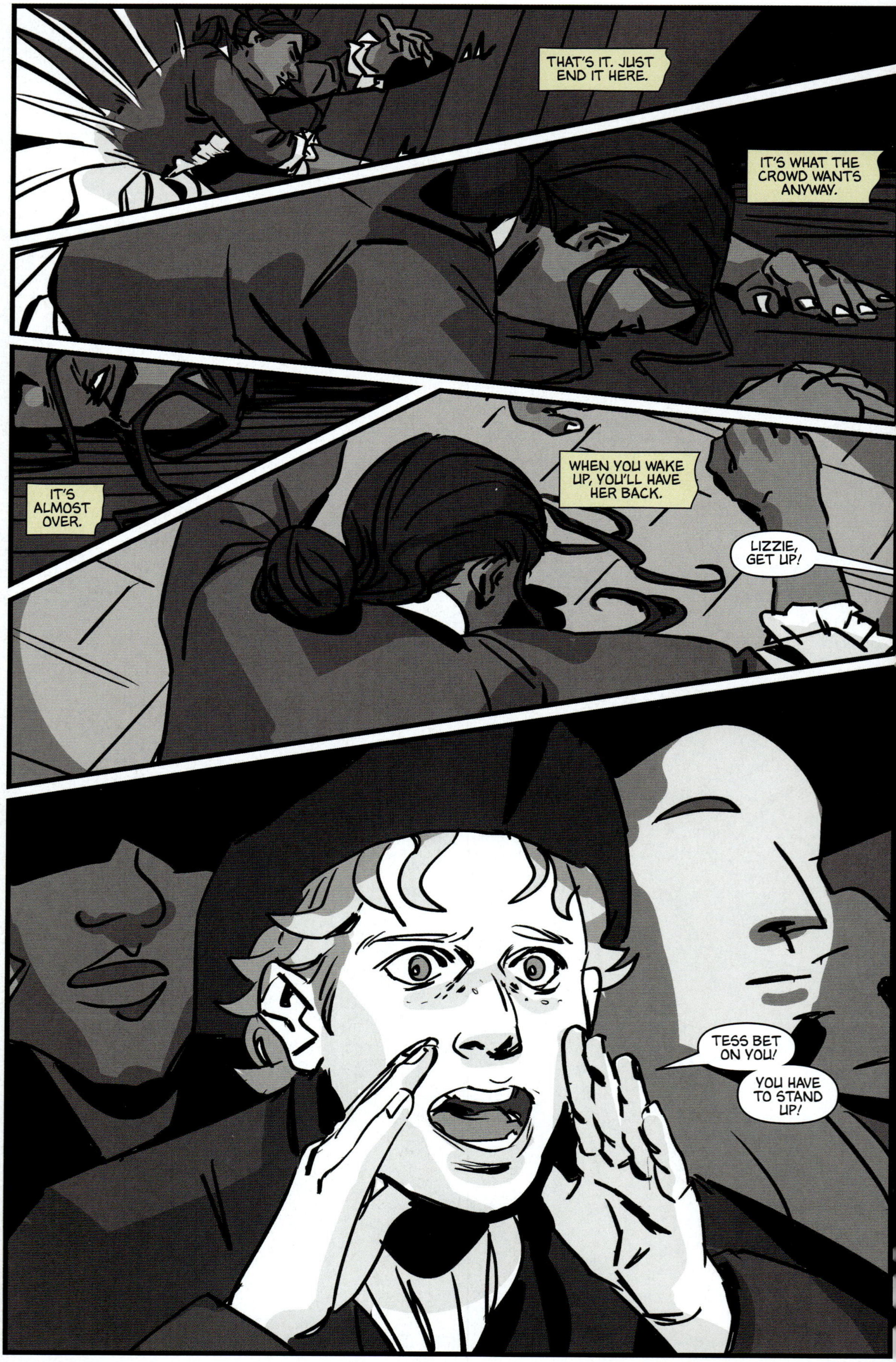
THAT'S IT. JUST END IT HERE.
IT'S WHAT THE CROWD WANTS ANYWAY.
IT'S ALMOST OVER.
WHEN YOU WAKE UP, YOU'LL HAVE HER BACK.
LIZZIE, GET UP!
TESS BET ON YOU!
YOU HAVE TO STAND UP!

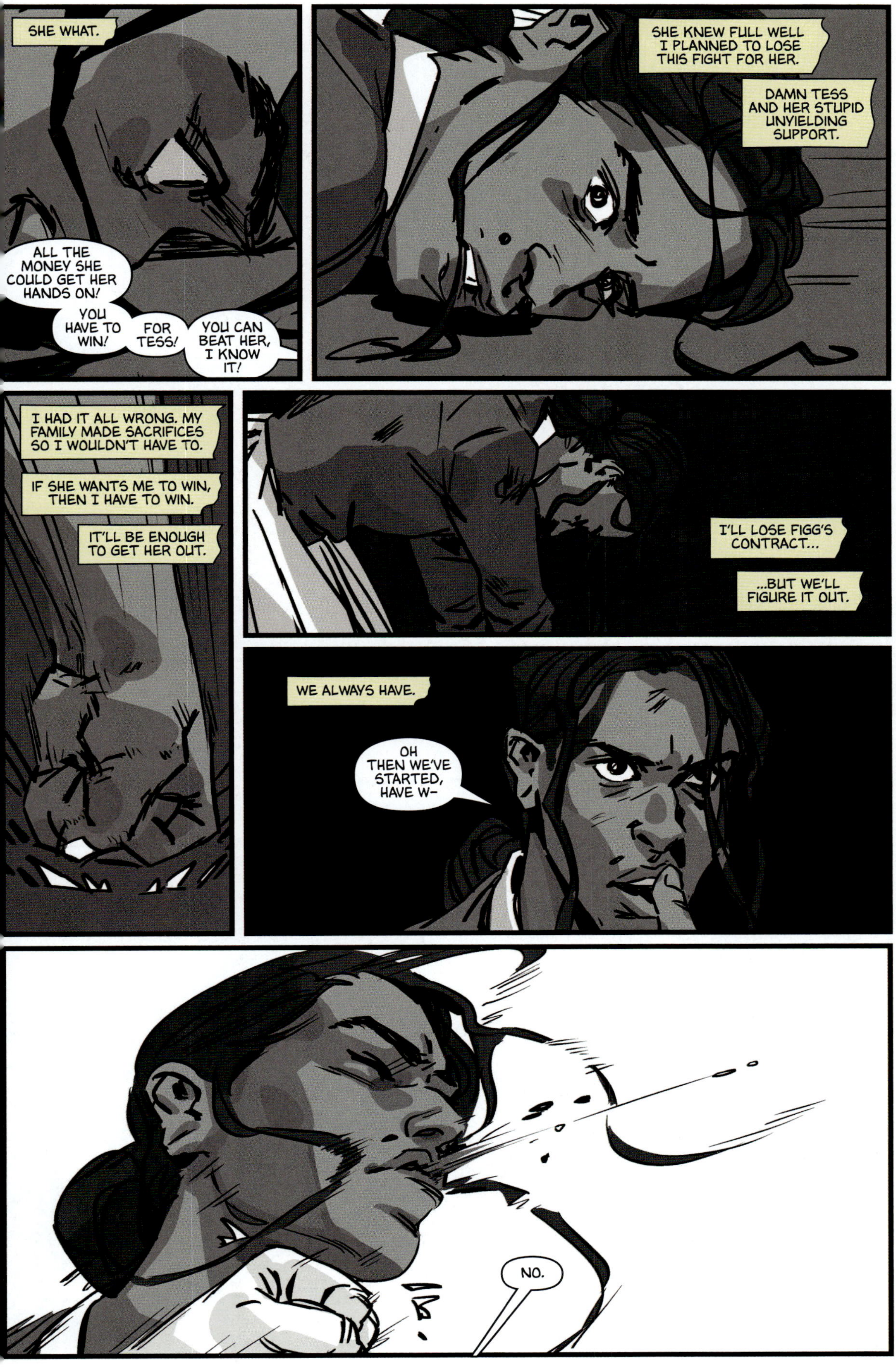
SHE WHAT.
ALL THE MONEY SHE COULD GET HER HANDS ON!
YOU HAVE TO WIN!
FOR TESS!
YOU CAN BEAT HER, I KNOW IT!
SHE KNEW FULL WELL I PLANNED TO LOSE THIS FIGHT FOR HER.
DAMN TESS AND HER STUPID UNYIELDING SUPPORT.
I HAD IT ALL WRONG. MY FAMILY MADE SACRIFICES SO I WOULDN'T HAVE TO.
IF SHE WANTS ME TO WIN, THEN I HAVE TO WIN.
IT'LL BE ENOUGH TO GET HER OUT.
I'LL LOSE FIGG'S CONTRACT...
...BUT WE'LL FIGURE IT OUT.
WE ALWAYS HAVE.
OH THEN WE'VE STARTED, HAVE W-
NO.

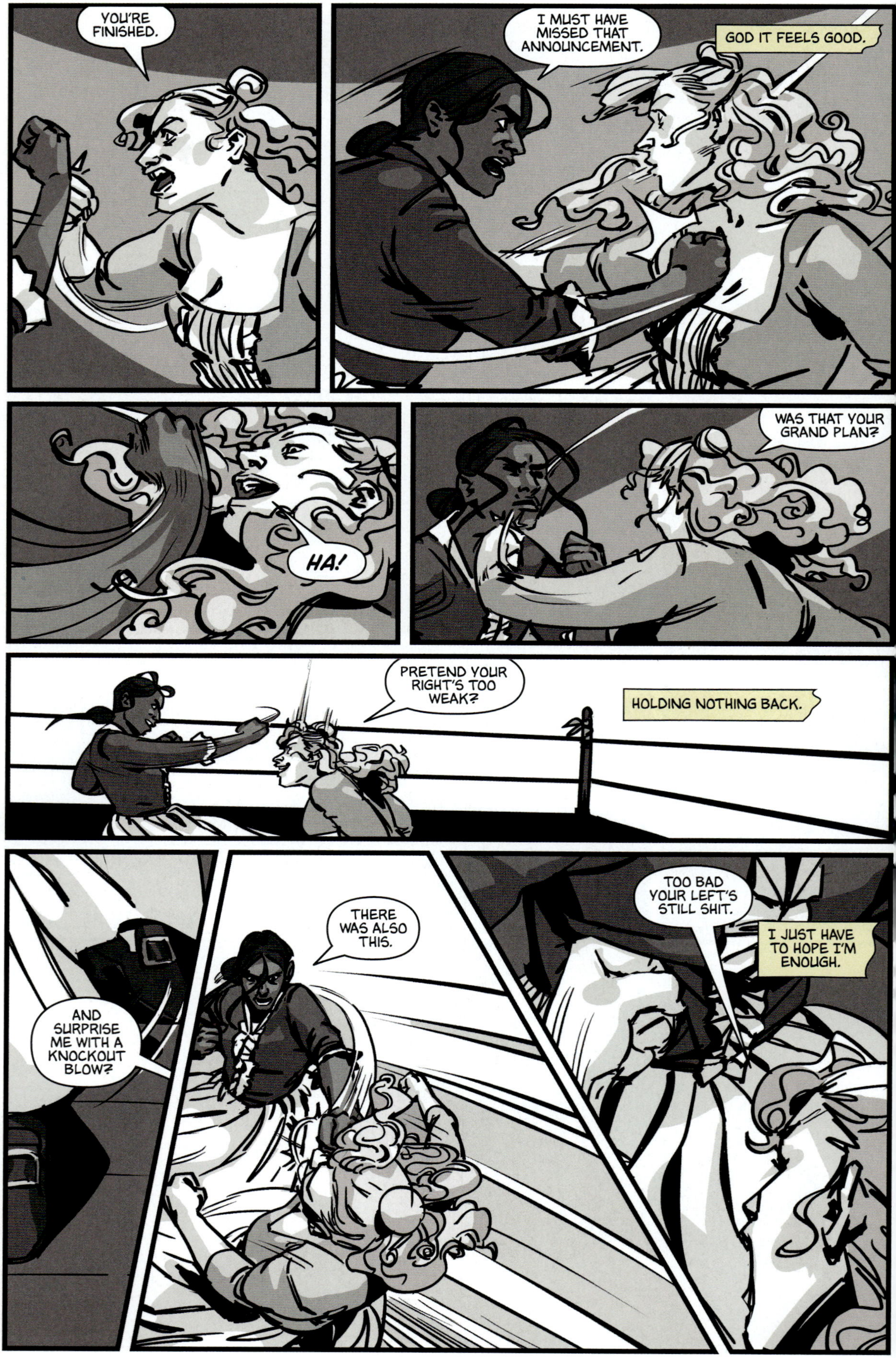

YOU'RE FINISHED.
I MUST HAVE MISSED THAT ANNOUNCEMENT.
GOD IT FEELS GOOD.
HA!
WAS THAT YOUR GRAND PLAN?
PRETEND YOUR RIGHT'S TOO WEAK?
HOLDING NOTHING BACK.
AND SURPRISE ME WITH A KNOCKOUT BLOW?
THERE WAS ALSO THIS.
TOO BAD YOUR LEFT'S STILL SHIT.
I JUST HAVE TO HOPE I'M ENOUGH.

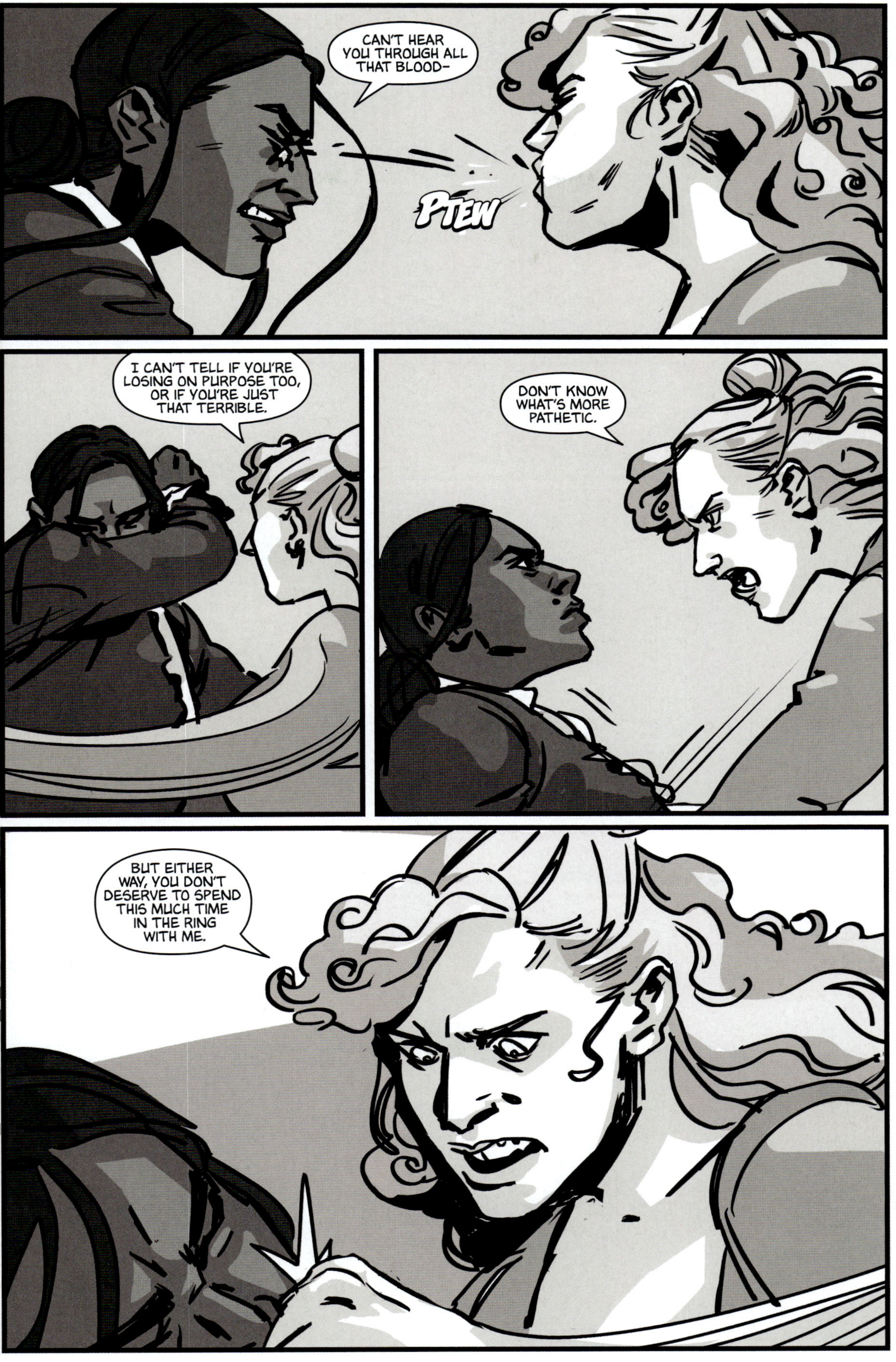
CAN'T HEAR YOU THROUGH ALL THAT BLOOD-
PTEW
I CAN'T TELL IF YOU'RE LOSING ON PURPOSE TOO, OR IF YOU'RE JUST THAT TERRIBLE.
DON'T KNOW WHAT'S MORE PATHETIC.
BUT EITHER WAY, YOU DON'T DESERVE TO SPEND THIS MUCH TIME IN THE RING WITH ME.

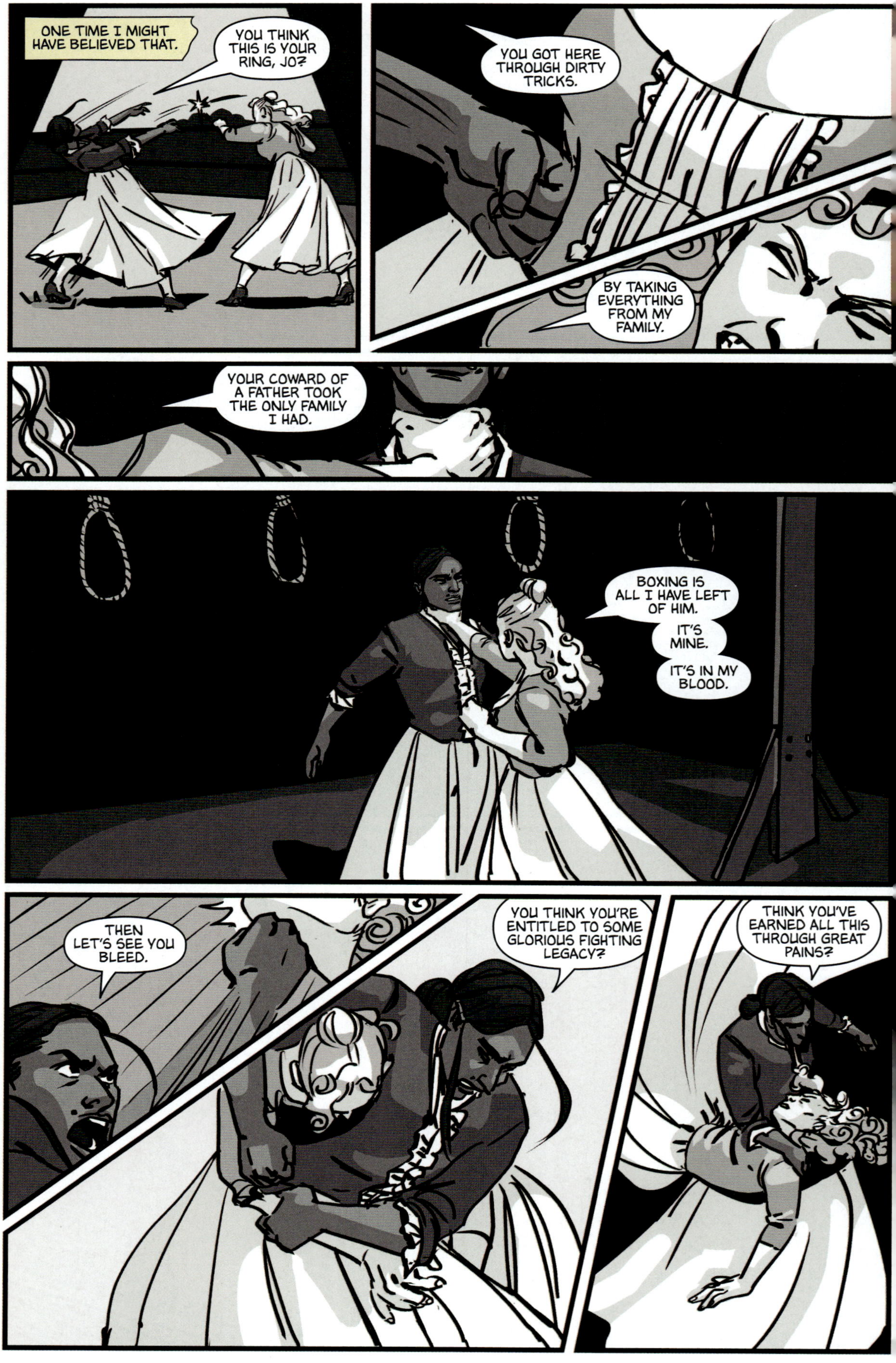
ONE TIME I MIGHT HAVE BELIEVED THAT.
YOU THINK THIS IS YOUR RING, JO?
YOU GOT HERE THROUGH DIRTY TRICKS.
BY TAKING EVERYTHING FROM MY FAMILY.
YOUR COWARD OF A FATHER TOOK THE ONLY FAMILY I HAD.
BOXING IS ALL I HAVE LEFT OF HIM.
IT'S MINE.
IT'S IN MY BLOOD.
THEN LET'S SEE YOU BLEED.
YOU THINK YOU'RE ENTITLED TO SOME GLORIOUS FIGHTING LEGACY?
THINK YOU'VE EARNED ALL THIS THROUGH GREAT PAINS?

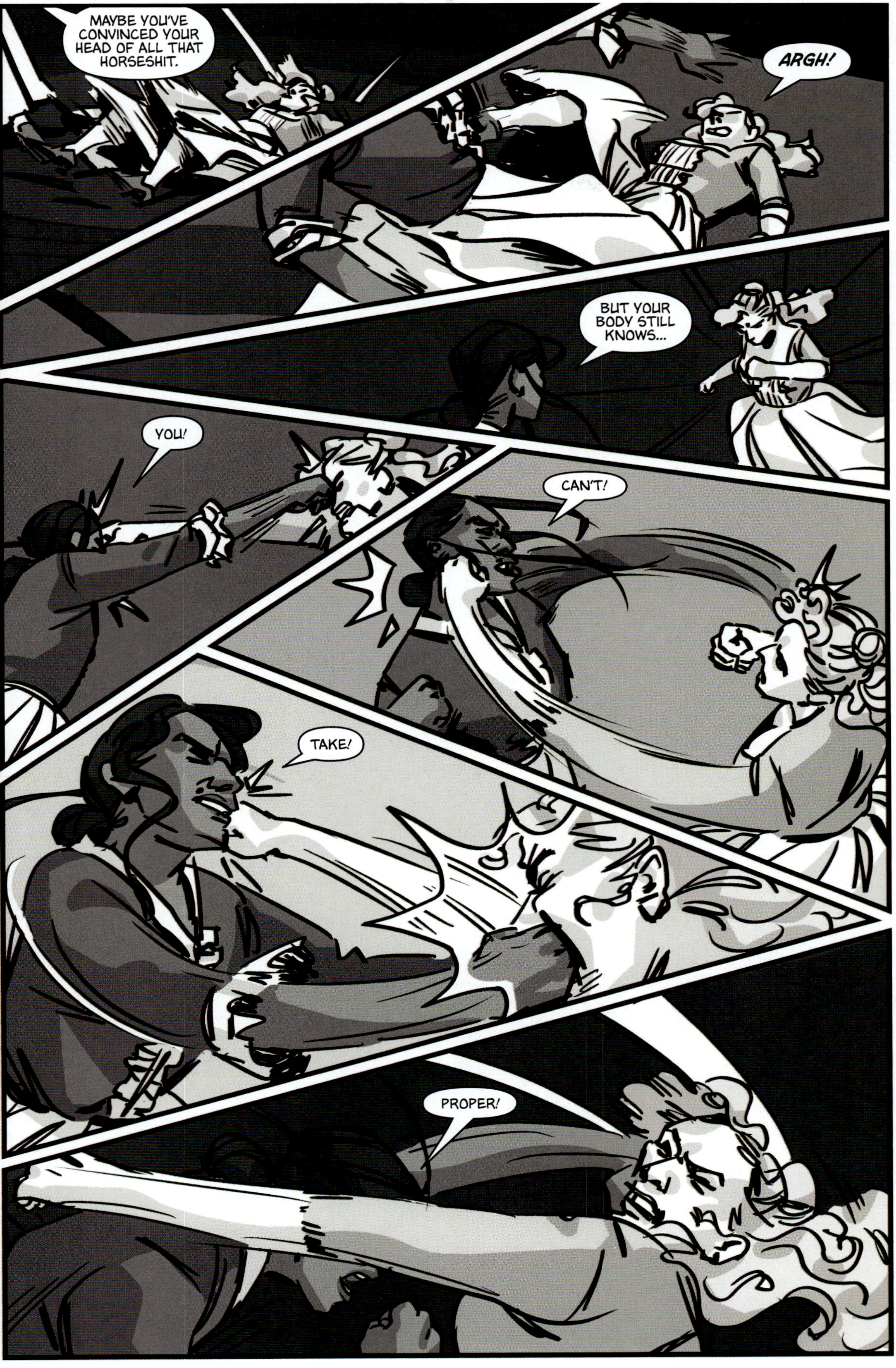
MAYBE YOU'VE CONVINCED YOUR HEAD OF ALL THAT HORSESHIT.
ARGH!
BUT YOUR BODY STILL KNOWS...
YOU!
CAN'T!
TAKE!
PROPER!

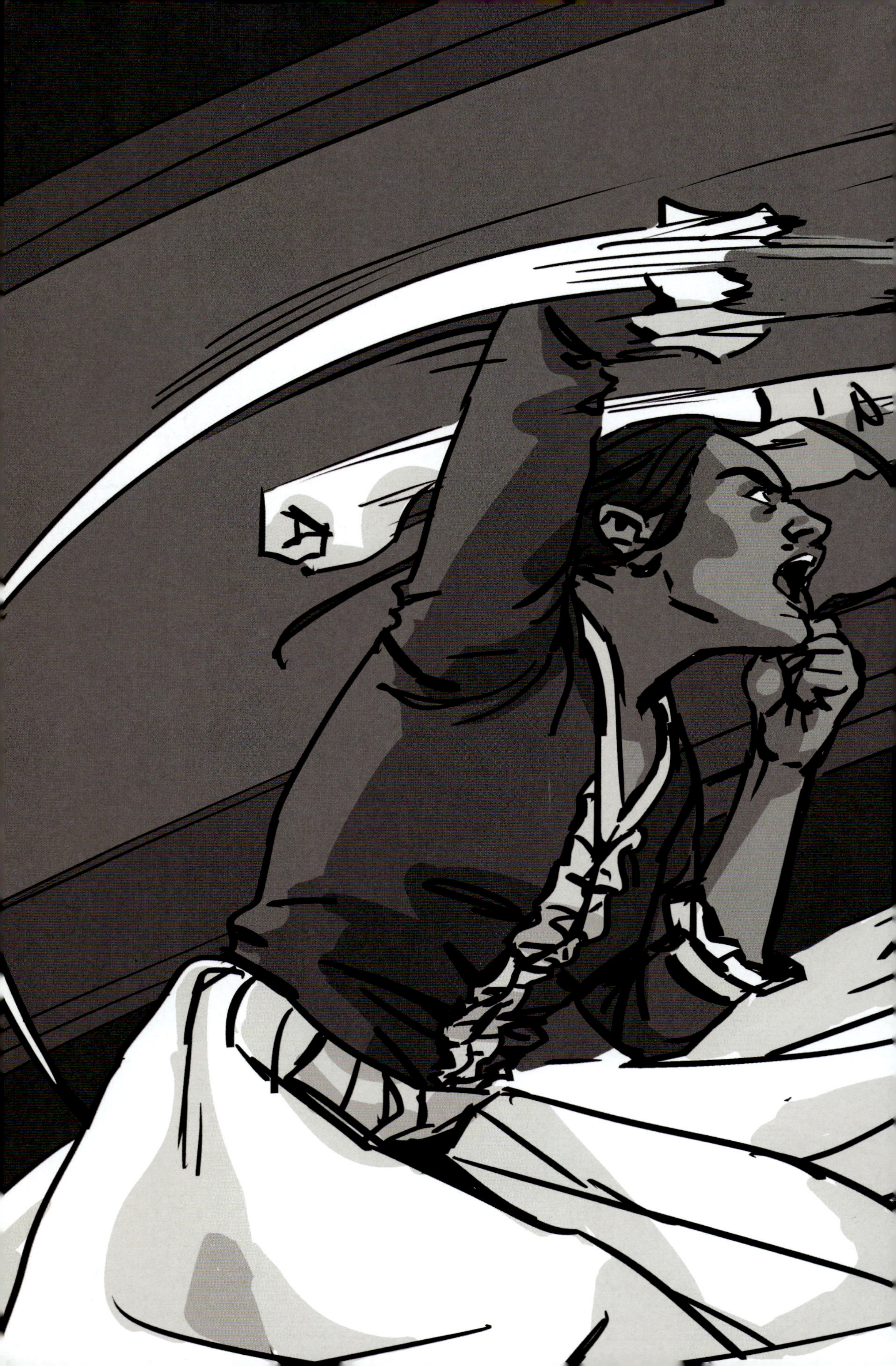

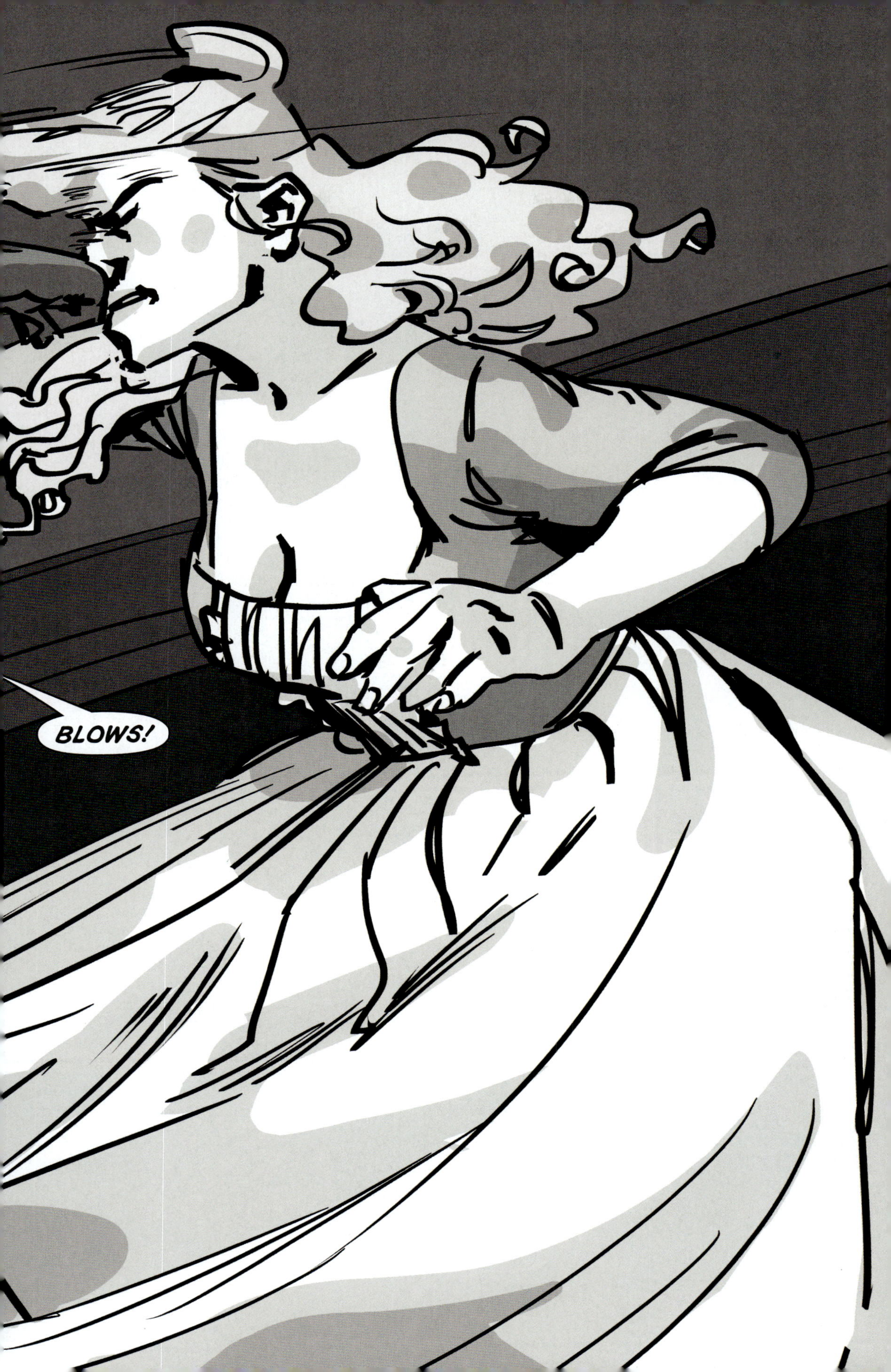
BLOWS!

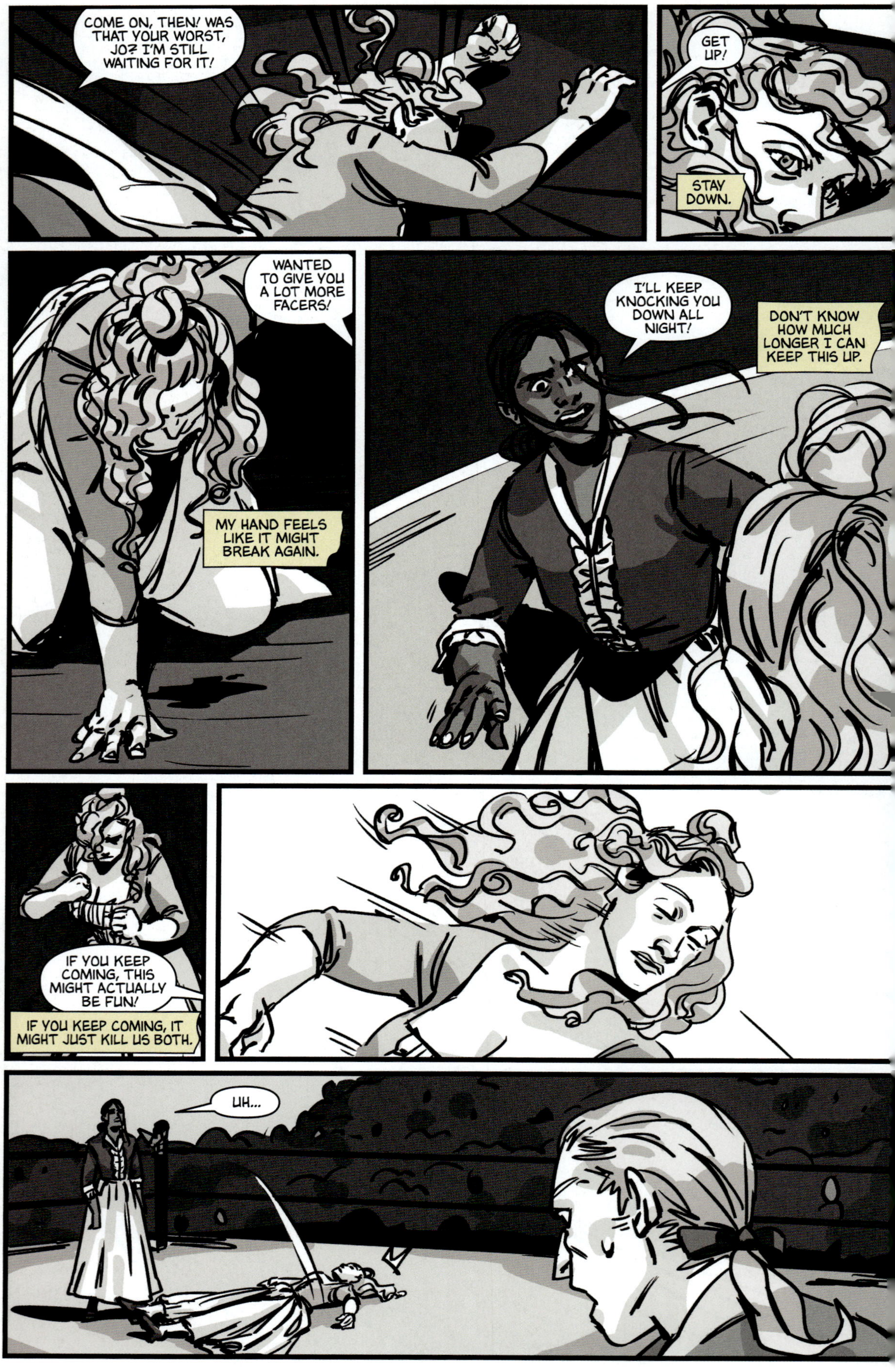

COME ON, THEN! WAS THAT YOUR WORST, JO? I'M STILL WAITING FOR IT!
GET UP!
STAY DOWN.
WANTED TO GIVE YOU A LOT MORE FACERS!
MY HAND FEELS LIKE IT MIGHT BREAK AGAIN.
I'LL KEEP KNOCKING YOU DOWN ALL NIGHT!
DON'T KNOW HOW MUCH LONGER I CAN KEEP THIS UP.
IF YOU KEEP COMING, THIS MIGHT ACTUALLY BE FUN!
IF YOU KEEP COMING, IT MIGHT JUST KILL US BOTH.
UH...

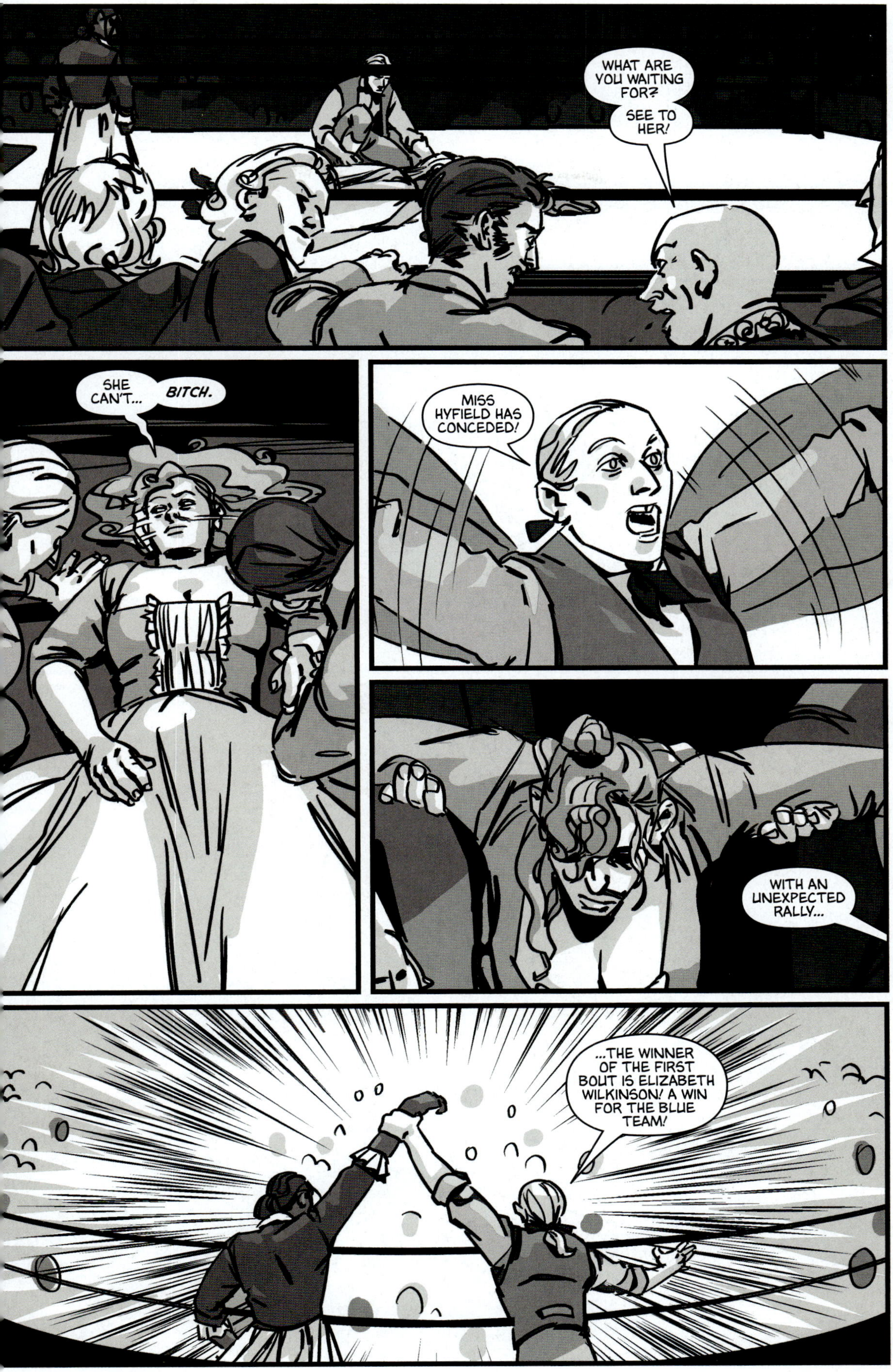
WHAT ARE YOU WAITING FOR?
SEE TO HER!
SHE CAN'T...
BITCH.
MISS HYFIELD HAS CONCEDED!
WITH AN UNEXPECTED RALLY...
...THE WINNER OF THE FIRST BOUT IS ELIZABETH WILKINSON! A WIN FOR THE BLUE TEAM!

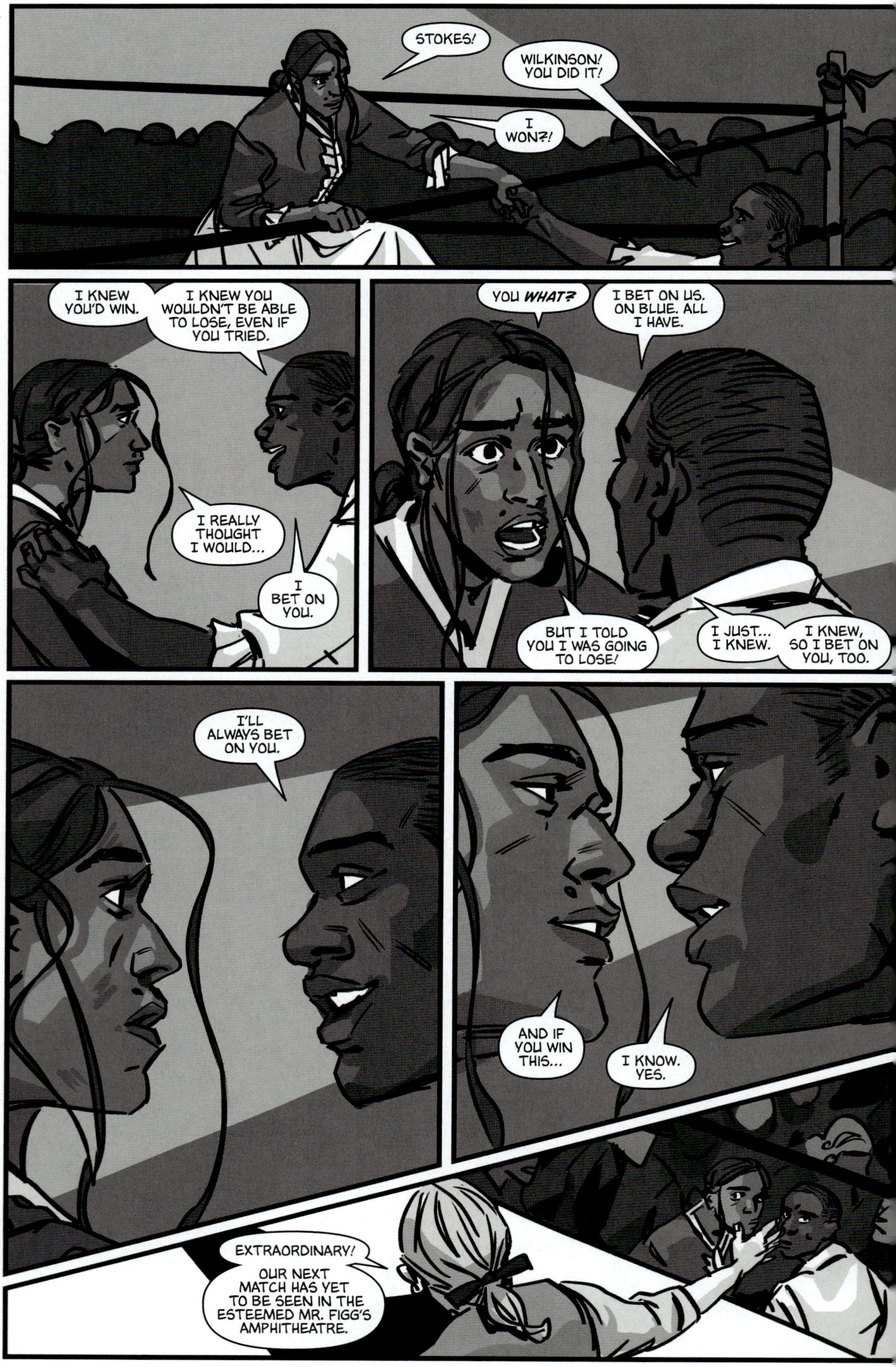
STOKES!
WILKINSON! YOU DID IT!
I WON?!
I KNEW YOU'D WIN.
I KNEW YOU WOULDN'T BE ABLE TO LOSE, EVEN IF YOU TRIED.
I REALLY THOUGHT I WOULD...
I BET ON YOU.
YOU *WHAT?*
I BET ON US. ON BLUE. ALL I HAVE.
BUT I TOLD YOU I WAS GOING TO LOSE!
I JUST... I KNEW.
I KNEW, SO I BET ON YOU, TOO.
I'LL ALWAYS BET ON YOU.
AND IF YOU WIN THIS...
I KNOW. YES.
EXTRAORDINARY!
OUR NEXT MATCH HAS YET TO BE SEEN IN THE ESTEEMED MR. FIGG'S AMPHITHEATRE.

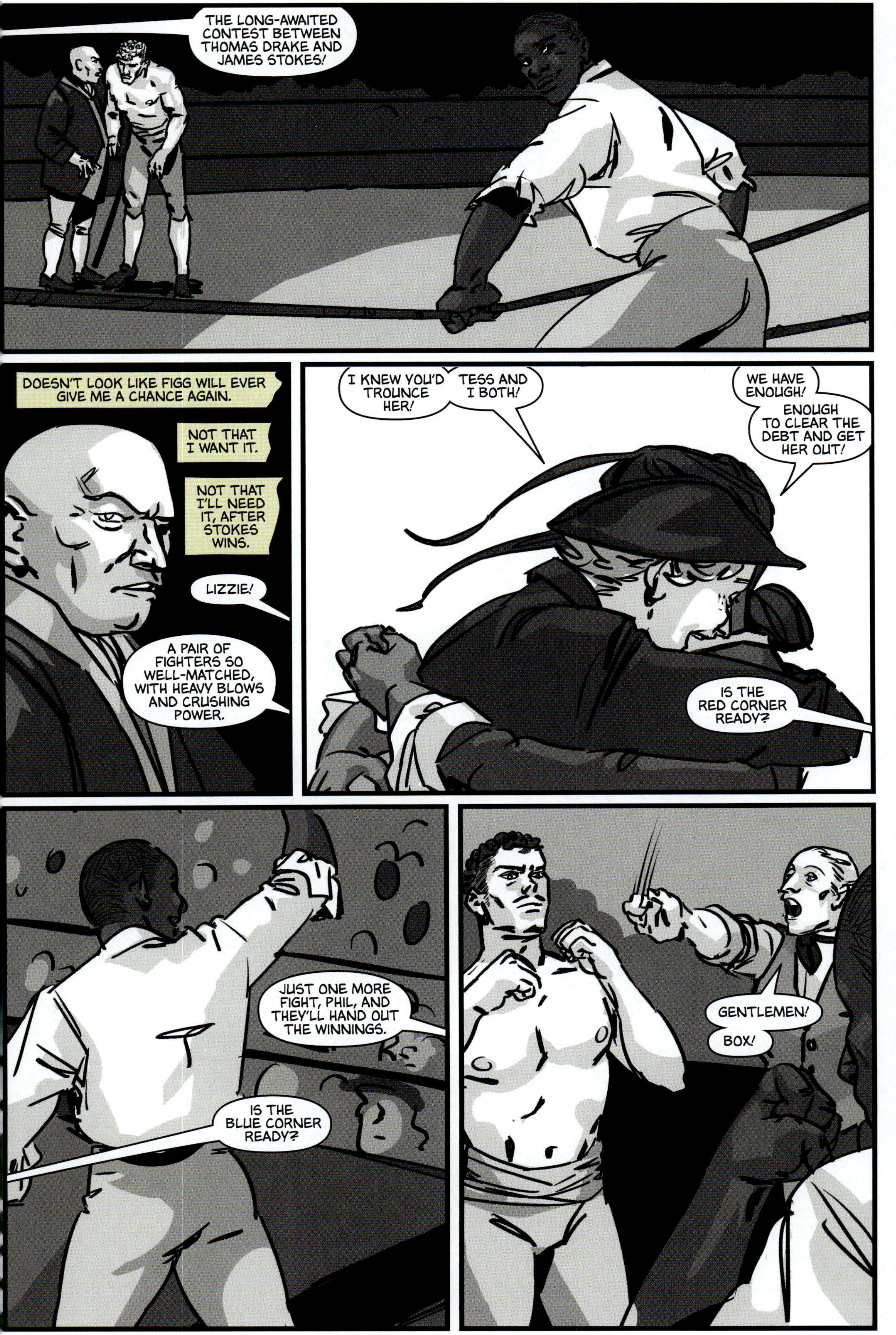
THE LONG-AWAITED CONTEST BETWEEN THOMAS DRAKE AND JAMES STOKES!
DOESN'T LOOK LIKE FIGG WILL EVER GIVE ME A CHANCE AGAIN.
NOT THAT I WANT IT.
NOT THAT I'LL NEED IT, AFTER STOKES WINS.
LIZZIE!
A PAIR OF FIGHTERS SO WELL-MATCHED, WITH HEAVY BLOWS AND CRUSHING POWER.
I KNEW YOU'D TROUNCE HER!
TESS AND I BOTH!
WE HAVE ENOUGH!
ENOUGH TO CLEAR THE DEBT AND GET HER OUT!
IS THE RED CORNER READY?
JUST ONE MORE FIGHT, PHIL, AND THEY'LL HAND OUT THE WINNINGS.
IS THE BLUE CORNER READY?
GENTLEMEN!
BOX!

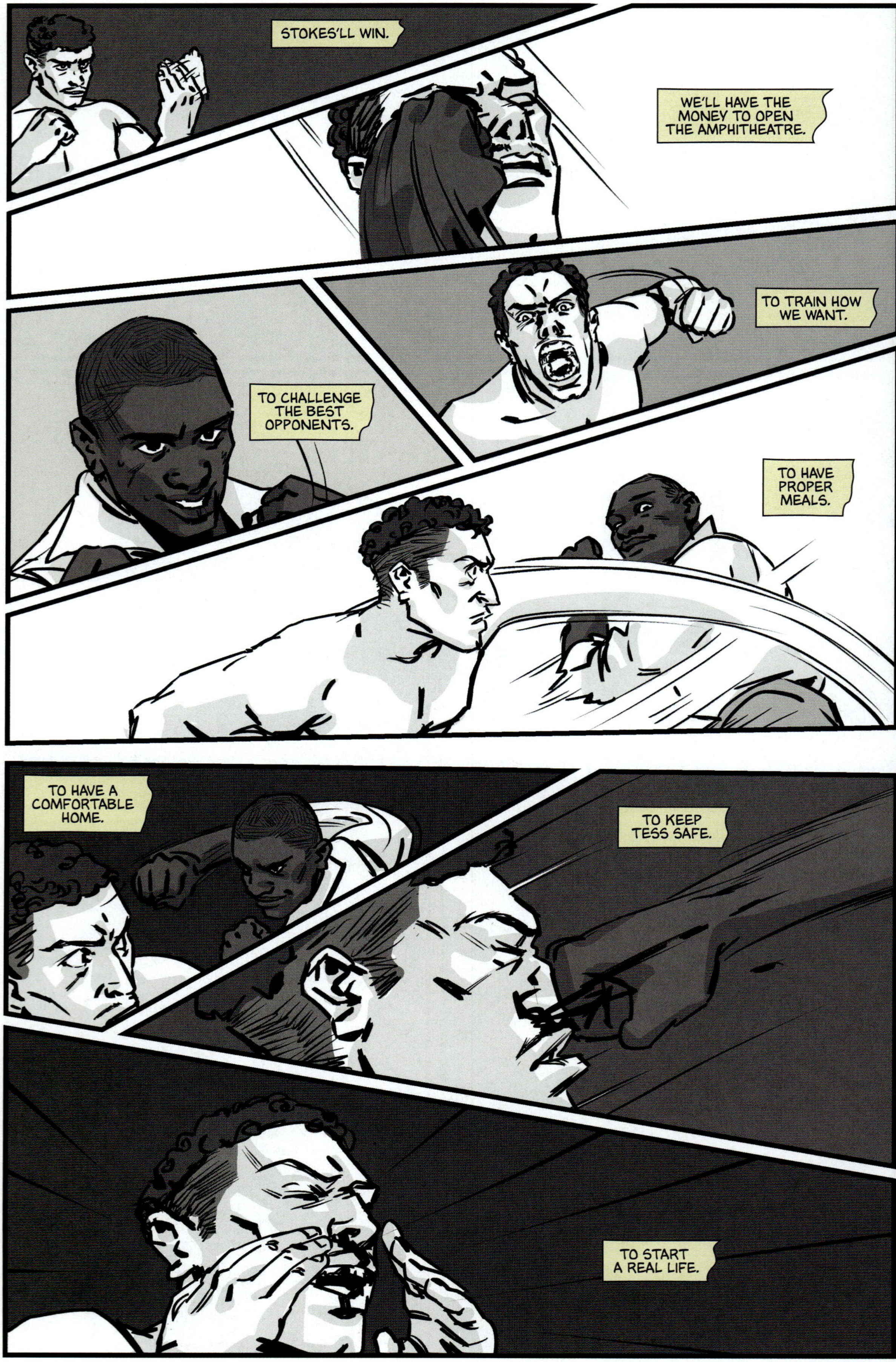
STOKES'LL WIN.
WE'LL HAVE THE MONEY TO OPEN THE AMPHITHEATRE.
TO TRAIN HOW WE WANT.
TO CHALLENGE THE BEST OPPONENTS.
TO HAVE PROPER MEALS.
TO HAVE A COMFORTABLE HOME.
TO KEEP TESS SAFE.
TO START A REAL LIFE.

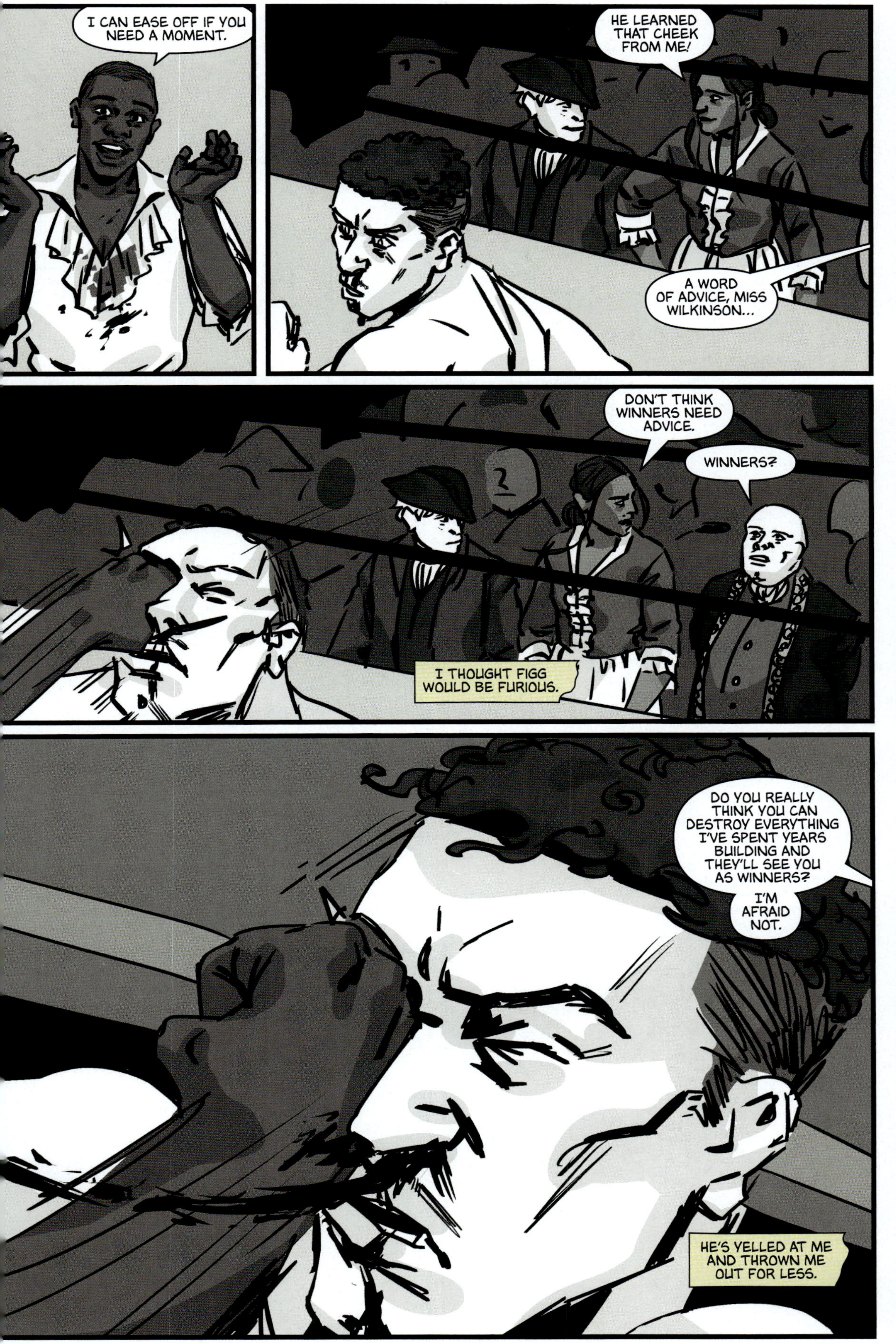
I CAN EASE OFF IF YOU NEED A MOMENT.
HE LEARNED THAT CHEEK FROM ME!
A WORD OF ADVICE, MISS WILKINSON...
DON'T THINK WINNERS NEED ADVICE.
WINNERS?
I THOUGHT FIGG WOULD BE FURIOUS.
DO YOU REALLY THINK YOU CAN DESTROY EVERYTHING I'VE SPENT YEARS BUILDING AND THEY'LL SEE YOU AS WINNERS?
I'M AFRAID NOT.
HE'S YELLED AT ME AND THROWN ME OUT FOR LESS.

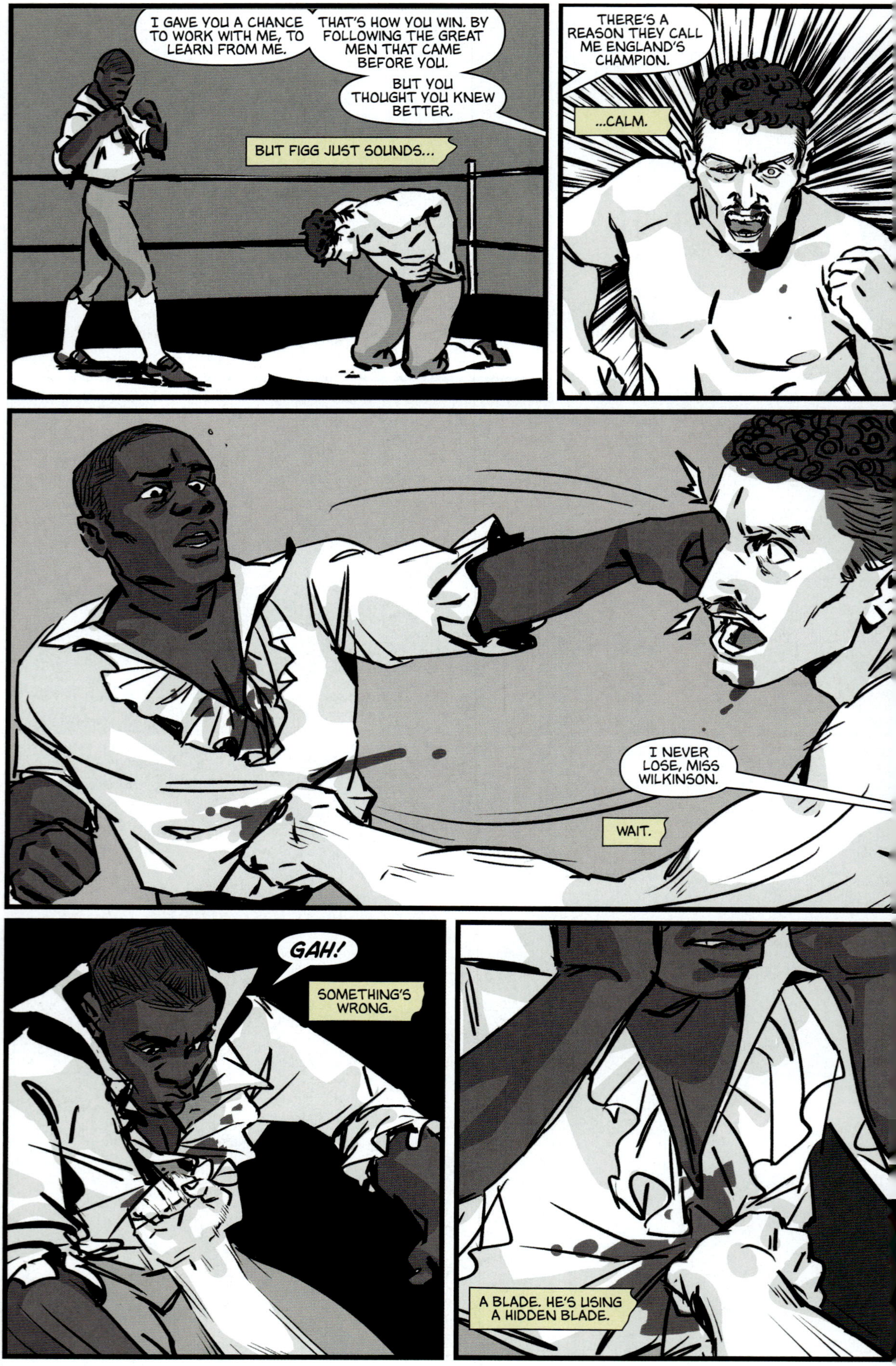
I GAVE YOU A CHANCE TO WORK WITH ME, TO LEARN FROM ME.
THAT'S HOW YOU WIN. BY FOLLOWING THE GREAT MEN THAT CAME BEFORE YOU.
BUT YOU THOUGHT YOU KNEW BETTER.
BUT FIGG JUST SOUNDS...
THERE'S A REASON THEY CALL ME ENGLAND'S CHAMPION.
...CALM.
I NEVER LOSE, MISS WILKINSON.
WAIT.
GAH!
SOMETHING'S WRONG.
A BLADE. HE'S USING A HIDDEN BLADE.

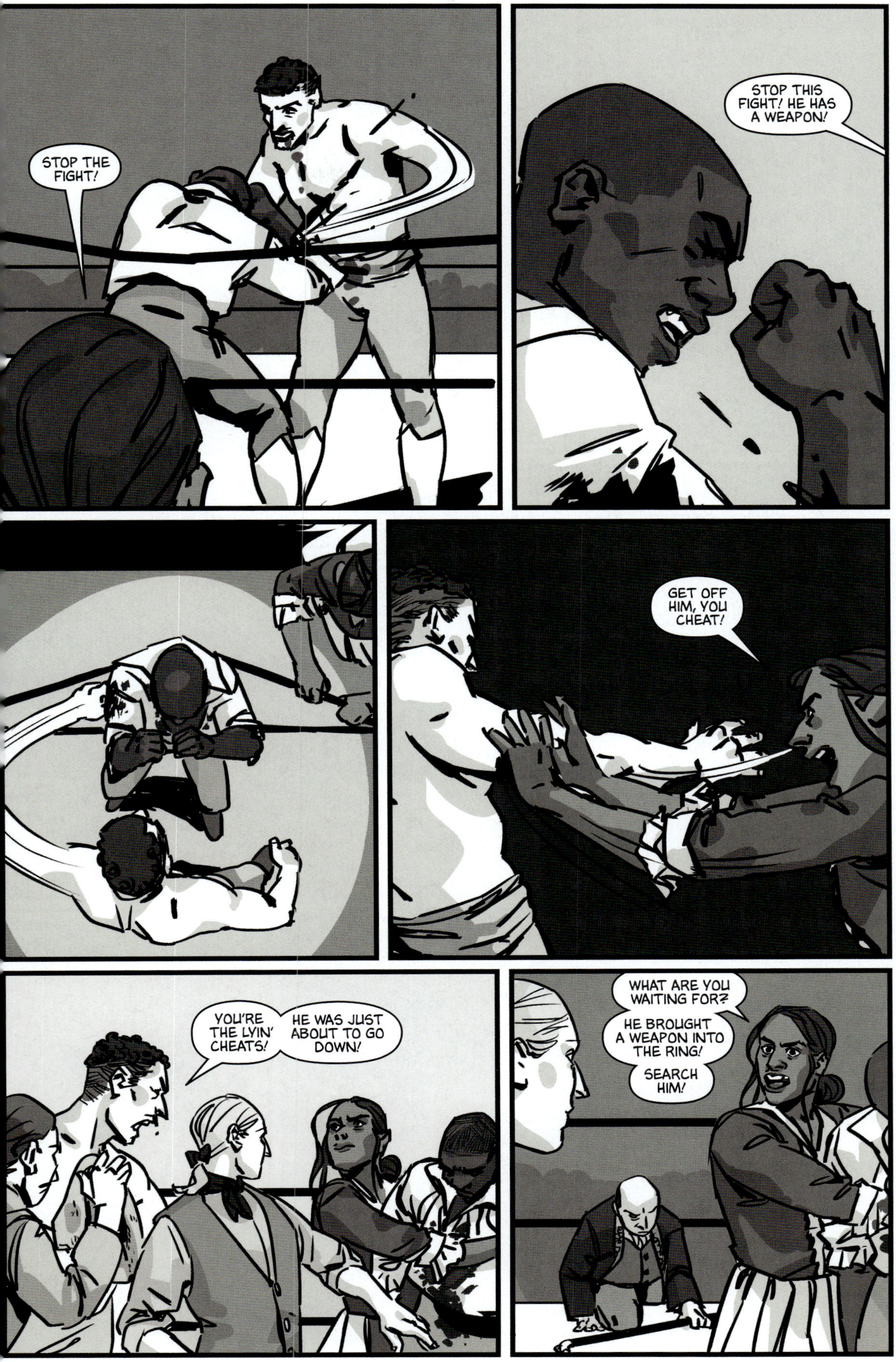
STOP THE FIGHT!
STOP THIS FIGHT! HE HAS A WEAPON!
GET OFF HIM, YOU CHEAT!
HE WAS JUST ABOUT TO GO DOWN!
YOU'RE THE LYIN' CHEATS!
WHAT ARE YOU WAITING FOR?
HE BROUGHT A WEAPON INTO THE RING!
SEARCH HIM!

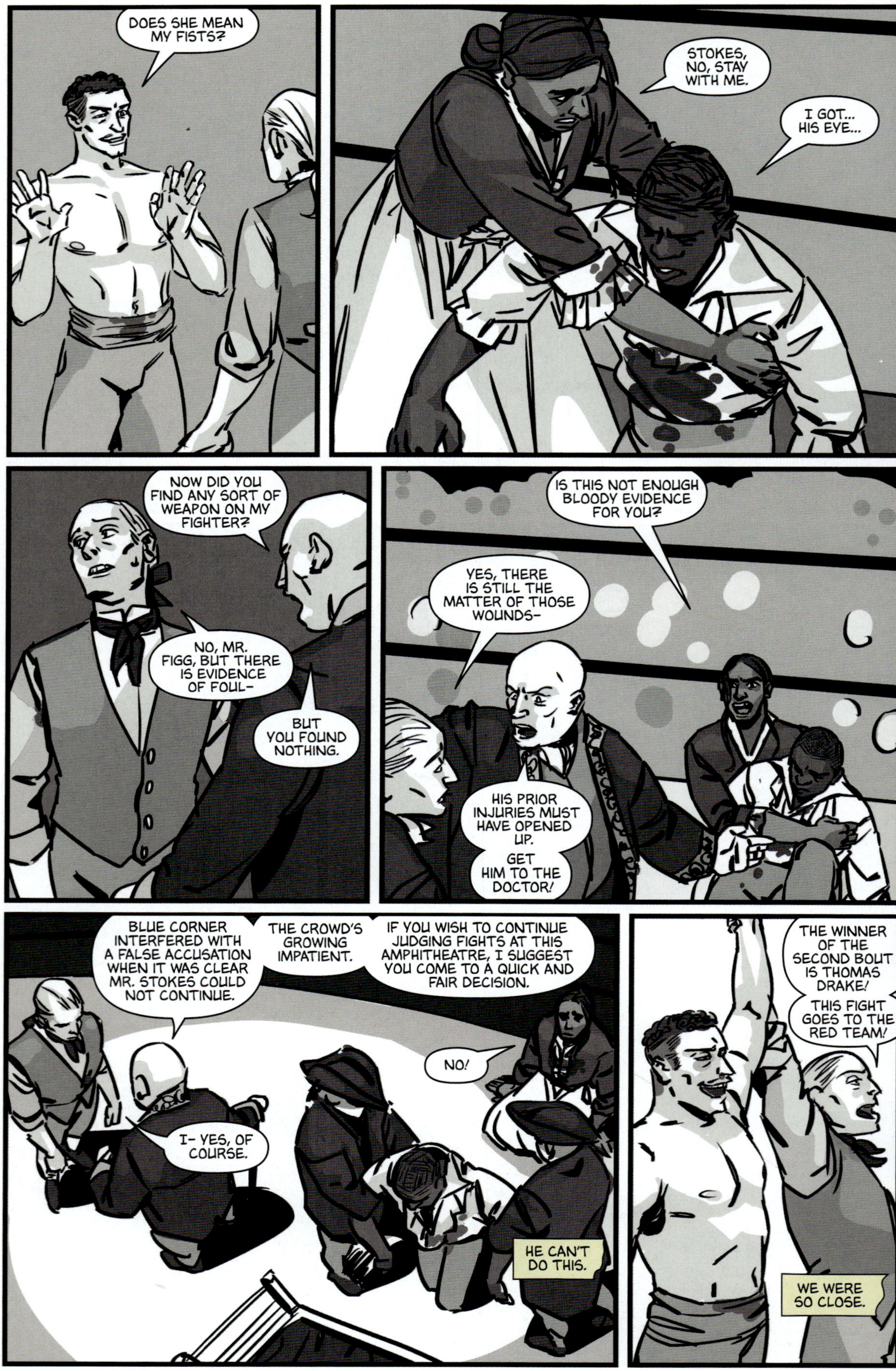
DOES SHE MEAN MY FISTS?
STOKES, NO, STAY WITH ME.
I GOT... HIS EYE...
NOW DID YOU FIND ANY SORT OF WEAPON ON MY FIGHTER?
NO, MR. FIGG, BUT THERE IS EVIDENCE OF FOUL-
BUT YOU FOUND NOTHING.
IS THIS NOT ENOUGH BLOODY EVIDENCE FOR YOU?
YES, THERE IS STILL THE MATTER OF THOSE WOUNDS-
HIS PRIOR INJURIES MUST HAVE OPENED UP.
GET HIM TO THE DOCTOR!
BLUE CORNER INTERFERED WITH A FALSE ACCUSATION WHEN IT WAS CLEAR MR. STOKES COULD NOT CONTINUE.
THE CROWD'S GROWING IMPATIENT.
IF YOU WISH TO CONTINUE JUDGING FIGHTS AT THIS AMPHITHEATRE, I SUGGEST YOU COME TO A QUICK AND FAIR DECISION.
NO!
I- YES, OF COURSE.
HE CAN'T DO THIS.
THE WINNER OF THE SECOND BOUT IS THOMAS DRAKE!
THIS FIGHT GOES TO THE RED TEAM!
WE WERE SO CLOSE.

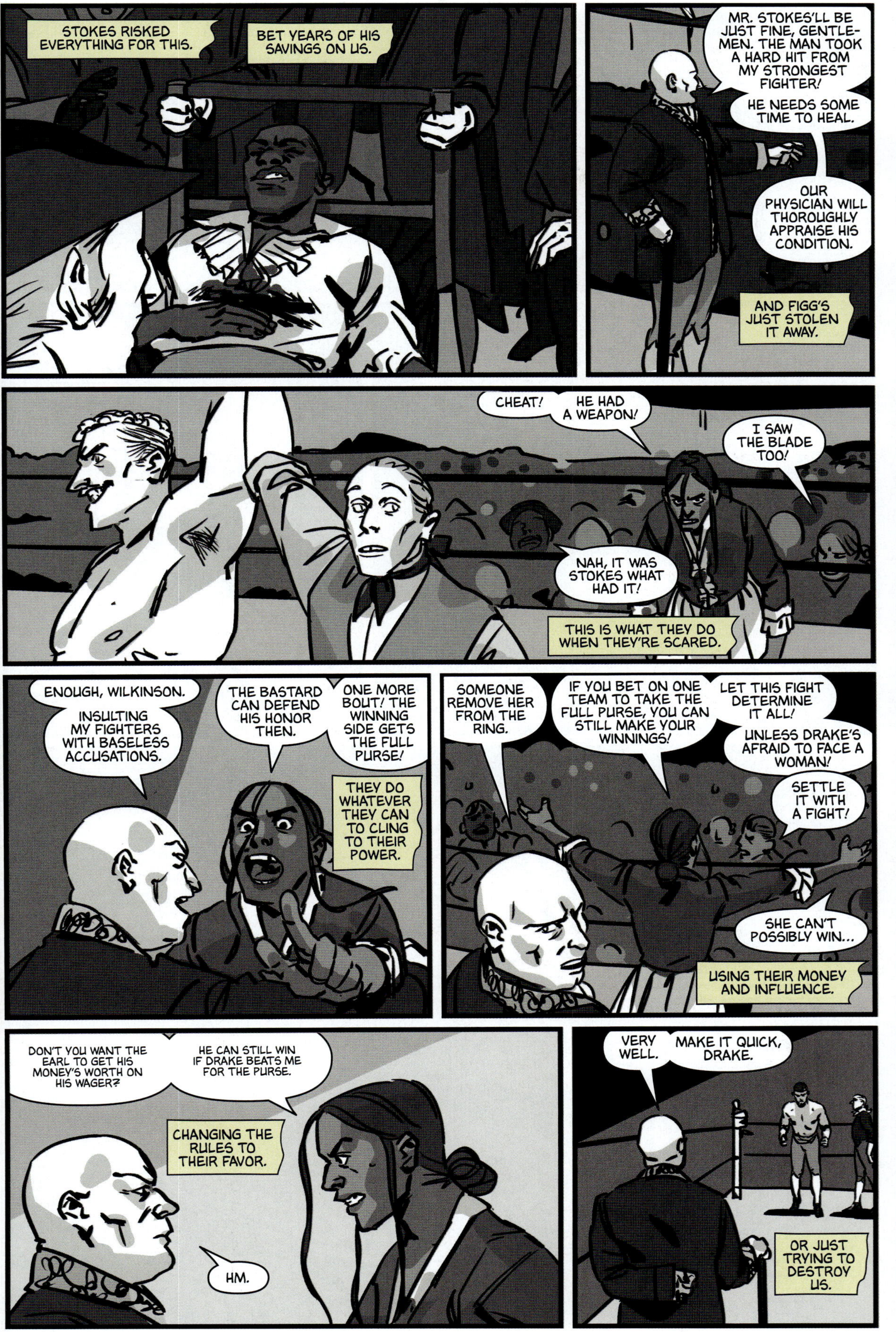
STOKES RISKED EVERYTHING FOR THIS.
BET YEARS OF HIS SAVINGS ON US.
MR. STOKES'LL BE JUST FINE, GENTLEMEN. THE MAN TOOK A HARD HIT FROM MY STRONGEST FIGHTER!
HE NEEDS SOME TIME TO HEAL.
OUR PHYSICIAN WILL THOROUGHLY APPRAISE HIS CONDITION.
AND FIGG'S JUST STOLEN IT AWAY.
CHEAT!
HE HAD A WEAPON!
I SAW THE BLADE TOO!
NAH, IT WAS STOKES WHAT HAD IT!
THIS IS WHAT THEY DO WHEN THEY'RE SCARED.
ENOUGH, WILKINSON.
INSULTING MY FIGHTERS WITH BASELESS ACCUSATIONS.
THE BASTARD CAN DEFEND HIS HONOR THEN.
ONE MORE BOUT! THE WINNING SIDE GETS THE FULL PURSE!
THEY DO WHATEVER THEY CAN TO CLING TO THEIR POWER.
SOMEONE REMOVE HER FROM THE RING.
IF YOU BET ON ONE TEAM TO TAKE THE FULL PURSE, YOU CAN STILL MAKE YOUR WINNINGS!
LET THIS FIGHT DETERMINE IT ALL!
UNLESS DRAKE'S AFRAID TO FACE A WOMAN!
SETTLE IT WITH A FIGHT!
SHE CAN'T POSSIBLY WIN...
USING THEIR MONEY AND INFLUENCE.
DON'T YOU WANT THE EARL TO GET HIS MONEY'S WORTH ON HIS WAGER?
HE CAN STILL WIN IF DRAKE BEATS ME FOR THE PURSE.
CHANGING THE RULES TO THEIR FAVOR.
HM.
VERY WELL.
MAKE IT QUICK, DRAKE.
OR JUST TRYING TO DESTROY US.

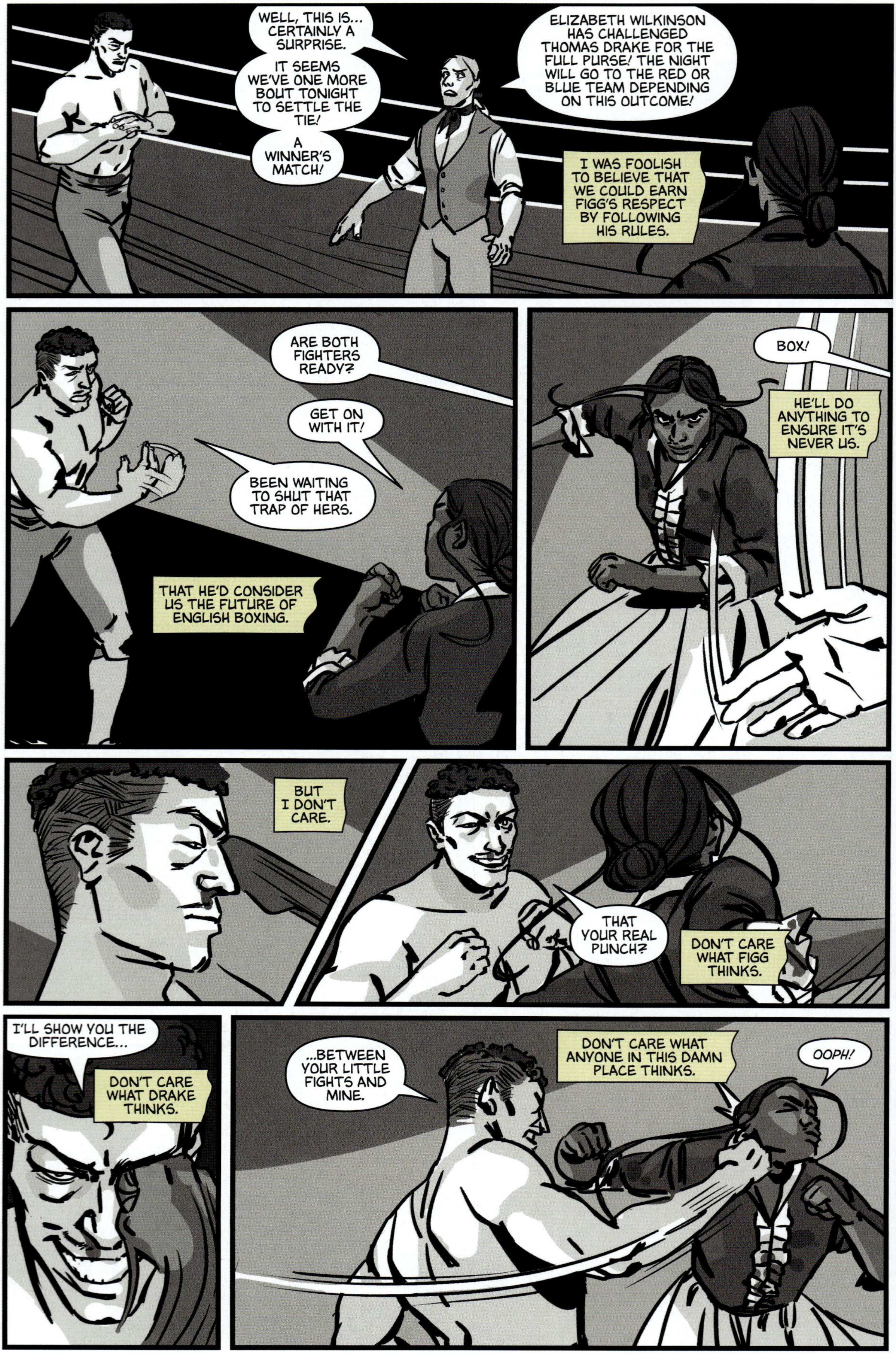

WELL, THIS IS... CERTAINLY A SURPRISE.
IT SEEMS WE'VE ONE MORE BOUT TONIGHT TO SETTLE THE TIE!
A WINNER'S MATCH!
ELIZABETH WILKINSON HAS CHALLENGED THOMAS DRAKE FOR THE FULL PURSE! THE NIGHT WILL GO TO THE RED OR BLUE TEAM DEPENDING ON THIS OUTCOME!
I WAS FOOLISH TO BELIEVE THAT WE COULD EARN FIGG'S RESPECT BY FOLLOWING HIS RULES.
ARE BOTH FIGHTERS READY?
GET ON WITH IT!
BEEN WAITING TO SHUT THAT TRAP OF HERS.
THAT HE'D CONSIDER US THE FUTURE OF ENGLISH BOXING.
BOX!
HE'LL DO ANYTHING TO ENSURE IT'S NEVER US.
BUT I DON'T CARE.
THAT YOUR REAL PUNCH?
DON'T CARE WHAT FIGG THINKS.
I'LL SHOW YOU THE DIFFERENCE...
DON'T CARE WHAT DRAKE THINKS.
...BETWEEN YOUR LITTLE FIGHTS AND MINE.
DON'T CARE WHAT ANYONE IN THIS DAMN PLACE THINKS.
OOPH!

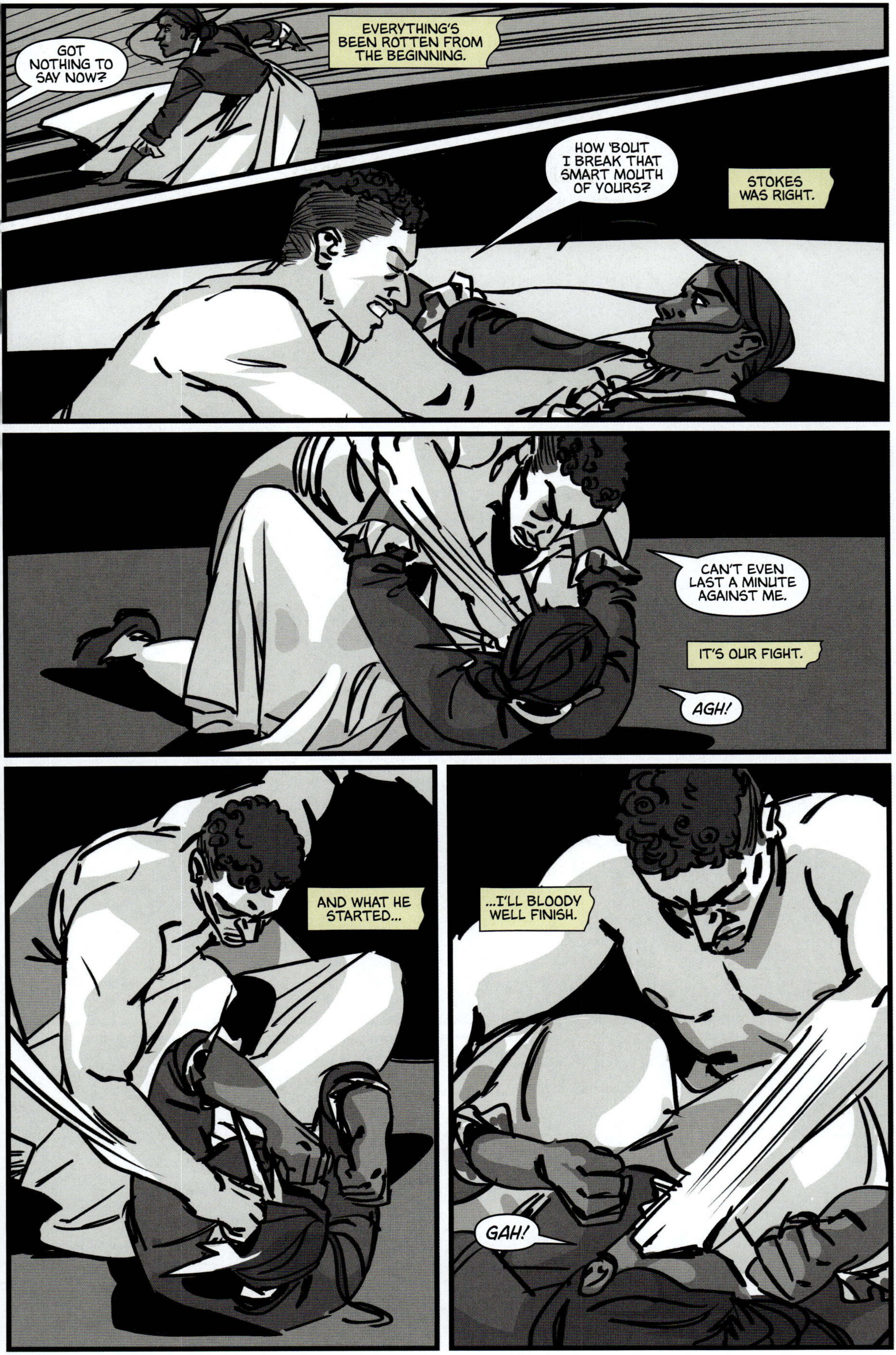
GOT NOTHING TO SAY NOW?
EVERYTHING'S BEEN ROTTEN FROM THE BEGINNING.
HOW 'BOUT I BREAK THAT SMART MOUTH OF YOURS?
STOKES WAS RIGHT.
CAN'T EVEN LAST A MINUTE AGAINST ME.
IT'S OUR FIGHT.
AGH!
AND WHAT HE STARTED...
...I'LL BLOODY WELL FINISH.
GAH!

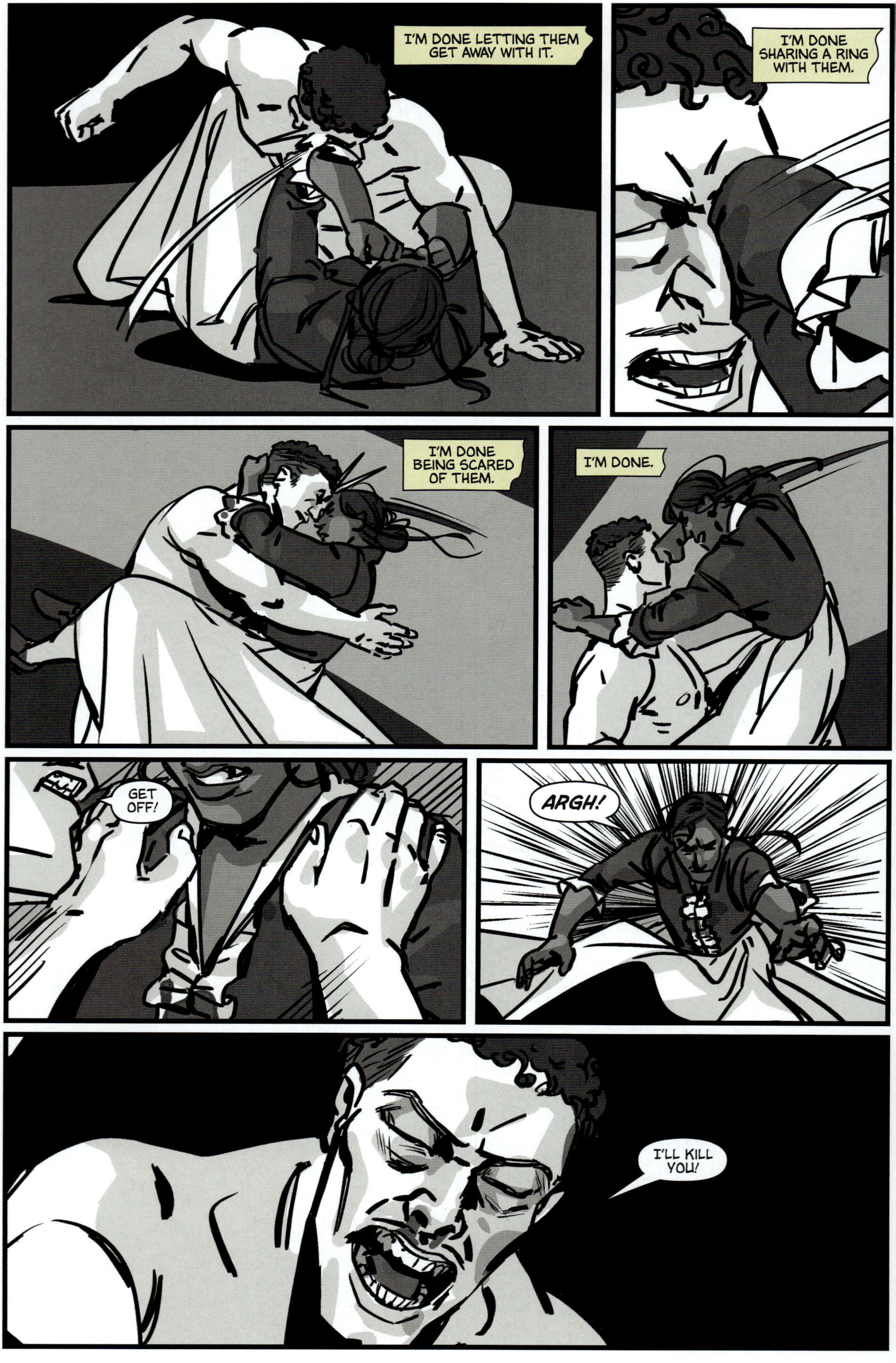
I'M DONE LETTING THEM GET AWAY WITH IT.
I'M DONE SHARING A RING WITH THEM.
I'M DONE BEING SCARED OF THEM.
I'M DONE.
GET OFF!
ARGH!
I'LL KILL YOU!

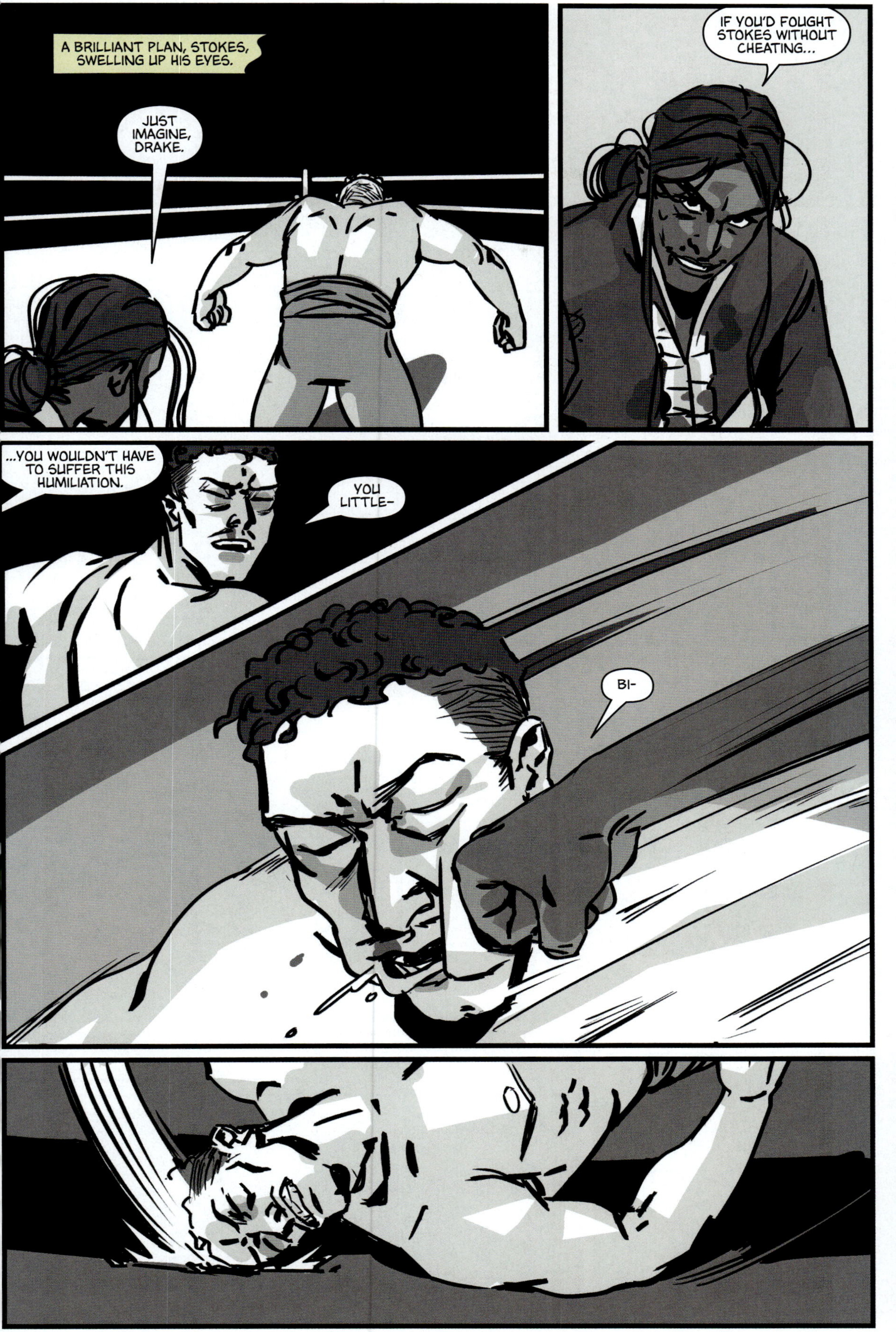
A BRILLIANT PLAN, STOKES, SWELLING UP HIS EYES.
JUST IMAGINE, DRAKE.
IF YOU'D FOUGHT STOKES WITHOUT CHEATING...
...YOU WOULDN'T HAVE TO SUFFER THIS HUMILIATION.
YOU LITTLE-
BI-

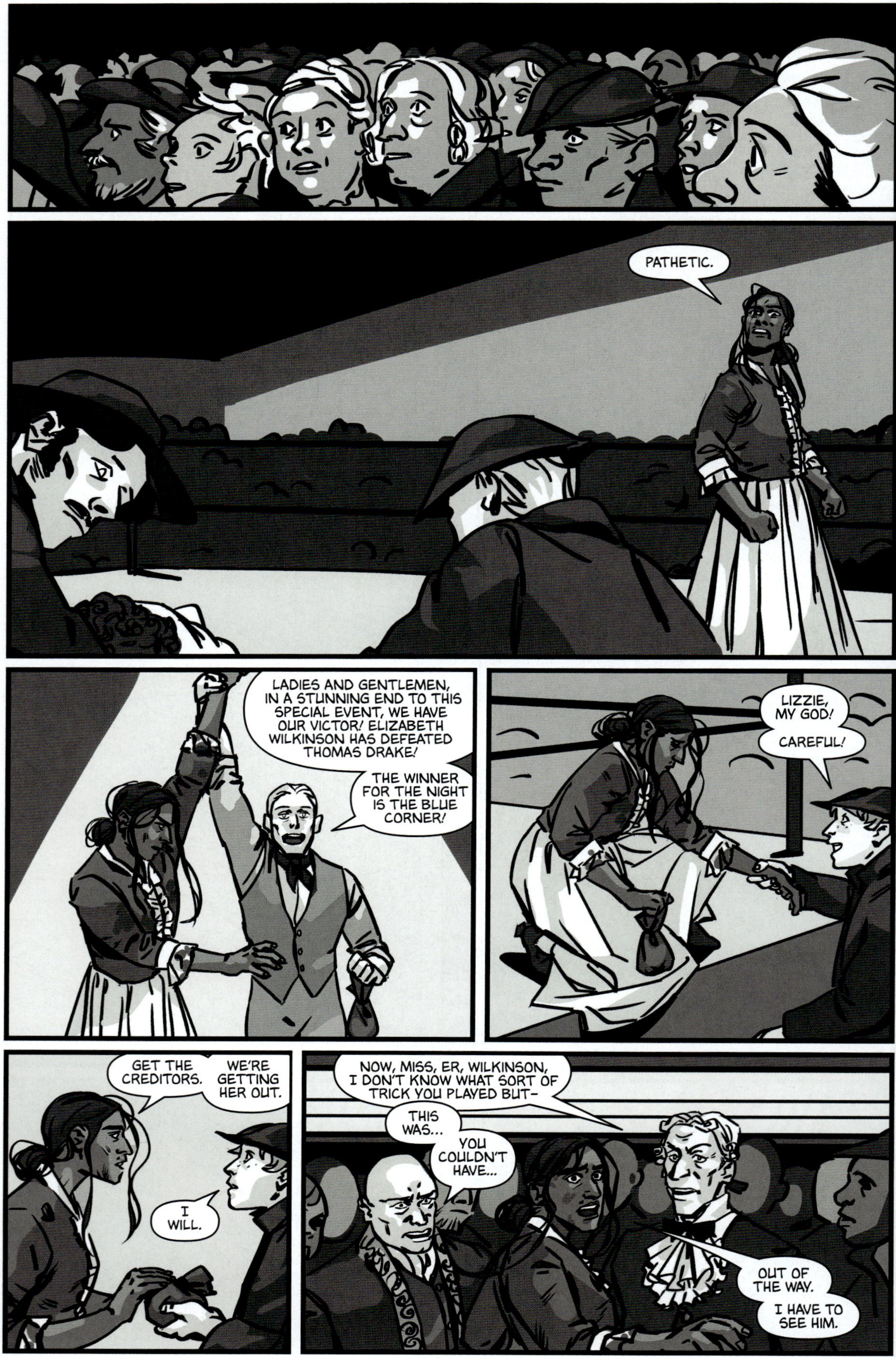
PATHETIC.
LADIES AND GENTLEMEN, IN A STUNNING END TO THIS SPECIAL EVENT, WE HAVE OUR VICTOR! ELIZABETH WILKINSON HAS DEFEATED THOMAS DRAKE!
THE WINNER FOR THE NIGHT IS THE BLUE CORNER!
LIZZIE, MY GOD!
CAREFUL!
GET THE CREDITORS.
WE'RE GETTING HER OUT.
I WILL.
NOW, MISS, ER, WILKINSON, I DON'T KNOW WHAT SORT OF TRICK YOU PLAYED BUT-
THIS WAS...
YOU COULDN'T HAVE...
OUT OF THE WAY.
I HAVE TO SEE HIM.

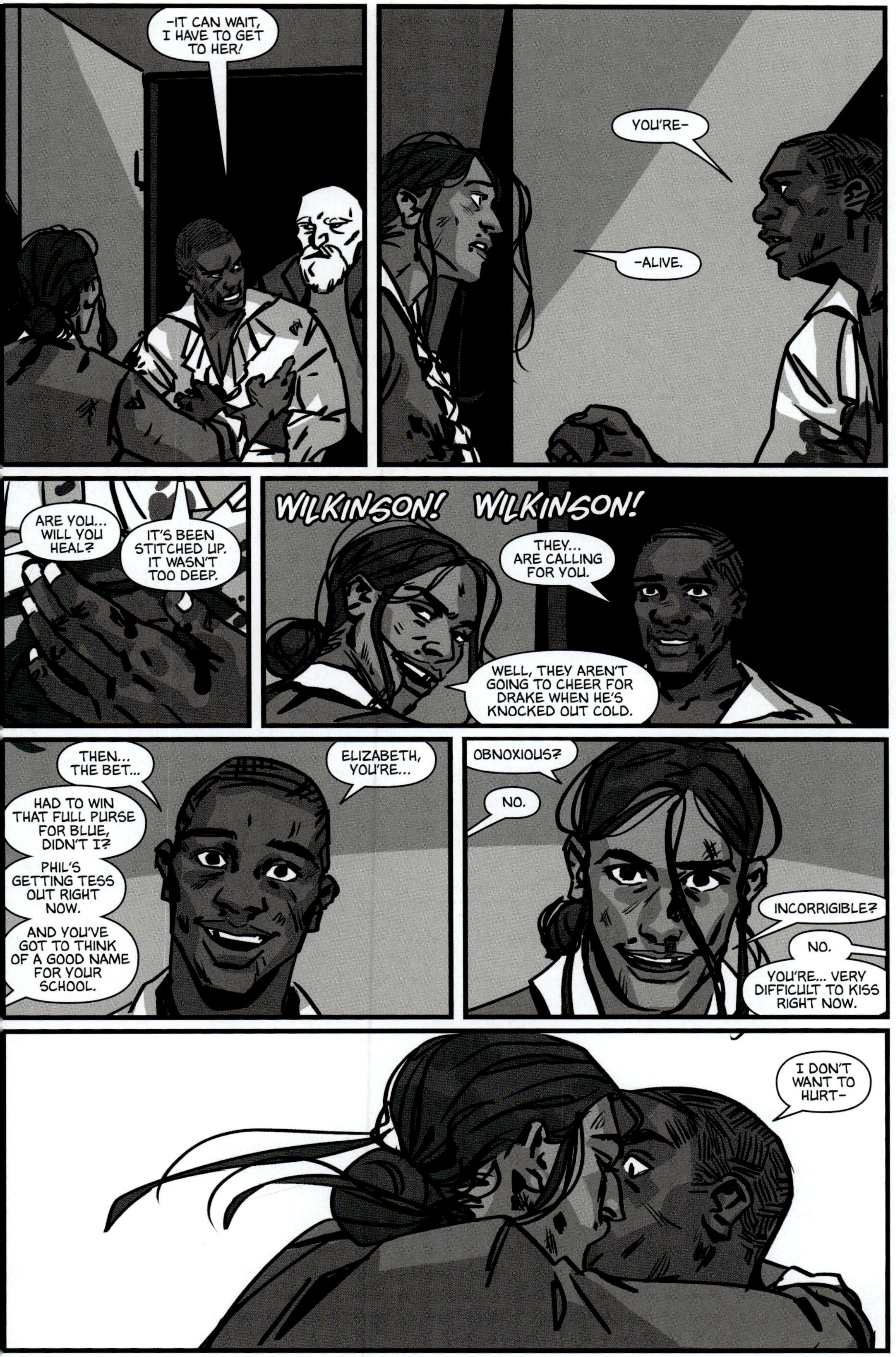

-IT CAN WAIT, I HAVE TO GET TO HER!
YOU'RE-
-ALIVE.
ARE YOU... WILL YOU HEAL?
IT'S BEEN STITCHED UP. IT WASN'T TOO DEEP.
WILKINSON! WILKINSON!
THEY... ARE CALLING FOR YOU.
WELL, THEY AREN'T GOING TO CHEER FOR DRAKE WHEN HE'S KNOCKED OUT COLD.
THEN... THE BET...
HAD TO WIN THAT FULL PURSE FOR BLUE, DIDN'T I?
PHIL'S GETTING TESS OUT RIGHT NOW.
AND YOU'VE GOT TO THINK OF A GOOD NAME FOR YOUR SCHOOL.
ELIZABETH, YOU'RE...
OBNOXIOUS?
NO.
INCORRIGIBLE?
NO.
YOU'RE... VERY DIFFICULT TO KISS RIGHT NOW.
I DON'T WANT TO HURT-

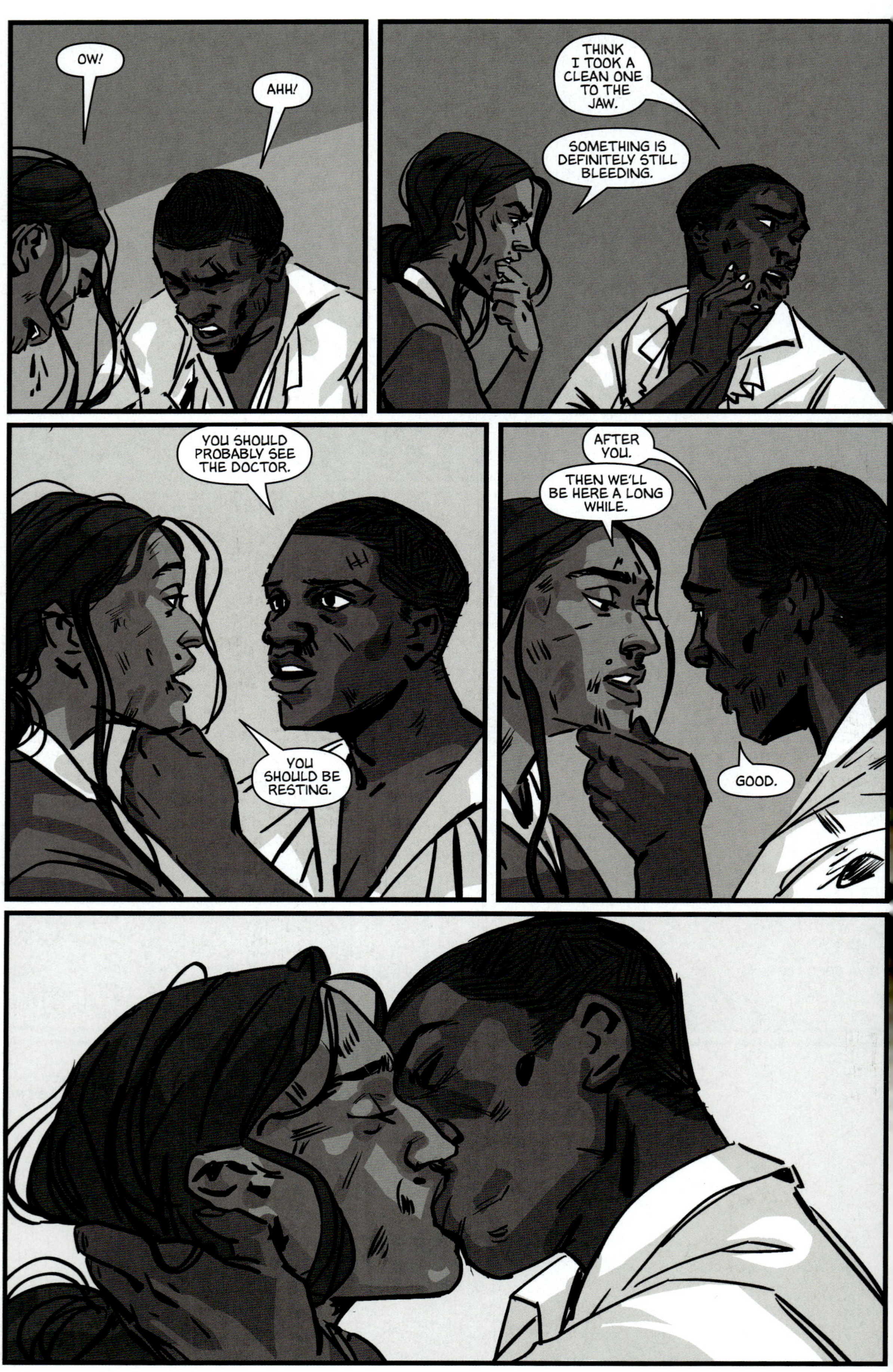
OW!
AHH!
THINK I TOOK A CLEAN ONE TO THE JAW.
SOMETHING IS DEFINITELY STILL BLEEDING.
YOU SHOULD PROBABLY SEE THE DOCTOR.
YOU SHOULD BE RESTING.
AFTER YOU.
THEN WE'LL BE HERE A LONG WHILE.
GOOD.

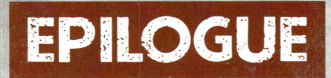

EPILOGUE

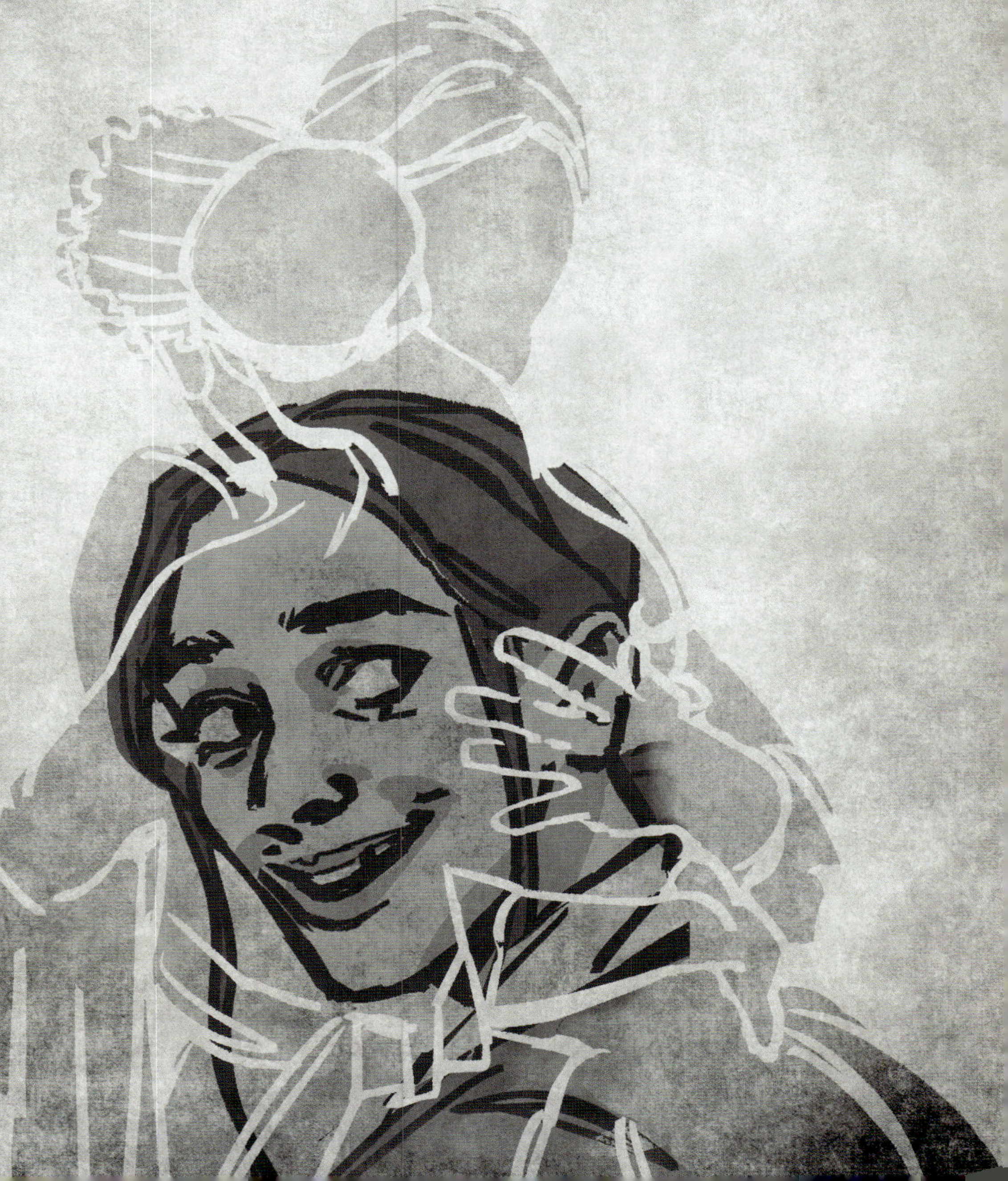

"I, Elizabeth Stokes, of the famous City of London, being well known by the Name of the Invincible City Championess for my Abilities and Judgement in the abovesaid science; having never engaged with any of my own Sex but I always came off with Victory and Applause, shall make no Apology for accepting the Challenge of this Irish Heroine..."

(Original response printed in The Weekly Journal, or The British Gazetteer, Issue 74)

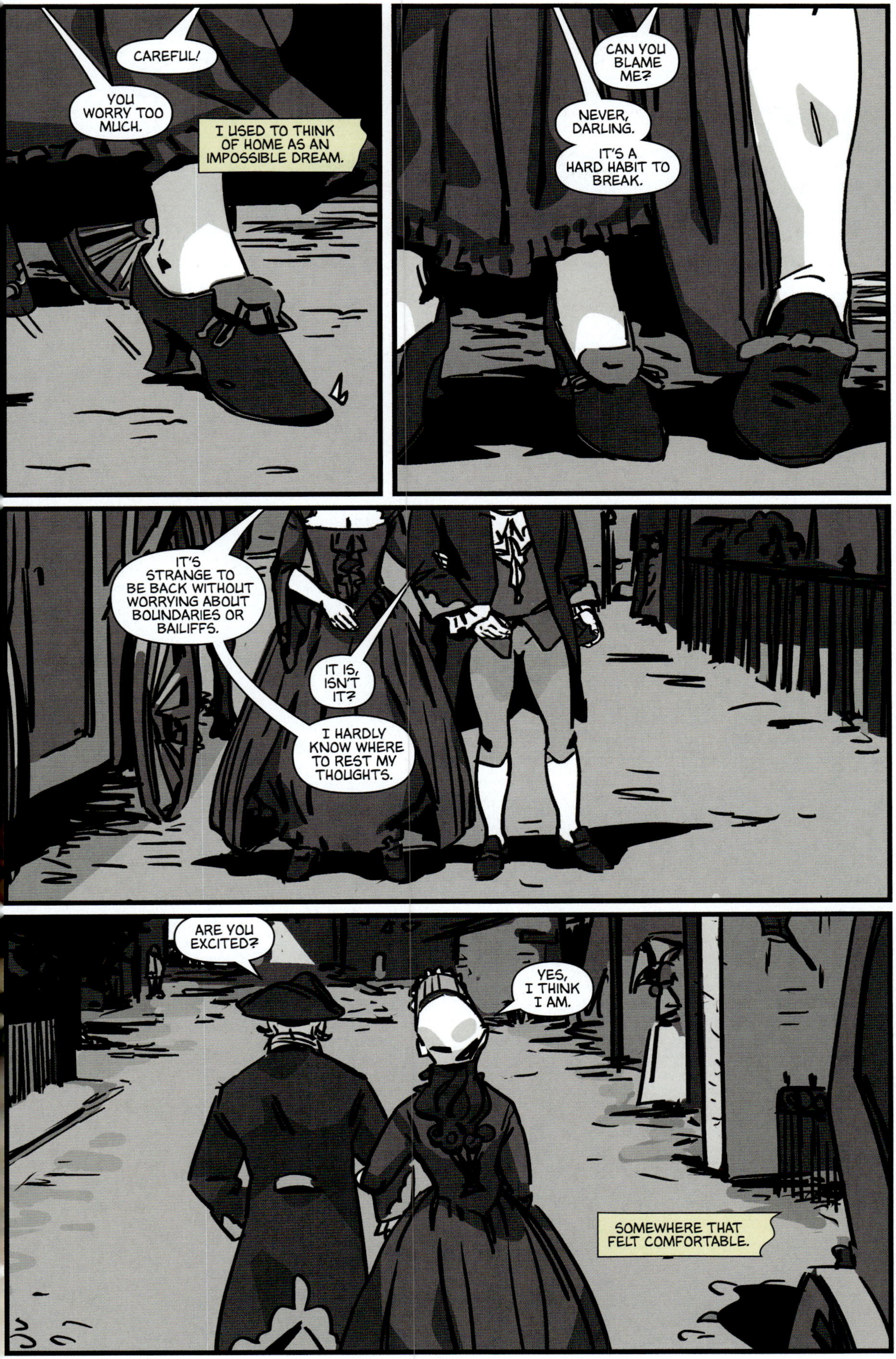
CAREFUL!
YOU WORRY TOO MUCH.
I USED TO THINK OF HOME AS AN IMPOSSIBLE DREAM.
CAN YOU BLAME ME?
NEVER, DARLING.
IT'S A HARD HABIT TO BREAK.
IT'S STRANGE TO BE BACK WITHOUT WORRYING ABOUT BOUNDARIES OR BAILIFFS.
IT IS, ISN'T IT?
I HARDLY KNOW WHERE TO REST MY THOUGHTS.
ARE YOU EXCITED?
YES, I THINK I AM.
SOMEWHERE THAT FELT COMFORTABLE.

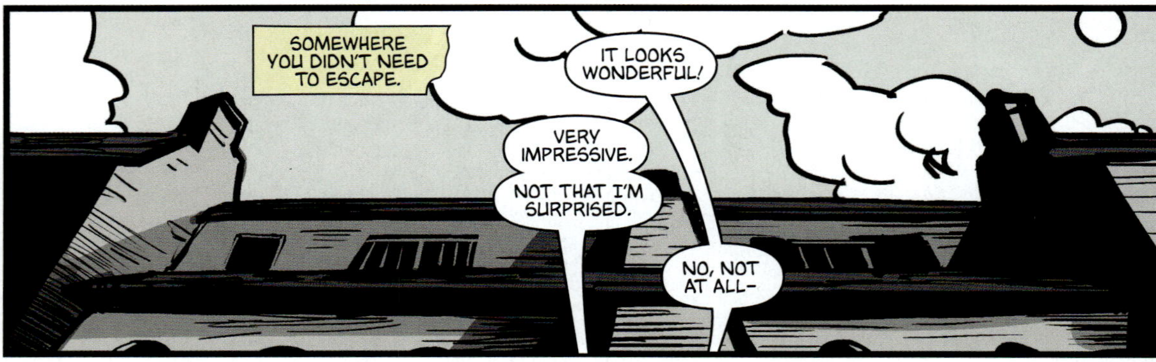
SOMEWHERE YOU DIDN'T NEED TO ESCAPE.
IT LOOKS WONDERFUL!
VERY IMPRESSIVE.
NOT THAT I'M SURPRISED.
NO, NOT AT ALL-

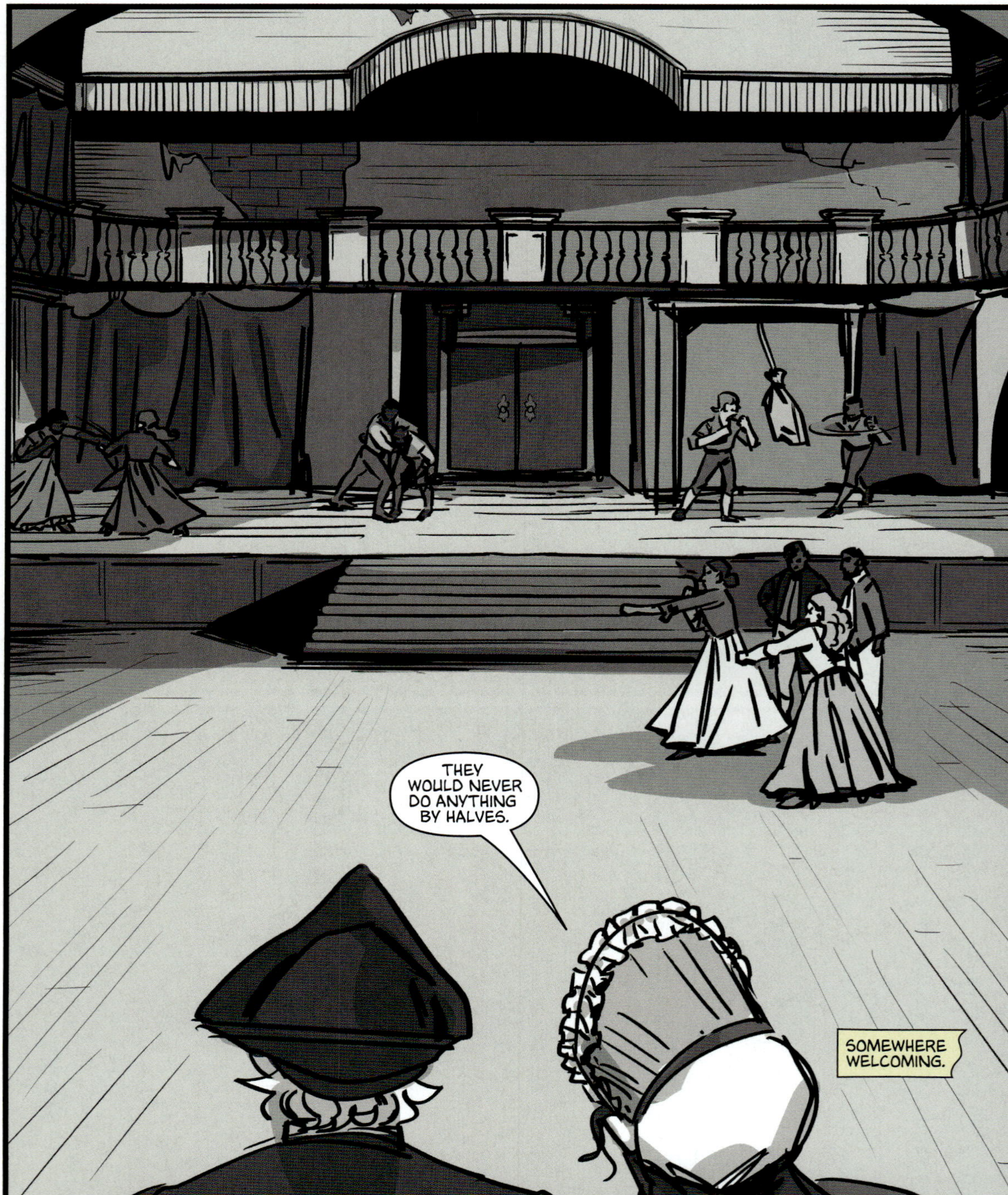
THEY WOULD NEVER DO ANYTHING BY HALVES.
SOMEWHERE WELCOMING.

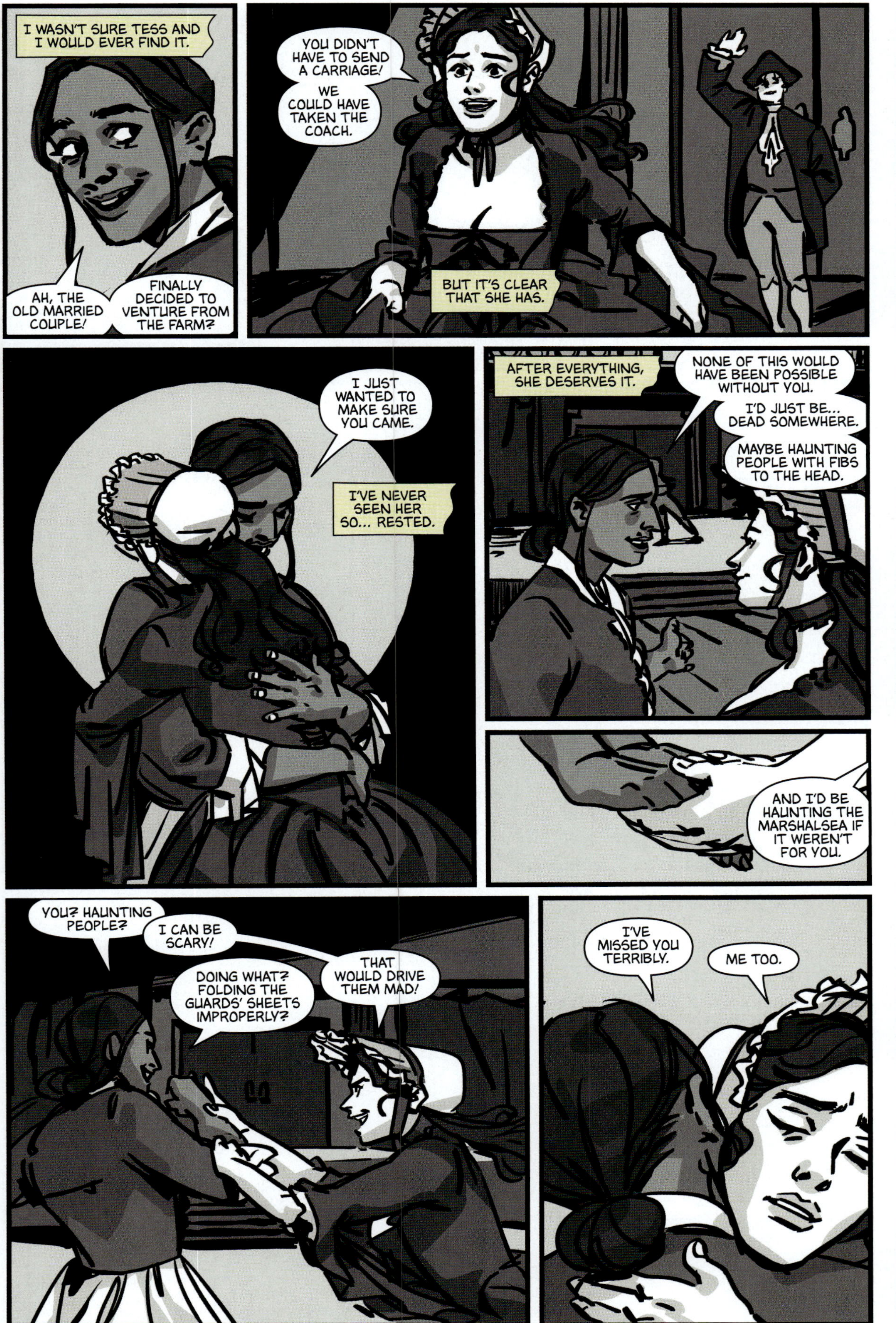

I WASN'T SURE TESS AND I WOULD EVER FIND IT.
AH, THE OLD MARRIED COUPLE!
FINALLY DECIDED TO VENTURE FROM THE FARM?
YOU DIDN'T HAVE TO SEND A CARRIAGE!
WE COULD HAVE TAKEN THE COACH.
BUT IT'S CLEAR THAT SHE HAS.
I JUST WANTED TO MAKE SURE YOU CAME.
I'VE NEVER SEEN HER SO... RESTED.
AFTER EVERYTHING, SHE DESERVES IT.
NONE OF THIS WOULD HAVE BEEN POSSIBLE WITHOUT YOU.
I'D JUST BE... DEAD SOMEWHERE.
MAYBE HAUNTING PEOPLE WITH FIBS TO THE HEAD.
AND I'D BE HAUNTING THE MARSHALSEA IF IT WEREN'T FOR YOU.
YOU? HAUNTING PEOPLE?
I CAN BE SCARY!
DOING WHAT? FOLDING THE GUARDS' SHEETS IMPROPERLY?
THAT WOULD DRIVE THEM MAD!
I'VE MISSED YOU TERRIBLY.
ME TOO.

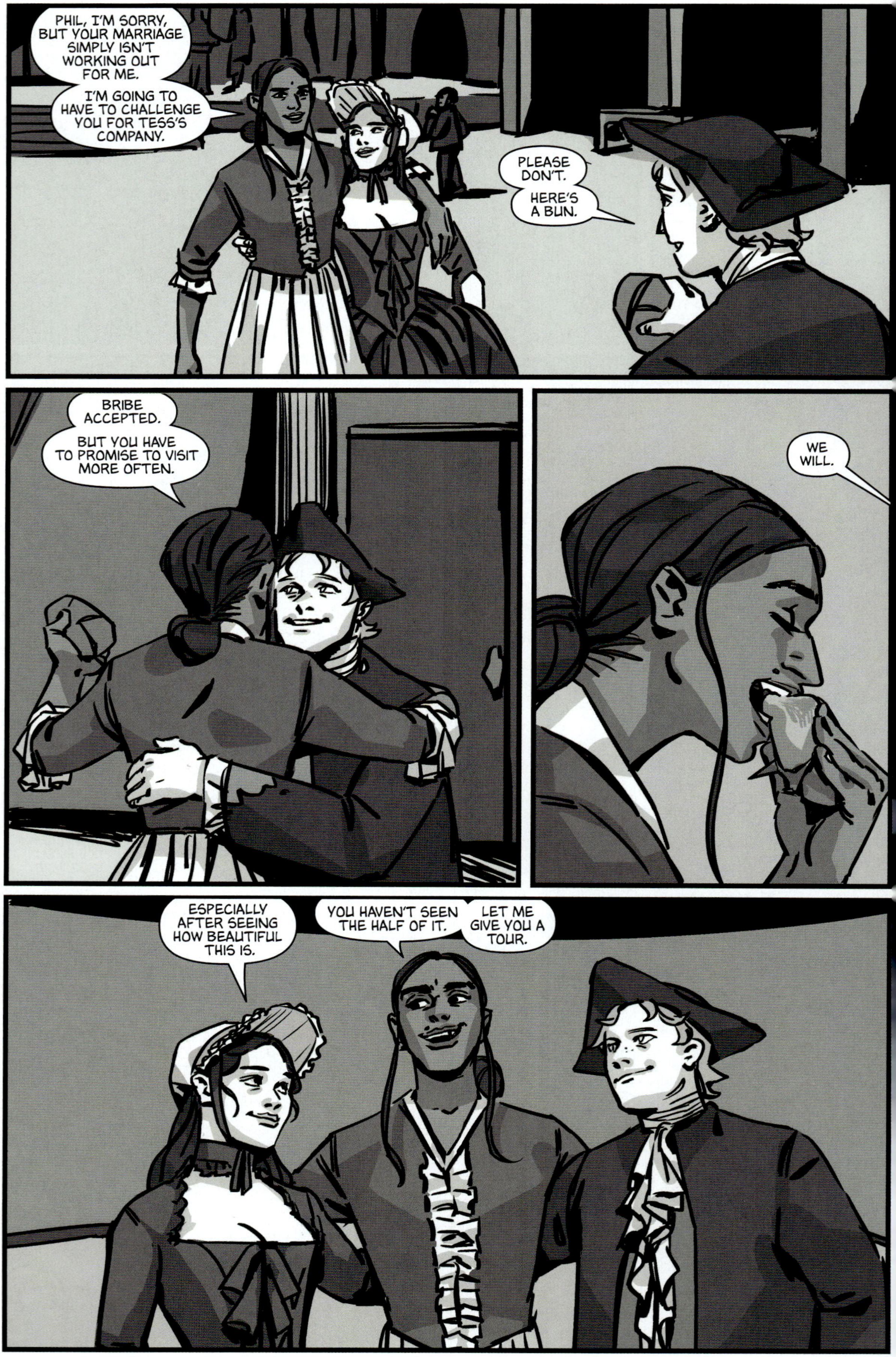
PHIL, I'M SORRY, BUT YOUR MARRIAGE SIMPLY ISN'T WORKING OUT FOR ME.
I'M GOING TO HAVE TO CHALLENGE YOU FOR TESS'S COMPANY.
PLEASE DON'T.
HERE'S A BUN.
BRIBE ACCEPTED.
BUT YOU HAVE TO PROMISE TO VISIT MORE OFTEN.
WE WILL.
ESPECIALLY AFTER SEEING HOW BEAUTIFUL THIS IS.
YOU HAVEN'T SEEN THE HALF OF IT.
LET ME GIVE YOU A TOUR.

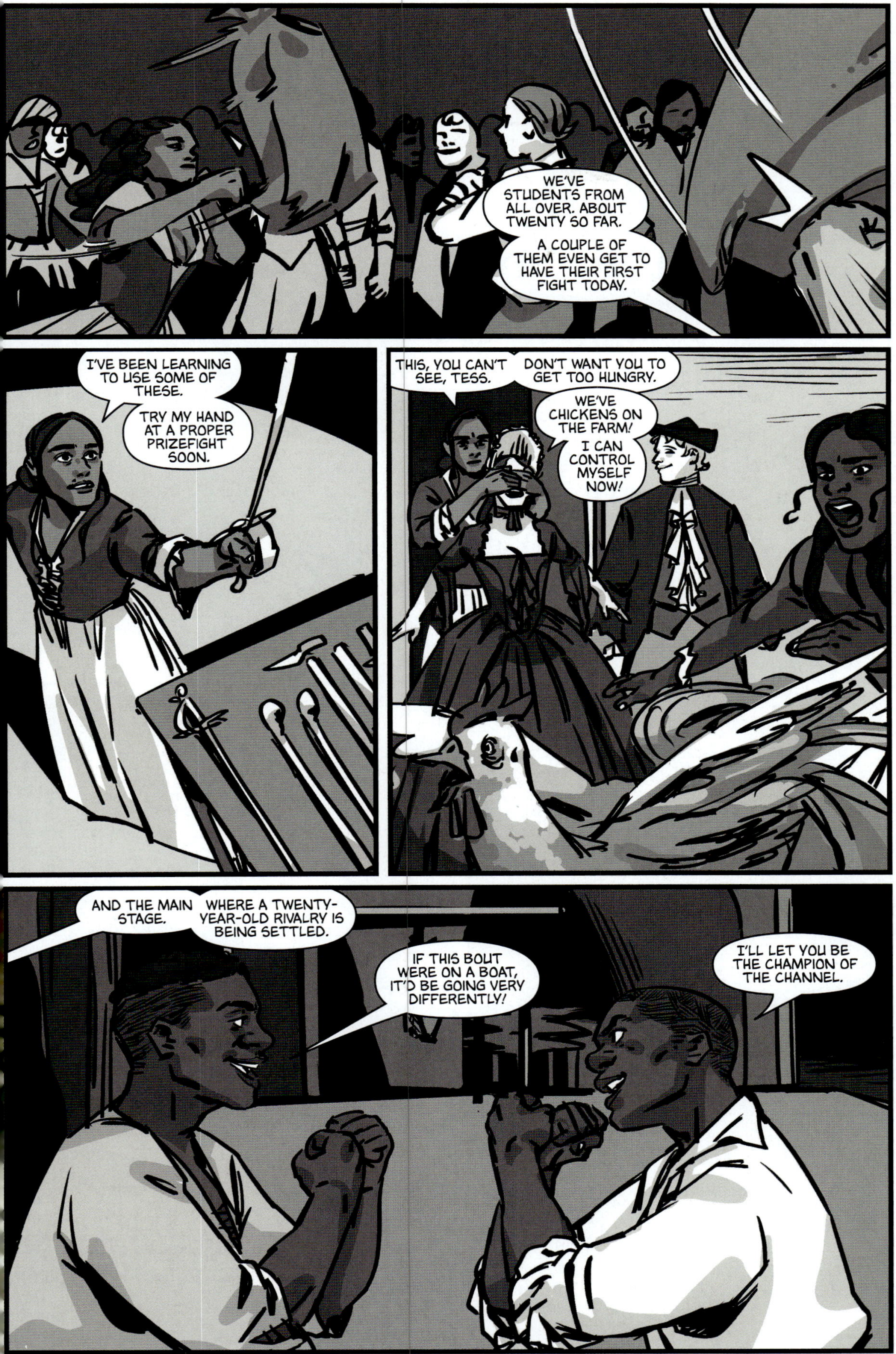
WE'VE STUDENTS FROM ALL OVER. ABOUT TWENTY SO FAR.
A COUPLE OF THEM EVEN GET TO HAVE THEIR FIRST FIGHT TODAY.
I'VE BEEN LEARNING TO USE SOME OF THESE.
TRY MY HAND AT A PROPER PRIZEFIGHT SOON.
THIS, YOU CAN'T SEE, TESS.
DON'T WANT YOU TO GET TOO HUNGRY.
WE'VE CHICKENS ON THE FARM!
I CAN CONTROL MYSELF NOW!
AND THE MAIN STAGE.
WHERE A TWENTY-YEAR-OLD RIVALRY IS BEING SETTLED.
IF THIS BOUT WERE ON A BOAT, IT'D BE GOING VERY DIFFERENTLY!
I'LL LET YOU BE THE CHAMPION OF THE CHANNEL.

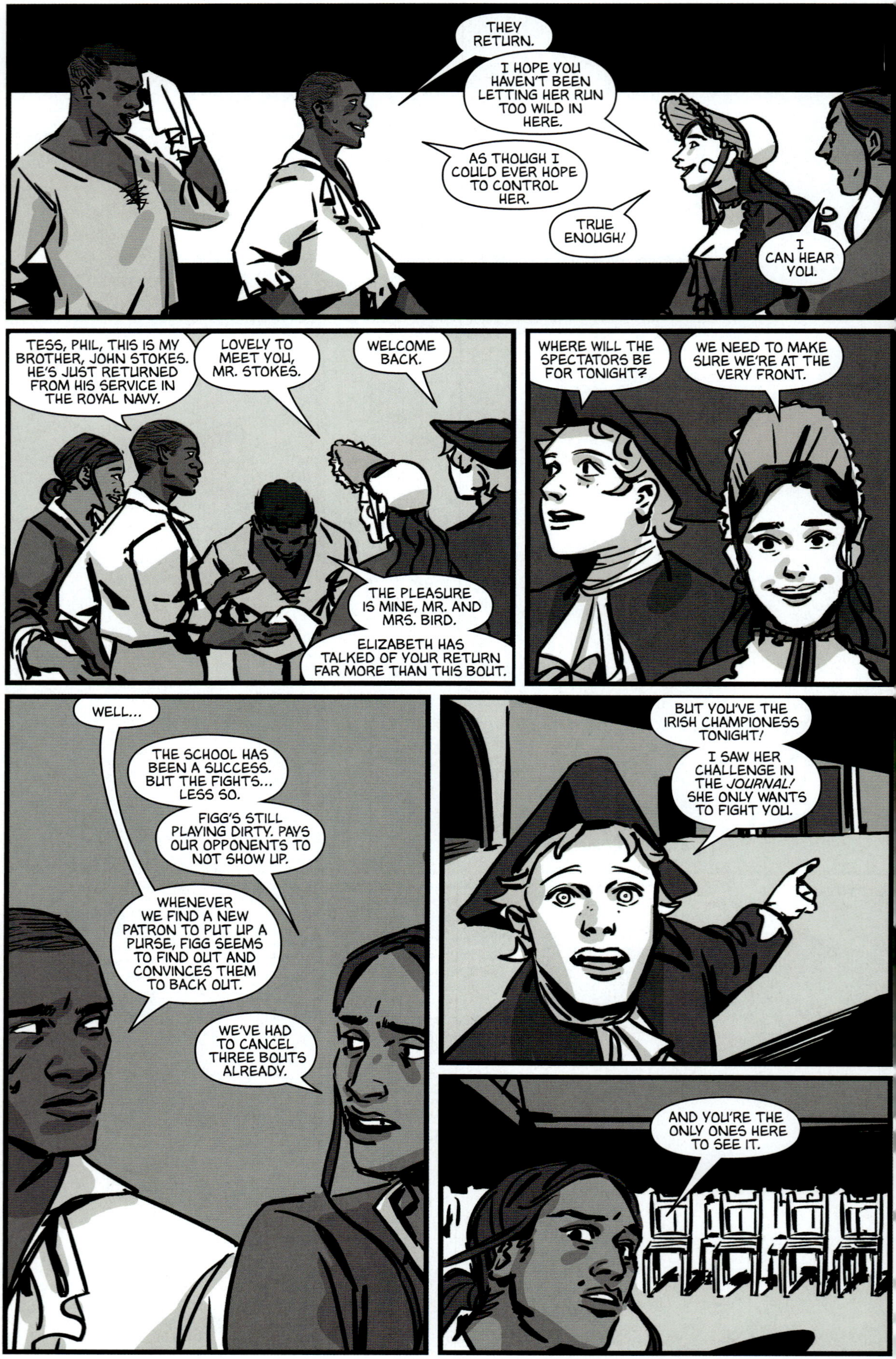
THEY RETURN.
I HOPE YOU HAVEN'T BEEN LETTING HER RUN TOO WILD IN HERE.
AS THOUGH I COULD EVER HOPE TO CONTROL HER.
TRUE ENOUGH!
I CAN HEAR YOU.
TESS, PHIL, THIS IS MY BROTHER, JOHN STOKES. HE'S JUST RETURNED FROM HIS SERVICE IN THE ROYAL NAVY.
LOVELY TO MEET YOU, MR. STOKES.
WELCOME BACK.
THE PLEASURE IS MINE, MR. AND MRS. BIRD.
ELIZABETH HAS TALKED OF YOUR RETURN FAR MORE THAN THIS BOUT.
WHERE WILL THE SPECTATORS BE FOR TONIGHT?
WE NEED TO MAKE SURE WE'RE AT THE VERY FRONT.
WELL...
THE SCHOOL HAS BEEN A SUCCESS. BUT THE FIGHTS... LESS SO.
FIGG'S STILL PLAYING DIRTY. PAYS OUR OPPONENTS TO NOT SHOW UP.
WHENEVER WE FIND A NEW PATRON TO PUT UP A PURSE, FIGG SEEMS TO FIND OUT AND CONVINCES THEM TO BACK OUT.
WE'VE HAD TO CANCEL THREE BOUTS ALREADY.
BUT YOU'VE THE IRISH CHAMPIONESS TONIGHT!
I SAW HER CHALLENGE IN THE *JOURNAL!* SHE ONLY WANTS TO FIGHT YOU.
AND YOU'RE THE ONLY ONES HERE TO SEE IT.

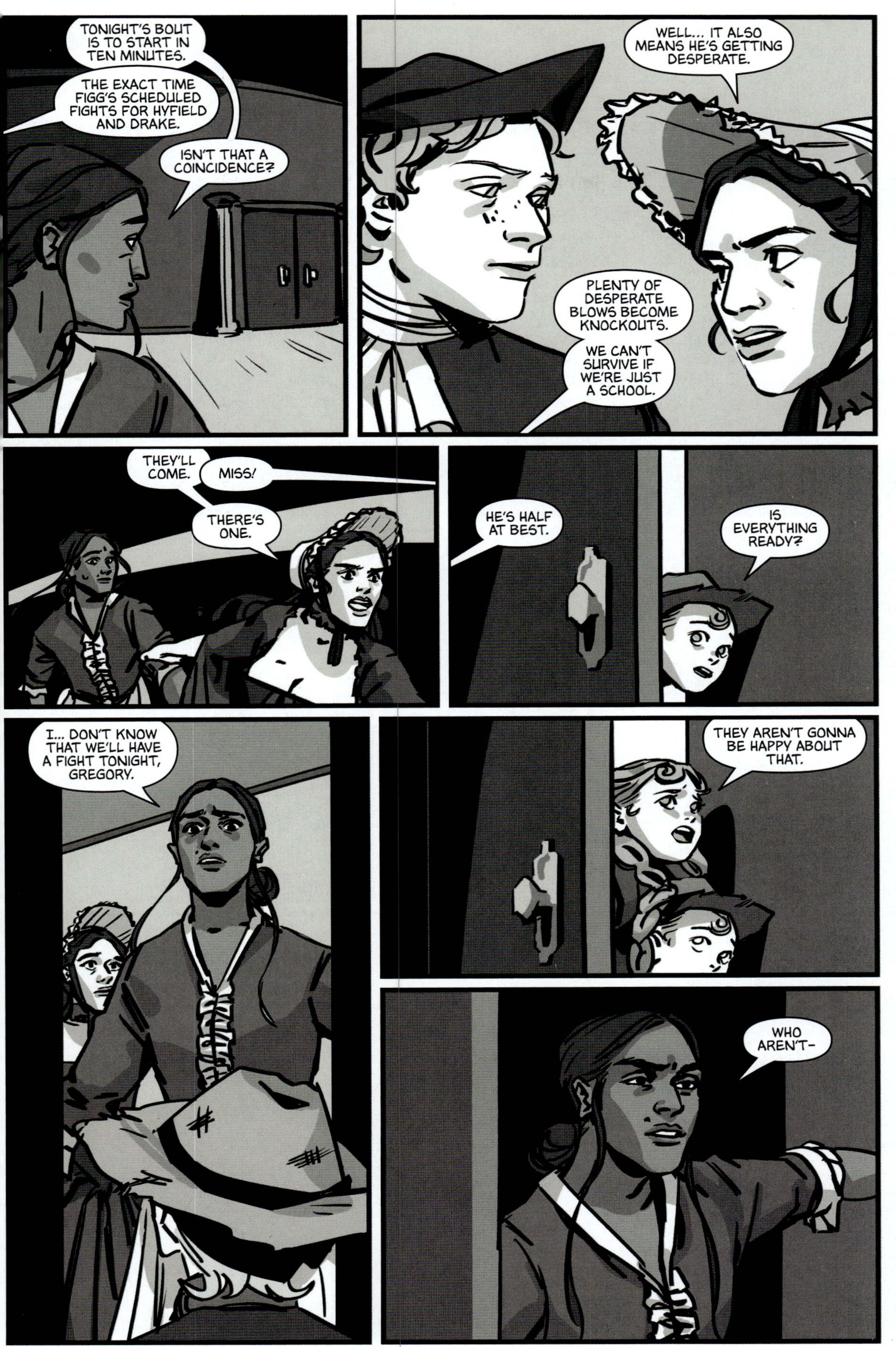
TONIGHT'S BOUT IS TO START IN TEN MINUTES.
THE EXACT TIME FIGG'S SCHEDULED FIGHTS FOR HYFIELD AND DRAKE.
ISN'T THAT A COINCIDENCE?
WELL... IT ALSO MEANS HE'S GETTING DESPERATE.
PLENTY OF DESPERATE BLOWS BECOME KNOCKOUTS.
WE CAN'T SURVIVE IF WE'RE JUST A SCHOOL.
THEY'LL COME.
MISS!
THERE'S ONE.
HE'S HALF AT BEST.
IS EVERYTHING READY?
I... DON'T KNOW THAT WE'LL HAVE A FIGHT TONIGHT, GREGORY.
THEY AREN'T GONNA BE HAPPY ABOUT THAT.
WHO AREN'T-

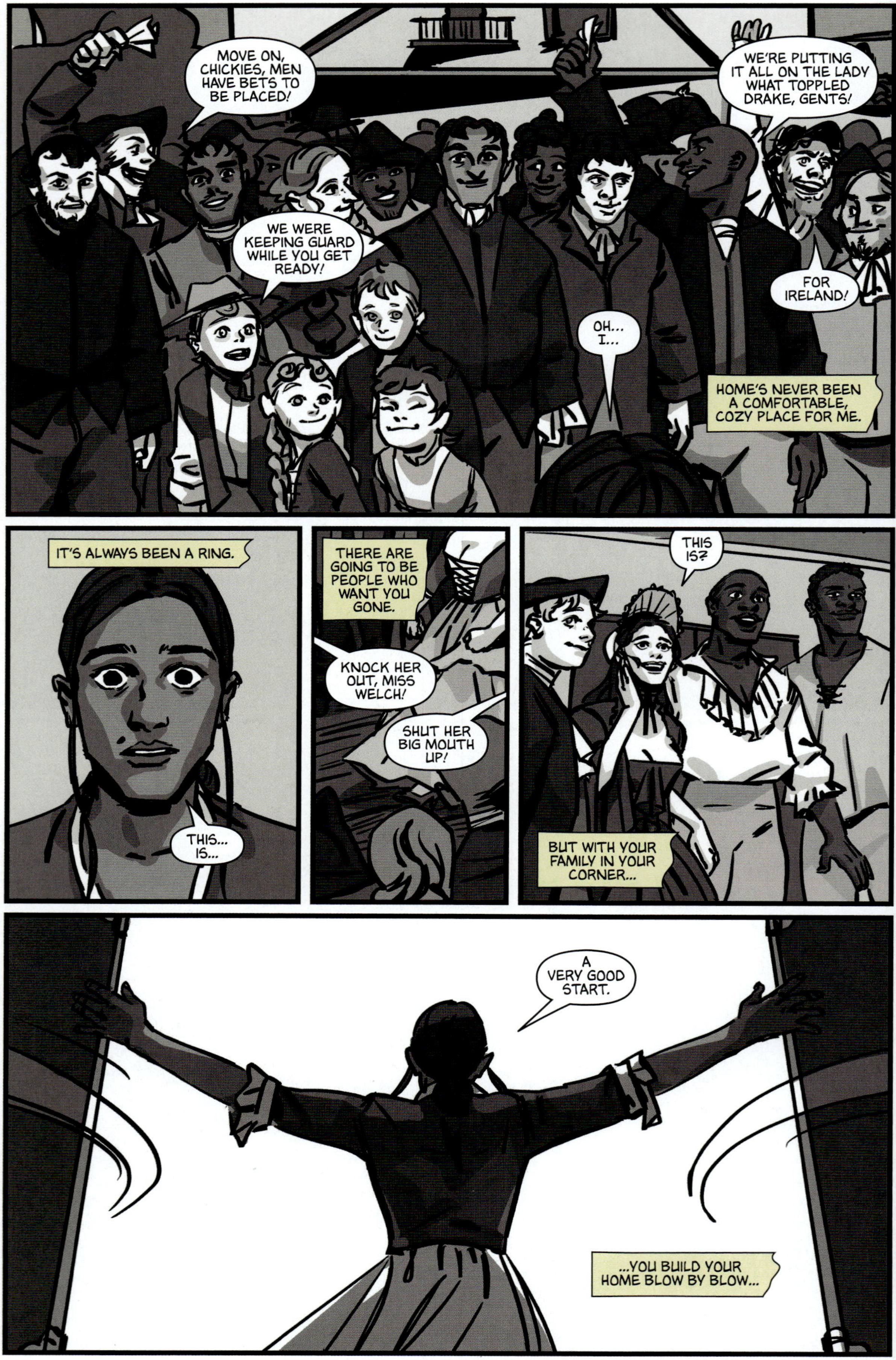
MOVE ON, CHICKIES, MEN HAVE BETS TO BE PLACED!
WE'RE PUTTING IT ALL ON THE LADY WHAT TOPPLED DRAKE, GENTS!
WE WERE KEEPING GUARD WHILE YOU GET READY!
FOR IRELAND!
OH... I...
HOME'S NEVER BEEN A COMFORTABLE, COZY PLACE FOR ME.
IT'S ALWAYS BEEN A RING.
THIS... IS...
THERE ARE GOING TO BE PEOPLE WHO WANT YOU GONE.
KNOCK HER OUT, MISS WELCH!
SHUT HER BIG MOUTH UP!
THIS IS?
BUT WITH YOUR FAMILY IN YOUR CORNER...
A VERY GOOD START.
...YOU BUILD YOUR HOME BLOW BY BLOW...

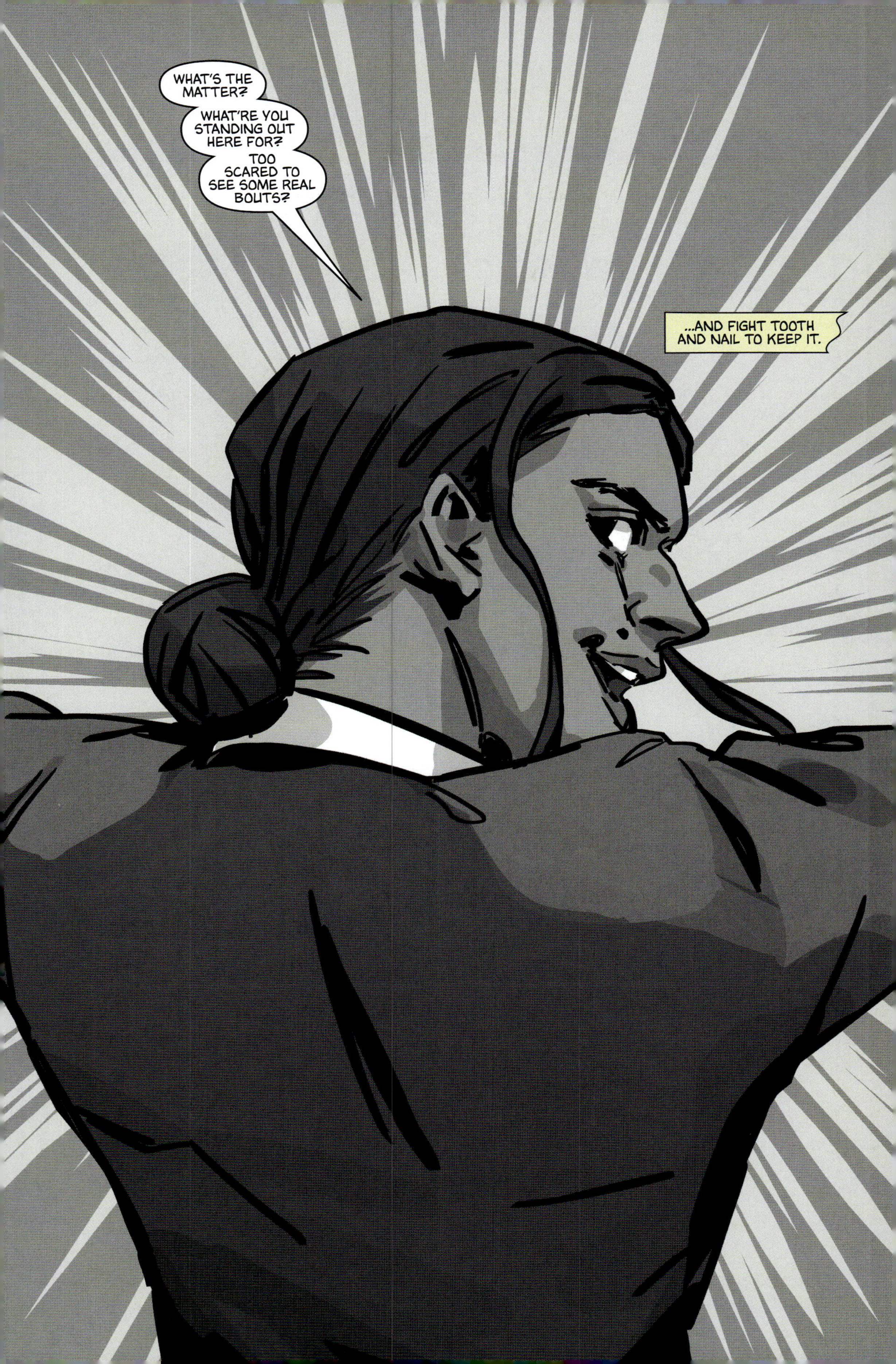
WHAT'S THE MATTER?
WHAT'RE YOU STANDING OUT HERE FOR?
TOO SCARED TO SEE SOME REAL BOUTS?
...AND FIGHT TOOTH AND NAIL TO KEEP IT.

SKETCHES

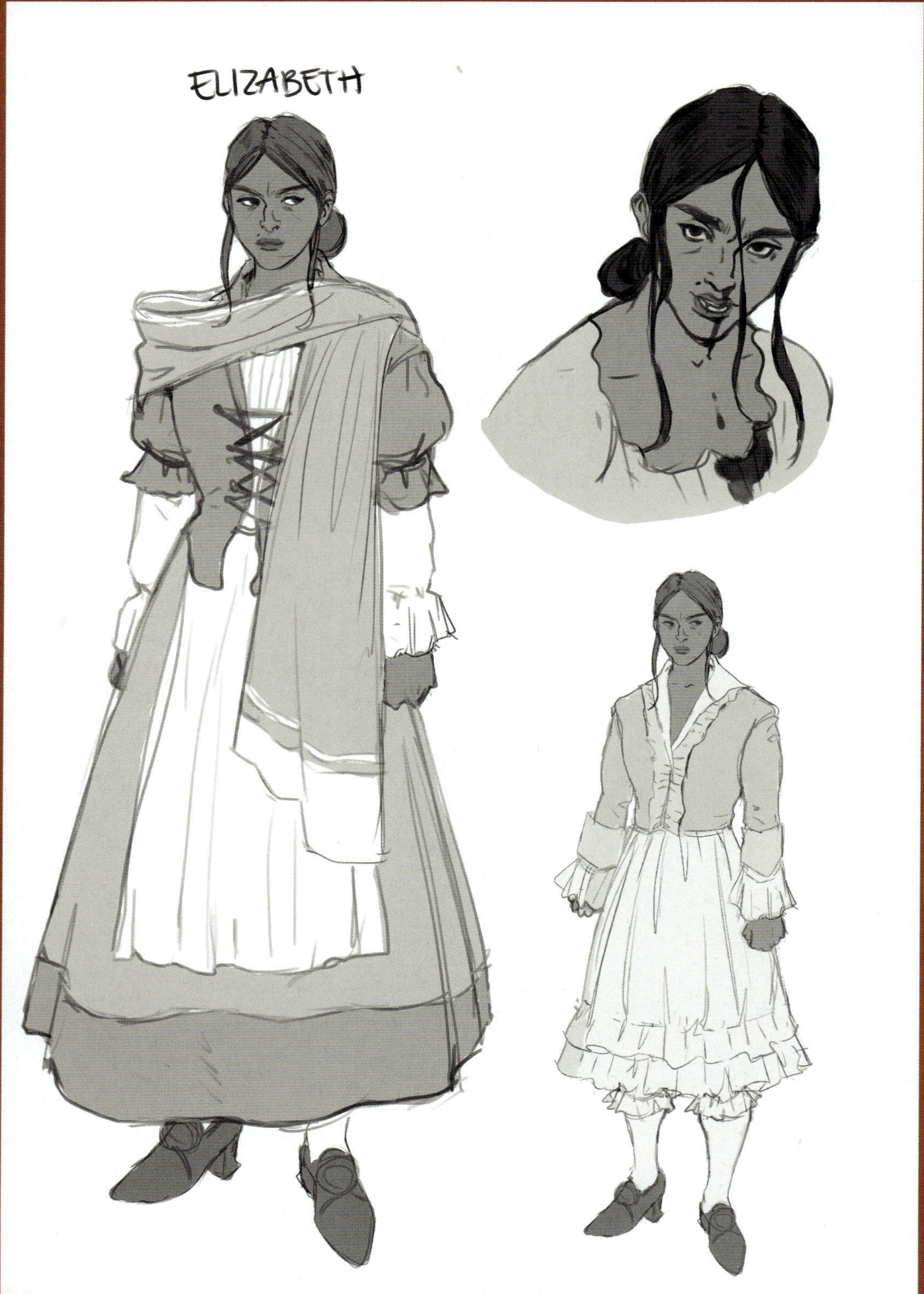
ELIZABETH

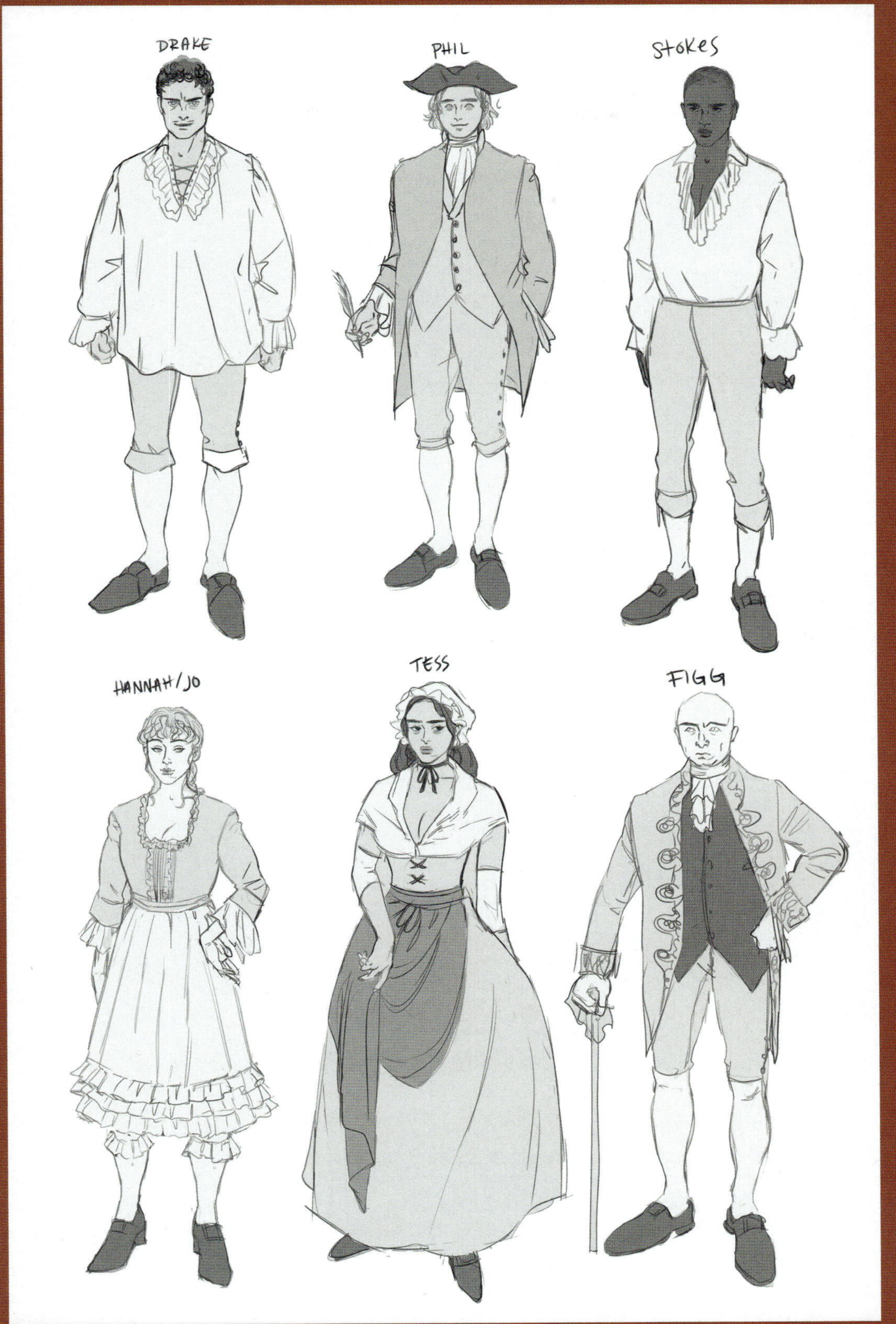
DRAKE
PHIL
STOKES
HANNAH/JO
TESS
FIGG

SCRIPT TO ART

CHAPTER 4 · PAGE 14 · 7 PANELS

Panel 1: Elizabeth looks sharply at her.
1. Elizabeth: Did you even hear what he said?
2. Elizabeth: I did it for you!
3. Tess: No, you didn't.

Panel 2: Tess gives a mirthless smile.
4. Tess: You act like you're doing something for me.
5. Tess: But you haven't for a while.

Panel 3: Tess and Elizabeth stop outside of their door on the street.
6. Tess: And I'm really scared.
7. Tess: I don't know how long I can hide when the Mint's gone.
8. Elizabeth: Just until my winnings-
9. Tess: Fuck your winnings!

Panel 4: Tess is furious. Elizabeth is devastated.
10. Tess: You've been talking about them forever!
11. Tess: Where are they?
12. Narration: They're coming.
13. Narration: I swear.
14. Elizabeth: I'm still a lot closer to clearing the debt than you've ever been.

Panel 5: The sisters stare at each other, hurt and angry.
15. Elizabeth: Even though you've always earned more.
16. Elizabeth: Even though no one ever refuses you work.
17. Elizabeth: If I had your advantages, I know we wouldn't still be stuck here!
18. Tess: I've been trying to keep us alive.

Panel 6: Tess, sad, opens their door.
19. Tess: But you're just... so desperate to prove something.
20. Tess: And all it does is make life harder.

Panel 7: Tess closes the door behind her, leaving a stunned Elizabeth in the street.

FROM AMANDA: It was particularly important that I pay close attention to the facial expressions in this scene, especially when it came to Tess. Their dialogue is angry and resentful, so I mirrored that in both sisters' postures and dramatic lighting, but there is an added layer of sadness that we wanted to communicate as well. It was a balancing act between capturing that sullen helplessness in Tess during the layout drafting process while also making sure that, as I laid out the tones, the harsh shadows from their lanterns wouldn't obscure those nuanced emotions in her face.

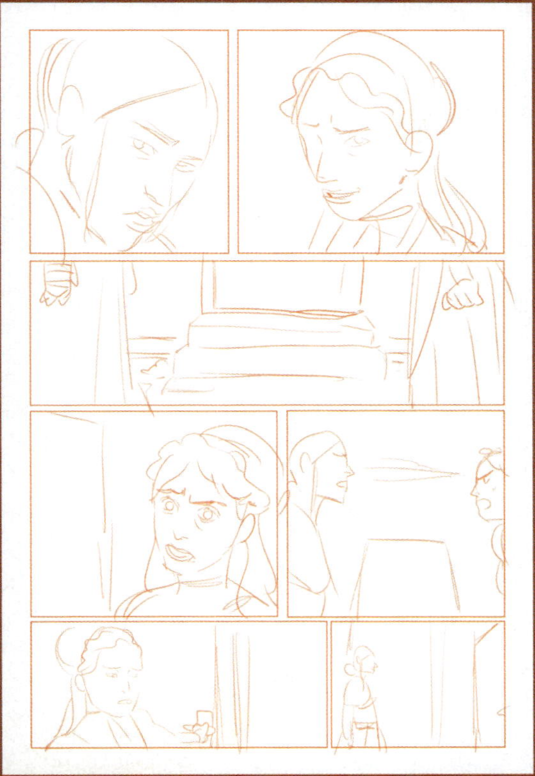

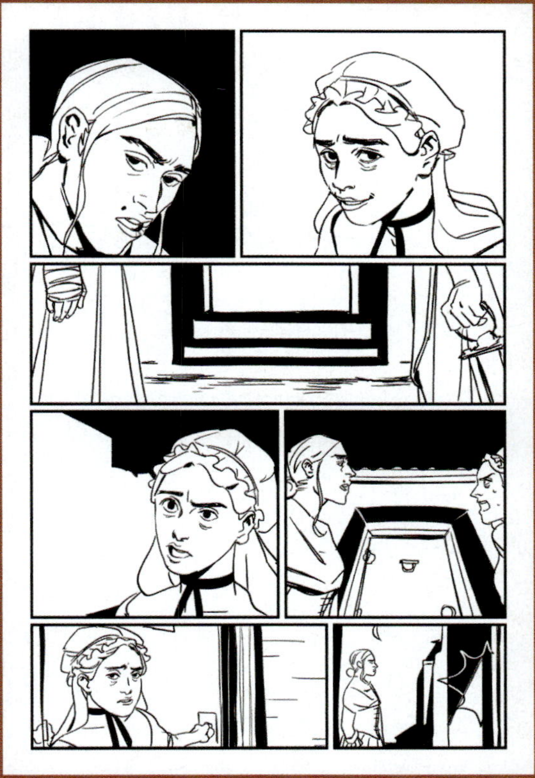

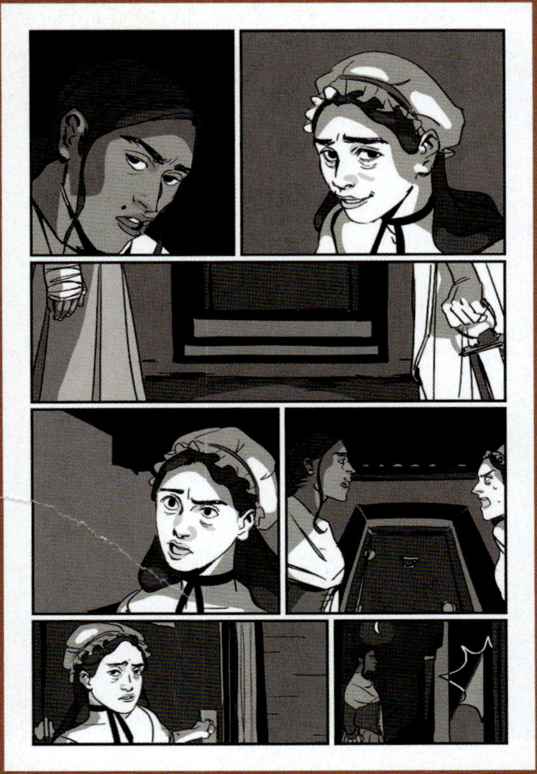

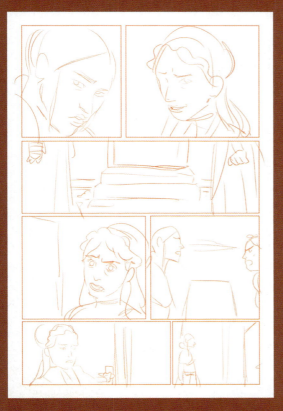

FROM KELLY AND TARUN:
Tess and Elizabeth's relationship is really special to us! As sister-less only children, we are fascinated by the incredible bonds people have with their siblings. But we also think there's truth in the idea that no one can hurt you quite like the person who knows you best. At this moment, both Tess and Elizabeth are scared like they never have been before, both grasping for some solution that will save them. For Tess, the dam finally breaks and all her nastiest thoughts and fears come tumbling out, which in turn, triggers Elizabeth to voice something she's left unsaid for a while. We wanted their argument to be a frustrating stalemate because neither of them are wrong, they've just had two very different perspectives their whole lives. At this point in working together, we knew Amanda well enough to give minimal direction and that she would highlight the pain and anger the sisters struggle through.

ALTERNATE COVER

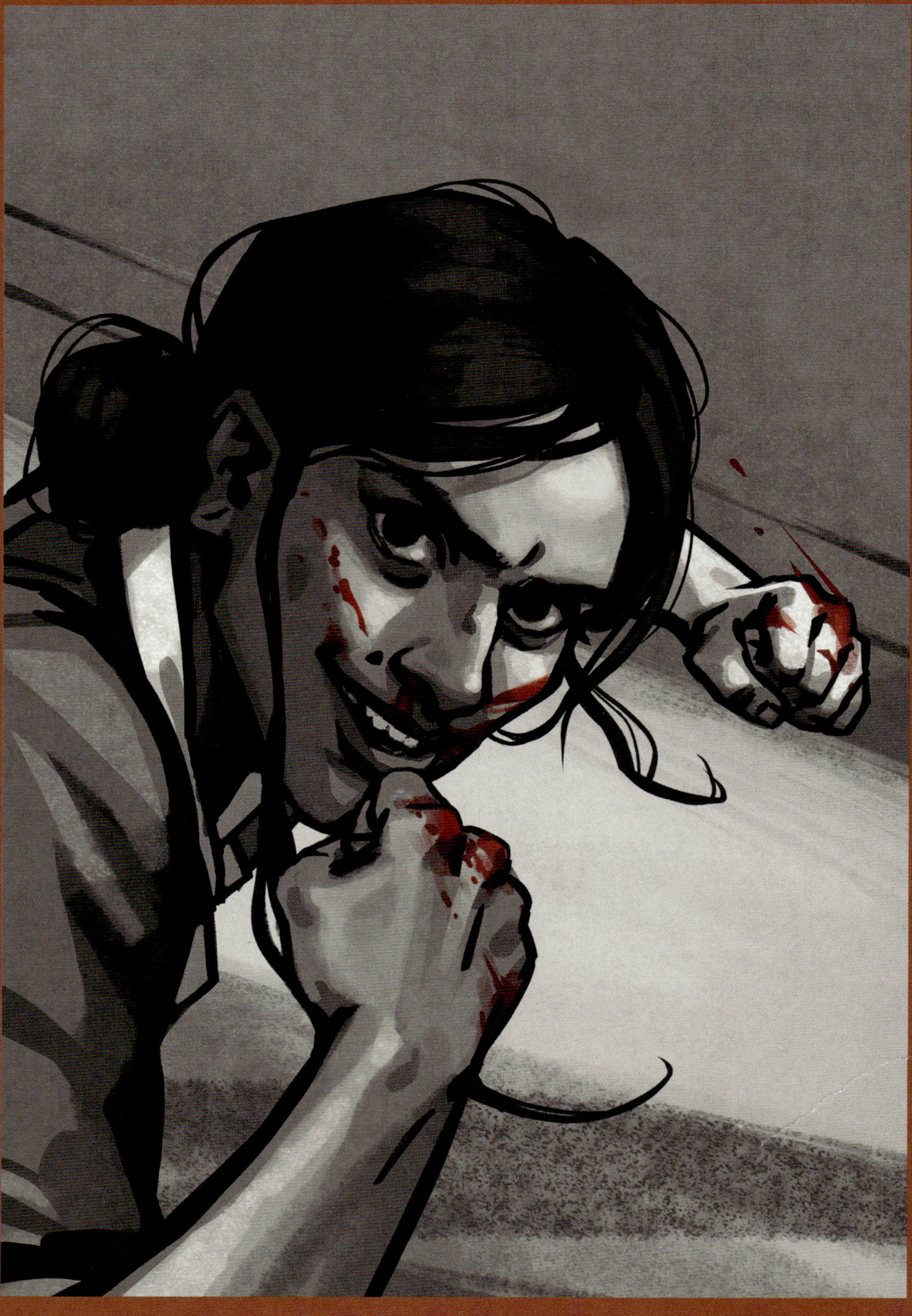